Murder-Go-Round

Murder-Go-Round

INCLUDING

THIRTEEN AT DINNER

THE A.B.C. MURDERS

FUNERALS ARE FATAL

by Agatha Christie

DODD, MEAD & COMPANY · NEW YORK

Contents

Thirteen at Dinner

I A Theatrical Performance

THE memory of the public is short. Already the intense interest and excitement aroused by the murder of George Alfred St. Vincent Marsh, fourth Baron Edgware, is a thing past and forgotten. Newer sensations have taken its place.

My friend, Hercule Poirot, was never openly mentioned in connection with the case. This, I may say, was entirely in accordance with his own wishes. He did not choose to appear in it. The credit went elsewhere—and that is how he wished it to be. Moreover, from Poirot's own peculiar private point of view, the case was one of his failures. He always swears that it was the chance remark of a stranger in the street that put him on the right track.

However that may be, it was his genius that discovered the truth of the affair. But for Hercule Poirot I doubt if the crime would have been brought home to its perpetrator.

I feel, therefore, that the time has come for me to set down all I know of the affair in black and white. I know the ins and outs of the case thoroughly, and I may also mention that I shall be fulfilling the wishes of a very fascinating lady in so doing.

I have often recalled that day in Poirot's prim, neat little sitting-room when, striding up and down a particular strip of carpet, my little friend gave us his masterly and astounding résumé of the case. I am going to begin my narrative where he did on that occasion—at a London theatre in June of last year.

Carlotta Adams was quite the rage in London at that moment. The year before she had given a couple of matinées which had been a wild success. This year she had had a three weeks season of which this was the last night but one.

Carlotta Adams was an American girl, with the most amazing talent for single-handed sketches, unhampered by make-up or scenery. She seemed to speak every language with ease. Her sketch of an evening in a foreign hotel was really wonderful. In turn, American tourists, German tourists, middle-class English families, questionable ladies, impoverished Russian aristocrats and weary, discreet waiters all flitted across the scene.

Her sketches went from grave to gay and back again. Her dying Czechoslovakian woman in hospital brought a lump to the throat. A minute later we were rocking with laughter as a dentist plied his trade and chatted amiably with his victims.

Her program closed with what she announced as "Some Imitations." Here again, she was amazingly clever. Without make-up of any kind, her features seemed to dissolve suddenly and re-form themselves into those of a famous politician, or a well-known actress, or a society beauty. In each character she gave a short, typical speech. These speeches, by the way, were remarkably clever. They seemed to hit off every weakness of the subject selected.

One of her last impersonations was Jane Wilkinson—a talented young American actress well known in London. It was really very clever. Inanities slipped off her tongue, charged with some powerful emotional appeal so that, in spite of yourself, you felt that each word was uttered with some potent and fundamental meaning. Her voice, exquisitely toned, with a deep, husky note in it, was intoxicating. The restrained gestures, each strangely significant, the slightly swaying body, the impression, even, of strong physical beauty—how she did it, I cannot think!

I had always been an admirer of the beautiful Jane Wilkinson. She had thrilled me in her emotional parts, and I had always maintained, in face of those who admitted her beauty but declared she was no actress, that she had considerable histrionic powers.

It was a little uncanny to hear that well-known, slightly husky voice, with the fatalistic drop in it that had stirred me so often, and to watch that seemingly poignant gesture of the slowly closing and unclosing hand and the sudden throw back of the head, with the hair shaken back from the face, that I realized she always gave at the close of a dramatic scene.

Jane Wilkinson was one of those actresses who had left the stage on her marriage, only to return to it a couple of years later.

Three years ago she had married the wealthy but slightly eccentric Lord Edgware. Rumour went that she left him shortly afterward. At any rate, eighteen months after the marriage, she was acting for the films in America and had this season appeared in a successful play in London.

Watching Carlotta Adams' clever but perhaps slightly malicious imitation, it occurred to me to wonder how such imitations were regarded by the subjects selected. Were they pleased at the notoriety—at the advertisement it afforded? Or were they annoyed at what was, after all, a deliberate exposing of the tricks of their trade? Was not Carlotta Adams in the position of the rival conjuror who says: "Oh! this is an old trick! Very simple. I'll show you how this one's done!"

I decided that if *I* were the subject in question, I should be very much annoyed. I should, of course, conceal my vexation, but decidedly I should not like it. One would need great broadmindedness and a distinct sense of humour to appreciate such a merciless exposé.

I had just arrived at these conclusions when the delightful husky laugh from the stage was echoed from behind me. I turned my head sharply. In the seat immediately behind mine, leaning forward with her lips slightly parted, was the subject of the present imitation—Lady Edgware, better known as Jane Wilkinson. I realized immediately that my deductions had been all wrong. She was leaning forward, her lips parted, with an expression of delight and excitement in her eyes.

As the "imitation" finished, she applauded loudly, laughing and turning to her companion, a tall, extremely good-looking man, of the Greek god type, whose face I recognized as one better known on the screen than on the stage. It was Bryan Martin, the hero of the screen most popular at the moment. He and Jane Wilkinson had been starred together in several screen productions.

"Marvellous, isn't she?" Lady Edgware was saying.

He laughed.

"Jane—you look all excited."

"Well, she really is too wonderful! Heaps better than I thought she'd be."

I did not catch Bryan Martin's amused rejoinder. Carlotta Adams had started on a fresh improvisation. What happened later is, I shall always think, a very curious coincidence.

After the theatre, Poirot and I went on to supper at the Savoy. At the very next table to ours were Lady Edgware, Bryan Martin, and two other people whom I did not know. I pointed them out to Poirot and, as I was doing so, another couple came and took their place at the table beyond that again. The woman's face was familiar; and yet, strangely enough, for the moment I could not place it. Then suddenly I realized that it was Carlotta Adams at whom I was staring! The man I did not know. He was well groomed, with a cheerful, somewhat vacuous face. Not a type that I admire.

Carlotta Adams was dressed very inconspicuously in black. Hers was not a face to command instant attention or recognition. It was one of those mobile, sensitive faces that pre-eminently lend themselves to the art of mimicry. It could take on an alien character easily, but it had no very recognizable character of its own.

I imparted these reflections of mine to Poirot. He listened attentively, his egg-shaped head cocked slightly to one side while he darted a sharp glance at the two tables in question.

"So that is Lady Edgware? Yes, I remember—I have seen her act. She is *belle femme.*"

"And a fine actress too."

"Possibly."

"You don't seem convinced."

"I think it would depend on the setting, my friend. If she is the centre of the play, if all revolves round her—yes, then she could play her part. I doubt if she could play a small part adequately, or even what is called a character part. The play must be written *about* her and *for* her. She appears to me of the type of women who are interested only in themselves." He paused and then added, rather unexpectedly, "Such people go through life in great danger."

"Danger?" I said, surprised.

"I have used a word that surprises you, I see, *mon ami.* Yes, danger. Because, you see, a woman like that sees only one thing

—herself. Such women see nothing of the dangers and hazards that surround them—the million conflicting interests and relationships of life. No, they see only their own forward path. And so—sooner or later—disaster."

I was interested. I confessed to myself that such a point of view would not have struck me.

"And the other?" I asked.

"Miss Adams?"

His gaze swept to her table.

"Well?" he said, smiling. "What do you want me to say about her?"

"Only how she strikes you."

"Moncher, am I tonight the fortune teller who reads the palm and tells the character?"

"You could do it better than most," I rejoined.

"It is a very pretty faith that you have in me, Hastings. It touches me. Do you not know, my friend, that each one of us is a dark mystery, a maze of conflicting passions and desires and aptitudes? *Mais oui, c'est vrai.* One makes one's little judgments —but nine times out of ten, one is wrong."

"Not Hercule Poirot," I said, smiling.

"Even Hercule Poirot! Oh! I know very well that you have always a little idea that I am conceited, but indeed, I assure you, I am really a very humble person."

I laughed.

"You—humble!"

"It is so. Except—I confess it—that I am a little proud of my moustaches. Nowhere in London have I observed anything to compare with them."

"You're quite safe," I said dryly. "You won't. So you are not going to risk judgment on Carlotta Adams."

"Elle est artiste!" said Poirot simply. "That covers nearly all, does it not?"

"Anyway, you don't consider that she walks through life in peril?"

"We all do that, my friend," said Poirot gravely. "Misfortune may always be waiting to rush out upon us. But, as to your question—Miss Adams, I think, will succeed. She is shrewd and she is ambitious."

"These make for success—that. Though there is still one avenue of danger—since it is of danger we are talking."

"You mean?"

"Love of the money that comes with success. Love of money might lead such a one from the prudent and cautious path."

"It might do that to all of us," I said.

"That is true, but at any rate you or I would see the danger involved. We could weigh the pros and cons. If you care for money too much, it is only the money you see; everything else is in shadow."

I laughed at his serious manner.

"Esmeralda, the gipsy queen, is in good form," I remarked teasingly.

"The psychology of character is interesting," returned Poirot, unmoved. "One cannot be interested in crime without being interested in psychology. It is not the mere act of killing; it is what lies *behind* it that appeals to the expert. You follow me, Hastings?"

I said that I followed him perfectly.

"I have noticed that, when we work on a case together, you are always urging me on to physical action, Hastings. You wish me to measure footprints, to analyze cigarette ash, to prostrate myself on my stomach for the examination of detail. You never realize that by lying back in an armchair, with the eyes closed, one can come nearer to the solution of any problem. One sees then with the eyes of the mind."

"I don't," I said. "When I lie back in an armchair with my eyes closed one thing happens to me and one thing only!"

"I have noticed it!" said Poirot. "It is strange. At such moments the brain should be working feverishly, not sinking into sluggish repose. The mental activity—it is so interesting, so stimulating! The employment of the little grey cells is a mental pleasure. They and they only can be trusted to lead one through fog to the truth."

I am afraid that I have got into the habit of averting my attention whenever Poirot mentions his little grey cells. I have heard it all so often before. In this instance my attention wandered to the four people sitting at the next table. When Poirot's monologue drew to a close I remarked with a chuckle:

"You have made a hit, Poirot. The fair Lady Edgware can hardly take her eyes off you."

"Doubtless she has been informed of my identity," said Poirot, trying to look modest, and failing.

"I think it is the famous moustaches," I said. "She is carried away by their beauty."

Poirot caressed them surreptitiously.

"It is true that they are unique," he admitted. "Oh, my friend —the 'toothbrush' as you call it, that you wear—it is a horror— an atrocity—a wilful stunting of the bounties of nature. Abandon it, my friend, I pray of you."

"By Jove," I said, disregarding Poirot's appeal, "the lady's getting up. I believe she's coming to speak to us. Bryan Martin is protesting, but she won't listen to him."

Sure enough, Jane Wilkinson swept impetuously from her seat and came over to our table. Poirot rose to his feet, bowing, and I rose also.

"M. Hercule Poirot, isn't it?" said the soft, husky voice.

"At your service."

"M. Poirot, I want to talk to you. I must talk to you."

"But certainly, madame, will you not sit down?"

"No, no, not here. I want to talk to you privately. We'll go right upstairs to my suite."

Bryan Martin had joined her. He spoke now with a deprecating laugh.

"You must wait a little, Jane. We're in the middle of supper. So is M. Poirot."

But Jane Wilkinson was not so easily turned from her purpose.

"Why, Bryan, what does that matter? We'll have supper sent up to the suite. Speak to them about it, will you? And, Bryan—"

She went after him as he was turning away and appeared to urge some course upon him. He stood out about it, I gathered, shaking his head and frowning. But she spoke even more emphatically, and finally, with a shrug of the shoulders, he gave way.

Once or twice during her speech to him she had glanced at the table where Carlotta Adams sat, and I wondered if what she was suggesting had anything to do with the American girl.

Her point gained, Jane came back, radiant.

"We'll go right up now," she said, and included me in a dazzling smile.

The question of our agreeing or not agreeing to her plan did not seem to occur to her mind. She swept us off without a shade of apology.

"It's the greatest luck just seeing you here this evening, M. Poirot," she said as she led the way to the lift. "It's wonderful how everything seems to turn out right for me. I'd just been thinking and wondering what on earth I was going to do, and I looked up and there you were at the next table, and I said to myself: 'M. Poirot will tell me what to do!'"

She broke off to say "Second floor" to the lift boy.

"If I can be of aid to you—" began Poirot.

"I'm sure you can. I've heard you're just the most marvellous man that ever existed. Somebody's got to get me out of the tangle I'm in, and I feel you're just the man to do it."

We got out at the second floor, and she led the way along the corridor, paused at a door and entered one of the most opulent of the Savoy suites.

Casting her white fur wrap on one chair, and her small jewelled bag on the table, the actress sank onto a chair and exclaimed:

"M. Poirot, somehow or other I've just *got* to get rid of my husband!"

II A Supper Party

AFTER a moment's astonishment Poirot recovered himself!

"But, madame," he said, his eyes twinkling. "Getting rid of husbands is not my speciality."

"Well, of course, I know that."

"It is a lawyer you require."

"That's just where you're wrong. I'm just about sick and tired of lawyers. I've had straight lawyers and crooked lawyers, and not one of them's done me any good. Lawyers just know the law; they don't seem to have any kind of natural sense."

"And you think I have?"

She laughed.

"I've heard that you're the cat's whiskers, M. Poirot."

"Comment? The cat's whiskers? I do not understand."

"Well—that you're *It.*"

"Madame, I may or may not have brains—as a matter of fact I have—why pretend? But your little affair, it is not my *genre.*"

"I don't see why not. It's a problem."

"Oh! a problem!"

"And it's difficult," went on Jane Wilkinson. "I should say you weren't the man to shy at difficulties."

"Let me compliment you on your insight, madame. But all the same, me, I do not make the investigations for divorce. It is not pretty—*ce métier là.*"

"My dear man, I'm not asking you to do spying work. It wouldn't be any good. But I've just got to get rid of the man, and I'm sure you could tell me how to do it."

Poirot paused awhile before replying. When he did, there was a new note in his voice.

"First tell me, madame, why you are so anxious to 'get rid' of Lord Edgware?"

There was no delay or hesitation about her answer. It came swift and pat.

"Why, of course. I want to get married again. What other reason could there be?"

Her great blue eyes opened ingenuously.

"But surely a divorce should be easy to obtain?"

"You don't know my husband, M. Poirot. He's—he's—" She shivered. "I don't know how to explain it. He's a queer man— he's not like other people." She paused and then went on: "He should never have married—anyone. I know what I'm talking about. I just can't describe him, but he's—queer. His first wife, you know, ran away from him—left a baby of three months behind. He never divorced her and she died miserably abroad somewhere. Then he married me. Well—I couldn't stick it. I was frightened. I left him and went to the States. I've no grounds for a divorce; and, if I've given him grounds for one, he won't take any notice of them. He's—he's a kind of fanatic."

"In certain American States you could obtain a divorce, madame."

"That's no good to me—not if I'm going to live in England."

"You want to live in England?"

"Yes."

"Who is the man you want to marry?"

"That's just it. The Duke of Merton."

I drew in my breath sharply. The Duke of Merton had so far been the despair of matchmaking mammas. A young man of monkish tendencies, a violent Anglo-Catholic, he was reported to be completely under the thumb of his mother, the redoubtable dowager duchess. His life was austere in the extreme. He collected Chinese porcelain and was reputed to be of æsthetic tastes. He was supposed to care nothing for women.

"I'm just crazy about him," said Jane sentimentally. "He's unlike anyone I ever met, and Merton Castle is too wonderful. The whole thing is the most romantic business that ever happened. He's so good-looking too—like a dreamy kind of monk."

She paused.

"I'm going to give up the stage when I marry. I just don't seem to care about it any more."

"In the meantime," said Poirot dryly, "Lord Edgware stands in the way of these romantic dreams."

"Yes, and it's driving me to distraction." She leaned back thoughtfully. "Of course if we were only in Chicago I could get him bumped off quite easily, but you don't seem to run to gunmen over here."

"Over here," said Poirot, smiling, "we consider that every human being has the right to live."

"Well, I don't know about that. I guess you'd be better off without some of your politicians; and knowing what I do of Edgware, I think he'd be no loss—rather the contrary."

There was a knock at the door and a waiter entered with supper dishes. Jane Wilkinson continued to discuss her problem, with no appreciation of his presence.

"But I don't want you to kill him for me, M. Poirot."

"*Merci,* madame."

"I thought perhaps you might argue with him in some clever way. Get him to give in to the idea of divorce. I'm sure you could."

"I think you overrate my persuasive powers, madame."

"Oh! but you can surely think of *something,* M. Poirot." She leaned forward. Her blue eyes opened wide again. "You'd like me to be happy, wouldn't you?"

Her voice was soft, low and deliciously seductive.

"I should like everybody to be happy," said Poirot cautiously.

"Yes, but I wasn't thinking of everybody. I was thinking of just me."

"I should say you always do that, madame." He smiled.

"You think I'm selfish?"

"Oh! I did not say so, madame."

"I dare say I am. But you see I do so hate being unhappy. It affects my acting, even. And I'm going to be ever so unhappy unless he agrees to a divorce—or dies."

"On the whole," she continued thoughtfully, "it would be much better if he died. I mean, I'd feel more finally quit of him."

She looked at Poirot for sympathy.

"You *will* help me, won't you, M. Poirot?" She rose, picking up the white wrap, and stood looking appealingly into his face.

I heard the noise of voices outside in the corridor. The door was ajar. "If you don't—" she went on.

"If I don't, madame?"

She laughed.

"I'll have to call a taxi and go round and bump him off myself."

Laughing, she disappeared through a door to an adjoining room just as Bryan Martin came in with the American girl, Carlotta Adams and her escort, and the two people who had been supping with him and Jane Wilkinson. They were introduced to me as Mr. and Mrs. Widburn.

"Hello!" said Bryan. "Where's Jane? I want to tell her I've succeeded in the commission she gave me."

Jane appeared in the doorway of the bedroom. She held a lipstick in one hand.

"Have you got her? How marvellous! Miss Adams, I do admire your performance so. I felt I just had to know you. Come in here and talk to me while I fix my face. It's looking too perfectly frightful."

Carlotta Adams accepted the invitation. Bryan Martin flung himself down in a chair.

"Well, M. Poirot," he said, "you were duly captured. Has our Jane persuaded you to fight her battles? You might as well give in sooner as later. She doesn't understand the word 'No.'"

"She has not come across it, perhaps."

"A very interesting character, Jane," said Bryan Martin. He lay back in his chair and puffed cigarette smoke idly towards the ceiling. "Taboos have no meaning for her. No morals whatever. I don't mean she's exactly immoral—she isn't. Amoral is the word, I believe. Just sees one thing only in life—what Jane wants."

He laughed.

"I believe she'd kill somebody quite cheerfully—and feel injured if they caught her and wanted to hang her for it. The trouble is that she *would* be caught. She hasn't any brains. Her idea of a murder would be to drive up in a taxi, sail in under her own name and shoot."

"Now I wonder what makes you say that?" murmured Poirot.

"Eh?"

"You know her well, monsieur?"

"I should say I did."

He laughed again, and it struck me that his laugh was unusually bitter.

"You agree, don't you?" he flung out to the others.

"Oh! Jane's an egoist," agreed Mrs. Widburn. "An actress has got to be, though. That is, if she wants to express her personality."

Poirot did not speak. His eyes were resting on Bryan Martin's face, dwelling there with a curious speculative expression that I could not quite understand.

At that moment Jane sailed in from the next room, Carlotta Adams behind her. I presume that Jane had now "fixed her face," whatever that term denoted, to her own satisfaction. It looked to me exactly the same as before and quite incapable of improvement.

The supper party that followed was quite a merry one, yet I sometimes had the feeling that there were undercurrents which I was incapable of appreciating.

Jane Wilkinson I acquitted of any subtleties. She was obviously a young woman who saw only one thing at a time. She had desired an interview with Poirot, and had carried her point and obtained her desire without delay. Now she was obviously in high good humour. Her desire to include Carlotta Adams in the party had been, I decided, a mere whim. She had been highly amused, as a child might be amused, by the clever counterfeit of herself.

No, the undercurrents that I sensed were nothing to do with Jane Wilkinson. In what direction did they lie? I studied the guests in turn. Bryan Martin? He was certainly not behaving quite naturally. But that, I told myself, might be merely characteristic of a film star, the exaggerated self-consciousness of a vain man, too accustomed to playing a part to lay it aside easily.

Carlotta Adams, at any rate, was behaving naturally enough. She was a quiet girl, with a pleasant low voice. I studied her with some attention, now that I had the chance to do so at close quarters. She had, I thought, distinct charm, but charm of a somewhat negative order. It consisted in an absence of any jarring or strident note. She was a kind of personified soft agreement. Her very appearance was negative. Soft, dark hair, eyes a rather colourless pale blue, pale face, and a mobile, sensitive mouth. A face that you liked but that you would find it hard to know again, if you were to meet her, say, in different clothes.

She seemed pleased at Jane's graciousness and complimentary sayings. Any girl would be, I thought—and then, just at that moment, something occurred that caused me to revise that rather too hasty opinion.

Carlotta Adams looked across the table at her hostess, who was at that moment turning her head to talk to Poirot. There was a curious scrutinizing quality in the girl's gaze—it seemed a deliberate summing up, and at the same time it struck me that there was a very definite hostility in those pale blue eyes.

Fancy, perhaps. Or possibly professional jealousy. Jane was a successful actress who had definitely arrived. Carlotta was merely climbing the ladder.

I looked at the three other members of the party. Mr. and Mrs. Widburn, what about them? He was a tall, cadaverous man; she, a plump, fair, gushing soul. They appeared to be wealthy people with a passion for everything connected with the stage. They were, in fact, unwilling to talk on any other subject. Owing to my recent absence from England they found me sadly ill-informed, and finally Mrs. Widburn turned a plump shoulder on me and remembered my existence no more.

The last member of the party was the dark young man with the round, cheerful face, who was Carlotta Adams' escort. I had had my suspicions from the first that the young man was not quite so sober as he might have been. As he drank more champagne, this became even more clearly apparent.

He appeared to be suffering from a profound sense of injury. For the first half of the meal he sat in gloomy silence. Towards the latter half he unbosomed himself to me, apparently under the impression that I was one of his oldest friends.

"What I mean to say," he said. "It isn't. No, dear old chap, it isn't—"

I omit the slight slurring together of the words.

"I mean to say," he went on, "I ask you? I mean, if you take a girl—well, I mean—butting in. Going round upsetting things. Not as though I'd ever said a word to her I shouldn't have done. She's not the sort. You know—Puritan Fathers—the *Mayflower* —all that. Dash it—the girl's straight. What I mean is—what was I saying?"

"That it was hard lines," I said soothingly.

"Well, dash it all, it is. Dash it, I had to borrow the money for this beano from my tailor. Very obliging chap, my tailor. I've owed him money for years. Makes a sort of bond between us. Nothing like a bond, is there, dear old fellow. You and I. You and I. Who the devil are you, by the way?"

"My name is Hastings."

"You don't say so. Now I could have sworn you were a chap called Spencer Jones. Dear old Spencer Jones. Met him at the Eton and Harrow and borrowed a fiver from him. What I say is one face is very like another face—that's what I say. If we were a lot of Chinks we wouldn't know each other apart."

He shook his head sadly, then cheered up suddenly and drank off some more champagne.

"Anyway," he said, "I'm not a damned foreigner."

This reflection seemed to cause him such elation that he presently made several remarks of a hopeful character.

"Look on the bright side, my boy," he adjured me. "What I say is, look on the bright side. One of these days—when I'm seventy-five or so—I'm going to be a rich man. When my uncle dies. Then I can pay my tailor."

He sat smiling happily at the thought. There was something strangely likable about the young man. He had a round face and an absurdly small black moustache that gave one the impression of being marooned in the middle of a dent.

Carlotta Adams, I noticed, had an eye on him, and it was after a glance in his direction that she rose and broke up the party.

"It was just sweet of you to come up here," said Jane. "I do so love doing things on the spur of the moment, don't you?"

"No," said Miss Adams. "I'm afraid I always plan a thing out very carefully before I do it. It saves—worry."

There was something faintly disagreeable in her manner.

"Well, at any rate the results justify you," laughed Jane. "I don't know when I enjoyed anything so much as I did your show tonight."

The American girl's face relaxed.

"Well, that's very sweet of you," she said warmly, "and I appreciate your telling me so. I need encouragement. We all do."

"Carlotta," said the young man with the black moustache, "shake hands and say thank you for the party to Aunt Jane and come along."

The way he walked straight through the door was a miracle of concentration. Carlotta followed him quickly.

"Well," said Jane, "what was that that blew in and called me Aunt Jane? I hadn't noticed him before."

"My dear," said Mrs. Widburn, "you mustn't take any notice of him. Most brilliant as a boy in the O.U.D.S. You'd hardly think so now, would you? I hate to see early promise come to nothing. But Charles and I positively must toddle."

The Widburns duly toddled, and Bryan Martin went with them.

"Well, M. Poirot?"

He smiled at her.

"*Eh bien*, Lady Edgware?"

"For goodness sake, don't call me that. Let me forget it! If you aren't the hardest-hearted little man in Europe!"

"But no, but no, I am not hard-hearted."

Poirot, I thought, had had quite enough champagne—possibly a glass too much.

"Then you'll go and see my husband? And make him do what I want?"

"I will go and see him," Poirot promised cautiously.

"And if he turns you down—as he will—you'll think of a clever plan. They say you're the cleverest man in England, M. Poirot."

"Madame, when I am hard-hearted, it is Europe you mention. But for cleverness you say only England."

"If you put this through I'll say the Universe."

Poirot raised a deprecating hand.

"Madame, I promise nothing. In the interests of the psychology I will endeavour to arrange a meeting with your husband."

"Psychoanalyze him as much as you like. Maybe it would do him good. But you've got to pull it off—for my sake. I've got to have my romance, M. Poirot."

She added dreamily: "Just think of the sensation it will make."

III The Man with the Gold Tooth

It was a few days later, when we were sitting at breakfast, that Poirot flung across to me a letter that he had just opened.

"Well, *mon ami,*" he said. "What do you think of that?"

The note was from Lord Edgware, and in stiff, formal language it made an appointment for the following day at eleven.

I must say that I was very much surprised. I had taken Poirot's words as uttered lightly in a convivial moment, and I had had no idea that he had actually taken steps to carry out his promise.

Poirot, who was very quick-witted, read my mind, and his eyes twinkled a little.

"But yes, *mon ami,* it was not solely the champagne."

"I didn't mean that."

"But yes—but yes—you thought to yourself: 'The poor old one, he has the spirit of the party, he promises things that he will not perform—that he has no intention of performing.' But, my friend, the promises of Hercule Poirot are sacred."

He drew himself up in a stately manner as he said the last words.

"Of course. Of course. I know that," I said hastily. "But I thought that perhaps your judgment was slightly—what shall I say?—influenced."

"I am not in the habit of letting my judgment be 'influenced' as you call it, Hastings. The best and driest of champagne, the most golden-haired and seductive of women—nothing influences the judgment of Hercule Poirot. No, *mon ami,* I am interested —that is all."

"In Jane Wilkinson's love affair?"

"Not exactly that. Her love affair, as you call it, is a very commonplace business. It is a step in the successful career of a very beautiful woman. If the Duke of Merton had neither a title nor wealth, his romantic likeness to a dreamy monk would no longer interest the lady. No, Hastings, what intrigues me is the psychology of the matter, the interplay of character. I welcome the chance of studying Lord Edgware at close quarters."

"You do not expect to be successful in your mission?"

"*Pourquoi pas?* Every man has his weak spot. Do not imagine, Hastings, that, because I am studying the case from a psychological standpoint, I shall not try my best to succeed in the commission entrusted to me. I always enjoy exercising my ingenuity."

I had feared an allusion to the little grey cells and was thankful to be spared it.

"So we go to Regent Gate at eleven tomorrow," I said.

"We?" Poirot raised his eyebrows quizzically.

"Poirot!" I cried. "You are not going to leave me behind. I always go with you."

"If it were a crime, a mysterious poisoning case, an assassination—ah! those are the things your soul delights in. But a mere matter of social adjustment?"

"Not another word," I said determinedly. "I'm coming."

Poirot laughed gently, and at that moment we were told that a gentleman had called. To our great surprise our visitor proved to be Bryan Martin.

The actor looked older by daylight. He was still handsome but it was a kind of ravaged handsomeness. It flashed across my mind that he might conceivably take drugs. There was a kind of nervous tension about him that suggested the possibility.

"Good morning, M. Poirot," he said in a cheerful manner. "You and Captain Hastings breakfast at a reasonable hour, I am glad to see. By the way, I suppose you are very busy just now?"

Poirot smiled at him amiably.

"No," he said. "At the moment I have practically no business of importance on hand."

"Come now," laughed Bryan. "Not called in by Scotland Yard? No delicate matters to investigate for Royalty? I can hardly believe it."

"You confound fiction with reality, my friend," said Poirot, smiling. "I am, I assure you, at the moment completely out of work, though not yet on the dole. *Dieu merci.*"

"Well, that's luck for me," said Bryan with another laugh. "Perhaps you'll take on something for me."

Poirot considered the young man thoughtfully.

"You have a problem for me—yes?" he said in a minute or two.

"Well—it's like this. I have and I haven't."

This time his laugh was rather nervous. Still considering him thoughtfully, Poirot indicated a chair. The young man took it. He sat facing us, for I had taken a seat by Poirot's side.

"And now," said Poirot, "let us hear all about it."

Bryan Martin still seemed to have a little difficulty in getting under way.

"The trouble is that I can't tell you quite as much as I'd like to." He hesitated. "It's difficult. You see the whole business started in America."

"In America? Yes?"

"A mere incident first drew my attention to it. As a matter of fact I was travelling by train and I noticed a certain fellow —ugly little chap, clean-shaven, glasses, and a gold tooth."

"Ah! a gold tooth."

"Exactly. That's really the crux of the matter."

Poirot nodded his head several times.

"I begin to comprehend. Go on."

"Well, as I say, I just noticed the fellow. I was travelling, by the way, to New York. Six months later, I was in Los Angeles, and I noticed the fellow again. Don't know why I should have —but I did. Still, nothing in that."

"Continue."

"A month afterward, I had occasion to go to Seattle; and shortly after I got there, whom should I see but my friend again, *only this time he wore a beard.*"

"Distinctly curious."

"Wasn't it? Of course I didn't fancy it had anything to do with me at that time, but when I saw the man again in Los Angeles, beardless, in Chicago with a moustache and different eyebrows, and in a mountain village disguised as a hobo—well, I began to wonder."

"Naturally."

"And at last—well, it seemed odd, but not a doubt about it. I was being what you call shadowed."

"Most remarkable."

"Wasn't it? After that I made sure of it. Wherever I was, there, somewhere near at hand, was my shadow, made up in different disguises. Fortunately, owing to the gold tooth, I could always spot him."

"Ah! that gold tooth; it was a very fortunate occurrence."

"It was."

"Pardon me, M. Martin, but did you never speak to the man? Question him as to the reason of his persistent shadowing?"

"No, I didn't." The actor hesitated. "I thought of doing so once or twice, but I always decided against it. It seemed to me that I should merely put the fellow on his guard and learn nothing. Possibly, once they had discovered that I had spotted him, they would have put someone else on my track—someone whom I might not recognize."

"*En effet*—someone without that useful gold tooth."

"Exactly. I may have been wrong, but that's how I figured it out."

"Now, M. Martin, you referred to 'they' just now. Whom did you mean by 'they'?"

"It was a mere figure of speech, used for convenience. I assumed—I don't know why—a nebulous 'they' in the background."

"Have you any reason for that belief?"

"None."

"You mean you have no conception of who could want you shadowed or for what purpose?"

"Not the slightest. At least—"

"*Continuez,*" said Poirot encouragingly.

"I *have* an idea," said Bryan Martin slowly. "It's a mere guess on my part, mind."

"A guess may be very successful sometimes, monsieur."

"It concerns a certain incident that took place in London about two years ago. It was a slight incident, but an inexplicable and an unforgettable one. I've often wondered and puzzled over it. Just because I could find no explanation of it at the time, I am inclined to wonder if this shadowing business might not be connected in some way with it—but for the life of me I can't see why or how."

"Perhaps I can."

"Yes, but you see—" Bryan Martin's embarrassment returned. "The awkward thing is that I can't tell you about it—not now, that is. In a day or so I might be able to."

Stung into further speech by Poirot's inquiring glance he continued desperately:

"You see—a girl was concerned in it."

"Ah! parfaitement! An English girl?"

"Yes. At least— Why?"

"Very simple. You cannot tell me now, but you hope to do so in a day or two. That means that you want to obtain the consent of the young lady. Therefore, she is in England. Also she must have been in England during the time you were shadowed, for if she had been in America you would have sought her out then and there. Therefore since she has been in England for the last eighteen months, she is probably, though not certainly, English. It is good reasoning that, eh?"

"Rather. Now tell me, M. Poirot; if I get her permission, will you look into the matter for me?"

There was a pause. Poirot seemed to be debating the matter in his mind. Finally he said:

"Why have you come to me before going to her?"

"Well, I thought—" He hesitated. "I wanted to persuade her to—to clear things up—I mean to let things be cleared up by you. What I mean is, if *you* investigate the affair, nothing need be made public, need it?"

"That depends," said Poirot calmly.

"What do you mean?"

"If there is any question of crime—"

"Oh! there's no crime concerned."

"You do not know. There may be."

"But you would do your best for her—for us?"

"That, naturally."

He was silent for a moment and then said:

"Tell me, this follower of yours—this shadow—of what age was he?"

"Oh! quite youngish. About thirty."

"Ah!" said Poirot. "That is indeed remarkable. Yes, that makes the whole thing very much more interesting."

I stared at him. So did Bryan Martin. This remark of his was, I am sure, equally inexplicable to us both. Bryan questioned me with a lift of his eyebrows. I shook my head.

"Yes," murmured Poirot. "It makes the whole story very interesting."

"He *may* have been older," said Bryan doubtfully, "but I don't think so."

"No, no, I am sure your observation is quite accurate, M. Martin. Very interesting—extraordinarily interesting."

Rather taken aback by Poirot's enigmatical words, Bryan Martin seemed at a loss what to say or do next. He started making desultory conversation.

"An amusing party the other night," he said. "Jane Wilkinson is the most high-handed woman that ever existed."

"She has the single vision," said Poirot, smiling. "One thing at a time."

"She gets away with it too," said Martin. "How people stand it, I don't know!"

"One will stand a good deal from a beautiful woman, my friend," said Poirot with a twinkle. "If she had the pug dog nose, the sallow skin, the greasy hair, then—ah! then she would not 'get away with it' as you put it."

"I suppose not," conceded Bryan. "But it makes me mad sometimes. All the same, I'm devoted to Jane, though in some ways, mind you, I don't think she's quite all there."

"On the contrary, I should say she was very much on the spot."

"I don't mean that, exactly. She can look after her interests all right. She's got plenty of business shrewdness. No, I meant morally."

"Ah! morally."

"She's what they call amoral. Right and wrong don't exist for her."

"Ah! I remember you said something of the kind the other evening."

"We were talking of crime just now—"

"Yes, my friend?"

"Well, it would never surprise me if Jane committed a crime."

"And you should know her well," murmured Poirot thoughtfully. "You have acted much with her, have you not?"

"Yes. I suppose I know her through and through, and up and down. I can see her killing anybody quite easily."

"Ah! she has the hot temper, yes?"

"No, no, not at all. Cool as a cucumber. I mean if anyone were in her way she'd just remove them—without a thought. And one couldn't really blame her—morally, I mean. She'd just think that anyone who interfered with Jane Wilkinson had got to go."

There was a bitterness in his last words that had been lacking heretofore. I wondered what memory he was recalling.

"You think she would do—murder?"

Poirot watched him intently. Bryan drew a deep breath.

"Upon my soul, I do. Perhaps, one of these days, you'll remember my words. I *know* her, you see. She'd kill as easily as she'd drink her morning tea. *I mean it, M. Poirot.*"

He had risen to his feet.

"Yes," said Poirot quietly. "I can see you mean it."

"I know her," said Bryan Martin again, "through and through."

He stood frowning for a minute, then with a change of tone, he said:

"As to this business we've been talking about—I'll let you know, M. Poirot, in a few days. You will undertake it, won't you?"

Poirot looked at him for a moment or two without replying.

"Yes," he said at last. "I will undertake it. I find it—interesting." There was something queer in the way he said the last word.

I went downstairs with Bryan Martin. At the door he said to me:

"Did you get the hang of what he meant about that fellow's age? I mean why was it interesting that he should be about thirty? I didn't get the hang of that at all."

"No more did I," I admitted.

"It doesn't seem to make sense. Perhaps he was just having a game with me."

"No," I said. "Poirot is not like that. Depend upon it, the point has significance, since he says so."

"Well, blessed if I can see it. Glad you can't either. I'd hate to feel I was a complete mutt."

He strode away. I rejoined my friend.

"Poirot," I said. "What was the point about the age of the shadower?"

"You do not see? My poor Hastings!" He smiled and shook his head. Then he asked: "What did you think of our interview on the whole?"

"There's so little to go upon. It seems difficult to say. If we knew more—"

"Even without knowing more, do not certain ideas suggest themselves to you, *mon ami?*"

The telephone ringing at that moment saved me from the ignominy of admitting that no ideas whatever suggested themselves to me. I took up the receiver.

A woman's voice spoke, a crisp, clear, efficient voice.

"This is Lord Edgware's secretary speaking. Lord Edgware regrets that he must cancel the appointment with M. Poirot for tomorrow morning. He has to go over to Paris tomorrow, unexpectedly. He could see M. Poirot for a few minutes at a quarter past twelve this morning, if that would be convenient."

I consulted Poirot.

"Certainly, my friend, we will go there this morning."

I repeated this into the mouthpiece.

"Very good," said the crisp businesslike voice. "A quarter past twelve this morning."

She rang off.

IV An Interview

I ARRIVED with Poirot at Lord Edgware's house in Regent Gate in a very pleasant state of anticipation. Though I had not Poirot's devotion to "the psychology," yet the few words in which Lady Edgware had referred to her husband had aroused my curiosity. I was anxious to see what my own judgment would be.

The house was an imposing one—well built, handsome and slightly gloomy. There were no window boxes or such frivolities.

The door was opened to us promptly, and by no aged, white-haired butler, such as would have been in keeping with the exterior of the house. On the contrary, it was opened by one of the handsomest young men I have ever seen. Tall, fair, he might have posed to a sculptor for Hermes or Apollo. Despite his good looks, there was something vaguely effeminate that I disliked about the softness of his voice. Also, in a curious way, he reminded me of someone—someone, too, whom I had met quite lately; but who it was I could not for the life of me remember.

We asked for Lord Edgware.

"This way, sir."

He led us along the hall, past the staircase, to a door at the rear of the hall. Opening it, he announced us in that same soft voice which I instinctively distrusted.

The room into which we were shown was a kind of library. The walls were lined with books; the furnishings were dark and sombre but handsome; the chairs were formal and not too comfortable.

Lord Edgware, who rose to receive us, was a tall man of about fifty. He had dark hair streaked with grey, a thin face and a sneering mouth. He looked bad-tempered and bitter. His eyes had a queer, secretive look about them. There was something, I thought, distinctly odd about those eyes. His manner was stiff and formal.

"M. Hercule Poirot? Captain Hastings? Please be seated."

We sat down. The room felt chilly. There was little light coming in from the one window, and the dimness contributed to the cold atmosphere.

Lord Edgware had taken up a letter which I saw to be in my friend's handwriting.

"I am familiar, of course, with your name, M. Poirot. Who is not?" Poirot bowed at the compliment. "But I cannot quite understand your position in this matter. You say that you wish to see me on behalf of—" he paused—"my wife."

He said the last two words in a peculiar way—as though it were an effort to get them out.

"That is so," said my friend.

"I understood that you were an investigator of—crime, M. Poirot?"

"Of problems, Lord Edgware. There are problems of crime, certainly. There are other problems."

"Indeed. And what may this one be?"

The sneer in his words was palpable by now. Poirot took no notice of it.

"I have the honour to approach you on behalf of Lady Edgware," he said. "Lady Edgware, as you may know, desires—a divorce."

"I am quite aware of that," said Lord Edgware coldly.

"Her suggestion was that you and I should discuss the matter."

"There is nothing to discuss."

"You refuse, then?"

"Refuse? Certainly not."

Whatever else Poirot had expected, he had not expected this. It is seldom that I have seen my friend utterly taken aback, but I did on this occasion. His appearance was ludicrous. His mouth fell open, his hands flew out, his eyebrows rose. He looked like a cartoon in a comic paper.

"*Comment?*" he cried. "What is this? You do not refuse?"

"I am at a loss to understand your astonishment, M. Poirot."

"*Ecoutez.* You are willing to divorce your wife?"

"Certainly I am willing. She knows that perfectly well. I wrote and told her so."

"You wrote and told her so?"

"Yes. Six months ago."

"But I do not understand. I do not understand at all."

Lord Edgware said nothing.

"I understood that you were opposed to the principle of divorce."

"I do not see that my principles are your business, M. Poirot. It is true that I did not divorce my first wife. My conscience would not allow me to do so. My second marriage, I will admit frankly, was a mistake. When my wife suggested a divorce, I refused point-blank. Six months ago she wrote to me again, urging the point. I have an idea she wanted to marry again—some film actor or fellow of that kind. My views had, by this time, undergone modification. I wrote to her at Hollywood telling her so. Why she has sent you to me I cannot imagine. I suppose it is a question of money."

His lips sneered again as he said the last words.

"Extremely curious," murmured Poirot. "Extremely curious. There is something here I do not understand at all."

"As regards money," went on Lord Edgware. "I have no intention of making any financial arrangement. My wife deserted me of her own accord. If she wishes to marry another man, I can set her free to do so, but there is no reason why she should receive a penny from me, and she will not do so."

"There is no question of any financial arrangement."

Lord Edgware raised his eyebrows.

"Jane must be marrying a rich man," he murmured cynically.

"There is something here that I do not understand," said Poirot. His face was perplexed and wrinkled with the effort of thought. "I understood from Lady Edgware that she had approached you repeatedly through lawyers?"

"She did," replied Lord Edgware dryly. "English lawyers, American lawyers, every kind of lawyer, down to the lowest kind of scallywag. Finally, as I say, she wrote to me herself."

"You having previously refused?"

"That is so."

"But, on receiving her letter, you changed your mind. Why did you change your mind, Lord Edgware?"

"Not on account of anything in that letter," he said sharply. "My views happened to have changed, that is all."

"The change was somewhat sudden."

Lord Edgware did not reply.

"What special circumstance brought about your change of mind, Lord Edgware?"

"That, really, is my own business, M. Poirot. I cannot enter into that subject. Shall we say that gradually I had perceived the advantages of severing what—you will forgive my plain speaking—I considered a degrading association. My second marriage was a mistake."

"Your wife says the same," said Poirot softly.

"Does she?"

There was a queer flicker for a moment in his eyes, but it was gone almost at once. He rose with an air of finality and, as we said good-bye, his manner became more unbending.

"You must forgive my altering the appointment. I have to go over to Paris tomorrow."

"Perfectly—perfectly."

"A sale of works of art as a matter of fact. I have my eye on a little statuette—a perfect thing in its way—a *macabre* way, perhaps. But I enjoy the *macabre*. I always have. My taste is peculiar."

Again that queer smile. I had been looking at the books in the shelves near. There were the Memoirs of Casanova, also a volume on the Comte de Sade, another on mediæval tortures.

I remembered Jane Wilkinson's little shudder as she spoke of her husband. That had not been acting. That had been real enough. I wondered exactly what kind of a man George Alfred St. Vincent Marsh, fourth Baron Edgware, was.

Very suavely he bade us farewell, touching the bell as he did so. We went out of the door. The Greek god of a butler was waiting in the hall. As I closed the library door behind me, I glanced back into the room. I almost uttered an exclamation as I did so.

That suave, smiling face was transformed. The lips were

drawn back from the teeth in a snarl, the eyes were alive with fury and an almost insane rage.

I wondered no longer that two wives had left Lord Edgware. What I did marvel at was the iron self-control of the man. To have gone through that interview with such frozen self-control, such aloof politeness!

Just as we reached the front door, a door on the right opened. A girl stood at the doorway of the room, shrinking back a little as she saw us. She was a tall, slender girl, with dark hair and a white face. Her eyes, dark and startled, looked for a moment into mine. Then, like a shadow, she shrank back into the room again, closing the door.

A moment later, we were out in the street. Poirot hailed a taxi. We got in and he told the man to drive to the Savoy.

"Well, Hastings," he said with a twinkle. "That interview did not go at all as I figured to myself it would."

"No, indeed. What an extraordinary man Lord Edgware is."

I related to him how I had looked back before closing the door of the study and what I had seen. He nodded his head slowly and thoughtfully.

"I fancy that he is very near the border line of madness, Hastings. I should imagine he practises many curious vices and that beneath his frigid exterior he hides a deep-rooted instinct of cruelty."

"It is no wonder both his wives left him."

"As you say."

"Poirot, did you notice a girl as we were coming out? A dark girl with a white face."

"Yes, I noticed her, *mon ami*. A young lady who was frightened and not happy."

His voice was grave.

"Who do you think she was?"

"Probably his daughter. He has one."

"She did look frightened," I said slowly. "That house must be a gloomy place for a young girl."

"Yes, indeed. Ah! here we are, *mon ami*. Now to acquaint her ladyship with the good news."

Jane was in, and, after telephoning, the clerk informed us that we were to go up. A page boy took us to the door.

It was opened by a neat middle-aged woman, with glasses and primly arranged grey hair. From the bedroom, Jane's voice, with its husky note, called to her.

"Is that M. Poirot, Ellis? Make him sit right down. I'll find a rag to put on and be there in a moment."

Jane Wilkinson's idea of a rag was a gossamer negligee which revealed more than it hid. She came in eagerly, saying: "Well?"

Poirot rose and bowed over her hand.

"Exactly the word, madame; it *is* well."

"Why—how do you mean?"

"Lord Edgware is perfectly willing to agree to a divorce."

"What?"

Either the stupefaction on her face was genuine, or else she was indeed a most marvellous actress.

"M. Poirot! You've managed it! At once! Like that! Why, you're a genius. How in mercy's name did you set about it?"

"Madame, I cannot take compliments where they are not earned. Six months ago, your husband wrote to you withdrawing his opposition."

"What's that you say? *Wrote* to *me?* Where?"

"It was when you were at Hollywood, I understand."

"I never got it. Must have gone astray, I suppose. And to think I've been thinking and planning and fretting and going nearly crazy all these months."

"Lord Edgware seemed to be under the impression that you wished to marry an actor."

"Naturally. That's what I told him." She gave a pleased child's smile. Suddenly it changed to a look of alarm. "Why, M. Poirot, you didn't go and tell him about me and the Duke?"

"No, no; reassure yourself. I am discreet. That would not have done, eh?"

"Well, you see he's got a queer mean nature. Marrying Merton, he'd feel, was perhaps a kind of leg up for me—so then naturally he'd queer the pitch. But a film actor's different. Though all the same I'm surprised. Yes, I am. Aren't you surprised, Ellis?"

I had noticed that the maid had come to and fro from the bedroom tidying away various outdoor garments which were lying flung over the backs of chairs. It had been my opinion that she had been listening to the conversation. Now it seemed that she was completely in Jane's confidence.

"Yes, indeed, m'lady. His lordship must have changed a good deal since we knew him," said the maid spitefully.

"Yes, he must."

"You cannot understand his attitude. It puzzles you?" suggested Poirot.

"Oh! it does. But anyway we needn't worry about that. What does it matter what made him change his mind, so long as he has changed it?"

"It may not interest you but it interests me, madame."

Jane paid no attention to him.

"The thing is that I'm free—at last."

"Not yet, madame."

She looked at him impatiently.

"Well, going to be free. It's the same thing."

Poirot looked as though he did not think it was.

"The Duke is in Paris," said Jane. "I must cable him right away. My—won't his old mother be wild!"

Poirot rose.

"I am glad, madame, that all is turning out as you wish."

"Good-bye, M. Poirot, and thanks awfully."

"I did nothing."

"You brought me the good news, anyway, M. Poirot, and I'm ever so grateful. I *really* am."

"And that is that," said Poirot to me, as we left the suite. "The single idea—herself! She has no speculation, no curiosity as to why that letter never reached her. You observe, Hastings, she is shrewd beyond belief in the business sense, but she has absolutely no intellect. Well, well, the good God cannot give everything."

"Except to Hercule Poirot," I said slyly.

"You mock yourself at me, my friend," he replied serenely. "But come, let us walk along the Embankment. I wish to arrange my ideas with order and method."

I maintained a discreet silence until such time as the oracle should speak.

"That letter," he resumed, when we were pacing along by the river. "It intrigues me. There are four solutions of that problem, my friend."

"Four?"

"Yes. First it was lost in the post. That *does* happen, you know. But not very often. No, not very often. Incorrectly addressed, it would have been returned to Lord Edgware long before this. No, I am inclined to rule out that solution—though of course it may be the true one.

"Solution two; our beautiful lady is lying when she says she never received it. That, of course, is quite possible. That charming lady is capable of telling any lie to her advantage, with the most childlike candour. But I cannot see, Hastings, how it could be to her advantage. If she knows that he will divorce her, why send me to ask him to do so? It does not make sense.

"Solution three. Lord Edgware is lying. And if anyone is lying it seems more likely that it is he than his wife. But I do not see much point in such a lie. Why invent a fictitious letter sent six months ago? Why not simply agree to my proposition? No, I am inclined to think that he *did* send that letter—though what the motive was for his sudden change of attitude I cannot guess.

"So we come to the fourth solution—that someone suppressed that letter. And there, Hastings, we enter on a very interesting field of speculation, because that letter could have been suppressed at either end—in America or England.

"Whoever suppressed it was someone who did not want that marriage dissolved. Hastings, I would give a great deal to know what is behind that affair. There is *something*—I swear there is something."

He paused and then added slowly:

"Something of which as yet I have only been able to get a glimpse."

V Murder

THE following day was the thirtieth of June. It was just half past nine when we were told that Inspector Japp was below and anxious to see us. It was some years since we had seen anything of the Scotland Yard Inspector.

"*Ah! ce bon Japp,*" said Poirot. "What does he want, I wonder?"

"Help," I snapped. "He's out of his depth over some case, and he's come to you."

I had not the indulgence for Japp that Poirot had. It was not so much that I minded his picking Poirot's brains. After all, Poirot enjoyed the process, it was a delicate flattery. What did annoy me was Japp's hypocritical pretence that he was doing nothing of the kind. I liked people to be straightforward. I said so, and Poirot laughed.

"You are the dog of the bulldog breed, eh, Hastings? But you must remember that the poor Japp, he has to save his face. So he makes his little pretence. It is very natural."

I thought it merely foolish and said so. Poirot did not agree.

"The outward form—it is a *bagatelle*—but it matters to people. It enables them to keep the *amour propre.*"

Personally I thought a dash of inferiority complex would do Japp no harm, but there was no point in arguing the matter. Besides I was anxious to learn what Japp had come about.

He greeted us both heartily.

"Just going to have breakfast, I see. Not got the hens to lay square eggs for you yet, M. Poirot?"

This was an illusion to a complaint from Poirot as to the varying sizes of eggs which had offended his sense of symmetry.

"As yet, no," said Poirot, smiling. "And what brings you to see us so early, my good Japp?"

"It's not early—not for me. I've been up and at work for a

good two hours. As to what brings me to see you—well, it's murder."

"Murder?"

Japp nodded.

"Lord Edgware was killed at his house in Regent Gate last night. Stabbed in the neck by his wife."

"By his wife?" I cried.

In a flash, I remembered Bryan Martin's words on the previous morning. Had he had a prophetic knowledge of what was going to happen? I remembered, too, Jane's easy reference to "bumping him off." Amoral, Bryan Martin had called her. She was the type, yes. Callous, egoistical and stupid. How right he had been in his judgment.

All this passed through my mind while Japp went on:

"Yes. Actress, you know. Well known. Jane Wilkinson. Married him three years ago. They didn't get on. She left him."

Poirot was looking puzzled and serious.

"What makes you believe that it was she who killed him?"

"No belief about it. She was recognized. Not much concealment about it, either. She drove up in a taxi—"

"A taxi—" I echoed involuntarily, her words at the Savoy that night coming back to me.

"Rang the bell, asked for Lord Edgware. It was ten o'clock. Butler said he'd see. 'Oh!' she says, cool as a cucumber. 'You needn't. I am Lady Edgware. I suppose he's in the library.' And with that she walks along and opens the door and goes in and shuts it behind her.

"Well, the butler thought it was queer, but all right. He went downstairs again. About ten minutes later he heard the front door shut. So anyway she hadn't stayed long. He locked up for the night about eleven. He opened the library door, but it was dark, so he thought his master had gone to bed. This morning the body was discovered by a housemaid. Stabbed in the back of the neck just at the roots of the hair."

"Was there no cry? Nothing heard?"

"They say not. That library's got pretty well soundproof doors, you know. And there's traffic passing, too. Stabbed in that way, death results amazing quick. Straight through the cistern into the medulla, that's what the doctor said—or something very like it. If you hit on exactly the right spot, it kills a man instantaneously."

"That implies a knowledge of exactly where to strike. It almost implies medical knowledge."

"Yes—that's true. A point in her favour as far as it goes. But ten to one it was a chance. She just struck lucky. Some people do have amazing luck, you know."

"Not so lucky if it results in her being hanged, *mon ami,*" observed Poirot.

"No. Of course she was a fool—sailing in like that and giving her name and all."

"Indeed very curious."

"Possibly she didn't intend mischief. They quarrelled and she whipped out a penknife and jabbed him one."

"Was it a penknife?"

"Something of that kind, the doctor says. Whatever it was, she took it away with her. It wasn't left in the wound."

Poirot shook his head in a dissatisfied manner.

"No, no, my friend, it was not like that. I know the lady. She would be quite incapable of such a hot-blooded, impulsive action. Besides she would be most unlikely to have a penknife with her. Few women have—and assuredly not Jane Wilkinson."

"You know her, you say, M. Poirot?"

"Yes. I know her."

He said no more for the moment. Japp was looking at him inquisitively.

"Got something up your sleeve, M. Poirot?" he ventured at last.

"Ah!" said Poirot. "That reminds me. What has brought you to me? Eh? It is not merely to pass the time of day with an old comrade? Assuredly not. You have here a nice straightforward murder. You have the criminal. You have the motive. What exactly is the motive, by the way?"

"Wanted to marry another man. She was heard to say so not a week ago. Also heard to make threats. Said she meant to call round in a taxi and bump him off."

"Ah!" said Poirot. "You are very well informed—very well informed. Someone has been very obliging."

I thought his eyes looked a question; but, if so, Japp did not respond.

"We get to hear things, M. Poirot," he said stolidly.

Poirot nodded. He had reached out for the daily paper. It had been opened by Japp, doubtless while he was waiting, and had been cast impatiently aside on our entry. In a mechanical manner, Poirot folded it back at the middle page, smoothed and arranged it. Though his eyes were on the paper, his mind was deep in some kind of puzzle.

"You have not answered," he said presently. "Since all goes in the swimming fashion, why come to me?"

"Because I heard you were at Regent Gate yesterday morning."

"I see."

"Now as soon as I heard that, I said to myself, 'Something here.' His lordship sent for M. Poirot. Why? What did he suspect? What did he fear? Before doing anything definite, I'd better go round and have a word with him."

"What do you mean by 'anything definite'? Arresting the lady, I suppose?"

"Exactly."

"You have not seen her yet?"

"Oh! yes, I have. Went round to the Savoy first thing. Wasn't going to risk her giving us the slip."

"Ah!" said Poirot. "So you—"

He stopped. His eyes, which had been fixed thoughtfully and up to now unseeingly on the paper in front of him, now took on a different expression. He lifted his head and spoke in a changed tone of voice.

"And what did she say? Eh! my friend. What did she say?"

"I gave her the usual stuff, of course, about wanting a statement and cautioning her. You can't say the English police aren't fair."

"In my opinion, foolishly so. But proceed. What did milady say?"

"Took hysterics—that's what she did. Rolled herself about,

threw up her arms and finally flopped down on the ground. Oh! she did it well—I'll say that for her. A pretty bit of acting."

"Ah!" said Poirot blandly. "You formed then, the impression that the hysterics were not genuine?"

Japp winked vulgarly.

"What do you think? I'm not to be taken in with those tricks. *She* hadn't fainted—not she! Just trying it on, she was. I'll swear she was enjoying it."

"Yes," said Poirot thoughtfully. "I should say that was perfectly possible. What next?"

"Oh! well, she came to—pretended to, I mean. And moaned, *and* groaned, and carried on; and that sour-faced maid of hers doped her with smelling salts; and at last she recovered enough to ask for her solicitor. Wasn't going to say anything without her solicitor. Hysterics one moment, solicitor the next, now I ask you, is that natural behaviour, sir?"

"In this case quite natural, I should say," said Poirot calmly.

"You mean because she's guilty and knows it."

"Not at all, I mean because of her temperament. First she gives you her conception of how the part of a wife suddenly learning of her husband's death should be played. Then, having satisfied her histrionic instinct, her native shrewdness makes her send for a solicitor. That she creates an artificial scene, and enjoys it, is no proof of her guilt. It merely indicates that she is a born actress."

"Well, she can't be innocent. That's sure."

"You are very positive," said Poirot. "I suppose that it must be so. She made no statement, you say? No statement at all?"

Japp grinned.

"Wouldn't say a word without her solicitor. The maid telephoned for him. I left two of my men there and came along to you. I thought it just as well to get put wise to whatever there was going on before I went on with things."

"And yet you are sure?"

"Of course I'm sure. But I like as many facts as possible. You see there's going to be a big splash made about this. No hole-and-corner business. All the papers will be full of it. And you know what papers are."

"Talking of papers," said Poirot, "how do you account for this, my dear friend? You have not read your morning paper very carefully."

He leant across the table, his finger on a paragraph in the Society news. Japp read the item aloud.

"Sir Montagu Corner gave a very successful dinner-party last night at his house on the river at Chiswick. Among those present were Sir George and Lady du Fisse, Mr. James Blunt, the well-known dramatic critic, Sir Oscar Hammerfeldt of the Overton Film Studios, Miss Jane Wilkinson (Lady Edgware) and others."

For a moment Japp looked taken aback. Then he rallied.

"What's that got to do with it? This thing was sent to the Press beforehand. You'll see. You'll find that our lady wasn't there, or that she came in late—eleven o'clock or so. Bless you, sir, you mustn't believe everything you see in the press to be gospel. You of all people ought to know better than that."

"Oh! I do, I do. It only struck me as curious, that was all."

"These coincidences do happen. Now, M. Poirot, close as an oyster I know you to be by bitter experience. But you'll come across with things, won't you? You'll tell me why Lord Edgware sent for you?"

Poirot shook his head.

"Lord Edgware did not send for me. It was I who requested him to give me an appointment."

"Really? And for what reason?"

Poirot hesitated a minute.

"I will answer your question," he said slowly, "but I should like to answer it in my own way."

Japp groaned. I felt a sneaking sympathy with him. Poirot can be intensely irritating at times.

"I will request," went on Poirot, "that you permit me to ring up a certain person and ask him to come here."

"What person?"

"Mr. Bryan Martin."

"The film star? What's he got to do with it?"

"I think," said Poirot, "that you may find what he has got to say interesting—and possibly helpful. Hastings, will you be so good?"

I took up the telephone book. The actor had a flat in a big block of buildings near St. James' Park.

"Victoria 49499."

The somewhat sleepy voice of Bryan Martin spoke after a few minutes.

"Hello—who's speaking?"

"What am I to say?" I whispered, covering the mouthpiece with my hand.

"Tell him," said Poirot, "that Lord Edgware has been murdered, and that I should esteem it a favour if he would come round here and see me immediately."

I repeated this meticulously. There was a startled exclamation at the other end.

"My God," said Martin. "So she's done it then! I'll come at once."

"What did he say?" asked Poirot.

I told him.

"Ah!" said Poirot. He seemed pleased. " *'So she's done it then.'* That is what he said? Then it is as I thought; it is as I thought."

Japp looked at him curiously.

"I can't make you out, M. Poirot. First you sound as though you thought the woman might not have done it after all. And now you make out that you knew it all along."

Poirot only smiled.

VI The Widow

BRYAN MARTIN was as good as his word. In less than ten minutes he had joined us. During the time that we awaited his arrival, Poirot would talk only of extraneous subjects and refused to satisfy Japp's curiosity in the smallest degree.

Evidently our news had upset the young actor terribly. His face was white and drawn.

"Good heavens, M. Poirot," he said as he shook hands, "this is a terrible business. I'm shocked to the core—and yet I can't say I'm surprised. I've always half suspected that something of this kind might happen. You may remember I was saying so yesterday."

"*Mais oui, mais oui,*" said Poirot. "I remember perfectly what you said to me yesterday. Let me introduce you to Inspector Japp who is in charge of the case."

Bryan Martin shot a glance of reproach at Poirot.

"I had no idea," he murmured. "You should have warned me."

He nodded coldly to the inspector.

He sat down, his lips pressed tightly together.

"I don't see," he objected, "why you asked me to come round. All this has nothing to do with me."

"I think it has," said Poirot gently. "In a case of murder one must put one's private repugnances behind one."

"No, no. I've acted with Jane. I know her well. Dash it all, she's a friend of mine."

"And yet the moment that you hear Lord Edgware is murdered, you jump to the conclusion that it is she who has murdered him," remarked Poirot dryly.

The actor started.

"Do you mean to say—?" His eyes seemed starting out of his

head. "Do you mean to say that I'm wrong? That she had nothing to do with it?"

Japp broke in.

"No, no, Mr. Martin. She did it right enough."

The young man sank back again in his chair.

"For a moment," he murmured, "I thought I'd made the most ghastly mistake."

"In a matter of this kind friendship must not be allowed to influence you," said Poirot decisively.

"That's all very well, but—"

"My friend, do you seriously wish to range yourself on the side of a woman who has murdered? Murder—the most repugnant of human crimes."

Bryan Martin sighed.

"You don't understand. Jane is not an ordinary murderess. She—she has no sense of right or wrong. Honestly she's not responsible."

"That'll be a question for the jury," said Japp.

"Come, come," said Poirot kindly. "It is not as though you were accusing her. She is already accused. You cannot refuse to tell us what you know. You have a duty to society, young man."

Bryan Martin sighed.

"I suppose you're right," he said. "What do you want me to tell you?"

Poirot looked at Japp.

"Have you ever heard Lady Edgware—or perhaps I'd better call her Miss Wilkinson—utter threats against her husband?" asked Japp.

"Yes, several times."

"What did she say?"

"She said that if he didn't give her her freedom she'd have to 'bump him off.'"

"And that was not a joke, eh?"

"No. I think she meant it seriously. Once she said she'd take a taxi and go round and kill him—*you* heard that, M. Poirot?"

He appealed pathetically to my friend. Poirot nodded. Japp went on with his questions.

"Now, Mr. Martin, we've been informed that she wanted her freedom in order to marry another man. Do you know who that man was?"

Bryan nodded.

"Who?"

"It was—the Duke of Merton."

"The Duke of Merton! Whew!" The detective whistled. "Flying at high game, eh? Why, he's said to be one of the richest men in England."

Bryan nodded more dejectedly than ever.

I could not quite understand Poirot's attitude. He was lying back in his chair, his fingers pressed together, and the rhythmic motion of his head suggested the complete approval of a man who has put a chosen record on the gramophone and is enjoying the result.

"Wouldn't her husband divorce her?"

"No, he refused absolutely."

"You know that for a fact?"

"Yes."

"And now," said Poirot, suddenly taking part once more in the proceedings, "you see where I come in, my good Japp. I was asked by Lady Edgware to see her husband and try to get him to agree to a divorce. I had an appointment for this morning."

Bryan Martin shook his head.

"It would have been of no use," he declared confidently. "Edgware would never have agreed."

"You think not?" said Poirot, turning an amiable glance on him.

"Sure of it. Jane knew that in her heart of hearts. She'd no real confidence that you'd succeed. She'd given up hope. The man was a monomaniac on the subject of divorce."

Poirot smiled. His eyes grew suddenly very green.

"You are wrong, my dear young man," he said gently. "I saw Lord Edgware yesterday, and he agreed to a divorce."

There was no doubt that Bryan Martin was completely dumbfounded by this piece of news. He stared at Poirot with his eyes almost starting out of his head.

"You—you saw him yesterday?" he spluttered.

"At a quarter past twelve," said Poirot in his methodical manner.

"And he agreed to a divorce?"

"He agreed to a divorce."

"You should have told Jane at once," cried the young man reproachfully.

"I did, M. Martin."

"You did?" cried Martin and Japp together.

Poirot smiled.

"It impairs the motive a little, does it not?" he murmured. "And now, M. Martin, let me call your attention to this."

He showed him the newspaper paragraph.

Bryan read it, but without much interest.

"You mean this makes an alibi?" he said. "I suppose Edgware was shot some time yesterday evening?"

"He was stabbed, not shot," said Poirot.

Martin laid the paper down slowly.

"I'm afraid this does no good," he said regretfully. "Jane didn't go to that dinner."

"How do you know?"

"I forget. Somebody told me."

"That is a pity," said Poirot thoughtfully.

Japp looked at him curiously.

"I can't make you out, Moosior. Seems now as though you don't want the young woman to be guilty."

"No, no, my good Japp. I am not the partisan you think. But frankly, the case as you present it, revolts the intelligence."

"What do you mean, revolts the intelligence? It doesn't revolt mine."

I could see words trembling on Poirot's lips. He restrained them.

"Here is a young woman who wishes, you say, to get rid of her husband. That point I do not dispute. She told me so frankly. *Eh bien,* how does she set about it? She repeats several times in the loud clear voice before witnesses that she is thinking of killing him. She then goes out one evening, calls at his house, has herself announced, stabs him and goes away. What do you call that, my good friend? Has it even the common sense?"

"It was a bit foolish, of course."

"Foolish? It is the imbecility!"

"Well," said Japp, rising. "It's all to the advantage of the police when criminals lose their heads. I must go back to the Savoy now."

"You permit that I accompany you?"

Japp made no demur, and we set out. Bryan Martin took a reluctant leave of us. He seemed to be in a great state of nervous excitement. He begged earnestly that any further development might be reported to him.

"Nervy sort of chap," was Japp's comment on him. Poirot agreed.

At the Savoy we found an extremely legal-looking gentleman who had just arrived, and we proceeded all together to Jane's suite. Japp spoke to one of his men.

"Anything?" he inquired laconically.

"She wanted to use the telephone!"

"Who did she telephone to?" inquired Japp eagerly.

"Jay's. For mourning."

Japp swore under his breath. We entered the suite.

The widowed Lady Edgware was trying on hats in front of the glass. She was dressed in a filmy creation of black and white. She greeted us with a dazzling smile.

"Why, M. Poirot, how good of you to come along. Mr. Moxon" (this was to the solicitor), "I'm so glad you've come. Just sit right by me and tell me what questions I ought to answer. This man here seems to think that I went out and killed George this morning."

"Last night, madam," said Japp.

"You said this morning. Ten o'clock."

"I said ten P.M."

"Well, I can never tell which is which—A.M.'s and P.M.'s."

"It's only just about ten o'clock now," added the inspector severely.

Jane's eyes opened very wide.

"Mercy," she murmured. "It's years since I've been awake as early as this. Why, it must have been early dawn when you came along."

"One moment, Inspector," said Mr. Moxon in his ponderous

legal voice. "When am I to understand that this—er—regrettable
—most shocking—occurrence took place?"

"Round about ten o'clock last night, sir."

"Why, that's all right," said Jane sharply. "I was at a party—
Oh!" she covered her mouth up suddenly. "Perhaps I oughtn't
to have said that."

Her eyes sought the solicitor's in timid appeal.

"If, at ten o'clock last night, you were—er—at a party, Lady
Edgware, I—er—I can see no objection to your informing the
inspector of the fact—no objection whatever."

"That's right," said Japp. "I only asked you for a statement of
your movements yesterday evening."

"You didn't. You said ten something M. And anyway you
gave me the most terrible shock. I fainted dead away, Mr.
Moxon."

"About this party, Lady Edgware?"

"It was at Sir Montagu Corner's—at Chiswick."

"What time did you go there?"

"The dinner was for eight-thirty."

"You left here—when?"

"I started about eight o'clock. I dropped in at the Piccadilly
Palace for a moment, to say good-bye to an American friend
who was leaving for the States—Mrs. Van Dusen. I got to
Chiswick at a quarter to nine."

"What time did you leave?"

"About half past eleven."

"You came straight back here?"

"Yes."

"In a taxi?"

"No. In my own car. I hire it from the Daimler people."

"And while you were at the dinner party you didn't leave it?"

"Well—I—"

"So you did leave it?"

It was like a terrier pouncing on a rat.

"I don't know what you mean. I was called to the telephone
when we were at dinner."

"Who called you?"

"I guess it was some kind of hoax. A voice said, 'Is that Lady

Edgware?' And I said, 'Yes, that's right,' and then they just laughed and rang off."

"Did you go outside the house to telephone?"

Jane's eyes opened wide in amazement.

"Of course not."

"How long were you away from the dinner table?"

"About a minute and a half."

Japp collapsed after that. I was fully convinced that he did not believe a word she was saying, but, having heard her story, he could do no more until he had confirmed or disproved it.

Having thanked her coldly, he withdrew. We also took our leave, but she called Poirot back.

"M. Poirot. Will you do something for me?"

"Certainly, madame."

"Send a cable for me to the Duke in Paris. He's at the Crillon. He ought to know about this. I don't like to send it myself. I guess I've got to look the bereaved widow for a week or two."

"It is quite unnecessary to cable, madame," said Poirot gently. "It will be in the papers over there."

"Why, what a headpiece you've got! Of course it will. Much better not to cable. I feel it's up to me to keep up my position, now everything's gone right. I want to act the way a widow should. Sort of dignified, you know. I thought of sending a wreath of orchids. They're about the most expensive things going. I suppose I shall have to go to the funeral. What do you think?"

"You will have to go to the inquest first, madame."

"Why, I suppose that's true." She considered for a moment or two. "I don't like that Scotland Yard inspector at all. He just scared me to death. M. Poirot?"

"Yes?"

"Seems it's kind of lucky I changed my mind and went to that party after all."

Poirot had been going towards the door. Suddenly, at these words, he wheeled round.

"What is that you say, madame? You changed your mind?"

"Yes. I meant to give it a miss. I had a frightful headache yesterday afternoon."

Poirot swallowed once or twice. He seemed to have a difficulty in speaking.

"Did you—say so to anyone?" he asked at last.

"Certainly I did. There was quite a crowd of us having tea and they wanted me to go on to a cocktail party and I said 'No.' I said my head was aching fit to split and that I was going right home and that I was going to cut the dinner too."

"And what made you change your mind, madame?"

"Ellis went on at me. Said I couldn't afford to turn it down. Old Sir Montagu pulls a lot of strings, you know, and he's a crotchety creature—takes offence easily. Well, I didn't care. Once I marry Merton I'm through with all this. But Ellis is always on the cautious side. She said there's many a slip, et cetera, and after all I guess she's right. Anyway, off I went."

"You owe Ellis a debt of gratitude, madame," said Poirot seriously.

"I suppose I do. That inspector had got it all taped out, hadn't he?"

She laughed. Poirot did not. He said in a low voice:

"All the same—this gives one furiously to think. Yes, furiously to think."

"Ellis," called Jane.

The maid came in from the next room.

"M. Poirot says it's very lucky you made me go to that party last night."

Ellis barely cast a glance at Poirot. She was looking grim and disapproving.

"It doesn't do to break engagements, m'lady. You're much too fond of doing it. People don't always forgive it. They turn nasty."

Jane picked up the hat she had been trying on when we came in. She tried it again.

"I hate black," she said disconsolately. "I never wear it. But, I suppose, as a correct widow, I've just got to. All those hats are too frightful. Ring up the other hat place, Ellis. I've got to be fit to be seen."

Poirot and I slipped quietly from the room.

VII The Secretary

WE had not seen the last of Japp. He reappeared about an hour later, flung down his hat on the table and said he was eternally blasted.

"You have made the inquiries?" asked Poirot sympathetically.

Japp nodded gloomily.

"And unless fourteen people are lying, she didn't do it," he growled. He went on: "I don't mind telling you, M. Poirot, that I expected to find a put-up job. On the face of it, it didn't seem likely that anyone else could have killed Lord Edgware. She's the only person who's got the ghost of a motive."

"I would not say that. *Mais continuez.*"

"Well, as I say, I expected to find a put-up job. You know what these theatrical crowds are—they'd all hang together to screen a pal. But this is rather a different proposition. The people there last night were all big guns; they were none of them close friends of hers, and some of them didn't know each other. Their testimony is independent and reliable. I hoped then to find that she'd slipped away for half an hour or so. She could easily have done that—powdering her nose or some excuse. But no. She did leave the dinner table, as she told us, to answer a telephone call, but the butler was with her—and by the way it was just as she told us. He heard what she said. 'Yes, quite right. This is Lady Edgware.' And then the other side rang off. It's curious, that, you know. Not that it's got anything to do with it."

"Perhaps not—but it is interesting. Was it a man or a woman who rang up?"

"A woman, I think she said."

"Curious," said Poirot thoughtfully.

"Never mind that," said Japp impatiently. "Let's get back to the important part. The whole evening went exactly as she said. She got there at a quarter to nine, left at half past eleven and got back here at a quarter to twelve. I've seen the chauffeur who drove her—he's one of Daimler's regular people. And the people at the Savoy saw her come in, and confirm the time."

"*Eh! bien,* that seems very conclusive."

"Then what about those two in Regent Gate? It isn't only the butler. Lord Edgware's secretary saw her too. They both swear by all that's holy that it was Lady Edgware who came there at ten o'clock."

"How long has the butler been there?"

"Six months. Handsome chap, by the way."

"Yes, indeed. *Eh bien,* my friend, if he has only been there six months he cannot have recognized Lady Edgware, since he had not seen her before."

"Well, he knew her from her pictures in the papers. And anyway, the secretary knew her. She's been with Lord Edgware five or six years, and she's the only one who's absolutely positive."

"Ah!" said Poirot. "I should like to see the secretary."

"Well, why not come along with me now?"

"Thank you, *mon ami,* I should be delighted to do so. You include Hastings in your invitation, I hope?"

Japp grinned.

"What do you think? Where the master goes, there the dog follows," he added, in what I could not think was the best of taste.

"Reminds me of the Elizabeth Canning Case," said Japp. "You remember? How at least a score of witnesses on either side swore they had seen the gipsy, Mary Squires, in two different parts of England. Good reputable witnesses, too. And she with such a hideous face there couldn't be two like it. That mystery was never cleared up. It's very much the same here. Here's a separate lot of people prepared to swear a woman was in two different places at the same time. Which of 'em is speaking the truth?"

"That ought not to be difficult to find out?"

"So you say—but this woman, Miss Carroll, really *knew* Lady

Edgware. I mean she'd lived in the house with her day after day. She wouldn't be likely to make a mistake."

"We shall soon see."

"Who comes into the title?" I asked.

"A nephew, Captain Ronald Marsh. Bit of a waster, I understand."

"What does the doctor say as to the time of death?" asked Poirot.

"We'll have to wait for the autopsy, to be exact, you know. See where the dinner had got to." Japp's way of putting things was, I am sorry to say, far from refined. "But ten o'clock fits in well enough. He was last seen alive at a few minutes past nine, when he left the dinner table and the butler took whisky and soda into the library. At eleven o'clock, when the butler went up to bed, the light was out—so he must have been dead then. He wouldn't have been sitting in the dark."

Poirot nodded thoughtfully. A moment or two later we drew up to the house, the blinds of which were now down. The door was opened to us by the handsome butler.

Japp took the lead and went in first. Poirot and I followed. The door opened to the left, so that the butler stood against the wall on that side. Poirot was on my right and, since he is smaller than I am, it was only just as we stepped into the hall that the butler saw him. Being close to him, I heard the sudden intake of his breath and looked sharply at the man to find him staring at Poirot with a kind of startled fear visible on his face. I put the fact away in my mind for what it might be worth.

Japp marched into the dining-room, which lay on our right, and called the butler in after him.

"Now then, Alton, I want to go into this again very carefully. It was ten o'clock when this lady came?"

"Her ladyship? Yes, sir."

"How did you recognize her?" asked Poirot.

"She told her name, sir; and besides I've seen her portrait in the papers. I've seen her act, too."

Poirot nodded.

"How was she dressed?"

"In black, sir. Black walking dress, and a small black hat. A string of pearls and grey gloves."

Poirot looked a question at Japp.

"White taffeta evening dress and ermine wrap," said the latter succinctly.

The butler proceeded. His tale tallied exactly with that which Japp had already passed on to us.

"Did anybody else come to see your master that evening?" asked Poirot.

"No, sir."

"How was the front door fastened?"

"It has a Yale lock, sir. I usually draw the bolts when I go to bed, sir. At eleven, that is. But last night Miss Geraldine was at the opera so it was left unbolted."

"How was it fastened this morning?"

"It was bolted, sir. Miss Geraldine had bolted it when she came in."

"When did she come in? Do you know?"

"I think it was about a quarter to twelve, sir."

"Then during the evening, until a quarter to twelve, the door could not be opened from outside without a key? From the inside it could be opened by simply drawing back the handle."

"Yes, sir."

"How many latchkeys were there?"

"His lordship had his, sir, and there was another key in the hall drawer, which Miss Geraldine took last night. I don't know if there were any others."

"Does nobody else in the house have a key?"

"No, sir. Miss Carroll always rings."

Poirot intimated that that was all he wished to ask, and we went in search of the secretary. We found her busily writing at a large desk.

Miss Carroll was a pleasant, efficient-looking woman of about forty-five. Her fair hair was turning grey, and she wore pince-nez, through which a pair of shrewd blue eyes gleamed out on us. When she spoke I recognized the clear, businesslike voice that had spoken to me through the telephone.

"Ah! M. Poirot," she said as she acknowledged Japp's introduction. "Yes. It was with you I made that appointment for yesterday morning."

"Precisely, mademoiselle."

I thought that Poirot was favourably impressed by her. Certainly she was neatness and precision personified.

"Well, Inspector Japp?" said Miss Carroll. "What more can I do for you?"

"Just this. Are you absolutely certain that it was Lady Edgware who came here last night?"

"That's the third time you've asked me. Of course, I'm sure. I saw her."

"Where did you see her, mademoiselle?"

"In the hall. She spoke to the butler for a minute, then she went along the hall and in at the library door."

"And where were you?"

"On the first floor—looking down."

"And you are positive you were not mistaken."

"Absolutely. I saw her face distinctly."

"You could not have been misled by a resemblance?"

"Certainly not. Jane Wilkinson's features are quite unique. It was her."

Japp threw a glance at Poirot as much to say: "You see."

"Had Lord Edgware any enemies?" asked Poirot suddenly.

"Nonsense," said Miss Carroll.

"How do you mean—nonsense, mademoiselle?"

"Enemies! People in these days don't have *enemies*. Not English people!"

"Yet Lord Edgware was murdered."

"That was his wife," said Miss Carroll.

"A wife is not an enemy—no?"

"I'm sure it was a most extraordinary thing to happen. I've never heard of such a thing happening—I mean to anyone in our class of life."

It was clearly Miss Carroll's idea that murders were only committed by drunken members of the lower classes.

"How many keys are there to the front door?"

"Two," replied Miss Carroll promptly. "Lord Edgware always carried one. The other was kept in the drawer in the hall, so that anybody who was going to be late in could take it. There was a third one, but Captain Marsh lost it. Very careless."

"Did Captain Marsh come much to the house?"

"He used to live here until three years ago."

"Why did he leave?" asked Japp.

"I don't know. He couldn't get on with his uncle, I suppose."

"I think you know a little more than that, mademoiselle," said Poirot gently.

She darted a quick glance at him.

"I am not one to gossip, M. Poirot."

"But you can tell us the truth concerning the rumours of a serious disagreement between Lord Edgware and his nephew."

"It wasn't so serious as all that. Lord Edgware was a difficult man to get on with."

"Even you found that?"

"I'm not speaking of myself. I never had any disagreements with Lord Edgware. He always found me perfectly reliable."

"But as regards Captain Marsh—"

Poirot stuck to it, gently continuing to goad her into further revelations.

Miss Carroll shrugged her shoulders.

"He was extravagant. Got into debt. There was some other trouble—I don't know exactly what. They quarrelled. Lord Edgware forbade him the house. That's all."

Her mouth closed firmly. Evidently she intended to say no more.

The room we had interviewed her in was on the first floor. As we left it, Poirot took me by the arm.

"A little minute. Remain here if you will, Hastings. I am going down with Japp. Watch till we have gone into the library, then join us there."

I have long ago given up asking Poirot questions beginning "Why?" Like the Light Brigade, "Mine not to reason why, mine but to do or die," though fortunately it has not yet come to dying! I thought that possibly he suspected the butler of spying on him and wanted to know if such were really the case.

I took up my stand looking over the banisters. Poirot and Japp went first to the front door—out of my sight. Then they reappeared, walking slowly along the hall. I followed their backs with my eye until they had gone into the library. I waited a minute or two, in case the butler appeared, but there was no sign of anyone, so I ran down the stairs and joined them.

The body had, of course, been removed. The curtains were drawn and the electric light was on. Poirot and Japp were standing in the middle of the room looking round them.

"Nothing here," Japp was saying.

And Poirot replied with a smile:

"Alas! not the cigarette ash—nor the footprint—nor a lady's glove—nor even a lingering perfume! Nothing that the detective of fiction so conveniently finds."

"The police are always made out to be as blind as bats in detective stories," said Japp with a grin.

"I found a clue once," said Poirot dreamily. "But since it was four feet long instead of four centimetres no one would believe in it."

I remembered the circumstance and laughed. Then I remembered my mission.

"It's all right, Poirot," I said. "I watched, but no one was spying upon you as far as I could see."

"The eyes of my friend Hastings," said Poirot in a kind of gentle mockery. "Tell me, my friend, did you notice the rose between my lips?"

"The rose between your lips?" I asked in astonishment. Japp turned aside spluttering with laughter.

"You'll be the death of me, M. Poirot," he said. "The death of me. A rose. What next?"

"I had the fancy to pretend I was Carmen," said Poirot quite undisturbed.

I wondered if they were going mad or if I was.

"You did not observe it, Hastings?" There was reproach in Poirot's voice.

"No," I said, staring. "But then I couldn't see your face."

"No matter." He shook his head gently.

Were they making fun of me?

"Well," said Japp. "No more to do here, I fancy. I'd like to see the daughter again if I could. She was too upset before for me to get anything out of her."

He rang the bell for the butler.

"Ask Miss Marsh if I can see her for a few moments?"

The man departed. It was not he, however, but Miss Carroll who entered the room a few minutes later.

"Geraldine is asleep," she said. "She's had a terrible shock, poor child. After you left I gave her something to make her sleep, and she's fast asleep now. In an hour or two, perhaps."

Japp agreed.

"In any case there's nothing she can tell you that I can't," said Miss Carroll firmly.

"What is your opinion of the butler?" asked Poirot.

"I don't like him much, and that's a fact," replied Miss Carroll. "But I can't tell you why."

We had reached the front door.

"It was up there that you stood, was it not, last night, mademoiselle?" said Poirot suddenly, pointing with his hand up the stairs.

"Yes. Why?"

"And you saw Lady Edgware go along the hall into the study?"

"Yes."

"And you saw her face distinctly?"

"Certainly."

"But you could not have seen her face, mademoiselle. You can only have seen the back of her head from where you were standing."

Miss Carroll flushed angrily. She seemed taken aback.

"Back of her head, her voice, her walk! It's all the same thing. Absolutely unmistakable! I tell you I *know* it was Jane Wilkinson—a thoroughly bad woman if there ever was one."

And turning away she flounced upstairs.

VIII Possibilities

JAPP had to leave us. Poirot and I turned into Regent's Park and found a quiet seat.

"I see the point of your rose between the lips now," I said, laughing. "At the moment I thought you had gone mad."

He nodded without smiling.

"You observe, Hastings, that the secretary is a dangerous witness. Dangerous because inaccurate. You notice that she stated positively that she saw the visitor's *face?* At the time I thought that impossible. Coming *from* the study—yes, but not going *to* the study. So I made my little experiment, which resulted as *I* thought, and then sprung my trap upon her. She immediately changed her ground."

"Her belief was quite unaltered, though," I argued. "And, after all, a voice and a walk are just as unmistakable."

"No, no."

"Why, Poirot, I think a voice and the general gait are about the most characteristic things about a person."

"I agree. And therefore they are the most easily counterfeited."

"You think—"

"Cast your mind back a few days. Do you remember one evening as we sat in the stalls of a theatre—"

"Carlotta Adams? Ah! but then she is a genius."

"A well-known person is not so difficult to mimic. But I agree she has unusual gifts. I believe she could carry a thing through without the aid of footlights and distance—"

A sudden thought flashed into my mind.

"Poirot," I cried. "You don't think that possibly—no, that would be too much of a coincidence."

"It depends how you look at it, Hastings. Regarded from one angle it would be no coincidence at all."

"But why should Carlotta Adams wish to kill Lord Edgware? She did not even know him."

"How do you know she did not know him? Do not assume things, Hastings. There may have been some link between them of which we know nothing. Not that that is precisely my theory."

"Then you have a theory?"

"Yes. The possibility of Carlotta Adams being involved struck me from the beginning."

"But, Poirot—"

"Wait, Hastings. Let me put together a few facts for you. Lady Edgware, with a complete lack of reticence, discusses the relations between her and her husband, and even goes so far as to talk of killing him. Not only you and I hear this. A waiter hears it, her maid probably has heard it many times, Bryan Martin hears it, and I imagine Carlotta Adams herself hears it. And there are the people to whom these people repeat it. Then, on that same evening, the excellence of Carlotta Adams' imitation of Jane is commented upon. Who had a motive for killing Lord Edgware? His wife.

"Now supposing that someone else wishes to do away with Lord Edgware. Here is a scapegoat ready to his hand. On the day when Jane Wilkinson announces that she has a headache and is going to have a quiet evening—the plan is put into operation.

"Lady Edgware must be seen to enter the house in Regent Gate. Well, she is seen. She even goes so far as to announce her identity. *Ah! c'est un peu trop, ça!* It would awaken suspicion in an oyster.

"And another point—a small point I admit. The woman who came to the house last night wore black. *Jane Wilkinson never wears black*. We heard her say so. Let us assume, then, that the woman who came to the house last night was *not* Jane Wilkinson—that it was a woman impersonating Jane Wilkinson. Did that woman kill Lord Edgware?

"Did a third person enter that house and kill Lord Edgware? If so, did the person enter before or after the supposed visit of Lady Edgware? If after, what did the woman say to Lord Edgware? How did she explain her presence? She might deceive the butler, who did not know her, and the secretary, who did not see her at close quarters, but she could not hope to deceive a husband. Or was there only a dead body in the room? Was Lord Edgware killed *before* she entered the house—some time between nine and ten?"

"Stop, Poirot!" I cried. "You are making my head spin."

"No, no, my friend. We are only considering possibilities. It is like trying on the clothes. Does this fit? No, it wrinkles on the shoulder? This one? Yes, that is better—but not quite large enough. This other one is too small. So on and so on, until we reach the perfect fit—the truth."

"Whom do you suspect of such a fiendish plot?" I asked.

"Ah! that is too early to say. One must go into the question of who has a motive for wishing Lord Edgware dead. There is, of course, the nephew who inherits. A little obvious, that, perhaps. And then, in spite of Miss Carroll's dogmatic pronouncement, there is the question of enemies. Lord Edgware struck me as a man who very easily might make enemies."

"Yes," I agreed. "That is so."

"Whoever it was must have fancied himself pretty safe. Remember, Hastings, but for her change of mind at the last minute, Jane Wilkinson would have had no alibi. She might have been in her room at the Savoy, and it would have been difficult to prove it. She would have been arrested, tried—probably hanged."

I shivered.

"But there is one thing that puzzles me," went on Poirot. "The desire to incriminate her is clear—but what then of the telephone call? Why did someone ring her up at Chiswick and, once satisfied of her presence there, immediately ring off? It looks, does it not, as if someone wanted to be sure of her presence there before proceeding to—what? That was at nine-thirty, almost certainly before the murder. The intention then seems—there is no other word for it—*beneficent*. It *cannot* be the murderer who rings up—the murderer has laid all his plans to incriminate Jane. Who, then, was it? It looks as though we have here two entirely different sets of circumstances."

I shook my head, utterly fogged.

"It might be just a coincidence," I suggested.

"No, no, everything cannot be a coincidence. Six months ago, a letter was suppressed. Why? There are too many things here unexplained. There must be some reason linking them together."

He sighed. Presently he went on:

"That story that Bryan Martin came to tell us—"

"Surely, Poirot, that has got no connection with this business."

"You are blind, Hastings, blind and wilfully obtuse. Do you not see that the whole thing makes a pattern? A pattern confused at present but which will gradually become clear."

I felt Poirot was being over optimistic. I did not feel that anything would ever become clear. My brain was frankly reeling.

"It's no good," I said suddenly. "I can't believe it of Carlotta Adams. She seemed such a—well, such a thoroughly nice girl."

Yet, even as I spoke, I remembered Poirot's words about love of money. Love of money! Was that at the root of the seemingly incomprehensible? I felt that Poirot had been inspired that night. He had seen Jane in danger—the result of her strange, egoistical temperament. He had seen Carlotta led astray by avarice.

"I do not think she committed the murder, Hastings. She is too cool and level-headed for that. Possibly she was not even told that murder would be done. She may have been used innocently. But then—"

He broke off, frowning.

"Even so, she's an accessory after the fact now. I mean, she will see the news today. She will realize—"

A hoarse sound broke from Poirot.

"Quick, Hastings. Quick! I have been blind—imbecile. A taxi. At once."

I stared at him.

He waved his arms.

"A taxi—at once."

One was passing. He hailed it and we jumped in.

"Do you know her address?"

"Carlotta Adams, do you mean?"

"*Mais oui, mais oui.* Quickly, Hastings, quickly. Every minute is of value."

"No," I said, "I don't."

Poirot swore under his breath.

"The telephone book? No, she would not be in it. The theatre."

At the theatre they were not disposed to give Carlotta's address, but Poirot managed it. It was a flat in a block of mansions near Sloane Square. We drove there, Poirot in a fever of impatience.

"If I am not too late, Hastings. If I am not too late."

"What is all this haste? I don't understand. What does it mean?"

"It means that I have been slow. Terribly slow to realize the obvious. Ah! *mon Dieu,* if only we may be in time."

IX The Second Death

THOUGH I did not understand the reason for Poirot's agitation, I knew him well enough to be sure that he had a reason for it.

We arrived at Rosedew Mansions. Poirot sprang out, paid the driver and hurried into the building. Miss Adams' flat was on the first floor, as a visiting card stuck on a board informed us.

Poirot hurried up the stairs not waiting to summon the lift which was at one of the upper floors. He knocked and rang. There was a short delay; then the door was opened by a neat, middle-aged woman with hair drawn tightly back from her face. Her eyelids were reddened as though with weeping.

"Miss Adams?" demanded Poirot eagerly.

The woman looked at him.

"Haven't you heard?"

"Heard? Heard what?"

His face had gone deadly pale, and I realized that this, whatever it was, was what he had feared.

The woman continued slowly to shake her head.

"She's dead. Passed away in her sleep. It's terrible."

Poirot leaned against the doorpost.

"Too late," he murmured.

His agitation was so apparent that the woman looked at him with more attention.

"Excuse me, sir, but are you a friend of hers? I do not remember seeing you come here before?"

Poirot did not reply to this directly. Instead he said:

"You have had a doctor? What did he say?"

"Took an overdose of a sleeping draught. Oh! the pity of it! Such a nice young lady. Nasty dangerous things—these drugs. Veronal, he said it was."

Poirot suddenly stood upright. His manner took on a new authority.

"I must come in," he said.

The woman was clearly doubtful and suspicious.

"I don't think—" she began.

But Poirot meant to have his way. He took probably the only course that would have obtained the desired result.

"You must let me in," he said. "I am a detective and I have got to inquire into the circumstances of your mistress's death."

The woman gasped. She stood aside and we passed into the flat. From there on Poirot took command of the situation.

"What I have told you," he said authoritatively, "is strictly confidential. It must not be repeated. Everyone must continue to think that Miss Adams' death was accidental. Please give me the name and address of the doctor you summoned."

"Dr. Heath, Seventeen Carlisle Street."

"And your own name?"

"Bennett—Alice Bennett."

"You were attached to Miss Adams, I can see, Miss Bennett."

"Oh! yes, sir. She were a nice young lady. I worked for her last year when she were over here. It wasn't as though she were one of those actresses. She were a real young lady. Dainty ways she had and liked everything just so."

Poirot listened with attention and sympathy. He had now no signs of impatience. I realized that to proceed gently was the best way of extracting the information he wanted.

"It must have been a great shock to you," he observed gently.

"Oh! it was, sir. I took her in her tea—at half past nine as usual—and there she was lying, asleep I thought. And I put the tray down. And I pulled the curtains. One of the rings caught, sir, and I had to jerk it hard. Such a noise it made. I was surprised when I looked round to see she hadn't woken. And then all of a sudden something seemed to take hold of me. Something not quite natural about the way she lay. And I went to the side of the bed, and I touched her hand. Icy cold it was, sir, and I cried out."

She stopped, tears coming into her eyes.

"Yes, yes," said Poirot sympathetically. "It must have been terrible for you. Did Miss Adams often take stuff to make her sleep?"

"She'd take something for a headache now and again, sir— some little tablets in a bottle—but it was some other stuff she took last night, or so the doctor said."

"Did anyone come to see her last night? A visitor?"

"No, sir. She was out yesterday evening, sir."

"Did she tell you where she was going?"

"No, sir. She went out about seven o'clock."

"Ah! How was she dressed?"

"She had on a black dress, sir. A black dress and a black hat."

Poirot looked at me.

"Did she wear any jewellery?"

"Just the string of pearls she always wore, sir."

"And gloves—grey gloves?"

"Yes, sir. Her gloves were grey."

"Ah! Now describe to me, if you will, what her manner was. Was she gay? Excited? Sad? Nervous?"

"It seemed to me she was pleased about something, sir. She kept smiling to herself, as though there were some kind of joke on."

"What time did she return?"

"A little after twelve o'clock, sir."

"And what was her manner then? The same?"

"She was terribly tired, sir."

"But not upset? Or distressed?"

"Oh! no, sir. I think she was pleased about something, but just done up, if you know what I mean. She started to ring someone up on the telephone, and then she said she couldn't bother. She'd do it tomorrow morning."

"Ah!" Poirot's eyes gleamed with excitement. He leaned forward and spoke in a would-be indifferent voice.

"Did you hear the name of the person she rang up?"

"No, sir. She just asked for the number and waited and then the Exchange must have said, 'I'm trying to get them,' as they do, sir, and she said, 'All right,' and then suddenly she yawned and said, 'Oh! I can't bother. I'm too tired,' and she put the receiver back and started undressing."

"And the number she called? Do you recollect that? Think. It may be important."

"I'm sorry I can't say, sir. It was a Victoria number, and that's all I can remember. I wasn't paying special heed, you see."

"Did she have anything to eat or drink before she went to bed?"

"A glass of hot milk, sir, like she always did."

"Who prepared it?"

"I did, sir."

"And nobody came to the flat that evening?"

"Nobody, sir."

"And earlier in the day?"

"Nobody came that I can remember, sir. Miss Adams was out to lunch and tea. She came in at six o'clock."

"When did the milk come? The milk she drank last night?"

"It was the new milk she had, sir. The afternoon delivery. The boy leaves it outside the door at four o'clock. But oh! sir, I'm sure there wasn't nothing wrong with the milk. I had it myself for tea this morning. And the doctor he said positive as she'd taken the nasty stuff herself."

"It is possible that I am wrong," said Poirot. "Yes, it is possible that I am entirely wrong. I will see the doctor. But, you see, Miss Adams had enemies. Things are very different in America—"

He hesitated, but the good Alice leapt at the bait.

"Oh! I know, sir, I've read about them gunmen and all that. It must be a wicked country; and what the police can be about, I can't think. Not like our policemen."

Poirot left it thankfully at that, realizing that Alice Bennett's insular proclivities would save him the trouble of explanations.

His eye fell on a small suitcase, more of an attaché case, that was lying on a chair.

"Did Miss Adams take that with her when she went out last night?"

"In the morning she took it, sir. She didn't have it when she came back at tea time, but she brought it back last thing."

"Ah! you permit that I open it?"

Alice Bennett would have permitted anything. Like most canny and suspicious women, once she had overcome her distrust she was child's play to manipulate. She would have assented to anything Poirot suggested.

The case was not locked. Poirot opened it. I came forward and looked over his shoulder.

"You see, Hastings, you see?" he murmured excitedly.

The contents were certainly suggestive.

There was a box of make-up materials, two objects which I recognized as elevators to place in shoes and raise the height an inch or so, there was a pair of grey gloves and, folded in tissue paper, an exquisitely made wig of golden hair, the exact shade of gold of Jane Wilkinson's, and dressed like hers, with a centre parting and curls in the back of the neck.

"Do you doubt now, Hastings?" asked Poirot.

I believe I had up to that moment. But now I doubted no longer.

Poirot closed the case again and turned to the maid.

"You do not know with whom Miss Adams dined yesterday evening?"

"No, sir."

"Do you know with whom she had lunch or tea?"

"I know nothing about tea, sir. I believe she lunched with Miss Driver."

"Miss Driver?"

"Yes, her great friend. She has a hat shop in Moffatt Street, just off Bond Street. Genevieve, it's called."

Poirot noted the address in his notebook, just below that of the doctor.

"One thing more, madame. Can you remember anything—*anything at all*—that Mademoiselle Adams said or did, after she came in at six o'clock, that strikes you as at all unusual or significant?"

The maid thought for a moment or two.

"I really can't say that I do, sir," she said at last. "I asked her if she would have tea and she said she'd had some."

"Oh! she said she had had it," interrupted Poirot. "Pardon. Continue."

"And after that she was writing letters till just on the time she went out."

"Letters, eh? You do not know to whom?"

"Yes, sir. It was just one letter—to her sister in Washington. She wrote her sister twice a week regular. She took the letter out with her to post because of catching the mail. But she forgot to post it."

"Then it is here still?"

"No, sir. I posted it. She remembered last night just as she was getting into bed. And I said I'd run out with it. By putting an extra stamp on it and putting it in the late fee box it would go all right."

"Ah! And is that far?"

"No, sir, the post office is just round the corner."

"Did you shut the door of the flat behind you?"

Bennett stared.

"No, sir. I just left it to—as I always do when I go out to post."

Poirot seemed about to speak. Then he checked himself.

"Would you like to look at her, sir?" asked the maid tearfully. "Looks beautiful she does."

We followed her into the bedroom.

Carlotta Adams looked strangely peaceful and much younger than she had appeared that night at the Savoy. She looked like a tired child asleep.

There was a strange expression on Poirot's face as he stood looking down on her. I saw him make the sign of the Cross.

"*J'ai fait un serment,* Hastings," he said as we went down the stairs.

I did not ask him what his vow was. I could guess. A minute or two later he said:

"There is one thing off my mind at least. I could not have saved her. By the time I heard of Lord Edgware's death she was already dead. That comforts me. Yes, that comforts me very much."

X Jenny Driver

OUR next proceeding was to call upon the doctor whose address the maid had given us.

He turned out to be a fussy elderly man somewhat vague in manner. He knew Poirot by repute and expressed a lively pleasure at meeting him in the flesh.

"And what can I do for you, M. Poirot?" he asked after this opening preamble.

"You were called this morning, M. le docteur, to the bedside of a Miss Carlotta Adams."

"Ah! yes, poor girl. Clever actress too. I've been twice to her show. A thousand pities it's ended this way. Why these girls must have drugs, I can't think."

"You think she was addicted to drugs, then?"

"Well, professionally, I should hardly have said so. At all events she didn't take them hypodermically. No marks of the needle. Evidently always took it by the mouth. Maid said she slept well naturally, but then maids never know. I don't suppose she took veronal every night, but she'd evidently taken it for some time."

"What makes you think so?"

"This. Dash it—where did I put the thing?"

He was peering into a small case.

"Ah! here it is."

He drew out a small black morocco handbag.

"There's got to be an inquest, of course. I brought this away so that the maid shouldn't meddle with it."

Opening the pochette he took out a small gold box. On it were the initials C. A. in rubies. It was a valuable and expensive trinket. The doctor opened it. It was nearly full of a white powder.

"Veronal," he explained briefly. "Now look what's written inside."

On the inside of the lid of the box was engraved:

C. A. from D. Paris, Nov. 10th.
Sweet Dreams.

"November 10th," said Poirot thoughtfully.

"Exactly, and we're now in June. That seems to show that she's been in the habit of taking the stuff for at least six months; and, as the year isn't given, it might be eighteen months or two years and a half—or any time."

"Paris. D," said Poirot, frowning.

"Yes. Convey anything to you? By the way, I haven't asked you what your interest is in the case. I'm assuming you've got good grounds. I suppose you want to know if it's suicide? Well, I can't tell you. Nobody can. According to the maid's account, she was perfectly cheerful yesterday. That looks like accident, and in my opinion accident it is. Veronal's very uncertain stuff. You can take a devil of a lot and it won't kill you, and you can take very little and off you go. It's a dangerous drug for that reason. I've no doubt they'll bring it in accidental death at the inquest. I'm afraid I can't be of any more help to you."

"May I examine the little bag of mademoiselle?"

"Certainly. Certainly."

Poirot turned out the contents of the pochette. There was a fine handkerchief with C. M. A. in the corner, a powder puff, a lipstick, a pound note and a little change, and a pair of pince-nez.

These last Poirot examined with interest. They were gold-rimmed and rather severe and academic in type.

"Curious," said Poirot. "I did not know that Miss Adams wore glasses. But perhaps they are for reading?"

The doctor picked them up.

"No, these are outdoor glasses," he affirmed. "Pretty powerful too. The person who wore these must have been very short-sighted."

"You do not know if Miss Adams—"

"I never attended her before. I was called in once to see a

poisoned finger of the maid's. Otherwise I have never been in
the flat. Miss Adams, whom I saw for a moment on that occasion, was certainly not wearing glasses then."

Poirot thanked the doctor and we took our leave.

Poirot wore a puzzled expression.

"It can be that I am mistaken," he admitted.

"About the impersonation?"

"No, no. That seems to me proved. No, I mean as to her
death. Obviously she had veronal in her possession. It is possible
that she was tired and strung up last night and determined to
ensure herself a good night's rest."

Then he suddenly stopped dead—to the great surprise of the
passers-by—and beat one hand emphatically on the other.

"No, no, no, no!" he declared emphatically. "Why should
that accident happen so conveniently? It was no accident. It
was not suicide. No, she played her part and in doing so she
signed her death warrant. Veronal may have been chosen simply
because it was known that she occasionally took it and that she
had that box in her possession. But if so, the murderer must
have been someone who knew her well. Who is D, Hastings?
I would give a good deal to know who D was."

"Poirot," I said, as he remained wrapt in thought, "hadn't
we better go on? Everyone is staring at us."

"Eh? Well, perhaps you are right. Though it does not in-
commode me that people should stare. It does not interfere in
the least with my train of thought."

"People were beginning to laugh," I murmured.

"That has no importance."

I did not quite agree. I have a horror of doing anything conspicuous. The only thing that affects Poirot is the possibility of
the damp or the heat affecting the set of his famous moustache.

"We will take a taxi," said Poirot, waving his stick.

One drew up by us, and Poirot directed it to go to Genevieve
in Moffatt Street.

Genevieve turned out to be one of those establishments where
one nondescript hat and a scarf display themselves in a glass
box downstairs and where the real centre of operations is one
floor up a flight of musty-smelling stairs.

Having climbed the stairs we came to a door with "Genevieve.
Please Walk In" on it, and, having obeyed this command, we
found ourselves in a small room full of hats while an imposing
blonde creature came forward with a suspicious glance at Poirot.

"Miss Driver?" asked Poirot.

"I do not know if modom can see you. What is your business,
please?"

"Please tell Miss Driver that a friend of Miss Adams would
like to see her."

The blonde beauty had no need to go on this errand. A black
velvet curtain was violently agitated and a small vivacious creature with flaming red hair emerged.

"What's that?" she demanded.

"Are you Miss Driver?"

"Yes. What's that about Carlotta?"

"You have heard the sad news?"

"What sad news?"

"Miss Adams died in her sleep last night. An overdose of
veronal."

The girl's eyes opened wide.

"How awful!" she exclaimed. "Poor Carlotta. I can hardly
believe it. Why, she was full of life yesterday."

"Nevertheless it is true, mademoiselle," said Poirot. "Now
see—it is just on one o'clock. I want you to do me the honour
of coming out to lunch with me and my friend. I want to ask
you several questions."

The girl looked him up and down. She was a pugilistic little
creature. She reminded me in some ways of a fox terrier.

"Who are you?" she demanded bluntly.

"My name is Hercule Poirot. This is my friend Captain
Hastings."

I bowed.

Her glance travelled from one to the other of us.

"I've heard of you," she said abruptly. "I'll come."

She called to the blonde:

"Dorothy?"

"Yes, Jenny."

"Mrs. Lester's coming in about that Rose Descartes model

we're making for her. Try the different feathers. By by, shan't be long, I expect."

She picked up a small black hat, affixed it to one ear, powdered her nose furiously, and then looked at Poirot.

"Ready," she said abruptly.

Five minutes afterward, we were sitting in a small restaurant in Dover Street. Poirot had given an order to the waiter and cocktails were in front of us.

"Now," said Jenny Driver. "I want to know the meaning of all this? What has Carlotta been getting herself mixed up in?"

"She had been getting herself mixed up in something then, mademoiselle?"

"Now then, who is going to ask the questions, you or me?"

"My idea was that I should," said Poirot, smiling. "I have been given to understand that you and Miss Adams were great friends."

"Right."

"*Eh bien*, then I ask you, mademoiselle, to accept my solemn assurance that, what I do, I am doing in the interests of your dead friend. I assure you that that is so."

There was a moment's silence while Jenny Driver considered this question. Finally she gave a quick assenting nod of the head.

"I believe you. Carry on. What do you want to know?"

"I understand, mademoiselle, that your friend lunched with you yesterday."

"She did."

"Did she tell you what her plans were for last night?"

"She didn't exactly mention last night."

"But she said something?"

"Well, she mentioned something that maybe is what you're driving at. Mind you, she spoke in confidence."

"That is understood."

"Well, let me see now. I think I'd better explain things in my own words."

"If you please, mademoiselle."

"Well, then. Carlotta was excited. She isn't often excited. She's not that kind. She wouldn't tell me anything definite, said she'd promised not to, but she'd got something on—something, I gathered, in the nature of a gigantic hoax."

"A hoax?"

"That's what she said. She didn't say how or when or where. Only—" She paused, frowning. "Well—you see—Carlotta's not the kind of person who enjoys practical jokes or hoaxes or things of that kind. She's one of those serious, nice-minded, hard-working girls. What I mean is somebody had obviously put her up to this stunt. And I think—she didn't say so, mind—"

"No, no, I quite understand. What was it that you thought?"

"I thought—I was sure—that in some way money was concerned. Nothing really ever excited Carlotta except money. She was made that way. She'd got one of the best heads for business I've ever met. She wouldn't have been so excited and so pleased unless money—quite a lot of money—had been concerned. My impression was that she'd taken on something for a bet, and that she was pretty sure of winning. And yet that isn't quite true. I mean, Carlotta didn't bet. I've never known her make a bet. But anyway, somehow or other, I'm sure money was concerned."

"She did not actually say so?"

"N-n-o. Just said that she'd be able to do this, that and the other in the near future. She was going to get her sister over from America to meet her in Paris. She was crazy about her little sister. Very delicate, I believe, and musical. Well, that's all I know. Is that what you want?"

Poirot nodded his head.

"Yes. It confirms my theory. I had hoped, I admit, for more. I had anticipated that Miss Adams would have been bound to secrecy. But I hoped that, being a woman, she would not have counted revealing the secret to her best friend."

"I tried to make her tell me," admitted Jenny, "but she only laughed and said she'd tell me all about it some day."

Poirot was silent for a moment. Then he said:

"You know the name of Lord Edgware?"

"What? The man who was murdered? On a poster half an hour ago."

"Yes. Do you know if Miss Adams was acquainted with him?"

"I don't think so. I'm sure she wasn't. Oh! wait a minute."

"Yes, mademoiselle?" said Poirot eagerly.

"What was it now?" she frowned, knitting her brow as she tried to remember. "Yes, I've got it now. She mentioned him once. Very bitterly."

"Bitterly?"

"Yes. She said—what was it?—that men like that shouldn't be allowed to ruin other people's lives by their cruelty and lack of understanding. She said—why, so she did—that he was the kind of man whose death would probably be a good thing for everybody."

"When was it she said this, mademoiselle?"

"Oh! about a month ago, I think it was."

"How did the subject come up?"

Jenny Driver racked her brains for some minutes and finally shook her head.

"I can't remember," she confessed. "His name cropped up or something. It might have been in the newspaper. Anyway, I remember thinking it odd that Carlotta should be so vehement all of a sudden when she didn't even know the man."

"Certainly it is odd," agreed Poirot thoughtfully. Then he asked:

"Do you know if Miss Adams was in the habit of taking veronal?"

"Not that I knew. I never saw her take it or mention taking it."

"Did you ever see in her bag a small gold box with the initials C. A. on it in rubies?"

"A small gold box—no, I am sure I didn't."

"Do you happen to know where Miss Adams was last November?"

"Let me see. She went back to the States in November, I think—towards the end of the month. Before that she was in Paris."

"Alone?"

"Alone of course! Sorry—perhaps you didn't mean that! I don't know why any mention of Paris always suggests the worst. And it's such a nice respectable place really. But Carlotta wasn't the week-ending sort, if that's what you're driving at."

"Now, mademoiselle, I am going to ask you a very important question. Was there any man Miss Adams was specially interested in?"

"The answer to that is 'No,'" said Jenny slowly. "Carlotta, since I've known her, has been wrapped up in her work and in her delicate sister. She's had the 'head of the family all depends on me' attitude very strongly. So the answer's No—strictly speaking."

"Ah! and not speaking so strictly?"

"I shouldn't wonder if—lately—Carlotta hadn't been getting interested in some man."

"Ah!"

"Mind you, that's entirely guesswork on my part. I've gone simply by her manner. She's been—different—not exactly dreamy, but abstracted. And she's looked different somehow. Oh! I can't explain. It's the sort of thing that another woman just feels, and of course may be quite wrong about."

Poirot nodded.

"Thank you, mademoiselle. One thing more. Is there any friend of Miss Adams whose initial is D?"

"D," said Jenny Driver thoughtfully. "D? No, I'm sorry. I can't think of anyone."

XI The Egoist

I DO not think Poirot had expected any other answer to his question. All the same he shook his head sadly. He remained lost in thought. Jenny Driver leant forward, her elbows on the table.

"And now," she said, "am I going to be told anything?"

"Mademoiselle," said Poirot, "first of all let me compliment you. Your answers to my questions have been singularly intelligent. Clearly you have brains, mademoiselle. You ask whether I am going to tell you anything. I answer—not very much. I will tell you just a few bare facts, mademoiselle."

He paused, and then said quietly:

"Last night Lord Edgware was murdered in his library. At ten o'clock yesterday evening a lady, whom I believe to have been your friend Miss Adams, came to the house, asked to see Lord Edgware, and announced herself as Lady Edgware. She wore a golden wig and was made up to resemble the real Lady Edgware who, as you probably know, is Miss Jane Wilkinson the actress. Miss Adams (if it were she) only remained a few moments. She left the house at five minutes past ten but she did not return home till after midnight. She went to bed, having taken an overdose of veronal. Now, mademoiselle, you see the point, perhaps, of some of the questions I have been asking you."

Jenny drew a deep breath.

"Yes," she said. "I see now. I believe you're right, M. Poirot. Right about its having been Carlotta, I mean. For one thing she bought a new hat off me yesterday."

"A new hat?"

"Yes. She said she wanted one to shade the left side of her face."

Here I must insert a few words of explanation, as I do not know when these words will be read. I have seen many fashions of hats in my time—the cloche that shaded the face so completely that one gave up in despair the task of recognizing one's friends. The tilted forward hat, the hat attached airily to the back of the head, the beret, and many other styles. In this particular June the hat of the moment was shaped like an inverted soup plate and was worn attached (as if by suction) over one ear, leaving the other side of the face and hair open to inspection.

"These hats are usually worn on the right side of the head?" asked Poirot.

The little modiste nodded.

"But we keep a few to be worn on the opposite side," she explained, "because there are people who much prefer their right profile to the left or who have a habit of parting the hair on one side only. Now would there be any special reason for Carlotta's wanting that side of her face to be in shadow?"

I remembered that the door of the house in Regent Gate opened to the left, so that anyone entering would be in full view of the butler that side. I remembered also that Jane Wilkinson (so I had noticed the other night) had a tiny mole at the corner of the left eye. I said as much, excitedly. Poirot agreed, nodding his head vigorously.

"It is so. It is so. *Vous avez parfaitement raison,* Hastings. Yes, that explains the purchase of the hat."

"M. Poirot?" Jenny sat suddenly bolt upright. "You don't think—you don't for one moment think—that Carlotta did it? Killed him, I mean. You can't think that? Not just because she spoke so bitterly about him."

"I do not think so, but it is curious all the same—that she should have spoken so, I mean. I would like to know the reason for it. What had he done—what did she know of him to make her speak in such a fashion?"

"I don't know, but she didn't kill him. She's—oh! she was—well—too refined."

Poirot nodded approvingly.

"Yes, yes. You put that very well. It is a point psychological. I agree. This was a scientific crime, but not a refined one."

"Scientific?"

"The murderer knew exactly where to strike so as to reach

the vital nerve centres at the base of the skull where it joins the spinal cord."

"Looks like a doctor," said Jenny thoughtfully.

"Did Miss Adams know any doctors? I mean was any particular doctor a friend of hers?"

Jenny shook her head.

"Never heard of one. Not over here, anyway."

"Another question. Did Miss Adams wear pince-nez?"

"Glasses? Never."

"Ah!" Poirot frowned.

A vision rose in my mind. A doctor, smelling of carbolic, with short-sighted eyes magnified by powerful lenses. Absurd!

"By the way, did Miss Adams know Bryan Martin, the film actor?"

"Why, yes. She used to know him as a child, she told me. I don't think she saw much of him, though. Just once in a while. She told me she thought he'd got very swollen headed."

She looked at her watch and uttered an exclamation.

"Goodness, I must fly. Have I helped you at all, M. Poirot?"

"You have. I shall ask you for further help by and by."

"It's yours. Someone staged this deviltry. We've got to find out who it is."

She gave us a quick shake of the hand, flashed her white teeth in a sudden smile and left us with characteristic abruptness.

"An interesting personality," said Poirot as he paid the bill.

"I like her," I said.

"It is always a pleasure to meet a quick mind."

"A little hard, perhaps," I reflected. "The shock of her friend's death did not upset her as much as I should have thought it would have done."

"She is not the sort that weeps, certainly," agreed Poirot dryly.

"Did you get what you hoped from the interview?"

He shook his head.

"No. I hoped—very much I hoped—to get a clue to the personality of D, the person who gave her the little gold box. There I have failed. Unfortunately Carlotta Adams was a reserved girl. She was not one to gossip about her friends or her possible love affairs. On the other hand, the person who suggested the hoax may not have been a friend at all. It may have been a mere acquaintance who proposed it—doubtless for some 'sporting' reason—on a money basis. This person may have seen the gold box she carried about with her and made some opportunity to discover what it contained."

"But how on earth did they get her to take it? And when?"

"Well, there was the time during which the flat door was open, when the maid was out posting a letter. Not that that satisfies me. It leaves too much to chance. But now—to work. We have still two possible clues."

"Which are?"

"The first is the telephone call to a Victoria number. It seems to me quite a probability that Carlotta Adams would ring up on her return to announce her success. On the other hand, where was she between five minutes past ten and midnight? She may have had an appointment with the instigator of the hoax. In that case the telephone call may have been merely one to a friend."

"What is the second clue?"

"Ah! that I do have hopes of. The letter, Hastings. The letter to the sister. It is possible—I only say possible—that in that she may have described the whole business. She would not regard it as a breach of faith, since the letter would not be read till a week later and in another country at that."

"Amazing, if that is so!"

"We must not build too much upon it, Hastings. It is a chance, that is all. No, we must work now from the other end."

"What do you call the other end?"

"A careful study of those who profit in any degree by Lord Edgware's death."

I shrugged my shoulders.

"Apart from his nephew and his wife—"

"And the man the wife wanted to marry," added Poirot.

"The Duke? He is in Paris."

"Quite so. But you cannot deny that he is an interested party. Then there are the people in the house—the butler, the servants. Who knows what grudges they may have had? But I think myself our first point of attack should be a further interview with

Mademoiselle Jane Wilkinson. She is shrewd. She may be able to suggest something."

Once more we made our way to the Savoy. We found the lady surrounded by boxes and tissue paper, while exquisite black draperies were strewn over the back of every chair. Jane had a rapt and serious expression and was just trying on yet another small black hat before the glass.

"Why, M. Poirot. Sit down. That is, if there's anything to sit on. Ellis, clear something, will you?"

"Madame, you look charming."

Jane looked serious.

"I don't want exactly to play the hypocrite, M. Poirot, but one must observe appearances, don't you think? I mean, I think I ought to be careful. Oh! by the way, I've had the sweetest telegram from the Duke."

"From Paris?"

"Yes, from Paris. Guarded, of course, and supposed to be condolences but put so that I can read between the lines."

"My felicitations, madame."

"M. Poirot." She clasped her hands; her husky voice dropped. She looked like an angel about to give event to thoughts of exquisite holiness. "I've been thinking. It all seems so *miraculous,* if you know what I mean. Here I am—all my troubles over. No tiresome business of divorce. No bothers. Just my path cleared and all plain sailing. It makes me feel almost religious—if you know what I mean."

I held my breath. Poirot looked at her, his head a little on one side. She was quite serious.

"That is how it strikes you, madame, eh?"

"Things happen right for me," said Jane in a sort of awed whisper. "I've thought and I've thought lately—if Edgware was to die. And there—he's dead! It's—it's almost like an answer to prayer."

Poirot cleared his throat.

"I cannot say I look at it quite like that, madame. Somebody killed your husband."

She nodded.

"Why of course."

"Has it not occurred to you to wonder who that someone was?" She stared at him.

"Does it matter? I mean—what's that to do with it? The Duke and I can be married in about four or five months."

With difficulty Poirot controlled himself.

"Yes, madame, I know that. But apart from that has it not occurred to you to ask yourself *who killed your husband?*"

"No." She seemed quite surprised by the idea. We could see her thinking about it.

"Does it not interest you to know?" asked Poirot.

"Not very much, I'm afraid," she admitted. "I suppose the police will find out. They're very clever, aren't they?"

"So it is said. I, too, am going to make it my business to find out."

"Are you? How funny."

"Why funny?"

"Well, I don't know." Her eyes strayed back to the clothes. She slipped on a satin coat and studied herself in the glass.

"You do not object, eh?" said Poirot, his eyes twinkling.

"Why, of course not, M. Poirot. I should just love you to be clever about it all. I wish you every success."

"Madame, I want your more than wishes. I want your opinion."

"Opinion?" said Jane absently, as she twisted her head over her shoulder. "What on?"

"Who do you think likely to have killed Lord Edgware?"

Jane shook her head.

"I haven't any idea."

She wriggled her shoulders experimentally and took up the hand glass.

"Madame!" said Poirot in a loud emphatic voice. "WHO DO *YOU* THINK KILLED YOUR HUSBAND?"

This time it got through. Jane threw him a startled glance.

"Geraldine, I expect," she said.

"Who is Geraldine?"

But Jane's attention had gone again.

"Ellis, take this up a little on the right shoulder. So. What, M. Poirot? Geraldine's his daughter. No, Ellis, the *right* shoulder.

That's better. Oh! must you go, M. Poirot? I'm terribly grateful for everything. I mean, for the divorce, even though it isn't necessary after all. I shall always think you were wonderful."

I saw Jane Wilkinson only twice again—once on the stage, once when I sat opposite her at a luncheon party. I always think of her as I saw her then, absorbed heart and soul in clothes, her lips carelessly throwing out the words that were to influence Poirot's further actions, her mind concentrated firmly and beatifically on herself.

"*Épatant*," said Poirot with reverence as we emerged into the Strand.

XII The Daughter

THERE was a letter sent by hand lying on the table when we got
back to our rooms. Poirot picked it up, slit it open with his usual
neatness and then laughed.

"What is it you say—'Talk of the devil'? See here, Hastings."
I took the note from him.

The paper was stamped 17 Regent Gate and was written in
very upright, characteristic handwriting which looked easy to
read and curiously enough was not.

Dear Sir, [it ran]
*I hear you were at the house this morning with the Inspector.
I am sorry not to have had the opportunity of speaking to you.
If convenient to yourself I should be much obliged if you could
spare me a few minutes any time this afternoon.*
Yours truly,
Geraldine Marsh.

"Curious," I said. "I wonder why she wants to see you?"

"Is it curious that she should want to see me? You are not
polite, my friend."

Poirot has the most irritating habit of joking at the wrong
moment.

"We will go round at once, my friend," he said; and, lovingly
brushing an imagined speck of dust from his hat, he put it on
his head.

Jane Wilkinson's careless suggestion that Geraldine might
have killed her father seemed to me particularly absurd. Only a
particularly brainless person could have suggested it. I said as
much to Poirot.

"Brains. Brains. What do we really mean by the term? In
your idiom you would say that Jane Wilkinson has the brains
of the rabbit. That is a term of disparagement. But consider

the rabbit for a moment. He exists and multiplies, does he not? That, in nature, is a sign of mental superiority. The lovely Lady Edgware she does not know history, or geography, or the classics *sans doute*. The name of Lao Tse would suggest to her a prize Pekingese dog, the name of Molière a *maison de couture*. But when it comes to choosing clothes, to making rich and advantageous marriages, and to getting her own way—her success is phenomenal. The opinion of a philosopher as to who murdered Lord Edgware would be no good to me; the motive for murder, from a philosopher's point of view, would be the greatest good of the greatest number, and, as that is difficult to decide, few philosophers are murderers. But a careless opinion from Lady Edgware *might* be useful to me, because her point of view would be materialistic and based on a knowledge of the worst side of human nature."

"Perhaps there's something in that," I conceded.

"*Nous voici,*" said Poirot. "I am curious to know why the young lady wishes so urgently to see me."

"It is a natural desire," I said, getting my own back. "You said so a quarter of an hour ago. The natural desire to see something unique at close quarters."

"Perhaps it is you, my friend, who made an impression on her heart the other day," replied Poirot as he rang the bell.

I recalled the startled face of the girl who had stood in the doorway. I could still see those burning dark eyes in the white face. That momentary glimpse had made a great impression on me.

We were shown upstairs to a big drawing-room and in a minute or two Geraldine Marsh came to us there. The impression of intensity which I had noticed before was heightened on this occasion. This tall, thin, white-faced girl, with her big haunting black eyes, was a striking figure. She was extremely composed—in view of her youth, remarkably so.

"It is very good of you to come so promptly, M. Poirot," she said. "I am sorry to have missed you this morning."

"You were lying down?"

"Yes. Miss Carroll—my father's secretary, you know—insisted. She has been very kind."

There was a queer grudging note in the girl's voice that puzzled me.

"In what way can I be of service to you, mademoiselle?" asked Poirot.

She hesitated a minute and then said:

"On the day before my father was killed you came to see him?"

"Yes, mademoiselle."

"Why? Did he—send for you?"

Poirot did not reply for a moment. He seemed to be deliberating. I believe, now, that it was a cleverly calculated move on his part. He wanted to goad her into further speech. She was, he realized, of the impatient type. She wanted things in a hurry.

"Was he afraid of something? Tell me! Tell me! I must know. Who was he afraid of? Why? What did he say to you? Oh! why can't you speak?"

I had thought that that forced composure was not natural. It had soon broken down. She was leaning forward now, her hands twisting themselves nervously on her lap.

"What passed between Lord Edgware and myself was in confidence," said Poirot slowly.

His eyes never left her face.

"Then it was about—I mean, it must have been something to do with—the family. Oh! you sit there and torture me. Why won't you tell me? It's necessary for me to know. It's necessary, I tell you."

Again, very slowly, Poirot shook his head, apparently a prey to deep perplexity.

"M. Poirot." She drew herself up. "I'm his daughter. It is my right to know—what my father dreaded on the last day but one of his life. It isn't fair to leave me in the dark. It isn't fair to him—not to tell me."

"Were you so devoted to your father, then, mademoiselle?" asked Poirot gently.

She drew back as though stung.

"Fond of him?" she whispered. "Fond of him. I—I—"

And suddenly her self-control snapped. Peals of laughter

broke from her. She lay back in her chair and laughed and laughed.

"It's so funny," she gasped. "It's so funny—to be asked that."

That hysterical laughter had not passed unheard. The door opened and Miss Carroll came in. She was firm and efficient.

"Now, now, Geraldine, my dear, that won't do. No, no. Hush, now. I insist. No. Stop it! I mean it. Stop it at once!"

Her determined manner had its effect. Geraldine's laughter grew fainter. She wiped her eyes and sat up.

"I'm sorry," she said in a low voice. "I've never done that before."

Miss Carroll was still looking at her anxiously.

"I'm all right now, Miss Carroll. It was idiotic."

She smiled suddenly, a queer bitter smile that twisted her lips. She sat up very straight in her chair and looked at no one.

"He asked me," she said in a cold, clear voice, "if I had been very fond of my father."

Miss Carroll made a sort of indeterminate cluck. It denoted irresolution on her part. Geraldine went on, her voice high and scornful:

"I wonder if it is better to tell lies or the truth? The truth, I think. I wasn't fond of my father. I hated him!"

"Geraldine dear."

"Why pretend? You didn't hate him, because he couldn't touch you! You were one of the few people in the world that he couldn't get at. You saw him as the employer who paid you so much a year. His rages and his queernesses didn't interest you. You ignored them. I know what you'd say: 'Everyone has got to put up with something.' You were cheerful and uninterested. You're a very strong woman. You're not really human. But then you could have walked out of the house any minute. I couldn't. I belonged."

"Really, Geraldine, I don't think it's necessary going into all this. Fathers and daughters often don't get on, but the less said in life the better, I've found."

Geraldine turned her back on her. She addressed herself to Poirot.

"M. Poirot, I *hated* my father! I am glad he is dead! It means freedom for me—freedom and independence. I am not in the least anxious to find his murderer. For all we know the person who killed him may have had reasons—ample reasons—justifying that action."

Poirot looked at her thoughtfully.

"That is a dangerous principle to adopt, mademoiselle."

"Will hanging someone else bring Father back to life?"

"No," said Poirot dryly, "but it may save other innocent people from being murdered."

"I don't understand."

"A person who has once killed, mademoiselle, nearly always kills again—sometimes again and again."

"I don't believe it. Not—not a real person."

"You mean—not a homicidal maniac? But yes, it is true. One life is removed—perhaps after a terrific struggle with the murderer's conscience. Then—danger threatens. The second murder is morally easier. At the slightest threatening of suspicion, a third follows. And little by little an artistic pride arises; it is a *métier*—to kill. It is done at last almost for pleasure."

The girl had hidden her face in her hands.

"Horrible! Horrible! It isn't true."

"And supposing I told you that it *had already happened?* That already—to save himself—*the murderer has killed a second time?*"

"What's that, M. Poirot?" cried Miss Carroll. "Another murder? Where? Who?"

Poirot gently shook his head.

"It was an illustration only. I ask pardon."

"Oh! I see. For a moment I really thought— Now, Geraldine, if you've finished talking arrant nonsense—"

"You are on my side, I see," said Poirot with a little bow.

"I don't believe in capital punishment," said Miss Carroll briskly. "Otherwise I am certainly on your side. Society must be protected."

Geraldine got up. She smoothed back her hair.

"I am sorry," she said. "I am afraid I have been making rather a fool of myself. You still refuse to tell me why my father called you in?"

"Called him in?" said Miss Carroll in lively astonishment.

"You misunderstand, Miss Marsh. I have not refused to tell you."

Poirot was forced to come out into the open.

"I was only considering how far that interview might have been said to be confidential. Your father did not call me in. *I* sought an interview with *him* on behalf of a client. That client was Lady Edgware."

"Oh! I see."

An extraordinary expression came over the girl's face. I thought at first it was disappointment. Then I saw it was relief.

"I have been very foolish," she said slowly. "I thought my father had perhaps thought himself menaced by some danger. It was stupid."

"You know, M. Poirot, you gave me quite a turn just now," said Miss Carroll, "when you suggested that woman had done a second murder."

Poirot did not answer her. He spoke to the girl.

"Do you believe Lady Edgware committed the murder, mademoiselle?"

She shook her head.

"No, I don't. I can't see her doing a thing like that. She's much too—well, artificial."

"I don't see who else can have done it," said Miss Carroll, "and I don't think women of that kind have got any moral sense."

"It needn't have been her," argued Geraldine. "She may have come here and just had an interview with him and gone away, and the real murderer may have been some lunatic who got in afterward."

"All murderers are mentally deficient—of that I am assured," said Miss Carroll. "Internal gland secretion."

At that moment the door opened and a man came in—then stopped awkwardly.

"Sorry," he said. "I didn't know anyone was in here."

Geraldine made a mechanical introduction.

"My cousin, Lord Edgware. M. Poirot. It's all right, Ronald. You're not interrupting."

"Sure, Dina? How do you do, M. Poirot? Are your grey cells functioning over our particular family mystery?"

I cast my mind back trying to remember. That round, pleasant, vacuous face, the eyes with slight pouches underneath them, the little moustache marooned like an island in the middle of the expanse of face.

Of course! It was Carlotta Adams' escort on the night of the supper party in Jane Wilkinson's suite.

Captain Ronald Marsh. Now Lord Edgware.

XIII The Nephew

THE new Lord Edgware's eye was a quick one. He noticed the slight start I gave.

"Ah! you've got it," he said amiably. "Aunt Jane's little supper party. Just a shade bottled, wasn't I? But I fancied it passed quite unperceived."

Poirot was saying good-bye to Geraldine Marsh and Miss Carroll.

"I'll come down with you," said Ronald genially.

He led the way down the stairs talking as he went.

"Rum thing—life. Kicked out one day, lord of the manor the next. My late unlamented uncle kicked me out, you know, three years ago. But I expect you know all about that, M. Poirot?"

"I had heard the fact mentioned, yes," replied Poirot composedly.

"Naturally. A thing of that kind is sure to be dug up. The earnest sleuth can't afford to miss it."

He grinned. Then he threw open the dining-room door.

"Have a spot before you go."

Poirot refused; so did I, but the young man mixed himself a drink and continued to talk.

"Here's to murder," he said cheerfully. "In the space of one short night I am converted from the creditor's despair to the tradesman's hope. Yesterday ruin stared me in the face, today all is affluence. God bless Aunt Jane."

He drained his glass. Then, with a slight change of manner, he spoke to Poirot.

"Seriously, though, M. Poirot, what *are* you doing here? Four days ago Aunt Jane was dramatically declaiming: 'Who will rid me of this insolent tyrant?' and lo and behold she is ridded! Not by your agency, I hope? The perfect crime, by Hercule Poirot, ex-sleuth hound."

Poirot smiled.

"I am here this afternoon in answer to a note from Miss Geraldine Marsh."

"A discreet answer, eh? No, M. Poirot, what are you really doing here? For some reason or other you are interesting yourself in my uncle's death."

"I am always interested in murder, Lord Edgware."

"But you don't commit it. Very cautious. You should teach Aunt Jane caution. Caution and a shade more camouflage. You'll excuse me calling her Aunt Jane. It amuses me. Did you see her blank face when I did it the other night? Hadn't the foggiest notion who I was."

"En verité?"

"No. I was kicked out of here three months before she came along."

The fatuous expression of good-nature on his face failed for a moment. Then he went on lightly:

"Beautiful woman. But no subtlety. Methods rather crude, eh?"

Poirot shrugged his shoulders.

"It is possible."

Ronald looked at him curiously.

"I believe you think she didn't do it. So she's got round you too, has she?"

"I have a great admiration for beauty," said Poirot evenly. "But also for—evidence."

He brought the last word out very quietly.

"Evidence?" said the other sharply.

"Perhaps you do not know, Lord Edgware, that Lady Edgware was at a party at Chiswick last night at the time she was supposed to have been seen here."

Ronald swore.

"So she went after all! How like a woman! At six o'clock she was throwing her weight about, declaring that nothing on earth would make her go, and I suppose about ten minutes after she'd changed her mind! When planning a murder never depend upon a woman doing what she says she'll do. That's how the best laid plans of murder gang agley. No, M. Poirot, I'm not incriminating myself. Oh! yes, don't think I can't read what's passing through your mind. Who is the Natural Suspect? The well-known Wicked Ne'er-do-Well Nephew."

He leaned back in his chair chuckling.

"I'm saving your little grey cells for you, M. Poirot. No need for you to hunt round for someone who saw me in the offing when Aunt Jane was declaring she never, never, never would go out that night, et cetera. I was there. So you ask yourself, did the wicked nephew in very truth come here last night disguised in a fair wig and a Paris hat?"

Seemingly enjoying the situation, he surveyed us both. Poirot, his head a little on one side, was regarding him with close attention. I felt rather uncomfortable.

"I had a motive—oh! yes, motive admitted. And I'm going to give you a present of a very valuable and significant piece of information. I called to see my uncle yesterday morning. Why? To ask for money. Yes, lick your lips over that. TO ASK FOR MONEY. And I went away without getting any. And that same evening—that very same evening—Lord Edgware dies. Good title that, by the way. Lord Edgware Dies. Look well on a bookstall."

He paused. Still Poirot said nothing.

"I'm really flattered by your attention, M. Poirot. Captain Hastings looks as though he had seen a ghost—or were going to see one any minute. Don't get so strung up, my dear fellow. Wait for the anticlimax. Well, where were we? Oh! yes, case against the Wicked Nephew. Guilt is to be thrown on the hated Aunt by Marriage. Nephew, celebrated at one time for acting female parts, does his supreme histrionic effort. In a girlish voice he announces himself as Lady Edgware and sidles past the butler with mincing steps. No suspicions are aroused. 'Jane,' cries my fond Uncle. 'George,' I squeak. I fling my arms about his neck and neatly insert the penknife. The next details are purely medical and can be omitted. Exit the spurious lady. And so to bed at the end of a good day's work."

He laughed and, rising, poured himself out another whisky and soda. He returned slowly to his chair.

"Works out well, doesn't it? But you see, here comes the crux

of the matter. The disappointment! The annoying sensation of
having been led up the garden. For now, M. Poirot, we come
to the alibi!"

He finished off his glass.

"I always find alibis very enjoyable," he remarked. "Whenever I happen to be reading a detective story I sit up and take
notice when the alibi comes along. This is a remarkably good
alibi. Three strong. In plainer language, Mr., Mrs., and Miss
Dortheimer. Extremely rich and extremely musical. They have
a box at Covent Garden. Into that box they invite young men
with prospects. I, M. Poirot, am a young man with prospects.
Do I like the opera? Frankly, no. But I enjoy the excellent dinner
in Grosvenor Square first, and I also enjoy an excellent supper
somewhere else afterward, even if I do have to dance with
Rachel Dortheimer and have a stiff arm for two days afterward.
So, you see, M. Poirot, there you are. When Uncle's life blood
is flowing, I am whispering cheerful nothings into the diamond-
encrusted ears of the fair Rachel in a box at Covent Garden.
And so you see, M. Poirot, why I can afford to be so frank."

He leaned back in his chair.

"I hope I have not bored you. Any questions to ask?"

"I can assure you that I have not been bored," said Poirot.
"Since you are so kind, there is one little question that I would
like to ask."

"Delighted."

"How long, Lord Edgware, have you known Miss Carlotta
Adams?"

Whatever the young man had expected, it certainly had not
been this. He sat up sharply with an entirely new expression
on his face.

"Why on earth do you want to know that? What's that got
to do with what we've been talking about?"

"I was curious, that was all. For the other, you have explained
so fully everything there is to explain that there is no need for
me to ask questions."

Ronald shot a quick glance at him. It was almost as though
he did not care for Poirot's amiable acquiescence. He would, I
thought, have preferred him to be more suspicious.

"Carlotta Adams? Let me see. About a year. A little more. I got to know her last year when she gave her first show."

"You knew her well?"

"Pretty well. She's not the sort of girl you ever get to know frightfully well. Reserved and all that."

"But you liked her?"

Ronald stared at him.

"I wish I knew why you are so interested in the lady. Is it because I was with her the other night? Yes, I like her very much. She's sympathetic—listens to a chap and makes him feel he's something of a fellow after all."

Poirot nodded.

"I comprehend. Then you will be sorry."

"Sorry? What about?"

"Sorry to hear the news."

"What news?"

"That she is dead."

"What?" Ronald sprang up in astonishment. "Carlotta dead?" He looked absolutely dumbfounded by the news.

"You're pulling my leg, M. Poirot. Carlotta was perfectly well the last time I saw her."

"When was that?" asked Poirot quickly.

"Day before yesterday, I think. I can't remember."

"*Tout de même,* she is dead."

"It must have been frightfully sudden. What was it? A street accident?"

Poirot looked at the ceiling.

"No. She took an overdose of veronal."

"Oh! I say. Poor kid. How frightfully sad."

"*N'est ce pas?*"

"I *am* sorry. And she was getting on so well. She was going to get her kid sister over and had all sorts of plans. Dash it, I'm more sorry than I can say."

"Yes," said Poirot. "It is sad to die when you are young— when you do not want to die—when all life is open before you and you have everything to live for."

Ronald looked at him curiously.

"I don't think I quite get you, M. Poirot?"

"No?"

Poirot rose and held out his hand.

"I express my thoughts a little strongly perhaps, for I do not like to see youth deprived of its right to live, Lord Edgware. I feel—very strongly about it. I wish you good-day."

"Oh!—er— Good-bye."

He looked rather taken aback.

As I opened the door I almost collided with Miss Carroll.

"Ah! M. Poirot, they told me you hadn't gone yet. I'd like a word with you if I may. Perhaps you wouldn't mind coming up to my room."

"It's about that child, Geraldine," she said when we had entered her sanctum and she had closed the door.

"Yes, mademoiselle?"

"She talked a lot of nonsense this afternoon. Now don't protest. Nonsense! That's what I call it and that's what it was. She broods."

"I could see that she was suffering from over strain," said Poirot gently.

"Well—to tell the truth—she hasn't had a very happy life. No, one can't pretend she has. Frankly, M. Poirot, Lord Edgware was a peculiar man—not the sort of man who ought to have had anything to do with the upbringing of children. Quite frankly, he terrorized Geraldine."

Poirot nodded.

"Yes, I should imagine something of the kind."

"He was a peculiar man. He—I don't quite know how to put it—but he enjoyed seeing anyone afraid of him. It seemed to give him a morbid kind of pleasure."

"Quite so."

"He was an extremely well-read man, and a man of considerable intellect; but in some ways—well, I didn't come across that side of him myself, but it was there. I'm not really surprised his wife left him. This wife, I mean. I didn't approve of her, mind. I've no opinion of that young woman at all, but in marrying Lord Edgware she got all and more than she deserved. Well, she left him—and no bones broken, as they say. But Geraldine couldn't leave him. For a long time he'd forget all about her, and then, suddenly, he'd remember. I sometimes think—though perhaps I shouldn't say it—"

"Yes, yes, mademoiselle, say it."

"Well, I sometimes thought he revenged himself on the mother—his first wife—that way. She was a gentle creature, I believe, with a very sweet disposition. I've always been sorry for her. I shouldn't have mentioned all this, M. Poirot, if it hadn't been for that very foolish outburst of Geraldine's just now. The things she said—about hating her father—they might sound peculiar to anyone who didn't know."

"Thank you very much, mademoiselle. Lord Edgware, I fancy, was a man who would have done much better not to marry."

"Much better."

"He never thought of marrying for a third time?"

"How could he? His wife was alive."

"By giving her her freedom, he would have been free himself."

"I should think he had had enough trouble with two wives as it was," said Miss Carroll grimly.

"So you think there would have been no question of a third marriage. There was no one? Think, mademoiselle. No one?"

Miss Carroll's colour rose.

"I cannot understand the way you keep harping on the point. Of course there was no one."

XIV Five Questions

"WHY did you ask Miss Carroll about the possibility of Lord Edgware's wanting to marry again?" I asked with some curiosity as we were driving home.

"It just occurred to me that there was the possibility of such a thing, *mon ami.*"

"Why?"

"I have been searching in my mind for something to explain Lord Edgware's sudden *volte face* regarding the matter of divorce. There is something curious there, my friend."

"Yes," I said thoughtfully. "It is rather odd."

"You see, Hastings, milor', he confirmed what madame had told us. She had employed the lawyers of all kinds, but he refused to budge the inch. No, he would not agree to the divorce. And then, all of a sudden, he yields!"

"Or so he says," I reminded him.

"Very true, Hastings. It is very just, the observation you make there. *So he says.* We have no proof, whatever, that that letter was written. *Eh bien,* on one part, *ce monsieur* is lying. For some reason he tells us the fabrication, the embroidery. Is it not so? Why, we do not know. But, on the hypothesis that he *did* write that letter, there must have been a *reason* for so doing. Now the reason that presents itself most naturally to the imagination is that he has suddenly met someone whom he desires to marry. That explains perfectly his sudden change of face. And so, naturally, I make the inquiries."

"Miss Carroll turned the idea down very decisively," I said.

"Yes. Miss Carroll," said Poirot in a meditative voice.

"Now what are you driving at?" I asked in exasperation.

Poirot is an adept at suggesting doubts by the tone of his voice.

"What reason should she have for lying about it?" I asked.

"*Aucune—aucune*. But, you see, Hastings, it is difficult to trust her evidence."

"You think she's lying? But why? She looks a most upright person."

"That is just it. Between the deliberate falsehood and the disinterested inaccuracy it is very hard to distinguish sometimes."

"What *do* you mean?"

"To deceive deliberately—that is one thing. But to be so sure of your facts, of your ideas, and of their essential truth, that the details do not matter—that, my friend, is a special characteristic of particularly honest persons. Already, mark you, she has told us one lie. She said she saw Jane Wilkinson's face when she could not possibly have done so. Now how did that come about? Look at it this way. She looks down and sees Jane Wilkinson in the hall. No doubt enters her head that it *is* Jane Wilkinson. She *knows* it is. She says she saw her face distinctly because—being so sure of her facts—exact details do not matter! It is pointed out to her that she could not have seen her face. Is that so? Well, what does it matter if she saw her face or not—it *was* Jane Wilkinson. And so with any other question. She *knows*. And so she answers questions in the light of her knowledge, not by reason of remembered facts. The positive witness should always be treated with suspicion, my friend. The uncertain witness, who doesn't remember, isn't sure, will think a minute—ah! yes, that's how it was—is infinitely more to be depended upon!"

"Dear me, Poirot," I said. "You upset all my preconceived ideas about witnesses."

"In reply to my question as to Lord Edgware's marrying again she ridicules the idea—simply because it has never occurred to her. She will not take the trouble to remember whether any infinitesimal signs may have pointed that way. Therefore we are exactly where we were before."

"She certainly did not seem at all taken aback when you pointed out that she could not have seen Jane Wilkinson's face," I remarked thoughtfully.

"No. That is why I decided that she was one of those honestly inaccurate persons, rather than a deliberate liar. I can see no motive for deliberate lying unless—true, that is an idea!"

"What is?" I asked eagerly.

But Poirot shook his head.

"An idea suggested itself to me, but it is too impossible—yes, much too impossible."

And he refused to say more.

"She seems very fond of the girl," I said.

"Yes. She certainly was determined to assist at our interview. What was your impression of Miss Geraldine Marsh, Hastings?"

"I was sorry for her—deeply sorry for her."

"You have always the tender heart, Hastings. Beauty in distress upsets you every time."

"Didn't you feel the same?"

He nodded gravely.

"Yes. She has not had a happy life. That is written very clearly on her face."

"At any rate," I said warmly, "you realize how preposterous Jane Wilkinson's suggestion was—that she should have had anything to do with the crime, I mean."

"Doubtless her alibi is satisfactory, but Japp has not communicated it to me as yet."

"My dear Poirot, do you mean to say that, even after seeing her and talking to her, you are still not satisfied and want an alibi?"

"*Eh bien,* my friend, what is the result of seeing and talking to her? We perceive that she has passed through great unhappiness; she admits that she hated her father and is glad that he is dead, and she is deeply uneasy about what he may have said to us yesterday morning. And after that you say—no alibi is necessary!"

"Her mere frankness proves her innocence," I said warmly.

"Frankness is a characteristic of the family. The new Lord Edgware—with what a gesture he laid his cards on the table."

"He did indeed," I said, smiling at the remembrance. "Rather an original method."

Poirot nodded.

"He—what do you say?—cuts the ground before our feet."

"From under," I corrected. "Yes, it made us look rather foolish."

"What a curious idea. You may have looked foolish. I did not feel foolish in the least, and I do not think I looked it. On the contrary, my friend, I put him out of countenance."

"Did you?" I said doubtfully, not remembering having seen signs of anything of the kind.

"*Si, si.* I listen—and listen, and at last I ask a question about something quite different; and that, you may have noticed, disconcerts our brave monsieur very much. You do not observe, Hastings."

"I thought his horror and astonishment at hearing of Carlotta Adams' death was genuine," I said. "I suppose you will say it was a piece of clever acting."

"Impossible to tell. I agree it *seemed* genuine."

"Why do you think he flung all those facts at our head in that cynical way? Just for amusement?"

"That is always possible. You English, you have the most extraordinary notions of humour. But it may have been policy. Facts that are concealed acquire a suspicious importance. Facts that are frankly revealed tend to be regarded as less important than they really are."

"The quarrel with his uncle that morning, for instance?"

"Exactly. He knows that the fact is bound to leak out. *Eh bien,* he will parade it."

"He is not so foolish as he looks."

"Oh! he is not foolish at all. He has plenty of brains when he cares to use them. He sees exactly where he stands and, as I said, he lays his cards on the table. You play the bridge, Hastings. Tell me, when does one do that?"

"You play bridge yourself," I said, laughing. "You know well enough—when all the rest of the tricks are yours and you want to save time and get on to a new hand."

"Yes, *mon ami,* that is all very true. But occasionally there is another reason. I have remarked it once or twice when playing with *les dames.* There is perhaps a little doubt. *Eh bien, la dame,* she throws down the cards, says 'and all the rest are mine' and gathers up the cards and cuts the new pack. And possibly the other players agree—especially if they are a little inexperienced. The thing is not obvious, mark you. It requires to be followed out. Half way through dealing the next hand, one of the players thinks: 'Yes, but she would have to have taken over that fourth diamond in dummy whether she wanted to or not, and then she would have had to lead a little club and my nine would have made.'"

"So you think?"

"I think, Hastings, that too much bravado is a very interesting thing. And I also think that it is time we dined. *Une petite omelette, n'est ce pas?* And after that, about nine o'clock, I have one more visit I wish to make."

"Where is that?"

"We will dine first, Hastings, and, until we drink our coffee, we will not discuss the case further. When engaged in eating, the brain should be the servant of the stomach."

Poirot was as good as his word. We went to a little restaurant in Soho where he was well known, and there we had a delicious omelette, a sole, a chicken and a baba au rhum of which Poirot was inordinately fond.

Then, as we sipped our coffee, Poirot smiled affectionately across the table at me.

"My good friend," he said. "I depend upon you more than you know."

I was confused and delighted by these unexpected words. He had never said anything of the kind to me before. Sometimes, secretly, I had felt slightly hurt. He seemed almost to go out of his way to disparage my mental powers.

Although I did not think his own powers were flagging, I did realize suddenly that perhaps he had come to depend on my aid more than he knew.

"Yes," he said dreamily, "you may not always comprehend just how it is so—but you do often and often point the way."

I could hardly believe my ears.

"Really, Poirot," I stammered, "I'm awfully glad. I suppose I've learnt a good deal from you one way or another—"

He shook his head.

"Mais non, ce n'est pas ça. You have learnt nothing."

"Oh!" I said, rather taken aback.

"That is as it should be. No human being should learn from

another. Each individual should develop his own powers to the uttermost, not try to imitate those of someone else. I do not wish you to be a second and inferior Poirot. I wish you to be the supreme Hastings. And you are the supreme Hastings. In you, Hastings, I find the normal mind almost perfectly illustrated."

"I'm not abnormal, I hope," I said.

"No, no. You are beautifully and perfectly balanced. In you sanity is personified. Do you realize what that means to me? When the criminal sets out to do a crime his first effort is to deceive. Whom does he seek to deceive? The image in his mind is that of the normal man. There is probably no such thing actually—it is a mathematical abstraction. But you come as near to realizing it as is possible. There are moments when you have flashes of brilliance, when you rise above the average, moments (I hope you will pardon me) when you descend to curious depths of obtuseness, but, take it all for all, you are amazingly normal. *Eh bien,* how does this profit me? Simply in this way. As in a mirror I see reflected in your mind exactly what the criminal wishes me to believe. That is terrifically helpful and suggestive."

I did not quite understand. It seemed to me that what Poirot was saying was hardly complimentary. However, he quickly disabused me of that impression.

"I have expressed myself badly," he said quickly. "You have an insight into the criminal mind, which I myself lack. You show me what the criminal wishes me to believe. It is a great gift."

"Insight," I said thoughtfully. "Yes, perhaps I have got insight."

I looked across the table at him. He was smoking his tiny cigarettes and regarding me with great kindliness.

"Ce cher Hastings," he murmured. "I have indeed much affection for you."

I was pleased but embarrassed and hastened to change the subject.

"Come," I said in a businesslike manner. "Let us discuss the case."

"*Eh bien.*" Poirot threw his head back, his eyes narrowed. He slowly puffed out smoke.

"*Je me pose des questions,*" he said.

"Yes?" I said eagerly.

"You, too, doubtless?"

"Certainly," I said. And also leaning back and narrowing my own eyes I threw out:

"Who killed Lord Edgware?"

Poirot immediately sat up and shook his head vigorously.

"No, no. Not at all. Is it a question, that? You are like someone who reads the detective story and who starts guessing each of the characters in turn without rhyme or reason. Once, I agree, I had to do that myself. It was a very exceptional case. I will tell you about it one of these days. It was a feather in my cap. But of what were we speaking?"

"Of the questions you were 'posing' to yourself," I replied dryly. It was on the tip of my tongue to suggest that my real use to Poirot was to provide him with a companion to whom he could boast, but I controlled myself. If he wished to instruct, then let him.

"Come on," I said. "Let's hear them."

That was all that the vanity of the man wanted. He leaned back again and resumed his former attitude.

"The first question we have already discussed. *Why did Lord Edgware change his mind on the subject of divorce?* One or two ideas suggest themselves to me on that subject. One of them you know.

"The second question I ask myself is *What happened to that letter?* To whose interest was it that Lord Edgware and his wife should continue to be tied together?

"Three, *What was the meaning of the expression on his face that you saw when you looked back yesterday morning on leaving the library?* Have you any answer to that, Hastings?"

I shook my head.

"I can't understand it."

"You are sure that you didn't imagine it? Sometimes, Hastings, you have the imagination *un peu vif.*"

"No, no." I shook my head vigorously. "I'm quite sure I wasn't mistaken."

"*Bien.* Then it is a fact to be explained. My fourth question concerns those pince-nez. Neither Jane Wilkinson nor Carlotta Adams wore glasses. *What, then, are the glasses doing in Carlotta Adams' bag?*

"And for my fifth question. *Why did someone telephone to find out if Jane Wilkinson were at Chiswick and who was it?*

"Those, my friend, are the questions with which I am tormenting myself. If I could answer those, I should feel happier in my mind. If I could even evolve a theory that explained them satisfactorily, my *amour propre* would not suffer so much."

"There are several other questions," I said.

"Such as?"

"Who incited Carlotta Adams to this hoax? Where was she that evening before and after ten o'clock? Who is D, who gave her the golden box?"

"Those questions are self-evident," said Poirot. "There is no subtlety about them. They are simply things we do not know. They are questions of *fact*. We may get to know them any minute. My questions, *mon ami,* are psychological. The little grey cells of the brain—"

"Poirot," I said desperately. I felt that I must stop him at all costs. I could not bear to hear it all over again. "You spoke of making a visit tonight?"

Poirot looked at his watch.

"True," he said. "I will telephone and find out if it is convenient."

He went away and returned a few minutes later.

"Come," he said. "All is well."

"Where are we going?" I asked.

"To the house of Sir Montagu Corner at Chiswick. I would like to know a little more about that telephone call."

XV Sir Montagu Corner

It was about ten o'clock when we reached Sir Montagu Corner's house on the river at Chiswick. It was a big house standing back in its own grounds. We were admitted into a beautifully panelled hall. On our right, through an open door, we saw the dining-room, with its long polished table lit with candles.

"Will you come this way, please?"

The butler led the way up a broad staircase and into a long room on the first floor overlooking the river.

"M. Hercule Poirot," announced the butler.

It was a beautifully proportioned room, and had an old-world air with its carefully shaded dim lamps. In one corner of the room was a bridge table, set near the open window, and round it sat four people. As we entered the room one of the four rose and came towards us.

"It is a great pleasure to make your acquaintance, M. Poirot."

I looked with some interest at Sir Montagu Corner. He had very small, intelligent black eyes and a carefully arranged toupee. He was a short man—five foot eight at most, I should say. His manner was affected to the last degree.

"Let me introduce you. Mr. and Mrs. Widburn."

"We've met before," said Mrs. Widburn brightly.

"And Mr. Ross."

Ross was a young fellow of about twenty-two, with a pleasant face and fair hair.

"I disturb your game. A million apologies," said Poirot.

"Not at all. We have not started. We were commencing to deal the cards only. Some coffee, M. Poirot?"

Poirot declined, but accepted an offer of old brandy. It was brought us in immense goblets.

As we sipped it, Sir Montagu discoursed. He spoke of Japanese prints, of Chinese lacquer, of Persian carpets, of the French impressionists, of modern music and of the theories of Einstein. Then he sat back and smiled at us beneficently. He had evidently thoroughly enjoyed his performance. In the dim light he looked like some genie of mediæval days. All round the room were exquisite examples of art and culture.

"And now, Sir Montagu," said Poirot. "I will trespass on your kindness no longer but will come to the object of my visit."

Sir Montagu waved a curious clawlike hand.

"There is no hurry. Time is infinite."

"One always feels that in this house," sighed Mrs. Widburn. "So wonderful."

"I would not live in London for a million pounds," said Sir Montagu. "Here one is in the old-world atmosphere of peace that, alas, we have put behind us in these jarring days."

A sudden impish fancy flashed over me that, if someone were really to offer Sir Montagu a million pounds, old-world peace might go to the wall, but I trod down such heretical sentiments.

"What is money, after all?" murmured Mrs. Widburn.

"Ah!" said Mr. Widburn thoughtfully and rattled some coins absent-mindedly in his trousers pocket.

"Archie," said Mrs. Widburn reproachfully.

"Sorry," said Mr. Widburn and stopped.

"To speak of crime in such an atmosphere is, I feel, unpardonable," began Poirot apologetically.

"Not at all." Sir Montagu waved a gracious hand. "A crime can be a work of art. A detective can be an artist. I do not refer, of course, to the police. An inspector has been here today. A curious person. He had never heard of Benvenuto Cellini, for instance."

"He came about Jane Wilkinson, I suppose," said Mrs. Widburn with instant curiosity.

"It was fortunate for that lady that she was at your house last night," said Poirot.

"So it seems," said Sir Montagu. "I asked her here knowing that she was beautiful and talented and hoping that I might be able to be of use to her. She was thinking of going into management. But it seems that I was fated to be of use to her in a very different way."

"Jane's got luck," said Mrs. Widburn. "She's been dying to get rid of Edgware, and here's somebody gone and saved her the trouble. She'll marry the young Duke of Merton now. Everyone says so. His mother's wild about it."

"I was favourably impressed by her," said Sir Montagu graciously. "She made several most intelligent remarks about Greek art."

I smiled to myself, picturing Jane saying, "Yes," and "No," "Really, how wonderful," in her magical husky voice. Sir Montagu was the type of man to whom intelligence consisted of the faculty of listening to his own remarks with suitable attention.

"Edgware was a queer fish, by all accounts," said Widburn. "I dare say he had a good few enemies."

"Is it true, M. Poirot," asked Mrs. Widburn, "that somebody ran a penknife into the back of his brain?"

"Perfectly true, madame. It was very neatly and efficiently done—scientific, in fact."

"I note your artistic pleasure, M. Poirot," said Sir Montagu.

"And now," said Poirot, "let me come to the object of my visit. Lady Edgware was called to the telephone when she was here at dinner. It is about that telephone call that I seek information. Perhaps you will allow me to question your domestics on the subject?"

"Certainly. Certainly. Just press that bell, will you, Ross?"

The butler answered the bell. He was a tall, middle-aged man of ecclesiastical appearance. Sir Montagu explained what was wanted. The butler turned to Poirot with polite attention.

"Who answered the telephone when it rang?" began Poirot.

"I answered it myself, sir. The telephone is in a recess leading out of the hall."

"Did the person calling ask to speak to Lady Edgware or to Miss Jane Wilkinson?"

"To Lady Edgware, sir."

"What did they say exactly?"

The butler reflected for a moment.

"As far as I remember, sir, I said, 'Hello.' A voice then asked

if I was Chiswick 43434. I replied that that was so. It then
asked me to hold the line. Another voice then asked if that was
Chiswick 43434 and on my replying, 'Yes,' it said, 'Is Lady
Edgware dining there?' I said her ladyship *was* dining here. The
voice said, 'I would like to speak to her please.' I went and informed her ladyship, who was at the dinner table. Her ladyship
rose, and I showed her where the phone was."

"And then?"

"Her ladyship picked up the receiver and said: 'Hello—who's
speaking?' Then she said, 'Yes—that's all right. Lady Edgware
speaking.' I was just about to leave her ladyship when she
called to me and said they had cut her off. She said someone
had laughed and evidently hung up the receiver. She asked me
if the person ringing up had given any name. They had not
done so. That was all that occurred, sir."

Poirot frowned to himself.

"Do you really think the telephone call has something to do
with the murder, M. Poirot?" asked Mrs. Widburn.

"Impossible to say, madame. It is just a curious circumstance."

"People do ring up for a joke sometimes. It's been done to
me."

"*C'est toujours possible, madame.*"

He spoke to the butler again.

"Was it a man's voice or a woman's who rang up?"

"A lady's, I think, sir."

"What kind of a voice, high or low?"

"Low, sir. Careful and rather distinct." He paused. "It may
be my fancy, sir, but it sounded like a *foreign* voice. The R's
were very noticeable."

"As far as that goes, it might have been a Scotch voice,
Donald," said Mrs. Widburn, smiling at Ross.

Ross laughed.

"Not guilty," he said. "I was at the dinner table."

Poirot spoke once again to the butler.

"Do you think," he asked, "that you would recognize that
voice if you were to hear it any time?"

The butler hesitated.

"I couldn't quite say, sir. I might do so. I think it is possible that I should do so."

"I thank you, my friend."

"Thank you, sir."

The butler inclined his head and withdrew, pontifical to the last.

Sir Montagu Corner continued to be very friendly and to play his rôle of old-world charm. He persuaded us to remain and play bridge. I excused myself—the stakes were bigger than I cared about. Young Ross seemed relieved also at the prospect of someone taking his hand. He and I sat looking on while the other four played. The evening ended in a heavy financial gain to Poirot and Sir Montagu.

Then we thanked our host and took our departure. Ross came with us.

"A strange little man," said Poirot as we stepped out into the night.

The night was fine and we had decided to walk until we picked up a taxi, instead of having one telephoned for.

"Yes, a strange little man," said Poirot again.

"A very rich little man," said Ross with feeling.

"I suppose so."

"He seems to have taken a fancy to me," said Ross. "Hope it will last. A man like that behind you means a lot."

"You are an actor, Mr. Ross?"

Ross said that he was. He seemed sad that his name had not brought instant recognition. Apparently he had recently won marvellous notices in some gloomy play translated from the Russian. When Poirot and I between us had soothed him down again, Poirot asked casually:

"You knew Carlotta Adams, did you not?"

"No. I saw her death announced in the paper tonight. Overdose of some drug or other. Idiotic the way all these girls dope."

"It is sad, yes. She was clever, too."

"I suppose so."

He displayed a characteristic lack of interest in anyone else's performance but his own.

"Did you see her show at all?" I asked.

"No. That sort of thing's not much in my line. Kind of craze for it at present, but I don't think it will last."

"Ah!" said Poirot. "Here is a taxi."

He waved a stick.

"Think I'll walk," said Ross. "I get a tube straight home from Hammersmith."

Suddenly he gave a nervous laugh.

"Odd thing," he said. "That dinner last night."

"Yes?"

"We were thirteen. Some fellow failed at the last minute. We never noticed it till just the end of dinner."

"And who got up first?" I asked.

He gave a queer little nervous cackle of laughter.

"I did," he said.

XVI Mainly Discussion

WHEN we got home we found Japp waiting for us.

"Thought I'd just call round and have a chat with you before turning in, M. Poirot," he said cheerfully.

"*Eh bien,* my good friend, how goes it?"

"Well, it doesn't go any too well, and that's a fact." He looked depressed. "Got any help for me, M. Poirot?"

"I have one or two little ideas that I should like to present to you," said Poirot.

"You and your ideas! In some ways, you know, you're a caution. Not that I don't want to hear them. I do. There's some good stuff in that funny shaped head of yours."

Poirot acknowledged the compliment somewhat coldly.

"Have you any ideas about the double lady problem? That's what I want to know. Eh, M. Poirot? What about it? Who was she?"

"That is exactly what I wish to talk to you about."

He asked Japp if he had ever heard of Carlotta Adams.

"I've heard the name. For the moment I can't just place it."

Poirot explained.

"Her! Does imitations, does she? Now what made you fix on her? What have you got to go on?"

Poirot related the steps we had taken and the conclusion we had drawn.

"By the Lord, it looks as though you were right. Clothes, hat, gloves, and the fair wig. Yes, it must be. I will say, you're the goods, M. Poirot. Smart work, that! Not that I think there's anything to show she was put out of the way. That seems a bit far fetched. I don't quite see eye to eye with you there. Your theory is a bit fantastical for me. I've more experience than you have. I don't believe in this villain-behind-the-scenes motif. Carlotta Adams was the woman all right, but I should put it

one of two ways. She went there for purposes of her own—
blackmail, maybe, since she hinted she was going to get money.
They had a bit of a dispute. He turned nasty, she turned nasty,
and she finished him off. And I should say that when she got
home she went all to pieces. She hadn't meant murder. It's my
belief she took an overdose on purpose, as the easiest way out."

"You think that covers all the facts?"

"Well, naturally there are a lot of things we don't know yet.
It's a good working hypothesis to go on with. The other explanation is that the hoax and the murder had nothing to do with
each other. It's just a damned queer coincidence."

Poirot did not agree, I knew, but he merely said
noncommittally:

"Mais oui, c'est possible."

"Or, look here, how's this? The hoax is innocent enough.
Someone gets to hear of it and thinks it will suit their purpose
jolly well. That's not a bad idea?" He paused, then went on:
"But personally I prefer idea number one. What the link was
between his lordship and the girl we'll find out somehow or
other."

Poirot told him of the letter to America, posted by the maid,
and Japp agreed that that might possibly be of great assistance.

"I'll get on to that at once," he said, making a note of it in his
little book.

"I'm the more in favour of the lady being the killer because
I can't find anyone else," he said, as he put the book away.
"Captain Marsh now, his lordship as now is. He's got a motive
sticking out a yard. A bad record too. Hard up and none too
scrupulous over money. What's more he had a row with his
uncle yesterday morning. He told me that himself, as a matter
of fact, which rather takes the taste out of it. Yes, he'd be a
likely customer. But he's got an alibi for yesterday evening. He
was at the opera with the Dortheimers. Rich Jews. Grosvenor
Square. I've looked into that and it's all right. He dined with
them, went to the opera and they went on to supper at Sobrani's.
So that's that."

"And mademoiselle?"

"The daughter, you mean? She was out of the house too.

Dined with some people called Carthew West. They took her
to the opera and saw her home afterward. Quarter to twelve
she got in. That disposes of *her*. The secretary woman seems
all right—very efficient, decent woman. Then there's the butler.
I can't say I take to him much. It isn't natural for a man to have
good looks like that. There's something fishy about him, and
something odd about the way he came to enter Lord Edgware's
service. Yes, I'm checking up on him all right. I can't see any
motive for murder, though."

"No fresh facts have come to light?"

"Yes, one or two. It's hard to say whether they mean anything or not. For one thing Lord Edgware's key's missing."

"The key to the front door?"

"Yes."

"That is interesting, certainly."

"As I say, it may mean a good deal or nothing at all. Depends.
What *is* a bit more significant to my mind is this. Lord Edgware
cashed a cheque yesterday—not a particularly large one—a hundred pounds, as a matter of fact. He took the money in French
notes. That's why he cashed the cheque, because of his journey
to Paris today. Well, that money has disappeared."

"Who told you of this?"

"Miss Carroll. She cashed the cheque and obtained the money.
She mentioned it to me, and then I found that it had gone."

"Where was it yesterday evening?"

"Miss Carroll doesn't know. She gave it to Lord Edgware
about half past three. It was in a bank envelope. He was in the
library at the time. He took it and laid it down beside him on
a table."

"That certainly gives one to think. It is a complication."

"Or a simplification. By the way—the wound."

"Yes?"

"The doctor says it wasn't made by an ordinary penknife.
Something of that kind but a different shaped blade. And it
was amazingly sharp."

"Not a razor?"

"No, no. Much smaller."

Poirot frowned thoughtfully.

"The new Lord Edgware seems to be fond of his joke," remarked Japp. "He seems to think it amusing to be suspected of murder. He made sure we *did* suspect him of murder, too. Looks a bit queer, that."

"It might be merely intelligence."

"More likely guilty conscience. His uncle's death came very pat for him. He's moved into the house, by the way."

"Where was he living before?"

"Martin Street, St. George's Road. Not a very swell neighbourhood."

"You might make a note of that, Hastings."

I did so, though I wondered a little. If Ronald had moved to Regent Gate, his former address was hardly likely to be needed.

"*I* think the Adams girl did it," said Japp, rising. "A fine bit of work on your part, M. Poirot, to tumble to that. But there, of course you go about to theatres and amusing yourself. Things strike you that don't get the chance of striking me. Pity there's no apparent motive, but a little spade work will soon bring it to light, I expect."

"There is one person with a motive to whom you have given no attention," remarked Poirot.

"Who's that, sir?"

"The gentleman who is reputed to have wanted to marry Lord Edgware's wife. I mean the Duke of Merton."

"Yes, I suppose there is a motive." Japp laughed. "But a gentleman in his position isn't likely to do murder. And anyway, he's over in Paris."

"You do not regard him as a serious suspect, then?"

"Well, M. Poirot, do you?"

And laughing at the absurdity of the idea, Japp left us.

XVII The Butler

THE following day was one of inactivity for us, and activity
for Japp. He came round to see us about tea time. He was red
and wrathful.

"I've made a bloomer."

"Impossible, my friend," said Poirot soothingly.

"Yes, I have. I've let that (here he gave way to profanity)
. . . of a butler slip through my fingers."

"He has disappeared?"

"Yes. Hooked it. What makes me kick myself for a double-
dyed idiot is that I didn't particularly suspect him."

"Calm yourself—but calm yourself then."

"All very well to talk. *You* wouldn't be calm if you'd been
hauled over the coals at headquarters. Oh! he's a slippery customer. It isn't the first time he's given anyone the slip. He's an
old hand."

Japp wiped his forehead and looked the picture of misery.
Poirot made sympathetic noises, somewhat suggestive of a hen
laying an egg. With more insight into the English character, I
poured out a stiff whisky and soda and placed it in front of the
gloomy inspector. He brightened a little.

"Well," he said. "I don't mind if I do."

Presently he began to talk more cheerfully.

"I'm not so sure even now that he's the murderer! Of course
it looks bad his bolting this way, but there might be other reasons
for that. I'd begun to get on to him, you see. Seems he's mixed
up with a couple of rather disreputable night clubs. Not the
usual thing. Something a great deal more recherché and nasty.
In fact, he's a real bad hat."

"*Tout de même,* that does not necessarily mean that he is a
murderer."

"Exactly! He may have been up to some funny business or

other, but not necessarily murder. No, I'm more than ever convinced it was the Adams girl. I've got nothing to prove it as yet, though. I've had men going all through her flat today, but we've found nothing that's helpful. She was a canny one. Kept no letters except a few business ones about financial contracts. They're all neatly docketed and labelled. Couple of letters from her sister in Washington. Quite straight and above board. One or two pieces of good old-fashioned jewellery—nothing new or expensive. She didn't keep a diary. Her pass book and cheque book don't show anything helpful. Dash it all, the girl doesn't seem to have had any private life at all!"

"She was of a reserved character," said Poirot thoughtfully. "From our point of view that is a pity."

"I've talked to the woman who did for her. Nothing there. I've been and seen that girl who keeps a hat shop and who, it seems, was a friend of hers."

"Ah! and what do you think of Miss Driver?"

"She seems a smart, wide-awake bit of goods. She couldn't help me, though. Not that that surprises me. The amount of missing girls I've had to trace, and their family and their friends always say the same things. 'She was of a bright and affectionate disposition and had no men friends.' That's never true. It's unnatural. Girls ought to have men friends. If not there's something wrong about them. It's the muddle-headed loyalty of friends and relations that makes a detective's life so difficult."

He paused for want of breath, and I replenished his glass.

"Thank you, Captain Hastings, I don't mind if I do. Well, there you are. You've got to hunt and hunt about. There's about a dozen young men she went out to supper and danced with, but nothing to show that one of them meant more than another. There's the present Lord Edgware; there's Mr. Bryan Martin, the film star, there's half a dozen others, but nothing special and particular. Your man-behind idea is all wrong. I think you'll find that she played a lone hand, M. Poirot. I'm looking now for the connection between her and the murdered man. That must exist. I think I'll have to go over to Paris. There was Paris written in that little gold box, and the late Lord Edgware ran over to Paris several times last autumn, so Miss Carroll tells me, attending sales and buying curios. Yes, I think I must go over to Paris. Inquest's tomorrow. It'll be adjourned, of course. After that I'll take the afternoon boat."

"You have a furious energy, Japp. It amazes me."

"Yes, you're getting lazy. You just sit here and *think!* What you call employing the little grey cells. No good; you've got to go out to things. They won't come to you."

The little maid servant opened the door.

"Mr. Bryan Martin, sir. Are you busy or will you see him?"

"I'm off, M. Poirot." Japp hoisted himself up. "All the stars of the theatrical world seem to consult you."

Poirot shrugged a modest shoulder, and Japp laughed.

"You must be a millionaire by now, M. Poirot. What do you do with the money? Save it?"

"Assuredly I practise the thrift. And talking of the disposal of money, how did Lord Edgware dispose of his?"

"Such property as wasn't entailed he left to his daughter. Five hundred to Miss Carroll. No other bequests. Very simple will."

"And it was made—when?"

"After his wife left him, just over two years ago. He expressly excludes her from participation, by the way."

"A vindictive man," murmured Poirot to himself.

With a cheerful "So long," Japp departed.

Bryan Martin entered. He was faultlessly attired and looked extremely handsome, yet I thought that he looked haggard and not too happy.

"I am afraid I have been a long time coming, M. Poirot," he said apologetically, "and, after all, I have been guilty of taking up your time for nothing."

"En verité?"

"Yes. I have seen the lady in question. I've argued with her, pleaded with her, but all to no purpose. She won't hear of my interesting you in the matter. So I'm afraid we'll have to let the thing drop. I'm very sorry—very sorry to have bothered you—"

"Du tout, du tout," said Poirot genially. "I expected this."

"Eh?" The young man seemed taken aback.

"You expected this?" he asked in a puzzled way.

"*Mais oui*. When you spoke of consulting your friend, I could have predicted that all would have arrived as it has done."

"You have a theory, then?"

"A detective, M. Martin, always has a theory. It is expected of him. I do not call it a theory myself. I say that I have a little idea. That is the first stage."

"And the second stage?"

"If the little idea turns out to be right, then I *know!* It is quite simple, you see."

"I wish you'd tell me what your theory—or your little idea—is?"

Poirot shook his head gently.

"That is another rule. The detective never tells."

"Can't you suggest it even?"

"No. I will only say that I formed my theory as soon as you mentioned a gold tooth."

Bryan Martin stared at him.

"I'm absolutely bewildered," he declared. "I can't make out what you are driving at. If you'd just give me a hint."

Poirot smiled and shook his head.

"Let us change the subject."

"Yes, but first, your fee—you must let me."

Poirot waved an imperious hand.

"*Pas un sou!* I have done nothing to aid you."

"I took up your time—"

"When a case interests me, I do not touch money. Your case interested me very much."

"I'm glad," said the actor uneasily. He looked supremely unhappy.

"Come," said Poirot kindly. "Let us talk of something else."

"Wasn't that the Scotland Yard man whom I met on the stairs?"

"Yes, Inspector Japp."

"The light was so dim, I wasn't sure. By the way, he came round and asked me some questions about that poor girl, Carlotta Adams, who died of an overdose of veronal."

"You knew her well, Miss Adams?"

"Not very well. I knew her as a child in America. I came

across her here once or twice, but I never saw very much of her. I was very sorry to hear of her death."

"You liked her?"

"Yes. She was extraordinarily easy to talk to."

"A personality very sympathetic. Yes, I found the same."

"I suppose they think it might be suicide? I knew nothing that could help the inspector. Carlotta was always very reserved about herself."

"I do not think it was suicide," said Poirot.

"Far more likely to be an accident, I agree."

There was a pause. Then Poirot said with a smile:

"The affair of Lord Edgware's death becomes intriguing, does it not?"

"Absolutely amazing. Do you know, have they any idea who did it—now that Jane is definitely out of it?"

"*Mais oui*, they have a very strong suspicion."

Bryan Martin looked excited.

"Really? Who?"

"The butler has disappeared. You comprehend—flight is as good as a confession."

"The butler! Really, you surprise me."

"A singularly good-looking man. *Il vous ressemble un peu.*" He bowed in a complimentary fashion.

Of course! I realized now why the butler's face had struck me as being faintly familiar when I first saw it.

"You flatter me," said Bryan Martin with a laugh.

"No, no, no. Do not all the young girls, the servant girls, the flappers, the typists, the girls of society, do they not all adore M. Bryan Martin? Is there one who can resist you?"

"A lot, I should think," said Martin. He got up abruptly.

"Well, thank you very much, M. Poirot. Let me apologize again for having troubled you."

He shook hands with us both. Suddenly, I noticed, he looked much older. The haggard look was more apparent.

I was devoured with curiosity, and as soon as the door closed behind him, I burst out with what I wanted to know.

"Poirot, did you really expect him to come back and relinquish all idea of investigating those queer things that happened to him in America?"

"You heard me say so, Hastings."

"But then—" I followed the thing out logically.

"Then you must know who this mysterious girl is that he had to consult?"

He smiled.

"I have a little idea, my friend. As I told you, it started from the mention of the gold tooth; and, if my little idea is correct, I know who the girl is; I know why she will not let M. Martin consult me; I know the truth of the whole affair. And so could you know it if you would only use the brains the good God has given you. Sometimes, I really am tempted to believe that by inadvertence he passed you by."

XVIII The Other Man

I DO not propose to describe either the inquest on Lord Edgware or that on Carlotta Adams. In Carlotta's case the verdict was death by misadventure. In the case of Lord Edgware the inquest was adjourned, after evidence of identification and the medical evidence had been given. As a result of the analysis of the stomach, the time of death was fixed as having occurred not less than an hour after the completion of dinner, with possible extension to an hour after that. This put it as between ten and eleven o'clock, with the probability in favour of the earlier time.

None of the facts concerning Carlotta's impersonation of Jane Wilkinson were allowed to leak out. A description of the butler was published in the press and the general impression seemed to be that the butler was the man wanted. His story of Jane Wilkinson's visit was looked upon as an impudent fabrication. Nothing was said of the secretary's corroborating testimony. There were columns concerning the murder in all the papers, but little real information.

Meanwhile Japp was actively at work, I knew. It vexed me a little that Poirot adopted such an inert attitude. The suspicion that approaching old age had something to do with it flashed across me—not for the first time. He made excuses to me which did not ring very convincingly.

"At my time of life one saves oneself the trouble," he explained.

"But, Poirot, my dear fellow, you mustn't think of yourself as old," I protested. I felt that he needed bracing. Treatment by suggestion—that, I know, is the modern idea.

"You are as full of vigour as ever you were," I said earnestly. "You're in the prime of life, Poirot, at the height of your powers.

You could go out and solve this case magnificently if you only would."

Poirot replied that he preferred to solve it sitting at home.

"But you can't do that, Poirot."

"Not entirely, it is true."

"What I mean is, we are doing nothing! Japp is doing everything."

"Which suits me admirably."

"It doesn't suit me at all. I want you to be doing things."

"So I am."

"What are you doing?"

"Waiting."

"Waiting for what?"

"Pour que mon chien de chasse me rapporte le gibier," replied Poirot with a twinkle.

"What *do* you mean?"

"I mean the good Japp. Why keep a dog and bark yourself? Japp brings us here the result of the physical energy you admire so much. He has various means at his disposal which I have not. He will have news for us very soon, I do not doubt."

By dint of persistent inquiry, it was true that Japp was slowly getting together material. He had drawn a blank in Paris, but a couple of days later he came in looking pleased with himself.

"It's slow work," he said, "but we're getting somewhere at last."

"I congratulate you, my friend. What has happened?"

"I've discovered that a fair-haired lady deposited an attaché case in the cloak room at Euston at nine o'clock that night. They've been shown Miss Adams' case and identify it positively. It's of American make and so just a little different."

"Ah! Euston. Yes, the nearest of the big stations to Regent Gate. She went there doubtless, made herself up in the lavatory, and then left the case. When was it taken out again?"

"At half past ten. The clerk says by the same lady."

Poirot nodded.

"And I've come on something else too. I've reason to believe that Carlotta Adams was in Lyons Corner House in the Strand at eleven o'clock."

"Ah! c'est très bien ça! How did you come across that?"

"Well, really more or less by chance. You see, there's been a mention in the papers of the little gold box with the ruby initials. Some reporter wrote it up. He was doing an article on the prevalence of dope-taking among young actresses. Sunday paper romantic stuff. The fatal little gold box with its deadly contents —pathetic figure of a young girl with all the world before her! And just a wonder expressed as to where she passed her last evening and how she felt and so on and so on.

"Well, it seems a waitress at the Corner House read this, and she remembered that a lady she had served that evening had had such a box in her hand. She remembered the C. A. on it. And she got excited and began talking to all her friends. Perhaps a paper would give her something?

"A young newspaper man soon got onto it, and there's going to be a good sobstuff article in tonight's *Evening Shriek*. The last hours of the talented actress. Waiting—for the man who never came—and a good bit about the waitress's sympathetic intuition that something was not well with her sister woman. You know the kind of bilge, M. Poirot?"

"And how has it come to your ears so quickly?"

"Oh, well, we're on very good terms with the *Evening Shriek*. It got passed on to me while their particular bright young man tried to get some news out of me about something else. So I rushed along to the Corner House straight away—"

Yes, that was the way things ought to be done. I felt a pang of pity for Poirot. Here was Japp getting all this news at first hand—quite possibly missing valuable details—and here was Poirot placidly content with stale news.

"I saw the girl, and I don't think there's much doubt about it. She couldn't pick out Carlotta Adams' photograph, but then she said she didn't notice the lady's face particularly. She was young and dark and slim, and very well dressed, the girl said. Had got on one of the new hats. I wish women looked at faces a bit more and hats a bit less."

"The face of Miss Adams was not an easy one to observe," said Poirot. "It had the mobility, the sensitiveness, the fluid quality."

"I dare say you're right. I don't go in for analyzing these things. Dressed in black the lady was, so the girl said, and she had an attaché case with her. The girl noticed that particularly, because it struck her as odd that a lady so well dressed should be carrying a case about. She ordered some scrambled eggs and some coffee, but the girl thinks she was putting in time and waiting for someone. She'd got a wrist watch on, and she kept looking at it. It was when the girl came to give her the bill that she noticed the box. The lady took it out of her handbag and had it on the table looking at it. She opened the lid and shut it down again. She was smiling in a pleased, dreamy sort of way. The girl noticed the box particular because it was such a lovely thing. 'I'd like to have a gold box with my initials in rubies on it!' she said.

"Apparently Miss Adams sat there some time after paying her bill. Then, finally, she looked at her watch once more, seemed to give it up, and went out."

Poirot was frowning.

"It was a rendezvous," he murmured. "A rendezvous with someone who did not turn up. Did Carlotta Adams meet that person afterward? Or did she fail to meet him and go home and try to ring him up? I wish I knew—oh! how I wish I knew."

"That's *your* theory, M. Poirot. Mysterious Man-in-the-Background. That Man-in-the-Background's a myth. I don't say she mayn't have been waiting for someone; that's possible. She may have made an appointment to meet someone there after her business with his lordship was settled satisfactorily. Well, we know what happened. She lost her head and stabbed him. But she's not one to lose her head for long. She changes her appearance at the station, gets out her case, goes to the rendezvous, and then what they call the 'reaction' gets her. Horror of what she's done. And when her friend doesn't turn up, that finishes her. He may be someone who knew she was going to Regent Gate that evening. She feels the game's up, so she takes out her little box of dope. An overdose of that and it'll be all over. At any rate she won't be hanged. Why, it's as plain as the nose on your face."

Poirot's hand strayed doubtfully to his nose, then his fingers dropped to his moustaches. He caressed them tenderly with a proud expression.

"There was no evidence at all of a mysterious Man-in-the-Background," said Japp, pursuing his advantage doggedly. "I haven't got evidence yet of a conversation between her and his lordship, but I shall do—it's only a question of time. I must say I'm disappointed about Paris, but nine months ago is a long time. I've still got someone making inquiries over there. Something may come to light yet. I know you don't think so. You're a pigheaded old boy, you know."

"You insult first my nose and then my head!"

"Figure of speech, that's all," said Japp soothingly. "No offence meant."

"The answer to that," I said, "is 'Nor taken.'"

Poirot looked from one to the other of us completely puzzled.

"Any orders?" inquired Japp facetiously from the door.

Poirot smiled forgivingly at him.

"An order, no. A suggestion, yes."

"Well, what is it? Out with it."

"A suggestion that you circularize the taxicabs. Find one that took a fare—or more probably two fares—yes, two fares—from the neighbourhood of Covent Garden to Regent Gate on the night of the murder. As to time it would probably be about twenty minutes to eleven."

Japp cocked an eye alertly. He had the look of a smart terrier dog.

"So that's the idea, is it?" he said. "Well, I'll do it. Can't do any harm, and you sometimes know what you're talking about."

No sooner had he left than Poirot arose and, with great energy, began to brush his hat.

"Ask me no questions, my friend. Instead bring me the benzine. A morsel of omelette this morning descended on my waistcoat."

I brought it to him.

"For once," I said, "I do not think I need to ask questions. It seems fairly obvious. But do you think it really is so?"

"*Mon ami,* at the moment I concern myself solely with the

toilet. If you will pardon me saying so your tie does not please me."

"It's a jolly good tie," I said.

"Possibly—once. It feels the old age as you have been kind enough to say I do. Change it, I beseech you, and also brush the right sleeve."

"Are we proposing to call on King George?" I inquired sarcastically.

"No. But I saw in the newspaper this morning that the Duke of Merton had returned to Merton House. I understand he is a premier member of the English aristocracy. I wish to do him all honour."

There is nothing of the Socialist about Poirot.

"Why are we going to call on the Duke of Merton?"

"I wish to see him."

That was all I could get out of him. When my attire was at last handsome enough to please Poirot's critical eye, we started out.

At Merton House, Poirot was asked by a footman if he had an appointment. Poirot replied in the negative. The footman bore away the card and returned shortly to say that His Grace was very sorry but he was extremely busy this morning. Poirot immediately sat down in a chair.

"*Très bien,*" he said. "I wait. I will wait several hours if need be."

This, however, was not necessary. Probably as the shortest way of getting rid of the importunate caller, Poirot was bidden to the presence of the gentleman he desired to see.

The Duke was about twenty-seven years of age. He was hardly prepossessing in appearance, being thin and weakly. He had nondescript hair, going bald at the temples, a small, bitter mouth and vague, dreamy eyes. There were several crucifixes in the room and various religious works of art. A wide shelf of books seemed to contain nothing but theological works. He looked far more like a weedy young haberdasher than like a duke.

He had, I knew, been educated at home, having been a terribly delicate child. He had succeeded to the dukedom as a boy of eight years old, and had grown up under the thumb of a strong-willed mother. This was the man who had fallen an immediate prey to Jane Wilkinson! It was really ludicrous in the extreme. His manner was priggish and his reception of us just short of courteous.

"You may, perhaps, know my name," began Poirot.

"I have no acquaintance with it."

"I study the psychology of crime."

The Duke was silent. He was sitting at a writing-table, an unfinished letter before him. He tapped impatiently on the desk with his pen.

"For what reason did you wish to see me?" he inquired coldly.

Poirot was sitting opposite him. His back was to the window. The Duke was facing it.

"I am at present engaged on investigating the circumstances connected with Lord Edgware's death."

Not a muscle of the weak yet obstinate face moved.

"Indeed? I was not acquainted with him."

"But you are, I think, acquainted with his wife—with Miss Jane Wilkinson?"

"That is so."

"You are aware that she is supposed to have had a strong motive for desiring the death of her husband?"

"I am really not aware of anything of the kind."

"I should like to ask you outright, your Grace, are you shortly going to marry Miss Jane Wilkinson?"

"When I am engaged to marry anyone the fact will be announced in the newspapers. I consider your question an impertinence." He stood up. "Good-morning."

Poirot stood up also. He looked awkward. He hung his head. He stammered.

"I did not mean—I— *Je vous demande pardon*—"

"Good-morning," repeated the Duke, a little louder.

This time Poirot gave it up. He made a characteristic gesture of hopelessness, and we left. It was an ignominious dismissal.

I felt rather sorry for Poirot. His usual bombast had not gone well. To the Duke of Merton a great detective was evidently lower than a black beetle.

"That didn't go too well," I said sympathetically. "What a

stiff-necked tartar the man is. What did you really want to see him for?"

"I wanted to know whether he and Jane Wilkinson are really going to marry."

"She said so."

"Ah! she said so; but, you realize, she is of those who say anything that suits their purpose. She might have decided to marry him and he—poor man—might not yet be aware of the fact."

"Well, he certainly sent you away with a flea in the ear."

"He gave me the reply he would give to a reporter—yes." Poirot chuckled. "But I know! I know exactly how the case stands."

"How do you know? By his manner?"

"Not at all. You saw he was writing a letter?"

"Yes."

"*Eh bien,* in my early days in the police force in Belgium I learned that it was very useful to read handwriting upside down. Shall I tell you what he was saying in that letter? *'My dearest, I can hardly bear to wait through the long months. Jane, my adored, my beautiful angel, how can I tell you what you are to me? You who have suffered so much! Your beautiful nature—'*"

"Poirot!" I cried, scandalized, stopping him.

"That was as far as he had got, *'Your beautiful nature—only I know it.'*"

I felt very upset. He was so naïvely pleased with his performance.

"Poirot," I cried. "You can't do a thing like that, overlook a private letter."

"You say the imbecilities, Hastings. Absurd to say I 'cannot do' a thing which I have just done!"

"It's not—not playing the game."

"I do not play games. You know that. Murder is not a game. It is serious. And anyway, Hastings, you should not use that phrase, playing the game. It is not said any more. I have discovered that. It is dead. Young people laugh when they hear it. *Mais oui,* young beautiful girls will laugh at you if you say 'playing the game' and 'not cricket.'"

I was silent. I could not bear this thing that Poirot had done so light-heartedly.

"It was so unnecessary," I said. "If you had only told him that you had gone to Lord Edgware at Jane Wilkinson's request, then he would have treated you very differently."

"Ah! but I could not do that. Jane Wilkinson was my client. I cannot speak of my client's affairs to another. I undertake a mission in confidence. To speak of it would not be honourable."

"Honourable!"

"Precisely."

"But she's going to marry him?"

"That does not mean that she has no secrets from him. Your ideas about marriage are very old-fashioned. No, what you suggest, I couldn't possibly have done. I have my honour as a detective to think of. The honour, it is a very serious thing."

"Well, I suppose it takes all kinds of honour to make a world."

XIX A Great Lady

THE visit that we received on the following morning was to my mind one of the most surprising things about the whole affair. I was in my room when Poirot slipped in with his eyes shining.

"Mon ami, we have a visitor."

"Who is it?"

"The Dowager Duchess of Merton."

"How extraordinary! What does she want?"

"If you accompany me downstairs, *mon ami,* you will know."

I hastened to comply. We entered the room together.

The Duchess was a small woman with a high bridged nose and autocratic eyes. Although she was short, one would not have dared to call her dumpy. Dressed though she was in unfashionable black, she was yet every inch a *grande dame.* She also impressed me as having an almost ruthless personality. Where her son was negative, she was positive. Her will power was terrific. I could almost feel waves of force emanating from her. No wonder this woman had always dominated all those with whom she came in contact!

She put up a lorgnette and studied first me and then my companion. Then she spoke to him. Her voice was clear and compelling, a voice accustomed to command and to be obeyed.

"You are M. Hercule Poirot?"

My friend bowed.

"At your service, Madame la Duchesse."

She looked at me.

"This is my friend, Captain Hastings. He assists me in my cases."

Her eyes looked momentarily doubtful. Then she bent her head in acquiescence. She took the chair that Poirot offered.

"I have come to consult you on a very delicate matter, M.

Poirot, and I must ask that what I tell you shall be understood to be entirely confidential."

"That without saying, madame."

"It was Lady Yardly who told me about you. From the way in which she spoke of you, and the gratitude she expressed, I felt that you were the only person likely to help me."

"Rest assured, I will do my best, madame."

Still she hesitated. Then, at last, with an effort, she came to the point, came to it with a simplicity that reminded me in an odd way of Jane Wilkinson on that memorable night at the Savoy.

"M. Poirot, I want to ensure that my son does not marry the actress, Jane Wilkinson."

If Poirot felt astonishment, he refrained from showing it. He regarded her thoughtfully and took his time about replying.

"Can you be a little more definite, madame, as to what you want me to do?"

"That is not easy. I feel that such a marriage would be a great disaster. It would ruin my son's life."

"Do you think so, madame?"

"I am sure of it. My son has very high ideals. He knows really very little of the world. He has never cared for the young girls of his own class. They have struck him as empty headed and frivolous. But as regards this woman—well, she is very beautiful, I admit that, and she has the power of enslaving men. She has bewitched my son. I have hoped that the infatuation would run its course. Mercifully she was not free. But now that her husband is dead—"

She broke off.

"They intend to be married in a few months' time. The whole happiness of my son's life is at stake." She spoke more peremptorily. "It must be stopped, M. Poirot."

Poirot shrugged his shoulders.

"I do not say that you are not right, madame. I agree that the marriage is not a suitable one. But what can one do?"

"It is for you to do something."

Poirot slowly shook his head.

"Yes, yes, you must help me."

"I doubt if anything would avail, madame. Your son, I should say, would refuse to listen to anything against the lady! And also, I do not think there is very much against her to say! I doubt if there are any discreditable incidents to be raked up in her past. She has been—shall we say—careful?"

"I know," said the Duchess grimly.

"Ah! So you have already made the inquiries in that direction."

She flushed a little under his keen glance.

"There is nothing I would not do, M. Poirot, to save my son from this marriage." She reiterated the word emphatically: *"Nothing!"*

She paused, then went on:

"Money is nothing in this matter. Name any fee you like. But the marriage must be stopped. You are the man to do it."

Poirot slowly shook his head.

"It is not a question of money. I can do nothing—for a reason which I will explain to you presently. But also, I may say, I do not see there is anything to be done. I cannot give you help, Madame la Duchesse. Will you think me impertinent if I give you advice?"

"What advice?"

"Do not antagonize your son! He is of an age to choose for himself. Because his choice is not your choice, do not assume that you must be right. If it is a misfortune, then accept misfortune. Be at hand to aid him when he needs aid. But do not turn him against you."

"You hardly understand."

She rose to her feet. Her lips were trembling.

"But, yes, Madame la Duchesse, I understand very well. I comprehend the mother's heart. No one comprehends it better than I, Hercule Poirot. And I say to you with authority, be patient. Be patient and calm, and disguise your feelings. There is yet a chance that the matter may break itself. Opposition will merely increase your son's obstinacy."

"Good-bye, M. Poirot," she said coldly. "I am disappointed."

"I regret infinitely, madame, that I cannot be of service to you.

I am in a difficult position. Lady Edgware, you see, has already done me the honour to consult me herself."

"Oh! I see." Her voice cut like a knife. "You are in the opposite camp. That explains, no doubt, why Lady Edgware has not yet been arrested for her husband's murder."

"Comment, Madame la Duchesse?"

"I think you heard what I said. Why is she not arrested? She was there that evening. She was seen to enter the house—to enter his study. No one else went near him, and he was found dead. And yet she is not arrested! Our police force must be corrupt through and through."

With shaking hands she arranged the scarf round her neck; then, with the slightest of bows, she swept out of the room.

"Whew!" I said. "What a tartar! I admire her, though, don't you?"

"Because she wishes to arrange the universe to her manner of thinking?"

"Well, she's only got her son's welfare at heart."

Poirot nodded his head.

"That is true enough, and yet, Hastings, will it really be such a bad thing for M. le Duc to marry Jane Wilkinson?"

"Why, you don't think she is really in love with him?"

"Probably not. Almost certainly not. But she is very much in love with his position. She will play her part carefully. She is an extremely beautiful woman and very ambitious. It is not such a catastrophe. The Duke might very easily have married a young girl of his own class who would have accepted him for the same reasons, but no one would have made the song and the dance about that."

"That is quite true, but—"

"And suppose he marries a girl who loves him passionately, is there such a great advantage in that? Often I have observed that it is a great misfortune for a man to have a wife who loves him. She creates the scenes of jealousy, she makes him look ridiculous, she insists on having all his time and attention. Ah! *non*, it is not the bed of roses."

"Poirot," I said, "you're an incurable old cynic."

"*Mais non, mais non,* I only make the reflections. See you, really, I am on the side of the good mamma."

I could not refrain from laughing at hearing the haughty Duchess described in this way.

Poirot remained quite serious.

"You should not laugh. It is of great importance, all this. I must reflect. I must reflect a great deal."

"I don't see what you can do in the matter," I said.

Poirot paid no attention.

"You observed, Hastings, how well informed the Duchess was? And how vindictive. She knew all the evidence there was against Jane Wilkinson."

"The case for the prosecution but not the case for the defence," I said, smiling.

"How did she come to know of it?"

"Jane told the Duke. The Duke told her," I suggested.

"Yes, that is possible. Yet I have—"

The telephone rang sharply. I answered it.

My part consisted of saying "Yes" at varying intervals. Finally I put down the receiver and turned excitedly to Poirot.

"That was Japp. Firstly, you're 'the goods,' as usual. Secondly, he's had a cable from America. Thirdly, he's got the taxi driver. Fourthly, would you like to come round and hear what the taxi driver says? Fifthly, you're 'the goods' again, and all along he's been convinced that you'd hit the nail on the head when you suggested that there was some man behind all this! I omitted to tell him that we'd just had a visitor here who says the police force is corrupt."

"So Japp is convinced at last," murmured Poirot. "Curious that the Man-in-the-Background theory should be proved just at the moment when I was inclining to another possible theory."

"What theory?"

"The theory that the motive for the murder might have nothing to do with Lord Edgware himself. Imagine someone who hated Jane Wilkinson, hated her so much that they would have even had her hanged for murder. *C'est une idee, ça!*"

He sighed, then he roused himself.

"Come, Hastings, let us hear what Japp has to say."

XX The Taxi Driver

WE found Japp interrogating an old man with a ragged moustache and spectacles. He had a hoarse, self-pitying voice.

"Ah! there you are," said Japp. "Well, things are all plain sailing, I think. This man—his name's Jobson—picked up two people in Long Acre on the night of June twenty-ninth."

"That's right," assented Jobson hoarsely. "Lovely night it were. Moon and all. The young lady and gentleman were by the tube station and hailed me."

"They were in evening dress?"

"Yes, gent in white waistcoat and the young lady all in white with birds embroidered on it. Come out of the Royal Opera, I guess."

"What time was this?"

"Sometime afore eleven."

"Well, what next?"

"Told me to go to Regent Gate—they'd tell me which house when they got there. And told me to be quick, too. People always says that. As though you wanted to loiter. Sooner you get there and get another fare the better for you. They never think of that. And, mind you, if there's an accident you'll get the blame for dangerous driving!"

"Cut it out," said Japp impatiently. "There wasn't an accident this time, was there?"

"No—no," agreed the man as though unwilling to abandon his claim to such an occurrence. "No, as a matter of fact, there weren't. Well, I got to Regent Gate—not above seven minutes it didn't take me—and there the gentleman rapped on the glass, and I stopped. About at Number Eight that were. Well, the gentleman and lady got out. The gentleman stopped where he was and told me to do the same. The lady crossed the road, and began walking back along the houses the other side. The gentleman stayed by the cab, standing on the sidewalk with his back to me, looking after her. Had his hands in his pockets. It was about five minutes when I heard him say something—kind of exclamation under his breath—and then off he goes too. I looks after him because I wasn't going to be bilked. It's been done afore to me, so I kept my eye on him. He went up the steps of one of the houses on the other side and went in."

"Did he push the door open?"

"No, he had a latchkey."

"What number was the house?"

"It would be Seventeen or Nineteen, I fancy. Well, it seemed odd to me my being told to stay where I was. So I kept watching. About five minutes later him and the young lady came out together. They got back into the cab and told me to drive back to Covent Garden Opera House. They stopped me just before I got there and paid me. Paid me handsome, I will say, though I expect I've got into trouble over it. Seems there's nothing but trouble."

"You're all right," said Japp. "Just run your eye over these, will you, and tell me if the young lady is among them."

There were half a dozen photographs, all fairly alike as to type. I looked with some interest over his shoulder.

"That were her," said Jobson. He pointed a decisive finger at one of Geraldine Marsh in evening dress.

"Sure?"

"Quite sure. Pale she was and dark."

"Now the man."

Another sheaf of photographs was handed to him.

He looked at them attentively and then shook his head.

"Well, I couldn't say—not for sure. Either of these two might be him."

The photographs included one of Ronald Marsh, but Jobson had not selected it. Instead he indicated two other men not unlike Marsh in type.

Jobson then departed and Japp flung the photographs on the table.

"Good enough. Wish I could have got a clearer identification of his lordship. Of course it's an old photograph, taken seven or eight years ago. The only one I could get hold of. Yes, I'd like a clearer identification, although the case is clear enough. Bang go a couple of alibis. Clever of you to think of it, M. Poirot."

Poirot looked modest.

"When I found that she and her cousin were both at the opera it seemed to me possible that they might have been together during one of the intervals. Naturally the parties they were with would assume that they had not left the Opera House. But a half hour interval gives plenty of time to get to Regent Gate and back. The moment the new Lord Edgware laid such stress upon his alibi, I was sure something was wrong with it."

"You're a nice suspicious sort of fellow, aren't you?" said Japp affectionately. "Well, you're about right. Can't be too suspicious in a world like this. His lordship is our man all right. Look at this."

He produced a paper.

"Cable from New York. They got into touch with Miss Lucie Adams. The letter was in the mail delivered to her this morning. She was not willing to give up the original unless absolutely necessary, but she willingly allowed the officer to take a copy of it and cable it to us. Here it is and it's as damning as you could hope for."

Poirot took the cable with great interest. I read it over his shoulder.

Following is text letter to Lucie Adams dated June 29th 8 Rosedew Mansions London S.W.3 Begins Dearest little Sister, I'm sorry I wrote you such a scrappy bit last week but things were rather busy and there was a lot to see to. Well, darling, it's been ever such a success! Notices splendid, box office good, and everybody most kind. I've got some real good friends over here and next year I'm thinking of taking a theatre for two months. The Russian dancer sketch went very well and the American woman in Paris too, but the Scenes at a Foreign Hotel are still the favourites, I think. I'm so excited that I hardly know what I'm writing, and you'll see why in a minute, but first I must tell you what people have said. Mr. Hergsheimer was ever so kind and he's going to ask me to lunch to meet Sir

Montagu Corner who might do great things for me. The other night I met Jane Wilkinson and she was ever so sweet about my show and my take-off of her which brings me round to what I am going to tell you. I don't really like her very much because I've been hearing a lot about her lately from someone I know and she's behaved cruelly, I think, and in a very underhand way—but I won't go into that now. You know that she really is Lady Edgware? I've heard a lot about him too lately and he's no beauty, I can tell you. He treated his nephew, the Captain Marsh I have mentioned to you, in the most shameful way— literally turned him out of the house and discontinued his allowance. He told me all about it and I felt awfully sorry for him. He enjoyed my show very much, he said, "I believe it would take in Lord Edgware himself. Look here, will you take something on for a bet?" I laughed and said, "How much?" Lucie, darling, the answer fairly took my breath away. Ten thousand dollars. Ten thousand dollars, think of it—just to help someone win a silly bet. "Why," I said, "I'd play a joke on the King in Buckingham Palace and risk lèse majesté for that." Well then, we laid our heads together and got down to details.

I'll tell you all about it next week—whether I'm spotted or not. But anyway, Lucie darling, whether I succeed or fail, I'm to have the ten thousand dollars. Oh! Lucie, little sister, what that's going to mean to us. No time for more—just going off to do my "hoax." Lots and lots and lots of love, little sister mine.

Yours,

Carlotta

Poirot laid down the letter. It had touched him, I could see. Japp, however, reacted in quite a different way.

"We've got him," said Japp exultantly.

"Yes," said Poirot.

His voice sounded strangely flat.

Japp looked at him curiously.

"What is it, M. Poirot?"

"Nothing," said Poirot. "It is not, somehow, just as I thought. That is all."

He looked acutely unhappy.

"But still it must be so," he said as though to himself. "Yes, it must be so."

"Of course it is so. Why, you've said so all along!"

"No, no. You misunderstood me."

"Didn't you say there was someone back of all this who got the girl into doing it innocently?"

"Yes, yes."

"Well, what more do you want?"

Poirot sighed and said nothing.

"You are an odd sort of cove. Nothing ever satisfies you. I say, it was a piece of luck the girl wrote this letter."

Poirot agreed with more vigour than he had yet shown.

"Mais oui, that is what the murderer did not expect. When Miss Adams accepted that ten thousand dollars she signed her death warrant. The murderer thought he had taken all pre-cautions—and yet in sheer innocence she outwitted him. The dead speak. Yes, sometimes the dead speak."

"I never thought she'd done it off her own bat," said Japp un-blushingly.

"No, no," said Poirot absently.

"Well, I must get on with things."

"You are going to arrest Captain Marsh—Lord Edgware, I mean?"

"Why not? The case against him seems proved up to the hilt."

"True."

"You seem very despondent about it, M. Poirot. The truth is you like things to be difficult. Here's your own theory proved, and even that does not satisfy you. Can you see any flaw in the evidence we've got?"

Poirot shook his head.

"Whether Miss Marsh was accessory or not, I don't know," said Japp. "Seems as though she must have known about it, going there with him from the opera. If she wasn't, why did he take her? Well, we'll hear what they've both got to say."

"May I be present?"

Poirot spoke almost humbly.

"Certainly you can. I owe the idea to you!"

He picked up the telegram on the table.

I drew Poirot aside.

"What is the matter, Poirot?"

"I am very unhappy, Hastings. This seems the plain sailing and the above board. But there is something wrong. Somewhere or other, Hastings, there is a fact that escapes us. It all fits together, it is as I imagined it, and yet, my friend, there is something wrong."

He looked at me piteously. I was at a loss what to say.

XXI Ronald's Story

I FOUND it hard to understand Poirot's attitude. Surely this was what he had predicted all along?

All the way to Regent Gate, he sat perplexed and frowning, paying no attention to Japp's self-congratulations. He came out of his reverie at last with a sigh.

"At all events," he murmured, "we can see what he has to say."

"Next to nothing, if he's wise," said Japp. "There's any amount of men that have hanged themselves by being too eager to make a statement. Well, no one can say as we don't warn them! It's all fair and above board. And the more guilty they are, the more anxious they are to pipe up and tell you the lies they've thought out to meet the case. They don't know that you should always submit your lies to a solicitor first."

He sighed and said:

"Solicitors and coroners are the worst enemies of the police. Again and again I've had a perfectly clear case messed up by the coroner fooling about and letting the guilty party get away with it. Lawyers you can't object to so much, I suppose. They're paid for their artfulness and twisting things this way and that."

On arrival at Regent Gate we found that our quarry was at home. The family were still at the luncheon table. Japp proffered a request to speak to Lord Edgware privately. We were shown into the library.

In a minute or two the young man came to us. There was an easy smile on his face which changed a little as he cast a quick glance over us. His lips tightened.

"Hello, Inspector," he said. "What's all this about?"

Japp said his little piece in the classic fashion.

"So that's it, is it?" said Ronald.

He drew a chair towards him and sat down. He pulled out a cigarette case.

"I think, Inspector, I'd like to make a statement."

"That's as you please, my lord."

"Meaning that it's damned foolish on my part. All the same, I think I will. 'Having no reason to fear the truth,' as the heroes in books always say."

Japp said nothing. His face remained expressionless.

"There's a nice handy table and chair," went on the young man. "Your minion can sit down and take it all down in shorthand."

I don't think that Japp was used to having his arrangements made for him so thoughtfully. Lord Edgware's suggestion was adopted.

"To begin with," said the young man. "Having some grains of intelligence I strongly suspect that my beautiful alibi has bust. Gone up in smoke. Exit the useful Dortheimers. Taxi driver, I suppose?"

"We know all about your movements on that night," said Japp woodenly.

"I have the greatest admiration for Scotland Yard. All the same, you know, if I had really been planning a deed of violence I shouldn't have hired a taxi and driven straight to the place and kept the fellow waiting. Have you thought of that? Ah! I see M. Poirot has."

"It had occurred to me, yes," said Poirot.

"Such is not the manner of premeditated crime," said Ronald. "Put on a red moustache and horn-rimmed glasses and drive to the next street and pay the man off. Take the tube—well—well, I won't go into it all. My counsel, at a fee of several thousand guineas will do it better than I can. Of course I see the answer. Crime was a sudden impulse. There was I, waiting in the cab, et cetera. It occurs to me, 'Now, my boy, up and doing.'

"Well, I'm going to tell you the truth. I was in a hole for money. That's been pretty clear, I think. It was rather a desperate business. I had to get it by the next day or drop out of things. I tried my uncle. He'd no love for me, but I thought he might care for the honour of his name. Middle-aged men sometimes do. My uncle proved to be lamentably modern in his cynical indifference.

"Well—it looked like just having to grin and bear it. I was going to try and have a shot at borrowing from Dortheimer, but I knew there wasn't a hope. And marry his daughter I couldn't. She's much too sensible a girl to take me, anyway. Then, by chance, I met my cousin at the opera. I don't often come across her, but she was always a decent kid when I lived in the house. I found myself telling her all about it. She'd heard something from her father, anyway. Then she showed her mettle. She suggested I should take her pearls. They'd belonged to her mother."

He paused. There was something like real emotion, I think, in his voice. Or else he suggested it better than I could have believed possible.

"Well—I accepted the blessed child's offer. I could raise the money I wanted on them, and I swore I'd turn to and redeem them, even if it meant working to manage it. But the pearls were at home in Regent Gate. We decided that the best thing to do would be to go and fetch them at once. We jumped in a taxi and off we went.

"We made the fellow stop on the opposite side of the street, in case anyone should hear the taxi draw up at the door. Geraldine got out and went across the road. She had her latchkey with her. She would go in quietly, get the pearls and bring them out to me. She didn't expect to meet anyone except possibly a servant. Miss Carroll, my uncle's secretary, usually went to bed at half past nine. He, himself, would probably be in the library.

"So off Dina went. I stood on the pavement smoking a cigarette. Every now and then I looked over towards the house to see if she was coming. And now I come to the part of the story that you may believe or not as you like. A man passed me on the sidewalk. I turned to look after him. To my surprise he went up the steps and let himself in to Number Seventeen. At least I thought it was Number Seventeen, but of course I was some distance away. That surprised me very much, for two reasons. One was that the man had let himself in with a key, and the second was that I thought I recognized in him a certain well-known actor.

"I was so surprised that I determined to look into matters. I happened to have my own key of Number Seventeen in my pocket. I'd lost it, or thought I'd lost it three years ago, had come across it unexpectedly a day or two ago and had been meaning to give it back to my uncle this morning. However, in the heat of our discussion, it had slipped my memory. I had transferred it with the other contents of my pockets when I changed.

"Telling the taxi man to wait, I strode hurriedly along the pavement, crossed the road, went up the steps of Number Seventeen and opened the door with my key. The hall was empty. There was no sign of any visitor having just entered. I stood for a minute looking about me. Then I went towards the library door. Perhaps the man was in with my uncle. If so, I should hear the murmur of voices. I stood outside the library door, but I heard nothing.

"I suddenly felt I had made the most abject fool of myself. Of course the man must have gone into some other house— the house beyond probably. Regent Gate is rather dimly lighted at night. I felt an absolute idiot. What on earth had possessed me to follow the fellow, I could not think. It had landed me here, and a pretty fool I should look if my uncle were to come suddenly out of the library and find me. I should get Geraldine into trouble and altogether the fat would be in the fire. All because something in the man's manner had made me imagine that he was doing something that he didn't want known. Luckily no one had caught me. I must get out of it as soon as I could.

"I tiptoed back towards the front door and at the same moment Geraldine came down the stairs with the pearls in her hand. She was very startled at seeing me, of course. I got her out of the house, and then explained."

He paused.

"We hurried back to the opera, got there just as the curtain was going up. No one suspected that we'd left it. It was a hot night and several people went outside to get a breath of air."

He paused.

"I know what you'll say: Why didn't I tell you this right away?

And now I put it to you: Would you, with a motive for murder sticking out a yard, admit light-heartedly that you'd actually been at the place the murder was committed on the night in question?

"Frankly, I funked it! Even if we were believed, it was going to be a lot of worry for me and for Geraldine. We'd had nothing to do with the murder; we'd seen nothing; we'd heard nothing. Obviously, I thought, Aunt Jane had done it. Well, why bring myself in? I told you about the quarrel and my lack of money, because I knew you'd ferret it out; and, if I'd tried to conceal all that, you'd be much more suspicious and you'd probably examine that alibi much more closely. As it was, I thought that if I bucked enough about it it would almost hypnotize you into thinking it all right. The Dortheimers were, I know, honestly convinced that I'd been at Covent Garden all the time. That I spent one interval with my cousin wouldn't strike them as suspicious. And she could always say she'd been with me there and that we hadn't left the place."

"Miss Marsh agreed to this—concealment?"

"Yes. Soon as I got the news, I got onto her and cautioned her for her life not to say anything about her excursion here last night. She'd been with me and I'd been with her during the last interval at Covent Garden. We'd walked in the street a little, that was all. She understood and she quite agreed."

He paused.

"I know it looks bad, coming out with this afterward, but the story's true enough. I can give you the name and address of the man who let me have the cash on Geraldine's pearls this morning. And if you ask her, she'll confirm every word I've told you."

He sat back in his chair and looked at Japp. Japp continued to look expressionless.

"You say you thought Jane Wilkinson had committed the murder, Lord Edgware?" he said.

"Well, wouldn't you have thought so? After the butler's story?"

"What about your wager with Miss Adams?"

"Wager with Miss Adams? With Carlotta Adams, do you mean? What has she got to do with it?"

"Do you deny that you offered her the sum of ten thousand dollars to impersonate Miss Jane Wilkinson at the house that night?"

Ronald stared.

"Offered her ten thousand dollars? Nonsense. Someone's been pulling your leg. I haven't got ten thousand dollars to offer. You've got hold of a mare's nest. Does *she* say so? Oh! dash it all—I forgot. She's dead, isn't she?"

"Yes," said Poirot quietly. "She is dead."

Ronald turned his eyes from one to the other of us. He had been debonair before. Now his face had whitened. His eyes looked frightened.

"I don't understand all this," he said. "It's true what I told you. I suppose you don't believe me—any of you."

And then to my amazement, Poirot stepped forward.

"Yes," he said. "I believe you."

XXII Strange Behaviour of Hercule Poirot

WE were in our rooms.

"What on earth—" I began.

Poirot stopped me with a gesture more extravagant than any gesture I had ever seen him make. Both arms whirled in the air.

"I implore of you, Hastings! Not now! Not now!"

And upon that, he seized his hat, clapped it on his head as though he had never heard of order and method, and rushed headlong from the room. He had not returned when, about an hour later, Japp appeared.

"Little man gone out?" he inquired.

I nodded.

Japp sank into a seat. He dabbed his forehead with a handkerchief. The day was warm.

"What the devil took him?" he inquired. "I can tell you, Captain Hastings, you could have knocked me over with a feather when he stepped up to the man and said: 'I believe you,' for all the world as though he were acting in a romantic melodrama. It beats me."

It beat me also, and I said so.

"And then he marches out of the house," said Japp. "What did he say about it to you?"

"Nothing," I replied.

"Nothing at all?"

"Absolutely nothing. When I was going to speak to him he waved me aside. I thought it best to leave him alone. When we got back here I started to question him. He waved his arms, seized his hat and rushed out again."

We looked at each other. Japp tapped his forehead significantly.

"Must be," he said.

For once I was disposed to agree. Japp had often suggested

before that Poirot was what he called "touched." In those cases he had simply not understood what Poirot was driving at. Here, I was forced to confess, I could not understand Poirot's attitude. If not touched, he was, at any rate, suspiciously changeable. Here was his own private theory triumphantly confirmed, and straight away he went back on it. It was enough to dismay and distress his warmest supporters. I shook my head in a discouraged fashion.

"He's always been what I call peculiar," said Japp. "Got his own particular angle of looking at things—and a very queer one it is. He's a kind of genius, I admit that. But they always say that geniuses are very near the border line and liable to slip over any minute. He's always been fond of having things difficult. A straightforward case is never good enough for him. No, it's got to be tortuous. He's got away from real life. He plays a game of his own. It's like an old lady playing patience. If it doesn't come out, she cheats. Well, it's the other way round with him. If it's coming out too easily, he cheats to make it more difficult! That's the way I look at it."

I found it difficult to answer him. I was too perturbed and distressed to be able to think clearly. I, also, found Poirot's behaviour unaccountable; and, since I was very attached to my strange little friend, it worried me more than I cared to express.

In the middle of a gloomy silence, Poirot walked into the room. He was, I was thankful to see, quite calm now. Very carefully, he removed his hat, placed it with his stick on a table and sat down in his accustomed chair.

"So you are here, my good Japp. I am glad. It was on my mind that I must see you as soon as possible."

Japp looked at him without replying. He saw that this was only the beginning. He waited for Poirot to explain himself. This my friend did, speaking slowly and carefully.

"*Ecoutez*, Japp. We are wrong. We are all wrong. It is grievous to admit it, but we have made a mistake."

"That's all right," said Japp confidently.

"But it is not all right. It is deplorable. It grieves me to the heart."

"You needn't be grieved about that young man. He richly deserves all he gets."

"It is not he I am grieving about; it is you."

"Me? You needn't worry about me."

"But I do. See you, who was it set you on this course? It was Hercule Poirot. *Mais oui,* I set you on the trail. I direct your attention to Carlotta Adams, I mention to you the matter of the letter to America. Every step of the way it is I who point it!"

"I was bound to get there anyway," said Japp coldly. "You got a bit ahead of me, that's all."

"*Cela ce peut.* But it does not console me. If harm, if loss of prestige comes to you through listening to my little ideas, I shall blame myself bitterly."

Japp merely looked amused. I think he credited Poirot with motives that were none too pure. He fancied that Poirot grudged him the credit resulting from the successful elucidation of the affair.

"That's all right," he said. "I shan't forget to let it be known that I owe something to you over this business."

He winked at me.

"Oh! it is not that at all." Poirot clicked his tongue with impatience. "I want no credit. And what is more, I tell you there will be no credit. It is a fiasco that you prepare for yourself, and I, Hercule Poirot, am the cause."

Suddenly, at Poirot's expression of extreme melancholy, Japp shouted with laughter. Poirot looked affronted.

"Sorry, M. Poirot." He wiped his eyes. "But you did look for all the world like a dying duck in a thunderstorm. Now look here, let's forget all this. I'm willing to shoulder the credit or the blame of this affair. It will make a big noise; you're right there. Well, I'm going out to get a conviction. It may be that a clever counsel will get his lordship off; you never know with a jury. But even so, it won't do me any harm. It will be known that we caught the right man, even if we couldn't get a conviction. And if, by any chance, the third housemaid has hysterics and owns up she did it—well, I'll take my medicine and I won't complain you led me up the garden. That's fair enough."

Poirot gazed at him mildly and sadly.

"You have the confidence—always the confidence! You never stop and say to yourself: 'Can it be so?' You never doubt—or wonder. You never think: 'This is too easy!'"

"You bet your life I don't. And that's just where, if you'll excuse me saying so, you go off the rails every time. Why shouldn't a thing be easy? What's the harm in a thing being easy?"

Poirot looked at him, sighed, half threw up his arms, then shook his head.

"*C'est fini!* I will say no more."

"Splendid," said Japp heartily. "Now let's get down to brass tacks. You'd like to hear what I've been doing?"

"Assuredly."

"Well, I saw Miss Marsh, and her story tallied exactly with his lordship's. They may both be in it together, but I think not. It's my opinion he bluffed her. She's three parts sweet on him anyway. Took on terribly when she found he was arrested."

"Did she now? And the secretary—Miss Carroll?"

"Wasn't too surprised, I fancy. However, that's only my idea."

"What about the pearls?" I asked. "Was that part of the story true?"

"Absolutely. He raised the money on them early the following morning. But I don't think that touches the main argument. As I see it, the plan came into his head when he came across his cousin at the opera. It came to him in a flash. He was desperate —here was a way out. I fancy he'd been meditating something of the kind; that's why he had the key with him. I don't believe that story of suddenly coming across it. Well, as he talks to his cousin, he sees that, by involving her, he gains additional security for himself. He plays on her feelings, hints at the pearls; she plays up, and off they go. As soon as she's in the house he follows her in and goes along to the library. Maybe his lordship had dozed off in his chair. Anyway, in two seconds he's done the trick and he's out again. I don't fancy he meant the girl to catch him in the house. He counted on being found pacing up and down near the taxi. And I don't think the taxi man was meant to see him go in. The impression was to be that he was walking up and down smoking while he waited for the girl. The taxi was facing the opposite direction, remember.

"Of course, the next morning, he has to pledge the pearls. He must still seem to be in need of the money. Then, when he hears of the crime, he frightens the girl into concealing their visit to the house. They will say that they spent that interval together at the Opera House."

"Then why did they not do so?" asked Poirot sharply.

Japp shrugged his shoulders.

"Changed his mind. Or judged that she wouldn't be able to go through with it. She's a nervous type."

"Yes," said Poirot meditatively. "She is a nervous type."

After a minute or two, he said:

"It does not strike you that it would have been easier and simpler for Captain Marsh to have left the opera during the interval by himself, to have gone in quietly with his key, killed his uncle, and returned to the opera—instead of having a taxi outside and a nervous girl coming down the stairs any minute who might lose her head and give him away."

Japp grinned.

"That's what you and I would have done. But then we're a shade brighter than Captain Ronald Marsh."

"I am not so sure. He strikes me as intelligent."

"But not so intelligent as M. Hercule Poirot! Come now, I'm sure of that!" Japp laughed.

Poirot looked at him coldly.

"If he isn't guilty, why did he persuade the Adams girl to take on that stunt?" went on Japp. "There can be only one reason for that stunt—to protect the real criminal."

"There I am of accord with you absolutely."

"Well, I'm glad we agree about something."

"It might be he who actually spoke to mademoiselle," mused Poirot, "while really—no, that is an imbecility."

Then, looking suddenly at Japp, he rapped out a quick question.

"What is your theory as to her death?"

Japp cleared his throat.

"I'm inclined to believe accident. A convenient accident, I

admit. I can't see that he could have had anything to do with it. His alibi is straight enough after the opera. He was at Sobranis' with the Dortheimers till after one o'clock. Long before that she was in bed and asleep. No, I think that was an instance of the infernal luck criminals sometimes have. Otherwise, if that accident hadn't happened, I think he had his plans for dealing with her. First, he'd put the fear of the Lord into her —tell her she'd be arrested for murder if she confessed the truth. And then he'd square her with a fresh lot of money."

"Does it strike you—" Poirot stared straight in front of him —"does it strike you that Miss Adams would let another woman be hanged when she herself held evidence that would acquit her?"

"Jane Wilkinson wouldn't have been hanged. The Montagu Corner party evidence was too strong for that."

"But the murderer did not know that. He would have had to count on Jane Wilkinson being hanged and Carlotta Adams keeping silence."

"You love talking, don't you, M. Poirot? And you're positively convinced now that Ronald Marsh is a white-headed boy who can do no wrong. Do you believe that story of his about seeing a man sneak surreptitiously into the house?"

Poirot shrugged his shoulders.

"Do you know who he says he thought it was?"

"I could guess, perhaps."

"He says he thought it was the film star, Bryan Martin. What do you think of that? A man who'd never even met Lord Edgware."

"Then it would certainly be curious if one saw such a man entering that house with a key."

"Chah!" said Japp. A rich noise expressive of contempt. "And now I suppose it will surprise you to hear that Mr. Bryan Martin wasn't in London that night. He took a young lady to dine down at Molesey. They didn't get back to London till midnight."

"Ah!" said Poirot mildly. "No, I am not surprised. Was the young lady also a member of the profession?"

"No. Girl who keeps a hat shop. As a matter of fact it was

Miss Adams' friend, Miss Driver. I think you'll agree her testimony is past suspicion."

"I am not disputing it, my friend."

"In fact, you're done down and you know it, old boy," said Japp, laughing. "Cock and bull story trumped up on the moment, that's what it was. Nobody entered Number Seventeen —and nobody entered either of the houses either side—so what does that show? That his lordship's a liar."

Poirot shook his head sadly.

Japp rose to his feet, his spirits restored.

"Come now, we're right, you know."

"Who was D, Paris, November?"

Japp shrugged his shoulders.

"Ancient history, I imagine. Can't a girl have a souvenir six months ago without its having something to do with this crime? We must have a sense of proportion."

"Six months ago," murmured Poirot, a sudden light in his eyes. *Dieu, que je suis bête!*"

"What's he saying?" inquired Japp of me.

"Listen." Poirot rose and tapped Japp on the chest. "Why does Miss Adams' maid not recognize that box? Why does Miss Driver not recognize it?"

"What do you mean?"

"Because the box was *new!* It had only just been given to her. Paris, November—that is all very well—doubtless that is the date of which the box is to be a souvenir. But it was given to her *now,* not *then.* It has just been bought! Only just been bought! Investigate that, I implore you, my good Japp. It is a chance, decidedly a chance. It was bought not here, but abroad. Probably Paris. If it had been bought here, some jeweller would have come forward. It has been photographed and described in the papers. Yes, yes, Paris. Possibly some other foreign town, but I think Paris. Find out, I implore you. Make the inquiries. I want—I so badly want to know who is this mysterious D."

"It will do no harm," said Japp good-naturedly. "Can't say I'm very excited about it myself, but I'll do what I can. The more we know the better."

Nodding cheerfully to us he departed.

XXIII The Letter

"AND now," said Poirot, "we will go out to lunch."

He put his hand through my arm. He was smiling at me.

"I have hope," he explained.

I was glad to see him restored to his old self, though I was none the less convinced myself of young Ronald's guilt. I fancied that Poirot himself had perhaps come round to this view, convinced by Japp's arguments. The search for the purchaser of the box was, perhaps, a last sally to save his face.

We went amicably to lunch together. Somewhat to my amusement, at a table the other side of the room, I saw Bryan Martin and Jenny Driver lunching together. Remembering what Japp had said, I suspected a possible romance. They saw us and Jenny waved a hand.

When we were sipping coffee, Jenny left her escort and came over to our table. She looked as vivid and dynamic as ever.

"May I sit here and talk to you a minute, M. Poirot?"

"Assuredly, mademoiselle. I am charmed to see you. Will not M. Martin join us also?"

"I told him not to. You see, I wanted to talk to you about Carlotta."

"Yes, mademoiselle?"

"You wanted to get a line onto some man friend of hers. Isn't that so?"

"Yes, yes."

"Well, I've been thinking and thinking. Sometimes you can't get at things straight away. To get them clear, you've got to think back—remember a lot of little words and phrases that perhaps you didn't pay much attention to at the time. Well, that's what I've been doing, thinking and thinking and remembering just what she said. And I've come to a certain conclusion."

"Yes, mademoiselle?"

"I think the man that she cared about—or was beginning to care about—was Ronald Marsh—you know, the one who has just succeeded to the title."

"What makes you think it was he, mademoiselle?"

"Well, for one thing, Carlotta was speaking in a general sort of way one day, about a man having hard luck, and how it might affect character. That a man might be a decent sort really and yet go down the hill. More sinned against than sinning— you know the idea. The first thing a woman kids herself with when she's getting soft about a man. I've heard the old wheeze so often! Carlotta had plenty of sense, yet here she was coming out with this stuff just like a complete ass who knew nothing of life. 'Hello,' I said to myself. 'Something's up.' She didn't mention a name; it was all general, but almost immediately after that she began to speak of Ronald Marsh and that she thought he'd been badly treated. She was very impersonal and off-hand about it. I didn't connect the two things at the time. But now, I wonder. It seems to me that it was Ronald she meant. What do you think, M. Poirot?"

Her face looked earnestly up into his.

"I think, mademoiselle, that you have perhaps given me some very valuable information."

"Good," Jenny clapped her hands.

Poirot looked kindly at her.

"Perhaps you have not heard; the gentleman of whom you speak—Ronald Marsh, Lord Edgware—has just been arrested."

"Oh!" Her mouth flew open in surprise. "Then my bit of thinking comes rather late in the day."

"It is never too late," said Poirot. "Not with me, you understand. Thank you, mademoiselle."

She left us to return to Bryan Martin.

"There, Poirot," I said. "Surely that shakes your belief."

"No, Hastings. On the contrary it strengthens it."

Despite that valiant assertion I believed myself that secretly he had weakened.

During the days that followed he never once mentioned the Edgware case. If I spoke of it, he answered monosyllabically and without interest. In other words, he had washed his hands of it. Whatever idea he had had lingering in his fantastic brain, he had now been forced to admit himself that it had not materialized—that his first conception of the case had been the true one, and that Ronald Marsh was only too truly accused of the crime. Only, being Poirot, he could not admit openly that such was the case! Therefore he pretended to have lost interest.

Such, I say, was my interpretation of his attitude. It seemed borne out by the facts. He took no faintest interest in the police court proceedings, which in any case were purely formal. He busied himself with other cases and, as I say, displayed no interest when the subject was mentioned.

It was nearly a fortnight later than the events mentioned in my last chapter when I came to realize that my interpretation of his attitude was entirely wrong. It was breakfast time. The usual heavy pile of letters lay by Poirot's plate. He sorted through them with nimble fingers. Then he uttered a quick exclamation of pleasure and picked up a letter with an American stamp on it. He opened it with his little letter opener. I looked on with interest, since he seemed so moved to pleasure about it. There was a letter and a fairly thick enclosure.

Poirot read the former through twice, then he looked up. "Would you like to see this, Hastings?"

I took it from him. It ran as follows:

Dear M. Poirot, I was much touched by your kind—your very kind letter. I have been feeling so bewildered by everything. Apart from my terrible grief, I have been so affronted by the things that seem to have been hinted about Carlotta—the dearest, sweetest sister that a girl ever had. No, M. Poirot, she did not take drugs. I'm sure of it. She had a horror of that kind of thing. I've often heard her say so. If she played a part in that poor man's death, it was an entirely innocent one—but of course her letter to me proves that. I am sending you the actual letter itself, since you ask me to do so. I hate parting with the last letter she ever wrote, but I know you will take care of it and let me have it back; and if it helps you to clear up some of the mystery about her death, as you say it may do, why, then, of course it must go to you.

You ask whether Carlotta mentioned any friend specially in her letters. She mentioned a great many people, of course, but nobody in a very outstanding way. Bryan Martin whom we used to know years ago, a girl called Jenny Driver, and a Captain Ronald Marsh were, I think, the ones she saw most of.

I wish I could think of something to help you. You write so kindly and with such understanding, and you seem to realize what Carlotta and I were to each other.

Gratefully yours,

Lucie Adams

P.S. An officer has just been here for the letter. I told him that I had already mailed it to you. This, of course, was not true, but I felt, somehow or other, that it was important you should see it first. It seems Scotland Yard need it as evidence against the murderer. You will take it to them. But Oh! please be sure they let you have it back again some day. You see, it is Carlotta's last words to me.

"So you wrote yourself to her," I remarked as I laid the letter down. "Why did you do that, Poirot? And why did you ask for the original of Carlotta Adams' letter?"

He was bending over the enclosed sheets of the letter I mentioned.

"In verity I could not say, Hastings, unless it is that I hoped against hope that the original letter might in some way explain the inexplicable."

"I don't see how you can get away from the text of that letter. Carlotta Adams gave it herself to the maid to post. There was no hocus pocus about it, and certainly it reads as a perfectly genuine ordinary epistle."

Poirot sighed.

"I know. I know. And that is what makes it so difficult, because, Hastings, as it stands, that letter is *impossible*."

"Nonsense."

"*Si, si*, it is so. See you, as I have reasoned it out, certain things *must* be; they follow each other with method and order in an understandable fashion. But then comes this letter. It does not accord. Who, then, is wrong? Hercule Poirot or the letter?"

"You don't think it possible that it could be Hercule Poirot?" I suggested as delicately as I was able.

Poirot threw me a glance of reproof.

"There are times when I have been in error, but this is not one of them. Clearly then, since the letter seems impossible, it *is* impossible. There is some fact about the letter which escapes us. I seek to discover what that fact is."

And thereupon he resumed his study of the letter in question, using a small pocket microscope. As he finished perusing each page, he passed it across to me. I, certainly, could find nothing amiss. It was written in a firm, fairly legible handwriting, and it was word for word as it had been telegraphed across.

Poirot sighed deeply.

"There is no forgery of any kind here. No, it is all written in the same hand. And yet, since, as I say, it is impossible—"

He broke off. With an impatient gesture he demanded the sheets from me. I passed them over, and once again he went slowly through them.

Suddenly he uttered a cry. I had left the breakfast table and was standing looking out of the window. At this sound, however, I turned sharply.

Poirot was literally quivering with excitement. His eyes were green like a cat's. His pointing finger trembled.

"See you, Hastings? Look here—quickly—come and look."

I ran to his side. Spread out before him was one of the middle sheets of the letter. I could see nothing unusual about it.

"See you not? All these other sheets they have the clean edge; they are single sheets. But this one—see—one side of it is ragged; it has been torn. Now do you see what I mean? *This was a double sheet*, and so, you comprehend, *one page of the letter is missing*."

I stared stupidly no doubt.

"But how can it be? It makes sense."

"Yes, yes, it makes sense. That is where the cleverness of the idea comes in. Read—and you will see."

I think I cannot do better than to append a facsimile of the page in question.

"You see it now?" said Poirot. "The letter breaks off where

he said I believe it would rate on Lord Edgware himself. Look here, will you rate something on from a bet?"

I laughed & said "How much?"

"Lu cri darling - the answer fairly took my breath away Ten thousand dollars!

she is talking of Captain Marsh. She is sorry for him, and then she says: 'He enjoyed my show very much.' Then on the new sheet she goes on 'he said—' But, *mon ami, a page is missing.* The 'he' of the new page may not be the 'he' of the old page. *In fact it is not the he of the old page.* It is another man altogether who proposed that hoax. Observe; nowhere after that is the name mentioned. Ah! *c'est épatant!* Somehow or other our murderer gets hold of this letter. It gives him away. No doubt he thinks to suppress it altogether, and then—reading it over—he sees another way of dealing with it. Remove one page, and the letter is capable of being twisted into a damning accusation of another man, a man, too, who has a motive for Lord Edgware's death. Ah! it was a gift! The money for the *confiture* as you say! He tears the sheet off and replaces the letter."

I looked at Poirot in some admiration. I was not perfectly convinced of the truth of his theory. It seemed to me highly possible that Carlotta had used an odd half sheet that was already torn, but Poirot was so transfigured with joy that I simply had not the heart to suggest this prosaic possibility. After all, he *might* be right.

I did, however, venture to point out one or two difficulties in the way of his theory.

"But how did the man, whoever he was, get hold of the letter? Miss Adams took it straight from her handbag and gave it herself to the maid to post. The maid told us so."

"Therefore we must assume one of two things. Either the maid was lying, or else, during that evening, Carlotta Adams met the murderer."

I nodded.

"It seems to me that that last possibility is the most likely one. We still do not know where Carlotta Adams was between the time she left her flat and nine o'clock when she left her suitcase at Euston station. During that time, I believe myself that she met the murderer in some appointed spot. They probably had some food together. He gave her some last instructions. What happened exactly in regard to the letter we do not know. One can make a guess. She may have been carrying it in her hand, meaning to post it. She may have laid it down on the table in the restaurant. He sees the address and scents a possible danger. He may have picked it up adroitly, made an excuse for leaving the table, opened it, read it, torn out the sheet, and then either replaced it on the table or perhaps given it to her as she left, telling her that she had dropped it without noticing. The exact way of it is not important, but one thing does seem clear—that Carlotta Adams met the murderer that evening, either before the murder of Lord Edgware or afterward (there was time after she left the Corner House for a brief interview). I have a fancy, though there I am perhaps wrong, that it was the murderer who gave her the gold box. It was possibly a sentimental memento of their first meeting. *If so the murderer is D.*"

"I don't see the point of the gold box."

"Listen, Hastings; Carlotta Adams was not addicted to veronal. Lucie Adams says so, and I, too, believe it to be true. She was a clear-eyed, healthy girl with no predilection for such things. None of her friends nor her maid recognized the box. Why, then, was it found in her possession after she died? To create the impression that she *did* take veronal and that she had taken it for a considerable time—that is to say, at least six months. Let us say that she met the murderer after the murder, if only for a few minutes. They had a drink together, Hastings, to celebrate the success of their plan, and in the girl's drink he put sufficient veronal to ensure that there should be no waking for her on the following morning."

"Horrible," I said with a shudder.

"Yes, it was not pretty," said Poirot dryly.

"Are you going to tell Japp all this?" I asked after a minute or two.

"Not at the moment. What have I got to tell? He would say, the excellent Japp, 'Another nest of the mare! The girl wrote on an odd sheet of paper!' *C'est tout.*"

I looked guiltily at the ground.

"What can I say to that? Nothing. It is a thing that might have happened. I only know it did not happen because *it is necessary that it should not have happened.*"

He paused. A dreamy expression stole across his face.

"Figure to yourself, Hastings; if only that man had had the

order and the method, he would have cut that sheet, not torn it. And we should have noticed nothing. But nothing!"

"So we deduce that he is a man of careless habits," I said, smiling.

"No, no. He might have been in a hurry. You observe it is very carelessly torn. Oh! assuredly he was pressed for time."

He paused and then said:

"One thing you do remark, I hope. This man—this D—he must have had a very good alibi for that evening."

"I can't see how he could have had any alibi at all, if he spent his time first at Regent Gate doing a murder and then with Carlotta Adams."

"Precisely," said Poirot. "That is what I mean. He is badly in need of an alibi, so no doubt he prepared one. Another point: Does his name really begin with D? Or does D stand for some nickname by which he was known to her?"

He paused and then said softly:

"A man whose initial or whose nickname is D. We have got to find him, Hastings. Yes, we have got to find him."

XXIV   News from Paris

On the following day we had an unexpected visit. Geraldine Marsh was announced. I felt sorry for her as Poirot greeted her and set a chair for her. Her large dark eyes seemed wider and darker than ever. There were black circles round them, as though she had not slept. Her face looked extraordinarily haggard and weary for one so young—little more, really, than a child.

"I have come to see you, M. Poirot, because I don't know how to go on any longer. I am so terribly worried and upset."

"Yes, mademoiselle?"

His manner was gravely sympathetic.

"Ronald told me what you said to him that day. I mean that dreadful day when he was arrested." She shivered. "He told me that you came up to him suddenly, just when he had said that he supposed no one would believe him, and that you said to him: 'I believe you.' Is that true, M. Poirot?"

"It is true, mademoiselle; that is what I said."

"I know, but I meant not was it true you said it, but were the words really true. I mean, *did* you believe his story?"

Terribly anxious she looked, leaning forward there, her hands clasped together.

"The words were true, mademoiselle," said Poirot quietly. "I do not believe your cousin killed Lord Edgware."

"Oh!" The colour came into her face, her eyes opened big and wide. "Then you must think—that someone else did it!"

"*Evidement*, mademoiselle." He smiled.

"I'm stupid. I say things badly. What I mean is—you think you know who that somebody is?"

She leaned forward eagerly.

"I have my little ideas, naturally, my suspicions, shall we say?"

"Won't you tell me? Please—please."

Poirot shook his head.

"It would be, perhaps, unfair."

"Then you *have* got a definite suspicion of somebody?"

Poirot merely shook his head noncommittally.

"If only I knew a little more," pleaded the girl, "it would make it so much easier for me. And I might perhaps be able to help you. Yes, really I might be able to help you."

Her pleading was very disarming, but Poirot continued to shake his head.

"The Duchess of Merton is still convinced it was my stepmother," said the girl thoughtfully. She gave a slight questioning glance at Poirot.

He showed no reaction.

"But I hardly see how that can be."

"What is your opinion of her? Of your stepmother?"

"Well—I hardly know her. I was at school in Paris when my father married her. When I came home, she was quite kind. I mean, she just didn't notice I was there. I thought her very empty-headed and—well, mercenary."

Poirot nodded.

"You spoke of the Duchess of Merton. You have seen much of her?"

"Yes. She has been very kind to me. I have been with her a great deal during the last fortnight. It has been terrible, with all the talk, and the reporters, and Ronald in prison and everything." She shivered. "I feel I have no real friends, but the Duchess has been wonderful, and he has been nice too—her son, I mean."

"You like him?"

"He is shy, I think, stiff and rather difficult to get on with. But his mother talks a lot about him, so that I feel that I know him better than I really do."

"I see. Tell me, mademoiselle, you are fond of your cousin?"

"Of Ronald? Of course. He—I haven't seen much of him the last two years, but before that he used to live in the house. I— I always thought he was wonderful, always joking and thinking of mad things to do. Oh! in that gloomy house of ours it made all the difference."

Poirot nodded sympathetically, but he went on to make a remark that shocked me in its crudity.

"You do not want to see him hanged then?"

"No, no." The girl shivered violently. "Not that. Oh! if only it were her—my stepmother. It *must* be her. The Duchess says it must."

"Ah!" said Poirot. "If only Captain Marsh had stayed in the taxi, eh?"

"Yes—at least, what do you mean?" Her brow wrinkled. "I don't understand."

"If he had not followed that man into the house. Did you hear anyone come in, by the way?"

"No, I didn't hear anything."

"What did you do when you came into the house?"

"I ran straight upstairs, to fetch the pearls, you know."

"Of course. It took you some time to fetch them."

"Yes. I couldn't find the key of my jewel-case all at once."

"So often is that the case. The more in haste, the less the speed. It was some time before you came down, and then—you found your cousin in the hall?"

"Yes, coming from the library." She swallowed.

"I comprehend. It gave you quite the turn."

"Yes, it did." She looked grateful for his sympathetic tone. "It startled me, you see."

"Quite, quite."

"Ronnie just said: 'Hello, Dina, got them?' from behind me, and it made me jump."

"Yes," said Poirot gently. "As I said before it is a pity he did not stay outside. Then the taxi driver would have been able to swear he never entered the house."

She nodded. Her tears began to fall, splashing unheeded on her lap. She got up. Poirot took her hand.

"You want me to save him for you. Is that it?"

"Yes, yes—oh! please, yes. You don't know—"

She stood there striving to control herself, clenching her hands.

"Life has not been easy for you, mademoiselle," said Poirot

gently. "I appreciate that. No, it has not been easy. Hastings, will you get mademoiselle a taxi?"

I went down with the girl and saw her into the taxi. She had composed herself by now and thanked me very prettily.

I found Poirot walking up and down the room, his brows knitted in thought. He looked unhappy. I was glad when the telephone bell rang to distract him.

"Who is that? Oh! it is Japp. *Bonjour, mon ami.*"

"What's he got to say?" I asked, drawing nearer the telephone.

Finally, after various ejaculations, Poirot spoke.

"Yes, and who called for it? Do they know?"

Whatever the answer, it was not what he expected. His face dropped ludicrously.

"Are you sure?"

". . . . ."

"No, it is a little upsetting, that is all."

". . . . ."

"Yes, I must rearrange my ideas."

". . . . ."

"Comment?"

". . . . ."

"All the same, I was right about it. Yes, a detail, as you say."

". . . . ."

"No, I am still of the same opinion. I would pray of you to make still further inquiries of the restaurants in the neighbourhood of Regent Gate and Euston, Tottenham Court Road and perhaps Oxford Street."

". . . . ."

"Yes, a woman and a man. And also in the neighbourhood of the Strand just before midnight. *Comment?"*

". . . . ."

"But, yes, I know that Captain Marsh was with the Dortheimers. But there are other people in the world besides Captain Marsh."

". . . . ."

"To say I have the head of the pig is not pretty. *Tout de même,* oblige me in this matter, I pray of you."

". . . . ."

He replaced the receiver.

"Well?" I asked impatiently.

"Is it well? I wonder. Hastings, that gold box *was* bought in Paris. It was ordered by letter and it comes from a well-known Paris shop which specializes in such things. The letter was supposedly from a Lady Ackerley—Constance Ackerley the letter was signed. Naturally there is no such person. The letter was received two days before the murder. It ordered the initials of (presumably) the writer in rubies and the inscription inside. It was a rush order—to be called for the following day. That is the day before the murder."

"And it was called for?"

"Yes, it was called for and paid for in notes."

"Who called for it?" I asked excitedly. I felt we were getting near to the truth.

"A woman called for it, Hastings."

"A woman?" I said, surprised.

"*Mais oui*. A woman—short, middle-aged and *wearing pince-nez*."

We looked at each other completely baffled.

XXV A Luncheon Party

It was, I think, on the day after that that we went to the Widburns' luncheon party at Claridge's. Neither Poirot nor I was particularly anxious to go. It was, as a matter of fact, about the sixth invitation we had received. Mrs. Widburn was a persistent woman and she liked celebrities. Undaunted by refusals, she finally offered such a choice of dates that capitulation was inevitable. Under those circumstances the sooner we went and got it over the better.

Poirot had been very uncommunicative ever since the news from Paris. To my remarks on the subject he returned always the same answer:

"There is something here I do not comprehend." And once or twice he murmured to himself: "Pince-nez. Pince-nez in Paris. Pince-nez in Carlotta Adams' bag."

I really felt glad of the luncheon party as a means of distraction.

Young Donald Ross was there and came up and greeted me cheerily. There were more men than women, and he was put next to me at table. Jane Wilkinson sat almost opposite us, and next to her, between her and Mrs. Widburn, sat the young Duke of Merton.

I fancied—of course it may have been only my fancy—that he looked slightly ill at ease. The company in which he found himself was, so I should imagine, little to his liking. He was a strictly conservative and somewhat reactionary young man, the kind of character that seemed to have stepped out of the Middle Ages by some regrettable mistake. His infatuation for the extremely modern Jane Wilkinson was one of those anachronistic jokes that Nature so loves to play.

Seeing Jane's beauty and appreciating the charm that her exquisite husky voice lent to the most trite utterances, I could

hardly wonder at his capitulation. But one can get used to perfect beauty and an intoxicating voice! It crossed my mind that
perhaps even now a ray of common sense was dissipating the
mists of intoxicated love. It was a chance remark, a rather hu-
miliating *gaffe* on Jane's part, that gave me that impression.

Somebody—I forget who—had uttered the phrase "judgment
of Paris," and straight away Jane's delightful voice was uplifted.

"Paris?" she said. "Why, Paris doesn't cut any ice nowadays.
It's London and New York that count."

As sometimes happens, the words fell in a momentary lull
of conversation. It was an awkward moment. On my right I
heard Donald Ross draw in his breath sharply. Mrs. Widburn
began to talk violently about Russian opera. Everyone hastily
said something to somebody else. Jane alone looked serenely up
and down the table without the least consciousness of having
said anything amiss.

It was then I noticed the Duke. His lips were drawn tightly
together, he had flushed, and it seemed to me as though he
drew slightly away from Jane. He must have had a foretaste of
the fact that for a man of his position to marry a Jane Wilkinson
might lead to some awkward contretemps.

As so often happens, I made the first remark that came into
my head to my left hand neighbour, a stout, titled lady who
arranged children's matinées. I remember that the remark in
question was: "Who is that extraordinarily got-up woman in
purple at the other end of the table?" It was, of course, the lady's
sister! Having stammered apologies I turned and chatted to
Ross, who answered in monosyllables.

It was then, rebuffed on both sides, that I noticed Bryan Martin. He must have come late, for I had not seen him before. He
was a little way further down the table on my side and was leaning forward and chatting with great animation to a pretty blonde
woman.

It was some time since I had seen him at close quarters, and
I was struck at once by the great improvement in his looks. The
haggard lines had almost disappeared. He looked younger and
in every way more fit. He was laughing and chaffing his vis-à-vis
and seemed in first rate spirits.

I did not have time to observe him further, for at that moment my stout neighbour forgave me and graciously permitted me to listen to a long monologue on the beauties of a children's matinée which she was organizing for charity.

Poirot had to leave early, as he had an appointment. He was investigating the strange disappearance of an ambassador's boots, and had a rendezvous fixed for half-past two. He charged me to make his adieus to Mrs. Widburn. While I was waiting to do so —not an easy matter, for she was at the moment closely surrounded by departing friends all breathing out "Darlings" at a great rate—somebody touched me on the shoulder. It was young Ross.

"Isn't M. Poirot here? I wanted to speak to him."

I explained that Poirot had just departed. Ross seemed taken aback. Looking more closely at him, I saw that something seemed to have upset him. He looked white and strained and he had a queer uncertain look in his eyes.

"Did you want to see him particularly?" I asked.

He answered slowly:

"I—don't know."

It was such a queer answer that I stared at him in surprise. He flushed.

"It sounds odd, I know. The truth is that something rather queer has happened, something that I can't make out. I—I'd like M. Poirot's advice about it, because, you see, I don't know what to do. I don't want to bother him, but—"

He looked so puzzled and unhappy that I hastened to reassure him.

"Poirot has gone to keep an appointment," I said, "but I know he means to be back at five o'clock. Why not ring him up then, or come and see him?"

"Thanks. Do you know, I think I will. Five o'clock?"

"Better ring up first," I said, "and make sure before coming round."

"All right, I will. Thanks, Hastings. You see I think it might —just might—be very important."

I nodded and turned again to where Mrs. Widburn was dispensing honied words and limp handshakes. My duty done, I was turning away when a hand was slipped through my arm.

"Don't cut me," said a merry voice. It was Jenny Driver—looking extremely chic, by the way.

"Hello," I said. "Where have you sprung from?"

"I was lunching at the next table to you."

"I didn't see you. How is business?"

"Booming, thank you."

"The soup plates going well?"

"Soup plates, as you rudely call them, are going very well. When everybody has got thoroughly laden up with them, there's going to be dirty work done. Something like a blister with a feather attached is going to be worn bang in the middle of the forehead."

"Unscrupulous," I said.

"Not at all. Somebody must come to the rescue of the ostriches. They're all on the dole."

She laughed and moved away.

"Good-bye. I'm taking an afternoon off from business. Going for a spin in the country."

"And very nice too," I said approvingly. "It's stifling in London today."

I myself walked leisurely through the Park. I reached home about four o'clock. Poirot had not yet come in. It was twenty minutes to five when he returned. He was twinkling and clearly in a good humour.

"I see, Holmes," I remarked, "that you have tracked the ambassadorial boots."

"It was a case of cocaine smuggling. Very ingenious. For the last hour I have been in a ladies' beauty parlour. There was a girl there with auburn hair who would have captured your susceptible heart at once."

Poirot always has the impression that I am particularly susceptible to auburn hair. I do not bother to argue about it.

The telephone rang.

"That's probably Donald Ross," I said as I went across to the instrument.

"Donald Ross?"

"Yes. The young man we met at Chiswick. He wants to see you about something."

I took down the receiver.

"Hello. Captain Hastings speaking."

It was Ross.

"Oh! is that you, Hastings? Has M. Poirot come in?"

"Yes, he's here now. Do you want to speak to him or are you coming round?"

"It's nothing much. I can tell him just as well over the telephone."

"Right. Hold on."

Poirot came forward and took the receiver. I was so close that I could hear, faintly, Ross's voice.

"Is that M. Poirot?" The voice sounded eager, excited.

"Yes, it is I."

"Look here, I don't want to bother you, but there's something that seems to me a bit odd. It's in connection with Lord Edgware's death."

I saw Poirot's figure go taut.

"Continue, continue."

"It may seem just nonsense to you—"

"No, no. Tell me, all the same."

"It was Paris set me off. You see—" Very faintly I heard a bell trilling.

"Half a second," said Ross.

There was the sound of the receiver being laid down.

We waited, Poirot at the mouthpiece, I standing beside him. I say we waited.

Two minutes passed—three minutes—four minutes—five minutes.

Poirot shifted his feet uneasily. He glanced up at the clock. Then he moved the hook up and down and spoke to the Exchange. He turned to me.

"The receiver is still off at the other end, but there is no reply. They cannot get an answer. Quick, Hastings, look up Ross's address in the telephone book. We must go there at once."

XXVI Paris?

A FEW minutes later we were jumping into a taxi. Poirot's face was very grave.

"I am afraid, Hastings," he said. "I am afraid."

"You don't mean—" I said and stopped.

"We are up against somebody who has already struck twice. That person will not hesitate to strike again. He is twisting and turning like a rat, fighting for his life. Ross is a danger. Then Ross will be eliminated."

"Was what he had to tell so important?" I asked doubtfully. "He did not seem to think so."

"Then he was wrong. Evidently what he had to tell was of supreme importance."

"But how could anyone know?"

"He spoke to you, you say. There, at Claridge's. With people all round. Madness—utter madness. Ah! why did you not bring him back with you—guard him—let no one near him till I had heard what he had to say?"

"I never thought—I never dreamt—" I stammered.

Poirot made a quick gesture.

"Do not blame yourself. How could you know? I—I would have known. The murderer, see you, Hastings, is as cunning as a tiger and as relentless. Ah! shall we never arrive?"

We were there at last. Ross lived in a maisonnette on the first floor of a house in a big square in Kensington. A card stuck in a little slot by the doorbell gave us the information. The hall door was open. Inside was a big flight of stairs.

"So easy to come in. None to see," murmured Poirot as he sprang up the stairs.

On the first floor was a kind of partition and a narrow door with a Yale lock. Ross's card was stuck in the centre of the door.

We paused there. Everywhere there was dead silence.

I pushed the door—to my surprise it yielded. We entered.

There was a narrow hall and an open door one side, another in front of us opening into what was evidently the sitting-room.

Into this sitting-room we went. It was the divided half of a big front drawing-room. It was cheaply but comfortably furnished, and it was empty. On a small table was the telephone; the receiver stood down beside the instrument.

Poirot took a swift step forward, looked round, then shook his head.

"Not here. Come, Hastings."

We retraced our steps and, going out into the hall, we passed through the other door. The room was a tiny dining-room. At one side of the table, fallen sideways from a chair and sprawled across the table, was Ross.

Poirot bent over him.

He straightened up. His face was white.

"He's dead. Stabbed at the base of the skull."

.   .   .   .

For long afterward the events of that afternoon remained like a nightmare in my mind. I could not rid myself of a dreadful feeling of responsibility.

Much later, that evening, when we were alone together, I stammered out to Poirot my bitter self-reproachings. He responded quickly:

"No, no, do not blame yourself. How could you have suspected? The good God has not given you a suspicious nature to begin with."

"*You* would have suspected?"

"That is different. All my life, see you, I have tracked down murderers. I know how, each time, the impulse to kill becomes stronger, till, at last, for a trivial cause—" He broke off.

He had been very quiet ever since our ghastly discovery. All through the arrival of the police, the questioning of the other people in the house, the hundred and one details of the dreadful routine following upon a murder, Poirot had remained aloof —strangely quiet—a far-away, speculative look in his eyes. Now, as he broke off his sentence, that same far-away, speculative look returned.

"We have no time to waste in regrets, Hastings," he said quietly. "No time to say 'If.' The poor young man who is dead had something to tell us, and we know now that that something must have been of great importance—otherwise he would not have been killed. Since he can no longer tell us, we have got to guess. We have got to guess, with only one little clue to guide us."

"Paris," I said.

"Yes, Paris." He got up and began to stroll up and down.

"There have been several mentions of Paris in this business, but unluckily in different connections. There is the word Paris engraved in the gold box. Paris in November last. Miss Adams was there then; perhaps Ross was there also. Was there some-one else there whom Ross knew, whom he saw with Miss Adams under somewhat peculiar circumstances?"

"We can never know," I said.

"Yes, yes, we can know. We *shall* know! The power of the human brain, Hastings, is almost unlimited. What other men-tions of Paris have we in connection with the case? There is the short woman with the pince-nez who called for the box at the jeweller's there. Was she known to Ross? The Duke of Merton was in Paris when the crime was committed. Paris, Paris, Paris. Lord Edgware was going to Paris— Ah! possibly we have some-thing there. Was he killed to prevent him going to Paris?"

He sat down again, his brows drawn together. I could almost feel the waves of his furious concentration of thought.

"What happened at that luncheon?" he murmured. "Some casual word or phrase must have shown to Donald Ross the significance of knowledge which was in his possession but which up to then he had not known was significant. Was there some mention of France? Of Paris? Up your end of the table, I mean."

"The word Paris was mentioned but not in that connection."

I told him about Jane Wilkinson's *"gaffe."*

"That probably explains it," he said thoughtfully. "The word Paris would be sufficient—taken in conjunction with something else. But what was that something else? At what was Ross looking? Or of what had he been speaking when that word was uttered?"

"He'd been talking about Scottish superstitions."

"And his eyes were where?"

"I'm not sure. I think he was looking up towards the head of the table where Mrs. Widburn was sitting."

"Who sat next to her?"

"The Duke of Merton, then Jane Wilkinson, then some fellow I didn't know."

"M. le Duc. It is possible that he was looking at M. le Duc when the word Paris was spoken. The Duke, remember, was in Paris, or was supposed to be in Paris, at the time of the crime. Suppose Ross suddenly remembered something which went to show that Merton was *not* in Paris."

"My dear Poirot!"

"Yes, you consider that an absurdity. So does everyone. Had M. le Duc a motive for the crime? Yes, a very strong one. But to suppose that he committed it—oh! absurd. He is so rich, of so assured a position, of such a well-known lofty character. No one will scrutinize his alibi too carefully. And yet to fake an alibi in a big hotel is not so difficult. To go across by the afternoon service—to return—it *could* be done. Tell me, Hastings, did Ross not say anything when the word Paris was mentioned. Did he show no emotion?"

"I do seem to remember that he drew in his breath rather sharply."

"And his manner when he spoke to you afterward. Was it bewildered? Confused?"

"That absolutely describes it."

"*Précisément.* An idea has come to him. He thinks it preposterous! Absurd! And yet— He hesitates to voice it. First he will speak to me. But alas! when he has made up his mind, I am already departed."

"If he had only said a little more to me," I lamented.

"Yes. If only— Who was near you at the time?"

"Well, everybody, more or less. They were saying good-bye to Mrs. Widburn. I didn't notice particularly."

Poirot got up again.

"Have I been all wrong?" he murmured as he began once more to pace the floor. "All the time, have I been wrong?"

I looked at him with sympathy. Exactly what the ideas were that passed through his head I did not know. "Close as an oyster," Japp had called him, and the Scotland Yard inspector's words were truly descriptive. I only knew that now, at this moment, he was at war with himself.

"At any rate," I said, "this murder cannot be put down to Ronald Marsh."

"It is a point in his favour," my friend said absent-mindedly. "But that does not concern us for the moment."

Abruptly, as before, he sat down.

"I cannot be entirely wrong. Hastings, do you remember that I once posed to myself five questions?"

"I seem to remember dimly something of the sort."

"They were: Why did Lord Edgware change his mind on the subject of divorce? What is the explanation of the letter he said he wrote to his wife and which she said she never got? Why was there that expression of rage on his face when we left his house that day? What were a pair of pince-nez doing in Carlotta Adams' handbag? Why did someone telephone to Lady Edgware at Chiswick and immediately ring off?"

"Yes, these were the questions," I said. "I remember now."

"Hastings, I have had in my mind all along a certain little idea. An idea as to who the man was—*the man behind*. Three of those questions I have answered, and the answers accord with my little idea. But two of the questions, Hastings, I cannot answer.

"You see what that means. Either I am wrong as to the person—*and it cannot be that reason*—or else the answer to the two questions that I cannot answer is there all the time. Which is it, Hastings? Which is it?"

Rising, he went to his desk, unlocked it and took out the letter Lucie Adams had sent him from America. He had asked Japp to let him keep it a day or two, and Japp had agreed. Poirot laid it on the table in front of him and pored over it.

The minutes went by. I yawned and picked up a book. I did not think that Poirot would get much result from his study. We had already gone over and over the letter. Granted that it was

not Ronald Marsh who was referred to, there was nothing whatever to show who else it might be.

I turned the pages of my book. Possibly I dozed off.

Suddenly Poirot uttered a low cry. I sat up abruptly. He was
looking at me with an indescribable expression, his eyes green
and shining.

"Hastings, Hastings."

"Yes, what is it?"

"Do you remember I said to you that if the murderer had been
a man of order and method he would have cut this page, not
torn it."

"Yes?"

"I was wrong. There is order and method throughout this
crime. The page had to be torn, not cut. Look for yourself."

I looked.

"Eh bien, you see?"

I shook my head.

"You mean he was in a hurry?"

"Hurry or no hurry, it would be the same thing. Do you not
see, my friend? *The page had to be torn."*

I shook my head.

In a low voice Poirot said:

"I have been foolish. I have been blind. But *now—now—*we
shall get on!"

XXVII Concerning Pince-Nez

A MINUTE later his mood had changed. He sprang to his feet.
I also sprang to mine—completely uncomprehending but willing.

"We will take a taxi. It is only nine o'clock, not too late to
make a visit."

I hurried after him down the stairs.

"Whom are we going to visit?"

"We are going to Regent Gate."

I judged it wisest to hold my peace. Poirot, I saw, was not in
the mood for being questioned. That he was greatly excited I
could see. As we sat side by side in the taxi, his fingers drummed
on his knee with a nervous impatience most unlike his usual
calm.

I went over in my mind every word of Carlotta Adams' letter
to her sister. By this time I almost knew it by heart. I repeated
again and again to myself Poirot's words about the torn page.
But it was no good. As far as I was concerned, Poirot's words
simply did not make sense. Why had a page *got* to be torn? No,
I could not see it.

A new butler opened the door to us at Regent Gate. Poirot
asked for Miss Carroll and, as we followed the butler up the
stairs, I wondered for the fiftieth time where the former "Greek
god" could be. So far the police had failed utterly to run him to
earth. A sudden shiver passed over me as I reflected that perhaps he, too, was dead.

The sight of Miss Carroll, brisk and neat and eminently sane,
recalled me from the fantastic speculations. She was clearly very
much surprised to see Poirot.

"I am glad to find you still here, mademoiselle," said Poirot
as he bowed over her hand. "I was afraid you might be no longer
in the house."

"Geraldine would not hear of my leaving," said Miss Carroll.

"She begged me to stay on. And really, at a time like this, the poor child needs someone. If she needs nothing else, she needs a buffer. And I can assure you, when need be, I make a very efficient buffer, M. Poirot."

Her mouth took on a grim line. I felt that she would have a short way with reporters or news hunters.

"Mademoiselle, you have always seemed to me the pattern of efficiency. The efficiency, I admire it very much. It is rare. Mademoiselle Marsh now, she has not got the practical mind."

"She's a dreamer," said Miss Carroll. "Completely impractical. Always has been. Lucky she hasn't got her living to get."

"Yes, indeed."

"But I don't suppose you came here to talk about people being practical or impractical. What can I do for you, M. Poirot?"

I do not think Poirot quite liked to be recalled to the point in this fashion. He was somewhat addicted to the oblique approach. With Miss Carroll, however, such a thing was not practicable. She blinked at him suspiciously through her strong glasses.

"There are a few points on which I should like definite information. I know I can trust your memory, Miss Carroll."

"I wouldn't be much use as a secretary if you couldn't," said Miss Carroll grimly.

"Was Lord Edgware in Paris last November?"

"Yes."

"Can you tell me the date of his visit?"

"I shall have to look it up."

She rose, unlocked a drawer, took out a small bound book, turned the pages and finally announced:

"Lord Edgware went to Paris on November third and returned on the seventh. He also went over on November twenty-ninth and returned on December fourth. Anything more?"

"Yes. For what purpose did he go?"

"On the first occasion he went to see some statuettes which he thought of purchasing and which were to be auctioned later. On the second occasion he had no definite purpose in view so far as I know."

"Did Mademoiselle Marsh accompany her father on either occasion?"

"She never accompanied her father on any occasion, M. Poirot. Lord Edgware would never have dreamed of such a thing. At that time she was at a convent in Paris, but I do not think her father went to see her or took her out—at least it would surprise me very much if he had."

"You yourself did not accompany him?"

"No."

She looked at him curiously and then said abruptly:

"Why are you asking me these questions, M. Poirot? What is the point of them?"

Poirot did not reply to this question. Instead he said:

"Miss Marsh is very fond of her cousin, is she not?"

"Really, M. Poirot, I don't see what that has got to do with you."

"She came to see me the other day. You knew that?"

"No, first I've heard of it." She seemed startled. "What did she say?"

"She told me—though not in actual words—that she was very fond of her cousin."

"Well, then, why ask me?"

"Because I seek your opinion."

This time Miss Carroll decided to answer.

"Much too fond of him in my opinion. Always has been."

"You do not like the present Lord Edgware?"

"I don't say that. I've no use for him, that's all. He's not serious. I don't deny he's got a pleasant way with him. He can talk you round. But I'd rather see Geraldine getting interested in someone with a little more backbone."

"Such as the Duke of Merton."

"I don't know the Duke. At any rate he seems to take the duties of his position seriously. But he's running after that woman—that precious Jane Wilkinson."

"His mother—"

"Oh! I dare say his mother would prefer him to marry Geraldine. But what can mothers do? Sons never want to marry the girls their mothers want them to marry."

"Do you think that Miss Marsh's cousin cares for her?"

"Doesn't matter whether he does or doesn't, in the position he's in."

"You think, then, that he will be condemned?"

"No, I don't. I don't think he did it."

"But he might be condemned all the same?"

Miss Carroll did not reply.

"I must not detain you." Poirot rose. "By the way, did you know Carlotta Adams?"

"I saw her act. Very clever."

"Yes, she was clever." He seemed lost in meditation. "Ah! I have put down my gloves."

Reaching forward to get them from the table where he had laid them, his cuff caught the chain of Miss Carroll's pince-nez and jerked them off. Poirot retrieved them and the gloves which he had dropped, uttering confused apologies.

"I must apologize also once more for disturbing you," he ended, "but I fancied there might be some clue in a dispute Lord Edgware had with someone last year. Hence my questions about Paris. A forlorn hope, I fear, but mademoiselle seemed so very positive she was. Well, good-night, mademoiselle, and a thousand pardons for disturbing you."

We had reached the door when Miss Carroll's voice recalled us.

"M. Poirot, these aren't my glasses. I can't see through them."

"*Comment?*" Poirot stared at her in amazement. Then his face broke up into smiles.

"Imbecile that I am! My own glasses fell out of my pocket as I stooped to get the gloves and pick up yours. I have mixed the two pairs. They look very alike, you see."

An exchange was made, with smiles on both sides, and we took our departure.

"Poirot," I said when we were outside. "You don't wear glasses."

He beamed at me.

"Penetrating! How quickly you see the point."

"Those were the pince-nez found in Carlotta Adams' handbag?"

"Correct."

"Why did you think they might be Miss Carroll's?"

Poirot shrugged his shoulders.

"She is the only person connected with the case who wears glasses."

"However, they are not hers," I said thoughtfully.

"So she affirms."

"You suspicious old devil."

"Not at all, not at all. Probably she spoke the truth. I think she did speak the truth. Otherwise I doubt if she would have noticed the substitution. I did it very adroitly, my friend."

We were strolling through the streets more or less at random. I suggested a taxi but Poirot shook his head.

"I have need to think, my friend. Walking aids me."

I said no more. The night was a close one and I was in no hurry to return home.

"Were your questions about Paris mere camouflage?" I asked curiously.

"Not entirely."

"We still haven't solved the mystery of the initial D," I said thoughtfully. "It's odd that nobody to do with the case has an initial D—either surname or Christian name—except—oh! yes, that's odd—except Donald Ross himself. And he's dead."

"Yes," said Poirot in a sombre voice. "He is dead."

I remembered another evening when three of us had walked at night, remembered something else, too, and drew my breath in sharply.

"By Jove, Poirot," I said. "Do you remember?"

"Remember what, my friend?"

"What Ross said about thirteen at table. *And he was the first to get up.*"

Poirot did not answer. I felt a little uncomfortable as one always does when superstition is proved justified.

"It is queer," I said in a low voice. "You must admit it is queer."

"Eh?"

"I said it was queer—about Ross and thirteen. Poirot, what are you thinking about?"

To my utter amazement and, I must admit, somewhat to my disgust, Poirot began suddenly to shake with laughter. He shook and he shook. Something was evidently causing him the most exquisite mirth.

"What the devil are you laughing at?" I said sharply.

"Oh! Oh! Oh!" gasped Poirot. "It is nothing. It is that I think of a riddle I hear the other day. I will tell it to you. What is it that has two legs, feathers, and barks like a dog?"

"A chicken, of course," I said wearily. "I knew that in the nursery."

"You are too well-informed, Hastings. You should say I do not know. And then me, I say, 'A chicken,' and then you say, 'But a chicken does not bark like a dog,' and I say, 'Ah! I put that in to make it more difficult.' Supposing, Hastings, that there we have the explanation of the letter D?"

"What nonsense!"

"Yes, to most people, but to a certain type of mind— Oh! if I had only someone I could ask—"

We were passing a big cinema. People were streaming out of it, discussing their own affairs, their servants, their friends of the opposite sex, and, occasionally, the picture they had just seen.

With a group of them we crossed the Euston Road.

"I loved it," a girl was sighing. "I think Bryan Martin's just wonderful. I never miss any picture he's in. The way he rode down that cliff and got there in time with the papers."

Her escort was less enthusiastic.

"Idiotic story. If they'd just had the sense to ask Ellis right away, which anyone with sense would have done—"

The rest was lost. Reaching the pavement I turned back to see Poirot standing in the middle of the road with buses bearing down on him from either side. Instinctively I put my hands over my eyes. There was a jarring of brakes, and some rich bus driver language. In a dignified manner Poirot walked to the curb. He looked like a man walking in his sleep.

"Poirot," I said. "Were you mad?"

"No, *mon ami*. It was just that—something came to me. There, at that moment."

"A damned bad moment," I said, "and very nearly your last one."

"No matter. Ah! *mon ami*—I have been blind, deaf, insensible. Now I see the answers to all those questions—yes, all five of them. Yes, I see it all—so simple, so childishly simple."

XXVIII Poirot Asks a Few Questions

WE had a curious walk home. Poirot was clearly following out some train of thought in his own mind. Occasionally he murmured a word under his breath. I heard one or two of them. Once he said "Candles" and another time he said something that sounded like *"douzaine."* I suppose if I had been really bright I should have seen the line his thoughts were taking. It was really such a clear trail. However, at the time, it sounded to me mere gibberish.

No sooner were we at home than he flew to the telephone. He rang up the Savoy and asked to speak to Lady Edgware.

"Not a hope, old boy," I said with some amusement.

Poirot, as I have often told him, is one of the worst informed men in the world.

"Don't you know?" I went on. "She's in a new play. She'll be at the theatre. It's only half past ten."

Poirot paid no attention to me. He was speaking to the hotel clerk who was evidently telling him exactly what I had just told him.

"Ah! is that so? I should like then to speak to Lady Edgware's maid."

In a few minutes the connection was made.

"Is that Lady Edgware's maid? This is M. Poirot speaking. M. Hercule Poirot. You remember me, do you not?"

".............."

"Très bien. Now, you understand, something of importance has arisen. I would like you to come and see me at once."

".............."

"But, yes, very important. I will give you the address. Listen carefully."

He repeated it twice, then hung up the receiver with a thoughtful face.

"What is the idea?" I asked curiously. "Have you really got a piece of information?"

"No, Hastings, it is she who will give me the information."

"What information?"

"Information about a certain person."

"Jane Wilkinson?"

"Oh! as to her, I have all the information I need. I know her back side before as you say."

"Who then?"

Poirot gave me one of his supremely irritating smiles and told me to wait and see. He then busied himself in tidying up the room in a fussy manner.

Ten minutes later the maid arrived. She seemed a little nervous and uncertain. A small, neat figure, dressed in black, she peered about her doubtfully.

Poirot bustled forward.

"Ah! you have come. That is most kind. Sit here, will you not, Mademoiselle—Ellis, I think?"

"Yes, sir. Ellis."

She sat down on the chair Poirot had drawn forward for her.

She sat with her hands folded on her lap looking from one to the other of us. Her small, bloodless face was quite composed, and her thin lips were pinched together.

"To begin with, Miss Ellis, you have been with Lady Edgware how long?"

"Three years, sir."

"That is as I thought. You know her affairs well."

Ellis did not reply. She looked disapproving.

"What I mean is, you should have a good idea of who her enemies are likely to be."

Ellis compressed her lips more tightly.

"Most women have tried to do her a spiteful turn, sir. Yes, they've been all against her. Nasty jealousy."

"Her own sex did not like her?"

"No, sir. She's too good-looking. And she always gets what she wants. There's a lot of nasty jealousy in the theatrical profession."

"What about men?"

Ellis allowed a sour smile to appear on her withered countenance.

"She can do what she likes with the gentlemen, sir, and that's a fact."

"I agree with you," said Poirot, smiling. "Yet, even allowing that, I can imagine circumstances arising—" He broke off.

Then he said in a different voice:

"You know Mr. Bryan Martin, the film actor?"

"Oh! yes, sir."

"Very well?"

"Very well indeed."

"I believe I am not mistaken in saying that a little less than a year ago, Mr. Bryan Martin was very deeply in love with your mistress."

"Head over ears, sir. And it's 'is' not 'was,' if you ask me."

"He believed at that time she would marry him, eh?"

"Yes, sir."

"Did she ever seriously consider marrying him?"

"She thought of it, sir. If she could have got her freedom from his lordship, I believe she would have married him."

"And then, I suppose, the Duke of Merton appeared on the scene?"

"Yes, sir. He was doing a tour through the States. Love at first sight it was with him."

"And so good-bye to Bryan Martin's chances."

Ellis nodded.

"Of course Mr. Martin made an enormous amount of money," she explained, "but the Duke of Merton had position as well, and her ladyship is very keen on position. Married to the Duke, she'd have been one of the first ladies in the land."

The maid's voice held a smug complacency. It amused me.

"So Mr. Bryan Martin was—how do you say—turned down? Did he take it badly?"

"He carried on something awful, sir."

"Ah!"

"He threatened her with a revolver once. And the scenes he made! It frightened me, it did. He was drinking a lot, too. He went all to pieces."

"But in the end he calmed down."

"So it seemed, sir, but he still hung about, and I didn't like the look in his eye. I've warned her ladyship about it, but she only laughed. She's one who enjoys feeling her power, if you know what I mean."

"Yes," said Poirot thoughtfully. "I think I know what you mean."

"We've not seen so much of him just lately, sir. A good thing in my opinion. He's beginning to get over it, I hope."

"Perhaps."

Something in Poirot's utterance of the word seemed to strike her. She asked anxiously:

"You don't think she's in danger, sir?"

"Yes," said Poirot gravely. "I think she is in great danger, but she has brought it on herself."

His hand, running aimlessly along the mantelshelf, caught a vase of roses and it toppled over. The water fell on Ellis's face and head. I had seldom known Poirot clumsy, and I could deduce from it that he was in a great state of mental perturbation. He was very upset—rushed for a towel—tenderly assisted the maid to dry her face and neck and was profuse in apologies.

Finally a treasury note changed hands and he escorted her towards the door thanking her for her goodness in coming.

"But it is still early," he said, glancing at the clock. "You will be back before your mistress returns."

"Oh! that is quite all right, sir. She is going out to supper, I think, and anyway she never expects me to sit up for her unless she says so special."

Suddenly Poirot flew off at a tangent.

"Mademoiselle, pardon me, but you are limping."

"That's nothing, sir. My feet are a little painful."

"The corns?" murmured Poirot in the confidential voice of one sufferer to another.

Corns, apparently it was. Poirot expatiated upon a certain remedy which according to him worked wonders.

Finally Ellis departed.

I was full of curiosity.

"Well, Poirot," I said. "Well?"

He smiled at my eagerness.

"Nothing more this evening, my friend. Tomorrow morning, early, we will ring up Japp. We will ask him to come round. We will also ring up Mr. Bryan Martin. I think he will be able to tell us something interesting. Also, I wish to pay him a debt that I owe him."

"Really?"

I looked at Poirot sideways. He was smiling to himself in a curious way.

"At any rate," I said, "you can't suspect *him* of killing Lord Edgware, especially after what we've heard tonight. That would be playing Jane's game with a vengeance. To kill off the husband so as to let the lady marry someone else is a little too disinterested for any man."

"What profound judgment!"

"Now don't be sarcastic," I said with some annoyance. "And what on earth are you fiddling with all the time?"

Poirot held the object in question up.

"With the pince-nez of the good Ellis, my friend. She left them behind."

"Nonsense, she had them on her nose when she went out."

He shook his head gently.

"Wrong! Absolutely wrong! What she had on, my dear Hastings, was the pair of pince-nez we found in Carlotta Adams' handbag."

I gasped.

XXIX Poirot Speaks

IT fell to me to ring up Inspector Japp the following morning. His voice sounded rather depressed.

"Oh! it's you, Captain Hastings. Well, what's in the wind now?"

I gave him Poirot's message.

"Come round at eleven? Well, I dare say I could. He's not got anything to help us over young Ross's death, has he? I don't mind confessing that we could do with something. There's not a clue of any kind. Most mysterious business."

"I think he's got something for you," I said noncommittally. "He seems very pleased with himself, at all events."

"That's more than I am, I can tell you. All right, Captain Hastings. I'll be there."

My next task was to ring up Bryan Martin. To him I said what I had been told to say: that Poirot had discovered something rather interesting which he thought Mr. Martin would like to hear. When asked what it was, I said that I had no idea. Poirot had not confided in me. There was a pause.

"All right," said Bryan at last. "I'll come."

He rang off.

Presently, somewhat to my surprise, Poirot rang up Jenny Driver and asked her, also, to be present. He was quiet and rather grave. I asked him no questions.

Bryan Martin was the first to arrive. He looked in good health and spirits, but—or it might have been my fancy—a shade uneasy. Jenny Driver arrived almost immediately afterward. She seemed surprised to see Bryan, and he seemed to share her surprise.

Poirot brought forward two chairs and urged them to sit down. He glanced at his watch.

"Inspector Japp will be here in one moment, I expect."

"Inspector Japp?" Bryan seemed startled.

"Yes. I have asked him to come here—informally—as a friend."

"I see."

He relapsed into silence. Jenny gave a quick glance at him, then glanced away. She seemed rather preoccupied about something this morning.

A moment later, Japp entered the room. He was, I think, a trifle surprised to find Bryan Martin and Jenny Driver there, but he made no sign. He greeted Poirot with his usual jocularity.

"Well, M. Poirot, what's it all about? You've got some wonderful theory or other, I suppose."

Poirot beamed at him.

"No, no, nothing wonderful. Just a little story, quite simple; so simple that I am ashamed not to have seen it at once. I want, if you permit, to take you with me through the case from the beginning."

Japp sighed and looked at his watch.

"If you won't be more than an hour—" he said.

"Reassure yourself," said Poirot. "It will not take as long as that. See here, you want to know, do you not, who it was killed Lord Edgware, who it was killed Miss Adams, who it was killed Donald Ross?"

"I'd like to know the last," said Japp cautiously.

"Listen to me and you shall know everything. See, I am going to be humble." (Not likely! I thought unbelievingly.) "I am going to show you every step of the way. I am going to reveal how I was hoodwinked, how I displayed the gross imbecility, how it needed the conversation of my friend Hastings and a chance remark by a total stranger to put me on the right track."

He paused and then, clearing his throat, he began to speak in what I called his "lecture" voice.

"I will begin at the supper party at the Savoy. Lady Edgware accosted me and asked for a private interview. She wanted to get rid of her husband. At the close of our interview she said—somewhat unwisely, I thought—that she might have to go round in a taxi and kill him herself. Those words were heard by Mr. Bryan Martin who came in at that moment."

He wheeled round.

"Eh? That is so, is it not?"

"We all heard," said the actor. "The Widburns, Marsh, Carlotta—all of us."

"Oh! I agree. I agree perfectly. *Eh bien,* I did not have a chance to forget those words of Lady Edgware's. Mr. Bryan Martin called on me the following morning for the express purpose of driving those words home."

"Not at all," cried Bryan Martin angrily; "I came—"

Poirot held up a hand.

"You came, ostensibly, to tell me a cock and bull story about being shadowed, a tale that a child might have seen through. You probably took it from an out-of-date film. A girl whose consent you had to obtain—a man whom you recognized by a gold tooth. *Mon ami,* no young man would have a gold tooth; it is not done in these days, and especially in America. The gold tooth, it is a hopelessly old-fashioned piece of dentistry. Oh! it was all of a piece—absurd! Having told your cock and bull story, you get down to the real purpose of your visit—to poison my mind against Lady Edgware. To put it clearly, you prepare the ground for the moment when she murders her husband."

"I don't know what you're talking about," muttered Bryan Martin. His face was deathly pale.

"You ridicule the idea that he will agree to a divorce! You think I am going to see him the following day, but actually the appointment is changed. I go to see him that morning and he *does* agree to a divorce. Any motive for a crime on Lady Edgware's part is gone. Moreover he tells me that he has already written to Lady Edgware to that effect.

"But Lady Edgware declares that she never got that letter. Either she lies, her husband lies, or somebody has suppressed it—who?

"Now I ask myself *why* does M. Bryan Martin give himself the trouble to come and tell me all these lies? What inner power drives him on? And I form the idea, monsieur, that you have been frantically in love with that lady. Lord Edgware says that his wife told him she wanted to marry an actor. Well, supposing that is so, but that the lady changes her mind. By the time Lord Edgware's letter agreeing to the divorce arrives, it is someone else she wants to marry—not you! There would be a reason, then, for your suppressing that letter."

"I never—"

"Presently you shall say all you want to say. Now you will attend to me.

"What then would be your frame of mind—you, a spoilt idol who has never known a rebuff? As I see it, a kind of baffled fury, a desire to do Lady Edgware as much harm as possible. And what greater harm could you do her than to have her accused—perhaps hanged—for murder."

"Good Lord!" said Japp.

Poirot turned to him.

"But yes, that was the little idea that began to shape itself in my mind. Several things came to support it. Carlotta Adams had two principal men friends—Captain Marsh and Bryan Martin. It was possible, then, that Bryan Martin, a rich man, was the one who suggested the hoax and offered her ten thousand dollars to carry it through. It has seemed to me unlikely all along that Miss Adams could ever have believed Ronald Marsh would have the ten thousand dollars to give her. She knew him to be extremely hard up. Bryan Martin was a far more likely solution."

"I didn't—I tell you I didn't—" came hoarsely from the film actor's lips.

"When the substance of Miss Adams' letter to her sister was wired from Washington— Oh! *là là!* I was very upset. It seemed that my reasoning was wholly wrong. But later I made a discovery. The actual letter itself was sent to me, and, instead of being continuous, a sheet of the letter was missing. *So 'he' might refer to someone who was not Captain Marsh.*

"There was one more piece of evidence. Captain Marsh, when he was arrested, distinctly stated that he thought he saw Bryan Martin enter the house. Coming from an accused man, that carried no weight. Also M. Martin had an alibi. That naturally! It was to be expected. If M. Martin did the murder, to have an alibi was absolutely necessary.

"That alibi was vouched for by one person only—Miss Driver."

"What about it?" said the girl sharply.

"Nothing, mademoiselle," said Poirot, smiling, "except that that same day I noticed you lunching with M. Martin and that you presently took the trouble to come over and try and make me believe that your friend Miss Adams was specially interested in Ronald Marsh, not, as I was sure was the case, in Bryan Martin."

"Not a bit of it," said the film star stoutly.

"You may have been unaware of it, monsieur," said Poirot quietly, "but I think it was true. It explains, as nothing else could, her feeling of dislike towards Lady Edgware. That dislike was on your behalf. You had told her all about your rebuff, had you not?"

"Well—yes—I felt I must talk to someone and she—"

"Was sympathetic. Yes, she was sympathetic; I noticed it myself. *Eh bien*, what happens next? Ronald Marsh, he is arrested. Immediately your spirits improve. Any anxiety you may have had is over. Although your plan has miscarried, owing to Lady Edgware's change of mind about going to a party at the last minute, yet somebody else has become the scapegoat and relieved you of all anxiety on your own account. And then—at a luncheon party—you hear Donald Ross—that pleasant but rather stupid young man—say something to Hastings that seems to show that you are not so safe after all."

"It isn't true," the actor howled. The perspiration was running down his face. His eyes looked wild with terror. "I tell you I heard nothing—nothing—I did nothing."

Then, I think, came the greatest shock of the morning.

"That is quite true," said Poirot quietly, "and I hope you have now been sufficiently punished for coming to me—*me*, Hercule Poirot, with a cock and bull story."

We all gasped. Poirot continued dreamily.

"You see—I am showing you all my mistakes. There were five questions I had asked myself. Hastings knows them. The answer to three of them fitted in very well. Who had suppressed that letter? Clearly Bryan Martin answered that question very well. Another question was what had induced Lord Edgware suddenly to change his mind and agree to a divorce? Well, I had an idea as to that. Either he wanted to marry again—but I could find no evidence pointing to that—or else some kind of blackmail was involved. Lord Edgware was a man of peculiar tastes. It was possible that facts about him had come to light which, while not entitling his wife to an English divorce, might yet be used by her as a lever, coupled with the threat of publicity. I think that is what happened. Lord Edgware did not want an open scandal attached to his name. He gave in, though his fury at having to do so was expressed in the murderous look on his face when he thought himself unobserved. It also explains the suspicious quickness with which he said, 'Not because of anything in the letter,' before I had even suggested that that might be the case.

"Two questions remained. The question of an odd pair of pince-nez in Miss Adams' bag, which did not belong to her, and the question of why Lady Edgware was rung up on the telephone while she was at dinner at Chiswick. In no way could I fit in M. Bryan Martin with either of those questions.

"So I was forced to the conclusion that either I was wrong about M. Martin, or wrong about the questions. In despair I once again read that letter of Miss Adams' through very carefully, and I found something! Yes, I found something!

"See for yourselves. Here it is. You see the sheet is torn? Unevenly, as often happens. Supposing now that before the 'h' at the top there was an 's.'

"Ah! you have it! You see. Not *he*—but *she*! It was a *woman* who suggested this hoax to Carlotta Adams.

"Well, I made a list of all the women who had been even remotely connected with the case. Besides Jane Wilkinson, there were four—Geraldine Marsh, Miss Carroll, Miss Driver and the Duchess of Merton.

"Of those four, the one that interested me most was Miss Carroll. She wore glasses, she was in the house that night, she had already been inaccurate in her evidence, owing to her desire to incriminate Lady Edgware, and she was also a woman of great efficiency and nerve who could have carried out such a crime. The motive was more obscure, but after all she had worked with Lord Edgware some years, and some motive might exist of which we were totally unaware.

"I also felt that I could not quite dismiss Geraldine Marsh from the case. She hated her father—she had told me so. She was a neurotic, highly strung type. Suppose when she went into the house that night she had deliberately stabbed her father and then coolly proceeded upstairs to fetch the pearls. Imagine her agony when she found that her cousin, whom she loved devotedly, had not remained outside in the taxi but had entered the house!

"Her agitated manner could be well explained on these lines. It could equally well be explained by her own innocence but by her fear that her cousin really had done the crime. There was another small point. The gold box found in Miss Adams' bag had the initial D in it. I had heard Geraldine addressed by her cousin as 'Dina.' Also she was in a Pensionnat in Paris last November and *might* possibly have met Carlotta Adams in Paris.

"You may think it fantastic to add the Duchess of Merton to the list. But she had called upon me and I recognized in her a fanatical type. The love of her whole life was centred on her son, and she might have worked herself up to contrive a plot to destroy the woman who was about to ruin her son's life.

"Then there was Miss Jenny Driver—"

He paused, looking at Jenny. She looked back at him, an impudent head on one side.

"And what have you got on me?" she asked.

"Nothing, mademoiselle, except that you were a friend of Bryan Martin's—and that your surname begins with D."

"That's not very much."

"There's one thing more. You have the brains and the nerve to commit such a crime. I doubt if anyone else had."

The girl lit a cigarette.

"Continue," she said cheerfully.

"Was M. Martin's alibi genuine or was it not? That was what I had to decide. If it was, who was it Ronald Marsh had seen go into the house? And suddenly I remembered something. The good-looking butler at Regent Gate bore a very marked resemblance to M. Martin. It was he whom Captain Marsh had seen, and I formed a theory as to that. It is my idea that he discovered his master killed. Beside his master was an envelope containing French banknotes to the value of a hundred pounds. He took these notes, slipped out of the house, left them in safe keeping with some rascally friend, and returned, letting himself in with Lord Edgware's key. He let the crime be discovered by the housemaid on the following morning. He felt in no danger himself, as he was quite convinced that Lady Edgware had done the murder, and the notes were out of the house and already changed before their loss was noticed. However, when Lady Edgware had an alibi and Scotland Yard began investigating his antecedents, he got the wind up and decamped."

Japp nodded approvingly.

"I still have the question of the pince-nez to settle. If Miss Carroll was the owner, then the case seemed settled. She could have suppressed the letter, and, in arranging details with Carlotta Adams, or in meeting her on the evening of the murder, the pince-nez might have inadvertently found their way into Carlotta Adams' bag.

"But the pince-nez were apparently nothing to do with Miss Carroll. I was walking home with Hastings here, somewhat depressed, trying to arrange things in my mind with order and method. And then the miracle happened!

"First Hastings spoke of things in a certain order. He mentioned Donald Ross having been one of thirteen at table at Sir Montagu Corner's and having been the first to get up. I was following out a train of thought of my own and did not pay much attention. It just flashed through my mind that, strictly speaking, that was not true. He may have got up first at the end of dinner, but actually Lady Edgware had been the first to get up, since she was called to the telephone. Thinking of her, a certain riddle occurred to me—a riddle that I fancied accorded well with her somewhat childish mentality. I told it to Hastings. He was, like Queen Victoria, not amused. I next fell to wondering whom I could ask for details about M. Martin's feeling for Jane Wilkinson. She herself would not tell me, I knew. And then a passer-by, as we were all crossing the road, uttered a simple sentence.

"He said to his girl companion that somebody or other 'should have asked Ellis.' And immediately the whole thing came to me in a flash!"

He looked round.

"Yes, yes, the pince-nez, the telephone call, the short woman who called for the gold box in Paris. *Ellis,* of course, Jane Wilkinson's maid. I followed every step of it—the candles—the dim light—Miss Van Dusen—everything. I *knew!*"

XXX The Story

HE looked round at us.

"Come, my friends," he said gently. "Let me tell you the real story of what happened that night.

"Carlotta Adams leaves her flat at seven o'clock. From there she takes a taxi and goes to the Piccadilly Palace."

"What?" I exclaimed.

"To the Piccadilly Palace. Earlier in the day she has taken a room there as Mrs. Van Dusen. She wears a pair of strong glasses which, as we all know, alters the appearance very much. As I say, she books a room, saying that she is going by the night boat train to Liverpool and that her luggage has gone on. At eight-thirty Lady Edgware arrives and asks for her. She is shown up to her room. There they change clothes. Dressed in a fair wig, a white taffeta dress and ermine wrap, *Carlotta Adams and not Jane Wilkinson leaves the hotel and drives to Chiswick.* Yes, yes, it is perfectly possible. I have been to the house in the evening. The dinner table is lit only with candles, the lamps are dim, no one there knows Jane Wilkinson very well. There is the golden hair, the well-known husky voice and manner. Oh! it was quite easy. And if it had not been successful—if someone had spotted the fake—well, that was all arranged for, too. Lady Edgware, wearing a dark wig, Carlotta's clothes and the pince-nez, pays her bill, has her suitcase put on a taxi, and drives to Euston. She removes the dark wig in the lavatory; she puts her suitcase in the cloakroom. Before going to Regent Gate she rings up Chiswick and asks to speak to Lady Edgware. This has been arranged between them. If all has gone well and Carlotta has not been spotted, she is to answer simply: 'That's right.' I need hardly say Miss Adams was ignorant of the real reason for the telephone call. Having heard the words, Lady Edgware goes ahead. She goes to Regent Gate, asks for Lord Edgware, proclaims her individuality, goes into the library, and commits the first murder. Of course she did not know that Miss Carroll was watching her from above. As far as she is aware it will be the butler's word (and he has never seen her, remember—and also she wears a hat which shields her from his gaze) against the word of twelve well-known and distinguished people.

"She leaves the house, returns to Euston, changes from fair to dark again and picks up her suitcase. She has now to put in time till Carlotta Adams returns from Chiswick. They have agreed as to the approximate time. She goes to the Corner House, occasionally glancing at her watch, for the time passes slowly. Then she prepares for the second murder. She puts the small gold box she has ordered from Paris in Carlotta Adams' bag which, of course, she is carrying. Perhaps it is then she finds the letter. Perhaps it was earlier. Anyway, as soon as she sees the address, she scents danger. She opens it—her suspicions are justified.

"Perhaps her first impulse is to destroy the letter altogether. But she soon sees a better way. By removing one page of the letter she makes it read like an accusation of Ronald Marsh—a man who had a powerful motive for the crime. Even if Ronald has an alibi, it will still read as an accusation of a man so long as she tears off the s of 'she.' So that is what she does, then replaces it in the envelope and the envelope back in the bag.

"Then, the time having come, she walks in the direction of the Savoy Hotel. As soon as she sees the car pass, with (presumably) herself inside, she quickens her pace, enters at the same time and goes straight up the stairs. She is inconspicuously dressed in black. It is unlikely that anyone will notice her.

"Upstairs, she goes to her room. Carlotta Adams has just reached it. The maid has been told to go to bed—a perfectly usual proceeding. They again change clothes, and then, I fancy, Lady Edgware suggests a little drink—to celebrate. In that drink is the veronal. She congratulates her victim, says she will send her the cheque tomorrow. Carlotta Adams goes home. She is very sleepy—tries to ring up a friend—possibly M. Martin or Captain Marsh, for both have Victoria numbers—but gives it up. She is too tired. The veronal is beginning to work. She goes to bed, and she never wakes again. The second crime has been carried through successfully.

"Now for the third crime. It is at a luncheon party. Sir Montagu Corner makes a reference to a conversation he had with Lady Edgware on the night of the murder. That is easy. She has only to murmur some flattering phrase. But Nemesis comes upon her later. There is a mention of the 'judgment of Paris' and she takes Paris to be the only Paris she knows—the Paris of fashions and frills!

"But opposite her is sitting a young man who was at that dinner at Chiswick—a young man who heard the Lady Edgware of that night discussing Homer and Greek civilization generally. Carlotta Adams was a cultured, well-read girl. He cannot understand. He stares. And suddenly it comes to him. *This is not the same woman.* He is terribly upset. He is not sure of himself. He must have advice. He thinks of me. He speaks to Hastings.

"But the lady overhears him. She is quick enough and shrewd enough to realize that in some way or other she has given herself away. She hears Hastings say that I will not be in till five. At twenty to five she goes to Ross's maisonnette. He opens the door, is very surprised to see her, but it does not occur to him to be afraid. A strong, able-bodied young man is not afraid of a woman. He goes with her into the dining-room. She pours out some story to him. Perhaps she goes on her knees and flings her arms round his neck. And then, swift and sure, she strikes—as before. Perhaps he gives a choked cry—no more. He, too, is silenced."

There was a silence. Then Japp spoke hoarsely.

"You mean—she did it all the time?"

Poirot bowed his head.

"But why, if he was willing to give her a divorce?"

"Because the Duke of Merton is a pillar of the Anglo-Catholics. Because he would not dream of marrying a woman whose husband was alive. He was a young man of fanatical principles. As a widow, she was pretty certain of being able to marry him. Doubtless she had tentatively suggested divorce but he had not risen to the bait."

"Then why send you to Lord Edgware?"

"*Ah! parbleu.*" Poirot from having been very correct and English, suddenly relapsed into his natural self. "To pull the cotton-wool over my eyes! To make me a witness to the fact that there was no motive for the murder! Yes, she dared to make me, Hercule Poirot, her cat's paw! *Ma foi,* she succeeded too! Oh! that strange brain—childlike and cunning. She can act! How well she acted surprise at being told of the letter her husband had written her which she swore she had never received. Did she feel the slightest pang of remorse for any of her three crimes? I can swear she did not."

"I told you what she was like," cried Bryan Martin. "I told you. I knew she was going to kill him. I felt it. And I was afraid that somehow she'd get away with it. She's clever—devilish clever in a kind of half-wit way. And I wanted her to suffer. I wanted her to suffer. I wanted her to hang for it."

His face was scarlet. His voice came thickly.

"Now, now," said Jenny Driver.

She spoke exactly as I have heard nursemaids speak to a small child in the Park.

"And the gold box with the initial D and Paris November inside?" said Japp.

"She ordered that by letter and sent Ellis, her maid, to fetch it. Naturally Ellis just called for a parcel which she paid for. She had no idea what was inside. Also, Lady Edgware borrowed a pair of Ellis's pince-nez to help in the Van Dusen impersonation. She forgot about them and left them in Carlotta Adams' handbag—her one mistake.

"Oh! it came to me—it all came to me as I stood in the middle of the road. It was not polite what the bus driver said to me, but it was worth it. Ellis! Ellis's pince-nez. Ellis calling for the box in Paris. Ellis, and therefore Jane Wilkinson. Very possibly, she borrowed something else from Ellis besides the pince-nez."

"What?"

"A corn knife."

I shivered. There was a momentary silence. Then Japp said with a strange reliance in the answer:

"M. Poirot. Is this *true?*"

"It is true, *mon ami.*"

Then Bryan Martin spoke, and his words were, I thought, very typical of him.

"But look here," he said peevishly. "What about *me?* Why bring *me* here today? Why nearly frighten me to death?"

Poirot looked at him coldly.

"To punish you, monsieur, for being impertinent! How dare you try and make the games with Hercule Poirot?"

And then Jenny Driver laughed. She laughed and laughed.

"Serves you right, Bryan," she said at last.

She turned to Poirot.

"I'm glad as I can be that it wasn't Ronnie Marsh," she said. "I've always liked him. And I'm glad, glad, *glad* that Carlotta's death won't go unpunished! As for Bryan here, well, I'll tell you something, M. Poirot. I'm going to marry him, and if he thinks he can get divorced and married every two or three years, in the approved Hollywood fashion, well, he never made a bigger mistake in his life. He's going to marry me and stick to me."

Poirot looked at her—looked at her determined chin and at her flaming hair.

"It is very possible, mademoiselle," he said, "that that may be so. I said that you had sufficient nerve for anything. Even to marry a film 'star.'"

XXXI A Human Document

A DAY or two after that I was suddenly recalled to the Argentine, so it happened that I never saw Jane Wilkinson again and only read in the paper of her trial and condemnation. Unexpectedly, at least unexpectedly to me, she went completely to pieces when charged with the truth. So long as she was able to be proud of her cleverness and act her part, she made no mistakes; but once her self-confidence failed her, owing to someone having found her out, she was as incapable as a child would be of keeping up a deception. Cross-examined, she went completely to pieces.

So, as I said before, that luncheon party was the last time I saw Jane Wilkinson. But when I think of her, I always see her the same way—standing in her room at the Savoy, trying on expensive black clothes with a serious, absorbed face. I am convinced that that was no pose. She was being completely natural. Her plan had succeeded, and therefore she had no further qualms and doubts. Neither do I think that she ever suffered one pang of remorse for the three crimes she had committed.

I reproduce here a document which she had directed was to be sent to Poirot after her death. It is, I think, typical of that very lovely and completely conscienceless lady.

Dear M. Poirot, I have been thinking things over and I feel that I should like to write this for you. I know that you sometimes publish reports of your cases. I don't really think that you've ever published a document by the person themselves. I feel, too, that I would like everyone to know just exactly how I did it all. I still think it was all very well planned. If it hadn't been for you everything would have been quite all right. I've felt rather bitter about that, but I suppose you couldn't help it. I'm sure, if I send you this, you'll give it plenty of prominence. You will, won't you? I should like to be remembered. And I do think I am really a unique person. Everybody here seems to think so.

It began in America when I got to know Merton. I saw at once that if only I were a widow he would marry me. Unfortunately he has got a queer sort of prejudice against divorce. I tried to overcome it but it was no good, and I had to be careful, because he was a very kinky sort of person.

I soon realized that my husband simply had got to die, but I didn't know how to set about it. You can manage things like that ever so much better in the States. I thought and I thought— but I couldn't see how to arrange it. And then, suddenly, I saw Carlotta Adams do her imitation of me and at once I began to see a way. With her help I could get an alibi. That same evening I saw you, and it suddenly struck me that it would be a good idea to send you to my husband to ask him for a divorce. At the same time I would go about talking of killing my husband, because I've always noticed that if you speak the truth in a rather silly way nobody believes you. I've often done it over contracts. And it's also a good thing to seem stupider than you are. At my second meeting with Carlotta Adams I broached the idea. I said it was a bet—and she fell for it at once. She was to pretend to be me at some party and if she got away with it she was to have ten thousand dollars. She was very enthusiastic and several of the ideas were hers—about changing clothes and all that. You see we couldn't do it here because of Ellis, and we couldn't do it at her place because of her maid. She, of course, didn't see why we couldn't. It was a little awkward. I just said "No." She thought me rather stupid about it, but she gave in and we thought of the hotel plan. I took a pair of Ellis's pince-nez.

Of course I realized quite soon that she would have to be got out of the way too. It was a pity, but, after all, those imitations of hers really were very impertinent. If mine hadn't happened to suit me I'd have been angry about it. I had some veronal myself, though I hardly ever take it, so that was quite easy. And then I had quite a brain wave. You see, it would be so much better if it could seem that she was in the habit of taking it. I ordered a box—the duplicate of one I'd been given—and I had her initials put on it and an inscription inside. I thought if I put some odd initial and Paris, November, inside it, it would make it all much more difficult. I wrote for the box from the Ritz when I was in there lunching one day. And I sent Ellis over to fetch it. She didn't know what it was, of course.

Everything went off quite well on the night. I took one of Ellis's corn knives, while she was over in Paris, because it was nice and sharp. She never noticed, because I put it back afterward. It was a doctor in San Francisco who showed me just where to stick it in. He'd been talking about lumbar and cistern punctures, and he said one had to be very careful, otherwise one went through the cistertia magna and into the medulla oblongata where all the vital nerve centres are and that that would cause immediate death. I made him show me the exact place several times. I thought it might perhaps come in useful one day. I told him I wanted to use the idea in a film.

It was very dishonourable of Carlotta Adams to write to her sister. She'd promised me to tell nobody. I do think it was clever of me to see what a good thing it would be to tear off that one page and leave he instead of she. I thought of that all by myself. I think I'm more proud of that than anything else. Everyone always says I haven't got brains—but I think it needed real brains to think of that.

I'd thought things out very carefully and I did exactly what I'd planned when the Scotland Yard man came. I rather enjoyed that part of it. I had thought, perhaps, that he'd really arrest me. I felt quite safe because I knew they'd have to believe all those people at the dinner and I didn't see how they could find out about me and Carlotta changing clothes.

After that I felt so happy and contented. My luck had held and I really felt everything was going to go right. The old Duchess was beastly to me, but Merton was sweet. He wanted to marry me as soon as possible and hadn't the least suspicion.

I don't think I've ever been so happy as I was those few weeks. My husband's nephew being arrested made me feel just as safe as anything. And I was more proud of myself than ever for having thought of tearing that page out of Carlotta Adams' letter.

The Donald Ross business was just sheer bad luck. I'm not

quite sure now just how it was he spotted me. Something about Paris being a person and not a place. Even now I don't know who Paris was—and I think it's a silly name for a man, anyway.

It's curious how when luck starts going against you, it keeps on going. I had to do something about Donald Ross quickly, and that did go all right. It mightn't have, because I hadn't time to be clever or think of making an alibi. I did think I was safe after that.

Of course Ellis told me you had sent for her and questioned her, but I gathered it was all something to do with Bryan Martin. I couldn't think what you were driving at. You didn't ask her whether she had called for the parcel in Paris. I suppose you thought if she repeated that to me I should smell a rat. As it was, it came as a complete surprise. I couldn't believe it. It was just uncanny the way you seemed to know everything I'd done.

I just felt it was no good. You can't fight against luck. It was bad luck, wasn't it? I wonder if you are ever sorry for what you did. After all, I only wanted to be happy in my own way. And if it hadn't been for me you would never have had anything to do with the case. I never thought you'd be so horribly clever. You didn't look clever.

It's funny, but I haven't lost my looks a bit. In spite of all that dreadful trial and the horrid things that man on the other side said to me, and the way he battered me with questions.

I look much paler and thinner, but it suits me somehow. They all say I'm wonderfully brave. They don't hang you in public any more, do they? I think that's a pity.

I'm sure there's never been a murderess like me before.

I suppose I must say Good-bye now. It's very queer. I don't seem to realize things a bit. I'm going to see the chaplain tomorrow.

Yours forgivingly (because I must forgive my enemies, mustn't I?)

Jane Wilkinson.

P.S.   Do you think they will put me in Madame Tussaud's?

The A.B.C.
Murders

FOREWORD

by CAPTAIN ARTHUR HASTINGS, O.B.E.

IN THIS narrative of mine I have departed from my usual practice of relating only those incidents and scenes at which I myself was present. Certain chapters, therefore, are written in the third person.

I wish to assure my readers that I can vouch for the occurrences related in these chapters. If I have taken a certain poetic licence in describing the thoughts and feelings of various persons, it is because I believe I have set them down with a reasonable amount of accuracy. I may add that they have been "vetted" by my friend Hercule Poirot himself.

In conclusion, I will say that if I have described at too great length some of the secondary personal relationships which arose as a consequence of this strange series of crimes, it is because the human and personal element can never be ignored. Hercule Poirot once taught me in a very dramatic manner that romance can be a by-product of crime.

As to the solving of the A.B.C. mystery, I can only say that in my opinion Poirot showed real genius in the way he tackled a problem entirely unlike any which had previously come his way.

I The Letter

IT WAS in June of 1935 that I came home from my ranch in South America for a stay of about six months. It had been a difficult time for us out there. Like every one else, we had suffered from world depression. I had various affairs to see to in England that I felt could only be successful if a personal touch was introduced. My wife remained to manage the ranch.

I need hardly say that one of my first actions on reaching England was to look up my old friend, Hercule Poirot.

I found him installed in one of the newest type of service flats in London. I accused him (and he admitted the fact) of having chosen this particular building entirely on account of its strictly geometrical appearance and proportions.

"But yes, my friend, it is of a most pleasing symmetry, do you not find it so?"

I said that I thought there could be too much squareness and, alluding to an old joke, I asked if in this super-modern hostelry they managed to induce hens to lay square eggs?

Poirot laughed heartily.

"Ah, you remember that? Alas! no—science has not yet induced the hens to conform to modern tastes, they still lay eggs of different sizes and colours!"

I examined my old friend with an affectionate eye. He was looking wonderfully well—hardly a day older than when I had last seen him.

"You're looking in fine fettle, Poirot," I said. "You've hardly aged at all. In fact, if it were possible, I should say that you had fewer grey hairs than when I saw you last."

Poirot beamed on me.

"And why is that not possible? It is quite true."

"Do you mean your hair is turning from grey to black instead of from black to grey?"

"Precisely."

"But surely that's a scientific impossibility!"

"Not at all."

"But that's very extraordinary. It seems against nature."

"As usual, Hastings, you have the beautiful and unsuspicious mind. Years do not change that in you! You perceive a fact and mention the solution of it in the same breath without noticing that you are doing so!"

I stared at him puzzled.

Without a word he walked into his bedroom and returned with a bottle in his hand which he handed to me.

I took it, for the moment uncomprehending.

It bore the words:

REVIVIT.—*To bring back the natural tone of the hair.* REVIVIT *is* NOT *a dye. In five shades, Ash, Chestnut, Titian, Brown, Black.*

"Poirot," I cried. "You have dyed your hair!"

"Ah, the comprehension comes to you!"

"So *that's* why your hair looks so much blacker than it did last time I was back."

"Exactly."

"Dear me," I said, recovering from the shock. "I suppose next time I come home I shall find you wearing false moustaches —or are you doing so now?"

Poirot winced. His moustaches had always been his sensitive point. He was inordinately proud of them. My words touched him on the raw.

"No, no, indeed, *mon ami*. That day, I pray the good God, is still far off. The false moustaches! *Quel horreur!*"

He tugged at them vigorously to assure me of their genuine character.

"Well, they are very luxuriant still," I said.

"*N'est-ce pas?* Never, in the whole of London, have I seen a pair of moustaches to equal mine."

A good job too, I thought privately. But I would not for the world have hurt Poirot's feelings by saying so.

Instead I asked if he still practised his profession on occasions.

"I know," I said, "that you actually retired years ago—"

"C'est vrai. To grow the vegetable marrows! And immediately a murder occurs—and I send the vegetable marrows to promenade themselves to the devil. And since then—I know very well what you will say—I am like the prima donna who makes positively the farewell performance! That farewell performance, it repeats itself an indefinite number of times!"

I laughed.

"In truth, it has been very like that. Each time I say: This is the end. But no, something else arises! And I will admit it, my friend, the retirement I care for it not at all. If the little grey cells are not exercised, they grow the rust."

"I see," I said. "You exercise them in moderation."

"Precisely. I pick and choose. For Hercule Poirot nowadays only the cream of crime."

"Has there been much cream about?"

"Pas mal. Not long ago I had a narrow escape."

"Of failure?"

"No, no." Poirot looked shocked. "But I—*I, Hercule Poirot,* was nearly exterminated."

I whistled.

"An enterprising murderer!"

"Not so much enterprising as careless," said Poirot. "Precisely that—careless. But let us not talk of it. You know, Hastings, in many ways I regard you as my mascot."

"Indeed?" I said. "In what ways?"

Poirot did not answer my question directly. He went on:

"As soon as I heard you were coming over I said to myself: Something will arise. As in former days we will hunt together, we two. But if so it must be no common affair. It must be something"—he waved his hands excitedly—"something *recherché*—delicate—*fine . . ."* He gave the last untranslatable word its full flavour.

"Upon my word, Poirot," I said. "Any one would think you were ordering a dinner at the Ritz."

"Whereas one cannot command a crime to order? Very true."

He sighed. "But I believe in luck—in destiny, if you will. It is your destiny to stand beside me and prevent me from committing the unforgivable error."

"What do you call the unforgivable error?"

"Overlooking the obvious."

I turned this over in my mind without quite seeing the point.

"Well," I said presently, smiling, "has this super crime turned up yet?"

"*Pas encore*. At least—that is—"

He paused. A frown of perplexity creased his forehead. His hands automatically straightened an object or two that I had inadvertently pushed awry.

"I am not sure," he said slowly.

There was something so odd about his tone that I looked at him in surprise.

The frown still lingered.

Suddenly with a brief decisive nod of the head he crossed the room to a desk near the window. Its contents, I need hardly say, were all neatly docketed and pigeon-holed so that he was able at once to lay his hand upon the paper he wanted.

He came slowly across to me, an open letter in his hand. He read it through himself, then passed it to me.

"Tell me, *mon ami,*" he said. "What do you make of this?"

I took it from him with some interest.

It was written on thickish white notepaper in printed characters:

Mr. HERCULE POIROT,—You fancy yourself, don't you, at solving mysteries that are too difficult for our poor thick-headed British police? Let us see, Mr. Clever Poirot, just how clever you can be. Perhaps you'll find this nut too hard to crack. Look out for Andover on the 21st of the month.

Yours, etc.,
A.B.C.

I glanced at the envelope. That also was printed.

"Postmarked W.C.1," said Poirot as I turned my attention to the postmark. "Well, what is your opinion?"

I shrugged my shoulders as I handed it back to him.

"Some madman or other, I suppose."

"That is all you have to say?"

"Well—doesn't it sound like a madman to you?"

"Yes, my friend, it does."

His tone was grave. I looked at him curiously.

"You take this very seriously, Poirot."

"A madman, *mon ami,* is to be taken seriously. A madman is a very dangerous thing."

"Yes, of course, that is true. . . . I hadn't considered that point. . . . But what I meant was, it sounds more like a rather idiotic kind of hoax. Perhaps some convivial idiot who had had one over the eight."

"*Comment?* Nine? Nine what?"

"Nothing—just an expression. I meant a fellow who was tight. No, damn it, a fellow who had had a spot too much to drink."

"*Merci*, Hastings—the expression 'tight' I *am* acquainted with it. As you say, there may be nothing more to it than that. . . ."

"But you think there is?" I asked, struck by the dissatisfaction of his tone.

Poirot shook his head doubtfully, but he did not speak.

"What have you done about it?" I inquired.

"What can one do? I showed it to Japp. He was of the same opinion as you—a stupid hoax—that was the expression he used. They get these things every day at Scotland Yard. I, too, have had my share. . . ."

"But you take this one seriously?"

Poirot replied slowly.

"There is something about that letter, Hastings, that I do not like. . . ."

In spite of myself, his tone impressed me.

"You think—what?"

He shook his head, and picking up the letter, put it away again in the desk.

"If you really take it seriously, can't you do something?" I asked.

"As always, the man of action! But what is there to do? The county police have seen the letter but they, too, do not take it seriously. There are no fingerprints on it. There are no local clues as to the possible writer."

"In fact there is only your own instinct?"

"Not instinct, Hastings. Instinct is a bad word. It is my *knowledge*—my *experience*—that tells me that something about that letter is wrong—"

He gesticulated as words failed him, then shook his head again.

"I may be making the mountain out of the anthill. In any case there is nothing to be done but wait."

"Well, the twenty-first is Friday. If a whacking great robbery takes place near Andover then—"

"Ah, what a comfort that would be—!"

"A *comfort?*" I stared. The word seemed to be a very extraordinary one to use.

"A robbery may be a *thrill* but it can hardly be a comfort!" I protested.

Poirot shook his head energetically.

"You are in error, my friend. You do not understand my meaning. A robbery would be a relief since it would dispossess my mind of the fear of something else."

"Of what?"

"*Murder,*" said Hercule Poirot.

II (Not from Captain Hastings' Personal Narrative)

MR. ALEXANDER BONAPARTE CUST rose from his seat and peered near-sightedly round the shabby bedroom. His back was stiff from sitting in a cramped position and as he stretched himself to his full height an onlooker would have realized that he was, in reality, quite a tall man. His stoop and his near-sighted peering gave a delusive impression.

Going to a well-worn overcoat hanging on the back of the door, he took from the pocket a packet of cheap cigarettes and some matches. He lit a cigarette and then returned to the table at which he had been sitting. He picked up a railway guide and consulted it, then he returned to the consideration of a type-written list of names. With a pen, he made a tick against one of the first names on the list.

It was Thursday, June 20th.

III Andover

I HAD been impressed at the time by Poirot's forebodings about the anonymous letter he had received, but I must admit that the matter had passed from my mind when the 21st actually arrived and the first reminder of it came with a visit paid to my friend by Chief Inspector Japp of Scotland Yard. The C.I.D. inspector had been known to us for many years and he gave me a hearty welcome.

"Well, I never," he exclaimed. "If it isn't Captain Hastings back from the wilds of the what do you call it! Quite like old days seeing you here with Monsieur Poirot. You're looking well, too. Just a little bit thin on top, eh? Well, that's what we're all coming to. I'm the same."

I winced slightly. I was under the impression that owing to the careful way I brushed my hair across the top of my head that thinness referred to by Japp was quite unnoticeable. However, Japp had never been remarkable for tact where I was concerned, so I put a good face upon it and agreed that we were none of us getting any younger.

"Except Monsieur Poirot here," said Japp. "Quite a good advertisement for a hair tonic, he'd be. Face fungus sprouting finer than ever. Coming out into the limelight, too, in his old age. Mixed up in all the celebrated cases of the day. Train mysteries, air mysteries, high society deaths—oh, he's here, there and everywhere. Never been so celebrated as since he retired."

"I have already told Hastings that I am like the prima donna who makes always one more appearance," said Poirot, smiling.

"Shouldn't wonder if you ended by detecting your own death," said Japp, laughing heartily. "That's an idea, that is. Ought to be put in a book."

"It will be Hastings who will have to do that," said Poirot, twinkling at me.

"Ha ha! That would be a joke, that would," laughed Japp.

I failed to see why the idea was so extremely amusing, and in any case I thought the joke was in poor taste. Poirot, poor old chap, is getting on. Jokes about his approaching demise can hardly be agreeable to him.

Perhaps my manner showed my feelings, for Japp changed the subject.

"Have you heard about Monsieur Poirot's anonymous letter?" he asked.

"I showed it to Hastings the other day," said my friend.

"Of course," I exclaimed. "It had quite slipped my memory. Let me see, what was the date mentioned?"

"The twenty-first," said Japp. "That's what I dropped in about. Yesterday was the twenty-first and just out of curiosity I rang up Andover last night. It was a hoax all right. Nothing doing. One broken shop window—kid throwing stones—and a couple of drunk and disorderlies. So just for once our Belgian friend was barking up the wrong tree."

"I am relieved, I must confess," acknowledged Poirot.

"You'd quite got the wind up about it, hadn't you?" said Japp affectionately. "Bless you, we get dozens of letters like that coming in every day! People with nothing better to do and a bit weak in the top story sit down and write 'em. They don't mean any harm! Just a kind of excitement."

"I have indeed been foolish to take the matter so seriously," said Poirot. "It is the nest of the horse that I put my nose into there."

"You're mixing up mares and wasps," said Japp.

"*Pardon?*"

"Just a couple of proverbs. Well, I must be off. Got a little business in the next street to see to—receiving stolen jewellery. I thought I'd just drop in on my way and put your mind at rest. Pity to let those grey cells function unnecessarily."

With which words and a hearty laugh, Japp departed.

"He does not change much, the good Japp, eh?" asked Poirot.

"He looks much older," I said. "Getting as grey as a badger," I added vindictively.

Poirot coughed and said:

"You know, Hastings, there is a little device—my hairdresser is a man of great ingenuity—one attaches it to the scalp and brushes one's own hair over it—it is not a wig, you comprehend—but—"

"Poirot," I roared. "Once and for all I will have nothing to do with the beastly inventions of your confounded hairdresser. What's the matter with the top of my head?"

"Nothing—nothing at all."

"It's not as though I were going *bald*."

"Of course not! Of course not!"

"The hot summers out there naturally cause the hair to fall out a bit. I shall take back a really good hair tonic."

"*Précisément*."

"And, anyway, what business is it of Japp's? He always was an offensive kind of devil. And no sense of humour. The kind of man who laughs when a chair is pulled away just as a man is about to sit down."

"A great many people would laugh at that."

"It's utterly senseless."

"From the point of view of the man about to sit, certainly it is."

"Well," I said, slightly recovering my temper. (I admit that I am touchy about the thinness of my hair.) "I'm sorry that anonymous letter business came to nothing."

"I have indeed been in the wrong over that. About that letter, there was, I thought, the odour of the fish. Instead a mere stupidity. Alas, I grow old and suspicious like the blind watchdog who growls when there is nothing there."

"If I'm going to co-operate with you, we must look about for some other 'creamy' crime," I said with a laugh.

"You remember your remark of the other day? If you could order a crime as one orders a dinner, what would you choose?"

I fell in with his humour.

"Let me see now. Let's review the menu. Robbery? Forgery? No, I think not. Rather too vegetarian. It must be murder—red-blooded murder—with trimmings, of course."

"Naturally. The *hors d'œuvres*."

"Who shall the victim be—man or woman? Man, I think.

Some bigwig. American millionaire. Prime Minister. Newspaper proprietor. Scene of the crime—well, what's wrong with the good old library? Nothing like it for atmosphere. As for the weapon—well, it might be a curiously twisted dagger—or some blunt instrument—a carved stone idol—"

Poirot sighed.

"Or, of course," I said, "there's poison—but that's always so technical. Or a revolver shot echoing in the night. Then there must be a beautiful girl or two—"

"With auburn hair," murmured my friend.

"Your same old joke. One of the beautiful girls, of course, must be unjustly suspected—and there's some misunderstanding between her and the young man. And then, of course, there must be some other suspects—an older woman—dark, dangerous type —and some friend or rival of the dead man's—and a quiet secretary—dark horse—and a hearty man with a bluff manner —and a couple of discharged servants or gamekeepers or something—and a damn fool of a detective rather like Japp—and well—that's about all."

"That is your idea of the cream, eh?"

"I gather you don't agree."

Poirot looked at me sadly.

"You have made there a very pretty résumé of nearly all the detective stories that have ever been written."

"Well," I said. "What would *you* order?"

Poirot closed his eyes and leaned back in his chair. His voice came purringly from between his lips.

"A very simple crime. A crime with no complications. A crime of quiet domestic life . . . very unimpassioned—very *intime.*"

"How can a crime be *intime?*"

"Supposing," murmured Poirot, "that four people sit down to play bridge and one, the odd man out, sits in a chair by the fire. At the end of the evening the man by the fire is found dead. One of the four, while he is dummy, has gone over and killed him, and, intent on the play of the hand, the other three have not noticed. Ah, there would be a crime for you! *Which of the four was it?*"

"Well," I said. "I can't see any excitement in that!"

Poirot threw me a glance of reproof.

"No, because there are no curiously twisted daggers, no black-mail, no emerald that is the stolen eye of a god, no untraceable Eastern poisons. You have the melodramatic soul, Hastings. You would like, not one murder, but a series of murders."

"I admit," I said, "that a second murder in a book often cheers things up. If the murder happens in the first chapter, and you have to follow up everybody's alibi until the last page but one—well, it does get a bit tedious."

The telephone rang and Poirot rose to answer.

"'Allo," he said. "'Allo. Yes, it is Hercule Poirot speaking."

He listened for a minute or two and then I saw his face change.

His own side of the conversation was short and disjointed.

"*Mais oui . . .*"

"Yes, of course . . ."

"But yes, we will come . . ."

"Naturally . . ."

"It may be as you say . . ."

"Yes, I will bring it. *A tout à l'heure* then."

He replaced the receiver and came across the room to me.

"That was Japp speaking, Hastings."

"Yes?"

"He had just got back to the Yard. There was a message from Andover. . . ."

"Andover?" I cried excitedly.

Poirot said slowly:

"An old woman of the name of Ascher who keeps a little tobacco and newspaper shop has been found murdered."

I think I felt ever so slightly damped. My interest, quickened by the sound of Andover, suffered a faint check. I had expected something fantastic—out of the way! The murder of an old woman who kept a little tobacco shop seemed, somehow, sordid and uninteresting.

Poirot continued in the same slow, grave voice:

"The Andover police believe they can put their hand on the man who did it—"

I felt a second throb of disappointment.

"It seems the woman was on bad terms with her husband. He drinks and is by way of being rather a nasty customer. He's threatened to take her life more than once.

"Nevertheless," continued Poirot, "in view of what has happened, the police there would like to have another look at the anonymous letter I received. I have said that you and I will go down to Andover at once."

My spirits revived a little. After all, sordid as this crime seemed to be, it was a *crime,* and it was a long time since I had had any association with crime and criminals.

I hardly listened to the next words Poirot said. But they were to come back to me with significance later.

"This is the beginning," said Hercule Poirot.

IV Mrs. Ascher

WE WERE received at Andover by Inspector Glen, a tall, fair-haired man with a pleasant smile.

For the sake of conciseness I think I had better give a brief résumé of the bare facts of the case.

The crime was discovered by Police Constable Dover at 1 A.M. on the morning of the 22nd. When on his round he tried the door of the shop and found it unfastened. He entered and at first thought the place was empty. Directing his torch over the counter, however, he caught sight of the huddled up body of the old woman. When the police surgeon arrived on the spot it was elicited that the woman had been struck down by a heavy blow on the back of the head, probably while she was reaching down a packet of cigarettes from the shelf behind the counter. Death must have occurred about nine to seven hours previously.

"But we've been able to get it down a bit nearer than that," explained the inspector. "We've found a man who went in and bought some tobacco at five-thirty. And a second man went in and found the shop empty, as he thought, at five minutes past six. That puts the time at between five-thirty and six-o-five. So far I haven't been able to find any one who saw this man Ascher in the neighbourhood, but, of course, it's early as yet. He was in the Three Crowns at nine o'clock pretty far gone in drink. When we get hold of him he'll be detained on suspicion."

"Not a very desirable character, inspector?" asked Poirot.

"Unpleasant bit of goods."

"He didn't live with his wife?"

"No, they separated some years ago. Ascher's a German. He was a waiter at one time, but he took to drink and gradually became unemployable. His wife went into service for a bit. Her last place was as cook-housekeeper to an old lady, Miss Rose. She allowed her husband so much out of her wages to keep himself, but he was always getting drunk and coming round and making scenes at the places where she was employed. That's why she took the post with Miss Rose at The Grange. It's three miles out of Andover, dead in the country. He couldn't get at her there so well. When Miss Rose died, she left Mrs. Ascher a small legacy, and the woman started this tobacco and newsagent business—quite a tiny place—just cheap cigarettes and a few newspapers—that sort of thing. She just about managed to keep going. Ascher used to come round and abuse her now and again and she used to give him a bit to get rid of him. She allowed him fifteen shillings a week regular."

"Had they any children?" asked Poirot.

"No. There's a niece. She's in service near Overton. Very superior, steady young woman."

"And you say this man Ascher used to threaten his wife?"

"That's right. He was a terror when he was in drink—cursing and swearing that he'd bash her head in. She had a hard time, did Mrs. Ascher."

"What age of woman was she?"

"Close on sixty—respectable and hard-working."

Poirot said gravely:

"It is your opinion, inspector, that this man Ascher committed the crime?"

The inspector coughed cautiously.

"It's a bit early to say that, Mr. Poirot, but I'd like to hear Franz Ascher's own account of how he spent yesterday evening. If he can give a satisfactory account of himself, well and good—if not—"

His pause was a pregnant one.

"Nothing was missing from the shop?"

"Nothing. Money in the till quite undisturbed. No signs of robbery."

"You think that this man Ascher came into the shop drunk, started abusing his wife and finally struck her down?"

"It seems the most likely solution. But I must confess, sir, I'd like to have another look at that very odd letter you received. I was wondering if it was just possible that it came from this man Ascher."

Poirot handed over the letter and the inspector read it with a frown.

"It doesn't read like Ascher," he said at last. "I doubt if Ascher would use the term 'our' British police—not unless he was trying to be extra cunning—and I doubt if he's got the wits for that. Then the man's a wreck—all to pieces. His hand's too shaky to print letters clearly like this. It's good quality notepaper and ink, too. It's odd that the letter should mention the twenty-first of the month. Of course it *might* be a coincidence."

"That is possible—yes."

"But I don't like this kind of concidence, Mr. Poirot. It's a bit too pat."

He was silent for a minute or two—a frown creasing his forehead.

"A.B.C. Who the devil could A.B.C. be? We'll see if Mary Drower (that's the niece) can give us any help. It's an odd business. But for this letter I'd have put my money on Franz Ascher for a certainty."

"Do you know anything of Mrs. Ascher's past?"

"She's a Hampshire woman. Went into service as a girl up in London—that's where she met Ascher and married him. Things must have been difficult for them during the war. She actually left him for good in 1922. They were in London then. She came back here to get away from him, but he got wind of where she was and followed her down here, pestering her for money—" A constable came in. "Yes, Briggs, what is it?"

"It's the man Ascher, sir. We've brought him in."

"Right. Bring him in here. Where was he?"

"Hiding in a truck on the railway siding."

"He was, was he? Bring him along."

Franz Ascher was indeed a miserable and unprepossessing specimen. He was blubbering and cringing and blustering alternately. His bleary eyes moved shiftily from one face to another.

"What do you want with me? I have not done nothing. It is a shame and a scandal to bring me here! You are swine, how dare you?" His manner changed suddenly. "No, no, I do not mean that—you would not hurt a poor old man—not be hard on him. Every one is hard on poor old Franz. Poor old Franz."

Mr. Ascher started to weep.

"That'll do, Ascher," said the inspector. "Pull yourself together. I'm not charging you with anything—yet. And you're not bound to make a statement unless you like. On the other hand, if you're *not* concerned in the murder of your wife—"

Ascher interrupted him—his voice rising to a scream.

"I did not kill her! I did not kill her! It is all lies! You are goddamned English pigs—all against me. I never kill her—never."

"You threatened to often enough, Ascher."

"No, no. You do not understand. That was just a joke—a good joke between me and Alice. She understood."

"Funny kind of joke! Do you care to say where you were yesterday evening, Ascher?"

"Yes, yes—I tell you everything. I did not go near Alice. I am with friends—good friends. We are at the Seven Stars— and then we are at the Red Dog—"

He hurried on, his words tumbling over each other.

"Dick Willows—he was with me—and old Curdie—and George —and Platt and lots of the boys. I tell you I do not never go near Alice. *Ach Gott,* it is the truth I am telling you."

His voice rose to a scream. The inspector nodded to his underling.

"Take him away. Detained on suspicion."

"I don't know what to think," he said as the unpleasant, shaking old man with the malevolent, mouthing jaw was removed. "If it wasn't for the letter, I'd say he did it."

"What about the men he mentions?"

"A bad crowd—not one of them would stick at perjury. I've no doubt he *was* with them the greater part of the evening. A lot depends on whether any one saw him near the shop between half-past five and six."

Poirot shook his head thoughtfully.

"You are sure nothing was taken from the shop?"

The inspector shrugged his shoulders. "That depends. A

packet or two of cigarettes might have been taken—but you'd hardly commit murder for that."

"And there was nothing—how shall I put it—introduced into the shop. Nothing that was odd there—incongruous?"

"There was a railway guide," said the inspector.

"A railway guide?"

"Yes. It was open and turned face downward on the counter. Looked as though some one had been looking up the trains from Andover. Either the old woman or a customer."

"Did she sell that type of thing?"

The inspector shook his head.

"She sold penny time-tables. This was a big one—kind of thing only Smith's or a big stationer would keep."

A light came into Poirot's eyes. He leant forward.

"A railway guide, you say. A Bradshaw—*or an A.B.C.?*"

A light came into the inspector's eye also.

"By the Lord," he said. "It *was* an A.B.C."

V Mary Drower

I THINK that I can date my interest in the case from that first mention of the A.B.C. railway guide. Up till then I had not been able to raise much enthusiasm. This sordid murder of an old woman in a back street shop was so like the usual type of crime reported in the newspapers that it failed to strike a significant note. In my own mind I had put down the anonymous letter with its mention of the 21st as a mere coincidence. Mrs. Ascher, I felt reasonably sure, had been the victim of her drunken brute of a husband. But now the mention of the railway guide (so familiarly known by its abbreviation of A.B.C., listing as it did all railway stations in their alphabetical order) sent a quiver of excitement through me. Surely—surely this could not be a second coincidence?

The sordid crime took on a new aspect.

Who was the mysterious individual who had killed Mrs. Ascher and left an A.B.C. railway guide behind him?

When we left the police station our first visit was to the mortuary to see the body of the dead woman. A strange feeling came over me as I gazed down on that wrinkled old face with the scanty grey hair drawn back tightly from the temples. It looked so peaceful, so incredibly remote from violence.

"Never knew who or what struck her," observed the sergeant. "That's what Dr. Kerr says. I'm glad it was that way, poor old soul. A decent woman she was."

"She must have been beautiful once," said Poirot.

"Really?" I murmured incredulously.

"But yes, look at the line of the jaw, the bones, the moulding of the head."

He sighed as he replaced the sheet and we left the mortuary.

Our next move was a brief interview with the police surgeon.

Dr. Kerr was a competent-looking middle-aged man. He spoke briskly and with decision.

"The weapon wasn't found," he said. "Impossible to say what it may have been. A weighted stick, a club, a form of sandbag —any of those would fit the case."

"Would much force be needed to strike such a blow?"

The doctor shot a keen glance at Poirot.

"Meaning, I suppose, could a shaky old man of seventy do it? Oh, yes, it's perfectly possible—given sufficient weight in the head of the weapon, quite a feeble person could achieve the desired result."

"Then the murderer could just as well be a woman as a man?"

The suggestion took the doctor somewhat aback.

"A woman, eh? Well, I confess it never occurred to me to connect a woman with this type of crime. But of course it's possible—perfectly possible. Only, psychologically speaking, I shouldn't say this was a woman's crime."

Poirot nodded his head in eager agreement.

"Perfectly, perfectly. On the face of it, highly improbable. But one must take all possibilities into account. The body was lying—how?"

The doctor gave us a careful description of the position of the victim. It was his opinion that she had been standing with her back to the counter (and therefore to her assailant) when the blow had been struck. She had slipped down in a heap behind the counter quite out of sight of any one entering the shop casually.

When we had thanked Dr. Kerr and taken our leave, Poirot said:

"You perceive, Hastings, that we have already one further point in favour of Ascher's innocence. If he had been abusing his wife and threatening her, she would have been *facing* him over the counter. Instead, she had her *back* to her assailant— obviously she is reaching down tobacco or cigarettes for a *customer*."

I gave a little shiver.

"Pretty gruesome."

Poirot shook his head gravely.

"Pauvre femme," he murmured.

Then he glanced at his watch.

"Overton is not, I think, many miles from here. Shall we run over there and have an interview with the niece of the dead woman?"

"Surely you will go first to the shop where the crime took place?"

"I prefer to do that later. I have a reason."

He did not explain further, and a few minutes later we were driving on the London road in the direction of Overton.

The address which the inspector had given us was that of a good-sized house about a mile on the London side of the village.

Our ring at the bell was answered by a pretty dark-haired girl whose eyes were red with recent weeping.

Poirot said gently:

"Ah! I think it is you who are Miss Mary Drower, the parlour-maid here?"

"Yes, sir, that's right. I'm Mary, sir."

"Then perhaps I can talk to you for a few minutes if your mistress will not object. It is about your aunt, Mrs. Ascher."

"The mistress is out, sir. She wouldn't mind, I'm sure, if you came in here."

She opened the door of a small morning-room. We entered and Poirot, seating himself on a chair by the window, looked up keenly into the girl's face.

"You have heard of your aunt's death, of course?"

The girl nodded, tears coming once more into her eyes.

"This morning, sir. The police came over. Oh! it's terrible! Poor auntie! Such a hard life as she'd had, too. And now this—it's too awful."

"The police did not suggest your returning to Andover?"

"They said I must come to the inquest—that's on Monday, sir. But I've nowhere to go there—I couldn't fancy being over the shop—now—and what with the housemaid being away, I didn't want to put the mistress out more than may be."

"You were fond of your aunt, Mary?" said Poirot gently.

"Indeed I was, sir. Very good she's been to me always, auntie has. I went to her in London when I was eleven years old, after mother died. I started in service when I was sixteen, but I usually went along to auntie's on my day out. A lot of trouble she went through with that German fellow. 'My old devil,' she used to call him. He'd never let her be in peace anywhere. Sponging, cadging old beast."

The girl spoke with vehemence.

"Your aunt never thought of freeing herself by legal means from this persecution?"

"Well, you see, he was her husband, sir, you couldn't get away from that."

The girl spoke simply but with finality.

"Tell me, Mary, he threatened her, did he not?"

"Oh, yes, sir, it was awful the things he used to say. That he'd cut her throat, and such like. Cursing and swearing too— both in German and in English. And yet auntie says he was a fine handsome figure of a man when she married him. It's dreadful to think, sir, what people come to."

"Yes, indeed. And so, I suppose, Mary, having actually heard these threats, you were not so very surprised when you learnt what had happened?"

"Oh, but I was, sir. You see, sir, I never thought for one moment that he meant it. I thought it was just nasty talk and nothing more to it. And it isn't as though auntie was afraid of him. Why, I've seen him slink away like a dog with its tail between its legs when she turned on him. *He* was afraid of *her* if you like."

"And yet she gave him money?"

"Well, he was her husband, you see, sir."

"Yes, so you said before." He paused for a minute or two. Then he said: "Suppose that, after all, he did *not* kill her."

"Didn't kill her?"

She stared.

"That is what I said. Supposing some one else killed her. . . . Have you any idea who that some one else could be?"

She stared at him with even more amazement.

"I've no idea, sir. It doesn't seem likely, though, does it?"

"There was no one your aunt was afraid of?"

Mary shook her head.

"Auntie wasn't afraid of people. She'd a sharp tongue and she'd stand up to anybody."

"You never heard her mention any one who had a grudge against her?"

"No, indeed, sir."

"Did she ever get anonymous letters?"

"What kind of letters did you say, sir?"

"Letters that weren't signed—or only signed by something like A.B.C." He watched her narrowly, but plainly she was at a loss. She shook her head wonderingly.

"Has your aunt any relations except you?"

"Not now, sir. One of ten she was, but only three lived to grow up. My uncle Tom was killed in the war, and my uncle Harry went to South America and no one's heard of him since, and mother's dead, of course, so there's only me."

"Had your aunt any savings? Any money put by?"

"She'd a little in the savings bank, sir—enough to bury her proper, that's what she always said. Otherwise she didn't more than just make ends meet—what with her old devil and all."

Poirot nodded thoughtfully. He said—perhaps more to himself than to her:

"At present one is in the dark—there is no direction—if things get clearer—" He got up. "If I want you at any time, Mary, I will write to you here."

"As a matter of fact, sir, I'm giving in my notice. I don't like the country. I stayed here because I fancied it was a comfort to auntie to have me near by. But now"—again the tears rose in her eyes—"there's no reason I should stay, and so I'll go back to London. It's gayer for a girl there."

"I wish that, when you do go, you would give me your address. Here is my card."

He handed it to her. She looked at it with a puzzled frown.

"Then you're not—anything to do with the police, sir?"

"I am a private detective."

She stood there looking at him for some moments in silence. She said at last:

"Is there anything—queer going on, sir?"

"Yes, my child. There is—something queer going on. Later you may be able to help me."

"I—I'll do anything, sir. It—it wasn't *right,* sir, auntie being killed."

A strange way of putting it—but deeply moving.

A few seconds later we were driving back to Andover.

VI The Scene of the Crime

THE street in which the tragedy had occurred was a turning off the main street. Mrs. Ascher's shop was situated about half-way down it on the right-hand side.

As we turned into the street Poirot glanced at his watch and I realized why he had delayed his visit to the scene of the crime until now. It was just on half-past five. He had wished to reproduce yesterday's atmosphere as closely as possible.

But if that had been his purpose it was defeated. Certainly at this moment the road bore very little likeness to its appearance on the previous evening. There were a certain number of small shops interspersed between private houses of the poorer class. I judged that ordinarily there would be a fair number of people passing up and down—mostly people of the poorer classes, with a good sprinkling of children playing on the pavements and in the road.

At this moment there was a solid mass of people standing staring at one particular house or shop and it took little perspicuity to guess which that was. What we saw was a mass of average human beings looking with intense interest at the spot where another human being had been done to death.

As we drew nearer this proved to be indeed the case. In front of a small dingy-looking shop with its shutters now closed stood a harassed-looking young policeman who was stolidly adjuring the crowd to "pass along there." By the help of a colleague, displacements took place—a certain number of people grudgingly sighed and betook themselves to their ordinary vocations, and almost immediately other persons came along and took up their stand to gaze their full on the spot where murder had been committed.

Poirot stopped a little distance from the main body of the crowd. From where we stood the legend painted over the door could be read plainly enough. Poirot repeated it under his breath.

"A. Ascher. *Oui, c'est peut-être la—*"

He broke off.

"Come, let us go inside, Hastings."

I was only too ready.

We made our way through the crowd and accosted the young policeman. Poirot produced the credentials which the inspector had given him. The constable nodded, and unlocked the door to let us pass within. We did so and entered to the intense interest of the lookers-on.

Inside it was very dark owing to the shutters being closed. The constable found and switched on the electric light. The bulb was a low-powered one so that the interior was still dimly lit.

I looked about me.

A dingy little place. A few cheap magazines strewn about, and yesterday's newspapers—all with a day's dust on them. Behind the counter a row of shelves reaching to the ceiling and packed with tobacco and packets of cigarettes. There were also a couple of jars of peppermint humbugs and barley sugar. A commonplace little shop, one of many thousand such others.

The constable in his slow Hampshire voice was explaining the *mise en scène.*

"Down in a heap behind the counter, that's where she was. Doctor says as how she never knew what hit her. Must have been reaching up to one of the shelves."

"There was nothing in her hand?"

"No, sir, but there was a packet of Players down beside her."

Poirot nodded. His eyes swept round the small space observing—noting.

"And the railway guide was—where?"

"Here, sir." The constable pointed out the spot on the counter. "It was open at the right page for Andover and lying face down. Seems as though he must have been looking up the trains to London. If so, 'twasn't an Andover man at all. But then, of course, the railway guide might have belonged to some one else what had nothing to do with the murder at all, but just forgot it here."

"Fingerprints?" I suggested.

The man shook his head.

"The whole place was examined straight away, sir. There weren't none."

"Not on the counter itself?" asked Poirot.

"A long sight too many, sir! All confused and jumbled up."

"Any of Ascher's among them?"

"Too soon to say, sir."

Poirot nodded, then asked if the dead woman lived over the shop.

"Yes, sir, you go through that door at the back, sir. You'll excuse me coming with you, but I've got to stay—"

Poirot passed through the door in question and I followed him. Behind the shop was a microscopic sort of parlour and kitchen combined—it was neat and clean but very dreary-looking and scantily furnished. On the mantelpiece were a few photographs. I went up and looked at them and Poirot joined me.

The photographs were three in all. One was a cheap portrait of the girl we had been with that afternoon, Mary Drower. She was obviously wearing her best clothes and had the self-conscious, wooden smile on her face that so often disfigures the expression in posed photography, and makes a snapshot preferable.

The second was a more expensive type of picture—an artistically blurred reproduction of an elderly woman with white hair. A high fur collar stood up round the neck.

I guessed that this was probably the Miss Rose who had left Mrs. Ascher the small legacy which had enabled her to start in business.

The third photograph was a very old one, now faded and yellow. It represented a young man and woman in somewhat old-fashioned clothes standing arm in arm. The man had a button-hole and there was an air of bygone festivity about the whole pose.

"Probably a wedding picture," said Poirot. "Regard, Hastings, did I not tell you that she had been a beautiful woman?"

He was right. Disfigured by old-fashioned hair-dressing and weird clothes, there was no disguising the handsomeness of the girl in the picture with her clear-cut features and spirited bearing. I looked closely at the second figure. It was almost impossible to recognize the seedy Ascher in this smart young man with the military bearing.

I recalled the leering drunken old man, and the worn, toil-worn face of the dead woman—and I shivered a little at the remorselessness of time. . . .

From the parlour a stair led to two upstairs rooms. One was empty and unfurnished, the other had evidently been the dead woman's bedroom. After being searched by the police it had been left as it was. A couple of old worn blankets on the bed—a little stock of well-darned underwear in a drawer—cookery recipes in another—a paper-backed novel entitled *The Green Oasis*—a pair of new stockings—pathetic in their cheap shininess—a couple of china ornaments—a Dresden shepherd much broken, and a blue and yellow spotted dog—a black rain-coat and a woolly jumper hanging on pegs—such were the worldly possessions of the late Alice Ascher.

If there had been any personal papers, the police had taken them.

"Pauvre femme," murmured Poirot. "Come, Hastings, there is nothing for us here."

When we were once more in the street, he hesitated for a minute or two, then crossed the road. Almost exactly opposite Mrs. Ascher's was a greengrocer's shop—of the type that has most of its stock outside rather than inside.

In a low voice Poirot gave me certain instructions. Then he himself entered the shop. After waiting a minute or two I followed him in. He was at the moment negotiating for a lettuce. I myself bought a pound of strawberries.

Poirot was talking animatedly to the stout lady who was serving him.

"It was just opposite you, was it not, that this murder occurred? What an affair! What a sensation it must have caused you!"

The stout lady was obviously tired of talking about the murder. She must have had a long day of it. She observed:

"It would be as well if some of that gaping crowd cleared off. What is there to look at, I'd like to know?"

"It must have been very different last night," said Poirot. "Possibly you even observed the murderer enter the shop—a tall, fair man with a beard, was he not? A Russian, so I have heard."

"What's that?" The woman looked up sharply. "A Russian did it, you say?"

"I understand that the police have arrested him."

"Did you ever now?" The woman was excited, voluble. "A foreigner."

"*Mais oui*. I thought perhaps you might have noticed him last night?"

"Well, I don't get much chance of noticing, and that's a fact. The evening's our busy time and there's always a fair few passing along and getting home after their work. A tall, fair man with a beard—no, I can't say I saw any one of that description anywhere about."

I broke in on my cue.

"Excuse me, sir," I said to Poirot. "I think you have been misinformed. A short *dark* man I was told."

An interested discussion intervened in which the stout lady, her lank husband and a hoarse-voiced shop-boy all participated. No less than four short dark men had been observed, and the hoarse boy had seen a tall fair one, "but he hadn't got no beard," he added regretfully.

Finally, our purchases made, we left the establishment, leaving our falsehoods uncorrected.

"And what was the point of all that, Poirot?" I demanded somewhat reproachfully.

"*Parbleu*, I wanted to estimate the chances of a stranger being noticed entering the shop opposite."

"Couldn't you simply have asked—without all that tissue of lies?"

"No, *mon ami.* If I had 'simply asked,' as you put it, I should have got no answer at all to my questions. You yourself are English and yet you do not seem to appreciate the quality of the English reaction to a direct question. It is invariably one of suspicion and the natural result is reticence. If I had asked those people for information they would have shut up like oysters. But by making a statement (and a somewhat out of the way and preposterous one) and by your contradiction of it, tongues are immediately loosened. We know also that that particular time was a 'busy time'—that is, that every one would be intent on their own concerns and that there would be a fair number of people passing along the pavements. Our murderer chose his time well, Hastings."

He paused and then added on a deep note of reproach:

"Is it that you have not in any degree the common sense, Hastings? I say to you: 'Make a purchase *quelconque*'—and you deliberately choose the strawberries! Already they commence to creep through their bag and endanger your good suit."

With some dismay, I perceived that this was indeed the case.

I hastily presented the strawberries to a small boy who seemed highly astonished and faintly suspicious.

Poirot added the lettuce, thus setting the seal on the child's bewilderment.

He continued to drive the moral home.

"At a cheap greengrocer's—*not* strawberries. A strawberry, unless fresh picked, is bound to exude juice. A banana—some apples—even a cabbage—but *strawberries—*"

"It was the first thing I thought of," I explained by way of excuse.

"That is unworthy of your imagination," returned Poirot sternly.

He paused on the sidewalk.

The house and shop on the right of Mrs. Ascher's was empty. A "To Let" sign appeared in the windows. On the other side was a house with somewhat grimy muslin curtains.

To this house Poirot betook himself and, there being no bell, executed a series of sharp flourishes with the knocker.

The door was opened after some delay by a very dirty child with a nose that needed attending to.

"Good-evening," said Poirot. "Is your mother within?"

"Ay?" said the child.

It stared at us with disfavour and deep suspicion.

"Your mother," said Poirot.

This took some twelve seconds to sink in, then the child turned and, bawling up the stairs, "Mum, you're wanted," retreated to some fastness in the dim interior.

A sharp-faced woman looked over the balusters and began to descend.

"No good you wasting your time—" she began, but Poirot interrupted her.

He took off his hat and bowed magnificently.

"Good-evening, madame. I am on the staff of the *Evening Flicker*. I want to persuade you to accept a fee of five pounds and let us have an article on your late neighbour, Mrs. Ascher."

The irate words arrested on her lips, the woman came down the stairs smoothing her hair and hitching at her skirt.

"Come inside, please—on the left there. Won't you sit down, sir."

The tiny room was heavily over-crowded with a massive pseudo-Jacobean suite, but we managed to squeeze ourselves in and on to a hard-seated sofa.

"You must excuse me," the woman was saying. "I am sure I'm sorry I spoke so sharp just now, but you'd hardly believe the worry one has to put up with—fellows coming along selling this, that and the other—vacuum cleaners, stockings, lavender bags and such like foolery—and all so plausible and civil spoken. Got your name, too, pat they have. It's Mrs. Fowler this, that and the other."

Seizing adroitly on the name, Poirot said:

"Well, Mrs. Fowler, I hope you're going to do what I ask."

"I don't know, I'm sure." The five pounds hung alluringly before Mrs. Fowler's eyes. "I *knew* Mrs. Ascher, of course, but as to *writing* anything."

Hastily Poirot reassured her. No labour on her part was required. He would elicit the facts from her and the interview would be written up.

Thus encouraged, Mrs. Fowler plunged willingly into reminiscence, conjecture and hearsay.

Kept to herself, Mrs. Ascher had. Not what you'd call really *friendly,* but there, she'd had a lot of trouble, poor soul, every one knew that. And by rights Franz Ascher ought to have been locked up years ago. Not that Mrs. Ascher had been afraid of him—a real tartar she could be when roused! Give as good as she got any day. But there it was—the pitcher could go to the well once too often. Again and again, she, Mrs. Fowler, had said to her: "One of these days that man will do for you. Mark my words." And he had done, hadn't he? And there had she, Mrs. Fowler, been right next door and never heard a sound.

In a pause Poirot managed to insert a question.

Had Mrs. Ascher ever received any peculiar letters—letters without a proper signature—just something like A.B.C.?

Regretfully, Mrs. Fowler returned a negative answer.

"I know the kind of thing you mean—anonymous letters they call them—mostly full of words you'd blush to say out loud. Well, I don't know, I'm sure, if Franz Ascher ever took to writing those. Mrs. Ascher never let on to me if he did. What's that? A railway guide, an A.B.C.? No, I never saw such a thing about—and I'm sure if Mrs. Ascher had been sent one I'd have heard about it. I declare you could have knocked me down with a feather when I heard about this whole business. It was my girl Edie what came to me. 'Mum,' she says, 'there's ever so many policemen next door.' Gave me quite a turn, it did. 'Well,' I said, when I heard about it, 'it does show that she ought never to have been alone in the house—that niece of hers ought to have been with her. A man in drink can be like a ravening wolf,' I said, 'and in my opinion a wild beast is neither more nor less than what that old devil of a husband of hers is. I've warned her,' I said, 'many times and now my words have come true. He'll do for you,' I said. And he has done for her! You can't rightly estimate what a man will do when he's in drink and this murder's a proof of it."

She wound up with a deep gasp.

"Nobody saw this man Ascher go into the shop, I believe?" said Poirot.

Mrs. Fowler sniffed scornfully.

"Naturally he wasn't going to show himself," she said.

How Mr. Ascher had got there without showing himself she did not deign to explain.

She agreed that there was no back way into the house and that Ascher was quite well known by sight in the district.

"But he didn't want to swing for it and he kept himself well hid."

Poirot kept the conversational ball rolling some little time longer but when it seemed certain that Mrs. Fowler had told all that she knew not once but many times over, he terminated the interview, first paying out the promised sum.

"Rather a dear five pounds' worth, Poirot," I ventured to remark when we were once more in the street.

"So far, yes."

"You think she knows more than she has told?"

"My friend, we are in the peculiar position of not knowing what questions to ask. We are like little children playing *Cache Cache* in the dark. We stretch out our hands and grope about. Mrs. Fowler has told us all that she *thinks* she knows—and has thrown in several conjectures for good measure! In the future, however, her evidence may be useful. It is for the future that I have invested that sum of five pounds."

I did not quite understand the point, but at this moment we ran into Inspector Glen.

VII Mr. Partridge and Mr. Riddell

INSPECTOR GLEN was looking rather gloomy. He had, I gathered, spent the afternoon trying to get a complete list of persons who had been noticed entering the tobacco shop.

"And nobody has seen any one?" Poirot inquired.

"Oh, yes, they have. Three tall men with furtive expressions —four short men with black moustaches—two beards—three fat men—all strangers—and all, if I'm to believe witnesses, with sinister expressions! I wonder somebody didn't see a gang of masked men with revolvers while they were about it!"

Poirot smiled sympathetically.

"Does anybody claim to have seen the man Ascher?"

"No, they don't. And that's another point in his favour. I've just told the Chief Constable that I think this is a job for Scotland Yard. I don't believe it's a local crime."

Poirot said gravely:

"I agree with you."

The inspector said:

"You know, Monsieur Poirot, it's a nasty business—a nasty business . . . I don't like it. . . ."

We had two more interviews before returning to London.

The first was with Mr. James Partridge. Mr. Partridge was the last person known to have seen Mrs. Ascher alive. He had made a purchase from her at 5.30.

Mr. Partridge was a small, spare man, a bank clerk by profession. He wore pince-nez, was very dry and spare-looking and extremely precise in all his utterances. He lived in a small house as neat and trim as himself.

"Mr.—er—Poirot," he said, glancing at the card my friend had handed to him. "From Inspector Glen? What can I do for you, Mr. Poirot?"

"I understand, Mr. Partridge, that you were the last person to see Mrs. Ascher alive."

Mr. Partridge placed his finger-tips together and looked at Poirot as though he were a doubtful cheque.

"That is a very debatable point, Mr. Poirot," he said. "Many people may have made purchases from Mrs. Ascher after I did so."

"If so, they have not come forward to say so."

Mr. Partridge coughed.

"Some people, Mr. Poirot, have no sense of public duty."

He looked at us owlishly through his spectacles.

"Exceedingly true," murmured Poirot. "You, I understand, went to the police of your own accord?"

"Certainly I did. As soon as I heard of the shocking occurrence I perceived that my statement might be helpful and came forward accordingly."

"A very proper spirit," said Poirot solemnly. "Perhaps you will be so kind as to repeat your story to me."

"By all means. I was returning to this house and at five-thirty precisely—"

"Pardon, how was it that you knew the time so accurately?"

Mr. Partridge looked a little annoyed at being interrupted.

"The church clock chimed. I looked at my watch and found I was a minute slow. That was just before I entered Mrs. Ascher's shop."

"Were you in the habit of making purchases there?"

"Fairly frequently. It was on my way home. About once or twice a week I was in the habit of purchasing two ounces of John Cotton mild."

"Did you know Mrs. Ascher at all? Anything of her circumstances or her history?"

"Nothing whatever. Beyond my purchase and an occasional remark as to the state of the weather, I had never spoken to her."

"Did you know she had a drunken husband who was in the habit of threatening her life?"

"No, I knew nothing whatever about her."

"You knew her by sight, however. Did anything about her

appearance strike you as unusual yesterday evening? Did she appear flurried or put out in any way?"

Mr. Partridge considered.

"As far as I noticed, she seemed exactly as usual," he said. Poirot rose.

"Thank you, Mr. Partridge, for answering these questions. Have you, by any chance, an A.B.C. in the house? I want to look up my return train to London."

"On the shelf just behind you," said Mr. Partridge.

On the shelf in question were an A.B.C., a Bradshaw, the Stock Exchange Year Book, Kelly's Directory, a Who's Who and a local directory.

Poirot took down the A.B.C., pretended to look up a train, then thanked Mr. Partridge and took his leave.

Our next interview was with Mr. Albert Riddell and was of a highly different character. Mr. Albert Riddell was a platelayer and our conversation took place to the accompaniment of the clattering of plates and dishes by Mr. Riddell's obviously nervous wife, the growling of Mr. Riddell's dog and the undisguised hostility of Mr. Riddell himself.

He was a big clumsy giant of a man with a broad face and small suspicious eyes. He was in the act of eating meat-pie, washed down by exceedingly black tea. He peered at us angrily over the rim of his cup.

"Told all I've got to tell once, haven't I?" he growled. "What's it to do with me, anyway? Told it to the blarsted police, I 'ave, and now I've got to spit it all out again to a couple of blarsted foreigners."

Poirot gave a quick, amused glance in my direction and then said:

"In truth I sympathize with you, but what will you? It is a question of murder, is it not? One has to be very, very careful."

"Best tell the gentleman what he wants, Bert," said the woman nervously.

"You shut your blarsted mouth," roared the giant.

"You did not, I think, go to the police of your own accord." Poirot slipped the remark in neatly.

"Why the hell should I? It were no business of mine."

"A matter of opinion," said Poirot indifferently. "There has been a murder—the police want to know who has been in the shop—I myself think it would have—what shall I say?—looked more natural if you had come forward."

"I've got my work to do. Don't say I shouldn't have come forward in my own time—"

"But as it was, the police were given your name as that of a person seen to go into Mrs. Ascher's and they had to come to you. Were they satisfied with your account?"

"Why shouldn't they be?" demanded Bert truculently.

Poirot merely shrugged his shoulders.

"What are you getting at, mister? Nobody's got anything against me? Every one knows who did the old girl in, that b—— of a husband of hers."

"But he was not in the street that evening and you were."

"Trying to fasten it on me, are you? Well, you won't succeed. What reason had I got to do a thing like that? Think I wanted to pinch a tin of her bloody tobacco? Think I'm a bloody homicidal maniac as they call it? Think I—?"

He rose threateningly from his seat. His wife bleated out: "Bert, Bert—don't say such things. Bert—they'll think—"

"Calm yourself, monsieur," said Poirot. "I demand only your account of your visit. That you refuse it seems to me—what shall we say—a little odd?"

"Who said I refused anything?" Mr. Riddell sank back again into his seat. "I don't mind."

"It was six o'clock when you entered the shop?"

"That's right—a minute or two after, as a matter of fact. Wanted a packet of Gold Flake. I pushed open the door—"

"It was closed, then?"

"That's right. I thought shop was shut, maybe. But it wasn't. I went in, there wasn't any one about. I hammered on the counter and waited a bit. Nobody came, so I went out again. That's all, and you can put it in your pipe and smoke it."

"You didn't see the body fallen down behind the counter?"

"No, no more would you have done—unless you was looking for it, maybe."

"Was there a railway guide lying about?"

"Yes, there was—face downwards. It crossed my mind like that the old woman might have had to go off sudden by train and forgot to lock shop up."

"Perhaps you picked up the railway guide or moved it along the counter?"

"Didn't touch the b—— thing. I did just what I said."

"And you did not see any one leaving the shop before you yourself got there?"

"Didn't see any such thing. What I say is, why pitch on me—?"

Poirot rose.

"Nobody is pitching upon you—yet. *Bon soir,* monsieur."

He left the man with his mouth open and I followed him. In the street he consulted his watch.

"With great haste, my friend, we might manage to catch the seven-o-two. Let us despatch ourselves quickly."

VIII The Second Letter

"WELL?" I demanded eagerly.

We were seated in a first-class carriage which we had to ourselves. The train, an express, had just drawn out of Andover.

"The crime," said Poirot, "was committed by a man of medium height with red hair and a cast in the left eye. He limps slightly on the right foot and has a mole just below the shoulder-blade."

"Poirot?" I cried.

For the moment I was completely taken in. Then the twinkle in my friend's eye undeceived me.

"Poirot!" I said again, this time in reproach.

"Mon ami, what will you? You fix upon me a look of doglike devotion and demand of me a pronouncement à la Sherlock Holmes! Now for the truth—I do not know what the murderer looks like, nor where he lives, nor how to set hands upon him."

"If only he had left some clue," I murmured.

"Yes, the clue—it is always the clue that attracts you. Alas that he did not smoke the cigarette and leave the ash, and then step in it with a shoe that has nails of a curious pattern. No—he is not so obliging. But at least, my friend, you have the *railway guide.* The A.B.C., that is a clue for you!"

"Do you think he left it by mistake then?"

"Of course not. He left it on purpose. The fingerprints tell us that."

"But there weren't any on it."

"That is what I mean. What was yesterday evening? A warm June night. Does a man stroll about on such an evening in *gloves?* Such a man would certainly have attracted attention. Therefore since there are no fingerprints on the A.B.C., it must have been carefully wiped. An innocent man would have left prints—a guilty man would not. So our murderer left it there for a purpose—but for all that it is none the less a clue. That A.B.C.

was bought by some one—it was carried by some one—there is a possibility there."

"You think we may learn something that way?"

"Frankly, Hastings, I am not particularly hopeful. This man, this unknown X, obviously prides himself on his abilities. He is not likely to blaze a trail that can be followed straight away."

"So that really the A.B.C. isn't helpful at all."

"Not in the sense you mean."

"In any sense?"

Poirot did not answer at once. Then he said slowly:

"The answer to that is yes. We are confronted here by an unknown personage. He is in the dark and seeks to remain in the dark. But in the very nature of things he cannot help throwing light upon himself. In one sense we know nothing about him—in another sense we know already a good deal. I see his figure dimly taking shape—a man who prints clearly and well—who buys good-quality paper—who is at great needs to express his personality. I see him as a child possibly ignored and passed over—I see him growing up with an inward sense of inferiority —warring with a sense of injustice. . . . I see that inner urge —to assert himself—to focus attention on himself ever becoming stronger, and events, circumstances—crushing it down—heaping, perhaps, more humiliations on him. And inwardly the match is set to the powder train. . . ."

"That's all pure conjecture," I objected. "It doesn't give you any practical help."

"You prefer the match end, the cigarette ash, the nailed boots! You always have. But at least we can ask ourselves some practical questions. Why the A.B.C.? Why Mrs. Ascher? Why Andover?"

"The woman's past life seems simple enough," I mused. "The interviews with those two men were disappointing. They couldn't tell us anything more than we knew already."

"To tell the truth, I did not expect much in that line. But we could not neglect two possible candidates for the murder."

"Surely you don't think—"

"There is at least a possibility that the murderer lives in or near Andover. That is a possible answer to our question: 'Why

Andover?' Well, here were two men known to have been in the shop at the requisite time of day. Either of them *might* be the murderer. And there is nothing as yet to show that one or other of them is *not* the murderer."

"That great hulking brute, Riddell, perhaps," I admitted.

"Oh, I am inclined to acquit Riddell off-hand. He was nervous, blustering, obviously uneasy—"

"But surely that just shows—"

"A nature diametrically opposed to that which penned the A.B.C. letter. Conceit and self-confidence are the characteristics that we must look for."

"Some one who throws his weight about?"

"Possibly. But some people, under a nervous and self-effacing manner, conceal a great deal of vanity and self-satisfaction."

"You don't think that little Mr. Partridge—?"

"He is more *le type*. One cannot say more than that. He acts as the writer of the letter would act—goes at once to the police —pushes himself to the fore—enjoys his position."

"Do you really think—?"

"No, Hastings. Personally I believe that the murderer came from outside Andover, but we must neglect no avenue of research. And although I say 'he' all the time, we must not exclude the possibility of a woman being concerned."

"Surely not!"

"The method of attack is that of a man, I agree. But anonymous letters are written by women rather than by men. We must bear that in mind."

I was silent for a few minutes, then I said:

"What do we do next?"

"My energetic Hastings," Poirot said and smiled at me.

"No, but what do we do?"

"Nothing."

"Nothing?" My disappointment rang out clearly.

"Am I the magician? The sorcerer? What would you have me do?"

Turning the matter over in my mind I found it difficult to give an answer. Nevertheless I felt convinced that something ought to be done and that we should not allow the grass to grow under our feet.

I said:

"There is the A.B.C.—and the notepaper and envelope—"

"Naturally everything is being done in that line. The police have all the means at their disposal for that kind of inquiry. If anything is to be discovered on those lines have no fear but that they will discover it."

With that I was forced to rest content.

In the days that followed I found Poirot curiously disinclined to discuss the case. When I tried to reopen the subject he waved it aside with an impatient hand.

In my own mind I was afraid that I fathomed his motive. Over the murder of Mrs. Ascher, Poirot had sustained a defeat. A.B.C. had challenged him—and A.B.C. had won. My friend, accustomed to an unbroken line of successes, was sensitive to his failure—so much so that he could not even endure discussion of the subject. It was, perhaps, a sign of pettiness in so great a man, but even the most sober of us is liable to have his head turned by success. In Poirot's case the head-turning process had been going on for years. Small wonder if its effects became noticeable at long last.

Understanding, I respected my friend's weakness and I made no further reference to the case. I read in the paper the account of the inquest. It was very brief, no mention was made of the A.B.C. letter, and a verdict was returned of murder by some person or persons unknown. The crime attracted very little attention in the press. It had no popular or spectacular features. The murder of an old woman in a side street was soon passed over in the press for more thrilling topics.

Truth to tell, the affair was fading from my mind also, partly, I think, because I disliked to think of Poirot as being in any way associated with a failure, when on July 25th it was suddenly revived.

I had not seen Poirot for a couple of days as I had been away in Yorkshire for the week-end. I arrived back on Monday afternoon and the letter came by the six o'clock post. I remember the sudden, sharp intake of breath that Poirot gave as he slit open that particular envelope.

"It has come," he said.

I stared at him—not understanding.

"What has come?"

"The second chapter of the A.B.C. business."

For a minute I looked at him uncomprehendingly. The matter had really passed from my memory.

"Read," said Poirot and passed me over the letter.

As before, it was printed on good-quality paper.

DEAR MR. POIROT,—Well, what about it? First game to me, I think. The Andover business went with a swing, didn't it?

But the fun's only just beginning. Let me draw your attention to Bexhill-on-Sea. Date, the 25th inst.

What a merry time we are having! Yours, etc.,

A.B.C.

"Good God, Poirot," I cried. "Does this mean that this fiend is going to attempt another crime?"

"Naturally, Hastings. What else did you expect? Did you think that the Andover business was an isolated case? Do you not remember my saying: 'This is the beginning'?"

"But this is horrible!"

"Yes, it is horrible."

"We're up against a homicidal maniac."

"Yes."

His quietness was more impressive than any heroics could have been. I handed back the letter with a shudder.

The following morning saw us at a conference of powers. The Chief Constable of Sussex, the Assistant Commissioner of the C.I.D., Inspector Glen from Andover, Superintendent Carter of the Sussex police, Japp and a younger inspector called Crome, and Dr. Thompson, the famous alienist, were all assembled together. The postmark on this letter was Hampstead, but in Poirot's opinion little importance could be attached to this fact.

The matter was discussed fully. Dr. Thompson was a pleasant middle-aged man who, in spite of his learning, contented himself with homely language, avoiding the technicalities of his profession.

"There's no doubt," said the Assistant Commissioner, "that the two letters are in the same hand. Both were written by the same person."

"And we can fairly assume that that person was responsible for the Andover murder."

"Quite. We've now got definite warning of a second crime scheduled to take place on the twenty-fifth—to-morrow—at Bexhill. What steps can be taken?"

The Sussex Chief Constable looked at his superintendent. "Well, Carter, what about it?"

The superintendent shook his head gravely.

"It's difficult, sir. There's not the least clue towards whom the victim may be. Speaking fair and square, what steps *can* we take?"

"A suggestion," murmured Poirot.

Their faces turned to him.

"I think it possible that the surname of the intended victim will begin with the letter B."

"That would be something," said the superintendent doubtfully.

"An alphabetical complex," said Dr. Thompson thoughtfully.

"I suggest it as a possibility—no more. It came into my mind when I saw the name Ascher clearly written over the shop door of the unfortunate woman who was murdered last month. When I got the letter naming Bexhill it occurred to me as a possibility that the victim as well as the place might be selected by an alphabetical system."

"It's possible," said the doctor. "On the other hand, it may be that the name Ascher was a coincidence—that the victim this time, no matter what her name is, will again be an old woman who keeps a shop. We're dealing, remember, with a madman. So far he hasn't given us any clue as to motive."

"Has a madman any motive, sir?" asked the superintendent sceptically.

"Of course he has, man. A deadly logic is one of the special characteristics of acute mania. A man may believe himself

divinely appointed to kill clergymen—or doctors—or old women
in tobacco shops—and there's always some perfectly coherent
reason behind it. We mustn't let the alphabetical business run
away with us. Bexhill succeeding to Andover *may* be a mere
coincidence."

"We can at least take certain precautions, Carter, and make
a special note of the B's, especially small shopkeepers, and
keep a watch on all small tobacconists and newsagents looked
after by a single person. I don't think there's anything more we
can do than that. Naturally keep tabs on all strangers as far
as possible."

The superintendent uttered a groan.

"With the schools breaking up and the holidays beginning?
People are fairly flooding into the place this week."

"We must do what we can," the Chief Constable said sharply.

Inspector Glen spoke in his turn.

"I'll have a watch kept on any one connected with the Ascher
business. Those two witnesses, Partridge and Riddell, and of
course on Ascher himself. If they show any signs of leaving
Andover they'll be followed."

The conference broke up after a few more suggestions and
a little desultory conversation.

"Poirot," I said as we walked along by the river, "surely this
crime can be prevented?"

He turned a haggard face to me.

"The sanity of a city full of men against the insanity of one?
I fear, Hastings—I very much fear. Remember the long-continued
successes of Jack the Ripper."

"It's horrible," I said.

"Madness, Hastings, is a terrible thing. . . . *I am afraid . . .
I am very much afraid. . . .*"

IX The Bexhill-on-Sea Murder

I STILL remember my awakening on the morning of the 25th of July. It must have been about seven-thirty.

Poirot was standing by my bedside gently shaking me by the shoulder. One glance at his face brought me from semi-consciousness into the full possession of my faculties.

"What is it?" I demanded, sitting up rapidly.

His answer came quite simply, but a wealth of emotion lay behind the three words he uttered.

"It has happened."

"What?" I cried. "You mean—but *to-day* is the twenty-fifth."

"It took place last night—or rather in the early hours of this morning."

As I sprang from bed and made a rapid toilet, he recounted briefly what he had just learnt over the telephone.

"The body of a young girl has been found on the beach at Bexhill. She has been identified as Elizabeth Barnard, a waitress in one of the cafés, who lived with her parents in a little recently built bungalow. Medical evidence gave the time of death as between eleven-thirty and one A.M."

"They're quite sure that this is *the* crime?" I asked, as I hastily lathered my face.

"An A.B.C. open at the trains to Bexhill was found actually under the body."

I shivered.

"This is horrible!"

"Faites attention, Hastings. I do not want a second tragedy in my rooms!"

I wiped the blood from my chin rather ruefully.

"What is our plan of campaign?" I asked.

"The car will call for us in a few moments' time. I will bring you a cup of coffee here so that there will be no delay in starting."

Twenty minutes later we were in a fast police car crossing the Thames on our way out of London.

With us was Inspector Crome, who had been present at the conference the other day, and who was officially in charge of the case.

Crome was a very different type of officer from Japp. A much younger man, he was the silent, superior type. Well educated and well read, he was, for my taste, several shades too pleased with himself. He had lately gained kudos over a series of child murders, having patiently tracked down the criminal who was now in Broadmoor.

He was obviously a suitable person to undertake the present case, but I thought that he was just a little too aware of the fact himself. His manner to Poirot was a shade patronizing. He deferred to him as a younger man to an older one—in a rather self-conscious, "public-school" way.

"I've had a good long talk with Dr. Thompson," he said. "He's very interested in the 'chain' or 'series' type of murder. It's the product of a particular distorted type of mentality. As a layman one can't, of course, appreciate the finer points as they present themselves to a medical point of view." He coughed. "As a matter of fact—my last case—I don't know whether you read about it—the Mabel Homer case, the Muswell Hill schoolgirl, you know—that man Capper was extraordinary. Amazingly difficult to pin the crime on to him—it was his third, too! Looked as sane as you or I. But there are various tests—verbal traps, you know—quite modern, of course, there was nothing of that kind in your day. Once you can induce a man to give himself again, you've got him! He knows that you know and his nerve goes. He starts giving himself away right and left."

"Even in my day that happened sometimes," said Poirot.

Inspector Crome looked at him and murmured conversationally:

"Oh, yes?"

There was silence between us for some time. As we passed
New Cross Station, Crome said:

"If there's anything you want to ask me about the case, pray
do so."

"You have not, I presume, a description of the dead girl?"

"She was twenty-three years of age, engaged as a waitress
at the Ginger Cat café—"

"*Pas ça.* I wondered—if she were pretty?"

"As to that I've no information," said Inspector Crome with
a hint of withdrawal. His manner said: "Really—these foreigners!
All the same!"

A faint look of amusement came into Poirot's eyes.

"It does not seem to you important, that? Yet, *pour une
femme,* it is of the first importance. Often it decides her destiny!"

Inspector Crome fell back on his conversational full stop.

"Oh, yes?" he inquired politely.

Another silence fell.

It was not until we were nearing Sevenoaks that Poirot
opened the conversation again.

"Were you informed, by any chance, how and with what the
girl was strangled?"

Inspector Crome replied briefly.

"Strangled with her own belt—a thick, knitted affair, I
gather."

Poirot's eyes opened very wide.

"Aha," he said. "At last we have a piece of information that
is very definite. That tells one something, does it not?"

"I haven't seen it yet," said Inspector Crome coldly.

I felt impatient with the man's caution and lack of imagination.

"It gives us the hall-mark of the murderer," I said. "The girl's
own belt. It shows the particular beastliness of his mind!"

Poirot shot me a glance I could not fathom. On the face of it
it conveyed humorous impatience. I thought that perhaps it was
a warning not to be too outspoken in front of the inspector.

I relapsed into silence.

At Bexhill we were greeted by Superintendent Carter. He had
with him a pleasant-faced, intelligent-looking young inspector

called Kelsey. The latter was detailed to work in with Crome over the case.

"You'll want to make your own inquiries, Crome," said the superintendent. "So I'll just give you the main heads of the matter and then you can get busy right away."

"Thank you, sir," said Crome.

"We've broken the news to her father and mother," said the superintendent. "Terrible shock to them, of course. I left them to recover a bit before questioning them, so you can start from the beginning there."

"There are other members of the family—yes?" asked Poirot.

"There's a sister—a typist in London. She's been communicated with. And there's a young man—in fact, she was supposed to be out with him last night, I gather."

"Any help from the A.B.C. guide?" asked Crome.

"It's there," the superintendent nodded towards the table. "No fingerprints. Open at the page for Bexhill. A new copy, I should say—doesn't seem to have been opened much. Not bought anywhere round here. I've tried all the likely stationers!"

"Who discovered the body, sir?"

"One of these fresh-air, early-morning old colonels. Colonel Jerome. He was out with his dog about six A.M. Went along the front in the direction of Cooden, and down on to the beach. Dog went off and sniffed at something. Colonel called it. Dog didn't come. Colonel had a look and thought something queer was up. Went over and looked. Behaved very properly. Didn't touch her at all and rang us up immediately."

"And the time of death was round about midnight last night?"

"Between midnight and one A.M.—that's pretty certain. Our homicidal joker is a man of his word. If he says the twenty-fifth, it is the twenty-fifth—though it may have been only by a few minutes."

Crome nodded.

"Yes, that's his mentality all right. There's nothing else? Nobody saw anything helpful?"

"Not as far as we know. But it's early yet. Every one who saw a girl in white walking with a man last night will be along to tell us about it soon, and as I imagine there were about four or five hundred girls in white walking with young men last night, it ought to be a nice business."

"Well, sir, I'd better get down to it," said Crome. "There's the café and there's the girl's home. I'd better go to both of them. Kelsey can come with me."

"And Mr. Poirot?" asked the superintendent.

"I will accompany you," said Poirot to Crome with a little bow.

Crome, I thought, looked slightly annoyed. Kelsey, who had not seen Poirot before, grinned broadly.

It was an unfortunate circumstance that the first time people saw my friend they were always disposed to consider him as a joke of the first water.

"What about this belt she was strangled with?" asked Crome. "Mr. Poirot is inclined to think it's a valuable clue. I expect he'd like to see it."

"*Du tout,*" said Poirot quickly. "You misunderstood me."

"You'll get nothing from that," said Carter. "It wasn't a leather belt—might have got fingerprints if it had been. Just a thick sort of knitted silk—ideal for the purpose."

I gave a shiver.

"Well," said Crome, "we'd better be getting along."

We set out forthwith.

Our first visit was to the Ginger Cat. Situated on the sea front, this was the usual type of small tea-room. It had little tables covered with orange-checked cloths and basket-work chairs of exceeding discomfort with orange cushions on them. It was the kind of place that specialized in morning coffee, five different kinds of teas (Devonshire, farmhouse, fruit, Carlton and plain), and a few sparing lunch dishes for females such as scrambled eggs and shrimps and macaroni au gratin.

The morning coffees were just getting under way. The manageress ushered us hastily into a very untidy back sanctum.

"Miss—er—Merrion?" inquired Crome.

Miss Merrion bleated out in a high, distressed gentlewoman voice:

"That is my name. This is a most distressing business. Most distressing. How it will affect our business I really cannot *think!*"

Miss Merrion was a very thin woman of forty with wispy orange hair (indeed she was astonishingly like a ginger cat herself). She played nervously with various fichus and frills that were part of her official costume.

"You'll have a boom," said Inspector Kelsey encouragingly. "You'll see! You won't be able to serve teas fast enough!"

"Disgusting," said Miss Merrion. "Truly disgusting. It makes one despair of human nature."

But her eye brightened nevertheless.

"What can you tell me about the dead girl, Miss Merrion?"

"Nothing," said Miss Merrion positively. "Absolutely nothing!"

"How long had she been working here?"

"This was the second summer."

"You were satisfied with her?"

"She was a good waitress—quick and obliging."

"She was pretty, yes?" inquired Poirot.

Miss Merrion, in her turn, gave him an "Oh, these foreigners" look.

"She was a nice, clean-looking girl," she said distantly.

"What time did she go off duty last night?" asked Crome.

"Eight o'clock. We close at eight. We do not serve dinners. There is no demand for them. Scrambled eggs and tea (Poirot shuddered) people come in for up to seven o'clock and sometimes after, but our rush is over by six-thirty."

"Did she mention to you how she proposed to spend her evening?"

"Certainly not," said Miss Merrion emphatically. "We were not on those terms."

"No one came in and called for her? Anything like that?"

"No."

"Did she seem quite her ordinary self? Not excited or depressed?"

"Really I could not say," said Miss Merrion aloofly.

"How many waitresses do you employ?"

"Two normally, and an extra two after the twentieth of July until the end of August."

"But Elizabeth Barnard was not one of the extras?"

"Miss Barnard was one of the regulars."

"What about the other one?"

"Miss Higley? She is a very nice young lady."

"Were she and Miss Barnard friends?"

"Really I could not say."

"Perhaps we'd better have a word with her."

"Now?"

"If you please."

"I will send her to you," said Miss Merrion, rising. "Please keep her as short a time as possible. This is the morning coffee rush hour."

The feline and gingery Miss Merrion left the room.

"Very refined," remarked Inspector Kelsey. He mimicked the lady's mincing tone. *"Really I could not say."*

A plump girl, slightly out of breath, with dark hair, rosy cheeks and dark eyes goggling with excitement, bounced in.

"Miss Merrion sent me," she announced breathlessly.

"Miss Higley?"

"Yes, that's me."

"You knew Elizabeth Barnard?"

"Oh, yes, I knew Betty. Isn't it *awful?* It's just too awful! I can't believe it's true. I've been saying to the girls all the morning I just *can't* believe it! 'You know, girls,' I said, 'it just doesn't seem *real.*' Betty! I mean, Betty Barnard, who's been here all along, *murdered!* 'I just can't believe it,' I said. Five or six times I've pinched myself just to see if I wouldn't wake up. Betty murdered . . . It's—well, you know what I mean—it doesn't seem real."

"You knew the dead girl well?" asked Crome.

"Well, she's worked here longer than I have. I only came this March. She was here last year. She was rather quiet, if you know what I mean. She wasn't one to joke or laugh a lot. I don't mean that she was exactly *quiet*—she'd plenty of fun in her and all that—but she didn't—well, she was quiet and she wasn't quiet, if you know what I mean."

I will say for Inspector Crome that he was exceedingly patient. As a witness the buxom Miss Higley was persistently maddening. Every statement she made was repeated and qualified half a dozen times. The net result was meagre in the extreme.

She had not been on terms of intimacy with the dead girl. Elizabeth Barnard, it could be guessed, had considered herself a cut above Miss Higley. She had been friendly in working hours, but the girls had not seen much of her out of them. Elizabeth Barnard had had a "friend"—worked in the estate agents near the station. Court and Brunskill. No, he wasn't Mr. Court nor Mr. Brunskill. He was a clerk there. She didn't know his name. But she knew him by sight well. Good-looking—oh, very good-looking, and always so nicely dressed. Clearly, there was a tinge of jealousy in Miss Higley's heart.

In the end it boiled down to this. Elizabeth Barnard had not confided in any one in the café as to her plans for the evening, but in Miss Higley's opinion she had been going to meet her "friend." She had had on a new white dress, "ever so sweet with one of the new necks."

We had a word with each of the other two girls but with no further results. Betty Barnard had not said anything as to her plans and no one had noticed her in Bexhill during the course of the evening.

X The Barnards

ELIZABETH BARNARD'S parents lived in a minute bungalow, one of fifty or so recently run up by a speculative builder on the confines of the town. The name of it was Llandudno.

Mr. Barnard, a stout, bewildered-looking man of fifty-five or so, had noticed our approach and was standing waiting in the doorway.

"Come in, gentlemen," he said.

Inspector Kelsey took the initiative.

"This is Inspector Crome of Scotland Yard, sir," he said. "He's come down to help us over this business."

"Scotland Yard?" said Mr. Barnard hopefully. "That's good. This murdering villain's got to be laid by the heels. My poor little girl—" His face was distorted by a spasm of grief.

"And this is Mr. Hercule Poirot, also from London, and er—"

"Captain Hastings," said Poirot.

"Pleased to meet you, gentlemen," said Mr. Barnard mechanically. "Come into the snuggery. I don't know that my poor wife's up to seeing you. All broken up, she is."

However, by the time that we were ensconced in the living-room of the bungalow, Mrs. Barnard had made her appearance. She had evidently been crying bitterly, her eyes were reddened and she walked with the uncertain gait of a person who had had a great shock.

"Why, Mother, that's fine," said Mr. Barnard. "You're sure you're all right—eh?"

He patted her shoulder and drew her down into a chair.

"The superintendent was very kind," said Mr. Barnard. "After he'd broken the news to us, he said he'd leave any questions till later when we'd got over the first shock."

"It is too cruel. Oh, it is too cruel," cried Mrs. Barnard tearfully. "The cruelest thing that ever was, it is."

Her voice had a faintly sing-song intonation that I thought for a moment was foreign till I remembered the name on the gate and realized that the "effer wass" of her speech was in reality proof of her Welsh origin.

"It's very painful, madam, I know," said Inspector Crome. "And we've every sympathy for you, but we want to know all the facts we can so as to get to work as quick as possible."

"That's sense, that is," said Mr. Barnard, nodding approval.

"Your daughter was twenty-three, I understand. She lived here with you and worked at the Ginger Cat café, is that right?"

"That's it."

"This is a new place, isn't it? Where did you live before?"

"I was in the ironmongery business in Kennington. Retired two years ago. Always meant to live near the sea."

"You have two daughters?"

"Yes. My elder daughter works in an office in London in the City."

"Weren't you alarmed when your daughter didn't come home last night?"

"We didn't know she hadn't," said Mrs. Barnard tearfully. "Dad and I always go to bed early. Nine o'clock's our time. We never knew Betty hadn't come home till the police officer came and said—and said—"

She broke down.

"Was your daughter in the habit of—er—returning home late?"

"You know what girls are nowadays, inspector," said Barnard. "Independent, that's what they are. These summer evenings they're not going to rush home. All the same, Betty was usually in by eleven."

"How did she get in? Was the door open?"

"Left the key under the mat—that's what we always did."

"There is some rumour, I believe, that your daughter was engaged to be married?"

"They don't put it as formally as that nowadays," said Mr. Barnard.

"Donald Fraser his name is, and I liked him. I liked him very much," said Mrs. Barnard. "Poor fellow, it'll be terrible for him—this news. Does he know yet, I wonder?"

"He works in Court and Brunskill's, I understand?"

"Yes, they're the estate agents."

"Was he in the habit of meeting your daughter most evenings after her work?"

"Not every evening. Once or twice a week would be nearer."

"Do you know if she was going to meet him yesterday?"

"She didn't say. Betty never said much about what she was doing or where she was going. But she was a good girl, Betty was. Oh, I can't believe—"

Mrs. Barnard started sobbing again.

"Pull yourself together, old lady. Try to hold up, Mother," urged her husband. "We've got to get to the bottom of this. . . ."

"I'm sure Donald would never—would never—" sobbed Mrs. Barnard.

"Now just you pull yourself together," repeated Mr. Barnard.

He turned to the two inspectors.

"I wish to God I could give you some help—but the plain fact is I know nothing—nothing at all that can help you to the dastardly scoundrel who did this. Betty was just a merry, happy girl—with a decent young fellow that she was—well, we'd have called it walking out with in my young days. Why any one should want to murder her simply beats me—it doesn't make sense."

"You're very near the truth there, Mr. Barnard," said Crome. "I tell you what I'd like to do—have a look over Miss Barnard's room. There may be something—letters—or a diary."

"Look over it and welcome," said Mr. Barnard, rising.

He led the way. Crome followed him, then Poirot, then Kelsey, and I brought up the rear.

I stopped for a minute to retie my shoelace, and as I did so, a taxi drew up outside and a girl jumped out of it. She paid the driver and hurried up the path to the house, carrying a small suitcase. As she entered the door she saw me and stopped dead. There was something so arresting in her pose that it intrigued me.

"Who are you?" she said.

I came down a few steps. I felt embarrassed as to how exactly to reply. Should I give my name? Or mention that I had come here with the police? The girl, however, gave me no time to make a decision.

"Oh, well," she said, "I can guess."

She pulled off the little white woollen cap she was wearing and threw it on the ground. I could see her better now as she turned a little so that the light fell on her.

My first impression was of the Dutch dolls that my sisters used to play with in my childhood. Her hair was black and cut in a straight bob and a bang across the forehead. Her cheekbones were high and her whole figure had a queer modern angularity that was not, somehow, unattractive. She was not good-looking—plain rather—but there was an intensity about her, a forcefulness that made her a person quite impossible to overlook.

"You are Miss Barnard?" I asked.

"I am Megan Barnard. You belong to the police, I suppose?"

"Well," I said, "not exactly—"

She interrupted me.

"I don't think I've got anything to say to you. My sister was a nice bright girl with no men friends. Good-morning."

She gave a short laugh as she spoke and regarded me challengingly.

"That's the correct phrase, I believe?" she said.

"I'm not a reporter, if that's what you're getting at."

"Well, what are you?" She looked round. "Where's mum and dad?"

"Your father is showing the police your sister's bedroom. Your mother's in there. She's very upset."

The girl seemed to make a decision.

"Come in here," she said.

She pulled open a door and passed through. I followed her and found myself in a small, neat kitchen.

I was about to shut the door behind me—but found an unexpected resistance. The next moment Poirot had slipped quietly into the room and shut the door behind him.

"Mademoiselle Barnard?" he said with a quick bow.

"This is M. Hercule Poirot," I said.

Megan Barnard gave him a quick, appraising glance.

"I've heard of you," she said. "You're the fashionable private sleuth, aren't you?"

"Not a pretty description—but it suffices," said Poirot.

The girl sat down on the edge of the kitchen table. She felt in her bag for a cigarette. She placed it between her lips, lighted it, and then said in between two puffs of smoke:

"Somehow, I don't see what M. Hercule Poirot is doing in our humble little crime."

"Mademoiselle," said Poirot, "what you do not see and what I do not see would probably fill a volume. But all that is of no practical importance. What *is* of practical importance is something that will not be easy to find."

"What's that?"

"Death, mademoiselle, unfortunately creates a *prejudice*. A prejudice in favour of the deceased. I heard what you said just now to my friend Hastings. 'A nice bright girl with no men friends.' You said that in mockery of the newspapers. And it is very true—when a young girl is dead, that is the kind of thing that is said. She was bright. She was happy. She was sweet-tempered. She had not a care in the world. She had no undesirable acquaintances. There is a great charity always to the dead. Do you know what I should like this minute? I should like to find some one who knew Elizabeth Barnard and who does not know she is dead! Then, perhaps, I should hear what is useful to me—the truth."

Megan Barnard looked at him for a few minutes in silence whilst she smoked. Then, at last, she spoke. Her words made me jump.

"Betty," she said, "was an unmitigated little ass!"

XI Megan Barnard

As I said, Megan Barnard's words, and still more the crisp business-like tone in which they were uttered, made me jump.

Poirot, however, merely bowed his head gravely.

"A la bonne heure," he said. "You are intelligent, mademoiselle."

Megan Barnard said, still in the same detached tone:

"I was extremely fond of Betty. But my fondness didn't blind me from seeing exactly the kind of silly little fool she was—and even telling her so upon occasions! Sisters are like that."

"And did she pay any attention to your advice?"

"Probably not," said Megan cynically.

"Will you, mademoiselle, be precise."

The girl hesitated for a minute or two.

Poirot said with a slight smile:

"I will help you. I heard what you said to Hastings. That your sister was a bright, happy girl with no men friends. It was— *un peu*—the *opposite* that was true, was it not?"

Megan said slowly:

"There wasn't any harm in Betty. I want you to understand that. She'd always go straight. She's not the week-ending kind. Nothing of that sort. But she liked being taken out and dancing and—oh, cheap flattery and compliments and all that sort of thing."

"And she was pretty—yes?"

This question, the third time I had heard it, met this time with a practical response.

Megan slipped off the table, went to her suitcase, snapped it open and extracted something which she handed to Poirot.

In a leather frame was a head and shoulders of a fair-haired, smiling girl. Her hair had evidently recently been permed, it stood out from her head in a mass of rather frizzy curls. The

smile was arch and artificial. It was certainly not a face that
you could call beautiful, but it had an obvious and cheap pretti-
ness.

Poirot handed it back, saying:

"You and she do not resemble each other, mademoiselle."

"Oh! I'm the plain one of the family. I've always known
that." She seemed to brush aside the fact as unimportant.

"In what way exactly do you consider your sister was behaving foolishly? Do you mean, perhaps, in relation to Mr. Donald
Fraser?"

"That's it, exactly. Don's a very quiet sort of person—but he—
well, naturally he'd resent certain things—and then—"

"And then what, mademoiselle?"

His eyes were on her very steadily.

It may have been my fancy but it seemed to me that she hesitated a second before answering.

"I was afraid that he might—chuck her altogether. And that
would have been a pity. He's a very steady and hard-working
man and would have made her a good husband."

Poirot continued to gaze at her. She did not flush under his
glance but returned it with one of her own equally steady and
with something else in it—something that reminded me of her
first defiant, disdainful manner.

"So it is like that," he said at last. "We do not speak the truth
any longer."

She shrugged her shoulders and turned towards the door.

"Well," she said, "I've done what I could to help you."

Poirot's voice arrested her.

"Wait, mademoiselle. I have something to tell you. Come
back."

Rather unwillingly, I thought, she obeyed.

Somewhat to my surprise, Poirot plunged into the whole
story of the A.B.C. letters, the murder at Andover, and the railway guide found by the bodies.

He had no reason to complain of any lack of interest on her
part. Her lips parted, her eyes gleaming, she hung on his words.

"Is this all true, M. Poirot?"

"Yes, it is true."

"You really mean my sister was killed by some horrible homicidal maniac?"

"Precisely."

She drew a deep breath.

"Oh! Betty—Betty— How—how *ghastly!*"

"You see, mademoiselle, that the information for which I ask you can give freely without wondering whether or no it will hurt any one."

"Yes, I see that now."

"Then let us continue our conversation. I have formed the idea that this Donald Fraser has, perhaps, a violent and jealous temper, is that right?"

Megan Barnard said quietly:

"I'm trusting you now, M. Poirot. I'm going to give you the absolute truth. Don is, as I say, a very quiet person—a bottled-up person, if you know what I mean. He can't always express what he feels in words. But underneath it all he minds things terribly. And he's got a jealous nature. He was always jealous of Betty. He was devoted to her—and of course she was very fond of him, but it wasn't in Betty to be fond of one person and not notice anybody else. She wasn't made that way. She'd got a —well, an eye for any nice-looking man who'd pass the time of day with her. And of course, working in the Ginger Cat, she was always running up against men—especially in the summer holidays. She was always very pat with her tongue and if they chaffed her she'd chaff back again. And then perhaps she'd meet them and go to the pictures or something like that. Nothing serious—never anything of that kind—but she just liked her fun. She used to say that as she'd got to settle down with Don one day she might as well have her fun now while she could."

Megan paused and Poirot said:

"I understand. Continue."

"It was just that attitude of mind of hers that Don couldn't understand. If she was really keen on him he couldn't see why she wanted to go out with other people. And once or twice they had flaming big rows about it."

"M. Don, he was no longer quiet?"

"It's like all those quiet people, when they do lose their tempers they lose them with a vengeance. Don was so violent that Betty was frightened."

"When was this?"

"There was one row nearly a year ago and another—a worse one—just over a month ago. I was home for the week-end—and I got them to patch it up again, and it was then that I tried to knock a little sense into Betty—told her she was a little fool. All she would say was that there hadn't been any harm in it. Well, that was true enough, but all the same she was riding for a fall. You see, after the row a year ago, she'd got into the habit of telling a few useful lies on the principle that what the mind doesn't know the heart doesn't grieve over. This last flare-up came because she'd told Don she was going to Hastings to see a girl pal—and he found out that she'd really been over to Eastbourne with some man. He was a married man, as it happened, and he'd been a bit secretive about the business anyway—and so that made it worse. They had an awful scene—Betty saying that she wasn't married to him yet and she had a right to go about with whom she pleased and Don all white and shaking and saying that one day—one day—"

"Yes?"

"He'd commit murder—" said Megan in a lowered voice.

She stopped and stared at Poirot.

He nodded his head gravely several times.

"And so, naturally, you were afraid . . ."

"I didn't think he'd actually done it—not for a minute! But I was afraid it might be brought up—the quarrel and all that he'd said—several people knew about it."

Again Poirot nodded his head gravely.

"Just so. And I may say, mademoiselle, that but for the egoistical vanity of a killer, that is just what would have happened. If Donald Fraser escapes suspicion, it will be thanks to A.B.C.'s maniacal boasting."

He was silent for a minute or two, then he said:

"Do you know if your sister met this married man, or any other man, lately?"

Megan shook her head.

"I don't know. I've been away, you see."

"But what do you think?"

"She mayn't have met that particular man again. He'd probably sheer off if he thought there was a chance of a row, but it wouldn't surprise me if Betty had—well, been telling Don a few lies again. You see, she did so enjoy dancing and the pictures, and of course, Don couldn't afford to take her all the time."

"If so, is she likely to have confided in any one? The girl at the café, for instance?"

"I don't think that's likely. Betty couldn't bear the Higley girl. She thought her common. And the others would be new. Betty wasn't the confiding sort anyway."

An electric bell trilled sharply above the girl's head.

She went to the window and leaned out. She drew back her head sharply.

"It's Don. . . ."

"Bring him in here," said Poirot quickly. "I would like a word with him before our good inspector takes him in hand."

Like a flash Megan Barnard was out of the kitchen, and a couple of seconds later she was back again leading Donald Fraser by the hand.

XII Donald Fraser

I FELT sorry at once for the young man. His white haggard face and bewildered eyes showed how great a shock he had had.

He was a well-made, fine-looking young fellow, standing close on six foot, not good-looking, but with a pleasant, freckled face, high cheek-bones and flaming red hair.

"What's this, Megan?" he said. "Why in here? For God's sake, tell me—I've only just heard—Betty . . ."

His voice trailed away.

Poirot pushed forward a chair and he sank down on it.

My friend then extracted a small flask from his pocket, poured some of its contents into a convenient cup which was hanging on the dresser and said:

"Drink some of this, Mr. Fraser. It will do you good."

The young man obeyed. The brandy brought a little colour back into his face. He sat up straighter and turned once more to the girl. His manner was quite quiet and self-controlled.

"It's true, I suppose?" he said. "Betty is—dead—killed?"

"It's true, Don."

He said as though mechanically:

"Have you just come down from London?"

"Yes. Dad phoned me."

"By the nine-twenty, I suppose?" said Donald Fraser.

His mind, shrinking from reality, ran for safety along these unimportant details.

"Yes."

There was silence for a minute or two, then Fraser said:

"The police? Are they doing anything?"

"They're upstairs now. Looking through Betty's things, I suppose."

"They've no idea who—? They don't know—?"

He stopped.

He had all a sensitive, shy person's dislike of putting violent facts into words.

Poirot moved forward a little and asked a question. He spoke in a business-like, matter-of-fact voice as though what he asked was an unimportant detail.

"Did Miss Barnard tell you where she was going last night?"

Fraser replied to the question. He seemed to be speaking mechanically.

"She told me she was going with a girl friend to St. Leonards."

"Did you believe her?"

"I—" Suddenly the automaton came to life. "What the devil do you mean?"

His face then, menacing, convulsed by sudden passion, made me understand that a girl might well be afraid of rousing his anger.

Poirot said crisply:

"Betty Barnard was killed by a homicidal murderer. Only by speaking the exact truth can you help us to get on his track."

His glance for a minute turned to Megan.

"That's right, Don," she said. "It isn't a time for considering one's own feelings or any one else's. You've got to come clean."

Donald Fraser looked suspiciously at Poirot.

"Who are you? You don't belong to the police?"

"I am better than the police," said Poirot. He said it without conscious arrogance. It was, to him, a simple statement of fact.

"Tell him," said Megan.

Donald Fraser capitulated.

"I—wasn't sure," he said. "I believed her when she said it. Never thought of doing anything else. Afterwards—perhaps it was something in her manner. I—I, well, I began to wonder."

"Yes?" said Poirot.

He had sat down opposite Donald Fraser. His eyes, fixed on the other man's, seemed to be exercising a mesmeric spell.

"I was ashamed of myself for being so suspicious. But—but I *was* suspicious . . . I thought of going down to the front and watching her when she left the café. I actually went there. Then I felt I couldn't do that. Betty would see me and she'd be angry. She'd realize at once that I was watching her."

"What did you do?"

"I went over to St. Leonards. Got over there by eight o'clock. Then I watched the buses—to see if she were in them. . . . But there was no sign of her. . . ."

"And then?"

"I—I lost my head rather. I was convinced she was with some man. I thought it probable he had taken her in his car to Hastings. I went on there—looked in hotels and restaurants, hung round cinemas—went on the pier. All damn foolishness. Even if she was there I was unlikely to find her, and anyway, there were heaps of other places he might have taken her to instead of Hastings."

He stopped. Precise as his tone had remained, I caught an undertone of that blind, bewildering misery and anger that had possessed him at the time he described.

"In the end I gave it up—came back."

"At what time?"

"I don't know. I walked. It must have been midnight or after when I got home. . . ."

"Then—"

The kitchen door opened.

"Oh, there you are," said Inspector Kelsey.

Inspector Crome pushed past him, shot a glance at Poirot and a glance at the two strangers.

"Miss Megan Barnard and Mr. Donald Fraser," said Poirot, introducing them.

"This is Inspector Crome from London," he explained.

Turning to the inspector, he said:

"While you pursued your investigations upstairs I have been conversing with Miss Barnard and Mr. Fraser, endeavouring if I could to find something that will throw light upon the matter."

"Oh, yes?" said Inspector Crome, his thoughts not upon Poirot but upon the two new-comers.

Poirot retreated to the hall. Inspector Kelsey said kindly as he passed:

"Get anything?"

But his attention was distracted by his colleague and he did not wait for a reply.

I joined Poirot in the hall.

"Did anything strike you, Poirot?" I inquired.

"Only the amazing magnanimity of the murderer, Hastings."

I had not the courage to say that I had not the least idea what he meant.

XIII A Conference

CONFERENCES!

Much of my memories of the A.B.C. case seem to be of conferences.

Conferences at Scotland Yard. At Poirot's rooms. Official conferences. Unofficial conferences.

This particular conference was to decide whether or no the facts relative to the anonymous letters should or should not be made public in the press.

The Bexhill murder had attracted much more attention than the Andover one.

It had, of course, far more elements of popularity. The victim was a young and good-looking girl to begin with. Also, it had taken place at a popular seaside resort.

All the details of the crime were reported fully and rehashed daily in thin disguises. The A.B.C. railway guide came in for its share of attention. The favourite theory was that it had been bought locally by the murderer and that it was a valuable clue to his identity. It also seemed to show that he had come to the place by train and was intending to leave for London.

The railway guide had not figured at all in the meagre accounts of the Andover murder so there seemed at present little likelihood of the two crimes being connected in the public eye.

"We've got to decide upon a policy," said the Assistant Commissioner. "The thing is—which way will give us the best results? Shall we give the public the facts—enlist their co-operation—after all, it'll be the co-operation of several million people, looking out for a madman—"

"He won't look like a madman," interjected Dr. Thompson.

"—looking out for sales of A.B.C.'s—and so on. Against that I suppose there's the advantage of working in the dark—not

letting our man know what we're up to, but then there's the fact
that *he knows very well that we know.* He's drawn attention to
himself deliberately by his letters. Eh, Crome, what's your
opinion?"

"I look at it this way, sir. If you make it public, you're playing
A.B.C.'s game. That's what he wants—publicity—notoriety.
That's what he's out after. I'm right, aren't I, doctor? He wants
to make a splash."

Thompson nodded.

The Assistant Commissioner said thoughtfully:

"So you're for baulking him. Refusing him the publicity he's
hankering after. What about you, M. Poirot?"

Poirot did not speak for a minute. When he did it was with
an air of choosing his words carefully.

"It is difficult for me, Sir Lionel," he said. "I am, as you
might say, an interested party. The challenge was sent to me.
If I say, 'Suppress that fact—do not make it public,' may it not
be thought that it is my vanity that speaks? That I am afraid
for my reputation? It is difficult! To speak out—to tell all—that
has its advantages. It is, at least, a warning. . . . On the other
hand, I am as convinced as Inspector Crome that it is what the
murderer wants us to do."

"H'm!" said the Assistant Commissioner, rubbing his chin.
He looked across at Dr. Thompson. "Suppose we refuse our
lunatic the satisfaction of the publicity he craves. What's he
likely to do?"

"Commit another crime," said the doctor promptly. "Force
your hand."

"And if we splash the thing about in headlines. Then what's
his reaction?"

"Same answer. One way you *feed* his megalomania, the
other you *baulk* it. The result's the same. Another crime."

"What do you say, M. Poirot?"

"I agree with Dr. Thompson."

"A cleft stick—eh? How many crimes do you think this—
lunatic has in mind?"

Dr. Thompson looked across at Poirot.

"Looks like A to Z," he said cheerfully.

"Of course," he went on, "he won't get there. Not nearly. You'll have him by the heels long before that. Interesting to know how he'd have dealt with the letter X." He recalled himself guiltily from this purely enjoyable speculation. "But you'll have him long before that. G or H, let's say."

The Assistant Commissioner struck the table with his fist.

"My God, are you telling me we're going to have five more murders?"

"It won't be as much as that, sir," said Inspector Crome. "Trust me."

He spoke with confidence.

"Which letter of the alphabet do you place it at, inspector?" asked Poirot.

There was a slight ironic note in his voice. Crome, I thought, looked at him with a tinge of dislike adulterating the usual calm superiority.

"Might get him next time, M. Poirot. At any rate I'd guarantee to get him by the time he gets to F."

He turned to the Assistant Commissioner.

"I think I've got the psychology of the case fairly clear. Dr. Thompson will correct me if I'm wrong. I take it that every time he brings a crime off, his self-confidence increases about a hundred per cent. Every time he feels 'I'm clever—they can't catch me!' he becomes so overweeningly confident that he also becomes careless. He exaggerates his own cleverness and every one else's stupidity. Very soon he'll be hardly bothering to take any precautions at all. That's right, isn't it, doctor?"

Thompson nodded.

"That's usually the case. In non-medical terms it couldn't have been put better. You know something about such things, M. Poirot. Don't you agree?"

I don't think that Crome liked Thompson's appeal to Poirot. He considered that he and he only was the expert on this subject.

"It is as Inspector Crome says," agreed Poirot.

"Paranœa," murmured the doctor.

Poirot turned to Crome.

"Are there any material facts of interest in the Bexhill case?"

"Nothing very definite. A waiter at the Splendide at East-bourne recognizes the dead girl's photograph as that of a young woman who dined there in company with a middle-aged man in spectacles. It's also been recognized at a roadhouse place called the Scarlet Runner, half-way between Bexhill and London. There they say she was with a man who looked like a naval officer. They can't both be right, but either of them's probable. Of course, there's a host of other identifications, but most of them not good for much. We haven't been able to trace the A.B.C."

"Well, you seem to be doing all that can be done, Crome," said the Assistant Commissioner. "What do you say, M. Poirot? Does any line of inquiry suggest itself to you?"

Poirot said slowly:

"It seems to me that there is one very important clue—the discovery of the motive."

"Isn't that pretty obvious? An alphabetical complex. Isn't that what you called it, doctor?"

"*Ça, oui,*" said Poirot. "There is an alphabetical complex. A madman in particular has always a very strong reason for the crimes he commits."

"Come, come, M. Poirot," said Crome. "Look at Stoneman in 1929. He ended by trying to do away with any one who annoyed him in the slightest degree."

Poirot turned to him.

"Quite so. But if you are a sufficiently great and important person, it is necessary that you should be spared small annoyances. If a fly settles on your forehead again and again, maddening you by its tickling—what do you do? You endeavour to kill that fly. You have no qualms about it. *You* are important —the fly is not. You kill the fly and the annoyance ceases. Your action appears to you sane and justifiable. Another reason for killing a fly is if you have a strong passion for hygiene. The fly is a potential source of danger to the community—the fly must go. So works the mind of the mentally deranged criminal. But consider now this case—if the victims are alphabetically selected, then they are not being removed because they are a source of annoyance to him personally. It would be too much of a coincidence to combine the two."

"That's a point," said Dr. Thompson. "I remember a case where a woman's husband was condemned to death. She started killing the members of the jury one by one. Quite a time before the crimes were connected up. They seemed entirely haphazard. But as M. Poirot says, there isn't such a thing as a murderer who commits crimes at random. Either he removes people who stand (however insignificantly) in his path, or else he kills by conviction. He removes clergymen, or policemen, or prostitutes because he firmly believes that they *should* be removed. That doesn't apply here either as far as I can see. Mrs. Ascher and Betty Barnard cannot be linked as members of the same class. Of course, it's possible that there is a sex complex. Both victims have been women. We can tell better, of course, after the next crime—"

"For God's sake, Thompson, don't speak so glibly of the next crime," said Sir Lionel irritably. "We're going to do all we can to prevent another crime."

Dr. Thompson held his peace and blew his nose with some violence.

"Have it your own way," the noise seemed to say. "If you won't face facts—"

The Assistant Commissioner turned to Poirot.

"I see what you're driving at, but I'm not quite clear yet."

"I ask myself," said Poirot, "what passes in itself exactly in the mind of the murderer? He kills, it would seem from his letters, *pour le sport*—to amuse himself. Can that really be true? And even if it is true, on what principle does he select his victims apart from the merely alphabetical one? If he kills merely to amuse himself he would not advertise the fact, since, otherwise, he could kill with impunity. But no, he seeks, as we all agree, to make the splash in the public eye—to assert his personality. In what way has his personality been suppressed that one can connect with the two victims he has so far selected? A final suggestion—Is his motive direct personal hatred of *me,* of Hercule Poirot? Does he challenge me in public because I have (unknown to myself) vanquished him somewhere in the course of my career? Or is his animosity impersonal—directed against a foreigner? And if so, what again has led to that? What injury has he suffered at a foreigner's hand?"

"All very suggestive questions," said Dr. Thompson.

Inspector Crome cleared his throat.

"Oh, yes? A little unanswerable at present, perhaps."

"Nevertheless, my friend," said Poirot, looking straight at him, "it is there in those questions that the solution lies. If we knew the exact reason—fantastic, perhaps, to us—but logical to him —of *why* our madman commits these crimes, we should know, perhaps, who the next victim is likely to be."

Crome shook his head.

"He selects them haphazard—that's my opinion."

"The magnanimous murderer," said Poirot.

"What's that you say?"

"I said—the magnanimous murderer! Franz Ascher would have been arrested for the murder of his wife—Donald Fraser might have been arrested for the murder of Betty Barnard—if it had not been for the warning letters of A.B.C. Is he, then, so soft-hearted that he cannot bear others to suffer for something they did not do?"

"I've known stranger things happen," said Dr. Thompson. "I've known men who've killed half a dozen victims all broken up because one of their victims didn't die instantaneously and suffered pain. All the same, I don't think that that is our fellow's reason. He wants the credit of these crimes for his own honour and glory. That's the explanation that fits best."

"We've come to no decision about the publicity business," said the Assistant Commissioner.

"If I may make a suggestion, sir," said Crome. "Why not wait till the receipt of the next letter? Make it public then—special editions, etc. It will make a bit of a panic in the particular town named, but it will put every one whose name begins with C on their guard, and it'll put A.B.C. on his mettle. He'll be determined to succeed. And that's when we'll get him."

How little we knew what the future held.

XIV The Third Letter

I WELL remember the arrival of A.B.C.'s third letter.

I may say that all precautions had been taken so that when A.B.C. resumed his campaign there should be no unnecessary delays. A young sergeant from Scotland Yard was attached to the house and if Poirot and I were out it was his duty to open anything that came so as to be able to communicate with headquarters without loss of time.

As the days succeeded each other we had all grown more and more on edge. Inspector Crome's aloof and superior manner grew more and more aloof and superior as one by one his more hopeful clues petered out. The vague descriptions of men said to have been seen with Betty Barnard proved useless. Various cars noticed in the vicinity of Bexhill and Cooden were either accounted for or could not be traced. The investigation of purchases of A.B.C. railway guides caused inconvenience and trouble to heaps of innocent people.

As for ourselves, each time the postman's familiar rat-tat sounded on the door, our hearts beat faster with apprehension. At least that was true for me, and I cannot but believe that Poirot experienced the same sensation.

He was, I knew, deeply unhappy over the case. He refused to leave London, preferring to be on the spot in case of emergency. In those hot dog days even his moustaches drooped—neglected for once by their owner.

It was on a Friday that A.B.C.'s third letter came. The evening post arrived about ten o'clock.

When we heard the familiar step and the brisk rat-tat, I rose and went along to the box. There were four or five letters, I remember. The last one I looked at was addressed in printed characters.

"Poirot," I cried. . . . My voice died away.

"It has come? Open it, Hastings. Quickly. Every moment may be needed. We must make our plans."

I tore open the letter (Poirot for once did not reproach me with untidiness) and extracted the printed sheet.

"Read it," said Poirot.

I read aloud:

POOR MR. POIROT,—Not so good at these little criminal matters as you thought yourself, are you? Rather past your prime, perhaps? Let us see if you can do any better this time. This time it's an easy one. Churston on the 30th. Do try and do something about it! It's a bit dull having it *all* my own way, you know!
Good hunting. Ever yours,

A.B.C.

"Churston," I said, jumping to our own copy of an A.B.C. "Let's see where it is."

"Hastings." Poirot's voice came sharply and interrupted me. "When was that letter written? Is there a date on it?"

I glanced at the letter in my hand.

"Written on the twenty-seventh," I announced.

"Did I hear you aright, Hastings? Did he give the date of the murder as the *thirtieth?*"

"That's right. Let me see, that's—"

"*Bon Dieu*, Hastings—do you not realize. *To-day is the thirtieth.*"

His eloquent hand pointed to the calendar on the wall. I caught up the daily paper to confirm it.

"But why—how—" I stammered.

Poirot caught up the torn envelope from the floor. Something unusual about the address had registered itself vaguely in my brain, but I had been too anxious to get at the contents of the letter to pay more than fleeting attention to it.

Poirot was at the time living in Whitehaven Mansions. The address ran: *M. Hercule Poirot, Whitehorse Mansions,* across the corner was scrawled: *"Not known at Whitehorse Mansions, E.C.1, nor at Whitehorse Court—try Whitehaven Mansions."*

"*Mon Dieu!*" murmured Poirot. "Does even chance aid this madman? *Vite—vite*—we must get on to Scotland Yard."

A minute or two later we were speaking to Crome over the wire. For once the self-controlled inspector did not reply "Oh, yes?" Instead a quickly stifled curse came to his lips. He heard what we had to say, then rang off in order to get a trunk connection to Churston as rapidly as possible.

"*C'est trop tard,*" murmured Poirot.

"You can't be sure of that," I argued, though without any great hope.

He glanced at the clock.

"Twenty minutes past ten? An hour and forty minutes to go. Is it likely that A.B.C. will have held his hand so long?"

I opened the railway guide I had previously taken from its shelf.

"Churston, Devon," I read, "from Paddington 204¾ miles. Population 544. It sounds a fairly small place. Surely our man will be bound to be noticed there."

"Even so, another life will have been taken," murmured Poirot. "What are the trains? I imagine train will be quicker than car."

"There's a midnight train—sleeping-car to Newton Abbot—gets there six-o-eight A.M., and to Churston at seven-fifteen."

"That is from Paddington?"

"Paddington, yes."

"We will take that, Hastings."

"You'll hardly have time to get news before we start."

"If we receive bad news to-night or to-morrow morning, does it matter which?"

"There's something in that."

I put a few things together in a suitcase whilst Poirot once more rang up Scotland Yard.

A few minutes later he came into the bedroom and demanded: "*Mais qu'est-ce que vous faites là?*"

"I was packing for you. I thought it would save time."

"*Vous éprouvez trop d'émotion, Hastings.* It affects your hands and your wits. Is that a way to fold a coat? And regard what you have done to my pyjamas. If the hairwash breaks what will befall them?"

"Good heavens, Poirot," I cried, "this is a matter of life and death. What does it matter what happens to our clothes?"

"You have no sense of proportion, Hastings. We cannot catch a train earlier than the time that it leaves, and to ruin one's clothes will not be the least helpful in preventing a murder."

Taking his suitcase from me firmly, he took the packing into his own hands.

He explained that we were to take the letter and envelope to Paddington with us. Some one from Scotland Yard would meet us there.

When we arrived on the platform the first person we saw was Inspector Crome.

He answered Poirot's look of inquiry.

"No news as yet. All men available are on the lookout. All persons whose name begins with C are being warned by phone when possible. There's just a chance. Where's the letter?"

Poirot gave it to him.

He examined it, swearing softly under his breath.

"Of all the damned luck. The stars in their courses fight for the fellow."

"You don't think," I suggested, "that it was done on purpose?"

Crome shook his head.

"No. He's got his rules—crazy rules—and abides by them. Fair warning. He makes a point of that. That's where his boastfulness comes in. I wonder now—I'd almost bet the chap drinks White Horse whisky."

"*Ah, c'est ingénieux ça!*" said Poirot, driven to admiration in spite of himself. "He prints the letter and the bottle is in front of him."

"That's the way of it," said Crome. "We've all of us done much the same thing one time or another: unconsciously copied something that's just under the eye. He started off White and went on horse instead of haven. . . ."

The inspector, we found, was also travelling by the train.

"Even if by some unbelievable luck nothing happened, Churston is the place to be. Our murderer is there, or has been there to-day. One of my men is on the phone here up to the last minute in case anything comes through."

Just as the train was leaving the station we saw a man running down the platform. He reached the inspector's window and called up something.

As the train drew out of the station Poirot and I hurried along the corridor and tapped on the door of the inspector's sleeper.

"You have news—yes?" demanded Poirot.

Crome said quietly:

"It's about as bad as it can be. Sir Carmichael Clarke has been found with his head bashed in."

Sir Carmichael Clarke, although his name was not very well known to the general public, was a man of some eminence. He had been in his time a very well-known throat specialist. Retiring from his profession very comfortably off, he had been able to indulge what had been one of the chief passions of his life—a collection of Chinese pottery and porcelain. A few years later, inheriting a considerable fortune from an elderly uncle, he had been able to indulge his passion to the full, and he was now the possessor of one of the best-known collections of Chinese art. He was married but had no children, and lived in a house he had built for himself near the Devon coast, only coming to London on rare occasions such as when some important sale was on.

It did not require much reflection to realize that his death, following that of the young and pretty Betty Barnard, would provide the best newspaper sensation for years. The fact that it was August and that the papers were hard up for subject matter would make matters worse.

"*Eh bien,*" said Poirot. "It is possible that publicity may do what private efforts have failed to do. The whole country now will be looking for A.B.C."

"Unfortunately," I said, "that's what he wants."

"True. But it may, all the same, be his undoing. Gratified by success, he may become careless. . . . That is what I hope —that he may be drunk with his own cleverness."

"How odd all this is, Poirot," I exclaimed, struck suddenly by an idea. "Do you know, this is the first crime of this kind that you and I have worked on together? All our murders have been—well, private murders, so to speak."

"You are quite right, my friend. Always, up to now, it has fallen to our lot to work from the *inside*. It has been the history of the victim that was important. The important points have been: 'Who benefited by the death? What opportunities had those round him to commit the crime?' It has always been the *'crime intime.'* Here, for the first time in our association, it is cold-blooded, impersonal murder. Murder from the *outside*."

I shivered.

"It's rather horrible. . . ."

"Yes. I felt from the first, when I read the original letter, that there was something wrong—misshapen. . . ."

He made an impatient gesture.

"One must not give way to the nerves. . . . This is no worse than any ordinary crime. . . ."

"It is. . . . It is. . . ."

"Is it worse to take the life or lives of strangers than to take the life of some one near and dear to you—some one who trusts and believes in you, perhaps?"

"It's worse because it's *mad*. . . ."

"No, Hastings. It is not *worse*. It is only more *difficult*."

"No, no, I do not agree with you. It's infinitely more frightening."

Hercule Poirot said thoughtfully:

"It should be easier to discover because it is mad. A crime committed by some one shrewd and sane would be far more complicated. Here, if one could but hit on the *idea* . . . This alphabetical business, it has discrepancies. If I could once see the *idea*—then everything would be clear and simple. . . ."

He sighed and shook his head.

"These crimes must not go on. Soon, soon, I must see the truth. . . . Go, Hastings. Get some sleep. There will be much to do to-morrow."

XV Sir Carmichael Clarke

CHURSTON, lying as it does between Brixham on the one side and Paignton and Torquay on the other, occupies a position about half-way round the curve of Torbay. Until about ten years ago it was merely a golf links and below the links a green sweep of countryside dropping down to the sea with only a farmhouse or two in the way of human occupation. But of late years there have been big building developments between Churston and Paignton and the coastline is now dotted with small houses and bungalows, new roads, et cetera.

Sir Carmichael Clarke had purchased a site of some two acres commanding an uninterrupted view of the sea. The house he had built was of modern design—a white rectangle that was not unpleasing to the eye. Apart from two big galleries that housed his collection it was not a large house.

Our arrival there took place about eight A.M. A local police officer had met us at the station and had put us *au courant* of the situation.

Sir Carmichael Clarke, it seemed, had been in the habit of taking a stroll after dinner every evening. When the police rang up—at some time after eleven—it was ascertained that he had not returned. Since his stroll usually followed the same course, it was not long before a search-party discovered his body. Death was due to a crashing blow with some heavy instrument on the back of the head. An open A.B.C. had been placed face downwards on the dead body.

We arrived at Combeside (as the house was called) at about eight o'clock. The door was opened by an elderly butler whose shaking hands and disturbed face showed how much the tragedy had affected him.

"Good-morning, Deveril," said the local police officer.

"Good-morning, Mr. Wells."

"These are the gentlemen from London, Deveril."

"This way, sir." He ushered us into a long dining-room where breakfast was laid. "I'll get Mr. Franklin, sir."

A minute or two later a big fair-haired man with a sunburnt face entered the room.

This was Franklin Clarke, the dead man's only brother.

He had the resolute competent manner of a man accustomed to meeting with emergencies.

"Good-morning, gentlemen."

Inspector Wells made the introductions.

"This is Inspector Crome of the C.I.D. Mr. Hercule Poirot and—er—Captain Hayter."

"Hastings," I corrected coldly.

Franklin Clarke shook hands with each of us in turn and in each case the handshake was accompanied by a piercing look.

"Let me offer you some breakfast," he said. "We can discuss the position as we eat."

There were no dissentient voices and we were soon doing justice to excellent eggs and bacon and coffee.

"Now for it," said Franklin Clarke. "Inspector Wells gave me a rough idea of the position last night—though I may say it seemed one of the wildest tales I have ever heard. Am I really to believe, Inspector Crome, that my poor brother is the victim of a homicidal maniac, that this is the third murder that has occurred and that in each case an A.B.C. railway guide has been deposited beside the body?"

"That is substantially the position, Mr. Clarke."

"But why? What earthly benefit can accrue from such a crime—even in the most diseased imagination?"

Poirot nodded his head in approval.

"You go straight to the point, Mr. Franklin," he said.

"It's not much good looking for motives at this stage, Mr. Clarke," said Inspector Crome. "That's a matter for an alienist —though I may say that I've had a certain experience of criminal lunacy and that the motives are usually grossly inadequate. There is a desire to assert one's personality, to make a splash in the public eye—in fact, to be a somebody instead of a nonentity."

"Is that true, M. Poirot?"

Clarke seemed incredulous. His appeal to the older man was too well received by Inspector Crome, who frowned.

"Absolutely true," replied my friend.

"At any rate such a man cannot escape detection long," said Clarke thoughtfully.

"*Vous croyez?* Ah, but they are cunning—*ces gens là!* And you must remember such a type has usually all the outer signs of insignificance—he belongs to the class of person who is usually passed over and ignored or even laughed at!"

"Will you let me have a few facts, please, Mr. Clarke," said Crome, breaking in on the conversation.

"Certainly."

"Your brother, I take it, was in his usual health and spirits yesterday? He received no unexpected letters? Nothing to upset him?"

"No. I should say he was quite his usual self."

"Not upset and worried in any way?"

"Excuse me, inspector. I didn't say that. To be upset and worried was my poor brother's normal condition."

"Why was that?"

"You may not know that my sister-in-law, Lady Clarke, is in very bad health. Frankly, between ourselves, she is suffering from an incurable cancer, and cannot live very much longer. Her illness has preyed terribly on my brother's mind. I myself returned from the East not long ago and I was shocked at the change in him."

Poirot interpolated a question.

"Supposing, Mr. Clarke, that your brother had been found shot at the foot of a cliff—or shot with a revolver beside him. What would have been your first thought?"

"Quite frankly, I should have jumped to the conclusion that it was suicide," said Clarke.

"*Encore!*" said Poirot.

"What is that?"

"A fact that repeats itself. It is of no matter."

"Anyway, it *wasn't* suicide," said Crome with a touch of

curtness. "Now I believe, Mr. Clarke, that it was your brother's habit to go for a stroll every evening?"

"Quite right. He always did."

"Every night?"

"Well, not if it was pouring with rain, naturally."

"And every one in the house knew of this habit?"

"Of course."

"And outside?"

"I don't quite know what you mean by outside. The gardener may have been aware of it or not, I don't know."

"And in the village?"

"Strictly speaking, we haven't got a village. There's a post office and cottages at Churston Ferrers—but there's no village or shops."

"I suppose a stranger hanging round the place would be fairly easily noticed?"

"On the contrary. In August all this part of the world is a seething mass of strangers. They come over every day from Brixham and Torquay and Paignton in cars and buses and on foot. Broadsands, which is down there (he pointed), is a very popular beach and so is Elbury Cove—it's a well-known beauty spot and people come there and picnic. I wish they didn't! You've no idea how beautiful and peaceful this part of the world is in June and the beginning of July."

"So you don't think a stranger would be noticed?"

"Not unless he looked—well, off his head."

"This man doesn't look off his head," said Crome with certainty. "You see what I'm getting at, Mr. Clarke. This man must have been spying out the land beforehand and discovered your brother's habit of taking an evening stroll. I suppose, by the way, that no strange man came up to the house and asked to see Sir Carmichael yesterday?"

"Not that I know of—but we'll ask Deveril."

He rang the bell and put the question to the butler.

"No, sir, no one came to see Sir Carmichael. And I didn't notice any one hanging about the house either. No more did the maids, because I've asked them."

The butler waited a moment, then inquired: "Is that all, sir?"

"Yes, Deveril, you can go."

The butler withdrew, drawing back in the doorway to let a young woman pass.

Franklin Clarke rose as she came.

"This is Miss Grey, gentlemen. My brother's secretary."

My attention was caught at once by the girl's extraordinary Scandinavian fairness. She had the almost colourless ash hair —light-grey eyes—and transparent glowing pallor that one finds amongst Norwegians and Swedes. She looked about twenty-seven and seemed to be as efficient as she was decorative.

"Can I help you in any way?" she asked as she sat down.

Clarke brought her a cup of coffee, but she refused any food.

"Did you deal with Sir Carmichael's correspondence?" asked Crome.

"Yes, all of it."

"I suppose he never received a letter or letters signed A.B.C.?"

"A.B.C.?" She shook her head. "No, I'm sure he didn't."

"He didn't mention having seen any one hanging about during his evening walks lately?"

"No. He never mentioned anything of the kind."

"And you yourself have noticed no strangers?"

"Not exactly hanging about. Of course, there are a lot of people what you might call *wandering* about at this time of year. One often meets people strolling with an aimless look across the golf links or down the lanes to the sea. In the same way, practically every one one sees this time of year is a stranger."

Poirot nodded thoughtfully.

Inspector Crome asked to be taken over the ground of Sir Carmichael's nightly walk. Franklin Clarke led the way through the French window, and Miss Grey accompanied us.

She and I were a little behind the others.

"All this must have been a terrible shock to you all," I said.

"It seems quite unbelievable. I had gone to bed last night when the police rang up. I heard voices downstairs and at last I came out and asked what was the matter. Deveril and Mr. Clarke were just setting out with lanterns."

"What time did Sir Carmichael usually come back from his walk?"

"About a quarter to ten. He used to let himself in by the side door and then sometimes he went straight to bed, sometimes to the gallery where his collections were. That is why, unless the police had rung up, he would probably not have been missed till they went to call him this morning."

"It must have been a terrible shock to his wife?"

"Lady Clarke is kept under morphia a good deal. I think she is in too dazed a condition to appreciate what goes on round her."

We had come out through a garden gate on to the golf links. Crossing a corner of them, we passed over a stile into a steep, winding lane.

"This leads down to Elbury Cove," explained Franklin Clarke. "But two years ago they made a new road leading from the main road to Broadsands and on to Elbury, so that now this lane is practically deserted."

We went on down the lane. At the foot of it a path led between brambles and bracken down to the sea. Suddenly we came out on a grassy ridge overlooking the sea and a beach of glistening white stones. All round dark green trees ran down to the sea. It was an enchanting spot—white, deep green—and sapphire blue.

"How beautiful!" I exclaimed.

Clarke turned to me eagerly.

"Isn't it? Why people want to go abroad to the Riviera when they've got this! I've wandered all over the world in my time and, honest to God, I've never seen anything as beautiful."

Then, as though ashamed of his eagerness, he said in a more matter-of-fact tone:

"This was my brother's evening walk. He came as far as here, then back up the path, and turning to the right instead of the left, went past the farm and across the fields back to the house."

We proceeded on our way till we came to a spot near the hedge, half-way across the field where the body had been found.

Crome nodded.

"Easy enough. The man stood here in the shadow. Your brother would have noticed nothing till the blow fell."

The girl at my side gave a quick shiver.

Franklin Clarke said:

"Hold up, Thora. It's pretty beastly, but it's no use shirking facts."

Thora Grey—the name suited her.

We went back to the house where the body had been taken after being photographed.

As we mounted the wide staircase the doctor came out of a room, black bag in hand.

"Anything to tell us, doctor?" inquired Clarke.

The doctor shook his head.

"Perfectly simple case. I'll keep the technicalities for the inquest. Anyway, he didn't suffer. Death must have been instantaneous."

He moved away.

"I'll just go in and see Lady Clarke."

A hospital nurse came out of a room further along the corridor and the doctor joined her.

We went into the room out of which the doctor had come.

I came out again rather quickly. Thora Grey was still standing at the head of the stairs.

There was a queer scared expression on her face.

"Miss Grey—" I stopped. "Is anything the matter?"

She looked at me.

"I was thinking," she said—"about D."

"About D?" I stared at her stupidly.

"Yes. The next murder. Something must be done. It's got to be stopped."

Clarke came out of the room behind me.

He said:

"What's got to be stopped, Thora?"

"These awful murders."

"Yes." His jaw thrust itself out aggressively. "I want to talk to M. Poirot sometime. . . . Is Crome any good?" He shot the words out unexpectedly.

I replied that he was supposed to be a very clever officer.

My voice was perhaps not as enthusiastic as it might have been.

"He's got a damned offensive manner," said Clarke. "Looks as though he knows everything—and what *does* he know? Nothing at all as far as I can make out."

He was silent for a minute or two. Then he said:

"M. Poirot's the man for my money. I've got a plan. But we'll talk of that later."

He went along the passage and tapped at the same door as the doctor had entered.

I hesitated a moment. The girl was staring in front of her.

"What are you thinking of, Miss Grey?"

She turned her eyes towards me.

"I'm wondering where he is now . . . the murderer, I mean. It's not twelve hours yet since it happened. . . . Oh! aren't there any *real* clairvoyants who could see where he is now and what he is doing . . . ?"

"The police are searching—" I began.

My commonplace words broke the spell. Thora Grey pulled herself together.

"Yes," she said. "Of course."

In her turn she descended the staircase. I stood there a moment longer conning her words over in my mind.

A.B.C. . . .

Where was he now . . . ?

XVI (Not from Captain Hastings' Personal Narrative)

MR. ALEXANDER BONAPARTE CUST came out with the rest of the audience from the Torquay Pavilion, where he had been seeing and hearing that highly emotional film, *Not a Sparrow*. . . .

He blinked a little as he came out into the afternoon sunshine and peered round him in that lost-dog fashion that was characteristic of him.

He murmured to himself: "It's an idea. . . ."

Newsboys passed along crying out:

"Latest . . . Homicidal Maniac at Churston . . ."

They carried placards on which was written:

CHURSTON MURDER. LATEST.

Mr. Cust fumbled in his pocket, found a coin, and bought a paper. He did not open it at once.

Entering the Princess Gardens, he slowly made his way to a shelter facing Torquay harbour. He sat down and opened the paper.

There were big headlines:

SIR CARMICHAEL CLARKE MURDERED
TERRIBLE TRAGEDY AT CHURSTON
WORK OF A HOMICIDAL MANIAC

And below them:

Only a month ago England was shocked and startled by the murder of a young girl, Elizabeth Barnard, at Bexhill. It may be remembered that an A.B.C. railway guide figured in the case. An A.B.C. was also found by the dead body of Sir Carmichael Clarke, and the police incline to the belief that both crimes were committed by the same person. Can it be possible that a homicidal murderer is going the round of our seaside resorts? . . .

A young man in flannel trousers and a bright blue aertex shirt who was sitting beside Mr. Cust remarked:

"Nasty business—eh?"

Mr. Cust jumped.

"Oh, very—very—"

His hands, the young man noticed, were trembling so that he could hardly hold the paper.

"You never know with lunatics," said the young man chattily. "They don't always look balmy, you know. Often they seem just the same as you or me. . . ."

"I suppose they do," said Mr. Cust.

"It's a fact. Sometimes it's the war what unhinged them—never been right since."

"I—I expect you're right."

"I don't hold with wars," said the young man.

His companion turned on him.

"I don't hold with plague and sleeping sickness and famine and cancer . . . but they happen all the same!"

"War's preventable," said the young man with assurance.

Mr. Cust laughed. He laughed for some time.

The young man was slightly alarmed.

"He's a bit batty himself," he thought.

Aloud he said:

"Sorry, sir, I expect you were in the war."

"I was," said Mr. Cust. "It—it—unsettled me. My head's never been right since. It aches, you know. Aches terribly."

"Oh! I'm sorry about that," said the young man awkwardly.

"Sometimes I hardly know what I'm doing. . . ."

"Really? Well, I must be getting along," said the young man and removed himself hurriedly. He knew what people were once they began to talk about their health.

Mr. Cust remained with his paper.

He read and reread. . . .

People passed to and fro in front of him.

Most of them were talking of the murder. . . .

"Awful . . . do you think it was anything to do with the Chinese? Wasn't the waitress in a Chinese café? . . ."

"Actually on the golf links . . ."

"I heard it was on the beach . . ."

"—but, darling, we took our tea to Elbury only *yesterday* . . ."

"—police are sure to get him . . ."

"—say he may be arrested any minute now . . ."

"—quite likely he's in Torquay . . . that other woman was who murdered the what do you call 'ems . . ."

Mr. Cust folded up the paper very neatly and laid it on the seat. Then he rose and walked sedately along towards the town.

Girls passed him, girls in white and pink and blue, in summery frocks and pyjamas and shorts. They laughed and giggled. Their eyes appraised the men they passed.

Not once did their eyes linger for a second on Mr. Cust. . . .

He sat down at a little table and ordered tea and Devonshire cream. . . .

XVII Marking Time

WITH the murder of Sir Carmichael Clarke the A.B.C. mystery leaped into the fullest prominence.

The newspapers were full of nothing else. All sorts of "clues" were reported to have been discovered. Arrests were announced to be imminent. There were photographs of every person or place remotely connected with the murder. There were interviews with any one who would give interviews. There were questions asked in Parliament.

The Andover murder was now bracketed with the other two.

It was the belief of Scotland Yard that the fullest publicity was the best chance of laying the murderer by the heels. The population of Great Britain turned itself into an army of amateur sleuths.

The *Daily Flicker* had the grand inspiration of using the caption:

He may be in *your* town!

Poirot, of course, was in the thick of things. The letters sent to him were published and facsimiled. He was abused wholesale for not having prevented the crimes and defended on the ground that he was on the point of naming the murderer.

Reporters incessantly badgered him for interviews.

What M. Poirot Says To-day.

Which was usually followed by a half-column of imbecilities.

M. Poirot Takes Grave View of Situation.

M. Poirot on the Eve of Success.

Captain Hastings, the great friend of M. Poirot, told our Special Representative . . .

"Poirot," I would cry. "Pray believe me. I never said anything of the kind."

My friend would reply kindly:

"I know, Hastings—I know. The spoken word and the written

—there is an astonishing gulf between them. There is a way of turning sentences that completely reverses the original meaning."

"I wouldn't like you to think I'd said—"

"But do not worry yourself. All this is of no importance. These imbecilities, even, may help."

"How?"

"Eh bien," said Poirot grimly. "If our madman reads what I am supposed to have said to the *Daily Blague* to-day, he will lose all respect for me as an opponent!"

I am, perhaps, giving the impression that nothing practical was being done in the way of investigations. On the contrary, Scotland Yard and the local police of the various counties were indefatigable in following up the smallest clues.

Hotels, people who kept lodgings, boarding-houses—all those within a wide radius of the crimes were questioned minutely.

Hundreds of stories from imaginative people who had "seen a man looking very queer and rolling his eyes," or "noticed a man with a sinister face slinking along," were sifted to the last detail. No information, even of the vaguest character, was neglected. Trains, buses, trams, railway porters, conductors, bookstalls, stationers—there was an indefatigable round of questions and verifications.

At least a score of people were detained and questioned until they could satisfy the police as to their movements on the night in question.

The net result was not entirely a blank. Certain statements were borne in mind and noted down as of possible value, but without further evidence they led nowhere.

If Crome and his colleagues were indefatigable, Poirot seemed to me strangely supine. We argued now and again.

"But what is it that you would have me do, my friend? The routine inquiries, the police make them better than I do. Always—always you want me to run about like the dog."

"Instead of which you sit at home like—like—"

"A sensible man! My force, Hastings, is in my *brain,* not in my *feet!* All the time, whilst I seem to you idle, I am reflecting."

"Reflecting?" I cried. "Is this a time for reflection?"

"Yes, a thousand times yes."

"But what can you possibly gain by reflection? You know the facts of the three cases by heart."

"It is not the facts I reflect upon—but the mind of the murderer."

"The mind of a madman!"

"Precisely. And therefore not to be arrived at in a minute. When I know what the murderer is like, I shall be able to find out who he is. And all the time I learn more. After the Andover crime, what did we know about the murderer? Next to nothing at all. After the Bexhill crime? A little more. After the Churston murder? More still. I begin to see—not what *you* would like to see—the outlines of a face and form—but the outlines of a *mind*. A mind that moves and works in certain definite directions. After the next crime—"

"Poirot!"

My friend looked at me dispassionately.

"But, yes, Hastings, I think it is almost certain there will be another. A lot depends on *la chance*. So far our *inconnu* has been lucky. This time the luck may turn against him. But in any case, after another crime, we shall know infinitely more. Crime is terribly revealing. Try and vary your methods as you will your tastes, your habits, your attitude of mind, and your soul is revealed by your actions. There are confusing indications —sometimes it is as though there were two intelligences at work—but soon the outline will clear itself, I shall know."

"Who it is?"

"No, Hastings, I shall not know his name and address! I shall know what kind of a man he is. . . ."

"And then?"

"Et alors, je vais à la pêche."

As I looked rather bewildered, he went on:

"You comprehend, Hastings, an expert fisherman knows exactly what flies to offer to what fish. I shall offer the right kind of fly."

"And then?"

"And then? And then? You are as bad as the superior Crome with his eternal 'Oh, yes?' *Eh bien,* and then he will take the bait and the hook and we will reel in the line. . . ."

"In the meantime people are dying right and left."

"Three people. And there are, what is it—about a hundred forty—road deaths every week?"

"That is entirely different."

"It is probably exactly the same to those who die. For the others, the relations, the friends—yes, there is a difference, but one thing at least rejoices me in this case."

"By all means let us hear anything in the nature of rejoicing."

"*Inutile* to be so sarcastic. It rejoices me that there is here no shadow of guilt to distress the innocent."

"Isn't this worse?"

"No, no, a thousand times no! There is nothing so terrible as to live in an atmosphere of suspicion—to see eyes watching you and the love in them changing to fear—nothing so terrible as to suspect those near and dear to you. . . . It is poisonous—a miasma. No, the poisoning of life for the innocent, that, at least, we cannot lay at A.B.C.'s door."

"You'll soon be making excuses for the man!" I said bitterly.

"Why not? He may believe himself fully justified. We may, perhaps, end by having sympathy with his point of view."

"Really, Poirot!"

"Alas! I have shocked you. First my inertia—and then my views."

I shook my head without replying.

"All the same," said Poirot after a minute or two. "I have one project that will please you—since it is active and not passive. Also, it will entail a lot of conversation and practically no thought."

I did not quite like his tone.

"What is it?" I asked cautiously.

"The extraction from the friends, relations and servants of the victims of all they know."

"Do you suspect them of keeping things back, then?"

"Not intentionally. But telling everything you know always implies *selection*. If I were to say to you, recount me your day yesterday, you would perhaps reply: 'I rose at nine, I breakfasted at half-past, I had eggs and bacon and coffee, I went to my club, etc.' You would not include: 'I tore my nail and had to cut it. I rang for shaving water. I spilt a little coffee on the table-cloth. I brushed my hat and put it on.' One cannot tell *every-thing*. Therefore one *selects*. At the time of a murder people select what *they* think is important. But quite frequently they think wrong!"

"And how is one to get at the right things?"

"Simply, as I said just now, by conversation. By talking! By discussing a certain happening, or a certain person, or a certain day, over and over again, extra details are bound to arise."

"What kind of details?"

"Naturally that I do not know or I should not want to find out! But enough time has passed now for ordinary things to reassume their value. It is against all mathematical laws that in three cases of murder there is no single fact or sentence with a bearing on the case. Some trivial happening, some trivial remark there *must* be which would be a pointer! It is looking for the needle in the haystack, I grant—*but in the haystack there is a needle*—of that I am convinced!"

It seemed to me extremely vague and hazy.

"You do not see it? Your wits are not so sharp as those of a mere servant girl."

He tossed me over a letter. It was neatly written in a sloping board-school hand.

DEAR SIR,—I hope you will forgive the liberty I take in writing to you. I have been thinking a lot since these awful two murders like poor Auntie's. It seems as though we're all in the same boat, as it were. I saw the young lady's picture in the paper, the young lady, I mean, that is the sister of the young lady that was killed at Bexhill. I made so bold as to write to her and tell her I was coming to London to get a place and asked if I could come to her or her mother as I said two heads might be better than one and I would not want much wages, but only to find out who this awful fiend is and perhaps we might get at it better if we could say what we knew something might come of it.

The young lady wrote very nicely and said as how she worked in an office and lived in a hostel, but she suggested I might write to you and she said she'd been thinking something of the same kind as I had. And she said we were in the same trouble and we ought to stand together. So I am writing, sir, to say I am coming to London and this is my address.

Hoping I am not troubling you, Yours respectfully,

MARY DROWER

"Mary Drower," said Poirot, "is a very intelligent girl."

He picked up another letter.

"Read this."

It was a line from Franklin Clarke, saying that he was coming to London and would call upon Poirot the following day if not inconvenient.

"Do not despair, *mon ami*," said Poirot. "Action is about to begin."

XVIII Poirot Makes a Speech

FRANKLIN CLARKE arrived at three o'clock on the following afternoon and came straight to the point without beating about the bush.

"M. Poirot," he said, "I'm not satisfied."

"No, Mr. Clarke?"

"I've no doubt that Crome is a very efficient officer, but, frankly, he puts my back up. That air of his of knowing best! I hinted something of what I had in mind to your friend here when he was down at Churston, but I've had all my brother's affairs to settle up and I haven't been free until now. My idea is, M. Poirot, that we oughtn't to let the grass grow under our feet—"

"Just what Hastings is always saying!"

"—but go right ahead. We've got to get ready for the next crime."

"So you think there will be a next crime?"

"Don't you?"

"Certainly."

"Very well, then. I want to get organized."

"Tell me your idea exactly?"

"I propose, M. Poirot, a kind of special legion—to work under your orders—composed of the friends and relatives of the murdered people."

"Une bonne idée!"

"I'm glad you approve. By putting our heads together I feel we might get at something. Also, when the next warning comes, by being on the spot, one of us might—I don't say it's probable—but we might recognize some person as having been near the scene of a previous crime."

"I see your idea, and I approve, but you must remember, Mr. Clarke, the relations and friends of the other victims are hardly in your sphere of life. They are employed persons and though they might be given a short vacation—"

Franklin Clarke interrupted.

"That's just it. I'm the only person in a position to foot the bill. Not that I'm particularly well off myself, but my brother died a rich man and it will eventually come to me. I propose, as I say, to enroll a special legion, the members to be paid for their services at the same rate as they get habitually, with, of course, the additional expenses."

"Who do you propose should form this legion?"

"I've been into that. As a matter of fact, I wrote to Miss Megan Barnard—indeed, this is partly her idea. I suggest myself, Miss Barnard, Mr. Donald Fraser, who was engaged to the dead girl. Then there is a niece of the Andover woman—Miss Barnard knows her address. I don't think the husband would be of any use to us—I hear he's usually drunk. I also think the Barnards— the father and mother—are a bit old for active campaigning."

"Nobody else?"

"Well—er—Miss Grey."

He flushed slightly as he spoke the name.

"Oh! Miss Grey?"

Nobody in the world could put a gentle nuance of irony into a couple of words better than Poirot. About thirty-five years fell away from Franklin Clarke. He looked suddenly like a shy schoolboy.

"Yes. You see, Miss Grey was with my brother for over two years. She knows the countryside and the people round, and everything. I've been away for a year and a half."

Poirot took pity on him and turned the conversation.

"You have been in the East? In China?"

"Yes. I had a kind of roving commission to purchase things for my brother."

"Very interesting it must have been. *Eh bien,* Mr. Clarke, I approve very highly of your idea. I was saying to Hastings only yesterday that a *rapprochement* of the people concerned was needed. It is necessary to pool reminiscences, to compare notes —*enfin* to talk the thing over—to talk—to talk—and again to talk. Out of some innocent phrase may come enlightenment."

A few days later the "Special Legion" met at Poirot's rooms.

As they sat round looking obediently towards Poirot, who had his place, like the chairman at a Board meeting, at the head of the table, I myself passed them, as it were, in review, confirming or revising my first impressions of them.

The three girls were all of them striking-looking—the extraordinary fair beauty of Thora Grey, the dark intensity of Megan Barnard, with her strange red Indian immobility of face—Mary Drower, neatly dressed in a black coat and skirt, with her pretty, intelligent face. Of the two men, Franklin Clarke, big, bronzed and talkative, Donald Fraser, self-contained and quiet, made an interesting contrast to each other.

Poirot, unable, of course, to resist the occasion, made a little speech.

"Mesdames and messieurs, you know what we are here for. The police are doing their utmost to track down the criminal. I, too, in my different way. But it seems to me a reunion of those who have a personal interest in the matter—and also, I may say, a personal knowledge of the victims—might have results that an outside investigation cannot pretend to attain.

"Here we have three murders—an old woman, a young girl, an elderly man. Only one thing links these three people together —*the fact that the same person killed them.* That means that *the same person was present in three different localities* and was seen necessarily by a large number of people. That he is a madman in an advanced stage of mania goes without saying. That his appearance and behaviour give no suggestion of such a fact is equally certain. This person—and though I say *he,* remember it may be a man or woman—has all the devilish cunning of insanity. He has succeeded so far in covering his traces completely. The police have certain vague indications but nothing upon which they can act.

"Nevertheless, there must exist indications which are not vague but certain. To take one particular point—this assassin he did not arrive at Bexhill at midnight and find conveniently on the beach a young lady whose name began with B—"

"Must we go into that?"

It was Donald Fraser who spoke—the words wrung from him, it seemed, by some inner anguish.

"It is necessary to go into everything, monsieur," said Poirot, turning to him. "You are here, not to save your feelings by refusing to think of details, but if necessary to harrow them by going into the matter *au fond*. As I say, it was not *chance* that provided A.B.C. with a victim in Betty Barnard. There must have been deliberate selection on his part—and therefore premeditation. That is to say, he must have reconnoitred the ground *beforehand*. There were facts of which he had informed himself —the best hour for the committing of the crime at Andover— the *mise en scène* at Bexhill—the habits of Sir Carmichael Clarke at Churston. Me, for one, I refuse to believe that there is *no* indication—no slightest hint—that might help to establish his identity.

"I make the assumption that one—or possibly *all* of you— knows something that they do not know they know.

"Sooner or later, by reason of your association with one another, something will come to light, will take on a significance as yet undreamed of. It is like the jigsaw puzzle—each of you may have a piece apparently without meaning, but which when reunited may show a definite portion of the picture as a whole."

"Words!" said Megan Barnard.

"Eh?" Poirot looked at her inquiringly.

"What you've been saying. It's just words. It doesn't mean anything."

She spoke with that kind of desperate dark intensity that I had come to associate with her personality.

"Words, mademoiselle, are only the outer clothing of ideas."

"Well, I think it's sense," said Mary Drower. "I do really, miss. It's often when you're talking over things that you seem to see your way clear. Your mind gets made up for you sometimes without your knowing how it's happened. Talking leads to a lot of things one way and another."

"If 'least said is soonest mended,' it's the converse we want here," said Franklin Clarke.

"What do you say, Mr. Fraser?"

"I rather doubt the practical applicability of what you say, M. Poirot."

"What do you think, Thora?" asked Clarke.

"I think the principle of talking things over is always sound."

"Suppose," suggested Poirot, "that you all go over your own remembrances of the time preceding the murder. Perhaps you'll start, Mr. Clarke."

"Let me see, on the morning of the day Car was killed I went off sailing. Caught eight mackerel. Lovely out there on the bay. Lunch at home. Irish stew, I remember. Slept in the hammock. Tea. Wrote some letters, missed the post, and drove into Paignton to post them. Then dinner and—I'm not ashamed to say it —reread a book of E. Nesbit's that I used to love as a kid. Then the telephone rang—"

"No further. Now reflect, Mr. Clarke, did you meet any one on your way down to the sea in the morning?"

"Lots of people."

"Can you remember anything about them?"

"Not a damned thing now."

"Sure?"

"Well—let's see—I remember a remarkably fat woman—she wore a striped silk dress and I wondered why—had a couple of kids with her . . . two young men with a fox terrier on the beach throwing stones for it— Oh, yes, a girl with yellow hair squeaking as she bathed—funny how things come back—like a photograph developing."

"You are a good subject. Now later in the day—the garden— going to the post—"

"The gardener watering . . . Going to the post? Nearly ran down a bicyclist—silly woman wobbling and shouting to a friend. That's all, I'm afraid."

Poirot turned to Thora Grey.

"Miss Grey?"

Thora Grey replied in her clear, positive voice:

"I did correspondence with Sir Carmichael in the morning— saw the housekeeper. I wrote letters and did needlework in the afternoon, I fancy. It is difficult to remember. It was quite an ordinary day. I went to bed early."

Rather to my surprise, Poirot asked no further. He said:

"Miss Barnard—can you bring back your remembrances of the last time you saw your sister?"

"It would be about a fortnight before her death. I was down for Saturday and Sunday. It was fine weather. We went to Hastings to the swimming pool."

"What did you talk about most of the time?"

"I gave her a piece of my mind," said Megan.

"And what else? She conversed of what?"

The girl frowned in an effort of memory.

"She talked about being hard up—of a hat and a couple of summer frocks she'd just bought. And a little of Don. . . . She also said she disliked Milly Higley—that's the girl at the café—and we laughed about the Merrion woman who keeps the café. . . . I don't remember anything else. . . ."

"She didn't mention any man—forgive me, Mr. Fraser—she might be meeting?"

"She wouldn't to me," said Megan dryly.

Poirot turned to the red-haired young man with the square jaw.

"Mr. Fraser—I want you to cast your mind back. You went, you said, to the café on the fatal evening. Your first intention was to wait there and watch for Betty Barnard to come out. Can you remember any one at all whom you noticed whilst you were waiting there?"

"There were a large number of people walking along the front. I can't remember any of them."

"Excuse me, but are you trying? However preoccupied the mind may be, the eye notices mechanically—unintelligently but accurately. . . ."

The young man repeated doggedly:

"I don't remember anybody."

Poirot sighed and turned to Mary Drower.

"I suppose you got letters from your aunt?"

"Oh, yes, sir."

"When was the last?"

Mary thought a minute.

"Two days before the murder, sir."

"What did it say?"

"She said the old devil had been round and that she'd sent him off with a flea in the ear—excuse the expression, sir—said she expected me over on the Wednesday—that's my day out, sir—and she said we'd go to the pictures. It was going to be my birthday, sir."

Something—the thought of the little festivity perhaps, suddenly brought the tears to Mary's eyes. She gulped down a sob. Then apologized for it.

"You must forgive me, sir. I don't want to be silly. Crying's no good. It was just the thought of her—and me—looking forward to our treat. It upset me somehow, sir."

"I know just what you feel like," said Franklin Clarke. "It's always the little things that get one—and especially anything like a treat or a present—something jolly and natural. I remember seeing a woman run over once. She'd just bought some new shoes. I saw her lying there—and the burst parcel with the ridiculous little high-heeled slippers peeping out—it gave me a turn—they looked so pathetic."

Megan said with a sudden eager warmth:

"That's true—that's awfully true. The same thing happened after Betty—died. Mum had bought some stockings for her as a present—bought them the very day it happened. Poor mum, she was all broken up. I found her crying over them. She kept saying: 'I bought them for Betty—I bought them for Betty—and she never even saw them.'"

Her own voice quivered a little. She leaned forward, looking straight at Franklin Clarke. There was between them a sudden sympathy—a fraternity in trouble.

"I know," he said. "I know exactly. Those are just the sort of things that are hell to remember."

Donald Fraser stirred uneasily.

Thora Grey diverted the conversation.

"Aren't we going to make any plans—for the future?" she asked.

"Of course." Franklin Clarke resumed his ordinary manner. "I think that when the moment comes—that is, when the fourth letter arrives—we ought to join forces. Until then, perhaps we might each try our luck on our own. I don't know whether there are any points M. Poirot thinks might repay investigation?"

"I could make some suggestions," said Poirot.

"Good. I'll take them down." He produced a notebook. "Go ahead, M. Poirot. A—?"

"I consider it just possible that the waitress, Milly Higley, might know something useful."

"A—Milly Higley," wrote down Franklin Clarke.

"I suggest two methods of approach. You, Miss Barnard, might try what I call the offensive approach."

"I suppose you think that suits my style?" said Megan dryly.

"Pick a quarrel with the girl—say you knew she never liked your sister—and that your sister had told you all about *her*. If I do not err, that will provoke a flood of recrimination. She will tell you just what she thought of your sister! Some useful fact may emerge."

"And the second method?"

"May I suggest, Mr. Fraser, that you should show signs of interest in the girl?"

"Is that necessary?"

"No, it is not necessary. It is just a possible line of exploration."

"Shall I try my hand?" asked Franklin. "I've—er—a pretty wide experience, M. Poirot. Let me see what I can do with the young lady."

"You've got your own part of the world to attend to," said Thora Grey rather sharply.

Franklin's face fell just a little.

"Yes," he said. "I have."

"*Tout de même,* I do not think there is much you can do down there for the present," said Poirot. "Mademoiselle Grey now, she is far more fitted—"

Thora Grey interrupted him.

"But you see, M. Poirot, I have left Devon for good."

"Ah? I did not understand."

"Miss Grey very kindly stayed on to help me clear up things," said Franklin. "But naturally she prefers a post in London."

Poirot directed a sharp glance from one to the other.

"How is Lady Clarke?" he demanded.

I was admiring the faint colour in Thora Grey's cheeks and almost missed Clarke's reply.

"Pretty bad. By the way, M. Poirot, I wonder if you could see your way to running down to Devon and paying her a visit? She expressed a desire to see you before I left. Of course, she often can't see people for a couple of days at a time, but if you would risk that—at my expense, of course."

"Certainly, Mr. Clarke. Shall we say, the day after to-morrow?"

"Good. I'll let nurse know and she'll arrange the dope accordingly."

"For you, my child," said Poirot, turning to Mary, "I think you might perhaps do good work in Andover. Try the children."

"The children?"

"Yes. Children will not chat readily to outsiders. But you are known in the street where your aunt lived. There were a good many children playing about. They may have noticed who went in and out of your aunt's shop."

"What about Miss Grey and myself?" asked Clarke. "That is, if I'm not to go to Bexhill."

"M. Poirot," said Thora Grey. "What was the postmark on the third letter?"

"Putney, mademoiselle."

She said thoughtfully: "S.W.15, Putney, that is right, is it not?"

"For a wonder, the newspapers printed it correctly."

"That seems to point to A.B.C. being a Londoner."

"On the face of it, yes."

"One ought to be able to draw him," said Clarke. "M. Poirot, how would it be if I inserted an advertisement—something after these lines: *A.B.C. Urgent. H.P. close on your track. A hundred for my silence. X.Y.Z.* Nothing quite so crude as that—but you see the idea. It might draw him."

"It is a possibility—yes."

"Might induce him to try and have a shot at me."

"I think it's very dangerous and silly," said Thora Grey sharply.

"What about it, M. Poirot?"

"It can do no harm to try. I think myself that A.B.C. will be too cunning to reply." Poirot smiled a little. "I see, Mr. Clarke, that you are—if I may say so without being offensive—still a boy at heart."

Franklin Clarke looked a little abashed.

"Well," he said, consulting his notebook, "we're making a start.

> A.—Miss Barnard and Milly Higley.
> B.—Mr. Fraser and Miss Higley.
> C.—Children in Andover.
> D.—Advertisement.

I don't feel any of it is much good, but it will be something to do whilst waiting."

He got up and a few minutes later the meeting had dispersed.

XIX By Way of Sweden

POIROT returned to his seat and sat humming a little tune to himself.

"Unfortunate that she is so intelligent," he murmured.

"Who?"

"Megan Barnard. Mademoiselle Megan. 'Words,' she snaps out. At once she perceives that what I am saying means nothing at all. Everybody else was taken in."

"I thought it sounded very plausible."

"Plausible, yes. It was just that that she perceived."

"Didn't you mean what you said, then?"

"What I said could have been comprised into one short sentence. Instead I repeated myself ad lib. without any one but Mademoiselle Megan being aware of the fact."

"But why?"

"*Eh bien*—to get things going! To imbue every one with the impression that there was work to be done! To start—shall we say—the conversations!"

"Don't you think any of these lines will lead to anything?"

"Oh, it is always possible."

He chuckled.

"In the midst of tragedy we start the comedy. It is so, is it not?"

"What do you mean?"

"The human drama, Hastings! Reflect a little minute. Here are three sets of human beings brought together by a common tragedy. Immediately a second drama commences—*tout à fait à part*. Do you remember my first case in England? Oh, so many years ago now. I brought together two people who loved one another—by the simple method of having one of them arrested for murder! Nothing less would have done it! In the midst of death we are in life, Hastings. . . . Murder, I have often noticed, is a great matchmaker."

"Really, Poirot," I cried, scandalized. "I'm sure none of those people was thinking of anything but—"

"Oh! my dear friend. And what about yourself?"

"I?"

"*Mais oui,* as they departed, did you not come back from the door humming a tune?"

"One may do that without being callous."

"Certainly, but that tune told me your thoughts."

"Indeed?"

"Yes. To hum a tune is extremely dangerous. It reveals the sub-conscious mind. The tune you hummed dates, I think, from the days of the war. *Comme ça,*" Poirot sang in an abominable falsetto voice:

> "Some of the time I love a brunette,
>   Some of the time I love a blonde (who comes
>   from Eden by way of Sweden).

"What could be more revealing? *Mais je crois que la blonde l'emporte sur la brunette!*"

"Really, Poirot," I cried, blushing slightly.

"*C'est tout naturel.* Did you observe how Franklin Clarke was suddenly at one and in sympathy with Mademoiselle Megan? How he leaned forward and looked at her? And did you also notice how very much annoyed Mademoiselle Thora Grey was about it? And Mr. Donald Fraser, he—"

"Poirot," I said, "your mind is incurably sentimental."

"That is the last thing my mind is. You are the sentimental one, Hastings."

I was about to argue the point hotly, but at that moment the door opened.

To my astonishment it was Thora Grey who entered.

"Forgive me for coming back," she said composedly. "But there was something that I think I would like to tell you, M. Poirot."

"Certainly, mademoiselle. Sit down, will you not?"

She took a seat and hesitated for just a minute as though choosing her words.

"It is just this, M. Poirot. Mr. Clarke very generously gave you to understand just now that I had left Combeside by my own wish. He is a very kind and loyal person. But as a matter of fact, it is not quite like that. I was quite prepared to stay on—there is any amount of work to be done in connection with the collections. It was Lady Clarke who wished me to leave! I can make allowances. She is a very ill woman, and her brain is somewhat muddled with the drugs they give her. It makes her suspicious and fanciful. She took an unreasoning dislike to me and insisted that I should leave the house."

I could not but admire the girl's courage. She did not attempt to gloss over facts, as so many might have been tempted to do, but went straight to the point with an admirable candour. My heart went out to her in admiration and sympathy.

"I call it splendid of you to come and tell us this," I said.

"It's always better to have the truth," she said with a little smile. "I don't want to shelter behind Mr. Clarke's chivalry. He is a very chivalrous man."

There was a warm glow in her words. She evidently admired Franklin Clarke enormously.

"You have been very honest, mademoiselle," said Poirot.

"It is rather a blow to me," said Thora ruefully. "I had no idea Lady Clarke disliked me so much. In fact, I always thought she was rather fond of me." She made a wry face. "One lives and learns."

She rose.

"That is all I came to say. Good-bye."

I accompanied her downstairs.

"I call that very sporting of her," I said as I returned to the room. "She has courage, that girl."

"And calculation."

"What do you mean—calculation?"

"I mean that she has the power of looking ahead."

I looked at him doubtfully.

"She really is a lovely girl," I said.

"And wears very lovely clothes. That crepe marocain and the silky fox collar—*dernier cri!*"

"You're a man milliner, Poirot. I never notice what people have on."

"You should join a nudist colony."

As I was about to make an indignant rejoinder, he said, with a sudden change of subject:

"Do you know, Hastings, I cannot rid my mind of the impression that already, in our conversations this afternoon, something was said that was significant. It is odd—I cannot pin down exactly what it was. . . . Just an impression that passed through my mind. . . . *That reminds me of something I have already heard or seen or noted. . . .*"

"Something at Churston?"

"No—not at Churston. . . . Before that. . . . No matter, presently it will come to me. . . ."

He looked at me (perhaps I had not been attending very closely), laughed and began once more to hum.

"She is an angel, is she not? From Eden, by way of Sweden. . . ."

"Poirot," I said. "Go to the devil!"

XX Lady Clarke

THERE was an air of deep and settled melancholy over Combeside when we saw it again for the second time. This may, perhaps, have been partly due to the weather—it was a moist September day with a hint of autumn in the air, and partly, no doubt, it was the semi-shut-up state of the house. The downstairs rooms were closed and shuttered, and the small room into which we were shown smelt damp and airless.

A capable-looking hospital nurse came to us there pulling down her starched cuffs.

"M. Poirot?" she said briskly. "I am Nurse Capstick. I got Mr. Clarke's letter saying you were coming."

Poirot inquired after Lady Clarke's health.

"Not at all bad really, all things considered."

"All things considered," I presumed meant considering she was under sentence of death.

"One can't hope for much improvement, of course, but some new treatment has made things a little easier for her. Dr. Logan is quite pleased with her condition."

"But it is true, is it not, that she can never recover?"

"Oh, we never actually *say* that," said Nurse Capstick, a little shocked by this plain speaking.

"I suppose her husband's death was a terrible shock to her?"

"Well, M. Poirot, if you understand what I mean, it wasn't as much of a shock as it would have been to any one in full possession of her health and faculties. Things are *dimmed* for Lady Clarke in her condition."

"Pardon my asking, but was she deeply attached to her husband and he to her?"

"Oh, yes, they were a very happy couple. He was very worried and upset about her, poor man. It's always worse for a doctor, you know. They can't buoy themselves up with false hopes. I'm afraid it preyed on his mind very much to begin with."

"To begin with? Not so much afterwards?"

"One gets used to everything, doesn't one? And then Sir Carmichael had his collection. A hobby is a great consolation to a man. He used to run up to sales occasionally, and then he and Miss Grey were busy recataloguing and rearranging the museum on a new system."

"Oh, yes—Miss Grey. She has left, has she not?"

"Yes—I'm very sorry about it—but ladies do take these fancies sometimes when they're not well. And there's no arguing with them. It's better to give in. Miss Grey was very sensible about it."

"Has Lady Clarke always disliked her?"

"No—that is to say, not *disliked*. As a matter of fact, I think she rather liked her to begin with. But there, I mustn't keep you gossiping. My patient will be wondering what has become of us."

She led us upstairs to a room on the first floor. What had at one time been a bedroom had been turned into a cheerful-looking sitting-room.

Lady Clarke was sitting in a big arm-chair near the window. She was painfully thin, and her face had the grey, haggard look of one who suffers much pain. She had a slightly far-away, dreamy look, and I noticed that the pupils of her eyes were mere pin-points.

"This is M. Poirot whom you wanted to see," said Nurse Capstick in her high, cheerful voice.

"Oh, yes, M. Poirot," said Lady Clarke vaguely.

She extended her hand.

"My friend Captain Hastings, Lady Clarke."

"How do you do? So good of you both to come."

We sat down as her vague gesture directed. There was a silence. Lady Clarke seemed to have lapsed into a dream.

Presently with a slight effort she roused herself.

"It was about Car, wasn't it? About Car's death. Oh, yes."

She sighed, but still in a far-away manner, shaking her head.

"We never thought it would be that way round . . . I was so

sure I should be the first to go. . . ." She mused a minute or two. "Car was very strong—wonderful for his age. He was never ill. He was nearly sixty—but he seemed more like fifty. . . . Yes, very strong. . . ."

She relapsed again into her dream. Poirot, who was well acquainted with the effects of certain drugs and of how they give their taker the impression of endless time, said nothing.

Lady Clarke said suddenly:

"Yes—it was good of you to come. I told Franklin. He said he wouldn't forget to tell you. I hope Franklin isn't going to be foolish . . . he's so easily taken in, in spite of having knocked about the world so much. Men are like that. . . . They remain boys . . . Franklin, in particular."

"He has an impulsive nature," said Poirot.

"Yes—yes. . . . And very chivalrous. Men are so foolish that way. Even Car—" Her voice trailed off.

She shook her head with a febrile impatience.

"Everything's so dim. . . . One's body is a nuisance, M. Poirot, especially when it gets the upper hand. One is conscious of nothing else—whether the pain will hold off or not—nothing else seems to matter."

"I know, Lady Clarke. It is one of the tragedies of this life."

"It makes me so stupid. I cannot even remember what it was I wanted to say to you."

"Was it something about your husband's death?"

"Car's death? Yes, perhaps. . . . Mad, poor creature—the murderer, I mean. It's all the noise and the speed nowadays—people can't stand it. I've always been sorry for mad people—their heads must feel so queer. And then, being shut up—it must be so terrible. But what else can one do? If they kill people . . ." She shook her head—gently pained. "You haven't caught him yet?" she asked.

"No, not yet."

"He must have been hanging round here that day."

"There were so many strangers about, Lady Clarke. It is the holiday season."

"Yes—I forgot. . . . But they keep down by the beaches, they don't come up near the house."

"No stranger came to the house that day."

"Who says so?" demanded Lady Clarke, with a sudden vigour.
Poirot looked slightly taken aback.

"The servants," he said. "Miss Grey."

Lady Clarke said very distinctly:

"That girl is a liar!"

I started on my chair. Poirot threw me a glance.

Lady Clarke was going on, speaking now rather feverishly.

"I didn't like her. I never liked her. Car thought all the world
of her. Used to go on about her being an orphan and alone in
the world. What's wrong with being an orphan? Sometimes it's
a blessing in disguise. You might have a good-for-nothing father
and a mother who drank—then you would have something to
complain about. Said she was so brave and such a good worker.
I dare say she did her work well! I don't know where all this
bravery came in!"

"Now don't excite yourself, dear," said Nurse Capstick, in-
tervening. "We mustn't have you getting tired."

"I soon sent her packing! Franklin had the impertinence to
suggest that she might be a comfort to me. Comfort to me indeed! The sooner I saw the last of her the better—that's what I
said! Franklin's a fool! I didn't want him getting mixed up with
her. He's a boy! No sense! 'I'll give her three months' salary, if
you like,' I said. 'But out she goes. I don't want her in the house
a day longer.' There's one thing about being ill—men can't argue
with you. He did what I said and she went. Went like a martyr,
I expect—with more sweetness and bravery!"

"Now, dear, don't get so excited. It's bad for you."

Lady Clarke waved Nurse Capstick away.

"You were as much of a fool about her as any one else."

"Oh! Lady Clarke, you mustn't say that. I did think Miss Grey
a very nice girl—so romantic-looking, like some one out of a
novel."

"I've no patience with the lot of you," said Lady Clarke feebly.

"Well, she's gone now, my dear. Gone right away."

Lady Clarke shook her head with feeble impatience but she
did not answer.

Poirot said:

"Why did you say that Miss Grey was a liar?"

"Because she is. She told you no strangers came to the house, didn't she?"

"Yes."

"Very well, then. I saw her—with my own eyes—out of this window—talking to a perfectly strange man on the front doorstep."

"When was this?"

"In the morning of the day Car died—about eleven o'clock."

"What did this man look like?"

"An ordinary sort of man. Nothing special."

"A gentleman—or a tradesman?"

"Not a tradesman. A shabby sort of person. I can't remember."

A sudden quiver of pain shot across her face.

"Please—you must go now—I'm a little tired— Nurse."

We obeyed the cue and took our departure.

"That's an extraordinary story," I said to Poirot as we journeyed back to London. "About Miss Grey and a strange man."

"You see, Hastings? It is, as I tell you: there is always something to be found out."

"Why did the girl lie about it and say she had seen no one?"

"I can think of seven separate reasons—one of them an extremely simple one."

"Is that a snub?" I asked.

"It is, perhaps, an invitation to use your ingenuity. But there is no need for us to perturb ourselves. The easiest way to answer the question is to ask her."

"And suppose she tells us another lie."

"That would indeed be interesting—and highly suggestive."

"It is monstrous to suppose that a girl like that could be in league with a madman."

"Precisely—so I do not suppose it."

I thought for some minutes longer.

"A good-looking girl has a hard time of it," I said at last with a sigh.

"*Du tout*. Disabuse your mind of that idea."

"It's true," I insisted. "Every one's hand is against her simply because she is good-looking."

"You speak the *bêtises,* my friend. Whose hand was against her at Combeside? Sir Carmichael's? Franklin's? Nurse Capstick's?"

"Lady Clarke was down on her, all right."

"Mon ami, you are full of charitable feeling towards beautiful young girls. Me, I feel charitable to sick old ladies. It may be that Lady Clarke was the clear-sighted one—and that her husband, Mr. Franklin Clarke and Nurse Capstick were all as blind as bats—and Captain Hastings.

"Realize, Hastings, that in the ordinary course of events those three separate dramas would never have touched each other. They would have pursued their course uninfluenced by each other. The permutations and combinations of life, Hastings—I never cease to be fascinated by them."

"This is Paddington," was the only answer I made.

It was time, I felt, that some one pricked the bubble.

On our arrival at Whitehaven Mansions we were told that a gentleman was waiting to see Poirot.

I expected it to be Franklin, or perhaps Japp, but to my astonishment it turned out to be none other than Donald Fraser.

He seemed very embarrassed and his inarticulateness was more noticeable than ever.

Poirot did not press him to come to the point of his visit, but instead suggested sandwiches and a glass of wine.

Until these made their appearance he monopolized the conversation, explaining where we had been, and speaking with kindliness and feeling of the invalid woman.

Not until we were finished the sandwiches and sipped the wine did he give the conversation a personal turn.

"You have come from Bexhill, Mr. Fraser?"

"Yes."

"Any success with Milly Higley?"

"Milly Higley? Milly Higley?" Fraser repeated the name wonderingly. "Oh, that girl! No, I haven't done anything there yet. It's—"

He stopped. His hands twisted themselves together nervously.

"I don't know why I've come to you," he burst out.

"I know," said Poirot.

"You can't. How can you?"

"You have come to me because there is something that you must tell to some one. You were quite right. I am the proper person. Speak!"

Poirot's air of assurance had its effect. Fraser looked at him with a queer air of grateful obedience.

"You think so?"

"*Parbleu*, I am sure of it."

"M. Poirot, do you know anything about dreams?"

It was the last thing I had expected him to say.

Poirot, however, seemed in no wise surprised.

"I do," he replied. "You have been dreaming—?"

"Yes. I suppose you'll say it's only natural that I should—should dream about—It. But it isn't an ordinary dream."

"No?"

"I've dreamed it now three nights running, sir. . . . I think I'm going mad. . . ."

"Tell me—"

The man's face was livid. His eyes were starting out of his head. As a matter of fact, he *looked* mad.

"It's always the same. I'm on the beach. Looking for Betty. She's lost—only lost, you understand. I've got to find her. I've got to give her her belt. I'm carrying it in my hand. And then—"

"Yes?"

"The dream changes . . . I'm not looking any more. She's there in front of me—sitting on the beach. She doesn't see me coming— It's—oh, I can't—"

"Go on."

Poirot's voice was authoritative—firm.

"I come up behind her . . . she doesn't hear me . . . I slip the belt round her neck and pull—oh—pull. . . ."

The agony in his voice was frightful . . . I gripped the arms of my chair. . . . The thing was too real.

"She's choking . . . she's dead . . . I've strangled her—and then her head falls back and I see her face . . . and it's *Megan* —not Betty!"

He leant back white and shaking. Poirot poured out another glass of wine and passed it over to him.

"What's the meaning of it, M. Poirot? Why does it come to me? Every night . . . ?"

"Drink up your wine," ordered Poirot.

The young man did so, then he asked in a calmer voice: "What does it mean? I—I didn't kill her, did I?"

What Poirot answered I do not know, for at that minute I heard the postman's knock and automatically I left the room.

What I took out of the letter-box banished all my interest in Donald Fraser's extraordinary revelations.

I raced back into the sitting-room.

"Poirot," I cried. "It's come. The fourth letter."

He sprang up, seized it from me, caught up his paper-knife and slit it open. He spread it out on the table.

The three of us read it together.

Still no success? Fie! Fie! What are you and the police doing? Well, well, isn't this fun? And where shall we go next for honey?

Poor Mr. Poirot. I'm quite sorry for you.

If at first you don't succeed, try, try, try again.

We've a long way to go still.

Tipperary? No—that comes farther on. Letter T.

The next little incident will take place at Doncaster on September 11th.

So long.

A.B.C.

XXI Description of a Murderer

IT WAS at this moment, I think, that what Poirot called the human element began to fade out of the picture again. It was as though, the mind being unable to stand unadulterated horror, we had had an interval of normal human interests.

We had, one and all, felt the impossibility of doing anything until the fourth letter should come revealing the projected scene of the D murder. That atmosphere of waiting had brought a release of tension.

But now, with the printed words jeering from the white stiff paper, the hunt was up once more.

Inspector Crome had come round from the Yard, and while he was still there, Franklin Clarke and Megan Barnard came in.

The girl explained that she, too, had come up from Bexhill.

"I wanted to ask Mr. Clarke something."

She seemed rather anxious to excuse and explain her procedure. I just noted the fact without attaching much importance to it.

The letter naturally filled my mind to the exclusion of all else.

Crome, was not, I think, any too pleased to see the various participants in the drama. He became extremely official and non-committal.

"I'll take this with me, M. Poirot. If you care to take a copy of it—"

"No, no, it is not necessary."

"What are your plans, inspector?" asked Clarke.

"Fairly comprehensive ones, Mr. Clarke."

"This time we've got to get him," said Clarke. "I may tell you, inspector, that we've formed an association of our own to deal with the matter. A legion of interested parties."

Inspector Crome said in his best manner:

"Oh, yes?"

"I gather you don't think much of amateurs, inspector?"

"You've hardly the same resources at your command, have you, Mr. Clarke?"

"We've got a personal axe to grind—and that's something."

"Oh, yes?"

"I fancy your own task isn't going to be too easy, inspector. In fact, I rather fancy old A.B.C. has done you again."

Crome, I had noticed, could often be goaded into speech when other methods would have failed.

"I don't fancy the public will have much to criticise in our arrangements this time," he said. "The fool has given us ample warning this time. The eleventh isn't till Wednesday of next week. That gives ample time for a publicity campaign in the press. Doncaster will be thoroughly warned. Every soul whose name begins with a D will be on his or her guard—that's so much to the good. Also, we'll draft police into the town on a fairly large scale. That's already been arranged for by consent of all the Chief Constables in England. The whole of Doncaster, police and civilians, will be out to catch one man—and with reasonable luck, we ought to get him!"

Clarke said quietly:

"It's easy to see you're not a sporting man, inspector."

Crome stared at him.

"What do you mean, Mr. Clarke?"

"Man alive, don't you realize that on next Wednesday the St. Leger is being run at Doncaster?"

The inspector's jaw dropped. For the life of him he could not bring out the familiar "Oh, yes?" Instead he said:

"That's true. Yes, that complicates matters. . . ."

"A.B.C. is no fool, even if he *is* a madman."

We were all silent for a minute or two, taking in the situation. The crowds on the race-course—the passionate, sport-loving English public—the endless complications.

Poirot murmured:

"*C'est ingénieux. Tout de même c'est bien imaginé, ça.*"

"It's my belief," said Clarke, "that the murder will take place on the race-course—perhaps actually while the Leger is being run."

For the moment his sporting instincts took a momentary pleasure in the thought. . . .

Inspector Crome rose, taking the letter with him.

"The St. Leger is a complication," he allowed. "It's unfortunate."

He went out. We heard a murmur of voices in the hallway. A minute later Thora Grey entered.

She said anxiously:

"The inspector told me there is another letter. Where this time?"

It was raining outside. Thora Grey was wearing a black coat and skirt and furs. A little black hat just perched itself on the side of her golden head.

It was to Franklin Clarke that she spoke and she came right up to him and, with a hand on his arm, waited for his answer.

"Doncaster—and on the day of the St. Leger."

We settled down to a discussion. It went without saying that we all intended to be present, but the race-meeting undoubtedly complicated the plans we had made tentatively beforehand.

A feeling of discouragement swept over me. What could this little band of six people do, after all, however strong their personal interest in the matter might be? There would be innumerable police, keen-eyed and alert, watching all likely spots. What could six more pairs of eyes do?

As though in answer to my thought, Poirot raised his voice. He spoke rather like a schoolmaster or a priest.

"*Mes enfants,*" he said, "we must not disperse the strength. We must approach this matter with method and order in our thoughts. We must look within and not without for the truth. We must say to ourselves—each one of us—what do *I* know about the murderer? And so we must build up a composite picture of the man we are going to seek."

"We know nothing about him," sighed Thora Grey helplessly.

"No, no, mademoiselle. That is not true. Each one of us knows something about him—if we only knew what it is we know. I am convinced that the knowledge is there if we could only get at it."

Clarke shook his head.

"We don't know anything—whether he's old or young, fair or dark! None of us has ever seen him or spoken to him! We've gone over everything we all know again and again."

"Not everything! For instance, Miss Grey here told us that she did not see or speak to any stranger on the day that Sir Carmichael Clarke was murdered."

Thora Grey nodded.

"That's quite right."

"Is it? Lady Clarke told us, mademoiselle, that from her window she saw you standing on the front door step talking to a man."

"She saw *me* talking to a strange man?" The girl seemed genuinely astonished. Surely that pure, limpid look could not be anything but genuine.

She shook her head.

"Lady Clarke must have made a mistake. I never— Oh!"

The exclamation came suddenly—jerked out of her. A crimson wave flooded her cheeks.

"I remember now! How stupid! I'd forgotten all about it. But it wasn't important. Just one of those men who come round selling stockings—you know, ex-Army people. They're very persistent. I had to get rid of him. I was just crossing the hall when he came to the door. He spoke to me instead of ringing but he was quite a harmless sort of person. I suppose that's why I forgot about him."

Poirot was swaying to and fro, his hands clasped to his head. He was muttering to himself with such vehemence that nobody else said anything, but stared at him instead.

"Stockings," he was murmuring. "Stockings . . . stockings . . . stockings . . . ça vient . . . stockings . . . stockings . . . It is the *motif*—yes . . . three months ago . . . and the other day . . . and now. *Bon Dieu*, I have it!"

He sat upright and fixed me with an imperious eye.

"You remember, Hastings? Andover. The shop. We go upstairs. The bedroom. On a chair. *A pair of new silk stockings.*

And now I know what it was that roused my attention two days ago. It was you, mademoiselle—" He turned on Megan. "You spoke of your mother who wept because she had bought your sister some new stockings on the very day of the murder. . . ."

He looked round on us all.

"You see? It is the same motif three times repeated. That cannot be coincidence. When mademoiselle spoke I had the feeling that what she said linked up with something. I know now with what. The words spoken by Mrs. Ascher's next-door neighbour, Mrs. Fowler. About people who were always trying to *sell* you things—and she mentioned *stockings*. Tell me, mademoiselle, it is true, is it not, that your mother bought those stockings, not at a shop, but from some one who came to the door?"

"Yes—yes—she did . . . I remember now. She said something about being sorry for these wretched men who go round and try to get orders."

"But what's the connection?" cried Franklin. "That a man came selling stockings proved nothing?"

"I tell you, my friends, it *cannot* be coincidence. Three crimes —and every time a man selling stockings and spying out the land."

He wheeled round on Thora.

"*A vous la parole!* Describe this man."

She looked at him blankly.

"I can't . . . I don't know how. . . . He had glasses, I think . . . and a shabby overcoat. . . ."

"*Mieux que ça, mademoiselle.*"

"He stooped . . . I don't know. I hardly looked at him. He wasn't the sort of man you'd notice. . . ."

Poirot said gravely:

"You are quite right, mademoiselle. The whole secret of the murders lies there in your description of the murderer—for without a doubt he *was* the murderer! '*He wasn't the sort of man you'd notice.*' Yes—there is no doubt about it. . . . You have described the murderer!"

XXII (Not from Captain Hastings' Personal Narrative)

MR. ALEXANDER BONAPARTE CUST sat very still. His breakfast lay cold and untasted on his plate. A newspaper was propped up against the teapot and it was this newspaper that Mr. Cust was reading with avid interest.

Suddenly he got up, paced to and fro for a minute, then sank into a chair by the window. He buried his head in his hands with a stifled groan.

He did not hear the sound of the opening door. His landlady, Mrs. Marbury, stood in the doorway.

"I was wondering, Mr. Cust, if you'd fancy a nice—why, whatever is it? Aren't you feeling well?"

Mr. Cust raised his head from his hands.

"Nothing. It's nothing at all, Mrs. Marbury. I'm not—feeling very well this morning."

Mrs. Marbury inspected the breakfast tray.

"So I see. You haven't touched your breakfast. Is it your head troubling you again?"

"No. At least, yes . . . I—I just feel a bit out of sorts."

"Well, I'm sorry, I'm sure. You'll not be going away to-day then?"

Mr. Cust sprang up abruptly.

"No, no. I have to go. It's business. Important. Very important."

His hands were shaking. Seeing him so agitated, Mrs. Marbury tried to soothe him.

"Well, if you must—you must. Going far this time?"

"No. I'm going to"—he hesitated for a minute or two— "Cheltenham."

There was something so peculiar about the tentative way he said the word that Mrs. Marbury looked at him in surprise.

"Cheltenham's a nice place," she said conversationally. "I went there from Bristol one year. The shops are ever so nice."

"I suppose so—yes."

Mrs. Marbury stooped rather stiffly—for stooping did not suit her figure—to pick up the paper that was lying crumpled on the floor.

"Nothing but this murdering business in the papers nowadays," she said as she glanced at the headlines before putting it back on the table. "Gives me the creeps, it does. I don't read it. It's like Jack the Ripper all over again."

Mr. Cust's lips moved, but no sound came from them.

"Doncaster—that's the place he's going to do his next murder," said Mrs. Marbury. "And to-morrow! Fairly makes your flesh creep, doesn't it? If I lived in Doncaster and my name began with a D, I'd take the first train away, that I would. I'd run no risks. What did you say, Mr. Cust?"

"Nothing, Mrs. Marbury—nothing."

"It's the races and all. No doubt he thinks he'll get his opportunity there. Hundreds of police, they say, they're drafting in and— Why, Mr. Cust, you *do* look bad. Hadn't you better have a little drop of something? Really, now, you oughtn't to go travelling to-day."

Mr. Cust drew himself up.

"It is necessary, Mrs. Marbury. I have always been punctual in my—engagements. People must have—must have confidence in you! When I have undertaken to do a thing, I carry it through. It is the only way to get on in—in—business."

"But if you're ill?"

"I am not ill, Mrs. Marbury. Just a little worried over—various personal matters. I slept badly. I am really quite all right."

His manner was so firm that Mrs. Marbury gathered up the breakfast things and reluctantly left the room.

Mr. Cust dragged out a suitcase from under the bed and began to pack. Pyjamas, sponge-bag, spare collar, leather slippers. Then unlocking a cupboard, he transferred a dozen or so flattish cardboard boxes about ten inches by seven from a shelf to the suitcase.

He just glanced at the railway guide on the table and then left the room, suitcase in hand.

Setting it down in the hall, he put on his hat and overcoat. As he did so he sighed deeply, so deeply that the girl who came out from a room at the side looked at him in concern.

"Anything the matter, Mr. Cust?"

"Nothing, Miss Lily."

"You were sighing so!"

Mr. Cust said abruptly:

"Are you at all subject to premonitions, Miss Lily? To presentiments?"

"Well, I don't know that I am, really. . . . Of course, there are days when you just feel everything's going wrong, and days when you feel everything's going right."

"Quite," said Mr. Cust.

He sighed again.

"Well, good-bye, Miss Lily. Good-bye. I'm sure you've been very kind to me always here."

"Well, don't say good-bye as though you were going away for ever," laughed Lily.

"No, no, of course not."

"See you Friday," laughed the girl. "Where are you going this time? Seaside again?"

"No, no—er—Cheltenham."

"Well, that's nice, too. But not quite as nice as Torquay. That must have been lovely. I want to go there for my holiday next year. By the way, you must have been quite near where the murder was—the A.B.C. murder. It happened while you were down there, didn't it?"

"Er—yes. But Churston's six or seven miles away."

"All the same, it must have been exciting! Why, you may have passed the murderer in the street! You may have been quite near to him!"

"Yes, I may, of course," said Mr. Cust with such a ghastly and contorted smile that Lily Marbury noticed it.

"Oh, Mr. Cust, you *don't* look well."

"I'm quite all right, quite all right. Good-bye, Miss Marbury."

He fumbled to raise his hat, caught up his suitcase and fairly hastened out of the front door.

"Funny old thing," said Lily Marbury indulgently. "Looks half batty to my mind."

Inspector Crome said to his subordinate:

"Get me out a list of all stocking manufacturing firms and circularize them. I want a list of all their agents—you know, fellows who sell on commission and tout for orders."

"This the A.B.C. case, sir?"

"Yes. One of Mr. Hercule Poirot's ideas." The inspector's tone was disdainful. "Probably nothing in it, but it doesn't do to neglect any chance, however faint."

"Right, sir. Mr. Poirot's done some good stuff in his time, but I think he's a bit gaga now, sir."

"He a mountebank," said Inspector Crome. "Always posing. Takes in some people. It doesn't take in *me*. Now then, about the arrangement for Doncaster. . . ."

Tom Hartigan said to Lily Marbury:

"Saw your old dugout this morning."

"Who? Mr. Cust?"

"Cust it was. At Euston. Looking like a lost hen, as usual. I think the fellow's half a loony. He needs some one to look after him. First he dropped his paper and then he dropped his ticket. I picked that up—he hadn't the faintest idea he'd lost it. Thanked me in an agitated sort of manner, but I don't think he recognized me."

"Oh, well," said Lily. "He's only seen you passing in the hall, and not very often at that."

They danced once round the floor.

"You dance something beautiful," said Tom.

"Go on," said Lily and wriggled yet a little closer.

They danced round again.

"Did you say Euston or Paddington?" asked Lily abruptly. "Where you saw old Cust, I mean?"

"Euston."

"Are you sure?"

"Of course I'm sure. What do you think?"

"Funny. I thought you went to Cheltenham from Paddington."

"So you do. But old Cust wasn't going to Cheltenham. He was going to Doncaster."

"Cheltenham."

"Doncaster. I know, my girl! After all, I picked up his ticket, didn't I?"

"Well, he told *me* he was going to Cheltenham. I'm sure he did."

"Oh, you've got it wrong. He was going to Doncaster all right. Some people have all the luck. I've got a bit on Firefly for the Leger and I'd love to see it run."

"I shouldn't think Mr. Cust went ro race-meetings; he doesn't look the kind. Oh, Tom, I hope he won't get murdered. It's Doncaster the A.B.C. murder's going to be."

"Cust'll be all right. His name doesn't begin with a D."

"He might have been murdered last time. He was down near Churston at Torquay when the last murder happened."

"Was he? That's a bit of a coincidence, isn't it?"

He laughed.

"He wasn't at Bexhill the time before, was he?"

Lily crinkled her brows.

"He was away. . . . Yes, I remember he was away . . . because he forgot his bathing-dress. Mother was mending it for him. And she said: 'There—Mr. Cust went away yesterday without his bathing-dress after all,' and I said: 'Oh, never mind the old bathing-dress—there's been the most awful murder,' I said, 'a girl strangled at Bexhill.'"

"Well, if he wanted his bathing-dress, he must have been going to the seaside. I say, Lily"—his face crinkled up with amusement. "What price your old dugout being the murderer himself?"

"Poor Mr. Cust? He wouldn't hurt a fly," laughed Lily.

They danced on happily—in their conscious minds nothing but the pleasure of being together.

In their unconscious minds something stirred. . . .

XXIII September 11th. Doncaster

DONCASTER!

I shall, I think, remember that 11th of September all my life.

Indeed, whenever I see a mention of the St. Leger my mind flies automatically not to horse-racing but to murder.

When I recall my own sensations, the thing that stands out most is a sickening sense of insufficiency. We were here—on the spot—Poirot, myself, Clarke, Fraser, Megan Barnard, Thora Grey and Mary Drower, and in the last resort what could any of us do?

We were building on a forlorn hope—on the chance of recognizing amongst a crowd of thousands of people a face or figure imperfectly seen on an occasion one, two or three months back.

The odds were in reality greater than that. Of us all, the only person likely to make such a recognition was Thora Grey.

Some of her serenity had broken down under the strain. Her calm, efficient manner was gone. She sat twisting her hands together, almost weeping, appealing incoherently to Poirot.

"I never really looked at him. . . . Why didn't I? What a fool I was. You're depending on me, all of you . . . and I shall let you down. Because even if I did see him again I mightn't recognize him. I've got a bad memory for faces."

Poirot, whatever he might say to me, and however harshly he might seem to criticize the girl, showed nothing but kindness now. His manner was tender in the extreme. It struck me that Poirot was no more indifferent to beauty in distress than I was.

He patted her shoulder kindly.

"Now then, *petite,* not the hysteria. We cannot have that. If you should see this man you would recognize him."

"How do you know?"

"Oh, a great many reasons—for one, because the red succeeds the black."

"What do you mean, Poirot?" I cried.

"I speak the language of the tables. At roulette there may be a long run on the black—but in the end red must turn up. It is the mathematical laws of chance."

"You mean that luck turns?"

"Exactly, Hastings. And that is where the gambler (and the murderer, who is, after all, only a supreme kind of gambler since what he risks is not his money but his life) often lacks intelligent anticipation. Because he *has* won he thinks he will *continue* to win! He does not leave the tables in good time with his pockets full. So in crime the murderer who is successful cannot conceive the possibility of not being successful! He takes to *himself* all the credit for a successful performance—but I tell you, my friends, however carefully planned, no crime can be successful without luck!"

"Isn't that going rather far?" demurred Franklin Clarke.

Poirot waved his hands excitedly.

"No, no. It is an even chance, if you like, but it must be in your favour. Consider! It might have happened that some one enters Mrs. Ascher's shop just as the murderer is leaving. That person might have thought of looking behind the counter, have seen the dead woman—and either laid hands on the murderer straight away or else been able to give such an accurate description of him to the police that he would have been arrested forthwith."

"Yes, of course, that's possible," admitted Clarke. "What it comes to is that a murderer's got to take a chance."

"Precisely. A murderer is always a gambler. And, like many gamblers, a murderer often does not know when to stop. With each crime his opinion of his own abilities is strengthened. His sense of proportion is warped. He does not say, 'I have been clever *and lucky!*' No, he says only, 'I have been clever!' And his opinion of his cleverness grows . . . and then, *mes amis,* the ball spins, and the run of colour is over—it drops into a new number and the croupier calls out *'Rouge.'*"

"You think that will happen in this case?" asked Megan, drawing her brows together in a frown.

"It *must* happen sooner or later! So far *the luck has been with the criminal*—sooner or later it must turn and be with us. I believe that it has turned! The clue of the stockings is the beginning. Now, instead of everything going *right* for him, everything will go *wrong* for him! And he, too, will begin to make mistakes. . . ."

"I will say you're heartening," said Franklin Clarke. "We all need a bit of comfort. I've had a paralyzing feeling of helplessness ever since I woke up."

"It seems to me highly problematical that we can accomplish anything of practical value," said Donald Fraser.

Megan rapped out:

"Don't be a defeatest, Don."

Mary Drower, flushing up a little, said:

"What I say is, you never know. That wicked fiend's in this place, and so are we—and after all, you do run up against people in the funniest way sometimes."

I fumed:

"If only we could do something more."

"You must remember, Hastings, that the police are doing everything reasonably possible. Special constables have been enrolled. The good Inspector Crome may have the irritating manner, but he is a very able police officer, and Colonel Anderson, the Chief Constable, is a man of action. They have taken the fullest measures for watching and patrolling the town and the race-course. There will be plain-clothes men everywhere. There is also the press campaign. The public is fully warned."

Donald Fraser shook his head.

"He'll never attempt it, I'm thinking," he said more hopefully. "The man would just be mad!"

"Unfortunately," said Clarke dryly, "he is mad! What do you think, M. Poirot? Will he give it up or will he try to carry it through?"

"In my opinion the strength of his obsession is such that he *must* attempt to carry out his promise! Not to do so would be to admit failure, and that his insane egoism would never allow.

That, I may say, is also Dr. Thompson's opinion. Our hope is that he may be caught in the attempt."

Donald shook his head again.

"He'll be very cunning."

Poirot glanced at his watch. We took the hint. It had been agreed that we were to make an all day session of it, patrolling as many streets as possible in the morning, and later, stationing ourselves at various likely points on the race-course.

I say "we." Of course, in my own case such a patrol was of little avail since I was never likely to have set eyes on A.B.C. However, as the idea was to separate so as to cover as wide an area as possible I had suggested that I should act as escort to one of the ladies.

Poirot had agreed—I am afraid with somewhat of a twinkle in his eye.

The girls went off to get their hats on. Donald Fraser was standing by the window looking out, apparently lost in thought.

Franklin Clarke glanced over at him, then evidently deciding that the other was too abstracted to count as a listener, he lowered his voice a little and addressed Poirot.

"Look here, M. Poirot. You went down to Churston, I know, and saw my sister-in-law. Did she say—or hint—I mean—did she suggest at all—?"

He stopped, embarrassed.

Poirot answered with a face of blank innocence that aroused my strongest suspicions.

"*Comment?* Did your sister-in-law say, hint or suggest—what?"

Franklin Clarke got rather red.

"Perhaps you think this isn't a time for butting in with personal things—"

"*Du tout!*"

"But I feel I'd like to get things quite straight."

"An admirable course."

This time I think Clarke began to suspect Poirot's bland face of concealing some inner amusement. He ploughed on rather heavily.

"My sister-in-law's an awfully nice woman—I've been very

"Yes. She's better."

"I find you, Hastings, singularly though transparently dishonest! All along you had made up your mind to spend the day with your blonde angel!"

"Oh, really, Poirot!"

"I am sorry to upset your plans, but I must request you to give your escort elsewhere."

"Oh, all right. I think you've got a weakness for that Dutch doll of a girl."

"The person you are to escort is Mary Drower—and I must request you not to leave her."

"But, Poirot, why?"

"Because, my dear friend, her name begins with a D. We must take no chances."

I saw the justice of his remark. At first it seemed far-fetched. But then I realized that if A.B.C. had a fanatical hatred of Poirot, he might very well be keeping himself informed of Poirot's movements. And in that case the elimination of Mary Drower might strike him as a very neat fourth stroke.

I promised to be faithful to my trust.

I went out leaving Poirot sitting in a chair near the window.

In front of him was a little roulette wheel. He spun it as I went out of the door and called after me:

"*Rouge*—that is a good omen, Hastings. The luck, it turns!"

XXIV (Not from Captain Hastings' Personal Narrative)

BELOW his breath Mr. Leadbetter uttered a grunt of impatience as his next-door neighbour got up and stumbled clumsily past him, dropping his hat over the seat in front, and leaning over to retrieve it.

All this at the culminating moment of *Not a Sparrow*, that all-star, thrilling drama of pathos and beauty that Mr. Leadbetter had been looking forward to seeing for a whole week.

The golden-haired heroine, played by Katherine Royal (in Mr. Leadbetter's opinion the leading film actress in the world), was just giving vent to a hoarse cry of indignation:

"Never. I would sooner starve. But I shan't starve. Remember those words: *not a sparrow falls—*"

Mr. Leadbetter moved his head irritably from right to left. People! Why on earth people couldn't wait till the *end* of a film . . . And to leave at this soul-stirring moment.

Ah, that was better. The annoying gentleman had passed on and out. Mr. Leadbetter had a full view of the screen and of Katherine Royal standing by the window in the Van Schreiner Mansion in New York.

And now she was boarding the train—the child in her arms. . . . What curious trains they had in America—not at all like English trains.

Ah, there was Steve again in his shack in the mountains. . . .

The film pursued its course to its emotional and semi-religious end.

Mr. Leadbetter breathed a sigh of satisfaction as the lights went up.

He rose slowly to his feet, blinking a little.

He never left the cinema very quickly. It always took him

a moment or two to return to the prosaic reality of everyday life.

He glanced round. Not many people this afternoon—naturally. They were all at the races. Mr. Leadbetter did not approve of racing or of playing cards or of drinking or of smoking. This left him more energy to enjoy going to the pictures.

Every one was hurrying towards the exit. Mr. Leadbetter prepared to follow suit. The man in the seat in front of him was asleep—slumped down in his chair. Mr. Leadbetter felt indignant to think that any one could sleep with such a drama as *Not a Sparrow* going on.

An irate gentleman was saying to the sleeping man whose legs were stretched out blocking the way:

"Excuse *me*, sir."

Mr. Leadbetter reached the exit. He looked back.

There seemed to be some sort of commotion. A commissionaire . . . a little knot of people. . . . Perhaps that man in front of him was dead drunk and not asleep. . . .

He hesitated and then passed out—and in so doing missed the sensation of the day—a greater sensation even than Not Half winning the St. Leger at 85 to 1.

The commissionaire was saying:

"Believe you're right, sir. . . . He's ill. . . . Why—what's the matter, sir?"

The other had drawn away his hand with an exclamation and was examining a red sticky smear.

"Blood. . . ."

The commissionaire gave a stifled exclamation.

He had caught sight of the corner of something yellow projecting from under the seat.

"Gor blimy!" he said. *"It's a b— A.B.C."*

XXV (Not from Captain Hastings' Personal Narrative)

MR. CUST came out of the Regal Cinema and looked up at the sky.

A beautiful evening. . . . A really beautiful evening. . . .

A quotation from Browning came into his head.

"God's in His heaven. All's right with the world."

He had always been fond of that quotation.

Only there were times, very often, when he had felt it wasn't true. . . .

He trotted along the street smiling to himself until he came to the Black Swan where he was staying.

He climbed the stairs to his bedroom, a stuffy little room on the second floor, giving over a paved inner court and garage.

As he entered the room, his smile faded suddenly. There was a stain on his sleeve near the cuff. He touched it tentatively—wet and red—blood. . . .

His hand dipped into his pocket and brought out something —a long, slender knife. The blade of that, too, was sticky and red. . . .

Mr. Cust sat there a long time.

Once his eyes shot round the room like those of a hunted animal.

His tongue passed feverishly over his lips. . . .

"It isn't my fault," said Mr. Cust.

He sounded as though he were arguing with somebody— a schoolboy pleading to his schoolmaster.

He passed his tongue over his lips again. . . .

Again, tentatively, he felt his coat sleeve.

His eyes crossed the room to the wash-basin.

A minute later he was pouring out water from the old-fashioned jug into the basin. Removing his coat, he rinsed the sleeve, carefully squeezing it out. . . .

Ugh! The water was red now. . . .

A tap on the door.

He stood there frozen into immobility—staring.

The door opened. A plump young woman—jug in hand.

"Oh, excuse me, sir. Your hot water, sir."

He managed to speak then.

"Thank you. . . . I've washed in cold. . . ."

Why had he said that? Immediately her eyes went to the basin.

He said frenziedly: "I—I've cut my hand. . . ."

There was a pause—yes, surely a very long pause—before she said: "Yes, sir."

She went out, shutting the door.

Mr. Cust stood as though turned to stone.

It had come—at last. . . .

He listened.

Were there voices—exclamations—feet mounting the stairs? He could hear nothing but the beating of his own heart. . . .

Then, suddenly, from frozen immobility he leaped into activity.

He slipped on his coat, tiptoed to the door and opened it. No noises as yet except the familiar murmur arising from the bar. He crept down the stairs. . . .

Still no one. That was luck. He paused at the foot of the stairs. Which way now?

He made up his mind, darted quickly along a passage and out by the door that gave into the yard. A couple of chauffeurs were there tinkering with cars and discussing winners and losers.

Mr. Cust hurried across the yard and out into the street.

Round the first corner to the right—then to the left—right again. . . .

Dare he risk the station?

Yes—there would be crowds there—special trains—if luck were on his side he would do it all right. . . .

If only luck were with him. . . .

XXVI (Not from Captain Hastings' Personal Narrative)

INSPECTOR CROME was listening to the excited utterances of Mr. Leadbetter.

"I assure you, inspector, my heart misses a beat when I think of it. He must actually have been sitting beside me all through the programme!"

Inspector Crome, completely indifferent to the behaviour of Mr. Leadbetter's heart, said:

"Just let me have it quite clear? This man went out towards the close of the big picture—"

"*Not a Sparrow*—Katherine Royal," murmured Mr. Leadbetter automatically.

"He passed you and in doing so stumbled—"

"He *pretended* to stumble, I see it now. Then he leaned over the seat in front to pick up his hat. He must have stabbed the poor fellow then."

"You didn't hear anything? A cry? Or a groan?"

Mr. Leadbetter had heard nothing but the loud, hoarse accents of Katherine Royal, but in the vividness of his imagination he invented a groan.

Inspector Crome took the groan at its face value and bade him proceed.

"And then he went out—"

"Can you describe him?"

"He was a very big man. Six foot at least. A giant."

"Fair or dark?"

"I—well—I'm not exactly sure. I think he was bald. A sinister-looking fellow."

"He didn't limp, did he?" asked Inspector Crome.

"Yes—yes, now you come to speak of it I think he did limp. Very dark, he might have been some kind of half-caste."

"Was he in his seat the last time the lights came up?"

"No. He came in after the big picture began."

Inspector Crome nodded, handed Mr. Leadbetter a statement to sign and got rid of him.

"That's about as bad a witness as you'll find," he remarked pessimistically. "He'd say anything with a little leading. It's perfectly clear that he hasn't the faintest idea what our man looks like. Let's have the commissionaire back."

The commissionaire, very stiff and military, came in and stood to attention, his eyes fixed on Colonel Anderson.

"Now, then, Jameson, let's hear your story."

Jameson saluted.

"Yes, sir. Close of the performance, sir. I was told there was a gentleman taken ill, sir. Gentleman was in the two and four-pennies, slumped down in his seat like. Other gentlemen standing round. Gentleman looked bad to me, sir. One of the gentlemen standing by put his hand to the ill gentleman's coat and drew my attention. Blood, sir. It was clear the gentleman was dead—stabbed, sir. My attention was drawn to an A.B.C. railway guide, sir, under the seat. Wishing to act correctly, I did not touch same, but reported to the police immediate that a tragedy had occurred."

"Very good, Jameson, you acted very properly."

"Thank you, sir."

"Did you notice a man leaving the two and fourpennies about five minutes earlier?"

"There were several, sir."

"Could you describe them?"

"Afraid not, sir. One was Mr. Geoffrey Parnell. And there was a young fellow, Sam Baker, with his young lady. I didn't notice anybody else particular."

"A pity. That'll do, Jameson."

"Yes, sir."

The commissionaire saluted and departed.

"The medical details we've got," said Colonel Anderson. "We'd better have the fellow that found him next."

A police constable came in and saluted.

"Mr. Hercule Poirot's here, sir, and another gentleman."

Inspector Crome frowned.

"Oh, well," he said. "Better have 'em in, I suppose."

XXVII The Doncaster Murder

COMING in hard on Poirot's heels, I just caught the fag end of Inspector Crome's remark.

Both he and the Chief Constable were looking worried and depressed.

Colonel Anderson greeted us with a nod of the head.

"Glad you've come, M. Poirot," he said politely. I think he guessed that Crome's remark might have reached our ears. "We've got it in the neck again, you see."

"Another A.B.C. murder?"

"Yes. Damned audacious bit of work. Man leaned over and stabbed the fellow in the back."

"Stabbed this time?"

"Yes, varies his methods a bit, doesn't he? Biff on the head, strangling, now a knife. Versatile devil—what? Here are the medical details if you care to see 'em."

He shoved a paper towards Poirot.

"A.B.C. down on the floor between the dead man's feet," he added.

"Has the dead man been identified?" asked Poirot.

"Yes. A.B.C.'s slipped up for once—if that's any satisfaction to us. Deceased's a man called Earlsfield—George Earlsfield. Barber by profession."

"Curious," commented Poirot.

"May have skipped a letter," suggested the Colonel.

My friend shook his head doubtfully.

"Shall we have in the next witness?" asked Crome. "He's anxious to get home."

"Yes, yes—let's get on."

A middle-aged gentleman strongly resembling the frog footman in *Alice in Wonderland* was led in. He was highly excited and his voice was shrill with emotion.

"Most shocking experience I have ever known," he squeaked. "I have a weak heart, sir—a very weak heart; it might have been the death of me."

"Your name, please," said the inspector.

"Downes. Roger Emmanuel Downes."

"Profession?"

"I am a master at Highfield School for boys."

"Now, Mr. Downes, will you tell us in your own words what happened."

"I can tell you that very shortly, gentlemen. At the close of the performance I rose from my seat. The seat on my left was empty but in the one beyond a man was sitting, apparently asleep. I was unable to pass him to get out as his legs were stuck out in front of him. I asked him to allow me to pass. As he did not move I repeated my request in—a—er—slightly louder tone. He still made no response. I then took him by the shoulder to waken him. His body slumped down further and I became aware that he was either unconscious or seriously ill. I called out: 'This gentleman is taken ill. Fetch the commissionaire.' The commissionaire came. As I took my hand from the man's shoulder I found it was wet and red. . . . I realized that the man had been stabbed. At the same moment the commissionaire noticed the A.B.C. railway guide. . . . I can assure you, gentlemen, the shock was terrific! Anything might have happened! For years I have suffered from cardiac weakness—"

Colonel Anderson was looking at Mr. Downes with a very curious expression.

"You can consider that you're a lucky man, Mr. Downes."

"I do, sir. Not even a palpitation!"

"You don't quite take my meaning, Mr. Downes. You were sitting two seats away, you say?"

"Actually I was sitting at first in the next seat to the murdered man—then I moved along so as to be behind an empty seat."

"You're about the same height and build as the dead man, aren't you, and you were wearing a woollen scarf round your neck just as he was?"

"I fail to see—" began Mr. Downes stiffly.

"I'm telling you, man," said Colonel Anderson, "just where your luck came in. Somehow or other, when the murderer followed you in, he got confused. He picked on the wrong back. I'll eat my hat, Mr. Downes, if that knife wasn't meant for you!"

However well Mr. Downes' heart had stood former tests, it was unable to stand up to this one. Mr. Downes sank on a chair, gasped, and turned purple in the face.

"Water," he gasped. "Water. . . ."

A glass was brought him. He sipped it whilst his complexion gradually returned to the normal.

"Me?" he said. "Why me?"

"It looks like it," said Crome. "In fact, it's the only explanation."

"You mean that this man—this—this fiend incarnate—this blood-thirsty madman has been following *me* about waiting for an opportunity?"

"I should say that was the way of it."

"But in heaven's name, why *me?*" demanded the outraged schoolmaster.

Inspector Crome struggled with the temptation to reply:

"Why not?" and said instead: "I'm afraid it's no good expecting a lunatic to have reasons for what he does."

"God bless me soul," said Mr. Downes, sobered into whispering.

He got up. He looked suddenly old and shaken.

"If you don't want me any more, gentlemen, I think I'll go home. I—I don't feel very well."

"That's quite all right, Mr. Downes. I'll send a constable with you—just to see you're all right."

"Oh, no—no, thank you. That's not necessary."

"Might as well," said Colonel Anderson gruffly.

His eyes slid sideways, asking an imperceptible question of the inspector. The latter gave an equally imperceptible nod.

Mr. Downes went out shakily.

"Just as well he didn't tumble to it," said Colonel Anderson. "There'll be a couple of them—eh?"

"Yes, sir. Your Inspector Rice has made arrangements. The house will be watched."

"You think," said Poirot, "that when A.B.C. finds out his mistake he might try again?"

Anderson nodded.

"It's a possibility," he said. "Seems a methodical sort of chap, A.B.C. It will upset him if things don't go according to programme."

Poirot nodded thoughtfully.

"Wish we could get a description of the fellow," said Colonel Anderson irritably. "We're as much in the dark as ever."

"It may come," said Poirot.

"Think so? Well, it's possible. Damn it all, hasn't any one got eyes in their head?"

"Have patience," said Poirot.

"You seem very confident, M. Poirot. Got any reason for this optimism?"

"Yes, Colonel Anderson. Up to now, the murderer has not made a mistake. He is bound to make one soon."

"If that's all you've got to go on," began the Chief Constable with a snort, but he was interrupted.

"Mr. Ball of the Black Swan is here with a young woman, sir. He reckons he's got summat to say might help you."

"Bring them along. Bring them along. We can do with anything helpful."

Mr. Ball of the Black Swan was a large, slow-thinking, heavily-moving man. He exhaled a strong odour of beer. With him was a plump young woman with round eyes clearly in a state of high excitement.

"Hope I'm not intruding or wasting valuable time," said Mr. Ball in a slow, thick voice. "But this wench, Mary here, reckons she's got something to tell as you ought to know."

Mary giggled in a half-hearted way.

"Well, my girl, what is it?" said Anderson. "What's your name?"

"Mary, sir—Mary Stroud."

"Well, Mary, out with it."

Mary turned her round eyes on her master.

"It's her business to take up hot water to the gents' bedrooms," said Mr. Ball, coming to the rescue. "About half a dozen gentle-

men we'd got staying. Some for the races and some just com-
mercials."

"Yes, yes," said Anderson impatiently.

"Get on, lass," said Mr. Ball. "Tell your tale. Nowt to be afraid
of."

Mary gasped, groaned and plunged in a breathless voice into
her narrative.

"I knocked on door and there wasn't no answer, otherwise
I wouldn't have gone in leastways not unless gentleman had
said 'Come in,' and as he didn't say nothing I went in and he
was there washing his hands."

She paused and breathed deeply.

"Go on, my girl," said Anderson.

Mary looked sideways at her master and as though receiving
inspiration from his slow nod, plunged on again.

" 'It's your hot water, sir,' I said, 'and I did knock,' but 'Oh,'
he says, 'I've washed in cold,' he said, and so, naturally, I looks
in basin, and oh! God help me, sir, *it were all red!*"

"Red?" said Anderson sharply.

Ball struck in.

"The lass told me that he had his coat off and that he was
holding the sleeve of it, and it was all wet—that's right, eh, lass?"

"Yes, sir, that's right, sir."

She plunged on:

"And his face, sir, it looked queer, mortal queer it looked.
Gave me quite a turn."

"When was this?" asked Anderson sharply.

"About a quarter after five, so near as I can reckon."

"Over three hours ago," snapped Anderson. "Why didn't you
come at once?"

"Didn't hear about it at once," said Ball. "Not till news came
along as there'd been another murder done. And then the lass
she screams out as it might have been blood in the basin, and
I asks her what she means, and she tells me. Well, it doesn't
sound right to me and I went upstairs myself. Nobody in the
room. I asks a few questions and one of the lads in courtyard
says he saw a fellow sneaking out that way and by his description it was the right one. So I says to the missus as Mary here

had best go to police. She doesn't like the idea, Mary doesn't, and I says I'll come along with her."

Inspector Crome drew a sheet of paper towards him.

"Describe this man," he said. "As quick as you can. There's no time to be lost."

"Medium-sized, he were," said Mary. "And stooped and wore glasses."

"His clothes?"

"A dark suit and a Homburg hat. Rather shabby-looking." She could add little to this description.

Inspector Crome did not insist unduly. The telephone wires were soon busy, but neither the inspector nor the Chief Constable were over optimistic.

Crome elicited the fact that the man, when seen sneaking across the yard, had had no bag or suitcase.

"There's a chance there," he said.

Two men were despatched to the Black Swan.

Mr. Ball, swelling with pride and importance, and Mary, somewhat tearful, accompanied them.

The sergeant returned about ten minutes later.

"I've brought the register, sir," he said. "Here's the signature."

We crowded round. The writing was small and cramped— not easy to read.

"A. B. Case—or is it Cash?" said the Chief Constable.

"A.B.C.," said Crome significantly.

"What about luggage?" asked Anderson.

"One good-sized suitcase, sir, full of small cardboard boxes."

"Boxes? What was in 'em?"

"Stockings, sir. Silk stockings."

Crome turned to Poirot.

"Congratulations," he said. "Your hunch was right."

XXVIII (Not from Captain Hastings' Personal Narrative)

INSPECTOR CROME was in his office at Scotland Yard.

The telephone on his desk gave a discreet buzz and he picked it up.

"Jacobs speaking, sir. There's a young fellow come in with a story that I think you ought to hear."

Inspector Crome sighed. On an average twenty people a day turned up with so-called important information about the A.B.C. case. Some of them were harmless lunatics, some of them were well-meaning persons who genuinely believed that their information was of value. It was the duty of Sergeant Jacobs to act as a human sieve—retaining the grosser matter and passing on the residue to his superior.

"Very well, Jacobs," said Crome. "Send him along."

A few minutes later there was a tap on the inspector's door and Sergeant Jacobs appeared, ushering in a tall, moderately good-looking young man.

"This is Mr. Tom Hartigan, sir. He's got something to tell us which may have a possible bearing on the A.B.C. case."

The inspector rose pleasantly and shook hands.

"Good-morning, Mr. Hartigan. Sit down, won't you? Smoke? Have a cigarette?"

Tom Hartigan sat down awkwardly and looked with some awe at what he called in his own mind "one of the bigwigs." The appearance of the inspector vaguely disappointed him. He looked quite an ordinary person!

"Now then," said Crome. "You've got something to tell us that you think may have a bearing on the case. Fire ahead."

Tom began nervously.

"Of course it may be nothing at all. It's just an idea of mine. I may be wasting your time."

Again Inspector Crome sighed imperceptibly. The amount of time he had to waste in reassuring people!

"We're the best judge of that. Let's have the facts, Mr. Hartigan."

"Well, it's like this, sir. I've got a young lady, you see, and her mother lets rooms. Up Camden Town way. Their second floor back has been let for over a year to a man called Cust."

"Cust—eh?"

"That's right, sir. A sort of middle-aged bloke what's rather vague and soft—and come down in the world a bit, I should say. Sort of creature who wouldn't hurt a fly, you'd say—and I'd never of dreamed of anything being wrong if it hadn't been for something rather odd."

In a somewhat confused manner and repeating himself once or twice, Tom described his encounter with Mr. Cust at Euston Station and the incident of the dropped ticket.

"You see, sir, look at it how you will, it's funny like. Lily, that's my young lady, sir—she was quite positive that it was Cheltenham he said, and her mother says the same—says she remembers distinct talking about it the morning he went off. Of course, I didn't pay much attention to it at the time. Lily—my young lady said as how she hoped he wouldn't cop it for this A.B.C. fellow going to Doncaster—and then she says it's rather a coincidence because he was down Churston way at the time of the last crime. Laughing like, I asks her whether he was at Bexhill the time before, and she says she don't know where he was, but he was away at the seaside—that she does know. And then I said to her it would be odd if he was the A.B.C. himself and she said poor Mr. Cust wouldn't hurt a fly—and that was all at the time. We didn't think no more about it. At least, in a sort of way I did, sir, underneath like. I began wondering about this Cust fellow and thinking that, after all, harmless as he seemed, he might be a bit batty."

Tom took a breath and then went on. Inspector Crome was listening intently now.

"And then after the Doncaster murder, sir, it was in all the papers that information was wanted as to the whereabouts of a certain A. B. Case or Cash, and it gave a description that fitted well enough. First evening off I had, I went round to Lily's and asked her what her Mr. Cust's initials were. She couldn't remember at first, but her mother did. Said they were A. B. right enough. Then we got down to it and tried to figure out if Cust had been away at the time of the first murder at Andover. Well, as you know, sir, it isn't too easy to remember things three months back. We had a job of it, but we got it fixed down in the end, because Mrs. Marbury had a brother come from Canada to see her on June twenty-first. He arrived unexpected like and she wanted to give him a bed, and Lily suggested that as Mr. Cust was away Bert Marbury might have his bed. But Mrs. Marbury wouldn't agree, because she said it wasn't acting right by her lodger, and she always liked to act fair and square. But we fixed the date all right because of Bert Marbury's ship docking at Southampton that day."

Inspector Crome had listened very attentively, jotting down an occasional note.

"That's all?" he asked.

"That's all, sir. I hope you don't think I'm making a lot of nothing."

Tom flushed slightly.

"Not at all. You were quite right to come here. Of course, it's very slight evidence—these dates may be mere coincidence and the likeness of the name, too. But it certainly warrants my having an interview with your Mr. Cust. Is he at home now?"

"Yes, sir."

"When did he return?"

"The evening of the Doncaster murder, sir."

"What's he been doing since?"

"He's stayed in mostly, sir. And he's been looking very queer, Mrs. Marbury says. He buys a lot of newspapers—goes out early and gets the morning ones, and then after dark he goes out and gets the evening ones. Mrs. Marbury says he talks a lot to himself, too. She thinks he's getting queerer."

"What is this Mrs. Marbury's address?"

Tom gave it to him.

"Thank you. I shall probably be calling round in the course

of the day. I need hardly tell you to be careful of your manner if you come across this Cust."

He rose and shook hands.

"You may be quite satisfied you did the right thing in coming to us. Good-morning, Mr. Hartigan."

"Well, sir?" asked Jacobs, re-entering the room a few minutes later. "Think it's the goods?"

"It's promising," said Inspector Crome. "That is, if the facts are as the boy stated them. We've had no luck with the stocking manufacturers yet. It was time we got hold of something. By the way, give me that file of the Churston case."

He spent some minutes looking for what he wanted.

"Ah, here it is. It's amongst the statements made to the Torquay police. Young man of the name of Hill. Deposes he was leaving the Torquay Pavilion after the film *Not a Sparrow* and noticed a man behaving queerly. He was talking to himself. Hill heard him say, 'That's an idea.' *Not a Sparrow*—that's the film that was on at the Regal in Doncaster?"

"Yes, sir."

"There may be something in that. Nothing to it at the time —but it's possible that the idea of the *modus operandi* for his next crime occurred to our man then. We've got Hill's name and address, I see. His description of the man is vague but it links up well enough with the descriptions of Mary Stroud and this Tom Hartigan. . . ."

He nodded thoughtfully.

"We're getting warm," said Inspector Crome—rather inaccurately, for he himself was always slightly chilly.

"Any instructions, sir?"

"Put on a couple of men to watch this Camden Town address, but I don't want our bird frightened. I must have a word with the A.C. Then I think it would be as well if Cust was brought along here and asked if he'd like to make a statement. It sounds as though he's quite ready to get rattled."

Outside Tom Hartigan had rejoined Lily Marbury who was waiting for him on the Embankment.

"All right, Tom?"

Tom nodded.

"I saw Inspector Crome himself. The one who's in charge of the case."

"What's he like?"

"A bit quiet and la-di-da—not my idea of a detective."

"That's Lord Trenchard's new kind," said Lily with respect. "Some of them are ever so grand. Well, what did he say?"

Tom gave her a brief résumé of the interview.

"So they think as it really was him?"

"They think it might be. Anyway, they'll come along and ask him a question or two."

"Poor Mr. Cust."

"It's no good saying poor Mr. Cust, my girl. If he's A.B.C., he's committed four terrible murders."

Lily sighed and shook her head.

"It does seem awful," she observed.

"Well, now you're going to come and have a bite of lunch, my girl. Just you think that if we're right I expect my name will be in the papers!"

"Oh, Tom, will it?"

"Rather. And yours, too. *And* your mother's. And I dare say you'll have your picture in, too."

"Oh, Tom." Lily squeezed his arm in an ecstasy.

"And in the meantime, what do you say to a bite at the Corner House?"

Lily squeezed tighter.

"Come on then!"

"All right—half a minute. I must just telephone from the station."

"Who to?"

"A girl I was going to meet."

She slipped across the road, and rejoined him three minutes later, looking rather flushed.

"Now then, Tom." She slipped her arm in his.

"Tell me more about Scotland Yard. You didn't see the other one there?"

"What other one?"

"The Belgian gentleman. The one that A.B.C. writes to always."

"No. He wasn't there."

"Well, tell me all about it. What happened when you got inside? Who did you speak to and what did you say?"

Mr. Cust put the receiver back very gently on the hook.

He turned to where Mrs. Marbury was standing in the doorway of a room, clearly devoured with curiosity.

"Not often you have a telephone call, Mr. Cust?"

"No—er—no, Mrs. Marbury. It isn't."

"Not bad news, I trust?"

"No—no." How persistent the woman was. His eye caught the legend on the newspaper he was carrying.

Births—Marriages—Deaths . . .

"My sister's just had a little boy," he blurted out.

He—who had never had a sister!

"Oh, dear! Now—well, that *is* nice, I am sure. ('And never once mentioned a sister all these years,' was her inward thought. 'If that isn't just like a man!') I was surprised, I'll tell you, when the lady asked to speak to Mr. Cust. Just at first I fancied it was my Lily's voice—something like hers, it was—but haughtier if you know what I mean—sort of high up in the air. Well, Mr. Cust, my congratulations, I'm sure. Is it the first one, or have you other little nephews and nieces?"

"It's the only one," said Mr. Cust. "The only one I've ever had or likely to have, and—er—I think I must go off at once. They—they want me to come. I—I think I can just catch a train if I hurry."

"Will you be away long, Mr. Cust?" called Mrs. Marbury as he ran up the stairs.

"Oh, no—two or three days—that's all."

He disappeared into his bedroom. Mrs. Marbury retired into the kitchen, thinking sentimentally of "the dear little mite."

Her conscience gave her a sudden twinge.

Last night Tom and Lily and all the hunting back over dates! Trying to make out that Mr. Cust was that dreadful monster, A.B.C. Just because of his initials and because of a few coincidences.

"I don't suppose they meant it seriously," she thought comfortably. "And now I hope they'll be ashamed of themselves."

In some obscure way that she could not have explained, Mr.

Cust's statement that his sister had had a baby had effectually removed any doubts Mrs. Marbury might have had of her lodger's *bona fides*.

"I hope she didn't have too bad a time of it, poor dear," thought Mrs. Marbury, testing an iron against her cheek before beginning to iron out Lily's silk slip.

Her mind ran comfortably on a well-worn obstetric track.

Mr. Cust came quietly down the stairs, a bag in his hand. His eyes rested a minute on the telephone.

That brief conversation re-echoed in his brain.

"Is that you, Mr. Cust? I thought you might like to know there's an inspector from Scotland Yard may be coming to see you. . . ."

What had he said? He couldn't remember.

"Thank you—thank you, my dear . . . very kind of you. . . ."

Something like that.

Why had she telephoned to him? Could she possibly have guessed? Or did she just want to make sure he would stay in for the inspector's visit?

But how did she know the inspector was coming?

And her voice—she'd disguised her voice from her mother. . . .

It looked—it looked—as though she *knew*. . . .

But surely if she knew, she wouldn't . . .

She might, though. Women were very queer. Unexpectedly cruel and unexpectedly kind. He'd seen Lily once letting a mouse out of a mouse trap.

A kind girl. . . .

A kind, pretty girl. . . .

He paused by the hall stand with its load of umbrellas and coats.

Should he—?

A slight noise from the kitchen decided him. . . .

No, there wasn't time. . . .

Mrs. Marbury might come out. . . .

He opened the front door, passed through and closed it behind him. . . .

Where . . . ?

XXIX At Scotland Yard

CONFERENCE again.

The Assistant Commissioner, Inspector Crome, Poirot and myself.

The A.C. was saying:

"A good tip that of yours, M. Poirot, about checking a large sale of stockings."

Poirot spread out his hands.

"It was indicated. This man could not be a regular agent. He sold outright instead of touting for orders."

"Got everything clear so far, inspector?"

"I think so, sir." Crome consulted a file. "Shall I run over the position to date?"

"Yes, please."

"I've checked up with Churston, Paignton and Torquay. Got a list of people where he went and offered stockings. I must say he did the thing thoroughly. Stayed at the Pitt, small hotel near Torre Station. Returned to the hotel at ten-thirty on the night of the murder. Could have taken a train from Churston at ten-o-five, getting to Paignton at ten-fifteen. No one answering to his description noticed on train or at stations, but that Thursday was Dartmouth Regatta and the trains back from Kingswear were pretty full.

"Bexhill much the same. Stayed at the Globe under his own name. Offered stockings to about a dozen addresses, including Mrs. Barnard and including the Ginger Cat. Left hotel early in the evening. Arrived back in London about eleven-thirty the following morning. As to Andover, same procedure. Stayed at the Feathers. Offered stockings to Mrs. Fowler, next door to Mrs. Ascher, and to half a dozen other people in the street. The pair Mrs. Ascher had I got from the niece (name of Drower) —they're identical with Cust's supply."

"So far, good," said the A.C.

"Acting on information received," said the inspector, "I went to the address given me by Hartigan, but found that Cust had left the house about half an hour previously. He received a telephone message, I'm told. First time such a thing had happened to him, so his landlady told me."

"An accomplice?" suggested the Assistant Commissioner.

"Hardly," said Poirot. "It is odd that—unless—"

We all looked at him inquiringly as he paused.

He shook his head, however, and the inspector proceeded.

"I made a thorough search of the room he had occupied. That search puts the matter beyond doubt. I found a block of notepaper similar to that on which the letters were written, a large quantity of hosiery and—at the back of the cupboard where the hosiery was stored—a parcel much the same shape and size but which turned out to contain—not hosiery—but eight new A.B.C. railway guides!"

"Proof positive," said the Assistant Commissioner.

"I've found something else, too," said the inspector—his voice becoming suddenly almost human with triumph. "Only found it this morning, sir. Not had time to report yet. There was no sign of the knife in his room—"

"It would be the act of an imbecile to bring that back with him," remarked Poirot.

"After all, he's not a reasonable human being," remarked the inspector. "Anyway, it occurred to me that he might just possibly have brought it back to the house and then realized the danger of hiding it (as M. Poirot points out) in his room, and have looked about elsewhere. What place in the house would he be likely to select? I got it straightaway. *The hall stand*—no one ever moves a hall stand. With a lot of trouble I got it moved out from the wall—and there it was!"

"The knife?"

"The knife. Not a doubt of it. The dried blood's still on it."

"Good work, Crome," said the A.C. approvingly. "We only need one thing more now."

"What's that?"

"The man himself."

"We'll get him, sir. Never fear."

The inspector's tone was confident.

"What do you say, M. Poirot?"

Poirot started out of a reverie.

"I beg your pardon?"

"We are saying that it was only a matter of time before we got our man. Do you agree?"

"Oh, that—yes. Without a doubt."

His tone was so abstracted that the others looked at him curiously.

"Is there anything worrying you, M. Poirot?"

"There is something that worries me very much. It is the *why?* The *motive.*"

"But, my dear fellow, the man's crazy," said the Assistant Commissioner impatiently.

"I understand what M. Poirot means," said Crome, coming graciously to the rescue. "He's quite right. There's got to be some definite obsession. I think we'll find the root of the matter in an intensified inferiority complex. There may be persecution mania, too, and if so he may possibly associate M. Poirot with it. He may have the delusion that M. Poirot is a detective employed on purpose to hunt him down."

"H'm," said the A.C. "That's the jargon that's talked nowadays. In my day if a man was mad he was mad and we didn't look about for scientific terms to soften it down. I suppose a thoroughly up-to-date doctor would suggest putting a man like A.B.C. in a nursing home, telling him what a fine fellow he was for forty-five days on end and then letting him out as a responsible member of society."

Poirot smiled but did not answer.

The conference broke up.

"Well," said the Assistant Commissioner. "As you say, Crome, pulling him in is only a matter time."

"We'd have had him before now," said the inspector, "if he wasn't so ordinary-looking. We've worried enough perfectly inoffensive citizens as it is."

"I wonder where he is at this minute," said the Assistant Commissioner.

XXX (Not from Captain Hastings' Personal Narrative)

MR. CUST stood by a greengrocer's shop.

He stared across the road.

Yes, that was it.

Mrs. Ascher. News agent and Tobacconist. . . .

In the empty window was a sign.

To Let.

Empty. . . .

Lifeless. . . .

"Excuse me, sir."

The greengrocer's wife, trying to get at some lemons.

He apologized, moved to one side.

Slowly he shuffled away—back towards the main street of the town. . . .

It was difficult—very difficult—now that he hadn't any money left. . . .

Not having had anything to eat all day made one feel very queer and light-headed. . . .

He looked at a poster outside a newsagent's shop.

The A.B.C. Case. Murderer Still at Large. Interview with Hercule Poirot.

Mr. Cust said to himself:

"Hercule Poirot. I wonder if *he* knows. . . ."

He walked on again.

It wouldn't do to stand staring at that poster. . . .

He thought:

"I can't go on much longer. . . ."

Foot in front of foot . . . what an odd thing walking was. . . .

Foot in front of foot—ridiculous.

Highly ridiculous. . . .

But man was a ridiculous animal anyway. . . .

And he, Alexander Bonaparte Cust, was particularly ridiculous. . . .

He always had been. . . .

People had always laughed at him. . . .

He couldn't blame them. . . .

Where was he going? He didn't know. He'd come to the end. He no longer looked anywhere but at his feet.

Foot in front of foot. . . .

He looked up. Lights in front of him. And letters . . . .

Police Station.

"That's funny," said Mr. Cust. He gave a little giggle.

Then he stepped inside. Suddenly, as he did so, he swayed and fell forward.

XXXI Hercule Poirot Asks Questions

IT WAS a clear November day. Dr. Thompson and Chief Inspector Japp had come round to acquaint Poirot with the result of the police court proceedings in the case of Rex *v.* Alexander Bonaparte Cust.

Poirot himself had had a slight bronchial chill which had prevented his attending. Fortunately he had not insisted on having my company.

"Committed for trial," said Japp. "So that's that."

"Isn't it unusual?" I asked, "for a defence to be offered at this stage? I thought prisoners always reserved their defence."

"It's the usual course," said Japp. "I suppose young Lucas thought he might rush it through. He's a trier, I will say. Insanity's the only defence possible."

Poirot shrugged his shoulders.

"With insanity there can be no acquittal. Imprisonment during His Majesty's pleasure is hardly preferable to death."

"I suppose Lucas thought there was a chance," said Japp. "With a first-class alibi for the Bexhill murder, the whole case might be weakened. I don't think he realized how strong our case is. Anyway, Lucas goes in for originality. He's a young man, and he wants to hit the public eye."

Poirot turned to Thompson.

"What's your opinion, doctor?"

"Of Cust? Upon my soul, I don't know what to say. He's playing the sane man remarkably well. He's an epileptic, of course."

"What an amazing dénouement that was," I said.

"His falling into the Andover police station in a fit? Yes—it was a fitting dramatic curtain to the drama. A.B.C. had always timed his effects well."

Take time
to smell
the flowers.

"Is it possible to commit a crime and be unaware of it?" I asked. "His denials seem to have a ring of truth in them."

Dr. Thompson smiled a little.

"You mustn't be taken in by that theatrical 'I swear by God' pose. It's my opinion that Cust knows perfectly well he committed the murders."

"When they're as fervent as that they usually do," said Crome.

"As to your question," went on Thompson, "it's perfectly possible for an epileptic subject in a state of somnambulism to commit an action and be entirely unaware of having done so. But it is the general opinion that such an action must 'not be contrary to the will of the person in the waking state.'"

He went on discussing the matter, speaking of *grand mal* and *petit mal* and, to tell the truth, confusing me hopelessly as is often the case when a learned person holds forth on his own subject.

"However, I'm against the theory that Cust committed these crimes without knowing he'd done them. You might put that theory forward if it weren't for the letters. The letters knock the theory on the head. They show premeditation and a careful planning of the crime."

"And of the letters we have still no explanation," said Poirot.

"That interests you?"

"Naturally—since they were written to me. And on the subject of the letters Cust is persistently dumb. Until I get at the reason for those letters being written to me, I shall not feel that the case is solved."

"Yes—I can understand that from your point of view. There doesn't seem to be any reason to believe that the man ever came up against you in any way?"

"None whatever."

"I might make a suggestion. Your name!"

"My name?"

"Yes. Cust is saddled—apparently by the whim of his mother (Œdipus complex there, I shouldn't wonder!)—with two extremely bombastic Christian names: Alexander and Bonaparte. You see the implications? Alexander—the popularly supposed undefeatable who sighed for more world to conquer. Bonaparte

—the great Emperor of the French. He wants an adversary—
an adversary, one might say, in his class. Well—there you are—
Hercules the strong."

"Your words are very suggestive, doctor. They foster
ideas. . . ."

"Oh, it's only a suggestion. Well, I must be off."

Dr. Thompson went out. Japp remained.

"Does this alibi worry you?" Poirot asked.

"It does a little," admitted the inspector. "Mind you, I don't believe in it, because I know it isn't true. But it is going to be the
deuce to break it. This man Strange is a tough character."

"Describe him to me."

"He's a man of forty. A tough, confident, self-opinionated
mining engineer. It's my opinion that it was he who insisted on
his evidence being taken now. He wants to get off to Chile. He
hoped the thing might be settled out of hand."

"He's one of the most positive people I've ever seen," I said.

"The type of man who would not like to admit he was mistaken," said Poirot thoughtfully.

"He sticks to his story and he's not one to be heckled. He
swears by all that's blue that he picked up Cust in the Whitecross
Hotel at Eastbourne on the evening of July 24th. He was lonely
and wanted some one to talk to. As far as I can see, Cust made
an ideal listener. He didn't interrupt! After dinner he and Cust
played dominoes. It appears Strange was a whale on
dominoes and to his surprise Cust was pretty hot stuff too.
Queer game, dominoes. People go mad about it. They'll play
for hours. That's what Strange and Cust did apparently. Cust
wanted to go to bed but Strange wouldn't hear of it—swore they'd
keep it up until midnight at least. And that's what they did do.
They separated at ten minutes past midnight. And if Cust was
in the Whitecross Hotel at Eastbourne at ten minutes past midnight on the morning of the twenty-fifth he couldn't very well be
strangling Betty Barnard on the beach at Bexhill between midnight and one o'clock."

"The problem certainly seems insuperable," said Poirot
thoughtfully. "Decidedly, it gives one to think."

"It's given Crome something to think about," said Japp.

"This man Strange is very positive?"

"Yes. He's an obstinate devil. And it's difficult to see just where the flaw is. Supposing Strange is making a mistake and the man wasn't Cust—why on earth should he *say* his name is Cust? And the writing in the hotel register is his all right. You can't say he's an accomplice—homicidal lunatics don't have accomplices! Did the girl die later? The doctor was quite firm in his evidence, and anyway it would take some time for Cust to get out of the hotel at Eastbourne without being seen and get over to Bexhill—fourteen miles away—"

"It is a problem—yes," said Poirot.

"Of course, strictly speaking, it oughtn't to matter. We've got Cust on the Doncaster murder—the blood-stained coat, the knife—not a loophole there. You couldn't bounce any jury into acquitting him. But it spoils a pretty case. He did the Doncaster murder. He did the Churston murder. He did the Andover murder. Then, by hell, he *must* have done the Bexhill murder. But I don't see how!"

He shook his head and got up.

"Now's your chance, M. Poirot," he said. "Crome's in a fog. Exert those cellular arrangements of yours I used to hear so much about. Show us the way he did it."

Japp departed.

"What about it, Poirot?" I said. "Are the little grey cells equal to the task?"

Poirot answered my question by another.

"Tell me, Hastings, do you consider the case ended?"

"Well—yes, practically speaking. We've got the man. And we've got most of the evidence. It's only the trimmings that are needed."

Poirot shook his head.

"The case is ended! The case! The case is the *man*, Hastings. Until we know all about the man, the mystery is as deep as ever. It is not victory because we have put him in the dock!"

"We know a fair amount about him."

"We know nothing at all! We know where he was born. We know he fought in the war and received a slight wound in the head and that he was discharged from the Army owing to epilepsy. We know that he lodged with Mrs. Marbury for nearly two years. We know that he was quiet and retiring—the sort of man that nobody notices. We know that he invented and carried out an intensely clever scheme of systemized murder. We know that he made certain incredibly stupid blunders. We know that he killed without pity and quite ruthlessly. We know, too, that he was kindly enough not to let blame rest on any other person for the crimes he committed. If he wanted to kill unmolested—how easy to let other persons suffer for his crimes. Do you not see, Hastings, that the man is a mass of contradictions? Stupid and cunning, ruthless and magnanimous—and that there must be some dominating factor that reconciles his two natures."

"Of course, if you treat him like a psychological study," I began.

"What else has the case been since the beginning? All along I have been groping my way—trying to get to know the murderer. And now I realize, Hastings, that I do not know him at all! I am at sea."

"The lust for power—" I began.

"Yes—that might explain a good deal. . . . But it does not satisfy me. There are things I want to know. *Why* did he commit these murders? *Why* did he choose those particular people—?"

"Alphabetically—" I began.

"Was Betty Barnard the only person in Bexhill whose name began with a B? Betty Barnard—I had an idea there. . . . It ought to be true—it must be true. But if so—"

He was silent for some time. I did not like to interrupt him.

As a matter of fact, I believe I fell asleep.

I woke to find Poirot's hand on my shoulder.

"Mon cher Hastings," he said affectionately. "My good genius."

I was quite confused by this sudden mark of esteem.

"It is true," Poirot insisted. "Always—always—you help me—you bring me luck. You inspire me."

"How have I inspired you this time?" I asked.

"While I was asking myself certain questions I remembered a remark of yours—a remark absolutely shimmering in its clear vision. Did I not say to you once that you had a genius for stating the obvious. It is the obvious that I have neglected."

"What is this brilliant remark of mine?" I asked.

"It makes everything as clear as crystal. I see the answers to all my questions. The reason for Mrs. Ascher (that, it is true, I glimpsed long ago), the reason for Sir Carmichael Clarke, the reason for the Doncaster murder, and finally and supremely important, the reason for Hercule Poirot."

"Could you kindly explain?" I asked.

"Not at the moment. I require first a little more information. That I can get from our Special Legion. And then—then, when I have got the answer to a certain question, I will go and see A.B.C. We will be face to face at last—A.B.C. and Hercule Poirot—the adversaries."

"And then?" I asked.

"And then," said Poirot, "we will talk! *Je vous assure, Hastings*—there is nothing so dangerous for any one who has something to hide as conversation! Speech, so a wise old Frenchman said to me once, is an invention of man's to prevent him from thinking. It is also an infallible means of discovering that which he wishes to hide. A human being, Hastings, cannot resist the opportunity to reveal himself and express his personality which conversation gives him. Every time he will give himself away."

"What do you expect Cust to tell you?"

Hercule Poirot smiled.

"A lie," he said. "And by it, I shall know the truth!"

XXXII And Catch a Fox

DURING the next few days Poirot was very busy. He made mysterious absences, talked very little, frowned to himself, and consistently refused to satisfy my natural curiosity as to the brilliance I had, according to him, displayed in the past.

I was not invited to accompany him on his mysterious comings and goings—a fact which I somewhat resented.

Towards the end of the week, however, he announced his intention of paying a visit to Bexhill and neighbourhood and suggested that I should come with him. Needless to say, I accepted with alacrity.

The invitation, I discovered, was not extended to me alone. The members of our Special Legion were also invited.

They were as intrigued by Poirot as I was. Nevertheless, by the the end of the day, I had at any rate an idea as to the direction in which Poirot's thoughts were tending.

He first visited Mr. and Mrs. Barnard and got an exact account from her as to the hour at which Mr. Cust had called on her and exactly what he had said. He then went to the hotel at which Cust had put up and extracted a minute description of that gentleman's departure. As far as I could judge, no new facts were elicited by his questions but he himself seemed quite satisfied.

Next he went to the beach—to the place where Betty Barnard's body had been discovered. Here he walked round in circles for some minutes studying the shingle attentively. I could see little point in this, since the tide covered the spot twice a day.

However I have learnt by this time that Poirot's actions are usually dictated by an idea—however meaningless they may seem.

He then walked from the beach to the nearest point at which a car could have been parked. From there again he went to the place where the Eastbourne buses waited before leaving Bexhill.

Finally he took us all to the Ginger Cat café, where we had

a somewhat stale tea served by the plump waitress, Milly Higley.

Her he complimented in a flowing Gallic style on the shape of her ankles.

"The legs of the English—always they are too thin! But you, mademoiselle, have the perfect leg. It has shape—it has an ankle!"

Milly Higley giggled a good deal and told him not to go on so. She knew what French gentlemen were like.

Poirot did not trouble to contradict her mistake as to his nationality. He merely ogled her in such a way that I was startled and almost shocked.

"*Voilà*," said Poirot, "I have finished in Bexhill. Presently I go to Eastbourne. One little inquiry there—that is all. Unnecessary for you all to accompany me. In the meantime come back to the hotel and let us have a cocktail. That Carlton tea, it was abominable!"

As we were sipping our cocktails Franklin Clarke said curiously:

"I suppose we can guess what you are after? You're out to break that alibi. But I can't see what you're so pleased about. You haven't got a new fact of any kind."

"No—that is true."

"Well, then?"

"Patience. Everything arranges itself, given time."

"You seem quite pleased with yourself anyway."

"Nothing so far has contradicted my little idea—that is why." His face grew serious.

"My friend Hastings told me once that he had, as a young man, played a game called The Truth. It was a game where every one in turn was asked three questions—two of which must be answered truthfully. The third one could be barred. The questions, naturally, were of the most indiscreet kind. But to begin with every one had to swear that they would indeed speak the truth, the whole truth, and nothing but the truth."

He paused.

"Well?" said Megan.

"*Eh bien*—me, I want to play that game. Only it is not necessary to have three questions. One will be enough. One question to each of you."

"Of course," said Clarke impatiently. "We'll answer anything."

"Ah, but I want it to be more serious than that. Do you all swear to speak the truth?"

He was so solemn about it that the others, puzzled, became solemn themselves. They all swore as he demanded.

"*Bon*," said Poirot briskly. "Let us begin—"

"I'm ready," said Thora Grey.

"Ah, but ladies first—this time it would not be the politeness. We will start elsewhere."

He turned to Franklin Clarke.

"What, *mon cher M. Clarke,* did you think of the hats the ladies wore at Ascot this year?"

Franklin Clarke stared at him.

"Is this a joke?"

"Certainly not."

"Is that seriously your question?"

"It is."

Clarke began to grin.

"Well, M. Poirot, I didn't actually go to Ascot, but from what I could see of them driving in cars, women's hats for Ascot were an even bigger joke than the hats they wear ordinarily."

"Fantastic?"

"Quite fantastic."

Poirot smiled and turned to Donald Fraser.

"When did you take your holiday this year, monsieur?"

It was Fraser's turn to stare.

"My holiday? The first two weeks in August."

His face quivered suddenly. I guessed that the question had brought the loss of the girl he loved back to him.

Poirot, however, did not seem to pay much attention to the reply. He turned to Thora Grey and I heard the slight difference in his voice. It had tightened up. His question came sharp and clear.

"Mademoiselle, in the event of Lady Clarke's death, would you have married Sir Carmichael if he had asked you?"

The girl sprang up.

"How dare you ask me such a question. It's—it's insulting!"

"Perhaps. But you have sworn to speak the truth. *Eh bien—* Yes or no?"

"Sir Carmichael was wonderfully kind to me. He treated me almost like a daughter. And that's how I felt to him—just affectionate and grateful."

"Pardon me, but that is not answering Yes or No, mademoiselle."

She hesitated.

"The answer, of course, is no!"

He made no comment.

"Thank you, mademoiselle."

He turned to Megan Barnard. The girl's face was very pale. She was breathing hard as though braced up for an ordeal.

Poirot's voice came out like the crack of a whip lash.

"Mademoiselle, what do you hope will be the result of my investigations? Do you want me to find out the truth—or not?"

Her head went back proudly. I was fairly sure of her answer. Megan, I knew, had a fanatical passion for truth.

Her answer came clearly—and it stupefied me.

"No!"

We all jumped. Poirot leant forward, studying her face.

"Mademoiselle Megan," he said, "you may not want the truth but—*ma foi*—you can speak it!"

He turned towards the door, then, recollecting, went to Mary Drower.

"Tell me, *mon enfant*, have you a young man?"

Mary, who had been looking apprehensive, looked startled and blushed.

"Oh, Mr. Poirot. I—I—well, I'm not sure."

He smiled.

"*Alors c'est bien, mon enfant.*"

He looked round for me.

"Come, Hastings, we must start for Eastbourne."

The car was waiting and soon we were driving along the coast road that leads through Pevensey to Eastbourne.

"Is it any use asking you anything, Poirot?"

"Not at this moment. Draw your own conclusions as to what I am doing."

I relapsed into silence.

Poirot, who seemed pleased with himself, hummed a little

tune. As we passed through Pevensey he suggested that we stop and have a look over the castle.

As we were returning towards the car, we paused a moment to watch a ring of children—Brownies, I guessed, by their get-up—who were singing a ditty in shrill, untuneful voices. . . .

"What is it that they say, Hastings? I cannot catch the words."

I listened—till I caught one refrain.

> "—And catch a fox
> And put him in a box
> And never let him go."

"And catch a fox and put him in a box and never let him go!" repeated Poirot.

His face had gone suddenly grave and stern.

"It is very terrible that, Hastings." He was silent a minute. "You hunt the fox here?"

"I don't. I've never been able to afford to hunt. And I don't think there's much hunting in this part of the world."

"I meant in England generally. A strange sport. The waiting at the covert side—then they sound the tally-ho, do they not?—and the run begins—across the country—over the hedges and ditches—and the fox he runs—and sometimes he doubles back—but the dogs—"

"Hounds!"

"—hounds are on his trail, and at last they catch him and he dies—quickly and horribly."

"I suppose it does sound cruel, but really—"

"The fox enjoys it? Do not say les bêtises, my friend. Tout de même—it is better that—the quick, cruel death—than what those children were singing. . . .

"To be shut away—in a box—for ever. . . . No, it is not good, that."

He shook his head. Then he said, with a change of tone:

"To-morrow, I am to visit the man Cust," and he added to the chauffeur:

"Back to London."

"Aren't you going to Eastbourne?" I cried.

"What need? I know—quite enough for my purpose."

XXXIII   Alexander Bonaparte Cust

I WAS not present at the interview that took place between Poirot and that strange man—Alexander Bonaparte Cust. Owing to his association with the police and the peculiar circumstances of the case, Poirot had no difficulty in obtaining a Home Office order —but that order did not extend to me, and in any case it was essential, from Poirot's point of view, that that interview should be absolutely private—the two men face to face.

He has given me, however, such a detailed account of what passed between them that I set it down with as much confidence on paper as though I had actually been present.

Mr. Cust seemed to have shrunk. His stoop was more apparent. His fingers plucked vaguely at his coat.

For some time, I gather, Poirot did not speak.

He sat and looked at the man opposite him.

The atmosphere became restful—soothing—full of infinite leisure. . . .

It must have been a dramatic moment—this meeting of the two adversaries in the long drama. In Poirot's place I should have felt the dramatic thrill.

Poirot, however, is nothing if not matter-of-fact. He was absorbed in producing a certain effect upon the man opposite him.

At last he said gently:

"Do you know who I am?"

The other shook his head.

"No—no—I can't say I do. Unless you are Mr. Lucas's— what do they call it?—junior. Or perhaps you come from Mr. Maynard?"

(Maynard and Cole were the defending solicitors.)

His tone was polite but not very interested. He seemed absorbed in some inner abstraction.

"I am Hercule Poirot. . . ."

Poirot said the words very gently . . . and watched for the effect.

Mr. Cust raised his head a little.

"Oh, yes?"

He said it as naturally as Inspector Crome might have said it—but without the superciliousness.

Then, a minute later, he repeated his remark.

"Oh, yes?" he said, and this time his tone was different—it held an awakened interest. He raised his head and looked at Poirot.

Hercule Poirot met his gaze and nodded his own head gently once or twice.

"Yes," he said. "I am the man to whom you wrote the letters."

At once the contact was broken. Mr. Cust dropped his eyes and spoke irritably and fretfully.

"I never wrote to you. Those letters weren't written by me. I've said so again and again."

"I know," said Poirot. "But if you did not write them, who did?"

"An enemy. I must have an enemy. They are all against me. The police—every one—all against me. It's a gigantic conspiracy."

Poirot did not reply.

Mr. Cust said:

"Every one's hand has been against me—always."

"Even when you were a child?"

Mr. Cust seemed to consider.

"No—no—not exactly then. My mother was very fond of me. But she was ambitious—terribly ambitious. That's why she gave me those ridiculous names. She had some absurd idea that I'd cut a figure in the world. She was always urging me to assert myself—talking about will power . . . saying any one could be master of his fate . . . she said I could do anything!"

He was silent for a minute.

"She was quite wrong, of course. I realized that myself quite soon. I wasn't the sort of person to get on in life. I was always doing foolish things—making myself look ridiculous. And I was timid—afraid of people. I had a bad time at school—the boys found out my Christian names—they used to tease me about them. . . . I did very badly at school—in games and work and everything."

He shook his head.

"Just as well poor mother died. She'd have been disappointed. . . . Even when I was at the Commercial College I was stupid—it took me longer to learn typing and shorthand than any one else. And yet I didn't *feel* stupid—if you know what I mean."

He cast a sudden appealing look at the other man.

"I know what you mean," said Poirot. "Go on."

"It was just the feeling that everybody else *thought* me stupid. Very paralyzing. It was the same thing later in the office."

"And later still—in the war?" prompted Poirot.

Mr. Cust's face lightened up suddenly.

"You know," he said, "I enjoyed the war. What I had of it, that was. I felt, for the first time, a man like anybody else. We were all in the same box. I was as good as any one else."

His smile faded.

"And then I got that wound on the head. Very slight. But they found out I had fits. . . . I'd always known, of course, that there were times when I hadn't been quite sure what I was doing. Lapses, you know. And of course, once or twice I'd fallen down. But I don't really think they ought to have discharged me for that. No, I don't think it was right."

"And afterwards?" asked Poirot.

"I got a place as a clerk. Of course there was good money to be got just then. And I didn't do so badly after the war. Of course, a smaller salary. . . . And—I didn't seem to get on. I was always being passed over for promotion. I wasn't go-ahead enough. It grew very difficult—really very difficult. . . . Especially when the slump came. To tell you the truth, I'd got hardly enough to keep body and soul together (and you've got to look presentable as a clerk) when I got the offer of this stocking job. A salary and commission!"

Poirot said gently:

"But you are aware, are you not, that the firm whom you say employed you deny the fact?"

Mr. Cust got excited again.

"That's because they're in the conspiracy—they must be in the conspiracy."

He went on:

"I've got written evidence—written evidence. I've got their letters to me, giving me instructions as to what places to go to and a list of people to call on."

"Not *written* evidence exactly—*typewritten* evidence."

"It's the same thing. Naturally a big firm of wholesale manufacturers typewrite their letters."

"Don't you know, Mr. Cust, that a typewriter can be identified? All those letters were typed by one particular machine."

"What of it?"

"And that machine was your own—the one found in your room."

"It was sent me by the firm at the beginning of my job."

"Yes, but these letters were received afterwards. So it looks, does it not, as though you typed them yourself and posted them to yourself?"

"No, no! It's all part of the plot against me!"

He added suddenly:

"Besides, their letters would be written on the same kind of machine."

"The same *kind,* but not the same *actual* machine."

Mr. Cust repeated obstinately:

"It's a plot!"

"And the A.B.C.'s that were found in the cupboard?"

"I know nothing about them. I thought they were all stockings."

"Why did you tick off the name of Mrs. Ascher in that first list of people in Andover?"

"Because I decided to start with her. One must begin somewhere."

"Yes, that is true. *One must begin somewhere.*"

"I don't mean that!" said Mr. Cust. "I don't mean what you mean!"

"But you know what I meant?"

Mr. Cust said nothing. He was trembling.

"I didn't do it!" he said. "I'm perfectly innocent! It's all a mistake. Why, look at that second crime—that Bexhill one. I was playing dominoes at Eastbourne. You've got to admit that!"

His voice was triumphant.

"Yes," said Poirot. His voice was meditative—silky. "But it's so easy, isn't it, to make a mistake of one day? And if you're an obstinate, positive man, like Mr. Strange, you'll never consider the possibility of having been mistaken. What you've said you'll stick to. . . . He's that kind of man. And the hotel register—it's very easy to put down the wrong date when you're signing it—probably no one will notice it at the time."

"I was playing dominoes that evening!"

"You play dominoes very well, I believe."

Mr. Cust was a little flurried by this.

"I—I—well, I believe I do."

"It is a very absorbing game, is it not, with a lot of skill in it?"

"Oh, there's a lot of play in it—a lot of play! We used to play a lot in the city, in the lunch hour. You'd be surprised the way total strangers come together over a game of dominoes."

He chuckled.

"I remember one man—I've never forgotten him because of something he told me—we just got talking over a cup of coffee, and we started dominoes. Well, I felt after twenty minutes that I'd known that man all his life."

"What was it that he told you?" asked Poirot.

Mr. Cust's face clouded over.

"It gave me a turn—a nasty turn. Talking of your fate being written in your hand, he was. And he showed me his hand and the lines that showed he'd have two near escapes of being drowned—and he had had two near escapes. And then he looked at mine and he told me some amazing things. Said I was going to be one of the most celebrated men in England before I died. Said the whole country would be talking about me. But he said—he said. . . ."

Mr. Cust broke down—faltered. . . .

"Yes?"

Poirot's gaze held a quiet magnetism. Mr. Cust looked at him, looked away, then back again like a fascinated rabbit.

"He said—he said—that it looked as though I might die a violent death—and he laughed and said: 'Almost looks as though you might die on the scaffold,' and then he laughed and said that was only his joke. . . ."

He was silent suddenly. His eyes left Poirot's face—they ran from side to side. . . .

"My head—I suffer very badly with my head . . . the headaches are something cruel sometimes. And then there are times when I don't know—when I don't know. . . ."

He broke down.

Poirot leant forward. He spoke very quietly but with great assurance.

"But you do know, don't you," he said, "that you committed the murders?"

Mr. Cust looked up. His glance was quite simple and direct. All resistance had left him. He looked strangely at peace.

"Yes," he said. "I know."

"But—I'm right, am I not?—you don't know why you did them?"

Mr. Cust shook his head.

"No," he said. "I don't."

XXXIV Poirot Explains

WE WERE sitting in a state of tense attention to listen to Poirot's final explanation of the case.

"All along," he said, "I have been worried over the *why* of this case. Hastings said to me the other day that the case was ended. I replied to him that the case was the *man!* The mystery was *not the mystery of the murders,* but the *mystery of A.B.C.* Why did he find it necessary to commit these murders? Why did he select *me* as his adversary?

"It is no answer to say that the man was mentally unhinged. To say a man does mad things because he is mad is merely unintelligent and stupid. A madman is as logical and reasoned in his actions as a sane man—given his peculiar biased point of view. For example, if a man insists on going out and squatting about in nothing but a loin cloth his conduct seems eccentric in the extreme. But once you know that the man himself is firmly convinced that he is Mahatma Gandhi, then his conduct becomes perfectly reasonable and logical.

"What was necessary in this case was to imagine a mind so constituted that it was logical and reasonable to commit four or more murders and to announce them beforehand by letters written to Hercule Poirot.

"My friend, Hastings, will tell you that from the moment I received the first letter I was upset and disturbed. It seemed to me at once that there was something very wrong about the letter."

"You were quite right," said Franklin Clarke dryly.

"Yes. But there, at the very start, I made a grave error. I permitted my feeling—my very strong feeling about the letter to remain a mere impression. I treated it as though it had been an intuition. In a well-balanced, reasoning mind there is no such thing as an intuition—an inspired guess! You *can* guess, of course—and a guess is either right or wrong. If it is right you call it an intuition. If it is wrong you usually do not speak of it again. But what is often called an intuition is really an impression based on logical deduction or experience. When an expert feels that there is something wrong about a picture or a piece of furniture or the signature on a cheque he is really basing that feeling on a host of small signs and details. He has no need to go into them minutely—his experience obviates that—the net result is the definite impression that something is wrong. But it is not a *guess,* it is an impression based on *experience.*

"*Eh bien,* I admit that I did not regard that first letter in the way I should. It just made me extremely uneasy. The police regarded it as a hoax. I myself took it seriously. I was convinced that a murder would take place in Andover as stated. As you know, a murder *did* take place.

"There was no means at that point, as I well realized, of knowing who the *person* was who had done the deed. The only course open to me was to try and understand just what *kind* of a person had done it.

"I had certain indications. The letter—the manner of the crime—the person murdered. What I had to discover was: the motive of the crime, the motive of the letter."

"Publicity," suggested Clarke.

"Surely an inferiority complex covers that," added Thora Grey.

"That was, of course, the obvious line to take. But why me? Why Hercule Poirot? Greater publicity could be ensured by sending the letters to Scotland Yard. More again by sending them to a newspaper. A newspaper might not print the first letter, but by the time the second crime took place, A.B.C. could have been assured of all the publicity the press could give. Why, then, Hercule Poirot? Was it for some personal reason? There was, discernible in the letter, a slight anti-foreign bias—but not enough to explain the matter to my satisfaction.

"Then the second letter arrived—and was followed by the murder of Betty Barnard at Bexhill. It became clear now (what I had already suspected) that the murders were to proceed on an alphabetical plan, but that fact, which seemed final to most people, left the main question unaltered to my mind. Why did A.B.C. *need* to commit these murders?"

Megan Barnard stirred in her chair.

"Isn't there such a thing as—as a blood lust?" she said.

Poirot turned to her.

"You are quite right, mademoiselle. There *is* such a thing. The lust to kill. But that did not quite fit the facts of the case. A homicidal maniac who desires to kill usually desires to kill as many victims as possible. It is a recurring craving. The great idea of such a killer is to hide his tracks—not to advertise them. When we consider the four victims selected—or at any rate three of them (for I know very little of Mr. Downes or Mr. Earlsfield), we realize that if he had chosen, the murderer could have done away with them without incurring any suspicion. Franz Ascher, Donald Fraser or Megan Barnard, possibly Mr. Clarke—those are the people the police would have suspected even if they had been unable to get direct proof. An unknown homicidal murderer would not have been thought of! Why, then, did the murderer feel it necessary to call attention to himself? Was it the necessity of leaving on each body a copy of an A.B.C. railway guide? Was *that* the compulsion? Was there some complex connected with the railway guide?

"I found it quite inconceivable at this point to enter into the mind of the murderer. Surely it could not be magnanimity? A horror of responsibility for the crime being fastened on an innocent person?

"Although I could not answer the main question, certain things I did feel I was learning about the murderer."

"Such as?" asked Fraser.

"To begin with—that he had a tabular mind. His crimes were listed by alphabetical progression—that was obviously important to him. On the other hand, he had no particular taste in victims —Mrs. Ascher, Betty Barnard, Sir Carmichael Clarke, they all differed widely from each other. There was no sex complex—no particular age complex, and that seemed to me to be a very curious fact. If a man kills indiscriminately it is usually because he removes any one who stands in his way or annoys him. But the alphabetical progression showed that such was not the case here. The other type of killer usually selects a particular type of victim—nearly always of the opposite sex. There was something haphazard about the procedure of A.B.C. that seemed to me to be at war with the alphabetical selection.

"The slight inferences I permitted myself to make. The choice of the A.B.C. suggested to me what I may call a *railway-minded man*. This is more common in men than women. Small boys love trains better than small girls do. It might be the sign, too, of an in some ways undeveloped mind. The 'boy' motif still predominated.

"The death of Betty Barnard and the manner of it gave me certain other indications. The manner of her death was particularly suggestive. (Forgive me, Mr. Fraser.) To begin with, she was strangled with her own belt—therefore she must almost certainly have been killed by some one with whom she was on friendly or affectionate terms. When I learnt something of her character a picture grew up in my mind.

"Betty Barnard was a flirt. She liked attention from a personable male. Therefore A.B.C., to persuade her to come out with him, must have had a certain amount of attraction—*of le sex appeal!* He must be able, as you English say, to 'get off.' He must be capable of the click! I visualize the scene on the beach thus: the man admires her belt. She takes it off, he passes it playfully round her neck—says, perhaps, 'I shall strangle you.' It is all very playful. She giggled—and he pulls—"

Donald Fraser sprang up. He was livid.

"M. Poirot—for God's sake."

Poirot made a gesture.

"It is finished. I say no more. It is over. We pass to the next murder, that of Sir Carmichael Clarke. Here the murderer goes back to his first method—the blow on the head. The same alphabetical complex—but one fact worries me a little. To be consistent the murderer should have chosen his towns in some definite sequence.

"If Andover is the 155th name under A, then the B crime should be the 155th also—or it should be the 156th and the C the 157th. Here again the towns seemed to be chosen in rather too *haphazard* a fashion."

"Isn't that because you're rather biased on that subject, Poirot?" I suggested. "You yourself are normally methodical and orderly. It's almost a disease with you."

"No, it is *not* a disease! *Quelle idée!* But I admit that I may be over-stressing that point. *Passons!*

"The Churston crime gave me very little extra help. We were unlucky over it, since the letter announcing it went astray, hence no preparations could be made.

"But by the time the D crime was announced, a very formidable system of defence had been evolved. It must have been obvious that A.B.C. could not much longer hope to get away with his crimes.

"Moreover, it was at this point that the clue of the stockings came into my hands. It was perfectly clear that the presence of an individual selling stockings on and near the scene of each crime could not be a coincidence. Hence the stocking-seller must be the murderer. I may say that his description, as given me by Miss Grey, did not quite correspond with my own picture of the man who strangled Betty Barnard.

"I will pass over the next stages quickly. A fourth murder was committed—the murder of a man named George Earlsfield—it was supposed in mistake for a man named Downes, who was something of the same build and who was sitting near him in the cinema.

"And now at last comes the turn of the tide. Events play against A.B.C. instead of into his hands. He is marked down—hunted—and at last arrested.

"The case, as Hastings says, is ended!

"True enough as far as the public is concerned. The man is in prison and will eventually, no doubt, go to Broadmoor. There will be no more murders. Exit! Finis! R.I.P.

"But not for me! I know nothing—nothing at all! Neither the *why* nor the *wherefore*.

"And there is one small vexing fact. The man Cust has an alibi for the night of the Bexhill crime."

"That's been worrying me all along," said Franklin Clarke.

"Yes. It worried me. For the alibi, it has the air of being

genuine. But it cannot be genuine unless—and now we come to two very interesting speculations.

"Supposing, my friends, that while Cust committed three of the crimes—the A, C and D crimes—*he did not commit the B crime.*"

"M. Poirot. It isn't—"

Poirot silenced Megan Barnard with a look.

"Be quiet, mademoiselle. I am for the truth, I am! I have done with lies. Supposing, I say, that A.B.C. did not commit the second crime. It took place, remember, in the early hours of the twenty-fifth—the day he had arrived for the crime. Supposing some one had forestalled him? What in those circumstances would he do? Commit a second murder, or lie low and accept the first as a kind of macabre present?"

"M. Poirot!" said Megan. "That's a fantastic thought! All the crimes *must* have been committed by the same person!"

He took no notice of her and went steadily on:

"Such a hypothesis had the merit of explaining one fact—the discrepancy between the personality of Alexander Bonaparte Cust (who could never have made the click with any girl) and the personality of Betty Barnard's murderer. And it has been known, before now, that would-be murderers *have* taken advantage of the crimes committed by other people. Not all the crimes of Jack the Ripper were committed by Jack the Ripper, for instance. So far, so good.

"But then I came up against a definite difficulty.

"Up to the time of the Barnard murder, no facts about the A.B.C. murders had been made public. The Andover murder had created little interest. The incident of the open railway guide had not even been mentioned in the press. It therefore followed that whoever killed Betty Barnard must have had access to facts known only to certain persons—myself, the police, and certain relations and neighbours of Mrs. Ascher.

"That line of research seemed to lead me up against a blank wall."

The faces that looked at him were blank too. Blank and puzzled.

Donald Fraser said thoughtfully:

"The police, after all, are human beings. And they're good-looking men—"

He stopped, looking at Poirot inquiringly.

Poirot shook his head gently.

"No—it is simpler than that. I told you that there was a second speculation.

"Supposing that Cust was *not* responsible for the killing of Betty Barnard? Supposing that *some one else* killed her. Could that some one else have been responsible *for the other murders too?*"

"But that doesn't make sense?" cried Clarke.

"Doesn't it? I did then what I ought to have done at first. I examined the letters I had received from a totally different point of view. I had felt from the beginning that there was something wrong with them—just as a picture expert knows a picture is wrong. . . .

"I had assumed, without pausing to consider, that what was wrong with them was the fact that they were written by a mad-man.

"Now I examined them again—and this time I came to a totally different conclusion. What was wrong with them was the fact that they were written by a sane man!"

"What?" I cried.

"But yes—just that precisely! They were wrong as a picture is wrong—because they were a fake! They pretended to be the letters of a madman—of a homicidal lunatic, but in reality they were nothing of the kind."

"It doesn't make sense," Franklin Clarke repeated.

"*Mais si!* One must reason—reflect. What would be the object of writing such letters? To focus attention on the writer, to call attention to the murders! *En vérité,* it did not seem to make sense at first sight. And then I saw light. It was to focus attention on several murders—on a *group* of murders. . . . Is it not your great Shakespeare who has said, 'You cannot see the trees for the wood'?"

I did not correct Poirot's literary reminiscences. I was trying to see his point. A glimmer came to me. He went on:

"When do you notice a pin least? When it is in a pin-cushion!

When do you notice an individual murder least? When it is one of *a series of related murders*.

"I had to deal with an intensely clever, resourceful murderer—reckless, daring and a thorough gambler. *Not* Mr. Cust! He could never have committed these murders! No, I had to deal with a very different stamp of man—a man with a boyish temperament (witness the schoolboy-like letters and the railway guide), an attractive man to women, and a man with a ruthless disregard for human life, a man who was necessarily a prominent person in *one* of the crimes!

"Consider when a man or woman is killed, what are the questions that the police ask? Opportunity. Where everybody was at the time of the crime? Motive. Who benefited by the deceased's death? If the motive and the opportunity are fairly obvious, what is a would-be murderer to do? Fake an alibi—that is, manipulate *time* in some way? But that is always a hazardous proceeding. Our murderer thought of a more fantastic defence. Create a *homicidal* murderer!

"I had now only to review the various crimes and find the possible guilty person. The Andover crime? The most likely suspect for that was Franz Ascher, but I could not imagine Ascher inventing and carrying out such an elaborate scheme, nor could I see him planning a premeditated murder. The Bexhill crime? Donald Fraser was a possibility. He had brains and ability, and a methodical turn of mind. But his motive for killing his sweetheart could only be jealousy—and jealousy does not tend to premeditation. Also I learned that he had his holiday *early* in August, which rendered it unlikely that he had anything to do with the Churston crime. We come to the Churston crime next—and at once we are on infinitely more promising ground.

"Sir Carmichael Clarke was an immensely wealthy man. Who inherits his money? His wife, who is dying, has a life interest in it, and it then goes to *his brother Franklin*."

Poirot turned slowly round till his eyes met those of Franklin Clarke.

"I was quite sure then. The man I had known a long time in my secret mind was the same as the man whom I had known as a person. *A.B.C. and Franklin Clarke were one and the same!* The daring adventurous character, the roving life, the partiality for England that had showed itself, very faintly, in the jeer at foreigners. The attractive free and easy manner—nothing easier for him than to pick up a girl in a café. The methodical tabular mind—he made a list here one day, ticked off over the headings A.B.C.—and finally, the boyish mind—mentioned by Lady Clarke and even shown by his taste in fiction—I have ascertained that there is a book in the library called *The Railway Children* by E. Nesbit. I had no further doubt in my own mind—A.B.C., the man who wrote the letters and committed the crimes, was *Franklin Clarke.*"

Clarke suddenly burst out laughing.

"Very ingenious! And what about our friend Cust, caught red-handed? What about the blood on his coat? And the knife he hid in his lodgings? He may deny he committed the crimes—"

Poirot interrupted.

"You are quite wrong. He admits the fact."

"What?" Clarke looked really startled.

"Oh, yes," said Poirot gently. "I had no sooner spoken to him than I was aware that Cust *believed himself to be guilty.*"

"And even that didn't satisfy M. Poirot?" said Clarke.

"No. Because as soon as I saw him *I also knew that he could not be guilty!* He has neither the nerve nor the daring—nor, I may add, the *brains* to plan! All along I have been aware of the dual personality of the murderer. Now I see wherein it consisted. Two people were involved—the real murderer, cunning, resourceful and daring—and the *pseudo* murderer, stupid, vacillating and suggestible.

"Suggestible—it is in that word that the mystery of Mr. Cust consists! It was not enough for you, Mr. Clarke, to devise this plan of a *series* to distract attention from a *single* crime. You had also to have a stalking horse.

"I think the idea first originated in your mind as the result of a chance encounter in a city coffee den with this odd personality with his bombastic Christian names. You were at that time turning over in your mind various plans for the murder of your brother."

"Really? And why?"

"Because you were seriously alarmed for the future. I do not know whether you realize it, Mr. Clarke, but you played into my hands when you showed me a certain letter written to you by your brother. In it he displayed very clearly his affection and absorption in Miss Thora Grey. His regard may have been a paternal one—or he may have preferred to think it so. Nevertheless, there was a very real danger that on the death of your sister-in-law he might, in his loneliness, turn to this beautiful girl for sympathy and comfort and it might end—as so often happens with elderly men—in his marrying her. Your fear was increased by your knowledge of Miss Grey. You are, I fancy, an excellent, if somewhat cynical judge of character. You judged, whether correctly or not, that Miss Grey was a type of young woman 'on the make.' You had no doubt that she would jump at the chance of becoming Lady Clarke. Your brother was an extremely healthy and vigorous man. There might be children and your chance of inheriting your brother's wealth would vanish.

"You have been, I fancy, in essence a disappointed man all your life. You have been the rolling stone—and you have gathered very little moss. You were bitterly jealous of your brother's wealth.

"I repeat then that, turning over various schemes in your mind, your meeting with Mr. Cust gave you an idea. His bombastic Christian names, his account of his epileptic seizures and of his headaches, his whole shrinking and insignificant personality, struck you as fitting him for the tool you wanted. The whole alphabetical plan sprang into your mind—Cust's initials —the fact that your brother's name began with a C and that he lived at Churston were the nucleus of the scheme. You even went so far as to hint to Cust at his possible end—though you could hardly hope that that suggestion would bear the rich fruit that it did!

"Your arrangements were excellent. In Cust's name you wrote for a large consignment of hosiery to be sent to him. You yourself sent a number of A.B.C.'s looking like a similar parcel. You wrote to him—a typed letter purporting to be from the same

firm offering him a good salary and commission. Your plans
were so well laid beforehand that you typed all the letters that
were sent subsequently, *and then presented him with the
machine on which they had been typed.*

"You had now to look about for two victims whose names
began with A and B respectively and who lived at places also
beginning with those same letters.

"You hit on Andover as quite a likely spot and your preliminary reconnaissance there led you to select Mrs. Ascher's
shop as the scene of the first crime. Her name was written clearly
over the door, and you found by experiment that she was usually
alone in the shop. Her murder needed nerve, daring and reasonable luck.

"For the letter B you had to vary your tactics. Lonely women
in shops might conceivably have been warned. I should imagine
that you frequented a few cafés and tea-shops, laughing and
joking with the girls there and finding out whose name began
with the right letter and who would be suitable for your purpose.

"In Betty Barnard you found just the type of girl you were
looking for. You took her out once or twice, explaining to her
that you were a married man, and that outings must therefore
take place in a somewhat hole and corner manner.

"Then, your preliminary plans completed, you set to work!
You sent the Andover list to Cust, directing him to go there on
a certain date, and you sent off the first A.B.C. letter to me.

"On the appointed day, you went to Andover—and killed
Mrs. Ascher—without anything occurring to damage your plans.

"Murder number one was successfully accomplished.

"For the second murder, you took the precaution of committing it, in reality, *the day before.* I am fairly certain that
Betty Barnard was killed well before midnight on the twenty-
fourth July.

"We now come to murder number three—the important—in
fact, the *real* murder from your point of view.

"And here a full meed of praise is due to Hastings, who
made a simple and obvious remark to which no attention was
paid.

"He suggested that the third letter went astray intentionally!

"And he was right! . . .

"In that one simple fact lies the answer to the question that has puzzled me so all along. Why were the letters addressed in the first place to Hercule Poirot, a private detective, and not to the police?

"Erroneously I imagined some personal reason.

"Not at all! The letters were sent to me because the essence of your plan was that one of them *should be wrongly addressed and go astray*—but you cannot arrange for a letter addressed to the Criminal Investigation Department of Scotland Yard to go astray! It is necessary to have a *private* address. You chose me as a fairly well-known person, and a person who was sure to take the letters to the police—and also, in your rather insular mind, you enjoyed scoring off a foreigner.

"You addressed your envelope very cleverly—Whitehaven—Whitehorse—quite a natural slip. Only Hastings was sufficiently perspicacious to disregard subtleties and go straight for the obvious!

"Of course the letter was *meant* to go astray! The police were to be set on the trail *only when the murder was safely over*. Your brother's nightly walk provided you with the opportunity. And so successfully had the A.B.C. terror taken hold on the public mind that the possibility of your guilt never occurred to any one.

"After the death of your brother, of course, your object was accomplished. You had no wish to commit any more murders. On the other hand, if the murders stopped without reason, a suspicion of truth might come to some one.

"Your stalking horse, Mr. Cust, had so successfully lived up to his rôle of the invisible—because insignificant—man, that so far no one had noticed that the same person had been seen in the vicinity of the three murders! To your annoyance, even his visit to Combeside had not been mentioned. The matter had passed completely out of Miss Grey's head.

"Always daring, you decided that one more murder must take place but that this time the trail must be well blazed.

"You selected Doncaster for the scene of operations.

"Your plan was very simple. You yourself would be on the

scene in the nature of things. Mr. Cust would be ordered to Doncaster by his firm. Your plan was to follow him round and trust to opportunity. Everything fell out well. Mr. Cust went to a cinema. That was simplicity itself. You sat a few seats away from him. When he got up to go, you did the same. You pretended to stumble, leaned over and stabbed a dozing man in the row in front, slid the A.B.C. on to his knees and managed to collide heavily with Mr. Cust in the darkened doorway, wiping the knife on his sleeve and slipping it into his pocket.

"You were not in the least at pains to choose a victim whose name began with D. Any one would do! You assumed—and quite rightly—that it would be considered to be a mistake. There was sure to be some one whose name began with D not far off in the audience. It would be assumed that he had been intended to be the victim.

"And now, my friends, let us consider the matter from the point of view of the false A.B.C.—from the point of view of Mr. Cust.

"The Andover crime means nothing to him. He is shocked and surprised by the Bexhill crime—why, he himself was there about the time! Then comes the Churston crime and the headlines in the newspapers. An A.B.C. crime at Andover when he was there, an A.B.C. crime at Bexhill, and now another close by. . . . Three crimes *and he has been at the scene of each of them.* Persons suffering from epilepsy often have blanks when they cannot remember what they have done. . . . Remember that Cust was a nervous, highly neurotic subject and extremely suggestible.

"Then he receives the order to go to Doncaster.

"Doncaster! And the next A.B.C. crime is to be in Doncaster. He must have felt as though it was fate. He loses his nerve, fancies his landlady is looking at him suspiciously, and tells her he is going to Cheltenham.

"He goes to Doncaster because it is his duty. In the afternoon he goes to a cinema. Possibly he dozes off for a minute or two.

"Imagine his feelings when on his return to his inn he discovers that there is blood on his coat sleeve and a blood-stained knife in his pocket. All his vague forebodings leap into certainty.

"*He—he himself—is the killer!* He remembers his headaches—his lapses of memory. He is quite sure of the truth—*he, Alexander Bonaparte Cust, is a homicidal lunatic.*

"His conduct after that is the conduct of a hunted animal. He gets back to his lodgings in London. He is safe there—known. They think he has been in Cheltenham. He has the knife with him still—a thoroughly stupid thing to do, of course. He hides it behind the hall stand.

"Then, one day, he is warned that the police are coming. It is the end! They *know!*

"The hunted animal does his last run. . . .

"I do not know why he went to Andover—a morbid desire, I think, to go and look at the place where the crime was committed—the crime *he* committed though he can remember nothing about it. . . .

"He has no money left—he is worn out . . . his feet lead him of his own accord to the police station.

"But even a cornered beast will fight. Mr. Cust fully believes that he did the murders but he sticks strongly to his plea of innocence. And he holds with desperation to that alibi for the second murder. At least that cannot be laid to his door.

"As I say, when I saw him, I knew at once that he was *not* the murderer and that my name meant nothing to him. I knew, too, that he *thought* himself the murderer!

"After he had confessed his guilt to me, I knew more strongly than ever that my own theory was right."

"Your theory," said Franklin Clarke, "is absurd!"

Poirot shook his head.

"No, Mr. Clarke. You were safe enough so long as no one suspected you. Once you *were* suspected proofs were easy to obtain."

"Proofs?"

"Yes. I found the stick that you used in the Andover and Churston murders in a cupboard at Combeside. An ordinary stick with a thick knob handle. A section of wood had been removed and melted lead poured in. Your photograph was picked out from half a dozen others by two people who saw you leaving the cinema when you were supposed to be on the race-course at

Doncaster. You were identified at Bexhill the other day by Milly Higley and a girl from the Scarlet Runner Roadhouse, where you took Betty Barnard to dine on the fatal evening. And finally—most damning of all—you overlooked a most elementary precaution. You left a fingerprint on Cust's typewriter—the typewriter that, if you are innocent, you *could never have handled.*"

Clarke sat quite still for a minute, then he said:

"*Rouge, impair, manque!*—you win, M. Poirot! But it was worth trying!"

With an incredibly rapid motion, he whipped out a small automatic from his pocket and held it to his head.

I gave a cry and involuntarily flinched as I waited for the report.

But no report came—the hammer clicked harmlessly.

Clarke stared at it in astonishment and uttered an oath.

"No, Mr. Clarke," said Poirot. "You may have noticed I had a new manservant to-day—a friend of mine—an expert sneak thief. He removed your pistol from your pocket, unloaded it, and returned it all without your being aware of the fact."

"You unutterable little jackanapes of a foreigner!" cried Clarke, purple with rage.

"Yes, yes, that is how you feel. No, Mr. Clarke, no easy death for you. You told Mr. Cust that you had had near escapes from drowning. You know what that means—that you were born for another fate."

"You—"

Words failed him. His face was livid. His fists clenched menacingly.

Two detectives from Scotland Yard emerged from the next room. One of them was Crome. He advanced and uttered his time-honoured formula: "I warn you that anything you say may be used as evidence."

"He has said quite enough," said Poirot, and he added to Clarke: "You are very full of an insular superiority, but for myself I consider your crime not an English crime at all—not above-board—not *sporting*—"

XXXV —

I AM sorry to relate that as the door closed behind Franklin Clarke I laughed hysterically.

Poirot looked at me in mild surprise.

"It's because you told him his crime was not sporting," I gasped.

"It was quite true. It was abominable—not so much the murder of his brother—but the cruelty that condemned an unfortunate man to a living death. *To catch a fox and put him in a box and never let him go! That is not le sport!*"

Megan Barnard gave a deep sigh.

"I can't believe it—I can't. Is it true?"

"Yes, mademoiselle. The nightmare is over."

She looked at him and her colour deepened.

Poirot turned to Fraser.

"Mademoiselle Megan, all along, was haunted by a fear that it was you who had committed the second crime."

Donald Fraser said quietly:

"I fancied so myself at one time."

"Because of your dream?" He drew a little nearer to the young man and dropped his voice confidentially. "Your dream has a very natural explanation. It is that you find that already the image of one sister fades in your memory and that its place is taken by the other sister. Mademoiselle Megan replaces her sister in your heart, but since you cannot bear to think of yourself being unfaithful so soon to the dead, you strive to stifle the thought to kill it! That is the explanation of the dream."

Fraser's eyes went toward Megan.

"Do not be afraid to forget," said Poirot gently. "She was not so well worth remembering. In Mademoiselle Megan you have one in a hundred—*un cœur magnifique!*"

Donald Fraser's eyes lit up.

"I believe you are right."

We all crowded round Poirot asking questions, elucidating this point and that.

"Those questions, Poirot? That you asked of everybody. Was there any point in them?"

"Some of them were *simplement une blague*. But I learnt one thing that I wanted to know—that Franklin Clarke was in London when the first letter was posted—and also I wanted to see his face when I asked my question of Mademoiselle Thora. He was off his guard. I saw all the malice and anger in his eyes."

"You hardly spared my feelings," said Thora Grey.

"I do not fancy you returned me a truthful answer, mademoiselle," said Poirot dryly. "And now your second expectation is disappointed. Franklin Clarke will not inherit his brother's money."

She flung up her head.

"Is there any need for me to stay here and be insulted?"

"None whatever," said Poirot and held the door open politely for her.

"That fingerprint clinched things, Poirot," I said thoughtfully. "He went all to pieces when you mentioned that."

"Yes, they are useful—fingerprints."

He added thoughtfully:

"I put that in to please you, *mon ami*."

"But, Poirot," I cried, "wasn't it *true*?"

"Not in the least, *mon ami*," said Hercule Poirot.

I must mention a visit we had from Mr. Alexander Bonaparte Cust a few days later. After wringing Poirot's hand and endeavouring very incoherently and unsuccessfully to thank him, Mr. Cust drew himself up and said:

"Do you know, a newspaper has actually offered me a hundred pounds—*a hundred pounds*—for a brief account of my life and history. I—I really don't know what to do about it."

"I should not accept a hundred," said Poirot. "Be firm. Say five hundred is your price. And do not confine yourself to one newspaper."

"Do you really think—that I might—"

"You must realize," said Poirot, smiling, "that you are a very famous man. Practically the most famous man in England to-day."

Mr. Cust drew himself up still further. A beam of delight irradiated his face.

"Do you know, I believe you're right! Famous! In all the papers. I shall take your advice, M. Poirot. The money will be most agreeable—most agreeable. I shall have a little holiday. . . . And then I want to give a nice wedding present to Lily Marbury—a dear girl—really a dear girl, M. Poirot."

Poirot patted him encouragingly on the shoulder.

"You are quite right. Enjoy yourself. And—just a little word —what about a visit to an oculist. Those headaches, it is probably that you want new glasses."

"You think that it may have been that all the time?"

"I do."

Mr. Cust shook him warmly by the hand.

"You're a very great man, M. Poirot."

Poirot, as usual, did not disdain the compliment. He did not even succeed in looking modest.

When Mr. Cust had strutted importantly out, my old friend smiled across at me.

"So, Hastings—we went hunting once more, did we not? *Vive le sport.*"

Funerals Are
Fatal

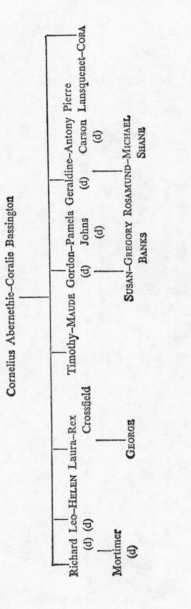

THE ABERNETHIE FAMILY.

Those designated in Capital and Small Cap letters were present at the funeral of RICHARD ABERNETHIE.

I

OLD LANSCOMBE moved totteringly from room to room, pulling up the blinds. Now and then he peered with screwed up rheumy eyes through the windows.

Soon they would be coming back from the funeral. He shuffled along a little faster. There were so many windows.

Enderby Hall was a vast Victorian house built in the Gothic style. In every room the curtains were of rich faded brocade or velvet. Some of the walls were still hung with faded silk. In the green drawing room, the old butler glanced up at the portrait above the mantelpiece of old Cornelius Abernethie for whom Enderby Hall had been built. Cornelius Abernethie's brown beard stuck forward aggressively, his hand rested on a terrestrial globe, whether by desire of the sitter, or as a symbolic conceit on the part of the artist, no one could tell.

A very forceful looking gentleman, so old Lanscombe had always thought, and was glad that he himself had never known him personally. Mr Richard had been *his* gentleman. A good master, Mr Richard. And taken very sudden, he'd been, though of course the doctor had been attending him for some little time. Ah, but the master had never recovered from the shock of young Mr Mortimer's death. The old man shook his head as he hurried through a connecting door into the White Boudoir. Terrible, that had been, a real catastrophe. Such a fine upstanding young gentleman, so strong and healthy. You'd never have thought such a thing likely to happen to him. Pitiful, it had been, quite pitiful. And Mr Gordon killed in the war. One thing on top of another. That was the way things went nowadays. Too much for the master, it had been. And yet he'd seemed almost himself a week ago.

The third blind in the White Boudoir refused to go up as it should. It went up a little way and stuck. The springs were weak—that's what it was—very old, these blinds were, like everything else in the house. And you couldn't get these old things mended nowadays. Too old fashioned, that's what they'd say, shaking their heads in that silly superior way—as if the old things weren't a great deal better than the new ones! *He* could tell them that! Gimcrack, half the new stuff was—came to pieces in your hand. The material wasn't good, or the craftsmanship either. Oh yes, *he* could tell them.

Couldn't do anything about this blind unless he got the steps. He didn't like climbing up the steps much, these days, made him come over giddy. Anyway, he'd leave the blind for now. It didn't matter since the White Boudoir didn't face the front of the house where it would be seen as the cars came back from the funeral—and it wasn't as though the room was ever used nowadays. It was a lady's room, this, and there hadn't been a lady at Enderby for a long while now. A pity Mr Mortimer hadn't married. Always going off to Norway for fishing and to Scotland for shooting and to Switzerland for those winter sports, instead of marrying some nice young lady and settling down at home with children running about the house. It was a long time since there had been any children in the house.

And Lanscombe's mind went ranging back to a time that stood out clearly and distinctly—much more distinctly than the last twenty years or so, which were all blurred and confused and he couldn't really remember who had come and gone or indeed what they looked like. But he could remember the old days well enough.

More like a father to those young brothers and sisters of his, Mr Richard had been. Twenty-four when his father had died, and he'd pitched in right away to the business, going off every day as punctual as clockwork, and keeping the house running and everything as lavish as it could be. A very happy household with all those young ladies and gentlemen growing up. Fights and quarrels now and again, of course, and those governesses had had a bad time of it! Poor spirited creatures, governesses, Lanscombe had always despised them. Very spirited the young ladies had been. Miss Geraldine in particular. Miss Cora, too, although she was so much younger. And now Mr

Leo was dead, and Miss Laura gone too. And Mr Timothy such a sad invalid. And Miss Geraldine dying somewhere abroad. And Mr Gordon killed in the war. Although he was the eldest, Mr Richard himself turned out the strongest of the lot. Outlived them all, he had—at least not quite because Mr Timothy was still alive and little Miss Cora who'd married that unpleasant artist chap. Twenty five years since he'd seen her and she'd been a pretty young girl when she went off with that chap, and now he'd hardly have known her, grown so stout—and so arty crafty in her dress! A Frenchman her husband had been, or nearly a Frenchman—and no good ever came of marrying one of *them!* But Miss Cora had always been a bit—well, *simple like* you'd call it if she'd lived in a village. Always one of them in a family.

She'd remembered *him* all right. "Why, it's Lanscombe!" she'd said and seemed ever so pleased to see him. Ah, they'd all been fond of him in the old days and when there was a dinner party they'd crept down to the pantry and he'd given them jelly and Charlotte Russe when it came out of the dining room. They'd all known old Lanscombe, and now there was hardly anyone who remembered. Just the younger lot whom he could never keep clear in his mind and who just thought of him as a butler who'd been there a long time. A lot of strangers, he had thought, when they all arrived for the funeral—and a seedy lot of strangers at that!

Not Mrs Leo—she was different. She and Mr Leo had come here off and on ever since Mr Leo married. She was a nice lady, Mrs Leo—a *real* lady. Wore proper clothes and did her hair well and looked what she was. And the master had always been fond of her. A pity that she and Mr Leo had never had any children . . .

Lanscombe roused himself; what was he doing standing here and dreaming about old days with so much to be done? The blinds were all attended to on the ground floor now, and he'd told Jane to go upstairs and do the bedrooms. He and Janet and the cook had gone to the funeral service in the church but instead of going on to the Crematorium they'd driven back to the house to get the blinds up and the lunch ready. Cold lunch, of course, it had to be. Ham and chicken and tongue and salad. With cold lemon soufflé and apple tart to follow. Hot soup first—and he'd better go along and see that Marjorie had got it on ready to serve, for they'd be back in a minute or two now for certain.

Lanscombe broke into a shuffling trot across the room. His gaze, abstracted and uncurious, just swept up to the picture over this mantelpiece—the companion portrait to the one in the green drawing room. It was a nice painting of white satin and pearls. The human being round whom they were draped and clasped was not nearly so impressive. Meek features, a rosebud mouth, hair parted in the middle. A woman both modest and unassuming. The only thing really worthy of note about Mrs Cornelius Abernethie had been her name—Coralie.

For over sixty years after their original appearance, Coral Cornplasters and the allied "Coral" foot preparations still held their own. Whether there had ever been anything outstanding about Coral Cornplasters nobody could say—but they had appealed to the public fancy. On a foundation of Coral Cornplasters there had arisen this neo Gothic palace, its acres of gardens, and the money that had paid out an income to seven sons and daughters and had allowed Richard Abernethie to die three days ago a very rich man.

ii

Looking into the kitchen with a word of admonition, Lanscombe was snapped at by Marjorie, the cook. Marjorie was young, only twenty seven, and was a constant irritation to Lanscombe as being so far removed from what his conception of a proper cook should be. She had no dignity and no proper appreciation of his, Lanscombe's, position. She frequently called the house "a proper old mausoleum" and complained of the immense area of the kitchen, scullery and larder saying that it was a "day's walk to get round them all." She had been at Enderby two years and only stayed because, in the first place the money was good, and in the second because Mr Abernethie had really appreciated her cooking. She cooked very well. Janet, who stood by the kitchen table, refreshing herself with a cup of tea, was an elderly housemaid who, although enjoying frequent acid disputes with Lanscombe, was nevertheless usually in alliance with him against the younger generation as represented by Marjorie. The fourth person in the kitchen was Mrs Jacks who "came in" to lend assistance where it was wanted and who had much enjoyed the funeral.

"Beautiful it was," she said with a decorous sniff as she replenished her cup. "Nineteen cars and the church quite full and the Canon read the service beautiful, I thought. A nice fine day for it, too. Ah, poor dear Mr Abernethie, there's not many like him left in the world. Respected by all, he was."

There was the note of a horn and the sound of a car coming up the drive, and Mrs Jacks put down her cup and exclaimed: "Here they are."

Marjorie turned up the gas under her large saucepan of creamy chicken soup. The large kitchen range of the days of Victorian grandeur stood cold and unused, like an altar to the past.

The cars drove up one after the other and the people issuing from them in their black clothes moved rather uncertainly across the hall and into the big green drawing room. In the big steel grate a fire was burning, tribute to the first chill of the Autumn days and calculated to counteract the further chill of standing about at a funeral.

Lanscombe entered the room, offering glasses of sherry on a silver tray.

Mr Entwhistle, senior partner of the old and respected firm of Bollard, Entwhistle, Entwhistle and Bollard, stood with his back to the fireplace warming himself. He accepted a glass of sherry, and surveyed the company with his shrewd lawyer's gaze. Not all of them were personally known to him, and he was under the necessity of sorting them out, so to speak. Introductions before the departure for the funeral had been hushed and perfunctory.

Appraising old Lanscombe first, Mr Entwhistle thought to himself, "Getting very shaky, poor old chap—going on for ninety I shouldn't wonder. Well, he'll have that nice little annuity. Nothing for *him* to worry about. Faithful soul. No such thing as old fashioned service nowadays. Household helps and baby sitters, God help us all! A sad world. Just as well, perhaps, poor Richard didn't last his full time. He hadn't much to live for."

To Mr Entwhistle who was seventy two, Richard Abernethie's death at sixty eight was definitely that of a man dead before his time. Mr Entwhistle had retired from active business two years ago, but as executor of Richard Abernethie's will and in respect for one of his oldest clients who was also a personal friend, he had made the journey to the North.

Reflecting in his own mind on the provisions of the will, he mentally appraised the family.

Mrs Leo, Helen, he knew well, of course. A very charming woman for whom he had both liking and respect. His eyes dwelt approvingly on her now as she stood near one of the windows. Black suited her. She had kept her figure well. He liked the clear cut features, the springing line of grey hair back from her temples and the eyes that had once been likened to cornflowers and which were still quite vividly blue.

How old was Helen now? About fifty one or two, he supposed. Strange that she had never married again after Leo's death. An attractive woman. Ah, but they had been very devoted, those two.

His eyes went on to Mrs Timothy. He had never known her very well. Black didn't suit her—country tweeds were her wear. A big sensible capable-looking woman. She'd always been a good devoted wife to Timothy. Looking after his health, fussing over him—fussing over him a bit too much, probably. Was there really anything the matter with Timothy? Just a hypochondriac, Mr Entwhistle suspected. Richard Abernethie had suspected so, too. "Weak chest, of course, when he was a boy," he had said. "But blest if I think there's much wrong with him now." Oh well, everybody had to have some hobby. Timothy's hobby was the all absorbing one of his own health. Was Mrs Tim taken in? Probably not—but women never admitted that sort of thing. Timothy must be quite comfortably off. He'd never been a spend-thrift. However, the extra would not come amiss—not in these days of taxation. He'd probably had to retrench his scale of living a good deal since the war.

Mr Entwhistle transferred his attention to George Crossfield, Laura's son. Dubious sort of fellow Laura had married. Nobody had ever known much about him. A stockbroker he had called himself. Young George was in a solicitor's office—not a very reputable firm. Good looking young fellow—but something a little shifty about him. He couldn't have too much to live on. Laura had been a complete fool over her investments. She'd left next to nothing when she died five years ago. A handsome romantic girl, she'd been, but no money sense.

Mr Entwhistle's eyes went on from George Crossfield. Which of the two girls was which? Ah yes, that was Rosamund, Geraldine's daughter, looking at the wax flowers on the malachite table. Pretty girl, beautiful, in fact—rather a silly face. On the stage. Repertory companies or some nonsense like that. Had married an actor, too. Good looking fellow. *"And* knows he is," thought Mr Entwhistle who was prejudiced against the stage as a profession. "Wonder what sort of a background *he* has and where he comes from."

He looked disapprovingly at Michael Shane with his fair hair and his haggard charm.

Now Susan, Gordon's daughter, would do much better on the stage than Rosamund. More personality. A little too much personality for everyday life, perhaps. She was quite near him and Mr Entwhistle studied her covertly. Dark hair, hazel—almost golden—eyes, a sulky attractive mouth. Beside her was the husband she had just married—a chemist's assistant, he understood. Really, a chemist's assistant! In Mr Entwhistle's creed girls did not marry young men who served behind a counter. But now of course, they married *anybody!* The young man who had a pale nondescript face and sandy hair seemed very ill at ease. Mr Entwhistle wondered why, but decided charitably that it was the strain of meeting so many of his wife's relations.

Last in his survey Mr Entwhistle came to Cora Lansquenet. There was a certain justice in that, for Cora had decidedly been an afterthought in the family. Richard's youngest sister, she had been born when her mother was just on fifty, and that meek woman had not survived her tenth pregnancy (three chil-

dren had died in infancy). Poor little Cora! All her life, Cora
had been rather an embarrassment—growing up tall and gawky,
and given to blurting out remarks that had always better have
remained unsaid. All her elder brothers and sisters had been
very kind to Cora, atoning for her deficiencies and covering
her social mistakes. It had never really occurred to anyone
that Cora would marry. She had not been a very attractive girl,
and her rather obvious advances to visiting young men had
usually caused the latter to retreat in some alarm. And then,
Mr Entwhistle mused, there had come the Lansquenet business
—Pierre Lansquenet, half French, whom she had come across
in an art school where she had been having very correct lessons
in painting flowers in water colours. But somehow she had got
into the life class and there she had met Pierre Lansquenet and
had come home and announced her intention of marrying him.
Richard Abernethie had put his foot down—he hadn't liked
what he saw of Pierre Lansquenet and suspected that the young
man was really in search of a rich wife. But whilst he was making a few researches into Lansquenet's antecedents, Cora had
bolted with the fellow and married him out of hand. They had
spent most of their married life in Brittany and Cornwall and
other painters' conventional haunts. Lansquenet had been a
very bad painter and not, by all accounts, a very nice man, but
Cora had remained devoted to him and had never forgiven her
family for their attitude to him. Richard had generously made
his young sister an allowance and on that they had, so Mr Entwhistle believed, lived. He doubted if Lansquenet had ever
earned any money at all. He must have been dead now twelve
years or more, thought Mr Entwhistle. And now here was his
widow, rather cushion-like in shape and dressed in wispy artistic
black with festoons of jet beads, back in the home of her girl-
hood, moving about and touching things and exclaiming with
pleasure when she recalled some childish memory. She made
very little pretence of grief at her brother's death. But then,
Mr Entwhistle reflected, Cora had never pretended.

Re-entering the room Lanscombe murmured in muted tones
suitable to the occasion:

"Luncheon is served."

II

AFTER THE delicious chicken soup, and plenty of cold viands accompanied by an excellent *chablis,* the funeral atmosphere lightened. Nobody had really felt any deep grief for Richard Abernethie's death since none of them had had any close ties with him. Their behaviour had been suitably decorous and subdued (with the exception of the uninhibited Cora who was clearly enjoying herself) but it was now felt that the decencies had been observed and that normal conversation could be resumed. Mr Entwhistle encouraged this attitude. He was experienced in funerals and knew exactly how to set correct funeral timing.

After the meal was over, Lanscombe indicated the library for coffee. This was his feeling for niceties. The time had come when business—in other words, The Will—would be discussed. The library had the proper atmosphere for that with its bookshelves and its heavy red velvet curtains. He served coffee to them there and then withdrew closing the door.

After a few desultory remarks, everyone began to look tentatively at Mr Entwhistle. He responded promptly after glancing at his watch.

"I have to catch the three-thirty train," he began.

Others, it seemed, also had to catch that train.

"As you know," said Mr Entwhistle, "I am the executor of Richard Abernethie's will—"

He was interrupted.

"*I* didn't know," said Cora Lansquenet brightly. "Are you? Did he leave me anything?"

Not for the first time, Mr Entwhistle felt that Cora was too apt to speak out of turn.

Bending a repressive glance at her he continued:

"Up to a year ago, Richard Abernethie's will was very simple. Subject to certain legacies he left everything to his son Mortimer."

"Poor Mortimer," said Cora. "I do think all this infantile paralysis is *dreadful*."

"Mortimer's death, coming so suddenly and tragically, was a great blow to Richard. It took him some months to rally from it. I pointed out to him that it might be advisable for him to make new testamentary dispositions."

Maude Abernethie asked in her deep voice:

"What would have happened if he *hadn't* made a new will? Would it—would it all have gone to Timothy—as the next of kin, I mean?"

Mr Entwhistle opened his mouth to give a disquisition on the subject of next of kin, thought better of it, and said crisply:

"On my advice, Richard decided to make a new will. First of all, however, he decided to get better acquainted with the younger generation."

"He had us up on appro," said Susan with a sudden rich laugh. "First George and then Greg and I, and then Rosamund and Michael."

Gregory Banks said sharply, his thin face flushing:

"I don't think you ought to put it like that, Susan. On appro, indeed!"

"But that was what it was, wasn't it, Mr Entwhistle?"

"Did he leave *me* anything?" repeated Cora.

Mr Entwhistle coughed and spoke rather coldly:

"I propose to send you all copies of the will. I can read it to you in full now if you like but its legal phraseology may seem to you rather obscure. Briefly it amounts to this: After certain small bequests and a substantial legacy to Lanscombe to purchase an annuity, the bulk of the estate—a very considerable one—is to be divided into six equal portions. Four of these, after all duties are paid, are to go to Richard's brother Timothy, his nephew George Crossfield, his niece Susan Banks, and his niece Rosamund Shane. The other two portions are to be held upon trust and the income from them paid to Mrs Helen Abernethie, the widow of his brother Leo; and to his sister Mrs Cora Lansquenet, during their lifetime. The capital after their death to be divided between the other four beneficiaries or their issue.

"That's *very* nice!" said Cora Lansquenet with real appreciation. "An income! How much?"

"I—er—can't say exactly at present. Death duties, of course will be heavy and—"

"Can't you give me any idea?"

Mr Entwhistle realised that Cora must be appeased.

"Possibly somewhere in the neighbourhood of three to four thousand a year."

"Goody!" said Cora. "I shall go to Capri."

Helen Abernethie said softly:

"How very kind and generous of Richard. I do appreciate his affection towards me."

"He was very fond of you," said Mr Entwhistle. "Leo was his favourite brother and your visits to him were always much appreciated after Leo died."

Helen said regretfully:

"I wish I had realised how ill he was—I came up to see him not long before he died, but although I knew he *had* been ill, I did not think it was serious."

"It was always serious," said Mr Entwhistle. "But he did not want it talked about and I do not believe that anybody expected the end to come as soon as it did. The doctor was quite surprised, I know."

"'*Suddenly, at his residence,*' that's what it said in the paper," said Cora nodding her head. "I wondered, then."

"It was a shock to all of us," said Maude Abernethie. "It upset poor Timothy dreadfully. So sudden, he kept saying. So *sudden.*"

"Still it's been hushed up very nicely, hasn't it?" said Cora.

Everybody stared at her and she seemed a little flustered.

"I think you're all quite right," she said hurriedly. "*Quite* right. I mean—it can't do any good—making it public. Very unpleasant for everybody. It should be kept strictly in the family."

The faces turned towards her looked even more blank.

Mr Entwhistle leaned forward:

"Really, Cora, I'm afraid I don't quite understand what you mean."

Cora Lansquenet looked round at the family in wide-eyed surprise. She tilted her head on one side with a birdlike movement.

"But he *was* murdered, wasn't he?" she said.

III

TRAVELLING TO LONDON in the corner of a first class carriage Mr Entwhistle gave himself up to somewhat uneasy thought over that extraordinary remark made by Cora Lansquenet. Of course Cora was a rather unbalanced and excessively stupid woman, and she had been noted, even as a girl, for the embarrassing manner in which she had blurted out unwelcome truths. At least, he didn't mean *truths*—that was *quite* the wrong word to use. Awkward statements—that was a much better term.

In his mind he went back over the immediate sequence to that unfortunate remark. The combined stare of many startled and disapproving eyes had roused Cora to a sense of the enormity of what she had said.

Maude had exclaimed, *"Really,* Cora!" George had said, "My dear Aunt Cora." Somebody else had said, "What *do* you mean?"

And at once Cora Lansquenet, abashed, and convicted of enormity, had burst into fluttering phrases.

"Oh I'm sorry—I didn't mean—oh, of course, it was very stupid of me, but I did think from what he said— Oh, of course I know it's quite all right, but his death was so *sudden*— Please forget that I said anything at all—I didn't mean to be so stupid—I know I'm always saying the wrong thing. . . ."

And then the momentary upset had died down and there had been a practical discussion about the disposition of the late Richard Abernethie's personal effects. The house and its contents Mr Entwhistle supplemented, would be put up for sale.

Cora's unfortunate *gaffe* had been forgotten. After all, Cora had always been, if not subnormal, at any rate embarrassingly *naive*. She had never had any idea of what should or should not be said. At nineteen it had not mattered so much. The mannerisms of an *enfant terrible* can persist to then, but an *enfant terrible* of nearly fifty is decidedly disconcerting. To blurt out unwelcome truths—

Mr Entwhistle's train of thought came to an abrupt check. It was the second time that that disturbing word had occurred. *Truths*. And why was it so disturbing? Because, of course, that had always been at the bottom of the embarrassment that Cora's outspoken comments had caused. It was because her *naive* statements had been either true or had contained some grain of truth that they had been so embarrassing!

Although in the plump woman of forty nine, Mr Entwhistle had been able to see little resemblance to the gawky girl of earlier days, certain of Cora's mannerisms had persisted—the slight birdlike twist of the head as she brought out a particularly outrageous remark—a kind of air of pleased expectancy. In just such a way had Cora once commented on the figure of the kitchenmaid. "Mollie can hardly get near the kitchen table, her stomach sticks out so. It's only been like that the last month or two. I wonder *why* she's getting so fat?"

Cora had been quickly hushed. The Abernethie household was Victorian in tone. The kitchenmaid had disappeared from the premises the next day, and after due inquiry the second gardener had been ordered to make an honest woman of her and had been presented with a cottage in which to do so.

Far off memories—but they had their point. . . .

Mr Entwhistle examined his uneasiness more closely. What was there in Cora's ridiculous remarks that had remained to tease his subconscious in this manner? Presently he isolated two phrases. "I did think from what he said—" and "his death was so sudden . . ."

Mr Entwhistle examined that last remark first. Yes, Richard's death could, in a fashion, be considered sudden. Mr Entwhistle had discussed Richard's health both with Richard himself and with his doctor. The latter had indicated plainly that a long life could not be expected. If Mr Abernethie took reasonable care of himself he might live two or even three years. Perhaps longer —but that was unlikely. In any case the doctor had anticipated no collapse in the near future.

Well, the doctor had been wrong—but doctors, as they were

the first to admit themselves, could never be sure about the individual reaction of a patient to disease. Cases given up, unexpectedly recovered. Patients on the way to recovery, relapsed and died. So much depended on the vitality of the patient. On his own inner urge to live.

And Richard Abernethie, though a strong and vigorous man, had had no great incentive to live.

For six months previously his only surviving son, Mortimer, had contracted infantile paralysis and had died within a week. His death had been a shock greatly augmented by the fact that he had been such a particularly strong and vital young man. A keen sportsman, he was also a good athlete and was one of those people of whom it was said that he had never had a day's illness in his life. He was on the point of becoming engaged to a very charming girl and his father's hopes for the future were centered in this dearly loved and thoroughly satisfactory son of his.

Instead had come tragedy. And besides the sense of personal loss, the future had held little to hold Richard Abernethie's interest. One son had died in infancy, the second without issue. He had no grandchildren. There was, in fact, no one of the Abernethie name to come after him, and he was the holder of a vast fortune with wide business interests which he himself still controlled to a certain extent. Who was to succeed to that fortune and to the control of those interests?

That this had worried the old man deeply, Entwhistle knew. His only surviving brother was very much of an invalid. There remained the younger generation. It had been in Richard's mind, the lawyer thought, though his friend had not actually said so, to choose one definite successor, though minor legacies would probably have been made. Anyway, as Entwhistle knew, within the last six months Richard Abernethie had invited to stay with him, in succession his nephew George, his niece Susan and her husband, his niece Rosamund and her husband, and his sister-in-law, Mrs Leo Abernethie. It was amongst the first three so the lawyer thought, that Abernethie had looked for his successor. Helen Abernethie, he thought, had been asked out of personal affection and even possibly as someone to consult, for

Richard had always held a high opinion of her good sense and practical judgment. Mr Entwhistle also remembered that some-time during that six months period Richard had paid a short visit to his brother Timothy.

The net result had been the will which the lawyer now carried in his brief case. An equable distribution of property. The only conclusion that could be drawn, therefore, was that he had been disappointed both in his nephew, and in his nieces—or perhaps in his nieces' husbands.

As far as Mr Entwhistle knew, he had not invited his sister, Cora Lansquenet to visit him—and that brought the lawyer back to that first disturbing phrase that Cora had let slip so incoherently—"but I did think from what he *said*—"

What had Richard Abernethie said? And when had he said it? If Cora had not been to Enderby, then Richard Abernethie must have visited her at the artistic village in Berkshire where she had a cottage. Or was it something that Richard had said in a letter?

Mr Entwhistle frowned. Cora, of course, was a very stupid woman. She could easily have misinterpreted a phrase, and twisted its meaning. But he did wonder what the phrase could have been. . . .

There was enough uneasiness in him to make him consider the possibility of approaching Mrs Lansquenet on the subject. Not too soon. Better not make it seem of importance. But he *would* like to know just what it was that Richard Abernethie had said to her which had led her to pipe up so briskly with that outrageous question:

"But he was murdered, wasn't he?"

ii

In a third class carriage, further along the train, Gregory Banks said to his wife:

"That aunt of yours must be completely bats!"

"Aunt Cora?" Susan was vague. "Oh, yes, I believe she was always a bit simple or something."

George Crossfield, sitting opposite, said sharply:

"She really ought to be stopped from going about saying things like that. It might put ideas into people's heads."

Rosamund Shane, intent on outlining the cupid's bow of her mouth with lipstick murmured vaguely:

"I don't suppose anyone would pay any attention to what a frump like that says. The most peculiar clothes and lashings and lashings of jet—"

"Well, I think it ought to be stopped," said George.

"All right, darling," laughed Rosamund, putting away her lipstick and contemplating her image with satisfaction in the mirror. "You stop it."

Her husband said unexpectedly:

"I think George is right. It's so easy to set people talking."

"Well, would it matter?" Rosamund contemplated the question. The cupid's bow lifted at the corners in a smile. "It might really be rather fun."

"Fun?" Four voices spoke.

"Having a murder in the family," said Rosamund. "Thrilling, you know!"

It occurred to that nervous and unhappy young man Gregory Banks that Susan's cousin, setting aside her attractive exterior might have some faint points of resemblance to her Aunt Cora. Her next words rather confirmed his impression.

"If he was murdered," said Rosamund, "who do you think did it?"

Her gaze travelled thoughtfully round the carriage.

"His death has been awfully convenient for all of us," she said thoughtfully. "Michael and I are absolutely on our beam ends. Mick's had a really good part offered to him in the Sandborne show if he can afford to wait for it. Now we'll be in clover. We'll be able to back our own show if we want to. As a matter of fact there's a play with a simply wonderful part—"

Nobody listened to Rosamund's ecstatic disquisition. Their attention had shifted to their own immediate future.

"Touch and go," thought George to himself. "Now I can put that money back and nobody will ever know. . . . But it's been a near shave."

Gregory closed his eyes as he lay back against the seat. Escape from bondage.

Susan said in her clear rather hard voice, "I'm very sorry, of course, for poor old Uncle Richard. But then he *was* very old, and Mortimer had died, and he'd nothing to live for and it would have been awful for him to go on as an invalid year after year. *Much* better for him to pop off suddenly like this with no fuss."

Her hard confident young eyes softened as they watched her husband's absorbed face. She adored Greg. She sensed vaguely that Greg cared for her less than she cared for him—but that only strengthened her passion. Greg was hers, she'd do anything for him. Anything at all. . . .

iii

Maude Abernethie, changing her dress for dinner at Enderby, (for she was staying the night) wondered if she ought to have offered to stay longer to help Helen out with the sorting and clearing of the house— There would be all Richard's personal things. . . . There might be letters. . . . All important papers, she supposed, had already been taken possession of by Mr Entwhistle. And it really was necessary for her to get back to Timothy as soon as possible. He fretted so when she was not there to look after him. She hoped he would be pleased about the will and not annoyed. He had expected, she knew, that most of Richard's fortune would come to *him*. After all, he was the only surviving Abernethie. Richard could surely have trusted *him* to look after the younger generation. Yes, she was afraid Timothy *would* be annoyed. . . . And that was so bad for his digestion. And really, when he was annoyed, Timothy could become quite unreasonable. There were times when he seemed to lose his sense of proportion. . . . She wondered if she ought to speak to Dr Barton about it. . . . Those sleeping pills—Timothy had been taking far too many of them lately— he got so angry when she wanted to keep the bottle for him. But they could be dangerous—Dr Barton had said so—you could get drowsy and forget you'd taken them—and then take more. And then anything might happen! There certainly weren't as

many left in the bottle as there ought to be. . . . Timothy was
really very naughty about medicines. He wouldn't listen to her.
. . . He was very difficult sometimes.

She sighed—then brightened— Things were going to be much
easier now. The garden, for instance—

iv

Helen Abernethie sat by the fire in the green drawing room
waiting for Maude to come down to dinner.

She looked round her, remembering old days here with Leo
and the others. It had been a happy house. But a house like this
needed *people*. It needed children and servants and big meals
and plenty of roaring fires in winter. It had been a sad house
when it had been lived in by one old man who had lost his
son. . . .

Who would buy it, she wondered? Would it be turned into
a Hotel, or an Institute, or perhaps one of those Hostels for
young people? That was what happened to these vast houses
nowadays. No one would buy them to live in. It would be
pulled down, perhaps, and the whole estate built over. It made
her sad to think of that, but she pushed the sadness aside
resolutely. It did one no good to dwell on the past. This house,
and happy days here, and Richard, and Leo, all that was good,
but it was over. She had her own activities and friends and
interests. Yes, her interests. . . . And now, with the income
Richard had left her, she would be able to keep on the villa
in Cyprus and do all the things she had planned to do.

How worried she had been lately over money—taxation—all
those investments going wrong. . . . Now, thanks to Richard's
money, all that was over. . . .

Poor Richard. To die in his sleep like that had been really
a great mercy. . . . *Suddenly on the 22nd*—she supposed that
that was what had put the idea into Cora's head. Really Cora
was outrageous! She always had been. Helen remembered meeting her once abroad, soon after her marriage to Pierre Lansquenet. She had been particularly foolish and fatuous that day,
twisting her head sideways and making dogmatic statements
about painting, and particularly about her husband's painting,

which must have been most uncomfortable for him. No man could like his wife appearing such a fool. And Cora was a fool! Oh, well, poor thing, she couldn't help it, and that husband of hers hadn't treated her too well.

Helen's gaze rested absently on a bouquet of wax flowers that stood on a round malachite table. Cora had been sitting beside it when they had all been sitting round waiting to start for the church. She had been full of reminiscences and delighted recognitions of various things and was clearly so pleased at being back in her old home that she had completely lost sight of the reason for which they were assembled.

"But perhaps," thought Helen, "she was just less of a hypocrite than the rest of us. . . ."

Cora had never been one for observing the conventions. Look at the way she had plumped out that question: "But he *was* murdered, wasn't he?"

The faces all round, startled, shocked, staring at her! Such a variety of expressions there must have been on those faces. . . .

And suddenly, seeing the picture clearly in her mind, Helen frowned. . . . There was something wrong with that picture . . .

Something . . . ?

Somebody . . . ?

Was it an expression on someone's face? Was that it? Something that—how could she put it?—ought not to have been there . . . ?

She didn't know . . . she couldn't place it . . . but there had been something—somewhere—*wrong*.

v

Meanwhile, in the buffet at Swindon, a lady in wispy mourning and festoons of jet was eating bath buns and drinking tea and looking forward to the future. She had no premonitions of disaster. She was happy.

These cross country journeys were certainly tiring. It would have been easier to get back to Lytchett St. Mary via London—and not so very much more expensive. Ah, but expense didn't matter now. Still, she would have had to travel with the family —probably having to talk all the way. Too much of an effort.

No, better to go home cross country. These bath buns were really excellent. Extraordinary how hungry a funeral made you feel. The soup at Enderby had been delicious—and so was the cold soufflé.

How smug people were—and what hypocrites! All those faces —when she'd said that about murder! The way they'd all looked at her!

Well, it had been the right thing to say. She nodded her head in satisfied approval of herself. Yes, it had been the right thing to do.

She glanced up at the clock. Five minutes before her train went. She drank up her tea. Not very good tea. She made a grimace.

For a moment or two she sat dreaming. Dreaming of the future unfolding before her. . . . She smiled like a happy child.

She was really going to enjoy herself at last. . . . She went out to the small branch line train busily making plans. . . .

IV

MR ENTWHISTLE passed a very restless night. He felt so tired and so unwell in the morning that he did not get up.

His sister who kept house for him, brought up his breakfast on a tray and explained to him severely how wrong he had been to go gadding off to the North of England at his age and in his frail state of health.

Mr Entwhistle contented himself with saying that Richard Abernethie had been a very old friend.

"Funerals!" said his sister with deep disapproval. "Funerals are absolutely fatal for a man of your age! You'll be taken off as suddenly as your precious Mr Abernethie was if you don't take more care of yourself."

The word "suddenly" made Mr Entwhistle wince. It also silenced him. He did not argue.

He was well aware of what had made him flinch at the word *suddenly*.

Cora Lansquenet! What she had suggested was definitely quite impossible, but all the same he would like to find out exactly why she had suggested it. Yes, he would go down to Lytchett St. Mary and see her. He could pretend that it was business connected with probate, that he needed her signature. No need to let her guess that he had paid any attention to her silly remark. But he would go down and see her—and he would do it soon.

He finished his breakfast and lay back on his pillows and read the *Times*. He found the *Times* very soothing.

It was about a quarter to six that evening when his telephone rang.

He picked it up. The voice at the other end of the wire was that of Mr James Parrott, the present second partner of Bollard, Entwhistle, Entwhistle and Bollard.

"Look here, Entwhistle," said Mr Parrott, "I've just been rung up by the police from a place called Lytchett St. Mary."

"Lytchett St. Mary?"

"Yes. It seems—" Mr Parrott paused a moment. He seemed embarrassed. "It's about a Mrs Cora Lansquenet. Wasn't she one of the heirs of the Abernethie estate?"

"Yes, of course. I saw her at the funeral yesterday."

"Oh? She was at the funeral, was she?"

"Yes. What about her?"

"Well," Mr Parrott sounded apologetic. "She's—it's really *most* extraordinary—she's been—well—*murdered.*"

Mr Parrott said the last word with the uttermost deprecation. It was not the sort of word, he suggested, that ought to mean anything to the firm of Bollard, Entwhistle, Entwhistle and Bollard.

"Murdered?"

"Yes—yes—I'm afraid so. Well, I mean, there's no doubt about it."

"How did the police get on to us?"

"Her companion, or housekeeper, or whatever she is—a Miss Gilchrist. The police asked for the name of her nearest relative or of her solicitors. And this Miss Gilchrist seemed rather doubtful about relatives and their addresses, but she knew about us. So they got through at once."

"What makes them think she was murdered?" demanded Mr Entwhistle.

Mr Parrott sounded apologetic again.

"Oh well, it seems there can't be any doubt about *that*—I mean it was a hatchet or something of that kind—a very violent sort of crime."

"Robbery?"

"That's the idea. A window was smashed and there are some trinkets missing and drawers pulled out and all that, but the police seem to think there might be something—well—phony about it."

"What time did it happen?"

"Sometime between two and four this afternoon."

"Where was the housekeeper?"

"Changing library books in Reading. She got back about five o'clock and found Mrs Lansquenet dead. The police want to know if we've any idea of who could have been likely to attack her. I said," Mr Parrott's voice sounded outraged, "that I thought it was a most unlikely thing to happen."

"Yes, of course."

"It *must* be some half-witted local oaf—who thought there might be something to steal and then lost his head and attacked her. That must be it—eh, don't you think so, Entwhistle?"

"Yes, yes . . ." Mr Entwhistle spoke absentmindedly.

Parrott was right, he told himself. That was what must have happened. . . .

But uncomfortably he heard Cora's voice saying brightly: "But he *was* murdered, wasn't he?"

Such a fool, Cora. Always had been. Rushing in where angels fear to tread. . . . Blurting out unpleasant truths. . . .

Truths!

That blasted word again . . .

ii

Mr Entwhistle and Inspector Morton looked at each other appraisingly.

In his neat precise manner Mr Entwhistle had placed at the Inspector's disposal all the relevant facts about Cora Lansquenet. Her upbringing, her marriage, her windowhood, her financial position, her relatives.

"Mr Timothy Abernethie is her only surviving brother and her next of kin, but he is a recluse and an invalid, and is quite unable to leave home. He has empowered me to act for him and to make all such arrangements as may be necessary."

The Inspector nodded. It was a relief for him to have this shrewd elderly solicitor to deal with. Moreover he hoped that the lawyer might be able to give him some assistance in solving what was beginning to look like a rather puzzling problem.

He said:

"I understand from Miss Gilchrist that Mrs Lansquenet had been North, to the funeral of an elder brother, on the day before her death?"

"That is so, Inspector. I myself was there."

"There was nothing unusual in her manner—nothing strange —or apprehensive?"

Mr Entwhistle raised his eyebrows in well simulated surprise.

"Is it customary for there to be something strange in the manner of a person who is shortly to be murdered?" he asked.

The Inspector smiled rather ruefully.

"I'm not thinking of her being 'fey' or having a premonition. No, I'm just hunting around for something—well, something out of the ordinary."

"I don't think I quite understand you, Inspector," said Mr Entwhistle.

"It's not a very easy case to understand, Mr Entwhistle. Say someone watched the Gilchrist woman come out of the house at about two o'clock and go along to the village and the bus stop. This someone then deliberately takes the hatchet that was lying by the woodshed, smashes the kitchen window with it, gets into the house, goes upstairs, attacks Mrs Lansquenet with the hatchet—and attacks her savagely. Six or eight blows were struck." Mr Entwhistle flinched—"Oh, yes, quite a brutal crime. Then the intruder pulls out a few drawers, scoops up a few trinkets—worth perhaps a tenner in all, and clears off."

"She was in bed?"

"Yes. It seems she returned late from the North the night before, exhausted and very excited. She'd come into some legacy as I understand?"

"Yes."

"She slept very badly and woke with a terrible headache. She had several cups of tea and took some dope for her head and then told Miss Gilchrist not to disturb her till lunch-time. She felt no better and decided to take two sleeping pills. She then sent Miss Gilchrist into Reading by the bus to change some library books. She'd have been drowsy, if not already asleep, when this man broke in. He could have taken what he wanted by means of threats, or he could easily have gagged her. A hatchet, deliberately taken up with him from the outside, seems excessive."

"He may just have meant to threaten her with it," Mr Entwhistle suggested. "If she showed fight then—"

"According to the medical evidence there is no sign that she did. Everything seems to show that she was lying on her side sleeping peacefully when she was attacked."

Mr Entwhistle shifted uneasily in his chair.

"One does hear of these brutal and rather senseless murders," he pointed out.

"Oh yes, yes, that's probably what it will turn out to be. There's an alert out, of course, for any suspicious character. Nobody local is concerned, we're pretty sure of that. The locals are all accounted for satisfactorily. Most people are at work at that time of day. Of course her cottage is up a lane outside the village proper. Anyone could get there easily without being seen. There's a maze of lanes all round the village. It was a fine morning and there has been no rain for some days so there aren't any distinctive car tracks to go by—in case anyone came by car."

"You think someone came by car?" Mr Entwhistle asked sharply.

The Inspector shrugged his shoulders. "I don't know. All I'm saying is there are curious features about the case. These, for instance—" He shoved across his desk a handful of things—a trefoil-shaped brooch with small pearls, a brooch set with amethysts, a small string of seed pearls, and a garnet bracelet.

"Those are the things that were taken from her jewel box. They were found just outside the house shoved into a bush."

"Yes—yes, that *is* rather curious. Perhaps if her assailant was frightened at what he had done—"

"Quite. But he would probably then have left them upstairs in her room . . . Of course a panic may have come over him between the bedroom and the front gate."

Mr Entwhistle said quietly:

"Or they may, as you are suggesting, have only been taken as a blind."

"Yes, several possibilities . . . Of course this Gilchrist woman may have done it. Two women living alone together—you never know what quarrels or resentments or passions may have been aroused. Oh yes, we're taking that possibility into consideration as well. But it doesn't seem very likely. From all accounts they seemed to be on quite amicable terms." He paused before going on. "According to you nobody stands to gain by Mrs Lansquenet's death?"

The lawyer shifted uneasily.

"I didn't quite say that."

Inspector Morton looked up sharply.

"I thought you said that Mrs Lansquenet's source of income was an allowance made to her by her brother and that as far as you knew she had no property or means of her own."

"That is so. Her husband died a bankrupt, and from what I knew of her as a girl and since, I should be surprised if she had ever saved or accumulated any money."

"The cottage itself is rented, not her own, and the few sticks of furniture aren't anything to write home about, even in these days. Some spurious 'cottage oak' and some arty painted stuff. Whoever she's left them to won't gain much—if she's made a will, that is to say."

Mr Entwhistle shook his head.

"I know nothing about her will. I had not seen her for many years, you must understand."

"Then what exactly did you mean just now? You had something in mind, I think?"

"Yes. Yes, I did. I wished to be strictly accurate."

"Were you referring to the legacy you mentioned? The one that her brother left her? Had she the power to dispose of that by will?"

"No, not in the sense you mean. She had no power to dispose of the capital. Now that she is dead, it will be divided amongst the five other beneficiaries of Richard Abernethie's will. That is what I meant. All five of them will benefit automatically by her death."

The Inspector looked disappointed.

"Oh, I thought we were on to something. Well, there certainly seems no motive there for anyone to come and swipe her with a hatchet. Looks though it's some chap with a screw loose—one of these adolescent criminals, perhaps—a lot of them about. And then he lost his nerve and bushed the trinkets and ran . . . Yes, it must be that. Unless it's the highly respectable Miss Gilchrist and I must say that seems unlikely."

"When did she find the body?"

"Not until just about five o'clock. She came back from Reading by the four-fifty bus. She arrived back at the cottage, let herself in by the front door, and went into the kitchen and put the kettle on for tea. There was no sound from Mrs Lansquenet's room, but Miss Gilchrist assumed that she was still sleeping. Then Miss Gilchrist noticed the kitchen window, the glass was all over the floor. Even then, she thought at first it might have been done by a boy with a ball or a catapult. She went upstairs and peeped very gently into Mrs Lansquenet's room to see if she were asleep or if she was ready for some tea. Then of course, she let loose, shrieked, and rushed down the lane to the nearest neighbour. Her story seems perfectly consistent and there was no trace of blood in her room or in the bathroom, or on her clothes. No, I don't think Miss Gilchrist had anything to do with it. The doctor got there at half past five. He puts the time of death not later than four o'clock—and probably much nearer to two o'clock, so it looks as though whoever it was, was hanging round waiting for Miss Gilchrist to leave the cottage."

The lawyer's face twitched slightly. Inspector Morton went on: "You'll be going to see Miss Gilchrist, I suppose?"

"I thought of doing so."

"I should be glad if you would. She's told us, I think, everything that she can, but you never know. Sometimes in conversation, some point or other may crop up. She's a trifle old-maidish—but quite a sensible practical woman—and she's really been most helpful and efficient."

He paused and then said:

"The body's at the mortuary. If you would like to see it—"

Mr Entwhistle assented though with no enthusiasm.

Some few minutes later he stood looking down at the mortal remains of Cora Lansquenet. She had been savagely attacked and the henna dyed fringe was clotted and stiffened with blood. Mr Entwhistle's lips tightened and he looked away queasily.

Poor little Cora. How eager she had been the day before

yesterday to know whether her brother had left her anything. What rosy anticipations she must have had of the future. What a lot of silly things she could have done—and enjoyed doing—with the money.

Poor Cora. . . . How short a time those anticipations had lasted.

No one had gained by her death—not even the brutal assailant who had thrust away those trinkets as he fled. Five people had a few thousands more of capital—but the capital they had already received was probably more than sufficient for them. No, there could be no motive there.

Funny that murder should have been running in Cora's mind the very day before she herself was murdered.

"It was murder, wasn't it?"

Such a ridiculous thing to say. Ridiculous! Quite ridiculous! Much too ridiculous to mention to Inspector Morton.

Of course, after he had seen Miss Gilchrist . . .

Supposing that Miss Gilchrist, although it was unlikely, could throw any light on what Richard had said to Cora.

"I thought from what he said—" What *had* Richard said?

"I must see Miss Gilchrist at once," said Mr Entwhistle to himself.

iii

Miss Gilchrist was a spare faded-looking woman with short iron grey hair. She had one of those indeterminate faces that women around fifty so often acquire.

She greeted Mr Entwhistle warmly.

"I'm *so* glad you have come, Mr Entwhistle. I really know *so little* about Mrs Lansquenet's family, and of course I've never never had anything to do with a *murder* before. It's too dreadful!"

Mr Entwhistle felt quite sure that Miss Gilchrist had never before had anything to do with murder. Indeed, her reaction to it was very much that of his partner.

"One *reads* about them, of course," said Miss Gilchrist, relegating crimes to their proper sphere. "And even *that* I'm not very fond of doing. So *sordid,* most of them."

Following her into the sitting room Mr Entwhistle was looking sharply about him. There was a strong smell of oil paint.
The cottage was overcrowded, less by furniture which was much
as Inspector Morton had described it, than by pictures. The
walls were covered with pictures, mostly very dark and dirty
oil paintings. But there were water colour sketches as well, and
one or two still lifes. Smaller pictures were stacked on the window seat.

"Mrs Lansquenet used to buy them at sales," Miss Gilchrist
explained. "It was a great interest to her, poor dear. She went
to all the sales round about. Pictures go so cheap, nowadays, a
mere song. She never paid more than a pound for any of them,
sometimes only a few shillings and there was a wonderful
chance, she always said, of picking up something worthwhile.
She used to say that this was an Italian Primitive that might
be worth a lot of money."

Mr Entwhistle looked at the Italian Primitive pointed out to
him dubiously. Cora, he reflected, had never really known
anything about pictures. He'd eat his hat if any of these daubs
were worth a five pound note!

"Of course," said Miss Gilchrist, noticing his expression, and
quick to sense his reaction. "I don't know much myself, though
my father was a painter—not a very successful one, I'm afraid.
But I used to do water colours myself as a girl and I heard a
lot of talk about painting and that made it nice for Mrs Lansquenet to have someone she could talk to about painting and
who'd understand. Poor dear soul, she cared so much about
artistic things."

"You were fond of her?"

A foolish question, he told himself. Could she possibly answer "no"? Cora, he thought, must have been a tiresome woman
to live with.

"Oh *yes*," said Miss Gilchrist. "We got on *very* well together.
In some ways, you know, Mrs Lansquenet was just like a child.
She said anything that came into her head. I don't know that
her *judgment* was always very good—"

One does not say of the dead—"She was a thoroughly silly

woman"— Mr Entwhistle said, "She was not in any sense an intellectual woman."

"No—no—perhaps not. But she was very shrewd, Mr Entwhistle. Really very shrewd. It quite surprised me sometimes—how she managed to hit the nail on the head."

Mr Entwhistle looked at Miss Gilchrist with more interest. He thought that she was no fool herself.

"You were with Mrs Lansquenet for some years, I think?"

"Three and a half."

"You—er—acted as companion and also did the—er—well—looked after the house?"

It was evident that he had touched on a delicate subject. Miss Gilchrist flushed a little.

"Oh yes, indeed. I did most of the cooking—I *quite* enjoy cooking—and did some dusting and light housework. None of the *rough,* of course." Miss Gilchrist's tone expressed a firm principle. Mr Entwhistle who had no idea what "the rough" was, made a soothing murmur.

"Mrs Panter from the village came in for that. Twice a week regularly. You see, Mr Entwhistle, I could not have contemplated being in any way a *servant.* When my little teashop failed —such a disaster—it was the war, you know. A delightful place. I called it the Willow Tree and all the china was blue willow pattern—sweetly pretty—and the cakes *really* good—I've always had a hand with cakes and scones. Yes I was doing really well and then the war came and supplies were cut down and the whole thing went bankrupt—a war casualty, that is what I always say, and I try to think of it like that. I lost the little money my father left me that I had invested in it, and of course I had to look round for something to do. I'd never been trained for anything. So I went to one lady but it didn't answer at all—she was so rude and overbearing and then I did some office work—but I didn't like that at all, and then I came to Mrs Lansquenet and we suited each other from the start—her husband being an artist and everything." Miss Gilchrist came to a breathless stop and added mournfully: "But how I loved my dear dear little teashop. Such *nice* people used to come to it!"

Looking at Miss Gilchrist, Mr Entwhistle felt a sudden stab

of recognition—a composite picture of hundreds of ladylike figures approaching him in numerous Bay Trees, Ginger Cats, Blue Parrots, Willow Trees and Cosy Corners, all chastely encased in blue or pink or orange overalls and taking orders for pots of china tea and cakes. Miss Gilchrist had a Spiritual Home —a ladylike teashop of Ye Olde Worlde variety with a suitable genteel clientele. There must, he thought, be large numbers of Miss Gilchrists all over the country, all looking much alike with mild patient faces and obstinate upper lips and slightly wispy grey hair.

Miss Gilchrist went on:

"But really I must not talk about myself. The police have been very kind and considerate. Very kind indeed. An Inspector Morton came over from headquarters and he was *most* understanding. He even arranged for me to go and spend the night at Mrs Lake's down the lane but I said 'No.' I felt it my duty to stay here with all Mrs Lansquenet's nice things in the house. They took the—the—" Miss Gilchrist gulped a little—"the body away, of course, and locked up the room, and the Inspector told me there would be a constable on duty in the kitchen all night—because of the broken window—it has been reglazed this morning, I am glad to say—where was I?—Oh yes, so I said I should be *quite* all right in my own room, though I must confess I *did* pull the chest of drawers across the door and put a big jug of water on the window-sill. One never knows—and if by any chance it *was* a maniac—one does hear of such things . . ."

Here Miss Gilchrist ran down. Mr Entwhistle said quickly:

"I am in possession of all the main facts. Inspector Morton gave them to me. But if it would not distress you too much to give me your own account—?"

"Of course, Mr Entwhistle. I know *just* what you feel. The police are so impersonal, are they not? Rightly so, of course."

"Mrs Lansquenet got back from the funeral the night before last," Mr Entwhistle prompted.

"Yes, her train didn't get in until quite late. I had ordered a taxi to meet it as she told me to. She was very tired, poor dear— as was only natural—but on the whole she was in quite good spirits."

"Yes, yes. Did she talk about the funeral at all?"

"Just a little. I made her a cup of Ovaltine—she didn't want anything else—and she told me that the church had been quite full and lots and lots of flowers—oh! and she said that she was sorry not to have seen her other brother—Timothy—was it?"

"Yes, Timothy."

"She said it was over twenty years since she had seen him and that she hoped he would have been there, but she quite realised he would have thought it better not to come under the circumstances, but that his wife was there and that she'd never been able to stand Maude—oh dear, I *do* beg your pardon, Mr Entwhistle—it just slipped out—I never meant—"

"Not at all. Not at all," said Mr Entwhistle encouragingly. "I am no relation, you know. And I believe that Cora and her sister-in-law never hit it off very well."

"Well, she almost said as much. 'I always knew Maude would grow into one of those bossy interfering women,' is what she said. And then she was very tired and said she'd go to bed at once—I'd got her hot water bottle in all ready—and she went up."

"She said nothing else that you can remember specially?"

"She had no *premonition,* Mr Entwhistle, if that is what you mean. I'm sure of that. She was really, you know, in remarkably good spirits—apart from tiredness and the—the sad occasion. She asked me how I'd like to go to Capri. To Capri! Of course I said it would be too wonderful—it's a thing I'd never dreamed I'd ever do—and she said, 'We'll go!' Just like that. I gathered —of course it wasn't actually *mentioned*—that her brother had left her an annuity or something of the kind."

Mr Entwhistle nodded.

"Poor dear. Well, I'm glad she had the pleasure of planning —at all events." Miss Gilchrist sighed and murmured wistfully, "I don't suppose I shall ever go to Capri now. . . ."

"And the next morning?" Mr Entwhistle prompted, oblivious of Miss Gilchrist's disappointments.

"The next morning Mrs Lansquenet wasn't at all well. Really, she looked dreadful. She'd hardly slept at all, she told me. Nightmares. 'It's because you were overtired yesterday,' I told her, and she said maybe it was. She had her breakfast in bed, and she didn't get up all the morning, but at lunchtime she told me that she still hadn't been able to sleep. 'I feel so restless,' she said. 'I keep thinking of things and wondering.' And then she said she'd take some sleeping tablets and try and get a good sleep in the afternoon. And she wanted me to go over by bus to Reading and change her two library books, because she'd finished them both on the train journey and she hadn't got anything to read. Usually two books lasted her nearly a week. So I went off just after two and that—and that—was the last time—" Miss Gilchrist began to sniff. "She must have been asleep, you know. She wouldn't have heard anything and the Inspector assures me that she didn't suffer. . . . He thinks the first blow killed her. Oh dear, it makes me quite sick even to *think* of it!"

"Please, please. I've no wish to take you any further over what happened. All I wanted was to hear what you could tell me about Mrs Lansquenet before the tragedy."

"Very natural, I'm sure. Do tell her relations that apart from having such a bad night she was really very happy and looking forward to the future."

Mr Entwhistle paused before asking his next question. He wanted to be careful not to lead the witness.

"She did not mention any of her relations in particular?"

"No, no, I don't think so." Miss Gilchrist considered. "Except what she said about being sorry not to see her brother Timothy."

"She did not speak at all about her brother's decease? The—er—cause of it? Anything like that?"

"No."

There was no sign of alertness in Miss Gilchrist's face. Mr Entwhistle felt certain there would have been if Cora had plumped out her verdict of murder.

"He'd been ill for some time, I think," said Miss Gilchrist vaguely, "though I must say I was surprised to hear it. He looked so very vigorous."

Mr Entwhistle said quickly:

"You saw him—when?"

"When he came down here to see Mrs Lansquenet. Let me see —that was about three weeks ago."

"Did he stay here?"

"Oh—no—just came for luncheon. It was quite a surprise. Mrs Lansquenet hadn't expected him. I gather there had been some family disagreement. She hadn't seen him for years, she told me."

"Yes, that is so."

"It quite upset her—seeing him again—and probably realising how ill he was—"

"She knew that he was ill?"

"Oh yes, I remember quite well. Because I wondered—only in my own mind, you understand—if perhaps Mr Abernethie might be suffering from softening of the brain. An aunt of mine—"

Mr Entwhistle deftly sidetracked the aunt.

"Something Mrs Lansquenet said caused you to think of softening of the brain?"

"Yes. Mrs Lansquenet said something like 'Poor Richard. Mortimer's death must have aged him a lot. He sounds quite senile. All these fancies about persecution and that someone is poisoning him. Old people get like that.' And of course, as I knew, that is only too *true*. This aunt that I was telling you about —convinced the servants were trying to poison her in her food and at last would eat only boiled eggs—because, she said, you couldn't get inside a boiled egg to poison it. We humoured her, but if it had been nowadays I don't know *what* we should have done. With eggs so scarce and mostly foreign at that, so that boiling is always risky."

Mr Entwhistle listened to the saga of Miss Gilchrist's aunt with deaf ears. He was very much disturbed.

He said at last, when Miss Gilchrist had twittered into silence:

"I suppose Mrs Lansquenet didn't take all this too seriously?"

"Oh no, Mr Entwhistle, she *quite* understood."

Mr Entwhistle found that remark disturbing too, though not quite in the sense in which Miss Gilchrist had used it.

Had Cora Lansquenet understood? Not then, perhaps, but later. Had she understood only too well?

Mr Entwhistle knew that there had been no senility about Richard Abernethie. Richard had been in full possession of his faculties. He was not the man to have persecution mania in any form. He was, as he always had been, a hard-headed business man—and his illness made no difference in that respect.

It seemed extraordinary that he should gave spoken to his sister in the terms that he had. But perhaps Cora, with her odd childlike shrewdness had read between the lines, and had crossed the t's and dotted the i's of what Richard Abernethie had actually said.

In most ways, thought Mr Entwhistle, Cora had been a complete fool. She had no judgment, no balance, and a crude childish point of view, but she had also the child's uncanny knack of sometimes hitting the nail on the head in a way that seemed quite startling.

Mr Entwhistle left it at that. Miss Gilchrist, he thought, knew no more than she had told him. He asked whether she knew if Cora Lansquenet had left a will. Miss Gilchrist replied promptly that Mrs Lansquenet's will was at the Bank.

With that and after making certain further arrangements he took his leave. He insisted on Miss Gilchrist's accepting a small sum in cash to defray present expenses and told her he would communicate with her again, and in the meantime he would be grateful if she would stay on at the cottage while she was looking about for a new post. That would be, Miss Gilchrist said, a great convenience and really she was not at all nervous.

He was unable to escape without being shown round the cottage by Miss Gilchrist, and introduced to various pictures by the late Pierre Lansquenet which were crowded into the small dining room and which made Mr Entwhistle flinch—they were mostly nudes executed with a singular lack of draughtsmanship but with much fidelity to detail. He was also made to admire various small oil sketches of picturesque fishing ports done by Cora herself.

"Polperro," said Miss Gilchrist proudly. "We were there last year and Mrs Lansquenet was delighted with its picturesqueness."

Mr Entwhistle, viewing Polperro from the southwest, from the northwest, and presumably from the several other points of the compass, agreed that Mrs Lansquenet had certainly been enthusiastic.

"Mrs Lansquenet promised to leave me her sketches," said

Miss Gilchrist wistfully. "I admired them so much. One can really see the waves breaking in this one, can't one? Even if she forgot, I might perhaps have just *one* as a souvenir, do you think?"

"I'm sure that could be arranged," said Mr Entwhistle graciously.

He made a few further arrangements and then left to interview the Bank Manager and to have a further consultation with Inspector Morton.

V

"WORN OUT, that's what you are," said Miss Entwhistle in the indignant and bullying tones adopted by devoted sisters towards brothers for whom they keep house. "You shouldn't do it, at your age. What's it all got to do with you, I'd like to know? You've retired, haven't you?"

Mr Entwhistle said mildly that Richard Abernethie had been one of his oldest friends.

"I daresay. But Richard Abernethie's dead, isn't he? So I see no reason for you to go mixing yourself up in things that are no concern of yours and catching your death of cold in these nasty draughty railway trains. And murder, too! *I* can't see why they sent for you at all."

"They communicated with me because there was a letter in the cottage signed by me, telling Cora the arrangements for the funeral."

"Funerals! One funeral after another, and that reminds me. Another of these precious Abernethies has been ringing you up—Timothy, I think he said. From somewhere in Yorkshire—and *that's* about a funeral, too! Said he'd ring again later."

A personal call for Mr Entwhistle came through that evening. Taking it, he heard Maude Abernethie's voice at the other end.

"Thank goodness I've got hold of you at last! Timothy has been in the most terrible state. This news about Cora has upset him dreadfully."

"Quite understandable," said Mr Entwhistle.

"What did you say?"

"I said it was quite understandable."

"I suppose so." Maude sounded more than doubtful. "Do you mean to say it was really murder?"

(*"It was murder, wasn't it?"* Cora had said. But this time there was no hesitation about the answer.)

"Yes, it was murder," said Mr Entwhistle.

"And with a hatchet, so the papers say?"

"Yes."

"It seems *quite* incredible to me," said Maude, "that Timothy's sister—his own sister—can have been murdered with a *hatchet!*"

It seemed no less incredible to Mr Entwhistle. Timothy's life was so remote from violence that even his relations, one felt, ought to be equally exempt.

"I'm afraid one has to face the fact," said Mr Entwhistle mildly.

"I am really *very* worried about Timothy. It's so bad for him all this! I've got him to bed now but he insists on my persuading you to come up and see him. He wants to know a hundred things —whether there will be an inquest, and who ought to attend, and how soon after that the funeral can take place, and where, and what funds there are, and if Cora expressed any wishes about being cremated or what, and if she left a will—"

Mr Entwhistle interrupted before the catalogue got too long.

"There is a will, yes. She left Timothy her executor."

"Oh dear, I'm afraid Timothy can't undertake anything—"

"The firm will attend to all the necessary business. The will's very simple. She left her own sketches and an amethyst brooch to her companion, Miss Gilchrist and everything else to Susan."

"To Susan? Now I wonder why Susan? I don't believe she ever saw Susan—not since she was a baby anyway."

"I imagine that it was because Susan was reported to have made a marriage not wholly pleasing to the family."

Maude snorted.

"Even Gregory is a great deal better than Pierre Lansquenet ever was! Of course marrying a man who serves in a shop would have been unheard of in my day—but a chemist's shop is much better than a haberdasher's—and at least Gregory seems quite respectable." She paused and added: "Does this mean that Susan gets the income Richard left to Cora?"

"Oh no. The capital of that will be divided according to the instructions of Richard's will. No, poor Cora had only a few hundred pounds and the furniture of her cottage to leave. When outstanding debts are paid and the furniture sold I doubt if the whole thing will amount to more than at most five hundred pounds." He went on: "There will have to be an inquest, of course. That is fixed for next Thursday. If Timothy is agreeable, we'll send down young Lloyd to watch the proceedings on behalf of the family." He added apologetically: "I'm afraid it may attract some notoriety owing to the—er—circumstances."

"How very unpleasant! Have they caught the wretch who did it?"

"Not yet."

"One of these dreadful half baked young men who go about the country roving and murdering, I suppose. The police are so incompetent."

"No, no," said Mr Entwhistle. "The police are by no means incompetent. Don't imagine that, for a moment."

"Well, it all seems to me quite extraordinary. And *so* bad for Timothy. I suppose you couldn't possibly come down here, Mr Entwhistle? I should be *most* grateful if you could. I think Timothy's mind might be set at rest if you were here to reassure him."

Mr Entwhistle was silent for a moment. The invitation was not unwelcome.

"There is something in what you say," he admitted. "And I shall need Timothy's signature as executor to certain documents. Yes, I think it might be quite a good thing."

"That is splendid. I am so relieved. Tomorrow? And you'll stay the night? The best train is the eleven-thirty from St. Pancras."

"It will have to be an afternoon train, I'm afraid. I have—" said Mr Entwhistle, "other business in the morning . . ."

ii

George Crossfield greeted Mr Entwhistle heartily but with, perhaps, just a shade of surprise.

Mr Entwhistle said, in an explanatory way, although it really explained nothing:

"I've just come up from Lytchett St. Mary."

"Then it really was Aunt Cora? I read about it in the papers and I just couldn't believe it. I thought it must be someone of the same name."

"Lansquenet is not a common name."

"No, of course it isn't. I suppose there is a natural aversion to believing that anyone of one's own family can be murdered. Sounds to me rather like that case last month on Dartmoor."

"Does it?"

"Yes. Same circumstances. Cottage in a lonely position. Two elderly women living together. Amount of cash taken really quite pitifully inadequate one would think."

"The value of money is always relative," said Mr Entwhistle. "It is the need that counts."

"Yes—yes, I suppose you're right."

"If you need ten pounds desperately—then fifteen is more than adequate. And inversely also. If your need is for a hundred pounds, forty five would be worse than useless. And if it's thousands you need, then hundreds are not enough."

George said with a sudden flicker of the eyes: "I'd say *any* money came in useful these days. Everyone's hard up."

"But not *desperate*," Mr Entwhistle pointed out. "It's the desperation that counts."

"Are you thinking of something in particular?"

"Oh no, not at all." He paused then went on. "It will be a little time before the estate is settled, would it be convenient for you to have an advance?"

"As a matter of fact, I *was* going to raise the subject. However, I saw the Bank this morning and referred them to you and they were quite obliging about an overdraft."

Again there came that flicker in George's eyes, and Mr Entwhistle, from the depths of his experience, recognised it. George, he felt certain, had been, if not desperate, then in very sore straits for money. He knew at that moment, what he had felt sub-consciously all along, that in money matters he would not trust George. He wondered if old Richard Abernethie, who also had had great experience in judging men, had felt that. Mr Entwhistle was almost sure that after Mortimer's death, Richard

Abernethie had formed the intention of making George his heir. George was not an Abernethie, but he was the only male of the younger generation. He was the natural successor to Mortimer. Richard Abernethie had sent for George, had had him staying in the house for some days. It seemed probable that at the end of the visit the older man had not found George satisfactory. Had he felt instinctively, as Mr Entwhistle felt, that George was not straight? George's father, so the family had thought, had been a poor choice on Laura's part. A stockbroker who had had other rather mysterious activities. George took after his father rather than after the Abernethies.

Perhaps misinterpreting the old lawyer's silence, George said with an uneasy laugh:

"Truth is, I've not been very lucky with my investments lately. I took a bit of a risk and it didn't come off. More or less cleaned me out. But I'll be able to recoup myself now. All one needs is a bit of capital. Ardens Consolidated are pretty good, don't you think?"

Mr Entwhistle neither agreed nor dissented. He was wondering if by any chance George had been speculating with money that belonged to clients and not with his own? If George had been in danger of criminal prosecution—

Mr Entwhistle said precisely:

"I tried to reach you the day after the funeral, but I suppose you weren't in the office."

"Did you? They never told me. As a matter of fact, I thought I was entitled to a day off after the good news!"

"The good news?"

George reddened.

"Oh look here, I didn't mean Uncle Richard's death. But knowing you've come into money does give one a bit of a kick. One feels one must celebrate. As a matter of fact I went to Hurst Park. Backed two winners. It never rains but it pours! If your luck's in, it's in! Only a matter of fifty quid, but it all helps."

"Oh yes," said Mr Entwhistle. "It all helps. And there will now be an additional sum coming to you as a result of your Aunt Cora's death."

George looked concerned.

"Poor old girl," he said. "It does seem rotten luck, doesn't it? Probably just when she was all set to enjoy herself."

"Let us hope the police will find the person responsible for her death," said Mr Entwhistle.

"I expect they'll get him all right. They're good, our police. They round up all the undesirables in the neighbourhood and go through 'em with a tooth comb—make them account for their actions at the time it happened."

"Not so easy if a little time has elapsed," said Mr Entwhistle. He gave a wintry little smile that indicated he was about to make a joke. "I myself was in Hatchard's bookshop at three-thirty on the day in question. Should I remember that if I were questioned by the police in ten days time? I very much doubt it. And you, George, you were at Hurst Park. Would you remember which day you went to the races in—say—a month's time?"

"Oh I could fix it by the funeral—the day after."

"True—true. And then you backed a couple of winners. Another aid to memory. One seldom forgets the name of a horse on which one has won money. Which were they, by the way?"

"Let me see. Gaymarck and Frogg II. Yes, I shan't forget them in a hurry."

Mr Entwhistle gave his dry little cackle of laughter and took his leave.

iii

"It's lovely to see you, of course," said Rosamund without any marked enthusiasm. "But it's frightfully early in the morning."

She yawned heavily.

"It's eleven o'clock," said Mr Entwhistle.

Rosamund yawned again. She said apologetically:

"We had the hell of a party last night. Far too much to drink. Michael's got a terrible hangover still."

Michael appeared at this moment, also yawning. He had a cup of black coffee in his hand and was wearing a very smart dressing gown. He looked haggard and attractive—and his smile had the usual charm. Rosamund was wearing a black skirt, a rather dirty yellow pullover, and nothing else as far as Mr Entwhistle could judge.

The precise and fastidious lawyer did not approve at all of the young Shanes' way of living. The rather ramshackle flat on the first floor of a Chelsea house—the bottles and glasses and cigarette ends that lay about in profusion—the stale air, and the general air of dust and dishevelment.

In the midst of this discouraging setting Rosamund and Michael bloomed with their wonderful good looks. They were certainly a very handsome couple and they seemed, Mr Entwhistle thought, very fond of each other. Rosamund was certainly adoringly fond of Michael.

"Darling," she said. "Do you think just a teeny sip of champagne? Just to pull us together and toast the future. Oh, Mr Entwhistle, it really is the most marvellous luck Uncle Richard leaving us all that lovely money just now—"

Mr Entwhistle noted the quick almost scowling frown that Michael gave, but Rosamund went on serenely:

"Because there's the most wonderful chance of a play. Michael's got an option on it. It's a most wonderful part for him and even a small part for me, too. It's about one of these young criminals, you know, that are really saints—it's absolutely full of the latest modern ideas."

"So it would seem," said Mr Entwhistle stiffly.

"He robs, you know, and he kills, and he's hounded by the police and by society—and then in the end, he does a miracle."

Mr Entwhistle sat in outraged silence. Pernicious nonsense these young fools talked! *And* wrote.

Not that Michael Shane was talking much. There was still a faint scowl on his face.

"Mr Entwhistle doesn't want to hear all our rhapsodies, Rosamund," he said. "Shut up for a bit and let him tell us why he's come to see us."

"There are just one or two little matters to straighten out," said Mr Entwhistle. "I have just come back from Lytchett St. Mary."

"Then it *was* Aunt Cora who was murdered? We saw it in

the paper. And I said it must be because it's a very uncommon name. Poor old Aunt Cora. I was looking at her at the funeral that day and thinking what a frump she was and that really one might as well be dead if one looked like that—and now she *is* dead. They absolutely wouldn't *believe* it last night when I told them that that murder with the hatchet in the paper was actually *my aunt!* They just laughed, didn't they, Michael?"

Michael Shane did not reply and Rosamund with every appearance of enjoyment said:

"Two murders one after another. It's almost too much, isn't it?"

"Don't be a fool, Rosamund, your Uncle Richard wasn't murdered."

"Well, Cora thought he was."

Mr Entwhistle intervened to ask:

"You came back to London after the funeral, didn't you?"

"Yes, we came by the same train as you did."

"Of course . . . of course. I ask because I tried to get hold of you," he shot a quick glance at the telephone—"on the following day—several times in fact, and couldn't get an answer."

"Oh dear—I'm so sorry. What were we doing that day? The day before yesterday. We were here until about twelve, weren't we? And then you went round to try and get hold of Rosenheim and you went on to lunch with Oscar and I went out to see if I could get some nylons and round the shops. I was to meet Janet but we missed each other. Yes, I had a lovely afternoon shopping—and then we dined at the *Castile*. We got back here about ten o'clock, I suppose."

"About that," said Michael. He was looking thoughtfully at Mr Entwhistle. "What did you want to get hold of us for, sir?"

"Oh! Just some points that had arisen about Richard Abernethie's estate—papers to sign—all that."

Rosamund asked: "Do we get the money now, or not for ages?"

"I'm afraid," said Mr Entwhistle, "that the law is prone to delays."

"But we can get an advance, can't we?" Rosamund looked

alarmed. "Michael said we could. Actually it's terribly important. Because of the play."

Michael said pleasantly:

"Oh, there's no real hurry. It's just a question of deciding whether or not to take up the option."

"It will be quite easy to advance you some money," said Mr Entwhistle. "As much as you need."

"Then that's all right." Rosamund gave a sigh of relief. She added as an afterthought: "Did Aunt Cora leave any money?"

"A little. She left it to your Cousin Susan."

"Why Susan, I should like to know! Is it much?"

"A few hundred pounds and some furniture."

"Nice furniture?"

"No," said Mr Entwhistle.

Rosamund lost interest. "It's all very odd, isn't it?" she said. "There was Cora, after the funeral, suddenly coming out with 'He *was* murdered!' and then, the very next day, *she* goes and gets *herself* murdered! I mean, it is *odd*, isn't it?"

There was a moment's rather uncomfortable silence before Mr Entwhistle said quietly:

"Yes, it is indeed very odd. . . ."

iv

Mr Entwhistle studied Susan Banks as she leant forward across the table talking in her animated manner.

None of the loveliness of Rosamund here. But it was an attractive face and its attraction lay, Mr Entwhistle decided, in its vitality. The curves of the mouth were rich and full. It was a woman's mouth and her body was very decidedly a woman's—emphatically so. Yet in many ways Susan reminded him of her uncle, Richard Abernethie. The shape of her head, the line of her jaw, the deep set reflective eyes. She had the same kind of dominant personality that Richard had had, the same driving energy, the same foresightedness and forthright judgment. Of the three members of the younger generation she alone seemed to be made of the metal that had raised up the vast Abernethie fortunes. Had Richard recognised in this niece a kindred spirit

to his own? Mr Entwhistle thought he must have done. Richard
had always had a keen appreciation of character. Here, surely,
were exactly the qualities of which he was in search. And yet,
in his will, Richard Abernethie had made no distinction in her
favour. Distrustful, as Mr Entwhistle believed, of George, passing
over that lovely dimwit, Rosamund—could he not have found
in Susan what he was seeking—an heir of his own mettle?

If not, the cause must be—yes, it followed logically—the husband. . . .

Mr Entwhistle's eyes slid gently over Susan's shoulder to
where Gregory Banks stood absently whittling at a pencil.

A thin pale nondescript young man with reddish sandy hair.
So overshadowed by Susan's colourful personality that it was
difficult to realise what he himself was really like. Nothing to
take hold of in the fellow—quite pleasant, ready to be agreeable—a yes man, as the modern term went. And yet that did not
seem to describe him satisfactorily. There was something vaguely
disquieting about the unobtrusiveness of Gregory Banks. He had
been an unsuitable match—yet Susan had insisted on marrying
him—had overborne all opposition—why? What had she seen
in him?

And now, six months after the marriage—"She's crazy about
the fellow," Mr Entwhistle said to himself. He knew the signs.
A large number of wives with matrimonial troubles had passed
through the office of Bollard, Entwhistle, Entwhistle and Bollard. Wives madly devoted to unsatisfactory and often what
appeared quite unprepossessing husbands, wives contemptuous
of, and bored by, apparently attractive and impeccable husbands. What any woman saw in some particular man was beyond the comprehension of the average intelligent male. It just
was so. A woman who could be intelligent about everything
else in the world could be a complete fool when it came to some
particular man. Susan, thought Mr Entwhistle, was one of those
women. For her the world revolved around Greg. And that
had its dangers in more ways than one.

Susan was talking with emphasis and indignation.

"—because it *is* disgraceful. You remember that woman who

was murdered in Yorkshire last year? Nobody was ever arrested.
And the old woman in the sweet shop who was killed with a
crowbar. They detained some man, and then they let him go!"

"There has to be evidence, my dear," said Mr Entwhistle.
Susan paid no attention.

"And that other case—a retired nurse—that was a hatchet
or an axe—just like Aunt Cora."

"Dear me, you appear to have made quite a study of these
crimes, Susan," said Mr Entwhistle mildly.

"Naturally one remembers these things—and when someone
in one's own family is killed—and in very much the same way—
well, it shows that there must be a lot of these sort of people
going round the countryside, breaking into places and attack-
ing lonely women—and that the police just don't *bother!*"

Mr Entwhistle shook his head.

"Don't belittle the police, Susan. They are a very shrewd and
patient body of men—persistent, too. Just because it isn't still
mentioned in the newspapers doesn't mean that a case is closed.
Far from it."

"And yet there are hundreds of unsolved crimes every year."

"Hundreds?" Mr Entwhistle looked dubious. "A certain number, yes. But there are many occasions when the police know
who has committed a crime but where the evidence is insufficient
for a prosecution."

"I don't believe it," said Susan. "I believe if you knew definitely *who* committed a crime you could always get the evidence."

"I wonder now." Mr Entwhistle sounded thoughtful. "I very
much wonder. . . ."

"Have they any idea *at all*—in Aunt Cora's case—of who it
might be?"

"That I couldn't say. Not as far as I know. But they would
hardly confide in me—and it's early days yet—the murder took
place only the day before yesterday, remember."

"It's definitely got to be a certain kind of person," Susan
mused. "A brutal, perhaps slightly half witted type—a discharged
soldier or a gaol bird. I mean, using a hatchet like that."

Looking slightly quizzical, Mr Entwhistle raised his eyebrows and murmured

> "Lizzie Borden with an axe
> Gave her father forty whacks
> When she saw what she had done
> She gave her mother forty-one."

"Oh," Susan flushed angrily, "Cora hadn't got any relations living with her—unless you mean the companion. And anyway Lizzie Borden was acquitted. Nobody knows for certain she killed her father and stepmother."

"The rhyme is quite definitely libellous," Mr Entwhistle agreed.

"You mean the companion *did* do it? Did Cora leave her anything?"

"An amethyst brooch of no great value and some sketches of fishing villages of sentimental value only."

"One has to have a motive for murder—unless one is half witted."

Mr Entwhistle gave a little chuckle.

"As far as one can see, the only person who had a motive is *you*, my dear Susan."

"What's that?" Greg moved forward suddenly. He was like a sleeper coming awake. An ugly light showed in his eyes. He was suddenly no longer a negligible feature in the background. "What's Sue got to do with it? What do you mean—saying things like that?"

Susan said sharply:

"Shut up, Greg. Mr Entwhistle doesn't mean anything—"

"Just my little joke," said Mr Entwhistle apologetically. "Not in the best taste, I'm afraid. Cora left her estate, such as it was, to you, Susan. But to a young lady who has just inherited several hundred thousand pounds, an estate, amounting at the most to a few hundreds, can hardly be said to represent a motive for murder."

"She left her money to me?" Susan sounded surprised. "How extraordinary. She didn't even know me. Why did she do it, do you think?"

"I think she had heard rumours that there had been a little

difficulty—er—over your marriage." Greg, back again at sharpening his pencil, scowled. "There had been a certain amount of trouble over her own marriage—and I think she experienced a fellow feeling."

Susan asked with a certain amount of interest:

"She married an artist, didn't she, whom none of the family liked? Was he a good artist?"

Mr Entwhistle shook his head very decidedly.

"Are there any of his paintings in the cottage?"

"Yes."

"Then I shall judge for myself," said Susan.

Mr Entwhistle smiled at the resolute tilt of Susan's chin.

"So be it. Doubtless I am an old fogey and hopelessly old fashioned in matters of art, but I really don't think you will dispute my verdict."

"I suppose I ought to go down there, anyway? And look over what there is. Is there anybody there now?"

"I have arranged with Miss Gilchrist to remain there until further notice."

Greg said: "She must have a pretty good nerve—to stay in a cottage where a murder's been committed."

"Miss Gilchrist is quite a sensible woman, I should say. Besides," added the lawyer drily, "I don't think she has anywhere else to go until she gets another situation."

"So Aunt Cora's death left her high and dry? Did she—were she and Aunt Cora—on intimate terms—"

Mr Entwhistle looked at her rather curiously, wondering just exactly what was in her mind.

"Moderately so, I imagine," he said. "She never treated Miss Gilchrist as a servant."

"Treated her a damned sight worse, I daresay," said Susan. "These wretched so called 'ladies' are the ones who get it taken out of them nowadays. I'll try and find her a decent post somewhere. It won't be difficult. Anyone who's willing to do a bit of housework and cook is worth their weight in gold—she does cook, doesn't she?"

"Oh yes. I gather it is something she called—er—*the rough*

that she objected to. I'm afraid I don't quite know what 'the rough' is."

Susan appeared to be a good deal amused.

Mr Entwhistle, glancing at his watch, said:

"Your Aunt left Timothy her executor."

"Timothy," said Susan with scorn. "Uncle Timothy is practically a myth. Nobody ever sees him."

"Quite." Mr. Entwhistle glanced at his watch. "I am travelling up to see him this afternoon. I will acquaint him with your decision to go down to the cottage."

"It will only take me a day or two, I imagine. I don't want to be long away from London. I've got various schemes in hand. I'm going into business."

Mr Entwhistle looked round him at the cramped sitting room of the tiny flat. Greg and Susan were evidently hard up. Her father, he knew, had run through most of his money. He had left his daughter badly off.

"What are your plans for the future, if I may ask?"

"I've got my eye on some premises in Cardigan Street. I suppose, if necessary, you can advance me some money? I may have to pay a deposit."

"That can be managed," said Mr Entwhistle. "I rang you up the day after the funeral several times—but could get no answer. I thought perhaps you might care for an advance. I wondered whether you might perhaps have gone out of town."

"Oh no," said Susan quickly. "We were in all day. Both of us. We didn't go out at all."

Greg said gently:

"You know, Susan, I think our telephone must have been out of order that day. You remember how I couldn't get through to Hard and Company in the afternoon? I meant to report it, but it was all right the next morning."

"Telephones," said Mr Entwhistle, "can be very unreliable sometimes."

Susan said suddenly:

"How did Aunt Cora know about our marriage? It was at a Registry Office and we didn't tell anyone until afterwards—"

"I fancy Richard may have told her about it. She remade

her will about three weeks ago. (It was formerly in favour of the Theosophical Society)—just about the time he had been down to see her."

Susan looked startled.

"Did Uncle Richard go down to see her? I'd no idea of that?"

"I hadn't any idea of it myself," said Mr Entwhistle.

"So that was when—"

"When what?"

"Nothing," said Susan.

VI

"VERY GOOD of you to come along," said Maude gruffly, as she greeted Mr Entwhistle on the platform of Bayham Compton station. "I can assure you that both Timothy and I much appreciate it. Of course the truth is that Richard's death was the worst thing possible for Timothy."

Mr Entwhistle had not yet considered his friend's death from this particular angle. But it was, he saw, the only angle from which Mrs Timothy Abernethie was likely to regard it.

As they proceeded towards the exit, Maude developed the theme.

"To begin with, it was a *shock*—Timothy was really very attached to Richard. And then unfortunately it put the idea of death into Timothy's head. Being such an invalid has made him rather nervous about himself. He realised that he was the only one of the brothers left alive—and he started saying that he'd be the next to go—and that it wouldn't be long now—all very morbid talk, as I told him."

They emerged from the station and Maude led the way to a dilapidated car of almost fabulous antiquity.

"Sorry about our old rattletrap," she said. "We've wanted a new car for years, but really we couldn't afford it. This has had a new engine twice—and these old cars really stand up to a lot of hard work—

"I hope it will start," she added. "Sometimes one has to wind it."

She pressed the starter several times but only a meaningless whirr resulted. Mr Entwhistle who had never cranked a car in his life, felt rather apprehensive, but Maude herself descended, inserted the starting handle and with a vigorous couple of turns woke the motor to life. It was fortunate, Mr Entwhistle reflected, that Maude was such a powerfully built woman.

"That's that," she said. "The old brute's been playing me up lately. Did it when I was coming back after the funeral. Had to walk a couple of miles to the nearest garage and they weren't good for much—just a village affair. I had to put up at the local Inn while they tinkered at it. Of course *that* upset Timothy too. I had to phone through to him and tell him I couldn't be back till the next day. Fussed him terribly. One tries to keep things from him as much as possible—but some things one can't do anything about—Cora's murder, for instance. I had to send for Dr Barton to give him a sedative. Things like murder are too much for a man in Timothy's state of health. I gather Cora was always a fool."

Mr Entwhistle digested this remark in silence. The inference was not quite clear to him.

"I don't think I'd seen Cora since our marriage," said Maude. "I didn't like to say to Timothy at the time: 'Your youngest sister's batty,' not just like that. But it's what I *thought*. There she was saying the most extraordinary things! One didn't know whether to resent them or whether to laugh. I suppose the truth is she lived in a kind of imaginary world of her own—full of melodrama and fantastic ideas about other people. Well, poor soul, she's paid for it now. She didn't have any protégés, did she?"

"Protégés? What do you mean?"

"I just wondered. Some young cadging artist, or musician—or something of that kind. Someone she might have let in that day, and who killed her for her loose cash. Perhaps an adolescent—they're so queer at that age sometimes—especially if they're the neurotic arty type. I mean, it seems so odd to break in and murder her in the middle of the afternoon. If you break into a house surely you'd do it at night."

"There would have been two women there then."

"Oh yes, the companion. But really I can't believe that anyone would deliberately wait until she was out of the way and then break in and attack Cora. What for? He can't have expected she'd have any cash or stuff to speak of, and there must have been times when both the women were out and the house was empty. That would have been much safer. It seems so stupid to go and commit a murder unless it's absolutely necessary."

"And Cora's murder, you feel, was unnecessary?"

"It all seems so stupid."

Should murder make sense? Mr Entwhistle wondered. Academically the answer was yes. But many pointless crimes were on record. It depended, Mr Entwhistle reflected, on the mentality of the murderer.

What did he really know about murderers and their mental processes? Very little. His firm had never had a criminal practice. He was no student of criminology himself. Murderers, as far as he could judge seemed to be of all sorts and kinds. Some had had over-weening vanity, some had had a lust for power, some, like Seddon, had been mean and avaricious, others, like Smith and Rowse had had an incredible fascination for women; some, like Armstrong, had been pleasant fellows to meet. Edith Thompson had lived in a world of violent unreality, Nurse Waddington had put her elderly patients out of the way with businesslike cheerfulness.

Maude's voice broke into his meditations.

"If I could only keep the newspapers from Timothy! But he will insist on reading them—and then, of course, it upsets him. You do understand, don't you, Mr Entwhistle, that there can be *no question* of Timothy's attending the inquest? If necessary, Dr Barton can write out a certificate or whatever it is."

"You can set your mind at rest about that."

"Thank goodness!"

They turned in through the gates of Stansfield Grange, and up a neglected drive. It had been an attractive small property once—but had now a doleful and neglected appearance. Maude sighed as she said:

"We had to let this go to seed during the war. Both gardeners called up. And now we've only got one old man—and he's not much good. Wages have gone up so terribly. I must say it's a blessing to realise that we'll be able to spend a little money on the place now. We're both so fond of it. I was really afraid that we might have to sell it. . . . Not that I suggested anything of the kind to Timothy. It would have upset him—dreadfully."

They drew up before the portico of a very lovely old Georgian house which badly needed a coat of paint.

"No servants," said Maude bitterly, as she led the way in. "Just a couple of women who come in. We had a resident maid until a month ago—slightly hunchbacked and terribly adenoidal and in many ways not too bright, but she was *there* which was such a comfort—and quite good at plain cooking. And would you believe it, she gave notice and went to a fool of a woman who keeps six pekinese dogs (it's a larger house than this and more work) because she was 'so fond of little doggies,' she said. Dogs, indeed! Being sick and making messes all the time I've no doubt! Really, these girls are *mental!* So there we are, and if I have to go out any afternoon, Timothy is left quite alone in the house and if anything should happen, how could he get help? Though I do leave the telephone close by his chair so that if he felt faint he could dial Dr Barton immediately."

Maude led the way into the drawing room where tea was laid ready by the fireplace, and establishing Mr Entwhistle there, disappeared, presumably to the back regions. She returned in a few minutes' time with a teapot and silver kettle, and proceeded to minister to Mr Entwhistle's needs. It was a good tea with homemade cake and fresh buns. Mr Entwhistle murmured:

"What about Timothy?" and Maude explained briskly that she had taken Timothy his tray before she set out for the station.

"And now," said Maude, "he will have had his little nap and it will be the best time for him to see you. Do try and not let him excite himself too much."

Mr Entwhistle assured her that he would exercise every precaution.

Studying her in the flickering firelight, he was seized by a feeling of compassion. This big stalwart matter of fact woman, so healthy, so vigorous, so full of common sense, and yet so strangely, almost pitifully, vulnerable in one spot. Her love for her husband was maternal love, Mr Entwhistle decided. Maude Abernethie had borne no child and she was a woman built for motherhood. Her invalid husband had become her child, to be shielded, guarded, watched over. And perhaps, being the stronger character of the two, she had unconsciously imposed

on him a state of invalidism greater than might otherwise have
been the case.

"Poor Mrs Tim," thought Mr Entwhistle to himself.

ii

"Good of you to come, Entwhistle."

Timothy raised himself up in his chair as he held out a hand.

He was a big man with a marked resemblance to his brother
Richard. But what was strength in Richard, in Timothy was
weakness. The mouth was irresolute, the chin very slightly re-
ceding, the eyes less deepset. Lines of peevish irritability showed
on his forehead.

His invalid status was emphasised by the rug across his knees
and a positive pharmacopeia of little bottles and boxes on a
table at his right hand."

"I mustn't exert myself," he said warningly. "Doctor's for-
bidden it. Keeps telling me not to worry! Worry! If *he*'d had a
murder in his family *he*'d do a bit of worrying, I bet! It's too
much for a man—first Richard's death—then hearing all about
his funeral and his will—what a will!—and on top of that poor
little Cora killed with a hatchet. Hatchet! Ugh! This country's
full of gangsters nowadays,—thugs—left over from the war!
Going about killing defenseless women. Nobody's got the guts
to put these things down—to take a strong hand. What's the
country coming to, I'd like to know? What's the damned country coming to?"

Mr Entwhistle was familiar with this gambit. It was a question almost invariably asked sooner or later by his clients for
the last twenty years and he had his routine for answering it.
The non-committal words he uttered could have been classified
under the heading of soothing noises.

"It all began with that damned Labour Government," said
Timothy. "Sending the whole Country to blazes. And the Government we've got now is no better. Mealy mouthed milk and
water socialists! Look at the state *we*'re in! Can't get a decent
gardener, can't get servants—poor Maude here has to work herself to a shadow messing about in the kitchen—(by the way
I think a custard pudding would go well with the sole tonight,

my dear—and perhaps a little clear soup first?) I've got to keep my strength up—Doctor Barton said so—let me see, where was I? Oh yes, *Cora*. It's a shock, I can tell you, to a man, when he hears his sister—his own sister—has been *murdered!* Why, I had palpitations for twenty minutes! You'll have to attend to everything for me, Entwhistle. *I* can't go to the inquest or be bothered by business of any kind connected with Cora's estate. I want to forget the whole thing. What happens, by the way, to Cora's share of Richard's money? Comes to me, I suppose?"

Murmuring something about clearing away tea, Maude left the room.

Timothy lay back in his chair and said:

"Good thing to get rid of the women. Now we can talk business without any silly interruptions."

"The sum left in trust for Cora," said Mr Entwhistle, "goes equally to you and the nieces and nephew."

"But look here," Timothy's cheeks assumed a purplish hue of indignation. "Surely I'm her next of kin? Only surviving brother."

Mr Entwhistle explained with some care the exact provisions of Richard Abernethie's will, reminding Timothy gently that he had had a copy sent him.

"Don't expect me to understand all that legal jargon, do you?" said Timothy ungratefully. "You lawyers! Matter of fact, I couldn't believe it when Maude came home and told me the gist of it. Thought she'd got it wrong. Women are never clear headed. Best woman in the world, Maude—but women don't understand finance. I don't believe Maude even realises that if Richard hadn't died when he did, we might have had to clear out of here. Fact!"

"Surely if you had applied to Richard—"

Timothy gave a short bark of harsh laughter.

"That's not my style. Our father left us all a perfectly reasonable share of his money—that is, if we didn't want to go into the family concern. I didn't. I've a soul above cornplasters, Entwhistle! Richard took my attitude a bit hard. Well, what with taxes, depreciation of income, one thing and another—it hasn't been easy to keep things going. I've had to realise a

good deal of capital. Best thing to do these days. I did hint once
to Richard that this place was getting a bit hard to run. He
took the attitude that we'd be much better off in a smaller place
altogether. Easier for Maude, he said, more labour saving—
labour saving, what a term! Oh no, I wouldn't have asked
Richard for help. But I can tell you, Entwhistle, that the worry
affected my health most unfavourably. A man in my state of
health oughtn't to have to worry. Then Richard died and though
of course naturally I was cut up about it—my brother and all
that—I couldn't help feeling relieved about future prospects.
Yes, it's all plain sailing now—and a great relief. Get the house
painted—get a couple of really good men on the garden—you
can get them at a price. Restock the rose garden completely.
And—where was I—"

"Detailing your future plans."

"Yes, yes—but I mustn't bother you with all that. What did
hurt me—and hurt me cruelly—were the terms of Richard's will."

"Indeed?" Mr Entwhistle looked enquiring. "They were not
—as you expected?"

"I should say they weren't! Naturally, after Mortimer's death,
I assumed that Richard would leave everything to *me*."

"Ah—did he—ever—indicate that to you?"

"He never said so—not in so many words. Reticent sort of
chap, Richard. But he asked himself here—not long after
Mortimer's death. Wanted to talk over family affairs generally.
We discussed young George—and the girls and their husbands.
Wanted to know my views—not that I could tell him much. I'm
an invalid and I don't get about, and Maude and I live out of
the world. Rotten silly marriages both of those girls made, if
you ask me. Well, I ask you, Entwhistle, naturally I thought
he was consulting me as the head of the family after he was gone
and naturally I thought the control of the money would be mine.
Richard could surely trust me to do the right thing by the
younger generation. And to look after poor old Cora. Dash
it all, Entwhistle, I'm an Abernethie—the last Abernethie. Full
control should have been left in my hands."

In his excitement Timothy had kicked aside his rug and had
sat up in his chair. There were no signs of weakness or fragility

about him. He looked, Mr Entwhistle thought, a perfectly healthy man, even if a slightly excitable one. Moreover the old lawyer realised very clearly that Timothy Abernethie had probably always been secretly jealous of his brother Richard. They had been sufficiently alike for Timothy to resent his brother's strength of character and firm grasp of affairs. When Richard had died, Timothy had exulted in the prospect of succeeding at this late date to the power to control the destinies of others.

Richard Abernethie had not given him that power. Had he thought of doing so and then decided against it?

A sudden squalling of cats in the garden brought Timothy up out of his chair. Rushing to the window he threw up the sash, bawled out "Stop it, you!" and picking up a large book hurled it out at the marauders.

"Beastly cats," he grumbled, returning to his visitor. "Ruin the flower beds and I can't stand that damned yowling."

He sat down again and asked:

"Have a drink, Entwhistle?"

"Not quite so soon. Maude has just given me an excellent tea."

Timothy grunted.

"Capable woman, Maude. But she does too much. Even has to muck about with the inside of that old car of ours—she's quite a mechanic in her way, you know."

"I hear she had a breakdown coming back from the funeral?"

"Yes. Car conked out. She had the sense to telephone through about it, in case I should be anxious, but that ass of a daily woman of ours wrote down the message in a way that didn't make sense. I was out getting a bit of fresh air— I'm advised by the doctor to take what exercise I can if I feel like it— I got back from my walk to find scrawled on a bit of paper: 'Madam's sorry car gone wrong got to stay night.' Naturally I thought she was still at Enderby. Put a call through and found Maude had left that morning. Might have had the breakdown *anywhere!* Pretty kettle of fish! Fool of a daily woman only left me a lumpy macaroni cheese for supper. I had to go down to the kitchen and warm it up *myself—and* make myself a cup of tea—to say nothing of stoking the boiler. I might have had a heart attack— but does that class of woman care? Not she. With any decent feelings she'd have come back that evening and looked after me properly. No loyalty any more in the lower classes—"

He brooded sadly.

"I don't know how much Maude told you about the funeral and the relatives," said Mr Entwhistle. "Cora produced rather an awkward moment. Said brightly that Richard had been murdered, hadn't he? Perhaps Maude told you."

Timothy chuckled easily.

"Oh yes, I heard about that. Everybody looked down their noses and pretended to be shocked. Just the sort of thing Cora would say! You know how she always managed to put her foot in it when she was a girl, Entwhistle? Said something at our wedding that upset Maude, I remember. Maude never cared for her very much. Yes, Maude rang me up that evening after the funeral to know if I was all right and if Mrs Jones had come in to give me my evening meal and then she told me it had all gone off very well, and I said 'What about the will?' and she tried to hedge a bit, but of course I had the truth out of her. I couldn't believe it, and I said she must have made a mistake, but she stuck to it. It hurt me, Entwhistle—it really *wounded* me, if you know what I mean. If you ask me, it was just *spite* on Richard's part. I know one shouldn't speak ill of the dead, but, upon my word—"

Timothy continued on this theme for some time.

Then Maude came back into the room and said firmly:

"I think, dear, Mr Entwhistle has been with you quite long enough. You really *must* rest. If you have settled everything—"

"Oh, we've settled things. I leave it all to you, Entwhistle. Let me know when they catch the fellow—if they ever do. I've no faith in the police nowadays—the Chief Constables aren't the right type. You'll see to the—er—interment—won't you? We shan't be able to come I'm afraid. But order an expensive wreath—and there must be a proper stone put up in due course —she'll be buried locally, I suppose? No point in bringing her North and I've no idea where Lansquenet is buried, somewhere in France I believe. I don't know what one puts on a stone when it's murder. . . . Can't very well say 'entered into rest' or anything like that. One will have to choose a text—something appropriate. R.I.P.? No, that's only for Catholics."

"O Lord thou hast seen my wrong. Judge thou my case," murmured Mr Entwhistle.

The startled glance Timothy bent on him made Mr Entwhistle smile faintly.

"From Lamentations," he said. "It seemed appropriate if somewhat melodramatic. However, it will be some time before the question of the Memorial stone comes up. The—er—ground has to settle, you know. Now don't worry about anything. We will deal with things and keep you fully informed."

Mr Entwhistle left for London by the breakfast train on the following morning.

When he got home, after a little hesitation, he rang up a friend of his.

VII

"I CAN'T TELL you how much I appreciate your invitation."
Mr Entwhistle pressed his host's hand warmly.

Hercule Poirot gestured hospitably to a chair by the fire.

Mr Entwhistle sighed as he sat down.

On one side of the room a table was laid for two.

"I returned from the country this morning," he said.

"And you have a matter on which you wish to consult me?"

"Yes. It's a long rambling story, I'm afraid."

"Then we will not have it until after we have dined. *Georges?*"

The efficient George materialised with some *Pâté de Foie Gras* accompanied by hot toast in a napkin.

"We will have our *Pâté* by the fire," said Poirot. "Afterwards we will move to the table."

It was an hour and a half later that Mr Entwhistle stretched himself comfortably out in his chair and sighed a contented sigh.

"You certainly know how to do yourself well, Poirot. Trust a Frenchman."

"I am a Belgian. But the rest of your remark applies. At my age the chief pleasure, almost the *only* pleasure that still remains, is the pleasure of the table. Mercifully I have an excellent stomach."

"Ah," murmured Mr Entwhistle.

They had dined off a *Sole Veronique,* followed by *Escalope de Veau Milanaise,* proceeding to *Poire Flambée* with ice cream.

They had drunk a *Pouilly Fuisse* followed by a *Corton* and a very good port now reposed at Mr Entwhistle's elbow. Poirot, who did not care for port, was sipping *Crème de Cacao.*

"I don't know," murmured Mr Entwhistle reminiscently, "how you manage to get hold of an escalope like that! It melted in the mouth!"

"I have a friend who is a Continental butcher. For him I solve a small domestic problem. He is appreciative—and ever since then he is most sympathetic to me in the matters of the stomach."

"A domestic problem." Mr Entwhistle sighed. "I wish you had not reminded me. . . . This is such a perfect moment. . . ."

"Prolong it, my friend. We will have presently the *demi tasse* and the fine brandy, and then, when digestion is peacefully under way, *then* you shall tell why you need my advice."

The clock struck the half hour after nine before Mr Entwhistle stirred in his chair. The psychological moment had come. He no longer felt reluctant to bring forth his perplexities —he was eager to do so.

"I don't know," he said, "whether I'm making the most colossal fool of myself. In any case I don't see that there's anything that can possibly be done. But I'd like to put the facts before you, and I'd like to know what you think."

He paused for a moment or two, then in his dry meticulous way, he told his story. His trained legal brain enabled him to put the facts clearly, to leave nothing out, and to add nothing extraneous. It was a clear succinct account, and as such appreciated by the little elderly man with the egg shaped head who sat listening to him.

When he had finished there was a pause. Mr Entwhistle was prepared to answer questions, but for some few moments no question came. Hercule Poirot was reviewing the evidence.

He said at last:

"It seems very clear. You have in your mind the suspicion that your friend, Richard Abernethie, may have been murdered? That suspicion, or assumption, rests on the basis of one thing only—*the words spoken by Cora Lansquenet at Richard Abernethie's funeral*. Take those away—and there is nothing left. The fact that she herself was murdered the day afterwards *may* be the purest coincidence. It is true that Richard Abernethie died suddenly, but he was attended by a reputable doctor who knew him well, and that doctor had no suspicions and gave a death certificate. Was Richard buried or cremated?"

"Cremated—according to his own request."

"Yes, that is the law. And it means that a second doctor signed the certificate—but there would be no difficulty about that. So we come back to the essential point, *what Cora Lansquenet said*. You were there and you heard her. She said: 'But he *was* murdered, wasn't he?'"

"Yes."

"And the real point is—that you believe she was speaking the truth."

The lawyer hesitated for a moment, then he said:

"Yes, I do."

"Why?"

"Why?" Entwhistle repeated the word, slightly puzzled.

"But yes, *why?* Is it because, already, deep down, you had an uneasiness about the manner of Richard's death?"

The lawyer shook his head. "No, no, not in the least."

"Then it is because of *her*—of Cora herself. You knew her well?"

"I had not seen her for—oh—over twenty years."

"Would you have known her if you had met her in the street?"

Mr Entwhistle reflected.

"I might have passed her by in the street without recognising her. She was a thin slip of a girl when I saw her last and she had turned into a stout shabby middle-aged woman. But I think that the moment I spoke to her face to face I should have recognised her. She wore her hair in the same way, a bang cut straight across the forehead and she had a trick of peering up at you through her fringe like a rather shy animal, and she had a very characteristic abrupt way of talking, and a way of putting her head on one side and then coming out with something quite outrageous. She had *character*, you see, and character is always highly individual."

"She was, in fact, the same Cora you had known years ago. And she still said outrageous things! The things, the outrageous things, she had said in the past—were they usually—justified?"

"That was always the awkward thing about Cora. When truth would have been better left unspoken, she spoke it."

"And that characteristic remained unchanged. Richard Abernethie was murdered—so Cora at once mentioned the fact."

Mr Entwhistle stirred.

"You think he *was* murdered?"

"Oh, no, no, my friend, we cannot go so fast. We agree on this—Cora *thought* he had been murdered. She was quite sure he had been murdered. It was, to her, more a certainty than a surmise. And so, we come to this, *she must have had some reason for the belief*. We agree, by your knowledge of her, that it was not just a bit of mischief making. Now tell me—when she said what she did, there was, at once, a kind of chorus of protest—that is right?"

"Quite right."

"And she then became confused, abashed, and retreated from the position—saying—as far as you can remember, something like 'But I thought—from what he told me—'"

The lawyer nodded.

"I wish I could remember more clearly. But I am fairly sure of that. She used the words 'he told me' or 'he said'—"

"And the matter was then smoothed over and everyone spoke of something else. You can remember, looking back, no special expression on anyone's face? Anything that remains in your memory as—shall we say—*unusual?*"

"No."

"And the very next day, *Cora is killed*—and you ask yourself: 'Can it be cause and effect?'"

The lawyer stirred.

"I suppose that seems to you quite fantastic?"

"Not at all," said Poirot. "Given that the original assumption is correct, it is logical. The perfect murder, the murder of Richard Abernethie, had been committed, all has gone off smoothly —and suddenly it appears that there is one person who has a knowledge of the truth! Clearly that person must be silenced *as quickly as possible*."

"Then you do think that—it was murder?"

Poirot said gravely:

"I think, *mon cher,* exactly as you thought—that there is a case for investigation. Have you taken any steps? You have spoken of these matters to the police?"

"No." Mr Entwhistle shook his head. "It did not seem to me that any good purpose could be achieved. My position is that I represent the family. If Richard Abernethie was murdered, there seems only one method by which it could be done."

"By poison?"

"Exactly. *And the body has been cremated.* There is now no evidence available. But I decided that I, myself, *must* be satisfied on the point. That is why, Poirot, I have come to *you.*"

"Who was in the house at the time of his death?"

"An old butler who has been with him for years, a cook and a housemaid. It would seem, perhaps, as though it must necessarily be one of them—"

"Ah! do not try to pull the wool upon my eyes. This Cora, she knows Richard Abernethie was killed, yet she acquiesces in the hushing up. She says 'I think you are all quite right.' Therefore it *must* be one of the family who is concerned, someone whom the victim himself might prefer not to have openly accused. Otherwise, since Cora was fond of her brother, she would not agree to let the sleeping murderer lie. You agree to that, yes?"

"It was the way I reasoned—yes," confessed Mr Entwhistle. "Though how any of the family could possibly—"

Poirot cut him short.

"Where poison is concerned there are all sorts of possibilities. It must, presumably, have been a narcotic of some sort if he died in his sleep and if there were no suspicious appearances. Possibly he was already having some narcotic administered to him."

"In any case," said Mr Entwhistle, "the *how* hardly matters. We shall never be able to prove anything."

"In the case of Richard Abernethie, no. But the murder of Cora Lansquenet is different. Once we know 'who' then evidence ought to be possible to get." He added with a sharp glance, "You have, perhaps, already done something."

"Very little. My purpose was mainly, I think, *elimination.* It is distasteful to me to think that one of the Abernethie family is a murderer. I still can't quite believe it. I hoped that by a few apparently idle questions I could exonerate certain members of the family beyond question. Perhaps, who knows, *all* of them? In which case, Cora would have been wrong in her assumption and her own death could be ascribed to some casual prowler who broke in. After all, the issue is very simple. What were the members of the Abernethie family doing on the afternoon that Cora Lansquenet was killed?"

"*Eh bien,*" said Poirot, "what were they doing?"

"George Crossfield was at Hurst Park races. Rosamund Shane was out shopping in London. Her husband—for one must include husbands—"

"Assuredly."

"Her husband was fixing up a deal about an option on a play, Susan and Gregory Banks were at home all day. Timothy Abernethie who is an invalid was at his home in Yorkshire, and his wife was driving herself home from Enderby."

He stopped.

Hercule Poirot looked at him and nodded comprehendingly.

"Yes, that is what they *say*. And is it all true?"

"I simply don't know, Poirot. Some of the statements are capable of proof or disproof—but it would be difficult to do so without showing one's hand pretty plainly. In fact to do so would be tantamount to an accusation. I will simply tell you certain conclusions of my own. George *may* have been at Hurst Park races, but I do not think he was. He was rash enough to boast that he had backed a couple of winners. It is my experience that so many offenders against the law ruin their own case by saying too much. I asked him the name of the winners, and he gave the names of two horses without any apparent hesitation. Both of them, I found, had been heavily tipped on the day in question and one had duly won. The other, though an odds on favourite, had unaccountably failed even to get a place."

"Interesting. Had this George any urgent need for money at the time of his uncle's death?"

"It is my impression that his need was very urgent. I have no evidence for saying so, but I strongly suspect that he has been speculating with his clients' funds and that he was in danger of prosecution. It is only my impression but I have some experience in these matters. Defaulting solicitors, I regret to say, are not entirely uncommon. I can only tell you that I would not have cared to entrust my own funds to George, and I suspect that Richard Abernethie, a very shrewd judge of men, was dissatisfied with his nephew and placed no reliance on him.

"His mother," the lawyer continued, "was a good looking rather foolish girl and she married a man of what I should call dubious character." He sighed. "The Abernethie girls were not good choosers."

He paused and then went on.

"As for Rosamund she is a lovely nit-wit. I really cannot see her smashing Cora's head in with a hatchet! Her husband, Michael Shane, is something of a dark horse—he's a man with ambition and also a man of overweening vanity I should say— But really I know very little about him. I have no reason to suspect him of a brutal crime or of a carefully planned poisoning, but until I know that he really was doing what he says he was doing I cannot rule him out."

"But you have no doubts about the wife?"

"No—no—there is a certain rather startling callousness . . . but no, I really cannot envisage the hatchet. She is a fragile looking creature."

"And beautiful!" said Poirot with a faint cynical smile. "And the other niece?"

"Susan? She is a very different type from Rosamund—a girl of remarkable ability, I should say. She and her husband were at home together that day. I said (falsely) that I had tried to get them on the telephone on the afternoon in question. Greg said very quickly that the telephone had been out of order all day. He had tried to get someone and failed."

"So again it is not conclusive. . . . You cannot eliminate as you hoped to do. . . . What is the husband like?"

"I find him hard to make out. He has a somewhat unpleasing personality though one cannot say exactly why he makes this impression. As for Susan—"

"Yes?"

"Susan reminds me of her uncle. She has the vigour, the drive, the mental capacity of Richard Abernethie. It may be my fancy that she lacks some of the kindliness and the warmth of my old friend."

"Women are never kind," remarked Poirot. "Though they can sometimes be tender. She loves her husband?"

"Devotedly, I should say. But really, Poirot, I can't believe —I *won't* believe for one moment that Susan—"

"You prefer George?" said Poirot. "It is natural! As for me, I am not so sentimental about beautiful young ladies. Now tell me about your visit to the older generation?"

Mr Entwhistle described his visit to Timothy and Maude at some length. Poirot summarised the result.

"So Mrs Abernethie is a good mechanic. She knows all about the inside of a car. And Mr Abernethie is not the invalid he likes to think himself. He goes out for walks and is according to you, capable of vigorous action. He is also a bit of an ego maniac and he resented his brother's success and superior character."

"He spoke very affectionately of Cora."

"And ridiculed her silly remark after the funeral. What of the sixth beneficiary?"

"Helen? Mrs Leo? I do not suspect her for a moment. In any case, her innocence will be easy to prove. She was at Enderby. With three servants in the house."

"*Eh bien,* my friend," said Poirot. "Let us be practical. What do you want me to do?"

"I want to know the truth, Poirot."

"Yes. Yes, I should feel the same in your place."

"And you're the man to find it out for me. I know you don't take cases any more, but I ask you to take this one. This is a matter of business. I will be responsible for your fees. Come now, money is always useful."

Poirot grinned.

"Not if it all goes in the taxes! But I will admit, your problem interests me! Because it is not easy. . . . It is all so nebulous. . . . One thing, my friend, had better be done by you. After that, I will occupy myself of everything. But I think it will be best if you yourself seek out the doctor who attended Mr Richard Abernethie. You know him?"

"Slightly."

"What is he like?"

"Middle-aged G.P. Quite competent. On very friendly terms with Richard. A thoroughly good fellow."

"Then seek him out. He will speak more freely to you than to me. Ask him about Mr Abernethie's illness. Find out what medicines Mr Abernethie was taking at the time of his death and before. Find out if Richard Abernethie ever said anything to his doctor about fancying himself being poisoned. By the way, this Miss Gilchrist is sure that he used the term *poisoned* in talking to his sister?"

Mr Entwhistle reflected.

"It was the word she used—but she is the type of witness who often changes the actual words used, because she is convinced she is keeping to the sense of them. If Richard had said he was afraid someone wanted to kill him, Miss Gilchrist might have assumed poison because she connected his fears with those of an aunt of hers who thought her food was being tampered with. I can take up the point with her again some time."

"Yes. Or I will do so." He paused and then said in a different voice: "Has it occurred to you, my friend, that your Miss Gilchrist may be in some danger herself?"

Mr Entwhistle looked surprised.

"I can't say that it had."

"But, yes. Cora voiced her suspicions on the day of the funeral. The question in the murderer's mind will be, did she voice them to anybody when she first heard of Richard's death? And the most likely person for her to have spoken to about them will be Miss Gilchrist. I think, *mon cher*, that she had better not remain alone in that cottage."

"I believe Susan is going down."

"Ah, so Mrs Banks is going down?"

"She wants to look through Cora's things."

"I see. . . . I see. . . . Well, my friend, do what I have asked of you. You might also prepare Mrs Abernethie—Mrs Leo Abernethie, for the possibility that I may arrive in the house. We will see. From now on I occupy myself of everything."

And Poirot twirled his moustaches with enormous energy.

VIII

MR ENTWHISTLE looked at Dr Larraby thoughtfully.

He had had a lifetime of experience in summing people up. There had been frequent occasions on which it had been necessary to tackle a difficult situation or a delicate subject. Mr Entwhistle was an adept by now in the art of how exactly to make the proper approach. How would it be best to tackle Dr Larraby on what was certainly a very difficult subject and one which the doctor might very well resent as reflecting upon his own professional skill?

Frankness, Mr Entwhistle thought—or at least a modified frankness. To say that suspicions had arisen because of a haphazard suggestion thrown out by a silly woman would be ill-advised. Dr Larraby had not known Cora.

Mr Entwhistle cleared his throat and plunged bravely.

"I want to consult you on a very delicate matter," he said. "You may be offended, but I sincerely hope not. You are a sensible man and you will realise, I'm sure, that a—er—preposterous suggestion is best dealt with by finding a reasonable answer and not by condemning it out of hand. It concerns my client, the late Mr Abernethie. I'll ask you my question flat out. Are you certain, *absolutely certain,* that he died what is termed a natural death?"

Dr Larraby's good humoured rubicund middle-aged face turned in astonishment on his questioner.

"What on earth— Of course he did. I gave a certificate, didn't I? If I hadn't been satisfied—"

Mr Entwhistle cut in adroitly:

"Naturally, naturally. I assure you that I am not assuming anything to the contrary. But I would be glad to have your positive assurance—in face of the—er—rumours that are flying around."

"Rumours? What rumours?"

"One doesn't know quite how these things start," said Mr Entwhistle mendaciously. "But my feeling is that they should be stopped—authoritatively, if possible."

"Abernethie was a sick man. He was suffering from a disease that would have proved fatal within, I should say, at the earliest, two years. It might have come much sooner. His son's death had weakened his will to live, and his powers of resistance. I admit that I did not expect his death to come so soon, or indeed so suddenly, but there are precedents—plenty of precedents. Any medical man who predicts exactly when a patient will die, or exactly how long he will live, is bound to make a fool of himself. The human factor is always incalculable. The weak have often unexpected powers of resistance, the strong sometimes succumb."

"I understand all that. I am not doubting your diagnosis. Mr Abernethie was, shall we say—(rather melodramatically, I'm afraid)—under sentence of death. All I'm asking you is, is it quite impossible that a man, knowing or suspecting that he is doomed, might of his own accord shorten that period of life? Or that someone else might do it for him?"

Dr Larraby frowned.

"Suicide, you mean? Abernethie wasn't a suicidal type."

"I see. You can assure me, medically speaking, that such a suggestion is impossible."

The doctor stirred uneasily.

"I wouldn't use the word impossible. After his son's death life no longer held the interest for Abernethie that it had done. I certainly don't feel that suicide is likely—but I can't say that it's *impossible*."

"You are speaking from the psychological angle. When I said *medically*, I really meant: do the circumstances of his death make such a suggestion impossible?"

"No, oh no. No, I can't say that. He died in his sleep, as people often do. There was no reason to suspect suicide, no evidence of his state of mind. If one were to demand an autopsy every time a man who is seriously ill died in his sleep—"

The doctor's face was getting redder and redder. Mr Entwhistle hastened to interpose.

"Of course. Of course. But if there *had* been evidence—evidence of which you yourself were not aware? If, for instance, he had said something to someone—"

"Indicating that he was contemplating suicide? Did he? I must say it surprises me."

"But if it *were* so—my case is purely hypothetical—could you rule out the possibility?"

Dr Larraby said slowly:

"No—no—I could not do that. But I say again, I should be very much surprised."

Mr Entwhistle hastened to follow up his advantage.

"If, then, we assume that his death was *not* natural—(all this is *purely* hypothetical)—what could have caused it? What kind of a drug, I mean?"

"Several. Some kind of a narcotic would be indicated. There was no sign of cyanosis, the attitude was quite peaceful."

"He had sleeping draughts or pills? Something of that kind."

"Yes. I had prescribed Slumberyl—a very safe and dependable hypnotic. He did not take it every night. And he only had a small bottle of tablets at a time. Three or even four times the prescribed dose would not have caused death. In fact, I remember seeing the bottle on his washstand after his death still nearly full."

"What else had you prescribed for him?"

"Various things—a medicine containing a small quantity of morphia to be taken when he had an attack of pain. Some vitamin capsules. An indigestion mixture."

Mr Entwhistle interrupted.

"Vitamin capsules? I think I was once prescribed a course of those. Small round capsules of gelatine."

"Yes. Containing adexoline."

"Could anything else have been introduced into—say—one of those capsules?"

"Something lethal, you mean?" The doctor was looking more and more surprised. "But surely no man would ever—look here,

Entwhistle, what are you getting at? My God, man, are you suggesting *murder?*"

"I don't quite know what I'm suggesting. . . . I just want to know what would be *possible*."

"But what evidence have you for even suggesting such a thing?"

"I haven't any evidence," said Mr Entwhistle in a tired voice. "Mr Abernethie is dead—and the person to whom he spoke is also dead. The whole thing is rumour—vague, unsatisfactory rumour, and I want to scotch it if I can. If you tell me that no one could possibly have poisoned Abernethie in any way whatsoever, I'll be delighted! It would be a big weight off my mind, I can assure you."

Dr Larraby got up and walked up and down.

"I can't tell you what you want me to tell you," he said at last. "I wish I could. Of course it could have been done. Anybody could have extracted the oil from a capsule and replaced it with—say—pure nicotine or half a dozen other things. Or something could have been put in his food or drink? Isn't that more likely?"

"Possibly. But you see there were only the servants in the house when he died—and I don't think it was any of them—in fact I'm quite sure it wasn't. So I'm looking for some delayed action possibility. There's no drug, I suppose, that you can administer and then the person dies weeks later?"

"A convenient idea—but untenable, I'm afraid," said the doctor drily. "I know you're a responsible person, Entwhistle, but who *is* making this suggestion? It seems to me wildly far-fetched."

"Abernethie never said anything to you? Never hinted that one of his relations might be wanting him out of the way?"

The doctor looked at him curiously.

"No, he never said anything to me. Are you sure, Entwhistle, that somebody hasn't been—well, playing up the sensational? Some hysterical subjects can give an appearance of being quite reasonable and normal, you know."

"I hope it was like that. It might well be."

"Let me understand. Someone claims that Abernethie told her—it was a woman, I suppose?"

"Oh yes, it was a woman."

"—told her that someone was trying to kill him?"

Cornered, Mr Entwhistle reluctantly told the tale of Cora's remark at the funeral. Dr Larraby's face lightened.

"My dear fellow. I shouldn't pay any attention! The explanation is quite simple. The woman's at a certain time of life—craving for sensation, unbalanced, unreliable—might say anything. They do, you know!"

Mr Entwhistle resented the doctor's easy assumption. He himself had had to deal with plenty of sensation-hunting and hysterical women.

"You may be quite right," he said, rising. "Unfortunately we can't tackle her on the subject, as she's been murdered herself."

"What's that—murdered?" Dr Larraby looked as though he had grave suspicions of Mr Entwhistle's own stability of mind.

"You've probably read about it in the paper. Mrs Lansquenet at Lytchett St. Mary in Berkshire."

"Of course— I'd no idea she was a relation of Richard Abernethie's!" Dr Larraby was looking quite shaken.

Feeling that he had revenged himself for the doctor's professional superiority, and unhappily conscious that his own suspicions had not been assuaged as a result of the visit, Mr Entwhistle took his leave.

ii

Back at Enderby, Mr Entwhistle decided to talk to Lanscombe. He started by asking the old butler what his plans were.

"Mrs Leo has asked me to stay on here until the house is sold, sir, and I'm sure I shall be very pleased to oblige her. We are all very fond of Mrs Leo." He sighed. "I feel it very much, sir, if you will excuse me mentioning it, that the house has to be sold. I've known it for so very many years, and seen all the young ladies and gentlemen grow up in it. I always thought that Mr Mortimer would come after his father and perhaps bring up a family here, too. It was arranged, sir, that I should go to the North Lodge when I got past doing my work here. A very nice little place, the North Lodge—and I looked forward to having it very spick and span. But I suppose that's all over now."

"I'm afraid so, Lanscombe. The estate will all have to be sold together. But with your legacy—"

"Oh I'm not complaining, sir, and I'm very sensible of Mr Abernethie's generosity. I'm well provided for, but it's not so easy to find a little place to buy nowadays and though my married niece has asked me to make my home with them, well, it won't be quite the same thing as living on the estate."

"I know," said Mr Entwhistle. "It's a hard new world for us old fellows. I wish I'd seen more of my old friend before he went. How did he seem those last few months?"

"Well, he wasn't himself, sir. Not since Mr Mortimer's death."

"No, it broke him up. And then he was a sick man—sick men have strange fancies sometimes. I imagine Mr Abernethie suffered from that sort of thing in his last days. He spoke of enemies sometimes, of somebody wishing to do him harm—perhaps? He may even have thought his food was being tampered with?"

Old Lanscombe looked surprised—surprised and offended. "I cannot recall anything of that kind, sir."

Entwhistle looked at him keenly.

"You're a very loyal servant, Lanscombe, I know that. But such fancies on Mr Abernethie's part would be quite—er—unimportant—a natural symptom in some—er—diseases."

"Indeed, sir? I can only say Mr Abernethie never said anything like that to me, or in my hearing."

Mr Entwhistle slid gently to another subject.

"He had some of his family down to stay with him, didn't he, before he died. His nephew and his two nieces and their husbands?"

"Yes, sir, that is so."

"Was he satisfied with those visits? Or was he disappointed?"

Lanscombe's eyes became remote, his old back stiffened.

"I really could not say, sir."

"I think you could, you know," said Mr Entwhistle gently. "It's not your place to say anything of that kind—that's what you really mean. But there are times when one has to do violence to one's sense of what is fitting. I was one of your master's oldest friends. I care for him very much. So did you. That's why I'm asking you for your opinion as a *man,* not as a butler."

Lanscombe was silent for a moment, then he said in a colourless voice:

"Is there anything—wrong, sir?"

Mr Entwhistle replied truthfully.

"I don't know," he said. "I hope not. I would like to make sure. Have you yourself felt that something was—wrong?"

"Only since the funeral, sir. And I couldn't say exactly what it is. But Mrs Leo and Mrs Timothy, too, they didn't seem quite themselves that evening after the others had gone."

"You know the contents of the will?"

"Yes, sir. Mrs Leo thought I would like to know. It seemed to me, if I may permit myself to comment, a very fair will."

"Yes, it was a fair will. Equal benefits. But it is not, I think, the will that Mr Abernethie originally intended to make after his son died. Will you answer now the question that I asked you just now?"

"As a matter of personal opinion—"

"Yes, yes, that is understood."

"The master, sir, was very much disappointed after Mr George had been here. . . . He had hoped, I think, that Mr George might resemble Mr Mortimer. Mr George, if I may say so, did not come up to standard. Miss Laura's husband was always considered unsatisfactory, and I'm afraid Mr George took after him." Lanscombe paused and then went on, "Then the young ladies came with their husbands. Miss Susan he took to at once—a very spirited and handsome young lady, but it's my opinion he couldn't abide her husband. Young ladies make funny choices nowadays, sir."

"And the other couple?"

"I couldn't say much about that. A very pleasant and good-looking young pair. I think the master enjoyed having them here—but I don't think—" the old man hesitated.

"Yes, Lanscombe?"

"Well, the master had never had much truck with the stage. He said to me one day, 'I can't understand why anyone gets stagestruck. It's a foolish kind of life. Seems to deprive people of what little sense they have. I don't know what it does to your moral sense. You certainly lose your sense of proportion.' Of course he wasn't referring directly—"

"No, no, I quite understand. Now after these visits, Mr Abernethie himself went away—first to his brother, and afterwards to his sister Mrs Lansquenet."

"That I did not know, sir. I mean he mentioned to me that he was going to Mr Timothy and afterwards to Something St. Mary."

"That is right. Can you remember anything he said on his return in regard to those visits?"

Lanscombe reflected.

"I really don't know—nothing direct. He was glad to be back. Travelling and staying in strange houses tired him very much— that I do remember his saying."

"Nothing else? Nothing about either of them?"

Lanscombe frowned.

"The master used to—well, to *murmur,* if you get my meaning—speaking to me and yet more to himself—hardly noticing I was there—because he knew me so well. . . ."

"Knew you and trusted you, yes."

"But my recollection is very vague as to what he said— something about he couldn't think what he'd done with his money—that was Mr Timothy, I take it. And then he said something about 'Women can be fools in ninety nine different ways but be pretty shrewd in the hundredth.' Oh yes, and he said, 'You can only say what you really think to some of your own generation. They don't think you're fancying things as the younger ones do.' And later he said—but I don't know in what connection—'It's not very nice to have to set traps for people, but I don't see what else I can do.' But I think it possible, sir, that he may have been thinking of the second gardener—a question of the peaches being taken."

But Mr Entwhistle did not think that it was the second gardener who had been in Richard Abernethie's mind. After a few more questions he let Lanscombe go and reflected on what he had learned. Nothing, really—nothing, that is, that he had not deduced before. Yet there were suggestive points. It was not his sister-in-law, Maude, but his sister Cora of whom he had been thinking when he made the remark about women who were fools and yet shrewd. And it was to her he had confided his "fancies." And he had spoken of setting a trap. For whom?

iii

Mr Entwhistle had meditated a good deal over how much he should tell Helen. In the end he decided to take her wholly into his confidence.

First he thanked her for sorting out Richard's things and for making various household arrangements. The house had been advertised for sale and there were one or two perspective buyers who would be shortly coming to look over it.

"Private buyers?"

"I'm afraid not. The Y.W.C.A. are considering it, and there is a young people's club, and the Trustees of the Jefferson Trust are looking for a suitable place to house their Collection."

"It seems sad that the house will not be lived in, but of course it is not a practicable proposition nowadays."

"I am going to ask you if it would be possible for you to remain here until the house is sold. Or would it be a great inconvenience?"

"No—actually it would suit me very well. I don't want to go to Cyprus until May, and I much prefer being here than to being in London as I had planned. I love this house, you know, Leo loved it, and we were always happy when we were here together."

"There is another reason why I should be grateful if you would stay on. There is a friend of mine, a man called Hercule Poirot—"

Helen said sharply: "Hercule Poirot? Then you think—"

"You know of him?"

"Yes. Some friends of mine—but I imagined that he was dead long ago."

"He is very much alive. Not young, of course."

"No, he could hardly be young."

She spoke mechanically. Her face was white and strained. She said with an effort:

"You think—that Cora was right? That Richard was—*murdered?*"

Mr Entwhistle unburdened himself. It was a pleasure to unburden himself to Helen with her clear calm mind.

When he had finished she said:

"One ought to feel it's fantastic—but one doesn't. Maude and I, that night after the funeral—it was in both our minds, I'm sure. Saying to ourselves what a silly woman Cora was—and yet being uneasy. And then—Cora was killed—and I told myself it was just coincidence—and of course it may be—but oh! if one can only be sure. It's all so difficult."

"Yes, it's difficult. But Poirot is a man of great originality and he has something really approaching genius. He understands perfectly what we need—assurance that the whole thing is a mare's nest."

"And suppose it isn't?"

"What makes you say that?" asked Mr Entwhistle sharply.

"I don't know. I've been uneasy. . . . Not just about what Cora said that day—something else. Something that I felt at the time to be wrong."

"Wrong? In what way?"

"That's just it. I don't know."

"You mean it was something about one of the people in the room?"

"Yes—yes—something of that kind. But I don't know who or what. . . . Oh, that sounds absurd—"

"Not at all. It is interesting—very interesting. You are not a fool, Helen. If you noticed something that something had significance."

"Yes, but I can't remember what it *was*. The more I think—"

"Don't think. That is the wrong way to bring anything back. Let it go. Sooner or later it will flash into your mind. And when it does—let me know—at once."

"I will."

IX

Miss Gilchrist pulled her black felt hat down firmly on her head and tucked in a wisp of grey hair. The inquest was set for twelve o'clock and it was not quite twenty past eleven. Her grey coat and skirt looked quite nice, she thought, and she had bought herself a black blouse. She wished she could have been all in black, but that would have been far beyond her means. She looked round the small neat bedroom and at the walls hung with representations of Brixham harbour, Cockington Forge, Anstey's Cove, Kynance Cove, Polflexan harbour, Babbacombe Bay, etcetera, all signed in a dashing way, Cora Lansquenet. Her eyes rested with particular fondness on Polflexan harbour. On the chest of drawers, a faded photograph, carefully framed, represented the Willow Teashop. Miss Gilchrist looked at it lovingly and sighed.

She was disturbed from her reverie by the sound of the door bell below.

"Dear me," murmured Miss Gilchrist, "I wonder who—"

She went out of her room and down the rather rickety stairs. The bell sounded again and there was a sharp knock.

For some reason Miss Gilchrist felt nervous. For a moment or two her steps slowed up, then she went rather unwillingly to the door, adjuring herself not to be so silly.

A young woman dressed smartly in black and carrying a small suitcase was standing on the step. She noticed the alarmed look on Miss Gilchrist's face and said quickly:

"Miss Gilchrist? I am Mrs Lansquenet's niece—Susan Banks."

"Oh dear, yes, of course. I didn't know. Do come in, Mrs Banks. Mind the hall stand—it sticks out a little. In here, yes. I didn't know you were coming down for the inquest. I'd have had something ready—some coffee or something."

Susan Banks said briskly:

"I don't want anything. I'm so sorry if I startled you."

"Well, you know you *did,* in a way. It's very silly of me. I'm not usually nervous. In fact, I told the lawyer that I wasn't nervous, and that I wouldn't be nervous staying on here alone, and really I'm not nervous. Only—perhaps it's just the inquest and—and thinking of things, but I have been jumpy all this morning. Just about half an hour ago the bell rang and I could hardly bring myself to open the door—which was really very stupid and so untimely that a murderer would come back—and why should he?—and actually it was only a nun, collecting for an orphanage—and I was so relieved I gave her two shillings although I'm *not* a Roman Catholic, though I believe the Little Sisters of the Poor do really do good work. But do please sit down, Mrs—Mrs—"

"Banks."

"Yes, of course, Banks. Did you come down by train?"

"No, I drove down. The lane seemed so narrow I ran the car on a little way and found a sort of old quarry I backed it into."

"This lane is very narrow, but there's hardly ever any traffic along here. It's rather a lonely road."

Miss Gilchrist gave a little shiver as she said those last words.

Susan Banks was looking round the room.

"Poor old Aunt Cora," she said. "She left what she had to me, you know."

"Yes, I know. Mr Entwhistle told me. I expect you'll be glad of the furniture. You're newly married, I understand, and furnishing is such an expense nowadays. Mrs Lansquenet had some very nice things."

Susan did not agree. Cora had had no taste for the antique. The contents varied between "modernistic" pieces and the "arty" type.

"I shan't want any of the furniture," she said. "I've got my own, you know. I shall put it up for auction. Unless—is there any of it you would like? I'd be very glad . . ."

She stopped, a little embarrassed. But Miss Gilchrist was not at all embarrassed. She beamed.

"Now really, that's *very* kind of you, Mrs Banks—yes, very kind indeed. I really do appreciate it. But actually, you know,

I have my own things. I put them in store in case—someday—
I should need them. There are some pictures my father left,
too. I had a small teashop at one time, you know—but then
the war came—it was all very unfortunate. But I didn't sell up
everything, because I did hope to have my own little home again
one day, so I put the best things in store with my father's pictures and some relics of our old home. But I *would* like very
much, if you *really* wouldn't mind, to have that little painted
tea table of dear Mrs Lansquenet's. Such a pretty thing and we
always had tea on it."

Susan, looking with a slight shudder at a small green table
painted with large purple clematis, said quickly that she would
be delighted for Miss Gilchrist to have it.

"Thank you *very* much, Mrs Banks. I feel a little greedy. I've
got all her beautiful pictures, you know, and a lovely amethyst
brooch, but I feel that perhaps I ought to give *that* back to you."

"No, no, indeed."

"You'll want to go through her things? After the inquest,
perhaps?"

"I thought I'd stay here a couple of days, go through things,
and clear everything up."

"Sleep here, you mean?"

"Yes. Is there any difficulty?"

"Oh no, Mrs Banks, of course not. I'll put fresh sheets on
my bed, and I can doss down here on the couch quite well."

"But there's Aunt Cora's room, isn't there? I can sleep in
that."

"You—you wouldn't mind?"

"You mean because she was murdered there? Oh no, I
wouldn't mind. I'm very tough, Miss Gilchrist. It's been—I mean
—it's all right again?"

Miss Gilchrist understood the question.

"Oh *yes*, Mrs Banks. All the blankets sent away to the cleaners and Mrs Panter and I scrubbed the whole room out
thoroughly. And there are plenty of spare blankets. But come
up and see for yourself."

She led the way upstairs and Susan followed her.

The room where Cora Lansquenet had died was clean and

fresh and curiously devoid of any sinister atmosphere. Like the sitting room it contained a mixture of modern utility and elaborately painted furniture. It represented Cora's cheerful tasteless personality. Over the mantelpiece an oil painting showed a buxom young woman about to enter her bath.

Susan gave a slight shudder as she looked at it and Miss Gilchrist said:

"That was painted by Mrs Lansquenet's husband. There are a lot more of his pictures in the dining room downstairs."

"How terrible."

"Well, I don't care very much for that style of painting *myself* —but Mrs Lansquenet was very proud of her husband as an artist and thought that his work was sadly unappreciated."

"Where are Aunt Cora's own pictures?"

"In my room. Would you like to see them?"

Miss Gilchrist displayed her treasures proudly.

Susan remarked that Aunt Cora seemed to have been fond of sea coast resorts.

"Oh yes. You see, she lived for many years with Mr Lansquenet at a small fishing village in Brittany. Fishing boats are always so picturesque, are they not?"

"Obviously," Susan murmured. A whole series of picture postcards could, she thought, have been made from Cora Lansquenet's paintings which were faithful to detail and very highly coloured. They gave rise to the suspicion that they might actually have been painted from picture postcards.

But when she hazarded this opinion Miss Gilchrist was indignant. Mrs Lansquenet *always* painted from Nature! Indeed once she had had a touch of the sun from reluctance to leave a subject when the light was just right.

"Mrs Lansquenet was a real artist," said Miss Gilchrist reproachfully.

She glanced at her watch and Susan said quickly:

"Yes, we ought to start for the inquest. Is it far? Shall I get the car?"

It was only five minutes' walk, Miss Gilchrist assured her. So they set out together on foot. Mr Entwhistle who had come down by train met them and shepherded them into the Village Hall.

There seemed to be a large number of strangers present. The inquest was not sensational. There was evidence of identification of the deceased. Medical evidence as to the nature of the wounds that had killed her. There were no signs of a struggle. Deceased was probably under a narcotic at the time she was attacked and would have been taken quite unawares. Death was unlikely to have occurred later than four thirty. Between two and four thirty was the nearest approximation. Miss Gilchrist testified to finding the body. A police constable and Inspector Morton gave their evidence. The Coroner summed up briefly. The jury made no bones about the verdict *"Murder by some person or persons unknown."*

It was over. They came out again into the sunlight. Half a dozen cameras clicked. Mr Entwhistle shepherded Susan and Miss Gilchrist into the King's Arms where he had taken the precaution to arrange for lunch to be served in a private room behind the bar.

"Not a very good lunch, I am afraid," he said apologetically.

But the lunch was not at all bad. Miss Gilchrist sniffed a little and murmured that "it was all so dreadful" but cheered up and tackled the Irish stew with appetite after Mr Entwhistle had insisted on her drinking a glass of sherry. He said to Susan:

"I'd no idea you were coming down today, Susan. We could have come together."

"I know I said I wouldn't. But it seemed rather mean for none of the family to be there. I rang up George but he said he was very busy and couldn't possibly make it, and Rosamund had an audition and Uncle Timothy, of course, is a crock. So it had to be me."

"Your husband didn't come with you?"

"Greg had to settle up with his tiresome shop."

Seeing a startled look in Miss Gilchrist's eye, Susan said: "My husband works in a chemist's shop."

A husband in retail trade did not quite square with Miss Gilchrist's impression of Susan's smartness, but she said valiantly:

"Oh yes, just like Keats."

"Greg's no poet," said Susan.

She added:

"We've got great plans for the future—a double barrelled establishment—Cosmetics and Beauty parlour and a laboratory for special preparations."

"That will be much nicer," said Miss Gilchrist approvingly. "Something like Elizabeth Arden who is really a Countess, so I have been told—or is that Helena Rubinstein? In any case," she added kindly, "a pharmacist's is not in the least like an ordinary shop—a *draper,* for instance, or a *grocer.*"

"You kept a tea shop, you said, didn't you?"

"Yes, indeed," Miss Gilchrist's face lit up. That the Willow Tree had ever been "trade" in the sense that a shop was trade, would never have occurred to her. To keep a tea shop was in her mind the essence of gentility. She started telling Susan about the Willow Tree.

Mr Entwhistle who had heard about it before let his mind drift to other matters. When Susan had spoken to him twice without his answering he hurriedly apologised.

"Forgive me, my dear, I was thinking, as a matter of fact, about your uncle Timothy. I am a little worried."

"About uncle Timothy? I shouldn't be. I don't believe really there's anything the matter with him. He's just a hypochondriac."

"Yes—yes, you may be right. I confess it was not his health that was worrying me. It's Mrs Timothy. Apparently she's fallen downstairs and twisted her ankle. She's laid up and your uncle is in a terrible state."

"Because he'll have to look after her instead of the other way about? Do him a lot of good," said Susan.

"Yes—yes, I daresay. But will your poor aunt *get* any looking after? That is really the question. With no servants in the house."

"Life is really hell for elderly people," said Susan. "They live in a kind of Georgian Manor house, don't they?"

Mr Entwhistle nodded.

They came rather warily out of the King's Arms, but the Press seemed to have dispersed.

A couple of reporters were lying in wait for Susan by the cottage door. Shepherded by Mr Entwhistle she said a few necessary and non-committal words. Then she and Miss Gilchrist went into the cottage and Mr Entwhistle returned to the King's Arms where he had booked a room. The funeral was to be on the following day.

"My car's still in the quarry," said Susan. "I'd forgotten about it. I'll drive it along to the village later."

Miss Gilchrist said anxiously:

"Not too late. You won't go out after dark, will you?"

Susan looked at her and laughed.

"You don't think there's a murderer still hanging about, do you?"

"No—no, I suppose not." Miss Gilchrist looked embarrassed.

"But it's exactly what she does think," thought Susan. "How amazing!"

Miss Gilchrist had vanished towards the kitchen.

"I'm sure you'd like tea early. In about half an hour, do you think, Mrs Banks?"

Susan thought that tea at half past three was overdoing it, but she was charitable enough to realise that "a nice cup of tea" was Miss Gilchrist's idea of restoration for the nerves and she had her own reasons for wishing to please Miss Gilchrist, so she said:

"Whenever you like, Miss Gilchrist."

A happy clatter of kitchen implements began and Susan went into the sitting room. She had only been there a few minutes when the bell sounded and was succeeded by a very precise little rat-tat-tat.

Susan came out into the hall and Miss Gilchrist appeared at the kitchen door wearing an apron and wiping floury hands on it.

"Oh dear, who do you think that can be?"

"More reporters, I expect," said Susan.

"Oh dear, how annoying for you, Mrs Banks."

"Oh well, never mind, I'll attend to it."

"I was just going to make a few scones for tea."

Susan went towards the front door and Miss Gilchrist hovered uncertainly. Susan wondered whether she thought a man with a hatchet was waiting outside.

The visitor, however, proved to be an elderly gentleman who raised his hat when Susan opened the door and said, beaming at her in avuncular style,

"Mrs Banks, I think?"

"Yes."

"My name is Guthrie—Alexander Guthrie. I was a friend—a very old friend, of Mrs Lansquenet's. You, I think, are her niece, formerly Miss Susan Abernethie?"

"That's quite right."

"Then since we know who we are, I may come in?"

"Of course."

Mr Guthrie wiped his feet carefully on the mat, stepped inside, divested himself of his overcoat, laid it down with his hat on a small oak chest and followed Susan into the sitting room.

"This is a melancholy occasion," said Mr Guthrie to whom melancholy did not seem to come naturally, his own inclination being to beam. "Yes, a very melancholy occasion. I was in this part of the world and I felt the least I could do was to attend the inquest—and of course the funeral. Poor Cora—poor foolish Cora. I have known her, my dear Mrs Banks, since the early days of her marriage. A high-spirited girl—and she took art very seriously—took Pierre Lansquenet seriously, too—as an artist, I mean. All things considered, he didn't make her too bad a husband. He strayed, if you know what I mean, yes, he strayed—but fortunately Cora took it as part of the artistic temperament. He was an artist and therefore immoral! In fact, I'm not sure she didn't go further: he was immoral and therefore he must be an artist! No kind of sense in artistic matters, poor Cora—though in other ways, mind you, Cora had a lot of sense—yes, a surprising lot of sense."

"That's what everybody seems to say," said Susan. "I didn't really know her."

"No, no, cut herself off from her family because they didn't appreciate her precious Pierre. She was never a pretty girl—but she had *something*. She was good company! You never knew what she'd say next and you never knew if her *naiveté* was genuine or whether she was doing it deliberately. She made us all laugh a good deal. The eternal child—that's what we always felt about her. And really the last time I saw her (I have seen her from time to time since Pierre died) she struck me as still behaving very much like a child."

Susan offered Mr Guthrie a cigarette, but the old gentleman shook his head.

"No thank you, my dear. I don't smoke. You must wonder why I've come? To tell you the truth I was feeling rather conscience-stricken. I promised Cora to come and see her some weeks ago. I usually called upon her once a year, and just lately she'd taken up the hobby of buying pictures at local sales, and wanted me to look at some of them. My profession is that of art critic, you know. Of course most of Cora's purchases were horrible daubs, but take it all in all, it isn't such a bad speculation. Pictures go for next to nothing at these country sales and the frames alone are worth more than you pay for the picture. Naturally any important sale is attended by dealers and one isn't likely to get hold of masterpieces. But only the other day, a small Cuyp was knocked down for a few pounds at a farmhouse sale. The history of it was quite interesting. It had been given to an old nurse by the family she had served faithfully for many years—they had no idea of its value. Old nurse gave it to farmer nephew who liked the horse in it but thought it was a dirty old thing! Yes, yes, these things sometimes happen, and Cora was convinced that she had an eye for pictures. She hadn't, of course. Wanted me to come and look at a Rembrandt she had picked up last year. A Rembrandt! Not even a respectable copy of one! But she had got hold of a quite nice Bartolozzi engraving— damp spotted unfortunately. I sold it for her for thirty pounds and of course that spurred her on. She wrote to me with great gusto about an Italian Primitive she had bought at some sale and I promised I'd come along and see it."

"That's it over there, I expect," said Susan, gesturing to the wall behind him.

Mr Guthrie got up, put on a pair of spectacles, and went over to study the picture.

"Poor dear Cora," he said at last.

"There are a lot more," said Susan.

Mr Guthrie proceeded to a leisurely inspection of the art treasures acquired by the hopeful Mrs Lansquenet. Occasionally he said, "Tchk tchk," occasionally he sighed.

Finally he removed his spectacles.

"Dirt," he said, "is a wonderful thing, Mrs Banks! It gives a patina of romance to the most horrible examples of the painter's art. I'm afraid that Bartolozzi was beginner's luck. Poor Cora. Still it gave her an interest in life. I am really thankful that I did not have to disillusion her."

"There are some pictures in the dining room," said Susan, "but I think they are all her husband's work."

Mr Guthrie shuddered slightly and held up a protesting hand.

"Do not force me to look at those again. Life classes have much to answer for! I always tried to spare Cora's feelings. A devoted wife—a very devoted wife. Well, dear Mrs Banks, I must not take up more of your time."

"Oh, do stay and have some tea. I think it's nearly ready."

"That is very kind of you." Mr Guthrie sat down again promptly.

"I'll just go and see."

In the kitchen, Miss Gilchrist was just lifting a last batch of scones from the oven. The teatray stood ready and the kettle was just gently rattling its lid.

"There's a Mr Guthrie here, and I've asked him to stay for tea."

"Mr Guthrie? Oh yes, he was a great friend of dear Mrs Lansquenet's. He's the celebrated art critic. How fortunate; I've made a nice lot of scones and that's some home made strawberry jam, and I just whipped up some little drop cakes. I'll just make the tea—I've warmed the pot. Oh please, Mrs Banks, don't carry that heavy tray. I can manage *everything*."

However Susan took in the tray and Miss Gilchrist followed with teapot and kettle, greeted Mr Guthrie, and they set to.

"Hot scones, that *is* a treat," said Mr Guthrie, "and what delicious jam! Really, the stuff one buys nowadays."

Miss Gilchrist was flushed and delighted. The little cakes

were excellent and so were the scones, and everyone did justice to them. The ghost of the Willow Tree hung over the party. Here, it was clear, Miss Gilchrist was in her element.

"Well, thank you, perhaps I will," said Mr Guthrie as he accepted the last cake, pressed upon him by Miss Gilchrist. "I do feel rather guilty, though—enjoying my tea, here, where poor Cora was so brutally murdered."

Miss Gilchrist displayed an unexpected Victorian reaction to this.

"Oh but Mrs Lansquenet would have wished you to make a good tea. You've got to keep your strength up."

"Yes, yes, perhaps you are right. The fact is, you know, that one cannot really bring oneself to believe that someone you knew—actually knew—*can* have been murdered!"

"I agree," said Susan. "It just seems—fantastic."

"And certainly not by some casual tramp who broke in and attacked her. I *can* imagine, you know, reasons why Cora might have been murdered—"

Susan said quickly, "Can you? What reasons?"

"Well, she wasn't discreet," said Mr Guthrie. "Cora was never discreet. And she enjoyed—how shall I put it—showing how sharp she could be? Like a child who's got hold of somebody's secret. If Cora got hold of a secret she'd want to talk about it. Even if she promised not to, she'd still do it. She wouldn't be able to help herself."

Susan did not speak. Miss Gilchrist did not either. She looked worried. Mr Guthrie went on.

"Yes, a little dose of arsenic in a cup of tea—*that* would not have surprised me, or a box of chocolates by post. But sordid robbery and assault—that seems highly incongruous. I may be wrong but I should have thought she had very little to take that would be worth a burglar's while. She didn't keep much money in the house, did she?"

Miss Gilchrist said, "Very little."

Mr Guthrie sighed and rose to his feet.

"Ah! well, there's a lot of lawlessness about since the war. Times have changed."

Thanking them for tea, he took a polite farewell of the two

women. Miss Gilchrist saw him out and helped him on with his overcoat. From the window of the sitting room, Susan watched him trot briskly down the front path to the gate.

Miss Gilchrist came back into the room with a small parcel in her hand.

"The postman must have been while we were at the inquest. He pushed it through the letter box and it had fallen in the corner behind the door. Now I wonder—why, of course, it must be wedding cake."

Happily Miss Gilchrist ripped off the paper. Inside was a small white box tied with silver ribbon.

"It is!" She pulled off the ribbon; inside was a modest wedge of rich cake with almond paste and white icing. "How nice! Now who—" she consulted the card attached. *"John and Mary—* Now who *can* that be? How silly to put no surname."

Susan, rousing herself from contemplation, said vaguely,

"It's quite difficult sometimes with people just using Christian names. I got a post-card the other day signed Joan. I counted up I knew eight Joans—and with telephoning so much, one often doesn't know their handwriting."

Miss Gilchrist was happily going over the possible Johns or Marys of her acquaintance.

"It might be Dorothy's daughter—*her* name was Mary, but I hadn't heard of an engagement, still less of a marriage. Then there's little John Banfield—I suppose he's grown up and old enough to be married—or the Enfield girl—no, her name was Margaret. No address or anything. Oh well, I daresay it will come to me . . ."

She picked up the tray and went out to the kitchen.

Susan roused herself and said:

"Well—I suppose I'd better go and put the car somewhere."

X

SUSAN RETRIEVED the car from the quarry where she had left it and drove it into the village. There was a petrol pump but no garage and she was advised to take it to the King's Arms. They had room for it there and she left it by a big Daimler which was preparing to go out. It was chauffeur driven and inside it, very much muffled up, was an elderly foreign gentleman with a large moustache.

The boy to whom Susan was talking about the car was staring at her with such rapt attention that he did not seem to be taking in half of what she said.

Finally he said in an awestricken voice:

"You're her niece, aren't you?"

"What?"

"You're the victim's niece," the boy repeated with relish.

"Oh—yes—yes, I am."

"Ar! Wondered where I'd seen you before."

"Ghoul," thought Susan as she retraced her steps to the cottage.

Miss Gilchrist greeted her with:

"Oh you're safely back," in tones of relief which further annoyed her. Miss Gilchrist added anxiously:

"You *can* eat spaghetti, can't you? I thought for tonight—"

"Oh yes, anything. I don't want much."

"I really flatter myself that I can make a very tasty spaghetti *au gratin.*"

The boast was not an idle one. Miss Gilchrist, Susan reflected, was really an excellent cook. Susan offered to help wash up but Miss Gilchrist, though clearly gratified by the offer, assured Susan that there was very little to do.

She came in a little while later with coffee. The coffee was less excellent, being decidedly weak. Miss Gilchrist offered Susan a piece of the wedding cake which Susan refused.

"It's really very good cake," Miss Gilchrist insisted, tasting it. She had settled to her own satisfaction that it must have been sent by someone whom she alluded to as "dear Ellen's daughter who I know was engaged to be married but I can't remember her name."

Susan let Miss Gilchrist chirrup away into silence before starting her own subject of conversation. This moment, after supper, sitting before the fire, was a companionable one.

She said at last:

"My uncle Richard came down here before he died, didn't he?"

"Yes, he did."

"When was that exactly?"

"Let me see—it must have been one, two—nearly three weeks before his death was announced."

"Did he seem—ill?"

"Well, no, I wouldn't say he seemed exactly ill. He had a very hearty vigorous manner. Mrs Lansquenet was very surprised to see him. She said, 'Well, really, Richard, after all these years!' And he said, 'I came to see for myself exactly how things are with you.' And Mrs Lansquenet said, 'I'm all right.' I think, you know, she was a teeny bit offended by his turning up so casually—after the long break. Anyway Mr Abernethie said, 'No use keeping up old grievances. You and I and Timothy are the only ones left—and nobody can talk to Timothy except about his own health.' And he said, 'Pierre seems to have made you happy, so it seems I was in the wrong. There, will that content you?' Very nicely he said it. A handsome man, though elderly, of course."

"How long was he here?"

"He stayed for lunch. Beef olives, I made. Fortunately it was the day the butcher called."

Miss Gilchrist's memory seemed to be almost wholly culinary.

"They seemed to be getting on well together?"

"Oh yes."

Susan paused and then said:

"Was Aunt Cora surprised when—he died?"

"Oh yes, it was quite sudden, wasn't it?"

"Yes, it was sudden . . . I meant—she *was* surprised. He hadn't given her any indication how ill he was."

"Oh—I see what you mean." Miss Gilchrist paused a moment. "No, no, I think perhaps you are right. She did say that he had got very old—I think she said senile . . ."

"But *you* didn't think he was senile?"

"Well, not to *look* at. But I didn't talk to him much. Naturally, I left them alone together."

Susan looked at Miss Gilchrist speculatively. Was Miss Gilchrist the kind of woman who listened at doors? She was honest, Susan felt sure, she wouldn't ever pilfer, or cheat over the house-keeping, or open letters. But inquisitiveness can drape itself in a mantle of rectitude. Miss Gilchrist might have found it necessary to garden near an open window, or to dust the hall . . . That would be within the permitted lengths. And then, of course, she could not have helped hearing something . . .

"You didn't hear any of their conversation?" Susan asked.

Too abrupt. Miss Gilchrist flushed angrily.

"No, indeed, Mrs Banks. It has never been my custom to listen at doors!"

That means she does, thought Susan, otherwise she'd just say "No."

Aloud she said: "I'm so sorry, Miss Gilchrist. I didn't mean it that way. But sometimes, in these small flimsily built cottages, one simply can't help hearing everything that goes on, and now that they are both dead, it's really rather important to the family to know just what was said at that meeting between them."

The cottage was anything but flimsily built—it dated from a sturdier era of building, but Miss Gilchrist accepted the bait, and rose to the suggestion held out.

"Of course what you say is quite true, Mrs Banks—this *is* a very small place and I do appreciate that you would want to know what passed between them, but really I'm afraid I can't help very much. I think they were talking about Mr Abernethie's health—and certain—well, *fancies* he had. He didn't look it, but he must have been a sick man and as is so often the case, he put his ill health down to *outside agencies*. A common symptom, I believe. My aunt—"

Miss Gilchrist described her aunt.

Susan, like Mr Entwhistle, sidetracked the aunt.

"Yes," she said. "That is just what we thought. My uncle's servants were all very attached to him and naturally they are upset by his thinking—" She paused.

"Oh of course! Servants are *very* touchy about anything of that kind. I remember that my aunt—"

Again Susan interrupted.

"It *was* the servants he suspected, I suppose? Of poisoning him, I mean?"

"I don't know . . . I—really—"

Susan noted her confusion.

"It wasn't the servants. Was it one particular person?"

"I don't know, Mrs Banks. Really I don't know—"

But her eye avoided Susan's. Susan thought to herself that Miss Gilchrist knew more than she was willing to admit.

It was possible that Miss Gilchrist knew a good deal. . . .

Deciding not to press the point for the moment, Susan said: "What are your own plans for the future, Miss Gilchrist?"

"Well, really, I was going to speak to you about that, Mrs Banks. I told Mr Entwhistle I would be willing to stay on until everything here was cleared up."

"I know. I'm very grateful."

"And I wanted to ask you how long that was likely to be, because, of course, I must start looking about for another post."

Susan considered.

"There's really not very much to be done here. In a couple of days I can get things sorted and notify the auctioneer."

"You have decided to sell up everything, then?"

"Yes. I don't suppose there will be any difficulty in letting the cottage?"

"*Oh no*—people will queue up for it, I'm sure. There are so few cottages to rent. One nearly always has to buy."

"So it's all very simple, you see." Susan hesitated a moment before saying, "I wanted to tell you—that I hope you'll accept three months' salary."

"That's very generous of you, I'm sure, Mrs Banks. I do appreciate it. And you would be prepared to—I mean I could ask you—if necessary—to—to recommend me? To say that I had been with a relation of yours and that I had—proved satisfactory?"

"Oh, of course."

"I don't know whether I ought to ask it." Miss Gilchrist's hands began to shake and she tried to steady her voice. "But would it be possible not to—to mention the circumstances—or even the *name?*"

Susan stared.

"I don't understand."

"That's because you haven't thought, Mrs Banks. It's *murder*. A murder that's been in the papers and that everybody has read about. Don't you see? People might think. 'Two women living together, and one of them is killed—and *perhaps the companion did it.*' Don't you see, Mrs Banks? I'm sure that if *I* was looking for someone, I'd—well, I'd think twice before engaging myself—if you understand what I mean. Because one never *knows!* It's been worrying me dreadfully, Mrs Banks; I've been lying awake at night thinking that perhaps I'll never get another job—not of this kind. And what else is there that I can do?"

The question came out with unconscious pathos. Susan felt suddenly stricken. She realised the desperation of this pleasant-spoken commonplace woman who was dependent for existence on the fears and whims of employers. And there was a lot of truth in what Miss Gilchrist had said. You wouldn't, if you could help it, engage a woman to share domestic intimacy who had figured, however innocently, in a murder case.

Susan said: "But if they find the man who did it—"

"Oh *then*, of course, it will be quite all right. But will they find him? I don't think, myself, the police have the *least idea*. And if he's *not* caught—well, that leaves me as—as not quite the most likely person, but as a person who *could* have done it."

Susan nodded thoughtfully. It was true that Miss Gilchrist did not benefit from Cora Lansquenet's death—but who was to know that? And besides there were so many tales—ugly tales —of animosity arising between women who lived together— strange pathological motives for sudden violence. Someone who had not known them might imagine that Cora Lansquenet and Miss Gilchrist had lived on those terms. . . .

Susan spoke with her usual decision.

"Don't worry, Miss Gilchrist," she said, speaking briskly and cheerfully. "I'm sure I can find you a post amongst my friends. There won't be the least difficulty."

"I'm afraid," said Miss Gilchrist, regaining some of her customary manner, "that I couldn't undertake any really *rough* work. Just a little plain cooking and housework—"

The telephone rang and Miss Gilchrist jumped.

"Dear me, I wonder who *that* can be."

"I expect it's my husband," said Susan, jumping up. "He said he'd ring me tonight."

She went to the telephone.

"Yes?—yes, this is Mrs Banks speaking personally . . ." There was a pause and then her voice changed. It became soft and warm. "Hullo, darling—yes, it's me. . . . Oh, quite well . . . Murder by someone unknown . . . the usual thing. . . . Only Mr Entwhistle. . . . What? . . . It's difficult to say, but I think so. . . . Yes, just as we thought. . . . Absolutely according to plan. . . . I shall sell the stuff. There's nothing *we'd* want. . . . Not for a day or two. . . . Absolutely frightful. . . . Don't fuss. I know what I'm doing. . . . Greg, you didn't . . . You were careful to . . . No, it's nothing. Nothing at all. Good night, darling."

She rang off. The nearness of Miss Gilchrist had hampered her a little. Miss Gilchrist could probably hear from the kitchen, where she had tactfully retired, exactly what went on. There were things she had wanted to ask Greg, but she hadn't liked to.

She stood by the telephone, frowning abstractedly. Then suddenly an idea came to her.

"Of course," she murmured. "Just the thing."

Lifting the receiver she asked for Trunk Enquiry.

Some quarter of an hour later a weary voice from the exchange was saying:

"I'm afraid there's no reply."

"Please go on ringing them."

Susan spoke autocratically. She listened to the far off buzzing of a telephone bell. Then, suddenly it was interrupted and a man's voice, peevish and slightly indignant, said:

"Yes, yes, what is it?"

"Uncle Timothy?"

"What's that? I can't hear you."

"Uncle Timothy? I'm Susan Banks."

"Susan who?"

"Banks. Formerly Abernethie. Your niece Susan."

"Oh, you're Susan, are you? What's the matter? What are you ringing up for at this time of night?"

"It's quite early still."

"It isn't. I was in bed."

"You must go to bed very early. How's Aunt Maude?"

"Is that all you rang up to ask? Your aunt's in a good deal of pain and she can't do a thing. Not a thing. She's helpless. We're in a nice mess, I can tell you. That fool of a doctor says he can't even get a nurse. He wanted to cart Maude off to hospital. I stood out against *that*. He's trying to get hold of someone for us. *I* can't do anything—I daren't even try. There's a fool from the village staying in the house tonight—but she's murmuring about getting back to her husband. Don't know *what* we're going to do."

"That's what I rang up about. Would you like Miss Gilchrist?"

"Who's she? Never heard of her."

"Aunt Cora's companion. She's very nice and capable."

"Can she cook?"

"Yes, she cooks very well, and she could look after Aunt Maude."

"That's all very well, but when could she come? Here I am, all on my own, with only these idiots of village women popping in and out at odd hours, and it's not good for me. My heart's playing me up."

"I'll arrange for her to get off to you as soon as possible. The day after tomorrow, perhaps?"

"Well, thanks very much," said the voice rather grudgingly. "You're a good girl, Susan—er—thank you."

Susan rang off and went into the kitchen.

"Would you be willing to go up to Yorkshire and look after my aunt? She fell and broke her ankle and my uncle is quite useless. He's a bit of a pest but Aunt Maude is a very good sort. They have help in from the village, but you could cook and look after Aunt Maude."

Miss Gilchrist dropped the coffee pot in her agitation.

"Oh thank you, thank you—that really is kind. I think I can say of myself that I am really good in the sickroom, and I'm sure I can manage your uncle and cook him nice little meals. It's really very kind of you, Mrs Banks, and I *do* appreciate it."

XI

Susan lay in bed and waited for sleep to come. It had been a long day and she was tired. She had been quite sure that she would go to sleep at once. She never had any difficulty in going to sleep. And yet here she lay, hour after hour, wide awake, her mind racing.

She had said she did not mind sleeping in this room, in this bed. This bed where Cora Abernethie—

No, no, she must put all that out of her mind. She had always prided herself on having no nerves. Why think of that afternoon less than a week ago? Think ahead—the future. Her future and Greg's. Those premises in Cardigan Street—just what they wanted. The business on the groundfloor and a charming flat upstairs. The room out at the back a laboratory for Greg. For purposes of income tax it would be an excellent set up. Greg would get calm and well again. There would be no more of those alarming brain storms. The times when he looked at her without seeming to know who she was. Once or twice she'd been quite frightened . . . And old Mr Cole—he'd hinted—threatened: "If this happens again . . ." And it might have happened again —it *would* have happened again. If Uncle Richard hadn't died just when he did . . .

Uncle Richard—but really why look at it like that? He'd nothing to live for. Old and tired and ill. His son dead. It was a mercy really. To die in his sleep quietly like that. Quietly . . . in his sleep. . . . If only she could sleep. It was so stupid lying awake hour after hour . . . hearing the furniture creak, and the rustling of trees and bushes outside the window and the occasional queer melancholy hoot—an owl, she supposed. How sinister the country was, somehow. So different from the big noisy indifferent town. One felt so safe there—surrounded by people—never alone. Whereas here . . .

Houses where a murder had been committed were sometimes haunted. Perhaps this cottage would come to be known as the haunted cottage. Haunted by the spirit of Cora Lansquenet . . . Aunt Cora. Odd, really, how ever since she had arrived she had felt as though Aunt Cora were quite close to her . . . within reach. All nerves and fancy. Cora Lansquenet was dead, to-morrow she would be buried. There was no one in the cottage except Susan herself and Miss Gilchrist. Then why did she feel that there was someone in this room, someone close beside her. . . .

She had lain on this bed when the hatchet fell . . . Lying there trustingly asleep . . . Knowing nothing till the hatchet fell . . . And now she wouldn't let Susan sleep. . . .

The furniture creaked again . . . was that a stealthy step? . . . Susan switched on the light. Nothing. Nerves, nothing but nerves. Relax . . . close your eyes. . . .

Surely that was a groan—a groan or a faint moan . . . Some-one in pain—someone dying. . . .

"I mustn't imagine things, I mustn't, I mustn't," Susan whis-pered to herself.

Death was the end—there was no existence after death. Under no circumstances could anyone come back. Or was she re-living a scene from the past—a dying woman groaning. . . .

There it was again . . . stronger . . . someone groaning in acute pain. . . .

But—this was real. Once again Susan switched on the light, sat up in bed and listened. The groans were real groans and she was hearing them through the wall. They came from the room next door.

Susan jumped out of bed, flung on a dressing gown and crossed to the door. She went out onto the landing, tapped for a moment on Miss Gilchrist's door and then went in. Miss Gil-christ's light was on. She was sitting up in bed. She looked ghastly. Her face was distorted with pain.

"Miss Gilchrist, what's the matter? Are you ill?"

"Yes. I don't know what—I—" she tried to get out of bed, was seized with a fit of vomiting and then collapsed back on the pillows.

She murmured: "Please—ring up doctor. Must have eaten something. . . ."

"I'll get you some bicarbonate. We can get the doctor in the morning if you're not better."

Miss Gilchrist shook her head.

"No, get doctor now. I—I feel dreadful."

"Do you know his number? Or shall I look in the book?"

Miss Gilchrist gave her the number. She was interrupted by another fit of retching.

Susan's call was answered by a sleepy male voice.

"Who? Gilchrist? In Mead's Lane. Yes, I know. I'll be right along."

He was as good as his word. Ten minutes later Susan heard his car draw up outside and she went to open the door to him.

She explained the case as she took him upstairs. "I think," she said, "she must have eaten something that disagreed with her. But she seems pretty bad."

The doctor had had the air of one keeping his temper in leash and who has had some experience of being called out unnecessarily on more than one occasion. But as soon as he examined the moaning woman his manner changed. He gave various curt orders to Susan and presently came down and telephoned. Then he joined Susan in the sitting room.

"I've sent for an ambulance. Must get her into hospital."

"She's really bad then?"

"Yes. I've given her a shot of morphia to ease the pain. But it looks—" he broke off. "What's she eaten?"

"We had macaroni *au gratin* for supper and a custard pudding. Coffee afterwards."

"You have the same things?"

"Yes."

"And you're all right? No pain or discomfort?"

"No."

"She's taken nothing else? No tinned fish? Or sausages?"

"No. We had lunch at the King's Arms—after the inquest."

"Yes, of course. You're Mrs Lansquenet's niece?"

"Yes."

"That was a nasty business. Hope they catch the man who did it."

"Yes, indeed."

The ambulance came. Miss Gilchrist was taken away and the doctor went with her. He told Susan he would ring her up in the morning. When he had left she went upstairs to bed.

This time she fell asleep as soon as her head touched the pillow.

ii

The funeral was well attended. Most of the village had turned out. Susan and Mr Entwhistle were the only mourners, but various wreaths had been sent by the other members of the family. Mr Entwhistle asked where Miss Gilchrist was, and Susan explained the circumstances in a hurried whisper. Mr Entwhistle raised his eyebrows.

"Rather an odd occurrence?"

"Oh, she's better this morning. They rang up from the hospital. People do get these bilious turns. Some make more fuss than others."

Mr Entwhistle said no more. He was returning to London immediately after the funeral.

Susan went back to the cottage. She found some eggs and made herself an omelette. Then she went up to Cora's room and started to sort through the dead woman's things.

She was interrupted by the arrival of the doctor.

The doctor was looking worried. He replied to Susan's inquiry by saying that Miss Gilchrist was much better.

"She'll be out and around in a couple of days," he said. "But it was lucky I got called in so promptly. Otherwise—it might have been a near thing."

Susan stared. "Was she really so bad?"

"Mrs Banks, will you tell me again exactly what Miss Gilchrist had to eat and drink yesterday. Everything."

Susan reflected and gave a meticulous account. The doctor shook his head in a dissatisfied manner.

"There must have been something she had and you didn't?"

"I don't think so . . . Cakes, scones, jam, tea—and then supper. No, I can't remember anything."

The doctor rubbed his nose. He walked up and down the
room.

"Was it definitely something she ate? Definitely food poisoning?"

The doctor threw her a sharp glance. Then he seemed to
come to a decision.

"It was arsenic," he said.

"Arsenic?" Susan stared. "You mean somebody gave her
arsenic?"

"That's what it looks like."

"Could she have taken it herself? Deliberately, I mean?"

"Suicide? She says not and she should know. Besides if she
wanted to commit suicide she wouldn't be likely to choose arsenic.
There are sleeping pills in this house. She could have taken an
overdose of them."

"Could the arsenic have got into something by accident?"

"That's what I am wondering. It seems very unlikely, but
such things have been known. But if you and she ate the same
things—"

Susan nodded. She said, "It all seems impossible—" then she
gave a sudden gasp. "Why, of course, the wedding cake!"

"What's that? Wedding cake?"

Susan explained. The doctor listened with close attention.

"Odd. And you say she wasn't sure who sent it? Any of it
left? Or is the box it came in lying around?"

"I don't know. I'll look."

They searched together and finally found the white cardboard box with a few crumbs of cake still in it lying on the
kitchen dresser. The doctor packed it away with some care.

"I'll take charge of this. Any idea where the wrapping paper
it came in might be?"

Here they were not successful and Susan said that it had
probably gone into the Ideal boiler.

"You won't be leaving here just yet, Mrs Banks?"

His tone was genial, but it made Susan feel a little uncomfortable.

"No, I have to go through my aunt's things. I shall be here for a few days."

"Good. You understand the police will probably want to ask some questions. You don't know of anyone who—well, might have had it in for Miss Gilchrist?"

Susan shook her head.

"I don't really know much about her. She was with my aunt for some years—that's all I know."

"Quite, quite. Always seemed a pleasant unassuming woman —quite ordinary. Not the kind, you'd say, to have enemies or anything melodramatic of that kind. Wedding cake through the post. Sounds like some jealous woman—but who'd be jealous of Miss Gilchrist? Doesn't seem to fit."

"No."

"Well, I must be on my way. I don't know what's happening to us in quiet little Lytchett St. Mary. First a brutal murder and now attempted poisoning through the post. Odd, the one following the other."

He went down the path to his car. The cottage felt stuffy and Susan left the door standing open as she went slowly upstairs to resume her task.

Cora Lansquenet had not been a tidy or methodical woman. Her drawers held a miscellaneous assortment of things. There were toilet accessories and letters and old handkerchiefs and paint brushes mixed up together in one drawer. There were a few old letters and bills thrust in amongst a bulging drawer of underclothes. In another drawer under some woollen jumpers was a cardboard box holding two false fringes. There was another drawer full of old photographs and sketching books. Susan lingered over a group taken evidently at some French place many years ago and which showed a younger thinner Cora clinging to the arm of a tall lanky man with a straggling beard dressed in what seemed to be a velveteen coat and whom Susan took to be the late Pierre Lansquenet.

The photographs interested Susan, but she laid them aside, sorted all the papers she had found into a heap and began to go through them methodically. About a quarter way through she came on a letter. She read it through twice and was still staring at it when a voice speaking behind her caused her to give a cry of alarm.

"And what may you have got hold of there, Susan? Hullo, what's the matter?"

Susan reddened with annoyance. Her cry of alarm had been quite involuntary and she felt ashamed and anxious to explain.

"George! How you startled me!"

Her cousin smiled lazily.

"So it seems."

"How did you get here?"

"Well, the door downstairs was open, so I walked in. There seemed to be nobody about on the ground floor, so I came up here. If you mean how did I get to this part of the world, I started down this morning to come to the funeral."

"I didn't see you there?"

"The old bus played me up. The petrol feed seemed choked. I tinkered with it for some time and finally it seemed to clear itself. I was too late for the funeral by then, but I thought I might as well come on down. I knew you were here."

He paused and then went on:

"I rang you up, as a matter of fact—and Greg told me you'd come down to take possession, as it were. I thought I might give you a hand."

Susan said, "Aren't you needed in the office? Or can you take days off whenever you like?"

"A funeral has always been a recognised excuse for absentee-ism. And this funeral is indubitably genuine. Besides a murder always fascinates people. Anyway, I shan't be going much to the office in future—not now that I'm a man of means. I shall have better things to do."

He paused and grinned. "Same as Greg," he said.

Susan looked at George thoughtfully. She had never seen much of this cousin of hers and when they did meet she had always found him rather difficult to make out.

She asked, "Why did you really come down here, George?"

"I'm not sure it wasn't to do a little detective work. I've been thinking a good deal about the last funeral we attended. Aunt Cora certainly threw a spanner into the works that day. I've wondered whether it was sheer irresponsibility and auntly *joie de vivre* that prompted her words, or whether she really had something to go upon. What actually is in that letter that you were reading so attentively when I came in?"

Susan said slowly, "It's a letter that Uncle Richard wrote to Cora after he'd been down here to see her."

How very black George's eyes were. She'd thought of them as brown but they were black, and there was something curiously impenetrable about black eyes. They concealed the thoughts that lay behind them.

George drawled slowly, "Anything interesting in it?"

"No, not exactly . . ."

"Can I see?"

She hesitated for a moment, then put the letter into his outstretched hand.

He read it, skimming over the contents in a low monotone.

"Glad to have seen you again after all these years . . . looking very well . . . had a good journey home and arrived back not too tired. . . ."

His voice changed suddenly, sharpened:

"Please don't say anything to anyone about what I told you. It may be a mistake. Your loving brother, Richard."

He looked up at Susan. "What does that mean?"

"It might mean anything. . . . It might be just about his health. Or it might be some gossip about a mutual friend."

"Oh yes, it might be a lot of things. It isn't conclusive—but it's suggestive. . . . What did he tell Cora? Does anyone know what he told her?"

"Miss Gilchrist might know," said Susan thoughtfully. "I think she listened."

"Oh yes, the companion help. Where is she, by the way?"

"In hospital, suffering from arsenic poisoning."

George stared.

"You don't mean it?"

"I do. Someone sent her some poisoned wedding cake."

George sat down on one of the bedroom chairs and whistled.

"It looks," he said, "as though Uncle Richard was not mistaken."

iii

On the following morning Inspector Morton called at the cottage.

He was a quiet middle-aged man with a soft country burr in his voice. His manner was quiet and unhurried, but his eyes were shrewd.

"You realise what this is about, Mrs Banks?" he said. "Dr Proctor has already told you about Miss Gilchrist. The few crumbs of wedding cake that he took from here have been analysed and show traces of arsenic."

"So somebody deliberately wanted to poison her?"

"That's what it looks like. Miss Gilchrist herself doesn't seem able to help us. She keeps repeating that it's impossible—that nobody would so such a thing. But somebody did. *You* can't throw any light on the matter?"

Susan shook her head.

"I'm simply dumbfounded," she said. "Can't you find out anything from the postmark? Or the handwriting?"

"You've forgotten—the wrapping paper was presumably burnt. And there's a little doubt whether it came through the post at all. Young Andrews, the driver of the postal van, doesn't seem able to remember delivering it. He's got a big round, and he can't be sure—but there it is—there's a doubt about it."

"But—what's the alternative?"

"The alternative, Mrs Banks, is that an old piece of brown paper was used that already had Miss Gilchrist's name and address on it and a cancelled stamp, and that the package was pushed through the letter box or deposited inside the door by hand to create the impression that it had come by post."

He added dispassionately:

"It's quite a clever idea, you know, to choose wedding cake. Lonely middle-aged women are sentimental about wedding cake, pleased at having been remembered. A box of sweets, or something of that kind *might* have awakened suspicion."

Susan said slowly:

"Miss Gilchrist speculated a good deal about who could have

sent it, but she wasn't at all suspicious—as you say, she was pleased and yes—flattered."

She added: "Was there enough poison in it to—kill?"

"That's difficult to say until we get the quantitative analysis. It rather depends on whether Miss Gilchrist ate the whole of the wedge. She seems to think that she didn't. Can you remember?"

"No—no, I'm not sure. She offered me some and I refused and then she ate some and said it was a very good cake, but I don't remember if she finished it or not."

"I'd like to go upstairs if you don't mind, Mrs Banks."

"Of course."

She followed him up to Miss Gilchrist's room. She said apologetically:

"I'm afraid it's in a rather disgusting state. But I didn't have time to do anything about it with my aunt's funeral and everything, and then after Dr Proctor came I thought perhaps I ought to leave it as it was."

"That was very intelligent of you, Mrs Banks. It's not everyone who would have been so intelligent."

He went to the bed and slipping his hand under the pillow raised it carefully. A slow smile spread over his face.

"There you are," he said.

A piece of wedding cake lay on the sheet looking somewhat the worse for wear.

"How extraordinary," said Susan.

"Oh no, it's not. Perhaps your generation doesn't do it. Young ladies nowadays mayn't set so much store on getting married. But it's an old custom. Put a piece of wedding cake under your pillow and you'll dream of your future husband."

"But surely Miss Gilchrist—"

"She didn't want to tell us about it because she felt foolish doing such a thing at her age. But I had a notion that's what it might be." His face sobered. "And if it hadn't been for an old maid's foolishness, Miss Gilchrist mightn't be alive today."

"But who could have possibly wanted to kill her?"

His eyes met hers, a curious speculative look in them that made Susan feel uncomfortable.

"You don't know?" he asked.

"No—of course I don't."

"It seems then as though we shall have to find out," said Inspector Morton.

XII

Two ELDERLY men sat together in a room whose furnishings were of the most modern kind. There were no curves in the room. Everything was square. Almost the only exception was Hercule Poirot himself who was full of curves. His stomach was pleasantly rounded, his head resembled an egg in shape, and his moustaches curved upwards in a flamboyant flourish.

He was sipping a glass of *sirop* and looking thoughtfully at Mr Goby.

Mr Goby was small and spare and shrunken. He had always been refreshingly nondescript in appearance and he was now so nondescript as practically not to be there at all. He was not looking at Poirot because Mr Goby never looked at anybody.

Such remarks as he was now making seemed to be addressed to the left hand corner of the chromium plated fireplace curb.

Mr Goby was famous for the acquiring of information. Very few people knew about him and very few employed his services —but those few were usually extremely rich. They had to be, for Mr Goby was very expensive. His speciality was the acquiring of information quickly. At the flick of Mr Goby's double jointed thumb, hundreds of patient questioning plodding men and women, old and young, of all apparent stations in life, were despatched to question, and probe, and achieve results.

Mr Goby had now practically retired from business. But he occasionally "obliged" a few old patrons. Hercule Poirot was one of these.

"I've got what I could for you," he told the fire curb in a soft confidential whisper. "I sent the boys out. They do what they can—good lads—good lads all of them, but not what they used to be in the old days. They don't come that way nowadays. Not willing to learn, that's what it is. Think they know everything after they've only been a couple of years on the job. And they work to time. Shocking the way they work to time."

He shook his head sadly and shifted his gaze to an electric plug socket.

"It's the Government," he told it. "And all this education racket. It gives them ideas. They come back and tell us what they think. They *can't* think, most of them, anyway. All they know is things out of books. That's no good in our business. Bring in the answers—that's all that's needed—no thinking."

Mr Goby flung himself back in his chair and winked at a lampshade.

"Mustn't crab the Government, though! Don't know really what we'd do without it. I can tell you that nowadays you can walk in most anywhere with a notebook and pencil, dressed right, and speaking B.B.C., and ask people all the most intimate details of their daily lives and all their back history, and what they had for dinner on November twenty-third because that was a test day for middle class incomes—or whatever it happens to be, (making it a grade above to butter them up!)—ask 'em any mortal thing you can; and nine times out of ten they'll come across pat, and even the tenth time though they may cut up rough, they won't doubt for a minute that you're what you say you are—and that the Government really wants to know—for some completely unfathomable reason! I can tell you, M. Poirot," said Mr Goby still talking to the lampshade, "that it's the best line we've ever had; much better than taking the electric meter or tracing a fault in the telephone—yes, or than calling as nuns, or the Girl Guides or the Boy Scouts asking for subscriptions—though we use all those too. Yes, Government snooping is God's gift to investigators and long may it continue!"

Poirot did not speak. Mr Goby had grown a little garrulous with advancing years, but he would come to the point in his own good time.

"Ar," said Mr Goby and took out a very scrubby little notebook. He licked his finger and flicked over the pages. "Here we are. Mr George Crossfield. We'll take him first. Just the plain facts. You won't want to know how I got them. He's been in Queer Street for quite a while now. Horses, mostly, and gambling—he's not a great one for women. Goes over to France now and then, and Monte too. Spends a lot of time at the Casino. Too downy to cash cheques there, but gets hold of a lot more money than his travelling allowance would account for. I didn't go into that, because it wasn't what you want to know. But he's not scrupulous about evading the law—and being a lawyer he knows how to do it. Some reason to believe that he's been using trust funds entrusted to him to invest. Plunging pretty wildly of late —on the Stock Exchange *and* on the gee-gees! Bad judgement and bad luck. Been off his feed badly for three months. Worried, bad tempered and irritable in the office. *But* since his uncle's death that's all changed. He's like the breakfast eggs (if we had 'em). Sunny side up!

"Now, as to particular information asked for. Statement that he was at Hurst Park races on day in question almost certainly untrue. Almost invariably places bets with one or other of two bookies on the course. They didn't see him that day. Possible that he left Paddington by train for destination unknown. Taxi driver who took fare to Paddington made doubtful identification of his photograph. But I wouldn't bank on it. He's a very common type—nothing outstanding about him. No success with porters etc., at Paddington. Certainly didn't arrive at Cholsey Station—which is nearest for Lytchett St. Mary. Small station, strangers noticeable. Could have got out at Reading and taken bus. Buses there crowded, frequent and several routes go within a mile or so of Lytchett St. Mary as well as the bus service that goes right into the village. He wouldn't take that—not if he meant business. All in all, he's a downy card. Wasn't seen in Lytchett St. Mary but he needn't have been. Other ways of approach than through the village. Was in the OUDS at Oxford, by the way. If he went to the cottage that day he mayn't have looked quite like the usual George Crossfield. I'll keep him in my book, shall I? There's a black market angle I'd like to play up."

"You may keep him in," said Hercule Poirot.

Mr Goby licked his finger and turned another page of his notebook.

"Mr Michael Shane. He's thought quite a lot of in the profession. Has an even better idea of himself than other people have. Wants to star and wants to star quickly. Fond of money and doing himself well. Very attractive to women. They fall for him right and left. He's partial to them himself—but business comes first, as you might say. He's been running around with Sorrel Dainton who was playing the lead in the last show he was in. He only had a minor part but made quite a hit in it, and Miss Dainton's husband doesn't like him. His wife doesn't know about him and Miss Dainton. Doesn't know much about anything, it seems. Not much of an actress, I gather, but easy on the eye. Crazy about her husband. Some rumour of a bust up likely between them not long ago, but that seems out now. Out since Mr Richard Abernethie's death."

Mr Goby emphasised the last point by nodding his head significantly at a cushion on the sofa.

"On the day in question, Mr Shane says he was meeting a Mr Rosenheim and a Mr Oscar Lewis to fix up some stage business. He didn't meet them. Sent them a wire to say he was terribly sorry he couldn't make it. What he *did* do was to go to the Emeraldo Car people, who hire out drive yourself cars. He hired a car about twelve o'clock and drove away in it. He returned it about six in the evening. According to the speedometer it had been driven just about the right number of miles for what we're after. No confirmation from Lytchett St. Mary. No strange car seems to have been observed there that day. Lots of places it could be left unnoticed a mile or so away. And there's even a disused quarry a few hundred yards down the lane from the cottage. Three market towns within walking distance where you can park in side streets, without the police bothering about you. All right, we keep Mr Shane in?"

"Most certainly."

"Now Mrs Shane." Mr Goby rubbed his nose and told his left cuff about Mrs Shane. "She says she was shopping. Just shopping . . ." Mr Goby raised his eyes to the ceiling. "Women who are shopping—just scatty, that's what they are. And she'd heard she'd come into money the day before. Naturally there'd be no holding her. She has one or two charge accounts but they're overdrawn and they've been pressing her for payment and she didn't put any more on the sheet. It's quite on the cards that she went in here and there and everywhere, trying on clothes, looking at jewellery, pricing this, that, and the other—and as likely as not, not buying anything! She's easy to approach—I'll say that. I had one of my young ladies who's knowledgeable on the theatrical line do a hook up. Stopped by her table in a restaurant and exclaimed the way they do: "Darling, I haven't seen you since 'Way Down Under.' You were *wonderful* in that! Have you seen Hubert lately?" That was the producer and Mrs Shane was a bit of a flop in the play—but that makes it go all the better. They're chatting theatrical stuff at once, and my girl throws the right names about, and then she says, 'I believe I caught a glimpse of you at so and so, on so and so, giving the day—and most ladies fall for it and say, 'Oh no, I was—' whatever it may be. But not Mrs Shane. Just looks vacant and says, 'Oh, I daresay.' What can you do with a lady like that?" Mr Goby shook his head severely at the radiator.

"Nothing," said Hercule Poirot with feeling. "Do I not have cause to know it? Never shall I forget the killing of Lord Edgware. I was nearly defeated—yes, I, Hercule Poirot—by the extremely simple cunning of a vacant brain. The very simple minded have often the genius to commit an uncomplicated crime and then leave it alone. Let us hope that our murderer—if there is a murderer in this affair—is intelligent and superior and thoroughly pleased with himself and unable to resist painting the lily. *Enfin*—but continue."

Once more Mr Goby applied himself to his little book.

"Mr and Mrs Banks—who said they were at home all day. *She* wasn't, anyway! Went around to the garage, got out her car, and drove off in it about one o'clock. Destination unknown. Back about five. Can't tell about mileage because she's had it out every day since and it's been nobody's business to check.

"As to Mr Banks, we've dug up something curious. To begin with, I'll mention that on the day in question we don't know *what* he did. He didn't go to work. Seems he'd already asked for a couple of days off on account of the funeral. And since then he's chucked his job—with no consideration for the firm. Nice, well established pharmacy, it is. They're not too keen on Master Banks. Seems he used to get into rather queer excitable states.

"Well, as I say, we don't know what he was doing on the day of Mrs L's death. He didn't go with his wife. It *could* be that he stopped in their little flat all day. There's no porter there, and nobody knows whether tenants are in or out. But his back history is interesting. Up till about four months ago—just before he met his wife, he was in a mental home. Not certified—just what they call a mental breakdown. Seems he made some slip up in dispensing a medicine. (He was working with a Mayfair firm then.) The woman recovered, and the firm were all over themselves apologising, and there was no prosecution. After all, these accidental slips do occur, and most decent people are sorry for a poor young chap who's done it—so long as there's no permanent harm done, that is. The firm didn't sack him, but he resigned—said it had shaken his nerve. But afterwards, it seems, he got into a very low state and told the doctor he was obsessed by guilt—that it had all been deliberate—the woman had been overbearing and rude to him when she came into the shop, had complained that her last prescription had been badly made up— and that he had resented this and had deliberately added a near lethal dose of some drug or other. He said 'She had to be punished for daring to speak to me like that!' And then wept and said he was too wicked to live and a lot of things like that. The medicos have a long word for that sort of thing—guilt complex or something—and don't believe it was deliberate at all, just carelessness, but that he wanted to make it important and serious."

"*Ca se peut,*" said Hercule Poirot.

"Pardon? Anyway, he went into this Sanitorium and they treated him and discharged him as cured, and he met Miss Abernethie as she was then. And he got a job in this respectable but rather obscure little chemist's shop. Told them he'd been out of England for a year and a half, and gave them his former reference from some shop in Eastbourne. Nothing against him in that shop, but a fellow dispenser said he had a very queer temper and was odd in his manner sometimes. There's a story about a customer saying once as a joke, 'Wish you'd sell me something to poison my wife, ha ha!' And Banks says to him, very soft and quiet: 'I could . . . It would cost you two hundred pounds.' The man felt uneasy and laughed it off. *May* have been all a joke, but it doesn't seem to me that Banks is the joking kind."

"*Mon ami,*" said Hercule Poirot. "It really amazes me how you get your information! Medical and highly confidential most of it!"

Mr Goby's eyes swivelled right round the room and he murmured, looking expectantly at the door, that there were *ways*. . . .

"Now we come to the country department. Mr and Mrs Timothy Abernethie. Very nice place they've got, but sadly needing money spent on it. Very straitened they seem to be, very straitened. Taxation and unfortunate investments. Mr Abernethie enjoys ill health and the emphasis is on the enjoyment. Complains a lot and has everyone running and fetching and carrying. Eats hearty meals, and seems quite strong physically if he likes to make the effort. There's no one in the house after the daily woman goes and no one's allowed into Mr Abernethie's room unless he rings his bell. He was in a very bad temper the morning of the day after the funeral. Swore at Mrs Jones. Ate only a little of his breakfast and said he wouldn't have any lunch—he'd had a bad night. He was in a worse temper still the next day and said the supper she had left out for him was unfit to eat and a good deal more. He was alone in the house and unseen by anybody from nine-thirty that morning until the following morning."

"And Mrs Abernethie?"

"She started off from Enderby by car at the time you mentioned. Arrived on foot at a small local garage in a place called Cathstone and explained her car had broken down a couple of miles away.

"A mechanic drove her out to it, made an investigation and said they'd have to tow it in and it would be a long job—couldn't promise to finish it that day. The lady was very put out, but went to a small inn, arranged to stay the night, and asked for some sandwiches as she said she'd like to see something of the countryside—it's on the edge of the moorland country. She didn't come back to the inn till quite late that evening. My informant said he didn't wonder. It's a sordid little place!"

"And the times?"

"She got the sandwiches at eleven. If she'd walked to the main road, a mile, she could have hitch-hiked into Wallcaster and caught a special South Coast express which stops at Reading West. I won't go into details of buses etcetera. It *could* just have been done if you could make the—er—attack fairly late in the afternoon."

"I understand the doctor stretched the time limit to possibly four-thirty."

"Mind you," said Mr Goby, "I shouldn't say it was likely. She seems to be a nice lady, liked by everybody. She's devoted to her husband, treats him like a child."

"Yes, yes, the maternal complex."

"She's strong and hefty, chops the wood and often hauls in great baskets of logs. Pretty good with the inside of a car, too."

"I was coming to that. What exactly *was* wrong with the car?"

"Do you want the exact details, M. Poirot?"

"Heaven forbid. I have no mechanical knowledge."

"It was a difficult thing to spot. And also to put right. And it *could* have been done maliciously by someone without very much trouble. By someone who was familiar with the insides of a car."

"*C'est magnifique!*" said Poirot with bitter enthusiasm. "All so convenient, all so possible. *Bon dieu,* can we eliminate *nobody?* And Mrs Leo Abernethie?"

"She's a very nice lady, too. Mr Abernethie deceased was very fond of her. She came there to stay about a fortnight before he died."

"After he had been to Lytchett St. Mary to see his sister?"

"No, just before. Her income is a good deal reduced since the war. She gave up her house in England and took a small flat in London. She has a villa in Cyprus and spends part of the year there. She has a young nephew whom she is helping to educate, and there seems to be one or two young artists whom she helps financially from time to time."

"St. Helen of the blameless life," said Poirot shutting his eyes.

"And it was quite impossible for her to have left Enderby that day without the servants knowing? Say that that is so, I implore you!"

Mr Goby brought his glance across to rest apologetically on Poirot's polished patent leather shoe, the nearest he had come to a direct encounter, and murmured:

"I'm afraid I can't say that, M. Poirot. Mrs Abernethie went to London to fetch some extra clothes and belongings as she had agreed with Mr Entwhistle to stay on and see to things."

"Il ne manquait que ça!" said Poirot with strong feeling.

XIII

WHEN THE card of Inspector Morton of the Berkshire County
Police was brought to Hercule Poirot, his eyebrows went up.

"Show him in, Georges, show him in. And bring—what is it
that the police prefer?"

"I would suggest beer, sir."

"How horrible! But how British. Bring beer, then."

Inspector Morton came straight to the point.

"I had to come to London," he said. "And I got hold of your
address, M. Poirot. I was interested to see you at the inquest on
Thursday."

"So you saw me there?"

"Yes. I was surprised—and, as I say, interested. You won't
remember me but I remember you very well. In that Pang-
bourne Case."

"Ah, you were connected with that?"

"Only in a very junior capacity. It's a long time ago but I've
never forgotten you."

"And you recognised me at once the other day?"

"That wasn't difficult, sir." Inspector Morton repressed a slight
smile. "Your appearance is—rather unusual."

His gaze took in Poirot's sartorial perfection and rested finally
on the curving moustaches.

"You stick out in a country place," he said.

"It is possible, it is possible," said Poirot with complacency.

"It interested me *why* you should be there. That sort of crime—
robbery—assault—doesn't usually interest you."

"Was it the usual ordinary brutal type of crime?"

"That's what I've been wondering."

"You have wondered from the beginning, have you not?"

"Yes, M. Poirot. There were some unusual features. Since
then we've worked along the routine lines. Pulled in one or two

people for questioning, but everyone has been able to account quite satisfactorily for his time that afternoon. It wasn't what you'd call an 'ordinary' crime, M. Poirot—we're quite sure of that. The Chief Constable agrees. It was done by someone who wished to make it appear that way. It could have been the Gilchrist woman, but there doesn't seem to be any motive—and there wasn't any emotional background. Mrs Lansquenet was perhaps a bit mental—or 'simple,' if you like to put it that way, but it was a household of mistress and dogsbody with no feverish feminine friendship about it. There are dozens of Miss Gilchrists about, and they're not usually the murdering type."

He paused.

"So it looks as though we'd have to look farther afield. I came to ask if you could help us at all. *Something* must have brought you down there, M. Poirot."

"Yes, yes, something did. An excellent Daimler car. But not only that."

"You had—information?"

"Hardly in your sense of the word. Nothing that could be used as evidence."

"But something that could be—a pointer?"

"Yes."

"You see, M. Poirot, there have been developments."

Meticulously, in detail, he told of the poisoned wedge of wedding cake.

Poirot took a deep hissing breath.

"Ingenious—yes, ingenious . . . I warned Mr Entwhistle to look after Miss Gilchrist. An attack on her was always a possibility. But I must confess that I did *not* expect poison. I anticipated a repetition of the hatchet *motif*. I merely thought that it would be inadvisable for her to walk alone in unfrequented lanes after dark."

"But *why* did you anticipate an attack on her? I think, M. Poirot, you ought to tell me that."

Poirot nodded his head slowly.

"Yes, I will tell you. Mr Entwhistle will not tell you, because he is a lawyer and lawyers do not like to speak of suppositions, of inferences made from the character of a dead woman, or from a few irresponsible words. But he will not be adverse to *my* telling you—no, he will be relieved. He does not wish to appear foolish or fanciful, but he wants you to know what may—only *may*—be the facts."

Poirot paused as George entered with a tall glass of beer.

"Some refreshment, Inspector. No, no, I insist."

"Won't you join me?"

"I do not drink the beer. But I will myself have a glass of *sirop de cassis*—the English they do not care for it, I have noticed."

Inspector Morton looked gratefully at his beer.

Poirot, sipping delicately from his glass of dark purple fluid, said:

"It begins, all this, at a funeral. Or rather, to be exact, *after* the funeral."

Graphically, with many gestures, he set forth the story as Mr Entwhistle had told it to him, but with such embellishments as his exuberant nature suggested. One almost felt that Hercule Poirot had himself been an eye-witness of the scene.

Inspector Morton had an excellent clear cut brain. He seized at once on what were, for his purposes, the salient points.

"This Mr Abernethie may have been poisoned?"

"It is a possibility."

"And the body has been cremated and there is no evidence?"

"Exactly."

Inspector Morton ruminated.

"Interesting. There's nothing in it for *us*. Nothing, that is, to make Richard Abernethie's death worth investigating. It would be waste of time."

"Yes."

"But there are the *people*—the people who were there—the people who heard Cora Lansquenet say what she did, and one of whom *may* have thought that she might say it again and with more detail."

"As she undoubtedly would have. There are, Inspector, as you say, *the people*. And now you see why I was at the inquest, why I interest myself in the case—because it is, always, *people* in whom I interest myself."

"Then the attack on Miss Gilchrist—"

"Was always indicated. Richard Abernethie had been down to the cottage. He had talked to Cora. He had, perhaps, actually mentioned a *name*. The only person who might possibly have known or overheard something was Miss Gilchrist. After Cora is silenced, the murderer might continue to be anxious. Does the other woman know something—anything? Of course, if the murderer is wise he will let well alone, but murderers, Inspector, are seldom wise. Fortunately for us. They brood, they feel uncertain, they desire to make sure—quite sure. They are pleased with their own cleverness. And so, in the end, they protrude their necks as you say."

Inspector Morton smiled faintly.

Poirot went on:

"This attempt to silence Miss Gilchrist, already it is a mistake. For now there are *two* occasions about which you make enquiry. There is the handwriting on the wedding label also. It is a pity the wrapping paper was burnt."

"Yes, I could have been certain, then, whether it came by post or whether it didn't."

"You have reason for thinking the latter, you say?"

"It's only what the postman thinks—he's not sure. If the parcel had gone through a village post office, it's ten to one the postmistress would have noticed it, but nowadays the mail is delivered by van from Market Keynes and of course the young chap does quite a round and delivers a lot of things. He thinks it was letters only and no parcel at the cottage—but he isn't sure. As a matter of fact he's having a bit of girl trouble and he can't think about anything else. I've tested his memory and he isn't reliable in any way. If he *did* deliver it, it seems to me odd that the parcel shouldn't have been noticed until after this Mr—whatshisname—Guthrie—"

"Ah, Mr Guthrie."

Inspector Morton smiled.

"Yes, M. Poirot. We're checking up on him. After all, it would be easy, wouldn't it, to come along with a plausible tale of having been a friend of Mrs Lansquenet's. Mrs Banks wasn't to know if he was or he wasn't. He could have dropped that little parcel, you know. It's easy to make a thing look as though it's been through the post. Lamp black a little smudged, makes quite a good postmark cancellation mark over a stamp."

He paused and then added:

"And there are other possibilities."

Poirot nodded.

"You think—?"

"Mr George Crossfield was down in that part of the world—but not until the next day. Meant to attend the funeral, but had a little engine trouble on the way. Know anything about him, M. Poirot?"

"A little. But not as much as I would like to know."

"Like that, is it? Quite a little bunch interested in the late Mr Abernethie's will, I understand. I hope it doesn't mean going after all of them."

"I have accumulated a little information. It is at your disposal. Naturally *I* have no authority to ask these people questions. In fact it would not be wise for me to do so."

"I shall go slowly myself. You don't want to fluster your bird too soon. But when you do fluster it, you want to fluster it well."

"A very sound technique. For you then, my friend, the routine—with all the machinery you have at your disposal. It is slow—but sure. For myself—"

"Yes, M. Poirot?"

"For myself, I go north. As I have told you, it is *people* in whom I interest myself. Yes—a little preparatory camouflage—and I go north.

"I intend," added Hercule Poirot, "to purchase a country mansion for foreign refugees. I represent U.N.A.R.C.O."

"And what's U.N.A.R.C.O.?"

"United Nations Aid for Refugee Centres Old Age. It sounds well, do you not think?"

Inspector Morton grinned.

XIV

HERCULE POIROT said to a grim-faced Janet:

"Thank you very much. You have been most kind."

Janet, her lips still fixed in a sour line, left the room. These foreigners! The questions they asked. Their impertinence! All very well to say that he was a specialist interested in unsuspected heart conditions such as Mr Abernethie must have suffered from. That was very likely true—gone very sudden the master had, and the doctor had been surprised. But what business was it of some foreign doctor coming along and nosing in?

All very well for Mrs Leo to say: "Please answer Monsieur Pontarlier's questions. He has a good reason for asking."

Questions. Always questions. Sheets of them sometimes to fill in as best you could—and what did the Government or anyone else want to know about your private affairs for? Asking your age at that census—downright impertinent and she hadn't told them, either! Cut off five years she had. Why not? If she only felt fifty four, she'd *call* herself fifty four!

At any rate Monsieur Pontarlier hadn't wanted to know her age. He'd had *some* decency. Just questions about the medicines the master had taken, and where they were kept, and if, perhaps, he might have taken too much of them if he was feeling not quite the thing—or if he'd been forgetful. As though she could remember all that rubbish—the master knew what he was doing! And asking if any of the medicines he took were still in the house. Naturally they'd all been thrown away. Heart condition—and some long word he'd used. Always thinking of something new they were, these doctors. Look at them telling old Rogers he had a disc or some such in his spine. Plain lumbago, that was all that was the matter with him. Her father had been a gardener and *he*'d suffered from lumbago. Doctors!

The self-appointed medical man sighed and went downstairs in search of Lanscombe. He had not got very much out of Janet but he had hardly expected to do so. All he had really wanted to do was to check such information as could unwillingly be extracted from her with that given him by Helen Abernethie and which had been obtained from the same source—but with much less difficulty, since Janet was ready to admit that Mrs Leo had a perfect right to ask such questions and indeed Janet herself had enjoyed dwelling at length on the last few weeks of her master's life. Illness and death were congenial subjects to her.

Yes, Poirot thought, he could have relied on the information that Helen had got for him. He had done so really. But by nature and long habit he trusted nobody until he himself had tried and proved them.

In any case the evidence was slight and unsatisfactory. It boiled down to the fact that Richard Abernethie had been prescribed vitamin oil capsules. That these had been in a large bottle which had been nearly finished at the time of his death. Anybody who had wanted to, could have operated on one or more of those capsules with a hypodermic syringe and could have rearranged the bottle so that the fatal dose would only be taken some weeks after that somebody had left the house. Or someone might have slipped into the house on the day before Richard Abernethie died and have doctored a capsule then—or, which was more likely—have substituted something else for a sleeping tablet in the little bottle that stood beside the bed. Or again might have quite simply tampered with the food or drink.

Hercule Poirot had made his own experiments. The front door was kept locked, but there was a side door giving on the garden which was not locked until evening. At about quarter past one, when the gardeners had gone to lunch and when the household was in the dining room Poirot had entered the grounds, come to the side door, and mounted the stairs to Richard Abernethie's bedroom without meeting anybody. As a variant he had pushed through a baize door and slipped into the larder. He had heard voices from the kitchen at the end of the passage but no one had seen him.

Yes, it could have been done. But had it been done? There was nothing to indicate that that was so. Not that Poirot was really looking for evidence—he wanted only to satisfy himself as to possibilities. The murder of Richard Abernethie could only be a hypothesis. It was Cora Lansquenet's murder for which evidence was needed. What he wanted was to study the people who had been assembled for the funeral that day, and to form his own conclusions about them. He already had his plan, but first he wanted a few more words with old Lanscombe.

Lanscombe was courteous but distant. Less resentful than Janet, he nevertheless regarded this upstart foreigner as the materialization of the Writing on the Wall. This was What We are Coming to!

He put down the leather with which he was lovingly polishing the Georgian teapot and straightened his back.

"Yes, sir?" he said politely.

Poirot sat down gingerly on a pantry stool.

"Mrs Abernethie tells me that you hoped to reside in the lodge by the North gate when you retired from service here?"

"That is so, sir. Naturally all that is changed now. When the property is sold—"

Poirot interrupted deftly:

"It might still be possible. There are cottages for the gardeners. The lodge is not needed for the guests or their attendants. It might be possible to make an arrangement of some kind."

"Well, thank you, sir, for the suggestion. But I hardly think— The majority of the—guests would be foreigners, I presume?"

"Yes, they will be foreigners. Amongst those who fled from Europe to this country are several who are old and infirm. There can be no future for them if they return to their own countries, for these persons, you understand, are those whose relatives there have perished. They cannot earn their living here as an able-bodied man or woman can do. Funds have been raised and are being administered by the organisation which I represent to endow various country homes for them. This place is, I think, eminently suitable. The matter is practically settled."

Lanscombe sighed.

"You'll understand, sir, that it's sad for me to think that this won't be a private dwelling house any longer. But I know how things are nowadays. None of the family could afford to live here—and I don't think the young ladies and gentlemen would even want to do so. Domestic help is too difficult to obtain these days, and even if obtained is expensive and unsatisfactory. I quite realise that these fine mansions have served their turn." Lanscombe sighed again. "If it has to be an—an institution of some kind, I'll be glad to think that it's the kind you're mentioning. We were Spared in This Country, sir, owing to our Navy and Air Force and our brave young men and being fortunate enough to be an island. If Hitler had landed here we'd all have turned out and given him short shrift. My sight isn't good enough for shooting, but I could have used a pitchfork, sir, and I intended to do so if necessary. We've always welcomed the unfortunate in this country, sir, it's been our pride. We shall continue so to do."

"Thank you, Lanscombe," said Poirot gently. "Your master's death must have been a great blow to you."

"It was, sir. I'd been with the master since he was quite a young man. I've been very fortunate in my life, sir. No one could have had a better master."

"I have been conversing with my friend and—er—colleague, Dr Larraby. We were wondering if your master could have had any extra worry—any unpleasant interview—on the day before he died? You do not remember if any visitors came to the house that day?"

"I think not, sir. I do not recall any."

"No one called at all just about that time?"

"The vicar was here to tea the day before. Otherwise—some nuns called for a subscription—and a young man came to the back door and wanted to sell Marjorie some brushes and saucepan cleaners. Very persistent he was. Nobody else."

A worried expression had appeared on Lanscombe's face. Poirot did not press him further. Lanscombe had already unburdened himself to Mr Entwhistle. He would be far less forthcoming with Hercule Poirot.

With Marjorie, on the other hand, Poirot had had instant success. Marjorie had none of the conventions of "good service." Marjorie was a first class cook and the way to her heart lay through her cooking. Poirot had visited her in the kitchen, praised certain dishes with discernment, and Marjorie, realising that here was someone who knew what he was talking about, hailed him immediately as a fellow spirit. He had no difficulty in finding out exactly what had been served the night before Richard Abernethie had died. Marjorie, indeed, was inclined to view the matter as "It was the night I made that chocolate soufflé that Mr Abernethie died. Six eggs I'd saved up for it. The dairyman he's a friend of mine. Got hold of some cream too. Better not ask how. Enjoyed it, Mr Abernethie did." The rest of the meal was likewise detailed. What had come out from the dining room had been finished in the kitchen. Ready as Marjorie was to talk, Poirot had learned nothing of value from her.

He went now to fetch his overcoat and a couple of scarves, and thus padded against the North Country air he went out on the terrace and joined Helen Abernethie who was clipping some late roses.

"Have you found out anything fresh?" she asked.

"Nothing. But I hardly expected to do so."

"I know. Ever since Mr Entwhistle told me you were coming, I've been ferreting round, but there's really been nothing."

She paused and said hopefully:

"Perhaps it *is* all a mare's nest?"

"To be attacked with a hatchet?"

"I wasn't thinking of Cora."

"But it is of Cora that I think. Why was it necessary for someone to kill her? Mr Entwhistle has told me that on that day, at the moment that she came out suddenly with her *gaffe,* you yourself felt that something was wrong. That is so?"

"Well—yes, but I don't know—"

Poirot swept on.

"How 'wrong'? Unexpected? Surprising? Or—what shall we say—uneasy? Sinister?"

"Oh no, not sinister. Just something that wasn't—oh, I don't know. I can't remember and it wasn't important."

"But why cannot you remember—because something else put it out of your head—something more important?"

"Yes—yes—I think you're right there. It was the mention of murder, I suppose. That swept away everything else."

"It was, perhaps, the reaction of some particular person to the word 'murder'?"

"Perhaps . . . But I don't remember looking at anyone in particular. We were all staring at Cora."

"It may have been something you heard—something dropped perhaps . . . or broken . . ."

Helen frowned in an effort of remembrance.

"No . . . I don't think so. . . ."

"Ah well, someday it will come back. And it may be of no consequence. Now tell me, madame, of those here, who knew Cora best?"

Helen considered.

"Lanscombe, I suppose. He remembers her from a child. The housemaid, Janet, only came after she had married and gone away."

"And next to Lanscombe?"

Helen said thoughtfully: "I suppose—*I* did. Maude hardly knew her at all."

"Then, taking you as the person who knew her best, why do you think she asked that question as she did?"

Helen smiled.

"It was very characteristic of Cora!"

"What I mean is, was it a *bêtise* pure and simple? Did she just blurt out what was in her mind without thinking? Or was she being malicious—amusing herself by upsetting everyone?"

Helen reflected.

"One can't ever be quite sure about a person, can you? I never have known whether Cora was just ingenuous—or whether she counted, childishly, on making an effect. That's what you mean, isn't it?"

"Yes. I was thinking: Suppose this Mrs Cora says to herself, 'What fun it would be to ask if Richard was murdered and see how they all look!' That would be like her, yes?"

Helen looked doubtful.

"It might be. She certainly had an impish sense of humour as a child. But what difference does it make?"

"It would underline the point that it is unwise to make jokes about murder," said Poirot drily.

Helen shivered.

"Poor Cora."

Poirot changed the subject.

"Mrs Timothy Abernethie stayed the night after the funeral?"

"Yes."

"Did she talk to you at all about what Cora had said?"

"Yes, she said it was outrageous and just like Cora!"

"She didn't take it seriously?"

"Oh no. No, I'm sure she didn't. . . ."

The second "no," Poirot thought, had sounded suddenly doubtful. But was not that almost always the case when you went back over something in your mind?

"And you, madame, did you take it seriously?"

Helen Abernethie, her eyes looking very blue and strangely young under the sideways sweep of crisp grey hair, said thoughtfully:

"Yes, M. Poirot, I think I did."

"Because of your feeling that something was wrong?"

"Perhaps."

He waited—but as she said nothing more, he went on:

"There had been an estrangement, lasting many years, between Mrs Lansquenet and her family?"

"Yes. None of us liked her husband and she was offended about it, and so the estrangement grew."

"And then, suddenly, your brother-in-law went to see her. Why?"

"I don't know—I suppose he knew, or guessed, that he hadn't very long to live and wanted to be reconciled—but I really don't know."

"He didn't tell you?"

"Tell *me?*"

"Yes. You were here, staying with him, just before he went there. He didn't even mention his intention to you?"

He thought a slight reserve came into her manner.

"He told me that he was going to see his brother Timothy—which he did. He never mentioned Cora at all. Shall we go in? It must be nearly lunchtime."

She walked beside him carrying the flowers she had picked. As they went in by the side door, Poirot said:

"You are sure, quite sure, that during your visit, Mr Abernethie said nothing to you about any member of the family which might be relevant?"

A faint resentment in her manner, Helen said:

"You are speaking like a policeman."

"I *was* a policeman—once. I have no status—no right to question you. But you want the truth—or so I have been led to believe?"

They entered the green drawing room. Helen said with a sigh:

"Richard was disappointed in the younger generation. Old men usually are. He disparaged them in various ways—but there was nothing—*nothing,* do you understand—that could possibly suggest a motive for murder."

"Ah," said Poirot. She reached for a Chinese bowl and began to arrange the roses in it. When they were disposed to her satisfaction she looked round for a place to put it.

"You arrange flowers admirably, madame," said Hercule. "I think that anything you undertook you would manage to do with perfection."

"Thank you. I am fond of flowers. I think this would look well on that green malachite table."

There was a bouquet of wax flowers under a glass shade on the malachite table. As she lifted it off, Poirot said casually:

"Did anyone tell Mr Abernethie that his niece Susan's husband had come near to poisoning a customer when making up a prescription? Ah, *pardon!*"

He sprang forward.

The Victorian ornament had slipped from Helen's fingers. Poirot's spring forward was not quick enough. It dropped on the floor and the glass shade broke. Helen gave an expression of annoyance.

"How careless of me. However, the flowers are not damaged. I can get a new glass shade made for it. I'll put it away in the big cupboard under the stairs."

It was not until Poirot had helped her to lift it onto a shelf in the dark cupboard and had followed her back to the drawing room that he said:

"It was my fault. I should not have startled you."

"What was it that you asked me? I have forgotten."

"Oh, there is no need to repeat my question. Indeed—I have forgotten what it was."

Helen came up to him. She laid her hand on his arm.

"M. Poirot, is there anyone whose life would really bear close investigation? *Must* people's lives be dragged into this when they have nothing to do with—with—"

"With the death of Cora Lansquenet? Yes. Because one has to examine *everything*. Oh! it is true enough—it is an old maxim —*everyone has something to hide*. It is true of all of us—it is perhaps true of you, too, madame. But I say to you, nothing can be ignored. That is why your friend, Mr Entwhistle, he has come to me. For I am not the police. I am discreet and what I learn does not concern me. But I have to *know*. And since in this matter is not so much *evidence* as *people*—then it is *people* with whom I occupy myself. I need, madame, to meet everyone who was here on the day of the funeral. And it would be a great convenience—yes, and it would be strategically satisfactory—if I could meet them *here*."

"I'm afraid," Helen said slowly, "that that would be too difficult—"

"Not so difficult as you think. Already I have devised a means. The house, it is sold. So Mr Entwhistle will declare. (*Entendu*, sometimes these things fall through!) He will invite the various members of the family to assemble here and to choose what they will from the furnishings before it is all put up to auction. A suitable weekend can be selected for that purpose."

He paused and then said:

"You see, it is easy, is it not?"

Helen looked at him. The blue eyes were cold—almost frosty.

"Are you laying a trap for someone, M. Poirot?"

"Alas! I wish I knew enough. No, I have still the open mind. "There may," Hercule Poirot added thoughtfully, "be certain tests . . ."

"Tests? What kind of tests?"

"I have not yet formulated them to myself. And in any case, madame, it would be better that you should not know them."

"So that I can be tested too?"

"You, madame, have been taken behind the scenes. Now there is one thing that is doubtful. The young people will, I think, come readily. But it may be difficult, may it not, to secure the presence here of Mr Timothy Abernethie. I hear that he never leaves home."

Helen smiled suddenly.

"I believe you may be lucky there, M. Poirot. I heard from Maude yesterday. The workmen are in painting the house and Timothy is suffering terribly from the smell of the paint. He says that it is seriously affecting his health. I think that he and Maude would both be pleased to come here—perhaps for a week or two. Maude is still not able to get about very well—you know she broke her ankle?"

"I had not heard. How unfortunate."

"Luckily they have got Cora's companion, Miss Gilchrist. It seems that she has turned out a perfect treasure."

"What is that?" Poirot turned sharply on Helen. "Did *they* ask for Miss Gilchrist to go to them? Who suggested it?"

"I think Susan fixed it up. Susan Banks."

"Aha," said Poirot in a curious voice. "So it was the little Susan who suggested it. She is fond of making the arrangements."

"Susan struck me as being a very competent girl."

"Yes. She is competent. Did you hear that Miss Gilchrist had a narrow escape from death with a piece of poisoned wedding cake?"

"No!" Helen looked startled. "I do remember now that Maude said over the telephone that Miss Gilchrist had just come out of hospital but I'd no idea why she had been in hospital. Poisoned? But, M. Poirot—*why?*"

"Do you really ask that?"

Helen said with sudden vehemence:

"Oh! get them all here! Find out the truth! There mustn't be any more murders."

"So you will co-operate?"

"Yes—I will co-operate."

XV

"THAT LINOLEUM does look nice, Mrs Jones. What a hand you have with lino. The teapot's on the kitchen table, so go and help yourself. I'll be there as soon as I've taken up Mr Abernethie's elevenses."

Miss Gilchrist trotted up the staircase, carrying a daintily set out tray. She tapped on Timothy's door, interpreted a growl from within as an invitation to enter, and tripped briskly in.

"Morning coffee and biscuits, Mr Abernethie. I do hope you're feeling brighter today. Such a lovely day."

Timothy grunted and said suspiciously:

"Is there skim on that milk?"

"Oh no, Mr Abernethie. I took it off very carefully, and anyway I've brought up the little strainer in case it should form again. Some people like it, you know, they say it's the *cream*—and so it is really."

"Idiots!" said Timothy. "What kind of biscuits are those?"

"They're those nice digestive biscuits."

"Digestive tripe. Ginger nuts are the only biscuits worth eating."

"I'm afraid the grocer hadn't got any this week. But these are really *very* nice. You try them and see."

"I know what they're like, thank you. Leave those curtains alone, can't you?"

"I thought you might like a little sunshine. It's such a nice sunny day."

"I want the room kept dark. My head's terrible. It's this paint. I've always been sensitive to paint. It's poisoning me."

Miss Gilchrist sniffed experimentally and said brightly:

"One really can't smell it much in here. The workmen are over on the other side."

"You're not sensitive like I am. Must I have *all* the books I'm reading taken out of my reach?"

"I'm so sorry, Mr Abernethie, I didn't know you were reading all of them."

"Where's my wife? I haven't seen her for over an hour."

"Mrs Abernethie's resting on the sofa."

"Tell her to come and rest up here."

"I'll tell her, Mr Abernethie. But she may have dropped off to sleep. Shall we say in about a quarter of an hour?"

"No, tell her I want her now. Don't monkey about with that rug. It's arranged the way I like it."

"I'm so sorry. I thought it was slipping off the far side."

"I like it slipping off. Go and get Maude. I want her."

Miss Gilchrist departed downstairs and tiptoed into the drawing room where Maude Abernethie was sitting with her leg up reading a novel.

"I'm so sorry, Mrs Abernethie," she said apologetically. "Mr Abernethie is asking for you."

Maude thrust aside her novel with a guilty expression.

"Oh dear," she said, "I'll go up at once."

She reached for her stick.

Timothy burst out as soon as his wife entered the room:

"So there you are at last!"

"I'm so sorry, dear, I didn't know you wanted me."

"That woman you've got into the house will drive me mad. Twittering and fluttering round like a demented hen. Real typical old maid, that's what she is."

"I'm sorry she annoys you. She tries to be kind, that's all."

"I don't want anybody kind. I don't want a blasted old maid always chirruping over me. She's so damned arch, too—"

"Just a little, perhaps."

"Treats me as though I was a confounded kid! It's maddening."

"I'm sure it must be. But please, *please,* Timothy, do try not to be rude to her. I'm really very helpless still—and you yourself say she cooks well."

"Her cooking's all right," Mr Abernethie admitted grudgingly. "Yes, she's a decent enough cook. But keep her in the kitchen, that's all I ask. Don't let her come fussing round me."

"No, dear, of course not. How are you feeling?"

"Not at all well. I think you'd better send for Barton to come and have a look at me. This paint affects my heart. Feel my pulse—the irregular way it's beating."

Maude felt it without comment.

"Timothy, shall we go to a hotel until the house painting is finished?"

"It would be a great waste of money."

"Does that matter so much—now?"

"You're just like all women—hopelessly extravagant! Just because we've come into a ridiculously small part of my brother's estate, you think we can go and live indefinitely at the Ritz."

"I didn't quite say that, dear."

"I can tell you that the difference Richard's money will make will be hardly appreciable. This bloodsucking Government will see to that. You mark my words, the whole lot will go in taxation."

Mrs Abernethie shook her head sadly.

"This coffee's cold," said the invalid, looking with distaste at the cup which he had not as yet tasted. "Why can't I ever get a cup of really hot coffee?"

"I'll take it down and warm it up."

In the kitchen Miss Gilchrist was drinking tea and conversing affably, though with slight condescension, with Mrs Jones.

"I'm so anxious to spare Mrs Abernethie all I can," she said. "All this running up and down stairs is so painful for her."

"Waits on him hand and foot, she does," said Mrs Jones stirring the sugar in her cup.

"It's very sad his being such an invalid."

"Not such an invalid either," Mrs Jones said darkly. "Suits him very well to lie up and ring bells and have trays brought up and down. But he's well able to get up and go about. Even seen him out in the village, I have, when *she's* been away. Walking as hearty as you please. Anything he *really* needs—like his tobacco or a stamp—he can come and get. And that's why when *she* was off at that funeral and got held up on the way back, and *he* told me I'd got to come in and stay the night again, I refused. 'I'm sorry, sir,' I said, 'but I've got my husband to think of. Going out to oblige in the mornings is all very well, but I've got

to be there to see to him when he comes back from work.' Nor I
wouldn't budge, I wouldn't. Do him good, I thought, to get about
the house and look after himself for once. Might make him see
what a lot he gets done for him. So I stood firm, I did. He
didn't half create."

Mrs Jones drew a deep breath and took a long satisfying
drink of sweet inky tea.

"Ar," she said.

Though deeply suspicious of Miss Gilchrist, and considering
her as a finicky thing, and a "regular fussy old maid" Mrs Jones
approved of the lavish way in which Miss Gilchrist dispensed
her employer's tea and sugar ration.

She set down the cup and said affably:

"I'll give the kitchen floor a nice scrub down and then I'll be
getting along. The potatoes is all ready peeled, dear, you'll find
them by the sink."

Though slightly affronted by the "dear," Miss Gilchrist was
appreciative of the good will which had divested an enormous
quantity of potatoes of their outer coverings.

Before she could say anything the telephone rang and she
hurried out in the hall to answer it. The telephone, in the style
of fifty odd years ago was situated inconveniently in a draughty
passage behind the staircase.

Maude Abernethie appeared at the top of the stairs, while
Miss Gilchrist was still speaking. The latter looked up and
said:

"It's Mrs—Leo—is it?—Abernethie speaking."

"Tell her I'm just coming."

Maude descended the stairs slowly and painfully.

Miss Gilchrist murmured, "I'm so sorry you've had to come
down again, Mrs Abernethie. Has Mr Abernethie finished his
elevenses? I'll just nip up and get the tray."

She trotted up the stairs as Mrs Abernethie said into the
receiver:

"Helen? This is Maude here."

The invalid received Miss Gilchrist with a baleful glare. As
she picked up the tray he asked fretfully:

"Who's that on the telephone?"

"Mrs Leo Abernethie."

"Oh? Suppose they'll go gossiping for about an hour. Women have no sense of time when they get on the phone. Never think of the money they're wasting."

Miss Gilchrist said brightly that it would be Mrs Leo who had to pay, and Timothy grunted.

"Just pull that curtain aside, will you? No, not that one, the *other* one. I don't want the light slap in my eyes. That's better. No reason because I'm an invalid that I should have to sit in the dark all day."

He went on:

"And you might look in that book case over there for a green— What's the matter now? What are you rushing off for?"

"It's the front door, Mr Abernethie."

"*I* didn't hear anything. You've got that woman downstairs, haven't you? Let her go and answer it."

"Yes, Mr Abernethie. What was the book you wanted me to find?"

The invalid closed his eyes.

"I can't remember now. You've put it out of my head. You'd better go."

Miss Gilchrist seized the tray and hurriedly departed. Putting the tray on the pantry table she hurried into the front hall, passing Mrs Abernethie who was still at the telephone.

She returned in a moment to ask in a muted voice:

"I'm so sorry to interrupt. It's a nun. Collecting. The Heart of Mary Fund, I think she said. She has a book. Half a crown or five shillings most people seem to have given."

Maude Abernethie said:

"Just a moment, Helen," into the telephone, and to Miss Gilchrist, "We have our own church charities."

Miss Gilchrist hurried away again.

Maude terminated her conversation after a few minutes with the phrase, "I'll talk to Timothy about it."

She replaced the receiver and came into the front hall. Miss Gilchrist was standing quite still by the drawing room door. She was frowning in a puzzled way and jumped when Maude Abernethie spoke to her.

"There's nothing the matter, is there, Miss Gilchrist?"

"Oh no, Mrs Abernethie, I'm afraid I was just wool gathering. So stupid of me when there's so much to be done."

Miss Gilchrist resumed her imitation of a busy ant and Maude Abernethie climbed the stairs slowly and painfully to her husband's room.

"That was Helen on the telephone. It seems that the place is definitely sold—some Institution for Foreign Refugees—"

She paused whilst Timothy expressed himself forcefully on the subject of Foreign Refugees, with side issues as to the house in which he had been born and brought up. "No decent standards left in this country. My old home! I can hardly bear to think of it."

Maude went on.

"Helen quite appreciates what you—we—will feel about it. She suggests that we might like to come there for a visit before it goes. She was very distressed about your health and the way the painting is affecting it. She thought you might prefer coming to Enderby to going to a hotel. The servants are there still, so you could be looked after comfortably."

Timothy, whose mouth had been open in outraged protests half way through this, had closed it again. His eyes had become suddenly shrewd. He now nodded his head approvingly.

"Thoughtful of Helen," he said. "Very thoughtful. I don't know, I'm sure, I'll have to think it over. . . . There's no doubt that this paint is poisoning me—there's arsenic in paint, I believe. I seem to have heard something of the kind. On the other hand the exertion of moving might be too much for me. It's difficult to know what would be the best."

"Perhaps you'd prefer a hotel, dear," said Maude. "A good hotel is very expensive, but where your health is concerned—"

Timothy interrupted.

"I wish I could make you understand, Maude, that we *are not millionaires*. Why go to a hotel when Helen has very kindly suggested that we should go to Enderby? Not that it's really for her to suggest! The house isn't hers. I don't understand legal subtleties, but I presume it belongs to us equally until it's sold and the proceeds divided. Foreign Refugees! It would have made

old Cornelius turn in his grave. Yes," he sighed, "I should like
to see the old place again before I die."

Maude played her last card adroitly.

"I understand that Mr Entwhistle has suggested that the members of the family might like to choose certain pieces of furniture
or china or something—before the contents are put up for
auction."

Timothy heaved himself briskly upright.

"We must certainly go. There must be a very exact valuation
of what is chosen by each person. Those men the girls have
married—I wouldn't trust either of them from what I've heard.
There might be some sharp practice. Helen is far too amiable.
As the head of the family, it is my duty to be present!"

He got up and walked up and down the room with a brisk
vigorous tread.

"Yes, it is an excellent plan. Write to Helen and accept. What
I am really thinking about is you, my dear. It will be a nice
rest and change for you. You have been doing far too much
lately. The decorators can get on with the painting while we are
away and that Gillespie woman can stay here and look after
the house."

"Gilchrist," said Maude.

Timothy waved a hand and said that it was all the same.

ii

"I can't do it," said Miss Gilchrist.

Maude looked at her in surprise.

Miss Gilchrist was trembling. Her eyes looked pleadingly
into Maude's.

"It's stupid of me, I know . . . But I simply can't. Not stay
here all alone in the house. If there was anyone who could
come and—and sleep here, too?"

She looked hopefully at the other woman, but Maude shook
her head. Maude Abernethie knew only too well how difficult
it was to get anyone in the neighbourhood to "live in."

Miss Gilchrist went on, a kind of desperation in her voice.

"I know you'll think it nervy and foolish—and I wouldn't
have dreamed once that I'd ever feel like this. I've never been

a nervous woman—or fanciful. But now it all seems different. I'd be terrified—yes, literally terrified—to be all alone here."

"Of course," said Maude. "It's stupid of me. After what happened at Lytchett St. Mary."

"I suppose that's it. . . . It's not logical, I know. And I didn't feel it at first. I didn't mind being alone in the cottage after— after it had happened. The feeling's grown up gradually. You'll have no opinion of me at all, Mrs Abernethie, but even since I've been here I've been feeling it—*frightened,* you know. Not of anything in particular—but just *frightened* . . . It's so silly and I really am ashamed. It's just as though all the time I was expecting something awful to happen. . . . Even that nun coming to the door startled me. Oh dear, I *am* in a bad way. . . ."

"I suppose it's what they call delayed shock," said Maude vaguely.

"Is it? I don't know. Oh dear, I'm so sorry to appear so— so ungrateful, and after all your kindness. What you will think—"

Maude soothed her.

"We must think of some other arrangement," she said.

XVI

GEORGE CROSSFIELD paused irresolutely for a moment as he watched a particular feminine back disappear through a doorway. Then he nodded to himself and went in pursuit.

The doorway in question was that of a double fronted shop —a shop that had gone out of business. The plate glass windows showed a disconcerting emptiness within. The door was closed, but George rapped on it. A vacuous faced young man with spectacles opened it and stared at George.

"Excuse me," said George. "But I think my cousin just came in here."

The young man drew back and George walked in.

"Hullo, Susan," he said.

Susan who was standing on a packing case and using a foot-rule turned her head in some surprise.

"Hullo, George. Where did you spring from?"

"I saw your back. I was sure it was yours."

"How clever of you. I suppose backs are distinctive."

"Much more so than faces. Add a beard and pads in your cheeks and do a few things to your hair and nobody will know you when you come face to face with them—but beware of the moment when you walk away."

"I'll remember. Can you remember seven feet fifteen inches until I've got time to write it down?"

"Certainly. What is this, book shelves?"

"No, cubicle space. Eight feet nineteen—and three twelve . . ."

The young man with the spectacles who had been fidgeting from one foot to the other, coughed apologetically.

"Excuse me, Mrs Banks, but if you want to be here for some time—"

"I do, rather," said Susan. "If you leave the keys, I'll lock the door and return them to the office when I go past. Will that be all right?"

"Yes, thank you. If it weren't that we're short staffed this morning—"

Susan accepted the apologetic intent of the half finished sentence and the young man removed himself to the outer world of the street.

"I'm glad we've got rid of him," said Susan. "House agents are a bother. They will keep talking just when I want to do sums."

"Ah," said George. "Murder in an empty shop. How exciting it would be for the passers by to see the dead body of a beautiful young woman displayed behind plate glass. How they would goggle. Like goldfish."

"There wouldn't be any reason for you to murder me, George."

"Well, I should get a fourth part of your share of our esteemed uncle's estate. If one were sufficiently fond of money that should be a reason."

Susan stopped taking measurements and turned to look at him. Her eyes opened a little.

"You look a different person, George. It's really—extraordinary."

"Different? How different?"

"Like an advertisement. *This is the same man that you saw overleaf, but now he has taken Uppington's Health Salts.*"

She sat down on another packing case and lit a cigarette.

"You must have wanted your share of old Richard's money pretty badly, George?"

"Nobody could honestly say that money isn't welcome these days."

George's tone was light.

Susan said: "You were in a jam, weren't you?"

"Hardly your business, is it, Susan?"

"I was just interested."

"Are you renting this shop as a place of business?"

"I'm buying the whole house."

"With possession?"

"Yes. The two upper floors were flats. One's empty and went with the shop. The other I'm buying the people out."

"Nice to have money, isn't it, Susan?"

There was a malicious tone in George's voice. But Susan merely took a deep breath and said:

"As far as I'm concerned, it's wonderful. An answer to prayer."

"Does prayer kill off elderly relatives?"

Susan paid no attention.

"This place is exactly *right*. To begin with it's a very good piece of period architecture. I can make the living part upstairs something quite unique. There are two lovely moulded ceilings and the rooms are a beautiful shape. This part down here which has already been hacked about I shall have completely modern."

"What is this? A dress business?"

"No. Beauty culture. Herbal preparations. Face creams!"

"The full racket?"

"The racket as before. It pays. It always pays. What you need to put it over is personality. I can do it."

George looked at his cousin appreciatively. He admired the slanting planes of her face, the generous mouth, the radiant colouring. Altogether an unusual and vivid face. And he recognised in Susan that odd, indefinable quality, the quality of success.

"Yes," he said, "I think you've got what it takes, Susan. You'll get back your outlay on this scheme and you'll get places with it."

"It's the right neighbourhood, just off a main shopping street *and* you can park a car right in front of the door."

Again George nodded.

"Yes, Susan, you're going to succeed. Have you had this in mind for a long time?"

"Over a year."

"Why didn't you put it up to old Richard? He might have staked you?"

"I did put it up to him."

"And he didn't see his way? I wonder why. I should have

thought he'd have recognised the same mettle that he himself was made of."

Susan did not answer, and into George's mind there leapt a swift bird's eye view of another figure. A thin nervous suspicious eyed young man.

"Where does—what's his name—Greg—come in on all this?" he asked. "He'll give up dishing out pills and powders, I take it?"

"Of course. There will be a laboratory built out at the back. We shall have our own formulas for face creams and beauty preparations."

George suppressed a grin. He wanted to say: "So baby is to have his play pen," but he did not say it. As a cousin he did not mind being spiteful, but he had an uneasy sense that Susan's feeling for her husband was a thing to be treated with care. It had all the qualities of a dangerous explosive. He wondered, as he had wondered on the day of the funeral, about that queer fish, Gregory. Something odd about the fellow. So nondescript in appearance—and yet, in some way, not nondescript . . .

He looked again at Susan, calmly and radiantly triumphant.

"You've got the true Abernethie touch," he said. "The only one of the family who has. Pity as far as old Richard was concerned that you're a woman. If you'd been a boy, I bet he'd have left you the whole caboodle."

Susan said slowly: "Yes, I think he would."

She paused and then went on:

"He didn't like Greg, you know. . . ."

"Ah." George raised his eyebrows. "His mistake."

"Yes."

"Oh well. Anyway things are going well now—all going according to plan."

As he said the words he was struck by the fact that they seemed particularly applicable to Susan.

The idea made him, just for a moment, a shade uncomfortable.

He didn't really like a woman who was so cold bloodedly efficient.

Changing the subject he said:

"By the way, did you get a letter from Helen? About Enderby?"

"Yes, I did. This morning. Did you?"

"Yes. What are you going to do about it?"

"Greg and I thought of going up the weekend after next—if that suits everyone else. Helen seemed to want us all together."

George laughed shrewdly.

"Or somebody might choose a more valuable piece of furniture than somebody else?"

Susan laughed.

"Oh, I suppose there is a proper valuation. But a valuation for probate will be much lower than the things would be in the open market. And besides I'd quite like to have a few relics of the founder of the family fortunes. Then I think it would be amusing to have one or two really absurd and charming specimens of the Victorian age in this place. Make a kind of *thing* of them! That period's coming in now. There was a green malachite table in the drawing room. You could build quite a colour scheme around it. And perhaps a case of stuffed humming birds—or one of those crowns made of waxed flowers. Something like that—just as a key note can be very effective."

"I trust your judgement."

"You'll be there I suppose?"

"Oh, I shall be there—to see fair play if nothing else."

Susan laughed.

"What do you bet there will be a grand family row?" she asked.

"Rosamund will probably want your green malachite table for a stage set!"

Susan did not laugh. Instead she frowned.

"Have you seen Rosamund lately?"

"I have not seen beautiful Cousin Rosamund since we all came back third class from the funeral."

"I've seen her once or twice. . . . She—she seemed rather odd—"

"What was the matter with her? Trying to think?"

"No. She seemed—well—upset."

"Upset about coming into a lot of money and being able

to put on some perfectly frightful play in which Michael can make an ass of himself?"

"Oh, that's going ahead. And it *does* sound frightful—but all the same it may be a success. Michael's good, you know. He can put himself across the footlights—or whatever the term is. He's not like Rosamund who's just beautiful and ham."

"Poor beautiful ham Rosamund."

"All the same Rosamund is not quite so dumb as one might think. She says things that are quite shrewd, sometimes. Things that you wouldn't have imagined she'd even noticed. It's—it's quite disconcerting."

"Quite like our Aunt Cora—"

"Yes . . ."

A momentary uneasiness descended on them both—conjured up, it seemed, by the mention of Cora Lansquenet.

Then George said with a rather elaborate air of unconcern:

"Talking of Cora—what about that companion woman of hers? I rather think something ought to be done about her."

"Done about her? What do you mean?"

"Well, it's up to the family so to speak. I mean I've been thinking Cora was our aunt—and it occurred to me that this woman mayn't find it easy to get another post."

"That occurred to you, did it?"

"Yes. People are so careful of their skins. I don't say they'd actually think that this Gilchrist female would take a hatchet to them—but at the back of their minds they feel that it might be unlucky. People are superstitious."

"How odd that you should have thought of all that, George? How would you know about things like that?"

George said drily:

"You forget that I'm a lawyer. I see a lot of the queer illogical side of people. What I'm getting at is, that I think we might do something about the woman, give her a small allowance or something, to tide her over, or find some office post for her if she's capable of that sort of thing. I feel rather as though we ought to keep in touch with her."

"You needn't worry," said Susan. Her voice was dry and ironic. "I've seen to things. She's gone to Timothy and Maude."

George looked startled.

"I say, Susan—is that wise?"

"It was the best thing I could think of—at the moment."

George looked at her curiously.

"You're very sure of yourself, aren't you, Susan? You know what you're doing and you don't have—regrets."

Susan said lightly:

"It's a waste of time—having regrets."

XVII

MICHAEL TOSSED the letter across the table to Rosamund.

"What about it?"

"Oh, we'll go. Don't you think so?"

Michael said slowly:

"It might be as well."

"There might be some jewellery . . . Of course all the things in the house are quite hideous—stuffed birds and wax flowers—ugh!"

"Yes. Bit of a mausoleum. As a matter of fact I'd like to make a sketch or two—particularly in that drawing room. The mantelpiece, for instance, and that very odd shaped couch. They'd be just right for *The Baronet's Progress*—if we revive it."

He got up and looked at his watch.

"That reminds me. I must go round and see Rosenheim. Don't expect me until rather late this evening. I'm dining with Oscar and we're going into the question of taking up that option and how it fits in with the American offer."

"Darling Oscar. He'll be pleased to see you after all this time. Give him my love."

Michael looked at her sharply. He no longer smiled and his face had an alert predatory look.

"What do you mean—after all this time? Anyone would think I hadn't seen him for months."

"Well, you haven't, have you?" murmured Rosamund.

"Yes, I have. We lunched together only a week ago."

"How funny. He must have forgotten about it. He rang up yesterday and said he hadn't seen you since the first night of *Tilly Looks West*."

"The old fool must be off his head."

Michael laughed. Rosamund, her eyes wide and blue, looked at him without emotion.

"You think I'm a fool, don't you, Mick?"

Michael protested.

"Darling, of course I don't."

"Yes, you do. But I'm not an absolute nit-wit. You didn't go near Oscar that day. I know where you did go."

"Rosamund darling—what do you mean?"

"I mean I know where you really were. . . ."

Michael, his attractive face uncertain, stared at his wife. She stared back at him, placid, unruffled.

How very disconcerting, he suddenly thought, a really empty stare could be.

He said rather unsuccessfully:

"I don't know what you're driving at. . . ."

"I just meant it's rather silly telling me a lot of lies."

"Look here, Rosamund—"

He had started to bluster—but he stopped, taken aback as his wife said softly:

"We do want to take up this option and put this play on, don't we?"

"Want to? It's the part I've always dreamed must exist somewhere."

"Yes—that's what I mean."

"Just what do you mean?"

"Well—it's worth a good deal, isn't it? But one mustn't take *too* many risks."

He stared at her and said slowly:

"It's your money—I know that. If you don't want to risk it—"

"It's *our* money, darling." Rosamund stressed it. "I think that's rather important."

"Listen, darling. The part of Eileen—it would bear writing up."

Rosamund smiled.

"I don't think—really—I want to play it."

"My dear girl." Michael was aghast. "What's come over you?"

"Nothing."

"Yes, there is, you've been different lately—moody—nervous, what is it?"

"Nothing. I only want you to be—careful, Mick."

"Careful about what? I'm always careful."

"No, I don't think you are. You always think you can get away with things and that everyone will believe whatever you want them to. You were stupid about Oscar that day."

Michael flushed angrily.

"And what about you? You said you were going shopping with Jane. You didn't. Jane's in America, has been for weeks."

"Yes," said Rosamund. "That was stupid, too. I really just went for a walk—in Regent's Park."

Michael looked at her curiously.

"Regent's Park? You never went for a walk in Regent's Park in your life. What's it all about? Have you got a boy friend? You may say what you like, Rosamund, you *have* been different lately. Why?"

"I've been—thinking about things. About what to do . . ."

Michael came round the table to her in a satisfying spontaneous rush. His voice held fervour as he cried:

"Darling—you know I love you madly!"

She responded satisfactorily to the embrace, but as they drew apart he was struck again disagreeably by the odd calculation in those beautiful eyes.

"Whatever I'd done, you'd always forgive me, wouldn't you?" he demanded.

"I suppose so," said Rosamund vaguely. "That's not the point. You see, it's all different now. We've got to think and plan."

"Think and plan—what?"

Rosamund, frowning, said:

"Things aren't over when you've done them. It's really a sort of beginning and then one's got to arrange what to do next, and what's important and what is not."

"Rosamund . . ."

She sat, her face perplexed, her wide gaze on a middle distance in which Michael, apparently, did not feature.

At the third repetition of her name, she started slightly and came out of her reverie.

"What did you say?"

"I asked you what you were thinking about. . . ."

"Oh? Oh yes, I was wondering if I'd go down to—what is it?

—Lytchett St. Mary, and see that Miss Somebody—the one who was with Aunt Cora."

"But why?"

"Well, she'll be going away soon, won't she? To relatives or someone. I don't think we ought to let her go away until we've asked her."

"Asked her what?"

"Asked her who killed Aunt Cora."

Michael stared.

"You mean—you think she *knows?*"

Rosamund said rather absently:

"Oh yes, I expect so. . . . She lived there, you see."

"But she'd have told the police."

"Oh, I don't mean she knows *that* way—I just mean that she's probably quite sure. Because of what Uncle Richard said when he went down there."

"But she wouldn't have heard what he said."

"Oh yes, she would, darling." Rosamund sounded like someone arguing with an unreasonable child.

"Nonsense, I can hardly see old Richard Abernethie discussing his suspicions of his family before an outsider."

"Well, of course. She'd have heard it through the door."

"Eavesdropping, you mean?"

"I expect so—in fact I'm sure. It must be so deadly dull shut up, two women in a cottage and nothing ever happening except washing up and the sink and putting the cat out and things like that. Of course she listened and read letters—anyone would."

Michael looked at her with something faintly approaching dismay.

"Would you?" he demanded bluntly.

"I wouldn't go and be a companion in the country." Rosamund shuddered. "I'd rather die."

"I meant—would you read letters and—and all that?"

Rosamund said calmly:

"If I wanted to know, yes. Everybody does, don't you think so?"

The limpid gaze met his.

"One just wants to know," said Rosamund. "One doesn't want

to do anything about it. I expect that's how *she* feels—Miss Gilchrist, I mean. But I'm certain she *knows*."

Michael said in a stifled voice:

"Rosamund, who do you think killed Cora? And old Richard?"

Once again that limpid blue gaze met his.

"Darling—don't be absurd. . . . You know as well as I do. But it's much much better *never* to mention it. So we won't."

XVIII

FROM HIS seat by the fireplace in the library, Hercule Poirot looked at the assembled company.

His eyes passed thoughtfully over Susan, sitting upright, looking vivid and animated, over her husband, sitting near her, his expression rather vacant and his fingers twisting a loop of string; they went on to George Crossfield, debonair and distinctly pleased with himself, talking about card sharpers on Atlantic cruises to Rosamund, who said mechanically, "How extraordinary, darling. But why?" in a completely uninterested voice; went on to Michael with his very individual type of haggard good looks and his very apparent charm; to Helen, poised and slightly remote; to Timothy comfortably settled in the best armchair with an extra cushion at his back and Maude, sturdy and thick-set, in devoted attendance, and finally to the figure sitting with a tinge of apology just beyond the range of the family circle—the figure of Miss Gilchrist wearing a rather peculiar "dressy" blouse. Presently, he judged, she would get up, murmur an excuse and leave the family gathering and go up to her room. Miss Gilchrist, he thought, knew her place. She had learned it the hard way.

Hercule Poirot sipped his after dinner coffee and between half closed lids made his appraisal.

He had wanted them there—all together, and he had got them. And what, he thought to himself, was he going to do with them now? He felt a sudden weary distaste for going on with the business. Why was that, he wondered? Was it the influence of Helen Abernethie? There was a quality of passive resistance about her that seemed unexpectedly strong. Had she, while apparently graceful and unconcerned, managed to impress her own reluctance upon him? She was averse to this raking up of the details of old Richard's death, he knew that. She wanted it left alone, left to die out into oblivion. Poirot was not surprised by that. What did surprise him was his own disposition to agree with her.

Mr Entwhistle's account of the family had, he realised, been admirable. He had described all these people shrewdly and well. With the old lawyer's knowledge and appraisal to guide him, Poirot had wanted to see for himself. He had fancied that, meeting these people intimately, he would have a very shrewd idea—not of *how* and *when*—(those were questions with which he did not propose to concern himself. Murder had been possible—that was all he needed to know!)—but of *who*. For Hercule Poirot had a lifetime of experience behind him, and as a man who deals with pictures can recognize the artist, so Poirot believed he could recognize a likely type of the amateur criminal who will—if his own particular need arises—be prepared to kill.

But it was not to be so easy.

Because he could visualise almost all of these people as a possible—though not a probable—murderer. George might kill —as the cornered rat kills. Susan calmly—efficiently—to further a plan. Gregory because he had that queer morbid streak which discounts and invites, almost craves, punishment. Michael because he was ambitious and had a murderer's cocksure vanity. Rosamund because she was frighteningly simple in outlook. Timothy because he had hated and resented his brother and had craved the power his brother's money would give. Maude because Timothy was her child and where her child was concerned she would be ruthless. Even Miss Gilchrist, he thought, might have contemplated murder if it could have restored to her The Willow Tree in its ladylike glory!

And Helen? He could not see Helen as committing murder. She was too civilised—too removed from violence. And she and her husband had surely loved Richard Abernethie.

Poirot sighed to himself. There were to be no short cuts to the truth. Instead he would have to adopt a longer, but a reasonably sure method. There would have to be conversation. Much conversation. For in the long run, either through a lie, or through truth, people were bound to give themselves away. . . .

He had been introduced by Helen to the gathering, and had

set to work to overcome the almost universal annoyance caused by his presence—a foreign stranger!—in this family gathering. He had used his eyes and his ears. He had watched and listened—openly and behind doors! He had noticed affinities, antagonisms, the unguarded words that arose as always when property was to be divided. He had engineered adroitly tête-à-têtes, walks upon the terrace, and had made his deductions and observations. He had talked with Miss Gilchrist about the vanished glories of her teashop and about the correct composition of *brioches* and chocolate *éclairs* and had visited the kitchen garden with her to discuss the proper use of herbs in cooking. He had spent some long half hours listening to Timothy talking about his own health and about the effect upon it of paint.

Paint? Poirot frowned. Somebody else had said something about paint—Mr Entwhistle?

There had also been discussion of a different kind of painting. Pierre Lansquenet as a painter. Cora Lansquenet's paintings, rapturized over by Miss Gilchrist, dismissed scornfully by Susan. "Just like picture postcards," she had said. "She did them from postcards, too."

Miss Gilchrist had been quite upset by that and had said sharply that dear Mrs Lansquenet always painted from Nature.

"But I bet she cheated," said Susan to Poirot when Miss Gilchrist had gone out of the room. "In fact I know she did, though I won't upset the old pussy by saying so."

"And how do you know?"

Poirot watched the strong confident line of Susan's chin.

"She will always be sure, this one," he thought. "And perhaps sometime, she will be too sure. . . ."

Susan was going on.

"I'll tell you, but don't pass it on to the Gilchrist. One picture is of Polflexan, the cove and the lighthouse and the pier—the usual aspect that all amateur artists sit down and sketch. But the pier was blown up in the war, and since Aunt Cora's sketch was done a couple of years ago, it can't very well be from Nature, can it? But the postcards they sell there still show the pier as it used to be. There was one in her bedroom drawer. So Aunt Cora started her 'rough sketch' down there, I expect, and then finished it surreptitiously later at home from a postcard! It's funny, isn't it, the way people get caught out?"

"Yes, it is, as you say, funny." He paused, and then thought that the opening was a good one.

"You do not remember me, madame," he said, "but I remember you. This is not the first time that I have seen you."

She stared at him. Poirot nodded with great gusto.

"Yes, yes, it is so. I was inside an automobile, well wrapped up and from the window I saw you. You were talking to one of the mechanics in the garage. You do not notice me—it is natural—I am inside the car—an elderly muffled-up foreigner! But *I* notice *you,* for you are young and agreeable to look at and you stand there in the sun. So when I arrive here, I say to myself, 'Tiens! what a coincidence!' "

"A garage? Where? When was this?"

"Oh a little time ago—a week—no, more. For the moment," said Poirot disingenuously and with a full recollection of the King's Arms Garage in his mind, "I cannot remember where. I travel so much all over this country."

"Looking for a suitable house to buy for your refugees?"

"Yes. There is so much to take into consideration, you see. Price—neighbourhood—suitability for conversion."

"I suppose you'll have to pull the house about a lot? Lots of horrible partitions."

"In the bedrooms, yes, certainly. But most of the ground floor rooms we shall not touch." He paused before going on. "Does it sadden you, madame, that this old family mansion of yours should go this way—to strangers?"

"Of course not." Susan looked amused. "I think it's an excellent idea. It's an impossible place for anybody to think of living in as it is. And I've nothing to be sentimental about. It's not *my* old home. My mother and father lived in London. We just came here for Christmas sometimes. Actually I've always thought it quite hideous—an almost indecent temple to wealth."

"The altars are different now. There is the building in, and the concealed lighting and the expensive simplicity. But wealth still has its temples, madame. I understand—I am not, I hope,

indiscreet—that you yourself are planning such an edifice?
Everything *de luxe*—and no expense spared."

Susan laughed.

"Hardly a temple—it's just a place of business."

"Perhaps the name does not matter. . . . But it will cost
much money—that is true, is it not?"

"Everything's wickedly expensive nowadays. But the initial
outlay will be worthwhile, I think."

"Tell me something about these plans of yours. It amazes me
to find a beautiful young woman so practical, so competent. In
my young days—a long time ago, I admit—beautiful women
thought only of their pleasures, of cosmetics, of *la toilette*."

"Women still think a great deal about their faces—that's where
I come in."

"Tell me."

And she had told him. Told him with a wealth of detail and
with a great deal of unconscious self-revelation. He appreciated
her business acumen, her boldness of planning and her grasp of
detail. A good bold planner, sweeping all side issues away. Perhaps a little ruthless as all those who plan boldly must be. . . .

Watching her, he had said:

"Yes, you will succeed. You will go ahead. How fortunate
that you are not restricted, as so many are, by poverty. One
cannot go far without the capital outlay. To have had these
creative ideas and to have been frustrated by lack of means—
that would have been unbearable."

"I couldn't have borne it! But I'd have raised money somehow or other—got someone to back me."

"Ah! of course. Your uncle, whose house this was, was rich.
Even if he had not died, he would, as you express it, have
'staked' you."

"Oh no, he wouldn't. Uncle Richard was a bit of a stick-in-
the-mud where women were concerned. If I'd been a man—"
A quick flash of anger swept across her face. "He made me very
angry."

"I see—yes, I see. . . ."

"The old shouldn't stand in the way of the young. I—oh, I
beg your pardon."

Hercule Poirot laughed easily and twirled his moustache.

"I am old, yes. But I do not impede youth. There is no one who needs to wait for my death."

"What a horrid idea."

"But you are a realist, madame. Let us admit without more ado that the world is full of the young—or even the middle-aged —who wait, patiently or impatiently, for the death of someone whose decease will give them, if not affluence—then opportunity."

"Opportunity!" Susan said, taking a deep breath. "That's what one needs."

Poirot who had been looking beyond her, said gaily:

"And here is your husband come to join our little discussion. . . . We talk, Mr Banks, of opportunity. Opportunity the golden —opportunity who must be grasped with both hands. How far in conscience can one go? Let us hear your views?"

But he was not destined to hear the views of Gregory Banks on opportunity or on anything else. In fact he had found it next to impossible to talk to Gregory Banks at all. Banks had a curious fluid quality. Whether by his own wish, or by that of his wife, he seemed to have no liking for tête-à-têtes or quiet discussions. No, "conversation" with Gregory had failed.

Poirot had talked with Maude Abernethie—also about paint (the smell of) and how fortunate it had been that Timothy had been able to come to Enderby, and how kind it had been of Helen to extend an invitation to Miss Gilchrist also.

"For really she is *most* useful. Timothy so often feels like a snack—and one cannot ask too much of other people's servants but there is a gas ring in a little room off the pantry, so that Miss Gilchrist can warm up Ovaltine or Benger's there without disturbing anybody. And she's so willing about fetching things, she's quite willing to run up and down stairs a dozen times a day. Oh yes, I feel that it was really quite providential that she should have lost her nerve about staying alone in the house as she did, though I admit it vexed me at the time."

"Lost her nerve?" Poirot was interested.

He listened whilst Maude gave him an account of Miss Gilchrist's sudden collapse.

"She was frightened, you say? And yet could not exactly say why? That is interesting. Very interesting."

"I put it down myself to delayed shock."

"Perhaps."

"Once, during the war, when a bomb dropped about a mile away from us, I remember Timothy—"

Poirot abstracted his mind from Timothy.

"Had anything particular happened that day?" he asked.

"On what day?" Maude looked blank.

"The day that Miss Gilchrist was upset."

"Oh, *that*—no, I don't think so. It seems to have been coming on ever since she left Lytchett St. Mary, or so she said. She didn't seem to mind when she was there."

And the result, Poirot thought, had been a piece of poisoned wedding cake. Not so very surprising that Miss Gilchrist was frightened after that. . . . And even when she had removed herself to the peaceful country round Stansfield Grange, the fear had lingered. More than lingered. Grown. Why grown? Surely attending on an exacting hypochondriac like Timothy must be so exhausting that nervous fears would be likely to be swallowed up in exasperation?

But something in that house had made Miss Gilchrist afraid. What? Did she know herself?

Finding himself alone with Miss Gilchrist for a brief space before dinner, Poirot had sailed into the subject with an exaggerated foreign curiosity.

"Impossible, you comprehend, for me to mention the matter of murder to members of the family. But I am intrigued. Who would not be? A brutal crime—a sensitive artist attacked in a lonely cottage. Terrible for her family. But terrible, also, I imagine, for *you*. Since Mrs Timothy Abernethie gives me to understand that you were there at the time?"

"Yes, I was. And if you'll excuse me, M. Pontarlier, I don't want to talk about it."

"I understand—oh yes, I completely understand."

Having said this, Poirot waited. And, as he had thought, Miss Gilchrist immediately *did* begin to talk about it.

He heard nothing from her that he had not heard before, but

he played his part with perfect sympathy, uttering little cries of comprehension and listening with an absorbed interest which Miss Gilchrist could not help but enjoy.

Not until she had exhausted the subject of what she herself had felt, and what the doctor had said, and how kind Mr Entwhistle had been, did Poirot proceed cautiously to the next point.

"You were wise, I think, not to remain alone down in that cottage."

"I couldn't have done it, M. Pontarlier. I really couldn't have done it."

"No. I understand even that you were afraid to remain alone in the house of Mr Timothy Abernethie whilst they came here?"

Miss Gilchrist looked guilty.

"I'm terribly ashamed about that. So foolish really. It was just a kind of panic I had—I really don't know *why*."

"But of course one knows why. You had just recovered from a dastardly attempt to poison you—"

Miss Gilchrist here sighed and said she simply couldn't understand it. Why should anyone try to poison her?

"But obviously, my dear lady, because this criminal, this assassin, thought that you knew something that might lead to his apprehension by the police."

"But what could *I* know? Some dreadful tramp, or semi-crazed creature."

"If it *was* a tramp. It seems to me unlikely—"

"Oh please, M. Pontarlier—" Miss Gilchrist became suddenly very upset. "Don't suggest such things. I don't want to believe it."

"You do not want to believe what?"

"I don't want to believe that it wasn't—I mean—that it was—" She paused, confused.

"And yet," said Poirot shrewdly, "you *do* believe."

"Oh I don't. I *don't!*"

"But I think you do. That is why you are frightened. . . . You are still frightened, are you not?"

"Oh no, not since I came here. So many people. And such a nice family atmosphere. Oh no, everything seems quite all right here."

"It seems to me—you must excuse my interest—I am an old man, somewhat infirm, and a great part of my time is given to idle speculation on matters which interest me—it seems to me that there must have been some definite occurrence at Stansfield Grange which, so to speak, brought your fears to a *head*. Doctors recognize nowadays how much takes place in our subconscious."

"Yes, yes—I know they say so."

"And I think your subconscious fears might have been brought to a point by some small concrete happening, something, perhaps, quite extraneous, serving, shall we say, as a focal point."

Miss Gilchrist seemed to lap this up eagerly.

"I'm sure you are right," she said.

"Now what, should you think, was this—er—extraneous circumstance?"

Miss Gilchrist pondered a moment, and then said, unexpectedly:

"I think, you know, M. Pontarlier, it was the *nun*."

Before Poirot could take this up, Susan and her husband came in, closely followed by Helen.

"A nun," thought Poirot. . . . "Now where, in all this, have I heard something about a nun?"

He resolved to lead the conversation to nuns sometime in the course of the evening.

XIX

THE FAMILY had all been polite to M. Pontarlier, the representative of N.A.R.C.O. And how right he had been to have chosen to designate himself by initials. Everyone had accepted N.A.R.C.O. as a matter of course—had even pretended to know all about it! How averse human beings were ever to admit ignorance! An exception had been Rosamund who had asked him wonderingly: "But what *is* it? I never heard of it?" Fortunately no one else had been there at the time. Poirot had explained the organisation in such a way that anyone but Rosamund would have felt abashed at having displayed ignorance of such a well-known, world wide institution. Rosamund, however, had only said vaguely, "Oh! refugees all over *again*. I'm so *tired* of refugees." Thus voicing the unspoken reaction of many, who were usually too conventional to express themselves so frankly.

M. Pontarlier was, therefore, now accepted—as a nuisance but also as a nonentity. He had become, as it were, a piece of foreign *décor*. The general opinion was that Helen should have avoided having him here this particular weekend, but as he was here they must make the best of it. Fortunately this queer little foreigner did not seem to know much English. Quite often he did not understand what you said to him, and when everyone was speaking more or less at once he seemed completely at sea. He appeared to be interested only in refugees and post war conditions, and his vocabulary only included those subjects. Ordinary chit chat appeared to bewilder him. More or less forgotten by all, Hercule Poirot leant back in his chair, sipped his coffee and observed, as a cat may observe, the twitterings, and comings and goings of a flock of birds. The cat is not ready yet to make its spring.

After twenty-four hours of prowling round the house and examining its contents, the heirs of Richard Abernethie were ready to state their preferences, and, if need be, to fight for them.

The subject of conversation was, first, a certain Spode dinner dessert service off which they had just been eating dessert.

"I don't suppose I have long to live," said Timothy in a faint melancholy voice. "And Maude and I have no children. It is hardly worth while our burdening ourselves with useless possessions. But for sentiment's sake I *should* like to have the old dessert service. I remember it in the dear old days. It's out of fashion, of course, and I understand dessert services have very little value nowadays—but there it is. I shall be *quite* content with that—and perhaps the Boule cabinet in the White Boudoir."

"You're too late, Uncle," George spoke with debonair insouciance. "I asked Helen to mark off the Spode service to me this morning."

Timothy became purple in the face.

"Mark it off—mark it off? What do you mean? Nothing's been settled yet. And what do *you* want with a dessert service? You're not married."

"As a matter of fact I collect Spode. And this is really a splendid specimen. But it's quite all right about the Boule cabinet, Uncle. I wouldn't have that as a gift."

Timothy waved aside the Boule cabinet.

"Now look here, young George. You can't go butting in, in this way. I'm an older man than you are—and I'm Richard's only surviving brother. That dessert service is *mine.*"

"Why not take the Dresden service, Uncle? A very fine example and I'm sure just as full of sentimental memories. Anyway, the Spode's mine. First come, first served."

"Nonsense—nothing of the kind!" Timothy spluttered.

Maude said sharply:

"Please don't upset your uncle, George. It's very bad for him. Naturally he will take the Spode if he wants to! The first choice is *his,* and you young people must come afterwards. He was Richard's brother, as he says, and you are only a nephew."

"And I can tell you this, young man." Timothy was seething with fury. "If Richard had made a proper will, the disposal of the contents of this place would have been entirely in my hands.

That's the way the property *should* have been left, and if it wasn't, I can only suspect *undue influence*. Yes—and I repeat it—*undue influence.*"

Timothy glared at his nephew.

"A preposterous will," he said. "Preposterous!"

He leant back, placed a hand to his heart, and groaned:

"This is very bad for me. If I could have—a little brandy."

Miss Gilchrist hurried to get it and returned with the restorative in a small glass.

"Here you are, Mr Abernethie. Please—please don't excite yourself. Are you sure you oughtn't to go up to bed?"

"Don't be a fool." Timothy swallowed the brandy. "Go to bed? I intend to protect my interests."

"Really, George, I'm surprised at you," said Maude. "What your uncle says is perfectly true. His wishes come first. If he wants the Spode dessert service he shall have it!"

"It's quite hideous anyway," said Susan.

"Hold your tongue, Susan," said Timothy.

The thin young man who sat beside Susan raised his head. In a voice that was a little shriller than his ordinary tones, he said:

"Don't speak like that to my wife!"

He half rose from his seat.

Susan said quickly: "It's all right, Greg. I don't mind."

"But *I* do."

Helen said: "I think it would be graceful on your part, George, to let your uncle have the dessert service."

Timothy spluttered indignantly: "There's no 'letting' about it!"

But George, with a slight bow to Helen said, "Your wish is law, Aunt Helen. I abandon my claim."

"You didn't really want it, anyway, did you?" said Helen.

He cast a sharp glance at her, then grinned:

"The trouble with you, Aunt Helen, is that you're too sharp by half! You see more than you're meant to see. Don't worry, Uncle Timothy, the Spode is yours. Just my idea of fun."

"Fun, indeed." Maude Abernethie was indignant. "Your uncle might have had a heart attack!"

"Don't you believe it," said George cheerfully. "Uncle Timothy will probably outlive us all. He's what is known as a creaking gate."

Timothy leaned forward balefully.

"I don't wonder," he said, "that Richard was disappointed in *you.*"

"What's that?" The good humour went out of George's face.

"You came up here after Mortimer died, expecting to step into his shoes—expecting that Richard would make you his heir, didn't you? But my poor brother soon took *your* measure. He knew where the money would go if you had control of it. I'm surprised that he even left you a part of his fortune. He knew where it would go. Horses, gambling, Monte Carlo, foreign casinos. Perhaps worse. He suspected you of not being straight, didn't he?"

George, a white dint appearing each side of his nose, said quietly:

"Hadn't you better be careful of what you are saying?"

"I wasn't well enough to come here for the funeral," said Timothy slowly, "but Maude told me what *Cora said.* Cora always was a fool—but there *may* have been something in it! And if so, I know who I'd suspect—"

"Timothy!" Maude stood up, solid, calm, a tower of forcefulness. "You have had a very trying evening. You must consider your health. I can't have you getting ill again. Come up with me. You must take a sedative and go straight to bed. Timothy and I, Helen, will take the Spode dessert service and the Boule cabinet as mementos of Richard. There is no objection to that, I hope?"

Her glance swept round the company. Nobody spoke, and she marched out of the room supporting Timothy with a hand under his elbow, waving aside Miss Gilchrist who was hovering half heartedly by the door.

George broke the silence after they had departed.

"Femme formidable!" he said. "That describes Aunt Maude exactly. I should hate ever to impede her triumphal progress."

Miss Gilchrist sat down again rather uncomfortably and murmured:

"Mrs Abernethie is always so kind."

The remark fell rather flat.

Michael Shane laughed suddenly and said: "You know, I'm enjoying all this! *The Voysey Inheritance* to the life. By the way, Rosamund and I want that malachite table in the drawing room."

"Oh no," cried Susan. "*I* want that."

"Here we go again," said George, raising his eyes to the ceiling.

"Well, we needn't get angry about it," said Susan. "The reason I want it is for my new beauty shop. Just a note of colour —and I shall put a great bouquet of wax flowers on it. It would look wonderful. I can find wax flowers easily enough, but a green malachite table isn't so common."

"But, darling," said Rosamund, "that's just why *we* want it. For the new set. As you say, a note of colour—and so *absolutely* period. And either wax flowers or stuffed humming birds. It will be absolutely *right*."

"I see what you mean, Rosamund," said Susan. "But I don't think you've got as good a case as I have. You could easily have a painted malachite table for the stage—it would look just the same. But for my *salon* I've *got* to have the genuine thing."

"Now, ladies," said George. "What about a sporting decision? Why not toss for it? Or cut the cards? All quite in keeping with the period of the table."

Susan smiled pleasantly.

"Rosamund and I will talk about it tomorrow," she said.

She seemed, as usual, quite sure of herself. George looked with some interest from her face to that of Rosamund. Rosamund's face had a vague, rather far away expression.

"Which one will you back, Aunt Helen?" he asked. "An even money chance, I'd say. Susan has determination, but Rosamund is so wonderfully single minded."

"Or perhaps *not* humming birds," said Rosamund. "One of those big Chinese vases would make a lovely lamp, with a gold shade."

Miss Gilchrist hurried into placating speech.

"This house is full of so many beautiful things," she said.

"That green table would look wonderful in your new establishment, I'm sure, Mrs Banks. I've never seen one like it. It must be worth a lot of money."

"It will be deducted from my share of the estate, of course," said Susan.

"I'm so sorry—I didn't mean—" Miss Gilchrist was covered with confusion.

"It may be deducted from *our* share of the estate," Michael pointed out. "With the wax flowers thrown in."

"They look so right on that table," Miss Gilchrist murmured. "Really artistic. Sweetly pretty."

But nobody was paying any attention to Miss Gilchrist's well meant trivialities.

Greg said, speaking again in that high nervous voice:

"Susan *wants* that table."

There was a momentary stir of unease, as though, by his words, Greg had set a different musical key.

Helen said quickly:

"And what do you really want, George? Leaving out the Spode service."

George grinned and the tension relaxed.

"Rather a shame to bait old Timothy," he said. "But he really is quite unbelievable. He's had his own way in everything so long that he's become quite pathological about it."

"You have to humour an invalid, Mr Crossfield," said Miss Gilchrist.

"Ruddy old hypochondriac, that's what he is," said George.

"Of course he is," Susan agreed. "I don't believe there's anything whatever the matter with him, do you, Rosamund?"

"What?"

"Anything the matter with Uncle Timothy."

"No—no, I shouldn't think so." Rosamund was vague. She apologised. "I'm sorry. I was thinking about what lighting would be right for the table."

"You see?" said George. "A woman of one idea. Your wife's a dangerous woman, Michael. I hope you realise it."

"I realise it," said Michael rather grimly.

George went on with every appearance of enjoyment.

"The Battle of the Table! To be fought tomorrow—politely—but with grim determination. We ought all to take sides. I back Rosamund who looks so sweet and yielding and isn't. Husbands presumably back their own wives. Miss Gilchrist? On Susan's side, obviously."

"Oh really, Mr Crossfield, I wouldn't venture to—"

"Aunt Helen?" George paid no attention to Miss Gilchrist's flutterings. "You have the casting vote. Oh er—I forgot. M. Pontarlier?"

"*Pardon?*" Hercule Poirot looked blank.

George considered explanations, but decided against it. The poor old boy hadn't understood a word of what was going on. He said: "Just a family joke."

"Yes, yes, I comprehend." Poirot smiled amiably.

"So yours is the casting vote, Aunt Helen. Whose side are you on?"

Helen smiled.

"Perhaps I want it myself, George."

She changed the subject deliberately, turning to her foreign guest.

"I'm afraid this is all very dull for you, M. Pontarlier?"

"Not at all, madame. I consider myself privileged to be admitted to your family life—" he bowed. "I would like to say—I cannot quite express my meaning—my regret that this house has to pass out of your hands into the hands of strangers. It is, without doubt—a great sorrow."

"No, indeed, we don't regret at all," Susan assured him.

"You are very amiable, madame. It will be, let me tell you, perfection here for my elderly sufferers of persecution. What a haven! What peace! I beg you to remember that, when the harsh feelings come to you as assuredly they must. I hear that there was also the question of a school coming here—not a regular school, a convent—run by *religeuses*—by 'nuns,' I think you say? You would have preferred that, perhaps?"

"Not at all," said George.

"The Sacred Heart of Mary," continued Poirot. "Fortunately, owing to the kindness of an unknown benefactor we were able to make a slightly higher offer." He addressed Miss Gilchrist directly. "You do not like nuns, I think?"

Miss Gilchrist flushed and looked embarrassed.

"Oh really, Mr Pontarlier, you mustn't—I mean, it's nothing *personal.* But I never do see that it's right to shut yourself up from the world in that way—not necessary, I mean, and really almost selfish, though not teaching ones, of course, or the ones that go about amongst the poor—because I'm sure they're thoroughly unselfish women and do a lot of good."

"I simply can't imagine wanting to be a nun," said Susan.

"It's very becoming," said Rosamund. "You remember—when they revived *The Miracle* last year. Sonia Wells looked absolutely too glamorous for *words.*"

"What beats me," said George, "is why it should be pleasing to the Almighty to dress oneself up in mediaeval dress. For after all, that's all a nun's dress is. Thoroughly cumbersome, unhygienic and impractical."

"And it makes them look so alike, doesn't it?" said Miss Gilchrist. "It's silly, you know, but I got quite a turn when I was at Mrs Abernethie's and a nun came to the door, collecting. I got it into my head she was the same as a nun who came to the door on the day of the inquest on poor Mrs Lansquenet at Lytchett St. Mary. I felt, you know, almost as though she had been following me round!"

"I thought nuns always collected in couples," said George. "Surely a detective story hinged on that point once?"

"There was only one this time," said Miss Gilchrist. "Perhaps they've got to economise," she added vaguely. "And anyway it couldn't have been the same nun, for the other one was collecting for an organ for St.—Barnabas, I think—and this one was for something quite different—something to do with children."

"But they both had the same type of features?" Hercule Poirot asked. He sounded interested. Miss Gilchrist turned to him.

"I suppose that must be it. . . . The upper lip—almost as though she had a moustache. I think, you know, that *that* is really what alarmed me—being in a rather nervous state at the time, and remembering those stories during the war of nuns who

were really men and in the Fifth Column and landed by para-
chute. Of course it was very foolish of me. I knew that afterwards."

"A nun would be a good disguise," said Susan thoughtfully.
"It hides your feet."

"The truth is," said George, "that one very seldom looks
properly at anyone. That's why one gets such wildly differing
accounts of a person from different witnesses in court. You'd
be surprised. A man is often described as tall—short; thin—
stout; fair—dark; dressed in a dark—light—suit; and so on.
There's usually *one* reliable observer, but one has to make up
one's mind who that is."

"Another queer thing," said Susan, "is that you sometimes
catch sight of yourself in a mirror unexpectedly and don't know
who it is. It just looks vaguely familiar. And you say to yourself, 'That's somebody I know quite well. . . .' and then suddenly realise it's yourself!"

George said: "It would be more difficult still if you could
really see yourself—and not a mirror image."

"Why?" asked Rosamund, looking puzzled.

"Because, don't you see, nobody ever sees themselves—*as
they appear to other people*. They always see themselves in a
glass—that is—as a reversed image."

"But does that look any different?"

"Oh yes," said Susan quickly. "It must. Because people's faces
aren't the same both sides. Their eyebrows are different, and
their mouths go up one side, and their noses aren't really
straight. You can see with a pencil—who's got a pencil?"

Somebody produced a pencil, and they experimented, holding a pencil each side of the nose and laughing to see the ridiculous variation in angle.

The atmosphere now had lightened a good deal. Everybody
was in a good humour. They were no longer the heirs of Richard
Abernethie gathered together for a division of property. They
were a cheerful and normal set of people gathered together for
a weekend in the country.

Only Helen Abernethie remained silent and abstracted.

With a sigh, Hercule Poirot rose to his feet and bade his hostess a polite good night.

"And perhaps, madame, I had better say goodbye. My train departs itself at nine o'clock tomorrow morning. That is very early. So I will thank you now for all your kindness and hospitality. The date of possession—that will be arranged with the good Mr Entwhistle. To suit your convenience, of course."

"It can be any time you please, M. Pontarlier. I—I have finished all that I came here to do."

"You will return now to your villa at Cyprus?"

"Yes." A little smile curved Helen Abernethie's lips.

Poirot said:

"You are glad, yes. You have no regrets?"

"At leaving England? Or leaving here, do you mean?"

"I meant—leaving here?"

"No—no. It's no good, is it, to cling on to the past? One must leave that behind one."

"If one can." Blinking his eyes innocently Poirot smiled apologetically round on the group of polite faces that surrounded him.

"Sometimes, is it not, the Past will not be left, will not suffer itself to pass into oblivion? It stands at one's elbow—it says *'I am not done with yet.'* "

Susan gave a rather doubtful laugh. Poirot said:

"But I am serious—yes."

"You mean," said Michael, "that your refugees when they come here will not be able to put their past sufferings completely behind them?"

"I did not mean my Refugees."

"He meant us, darling," said Rosamund. "He means Uncle Richard and Aunt Cora and the hatchet, and all that."

She turned to Poirot.

"Didn't you?"

Poirot looked at her with a blank face. Then he said:

"Why do you think that, madame?"

"Because you're a detective, aren't you? That's why you're here. N.A.R.C.O., or whatever you call it, is just nonsense, isn't it?"

XX

THERE WAS a moment of extraordinary tenseness. Poirot felt it, though he himself did not remove his eyes from Rosamund's lovely placid face.

He said with a little bow, "You have great perspicacity, madame."

"Not really," said Rosamund. "You were pointed out to me once in a restaurant. I remembered."

"But you have not mentioned it—until now?"

"I thought it would be more fun not to," said Rosamund.

Michael said in an imperfectly controlled voice:

"My—dear girl."

Poirot shifted his gaze then to look at him.

Michael was angry. Angry and something else—apprehensive?

Poirot's eyes went slowly round all the faces. Susan's, angry and watchful; Gregory's, dead and shut in; Miss Gilchrist's, foolish, her mouth wide open; George, wary; Helen, dismayed and nervous. . . .

All those expressions were normal ones under the circumstances. He wished he could have seen their faces a split second earlier, when the words "a detective" fell from Rosamund's lips. For now, inevitably, it could not be quite the same. . . .

He squared his shoulders and bowed to them. His language and his accent became less foreign.

"Yes," he said. "I am a detective."

George Crossfield said, the white dints showing once more each side of his nose:

"Who sent you here?"

"I was commissioned to enquire into the circumstances of Richard Abernethie's death."

"By whom?"

"For the moment, that does not concern you. But it would

be an advantage, would it not, if you could be assured beyond any possible doubt that Richard Abernethie died a natural death?"

"Of course he died a natural death. Who says anything else?"

"Cora Lansquenet said so. And Cora Lansquenet is dead herself."

A little wave of uneasiness seemed to sigh through the room like an evil breeze.

"She said it here—in this room," said Susan. "But I didn't really think—"

"Didn't you, Susan?" George Crossfield turned his sardonic glance upon her. "Why pretend any more? You won't take M. Pontarlier in?"

"We all thought so really," said Rosamund. "And his name isn't Pontarlier—it's Hercules something."

"Hercule Poirot—at your service."

Poirot bowed.

There were no gasps of astonishment or of apprehension. His name seemed to mean nothing at all to them.

They were less alarmed by it than they had been by the single word 'detective.'

"May I ask what conclusions you have come to?" asked George.

"He won't tell you, darling," said Rosamund. "Or if he does tell you, what he says won't be true."

Alone of the company she appeared to be amused.

Hercule Poirot looked at her thoughtfully.

ii

Hercule Poirot did not sleep well that night. He was perturbed, and he was not quite sure *why* he was perturbed. Elusive snatches of conversation, various glances, odd movements—all seemed fraught with a tantalising significance in the loneliness of the night. He was on the threshold of sleep, but sleep would not come. Just as he was about to drop off, something flashed into his mind and woke him up again. Paint—Timothy and paint. Oil paint—the smell of oil paint—connected somehow with Mr Entwhistle. Paint and Cora. Cora's paintings—picture postcards . . . Cora was deceitful about her painting. . . . No, back to Mr Entwhistle—something Mr Entwhistle had said—or was it Lanscombe? A nun who came to the house on the day that Richard Abernethie died. A nun with a moustache. A nun at Stansfield Grange—and at Lytchett St. Mary. Altogether too many nuns! Rosamund looking glamorous as a nun on the stage. Rosamund—saying that he was a detective—and everyone staring at her when she said it. That was the way they must all have stared at Cora that day when she said "But he was murdered, wasn't he?" What was it Helen Abernethie had felt to be "wrong" on that occasion? Helen Abernethie—leaving the past behind—going to Cyprus . . . Helen dropping the wax flowers with a crash when he had said—*what* was it he had said? He couldn't quite remember. . . .

He slept then, and as he slept he dreamed. . . .

He dreamed of the green malachite table. On it was the glass covered stand of wax flowers—only the whole thing had been painted over with thick crimson oil paint. Paint the colour of blood. He could smell the paint, and Timothy was groaning, was saying "I'm dying—dying . . . this is the end." And Maude, standing by, tall and stern, with a large knife in her hand was echoing him, saying "Yes, it's the end. . . ." The end—a death-bed, with candles and a nun praying. If he could just see the nun's face, he would know. . . .

Hercule Poirot woke up—and he did know!

Yes, it *was* the end. . . .

Though there was still a long way to go.

He sorted out the various bits of the mosaic.

Mr Entwhistle, the smell of paint, Timothy's house and some-thing that must be in it—or might be in it . . . the wax flowers . . . Helen . . . Broken glass . . .

iii

Helen Abernethie, in her room, took some time in going to bed. She was thinking.

Sitting in front of her dressing table, she stared at herself unseeingly in the glass.

She had been forced into having Hercule Poirot in the house.

She had not wanted it. But Mr Entwhistle had made it hard for her to refuse. And now the whole thing had come out into the open. No question any more of letting Richard Abernethie lie quiet in his grave. All started by those few words of Cora's. . . .

That day after the funeral . . . How had they all looked, she wondered? How had they looked to Cora? How had she herself looked?

What was it George had said? About seeing oneself?

There was some quotation, too. *To see ourselves as others see us* . . . As others see us.

The eyes that were staring into the glass unseeingly suddenly focussed. She was seeing herself—but not really herself—not herself as others saw her—not as Cora had seen her that day.

Her right—no, her left eyebrow was arched a little higher than the right. The mouth? No, the curve of the mouth was symmetrical. If she met herself she would surely not see much difference from this mirror image. Not like Cora.

Cora—the picture came quite clearly . . . Cora, on the day of the funeral, her head tilted sideways—asking her question—looking at Helen . . .

Suddenly Helen raised her hands to her face. She said to herself. *"It doesn't make sense . . . it can't make sense . . ."*

iv

Miss Entwhistle was aroused from a delightful dream, in which she was playing Piquet with Queen Mary, by the ringing of the telephone.

She tried to ignore it—but it persisted. Sleepily she raised her head from the pillow and looked at the watch beside her bed. Five minutes to seven—who on earth could be ringing up at that hour? It must be a wrong number.

The irritating ding-ding continued. Miss Entwhistle sighed, snatched up a dressing gown and marched into the sitting room.

"This is Kensington 675498," she said with asperity as she picked up the receiver.

"This is Mrs Abernethie speaking. Mrs *Leo* Abernethie. Can I speak to Mr Entwhistle?"

"Oh, good morning, Mrs Abernethie." The 'good morning' was not cordial. "This is Miss Entwhistle. My brother is still asleep I'm afraid. I was asleep myself."

"I'm so sorry," Helen was forced to the apology. "But it's very important that I should speak to your brother at once."

"Wouldn't it do later?"

"I'm afraid not."

"Oh, very well then."

Miss Entwhistle was tart.

She tapped at her brother's door and went in.

"Those Abernethies again!" she said bitterly.

"Eh! The Abernethies?"

"Mrs Leo Abernethie. Ringing up before seven in the morning! Really!"

"Mrs Leo is it? Dear me. How remarkable. Where is my dressing gown? Ah, thank you."

Presently he was saying:

"Entwhistle speaking. Is that you, Helen?"

"Yes. I'm terribly sorry to get you out of bed like this. But you did tell me once to ring you up at once if I remembered what it was that struck me as having been wrong somehow on the day of the funeral when Cora electrified us all by suggesting that Richard had been murdered."

"Ah! You *have* remembered?"

Helen said in a puzzled voice:

"Yes, but it doesn't make sense."

"You must allow me to be the judge of that. Was it something you noticed about one of the people?"

"Yes."

"Tell me."

"It seems absurd." Helen's voice sounded apologetic. "But I'm quite sure of it. It came to me when I was looking at myself in the glass last night. Oh . . ."

The little startled half cry was succeeded by a sound that came oddly through the wires—a dull heavy sound that Mr Entwhistle couldn't place at all—

He said urgently:

"Hullo—hullo—are you there? Helen, are you there? . . . Helen . . ."

XXI

IT WAS NOT until nearly an hour later that Mr Entwhistle after a great deal of conversation with supervisors and others found himself at last speaking to Hercule Poirot.

"Thank heaven!" said Mr Entwhistle with pardonable exasperation. "The Exchange seems to have had the greatest difficulty in getting the number."

"That is not surprising. The receiver was off the hook."

There was a grim quality in Poirot's voice which carried through to the listener.

Mr Entwhistle said sharply:

"Has something happened?"

"Yes. Mrs Leo Abernethie was found by the housemaid about twenty minutes ago lying by the telephone extension in the study. She was unconscious. A serious concussion."

"Do you mean she was struck on the head?"

"I think so. It is *just* possible that she fell and struck her head on a marble doorstop, but me I do not think so, and the doctor, he does not think so either."

"She was telephoning to me at the time. I wondered when we were cut off so suddenly."

"So it was to you she was telephoning. What did she say?"

"She mentioned to me some time ago that on the occasion when Cora Lansquenet suggested her brother had been murdered, she herself had a feeling of something being wrong—odd —she did not quite know how to put it—unfortunately she could not remember *why* she had that impression."

"And suddenly, she did remember?"

"Yes."

"And rang you up to tell you?"

"Yes."

"Eh bien?"

"There's no *eh bien* about it," said Mr Entwhistle testily. "She started to tell me, but was interrupted."

"How much had she said?"

"Nothing pertinent."

"You will excuse me, *mon ami,* but *I* am the judge of that, not you. What exactly did she say?"

"She reminded me that I had asked her to let me know at once if she remembered what it was that had struck her as peculiar. She said she had remembered—but that it 'didn't make sense.'

"I asked her if it was something about one of the people who were there that day, and she said, yes, it was. She said it had come to her when she was looking in the glass—"

"Yes?"

"That was all."

"She gave no hint as to—which of the people concerned it was?"

"I should hardly fail to let you know if she had told me *that,*" said Mr Entwhistle acidly.

"I apologise, *mon ami.* Of course you would have told me."

Mr Entwhistle said:

"We shall have to wait until she recovers consciousness before we know."

Poirot said gravely:

"That may not be for a very long time. Perhaps—never."

"Is it as bad as that?" Mr Entwhistle's voice shook a little.

"Yes, it is as bad as that."

"But—that's terrible, Poirot."

"Yes, it is terrible. And it is why we cannot afford to wait! For it shows that we have to deal with someone who is either completely ruthless or so frightened that it comes to the same thing."

"But look here, Poirot, what about Helen? I feel worried. Are you sure she will be safe at Enderby?"

"No, she would not be safe. So she is not at Enderby. Already the ambulance has come and is taking her to a nursing home where she will have special nurses and where *no one,* family or otherwise, will be allowed in to see her."

Mr Entwhistle sighed.

"You relieve my mind. She might have been in danger."

"She assuredly would have been in danger!"

Mr Entwhistle's voice sounded deeply moved.

"I have a great regard for Helen Abernethie. I always have had. A woman of very exceptional character. She may have had certain—what shall I say?—reticences in her life?"

"Ah, there were reticences?"

"I have always had an idea that such was the case."

"Hence the villa in Cyprus. Yes, that explains a good deal. . . ."

"I don't want you to begin thinking—"

"You cannot stop me thinking. But now, there is a little commission that I have for you. One moment."

There was a pause, then Poirot's voice spoke again.

"I had to make sure that nobody was listening. All is well. Now here is what I want you to do for me. You must prepare to make a journey."

"A journey?" Mr Entwhistle sounded faintly dismayed. "Oh, I see—you want me to come down to Enderby?"

"Not at all. _I_ am in charge here. No, you will not have to travel so far. Your journey will not take you very far from London. You will travel to Bury St. Edmunds—(_Ma foi!_ what names your English towns have!) and there you will hire a car and drive to Forsdyke House. It is a mental home. Ask for Dr Penrith and inquire of him particulars about a patient who was recently discharged."

"What patient? Anyway, surely—"

Poirot broke in:

"The name of the patient is Gregory Banks. Find out for what form of insanity he was being treated."

"Do you mean that Gregory Banks is insane?"

"Sh. Be careful what you say. And now—I have not yet breakfasted and you, too, I suspect have not breakfasted?"

"Not yet. I was too anxious—"

"Quite so. Then, I pray you, eat your breakfast, repose yourself. There is a good train to Bury St. Edmunds at twelve o'clock. If I have any more news I will telephone you before you start."

"Be careful of *yourself*, Poirot," said Mr Entwhistle with some concern.

"Ah that, yes! Me, I do not want to be hit on the head with a marble doorstop. You may be assured that I will take every precaution. And now—for the moment—goodbye."

Poirot heard the sound of the receiver being replaced at the other end, then he heard a very faint second click—and smiled to himself. Somebody had replaced the receiver on the telephone in the hall.

He went out there. There was no one about. He tiptoed to the cupboard at the back of the stairs and looked inside. At that moment Lanscombe came through the service door carrying a tray with toast and a silver coffee pot. He looked slightly surprised to see Poirot emerge from the cupboard.

"Breakfast is ready in the dining room, sir," he said.

Poirot surveyed him thoughtfully.

The old butler looked white and shaken.

"Courage," said Poirot, clapping him on the shoulder. "All will yet be well. Would it be too much trouble to serve me a cup of coffee in my bedroom?"

"Certainly, sir. I will send Janet up with it, sir."

Lanscombe looked disapprovingly at Hercule Poirot's back as the latter climbed the stairs. Poirot was attired in an exotic silk dressing gown with a pattern of triangles and squares.

"Foreigners!" thought Lanscombe bitterly. "Foreigners in the house! And Mrs Leo with concussion! I don't know what we're coming to. Nothing's the same since Mr Richard died."

Hercule Poirot was dressed by the time he received his coffee from Janet. His murmurs of sympathy were well received, since he stressed the shock her discovery must have given her.

"Yes, indeed, sir, what I felt when I opened the door of the study and came in with the Hoover and saw Mrs Leo lying there I never shall forget. There she lay—and I made sure she was dead. She must have been taken faint as she stood at the phone—and fancy her being up at that time in the morning! I've never known her do such a thing before."

"Fancy, indeed!" He added casually: "No one else was up, I suppose?"

"As it happens, sir, Mrs Timothy was up and about. She's a very early riser always—often goes for a walk before breakfast."

"She is of the generation that rises early," said Poirot nodding his head. "The younger ones, now—*they* do not get up so early?"

"No, indeed, sir, all fast asleep when I brought them their tea—and very late I was, too, what with the shock and getting the doctor to come and having to have a cup first to steady myself."

She went off and Poirot reflected on what she had said.

Maude Abernethie had been up and about, and the younger generation had been in bed—but that, Poirot reflected, meant nothing at all. Anyone could have heard Helen's door open and close, and have followed her down to listen—and would afterwards have made a point of being fast asleep in bed.

"But if I am right," thought Poirot. "And after all, it is natural to me to be right—it is a habit I have!—then there is no need to go into who was here and who was there. First, I must seek a proof where I have deduced the proof may be. And then—I make my little speech. And I sit back and see what happens . . ."

As soon as Janet had left the room, Poirot drained his coffee cup, put on his overcoat and his hat, left his room, ran nimbly down the back stairs and left the house by the side door. He walked briskly the quarter mile to the post office where he demanded a trunk call. Presently he was once more speaking to Mr Entwhistle.

"Yes, it is I yet again! Pay no attention to the commission with which I entrusted you. *C'etait une blague!* Someone was listening. Now, *mon vieux,* to the real commission. You must, as I said, take a train. But not to Bury St. Edmunds. I want you to proceed to the house of Mr Timothy Abernethie."

"But Timothy and Maude are at Enderby."

"Exactly. There is no one in the house but a woman by the name of Jones who has been persuaded by the offer of considerable *largesse* to guard the house whilst they are absent. What I want you to do is to take something out of that house!"

"My dear Poirot! I really can't stoop to burglary!"

"It will not seem like burglary. You will say to the excellent Mrs Jones who knows you, that you have been asked by Mr or Mrs Abernethie to fetch this particular object and take it to London. She will not suspect anything amiss."

"No, no, probably not. But I don't like it." Mr Entwhistle sounded most reluctant. "Why can't you go and get whatever it is yourself."

"Because, my friend, I should be a stranger of foreign appearance and as such a suspicious character, and Mrs Jones would at once raise the difficulties! With you, she will not."

"No, no—I see that. But what on earth are Timothy and Maude going to think when they hear about it? I have known them for forty odd years."

"And you knew Richard Abernethie for that time also! And you knew Cora Lansquenet when she was a little girl!"

In a martyred voice Mr Entwhistle asked:

"You're sure this is really *necessary,* Poirot?"

"The old question they asked in the war time on the posters. *Is your journey really necessary?* I say to you, it *is* necessary. It is vital!"

"And what is this object I've got to get hold of?"

Poirot told him.

"But really, Poirot, I don't see—"

"It is not necessary for *you* to see. *I* am doing the seeing."

"And what do you want me to do with the damned thing?"

"You will take it to London, to an address in Elm Park Gardens. If you have a pencil, note it down."

Having done so, Mr Entwhistle said, still in his martyred voice:

"I hope you know what you are doing, Poirot?"

He sounded very doubtful—but Poirot's reply was not doubtful at all.

"Of course I know what I am doing. We are nearing the end."

Mr Entwhistle sighed.

"If we could only guess what Helen was going to tell me."

"No need to guess. I *know.*"

"You know? But my dear Poirot—"

"Explanations must wait. But let me assure you of this. *I know what Helen Abernethie saw when she looked in her mirror.*"

ii

Breakfast had been an uneasy meal. Neither Rosamund nor Timothy had appeared, but the others were there and had talked in rather subdued tones, and eaten a little less than they normally would have done.

George was the first one to recover his spirits. His temperament was mercurial and optimistic.

"I expect Aunt Helen will be all right," he said. "Doctors always like to pull a long face. After all, what's concussion? Often clears up completely in a couple of days."

"A woman I knew had concussion during the war," said Miss Gilchrist conversationally. "A brick or something hit her as she was walking down Tottenham Court Road—it was during fly bomb time—and she never felt *anything* at all. Just went on with what she was doing—and collapsed in a train to Liverpool twelve hours later. And would you believe it, she had no recollection at all of going to the station and catching the train or *anything*. She just couldn't understand it when she woke up in hospital. She was there for nearly three weeks."

"What I can't make out," said Susan, "is what Helen was doing telephoning at that unearthly hour, and who she was telephoning to?"

"Felt ill," said Maude with decision. "Probably woke up feeling queer and came down to ring up the doctor. Then had a giddy fit and fell. That's the only thing that makes sense."

"Bad luck hitting her head on that doorstop," said Michael. "If she'd just pitched over onto that thick pile carpet she'd have been all right."

The door opened and Rosamund came in, frowning.

"I can't find those wax flowers," she said. "I mean the ones that were standing on the malachite table the day of Uncle Richard's funeral." She looked accusingly at Susan. *"You* haven't taken them?"

"Of course I haven't! Really, Rosamund, you're not *still* thinking about malachite tables with poor old Helen carted off to hospital with concussion?"

"I don't see why I shouldn't think about them. If you've got concussion you don't know what's happening and it doesn't matter to you. We can't do anything for Aunt Helen, and Michael and I have got to get back to London by tomorrow lunch-time because we're seeing Jackie Lygo about opening dates for *The Baronet's Progress*. So I'd like to fix up definitely about the table. But I'd like to have a look at those wax flowers again. There's a kind of Chinese vase on the table now—nice— but not nearly so period. I do wonder where they are—perhaps Lanscombe knows."

Lanscombe had just looked in to see if they had finished breakfast.

"We're all through, Lanscombe," said George getting up. "What's happened to our foreign friend?"

"He is having his coffee and toast served upstairs."

"Petit dejeuner for N.A.R.C.O."

"Lanscombe, do you know where those wax flowers are that used to be on that green table in the drawing room?" asked Rosamund.

"I understand Mrs Leo had an accident with them, m'am. She was going to have a new glass shade made, but I don't think she has seen about it yet."

"Then where is the thing?"

"It would probably be in the cupboard behind the staircase, m'am. That is where things are usually placed when awaiting repair. Shall I ascertain for you?"

"I'll go and look myself. Come with me, Michael sweetie. It's dark there, and I'm not going in any dark corners by myself after what happened to Aunt Helen."

Everybody showed a sharp reaction. Maude demanded in her deep voice:

"What *do* you mean, Rosamund?"

"Well, she was coshed by someone, wasn't she?"

Gregory Banks said sharply:

"She was taken suddenly faint and fell."

Rosamund laughed.

"Did she tell you so? Don't be silly, Greg, of course she was coshed."

George said sharply:

"You shouldn't say things like that, Rosamund."

"Nonsense," said Rosamund. "She *must* have been. I mean, it all adds up. A detective in the house looking for clues, and Uncle Richard poisoned, and Aunt Cora killed with a hatchet, and Miss Gilchrist given poisoned wedding cake, and now Aunt Helen struck down with a blunt instrument. You'll see, it will go on like that. One after another of us will be killed and the one that's left will be It—the murderer, I mean. But it's not going to be *me*—who's killed, I mean."

"And why should anyone want to kill you, beautiful Rosamund?" asked George lightly.

Rosamund opened her eyes very wide.

"Oh," she said. "Because I know too much, of course."

"What do you know?" Maude Abernethie and Gregory Banks spoke almost in unison.

Rosamund gave her vacant and angelic smile.

"Wouldn't you all like to know?" she said agreeably. "Come on, Michael."

XXII

At eleven o'clock, Hercule Poirot called an informal meeting in the library. Everyone was there and Poirot looked thoughtfully round the semi-circle of faces.

"Last night," he said, "Mrs Shane announced to you that I was a private detective. For myself, I hoped to retain my—*camouflage,* shall we say?—a little longer. But no matter! Today —or at most the day after—I would have told you the truth. Please listen carefully now to what I have to say.

"I am in my own line a celebrated person—I may say a *most* celebrated person. My gifts, in fact, are unequalled!"

George Crossfield grinned and said:

"That's the stuff, M. Pont—no, it's M. Poirot, isn't it? Funny, isn't it, that I've never even heard of you?"

"It is not funny," said Poirot severely. "It is lamentable! Alas, there is no proper education nowadays. Apparently one learns nothing but economics—and how to set intelligence tests! But to continue. I have been a friend for many years of Mr Entwhistle's—"

"So *he's* the nigger in the wood pile!"

"If you like to put it that way, Mr Crossfield. Mr Entwhistle was greatly upset by the death of his old friend, Mr Richard Abernethie. He was particularly perturbed by some words spoken on the day of the funeral by Mr Abernethie's sister, Mrs Lansquenet. Words spoken in this very room."

"Very silly—and just like Cora," said Maude. "Mr Entwhistle should have had more sense than to pay attention to them!"

Poirot went on:

"Mr Entwhistle was even more perturbed after the—the coincidence, shall I say?—of Mrs Lansquenet's death. He wanted one thing only—to be assured that that death *was* a coincidence. In other words he wanted to feel assured that Richard Abernethie had died a natural death. To that end he commissioned me to make the necessary investigations."

There was a pause.

"I have made them. . . ."

Again there was a pause. No one spoke.

Poirot threw back his head.

"*Eh bien,* you will all be delighted to hear that as a result of my investigations—there is absolutely no reason to believe that Mr Abernethie died anything but a natural death. There is no reason *at all* to believe that he was murdered!" He smiled. He threw out his hands in a triumphant gesture.

"That is good news, is it not?"

It hardly seemed to be, the way they took it. They stared at him and in all but the eyes of one person there still seemed to be doubt and suspicion.

The exception was Timothy Abernethie who was nodding his head in violent agreement.

"Of course Richard wasn't murdered," he said angrily. "Never could understand why anybody ever even thought of such a thing for a moment! Just Cora up to her tricks, that was all. Wanting to give you all a scare. Her idea of being funny. Truth is that although she was my own sister, she was always a bit mental, poor girl. Well, Mr whatever your name is, I'm glad you've had the sense to come to the right conclusion, though if you ask me, I call it damned cheek of Entwhistle to go commissioning you to come prying and poking about. And if he thinks he's going to charge the estate with your fee, I can tell you he won't get away with it! Damned cheek, and most uncalled for! Who's Entwhistle to set himself up? If the family's satisfied—"

"But the family wasn't, Uncle Timothy," said Rosamund.

"Hey—what's that?"

Timothy peered at her under beetling brows of displeasure.

"We weren't satisfied. And what about Aunt Helen this morning?"

Maude said sharply:

"Helen's just the age when you're liable to get a stroke. That's all there is to that."

"I see," said Rosamund. "Another coincidence, you think?" She looked at Poirot.

"Aren't there rather too many coincidences?"

"Coincidences," said Hercule Poirot, "do happen."

"Nonsense," said Maude. "Helen felt ill, came down and rang up the doctor, and then—"

"But she didn't ring up the doctor," said Rosamund. "I asked him—"

Susan said sharply:

"Who did she ring up?"

"I don't know," said Rosamund, a shade of vexation passing over her face. "But I daresay I can find out," she added hopefully.

ii

Hercule Poirot was sitting in the Victorian summerhouse. He drew his large watch from his pocket and laid it on the table in front of him.

He had announced that he was leaving by the twelve o'clock train. There was still half an hour to go. Half an hour for someone to make up their minds and come to him. Perhaps more than one person . . .

The summerhouse was clearly visible from most of the windows of the house. Surely, soon, someone would come?

If not, his knowledge of human nature was deficient, and his main premises incorrect.

He waited—and above his head a spider in its web waited for a fly.

It was Miss Gilchrist who came first. She was flustered and upset and rather incoherent.

"Oh, Mr Pontarlier—I can't remember your other name," she said. "I had to come and speak to you although I *don't* like doing it—but really I feel I *ought* to. I mean, after what happened to poor Mrs Leo this morning—and I think myself Mrs Shane was *quite right*—and *not* coincidence, and certainly not a *stroke*—as Mrs Timothy suggested, because my own father had a stroke and it was quite a different appearance, and anyway the doctor *said* concussion quite clearly!"

She paused, took breath and looked at Poirot with appealing eyes.

"Yes," said Poirot gently and encouragingly. "You want to tell me something?"

"As I say, I don't like doing it—because she's been so kind. She found me the position with Mrs Timothy and everything. She's been really *very* kind. That's why I feel so ungrateful. And even gave me Mrs Lansquenet's musquash jacket which is really *most* handsome and fits beautifully because it never matters if fur is a little on the large side. And when I wanted to return her the amethyst brooch she wouldn't *hear* of it—"

"You are referring," said Poirot gently, "to Mrs Banks?"

"Yes, you see—" Miss Gilchrist looked down, twisting her fingers unhappily. She looked up and said with a sudden gulp: "You see, I *listened!*"

"You mean you happened to overhear a conversation—"

"No." Miss Gilchrist shook her head with an air of heroic determination. "I'd rather speak the truth. And it's not so bad telling you because you're not English."

Hercule Poirot understood her without taking offence.

"You mean that to a foreigner it is natural that people should listen at doors and open letters, or read letters that are left about?"

"Oh, I'd never open anybody else's letters," said Miss Gilchrist in a shocked tone. "Not *that*. But I *did* listen that day—the day that Mr Richard Abernethie came down to see his sister. I was curious, you know, about his turning up suddenly after all those years. And I did wonder why—and—and—you see when you haven't much life of your own or very many friends, you do tend to get interested—when you're living *with* anybody, I mean."

"Most natural," said Poirot.

"Yes, I do think it was natural. . . . Though not, of course, at all *right*. But I did it! And I heard what he said!"

"You heard what Mr Abernethie said to Mrs Lansquenet?"

"Yes. He said something like—'It's no good talking to Timothy. He poohs-poohs everything. Simply won't listen. But I thought I'd like to get it off my chest to you, Cora. We three are the only ones left. And though you've always liked to play the simpleton you've got a lot of common sense. So what would *you* do about it, if you were me?'

"I couldn't quite hear what Mrs Lansquenet said, but I caught the word *police*—and then Mr Abernethie burst out quite loud, and said, 'I can't do that. Not when it's a question of *my own niece.*' And then I had to run in the kitchen for something boiling over and when I got back Mr Abernethie was saying, 'Even if I die an unnatural death I don't want the police called in, if it can possibly be avoided. You understand that, don't you, my dear girl? But don't worry. Now that I *know,* I shall take all possible precautions.' And he went on, saying he'd made a new will, and that she, Cora, would be quite all right. And then he said about her having been happy with her husband and how perhaps he'd made a mistake over that in the past."

Miss Gilchrist stopped.

Poirot said: "I see—I see . . ."

"But I never wanted to say—to tell. I didn't think Mrs Lansquenet would have wanted me to. . . . But now—after Mrs Leo being attacked this morning—and then you saying so calmly it was coincidence. But, oh, M. Pontarlier, it *wasn't* coincidence!"

Poirot smiled. He said:

"No, it wasn't coincidence. . . . Thank you, Miss Gilchrist, for coming to me. It was very necessary that you should."

iii

He had a little difficulty in getting rid of Miss Gilchrist, and it was urgent that he should, for he hoped for further confidences.

His instinct was right. Miss Gilchrist had hardly gone before Gregory Banks, striding across the lawn, came impetuously into the summerhouse. His face was pale and there were beads of perspiration on his forehead. His eyes were curiously excited.

"At last!" he said. "I thought that stupid woman would never go. You're all wrong in what you said this morning. You're wrong about everything. Richard Abernethie *was* killed. *I* killed him."

Hercule Poirot let his eyes move up and down over the excited young man. He showed no surprise.

"So you killed him, did you? How?"

Gregory Banks smiled.

"It wasn't difficult for *me*. You can surely realise that. There were fifteen or twenty different drugs I could lay my hands on that would do it. The method of administration took rather more thinking out, but I hit on a very ingenious idea in the end. The beauty of it was that *I* didn't need to be anywhere near at the time."

"Clever," said Poirot.

"Yes." Gregory Banks cast his eyes down modestly. He seemed pleased. "Yes—I *do* think it was ingenious."

Poirot asked with interest:

"Why did you kill him? For the money that would come to your wife?"

"No. No, of course not." Greg was suddenly excitedly indignant. "I'm not a money grubber. I didn't marry Susan for her *money!*"

"Didn't you, Mr Banks?"

"That's what *he* thought," Greg said with sudden venom. "Richard Abernethie! He liked Susan, he admired her, he was proud of her as an example of Abernethie blood! But he thought she'd married beneath her—he thought *I* was no good—he despised me! I daresay I hadn't the right accent—I didn't wear my clothes the right way. He was a snob—a filthy snob!"

"I don't think so," said Poirot mildly. "From all I have heard, Richard Abernethie was no snob."

"He was. He was." The young man spoke with something approaching hysteria. "He thought nothing of me. He sneered at me—always very polite but underneath I could *see* that he didn't like me!"

"Possibly."

"People can't treat me like that and get away with it! They've tried it before! A woman who used to come and have her medicines made up. She was rude to me. Do you know what I did?"

"Yes," said Poirot.

Gregory looked startled.

"So you know that?"

"Yes."

"She nearly died." He spoke in a satisfied manner. "That shows you I'm not the sort of person to be trifled with! Richard Abernethie despised me—and what happened to him? He died."

"A most successful murder," said Poirot with grave congratulation.

He added: "But why come and give yourself away—to me?"

"Because you said you were through with it all! You said he *hadn't* been murdered. I had to show you that you're not as clever as you think you are—and besides—besides—"

"Yes," said Poirot. "And besides?"

Greg collapsed suddenly onto the bench. His face changed. It took on a sudden ecstatic quality.

"It was wrong—wicked. . . . I must be punished. . . . I must go back there—to the place of punishment . . . to atone . . . Yes, to *atone!* Repentance! Retribution!"

His face was alight now with a kind of glowing ecstasy. Poirot studied him for a moment or two curiously.

Then he asked:

"How badly do you want to get away from your wife?"

Gregory's face changed.

"Susan? Susan is wonderful—wonderful!"

"Yes. Susan is wonderful. That is a grave burden. Susan loves you devotedly. That is a burden, too?"

Gregory sat looking in front of him. Then he said, rather in the manner of a sulky child:

"Why couldn't she let me alone?"

He sprang up.

"She's coming now—across the lawn. I'll go now. But you'll tell her what I told you? Tell her I've gone to the police station. To confess."

iv

Susan came in breathlessly.

"Where's Greg? He was here! I saw him."

"Yes." Poirot paused a moment—before saying: "He came to tell me that it was he who poisoned Richard Abernethie . . ."

"What absolute *nonsense!* You didn't believe him, I hope?"

"Why should I not believe him?"

"He wasn't even near this place when Uncle Richard died!"

"Perhaps not. Where was he when Cora Lansquenet died?"

"In London. We both were."

Hercule Poirot shook his head.

"No, no, that will not do. You, for instance, took out your car that day and were away all afternoon. I think I know where you went. You went to Lytchett St. Mary."

"I did no such thing!"

Poirot smiled.

"When I met you here, madame, it was not, as I told you, the first time I had seen you. After the inquest on Mrs Lansquenet you were in the garage of the King's Arms. You talk there to a mechanic and close by you is a car containing an elderly foreign gentleman. You did not notice him, but he noticed you."

"I don't see what you mean. That was the day of the inquest."

"Ah, but remember what that mechanic said to you! He asked you if you were a relative of the victim, and you said you were her niece."

"He was just being a ghoul. They're all ghouls."

"And his next words were, 'Ah, wondered where I'd seen you before.' Where did he see you before, madame? It must have been in Lytchett St. Mary, since in his mind his seeing you before was accounted for by your being Mrs Lansquenet's niece. Had he seen you near her cottage? And when? It was a matter, was it not, that demands inquiry. And the result of the inquiry is, that you were there—in Lytchett St. Mary—on the afternoon Cora Lansquenet died. You parked your car in the same quarry where you left it the morning of the inquest. The car was seen and the number was noted. By this time Inspector Morton knows whose car it was."

Susan stared at him. Her breath came rather fast, but she showed no signs of discomposure.

"You're talking nonsense, M. Poirot. And you're making me forget what I came here to say—I wanted to try and find you alone—"

"To confess to me that it was you and not your husband who committed the murder?"

"No, of course not. What kind of fool do you think I am? And I've already told you that Gregory never left London that day."

"A fact which you cannot possibly know since you were away yourself. Why did you go down to Lytchett St. Mary, Mrs Banks?"

Susan drew a deep breath.

"All right, if you must have it! What Cora said at the funeral worried me. I kept on thinking about it. Finally I decided to run down in the car and see her, and ask her what had put the idea into her head. Greg thought it a silly idea, so I didn't even tell him where I was going. I got there about three o'clock, knocked and rang, but there was no answer, so I thought she must be out or gone away. That's all there is to it. I didn't go round to the back of the cottage. If I had, I might have seen the broken window. I just went back to London without the faintest idea there was anything wrong."

Poirot's face was non-committal. He said:

"Why does your husband accuse himself of the crime?"

"Because he's—" a word trembled on Susan's tongue and was rejected. Poirot seized on it.

"You were going to say 'because he is batty' speaking in jest —but the jest was too near the truth, was it not?"

"Greg's all right. He is. He *is*."

"I know something of his history," said Poirot. "He was for some months in Forsdyke House Mental Home before you met him."

"He was never certified. He was a voluntary patient."

"That is true. He is not, I agree, to be classed as insane. But he is, very definitely, unbalanced. He has a punishment complex —has had it, I suspect, since infancy."

Susan spoke quickly and eagerly:

"You don't understand, M. Poirot. Greg has never had a *chance*. That's why I wanted Uncle Richard's money so badly. Uncle Richard was so matter of fact. He couldn't understand. I knew Greg had got to set up for himself. He had got to feel he was *someone*—not just a chemist's assistant, being pushed around. Everything will be different now. He will have his own laboratory. He can work out his own formulas."

"Yes, yes—you will give him the earth—because you love him. Love him too much for safety or for happiness. But you cannot give to people what they are incapable of receiving. At the end of it all, he will still be something that he does not want to be. . . ."

"What's that?"

"Susan's husband."

"How cruel you are! And what nonsense you talk!"

"Where Gregory Banks is concerned you are unscrupulous. You wanted your uncle's money—not for yourself—but for your husband. *How badly did you want it?*"

Angrily, Susan turned and dashed away.

v

"I thought," said Michael Shane lightly, "that I'd just come along and say goodbye."

He smiled, and his smile had a singularly intoxicating quality. Poirot was aware of the man's vital charm.

He studied Michael Shane for some moments in silence. He felt as though he knew this man least well of all the house party, for Michael Shane only showed the side of himself that he wanted to show.

"Your wife," said Poirot conversationally, "is a very unusual woman."

Michael raised his eyebrows.

"Do you think so? She's lovely, I agree. But not, or so I've found, conspicuous for brains."

"She will never try to be too clever," Poirot agreed. "But she knows what she wants." He sighed. "So few people do."

"Ah!" Michael's smile broke out again. "Thinking of the malachite table?"

"Perhaps," Poirot paused and added: "And of what was on it."

"The wax flowers, you mean?"

"The wax flowers."

Michael frowned.

"I don't always quite understand you, M. Poirot. However," the smile was switched on again. "I'm more thankful than I can say that we're all out of the wood. It's unpleasant, to say the least of it, to go around with the suspicion that somehow or other one of us murdered poor old Uncle Richard."

"That is how he seemed to you when you met him?" Poirot inquired. "Poor old Uncle Richard?"

"Of course he was very well preserved and all that—"

"And in full possession of his faculties—"

"Oh yes."

"And, in fact, quite *shrewd?*"

"I daresay."

"A shrewd judge of character."

The smile remained unaltered.

"You can't expect me to agree with *that,* M. Poirot. He didn't approve of *me.*"

"He thought you, perhaps, the unfaithful type?" Poirot suggested.

Michael laughed.

"What an old-fashioned idea!"

"But it is true, isn't it?"

"Now I wonder what you mean by *that?*"

Poirot placed the tips of his fingers together.

"There have been inquiries made, you know," he murmured.

"By you?"

"Not only by me."

Michael Shane gave him a quick searching glance. His reactions, Poirot noted, were quick. Michael Shane was no fool.

"You mean—the police are interested?"

"They have never been quite satisfied, you know, to regard the murder of Cora Lansquenet as a casual crime."

"And they've been making inquiries about me?"

Poirot said primly:

"They are interested in the movements of Mrs Lansquenet's relations on the day that she was killed."

"That's extremely awkward." Michael spoke with a charming, confidential, rueful air.

"Is it, Mr Shane?"

"More so than you can imagine! I told Rosamund, you see, that I was lunching with a certain Oscar Lewis on that day."

"When, in actual fact, you were not?"

"No. Actually I motored down to see a woman called Sorrel Dainton—quite a well-known actress. I was with her in her last show. Rather awkward, you see—for though it's quite satisfactory as far as the police are concerned, it won't go down very well with Rosamund."

"Ah!" Poirot looked discreet. "There has been a little trouble over this friendship of yours?"

"Yes . . . In fact—Rosamund made me promise I wouldn't see her any more."

"Yes, I can see that may be awkward. . . . *Entre nous*, you had an affair with the lady?"

"Oh, just one of those things! It's not as though I cared for the woman at all."

"But she cares for you?"

"Well, she's been rather tiresome. . . . Women do cling so. However, as you say, the police at any rate will be satisfied."

"You think so?"

"Well, I could hardly be taking a hatchet to Cora if I was dallying with Sorrel miles and miles away. She's got a cottage in Kent."

"I see—I see—and this Miss Dainton, she will testify for you?"

"She won't like it—but as it's murder, I suppose she'll have to do it."

"She will do it, perhaps, even if you were *not* dallying with her."

"What do you mean?" Michael looked suddenly black as thunder.

"The lady is fond of you. When they are fond, women will swear to what is true—and also to what is untrue."

"Do you mean to say that you don't believe me?"

"It does not matter if *I* believe you or not. It is not *I* you have to satisfy."

"Who then?"

Poirot smiled.

"Inspector Morton—who has just come out on the terrace through the side door."

Michael Shane wheeled round sharply.

XXIII

"I HEARD YOU were here, M. Poirot," said Inspector Morton.

The two men were pacing the terrace together.

"I came over with Superintendent Parwell from Matchfield. Dr Larraby rang him up about Mrs Leo Abernethie and he's come over here to make a few inquiries. The doctor wasn't satisfied."

"And you, my friend," inquired Poirot, "where do you come in? You are a long way from your native Berkshire."

"I wanted to ask a few questions—and the people I wanted to ask them of seemed very conveniently assembled here." He paused before adding, "Your doing?"

"Yes, my doing."

"And as a result Mrs Leo Abernethie gets knocked out."

"You must not blame me for that. If she had come to *me* . . . But she did not. Instead she rang up her lawyer in London."

"And was in process of spilling the beans to him when— Wonk!"

"When—as you say—Wonk!"

"And what had she managed to tell him?"

"Very little. She had only got as far as telling him that she was looking at herself in the glass."

"Ah! well," said Inspector Morton philosophically. "Women will do it." He looked sharply at Poirot. "That suggests something to you?"

"Yes, I think I know what it was she was going to tell him."

"Wonderful guesser, aren't you? You always were. Well, what was it?"

"Excuse me, are you inquiring into the death of Richard Abernethie?"

"Officially, no. Actually, of course, if it has a bearing on the murder of Mrs Lansquenet—"

"It has a bearing on that, yes. But I will ask you, my friend, to give me a few more hours. I shall know by then if what I have imagined—imagined only, you comprehend—is correct. If it *is*—"

"Well, if it is?"

"Then I may be able to place in your hands a piece of concrete evidence."

"We could certainly do with it," said Inspector Morton with feeling. He looked askance at Poirot. "What have you been holding back?"

"Nothing. Absolutely nothing. Since the piece of evidence I have imagined may not in fact exist. I have only deduced its existence from various scraps of conversation. I may," said Poirot in a completely unconvinced tone, "be wrong."

Morton smiled.

"But that doesn't often happen to you?"

"No. Though I will admit—yes, I am forced to admit—that it *has* happened to me."

"I must say I'm glad to hear it! To be always right must be sometimes monotonous."

"I do not find it so," Poirot assured him.

Inspector Morton laughed.

"And you're asking me to hold off with my questioning?"

"No, no, not at all. Proceed as you had planned to do. I suppose you were not actually contemplating an arrest?"

Morton shook his head.

"Much too flimsy for that. We'd have to get a decision from the Public Prosecutor first—and we're a long way from that. No, just statements from certain parties of their movements on the day in question—in one case with a caution, perhaps."

"I see. Mrs Banks?"

"Smart, aren't you? Yes. She was there that day. Her car was parked in that quarry."

"She was not seen actually *driving* the car?"

"No."

The Inspector added, "It's bad, you know, that she's never said a word about being down there that day. She's got to explain that satisfactorily."

"She is quite skilful at explanations," said Poirot drily.

"Yes. Clever young lady. Perhaps a thought too clever."

"It is never wise to be too clever. That is how murderers get caught. Has anything more come up about George Crossfield?"

"Nothing definite. He's a very ordinary type. There are a lot of young men like him going about the country in trains and buses or on bicycles. People find it hard to remember when a week or so has gone by if it was Wednesday or Thursday when they were at a certain place or noticed a certain person."

He paused and went on: "We've had one piece of rather curious information—from the Mother Superior of some convent or other. Two of her nuns had been out collecting from door to door. It seems that they went to Mrs Lansquenet's cottage on the day *before* she was murdered, but couldn't make anyone hear when they knocked and rang. That's natural enough—she was up North at the Abernethie funeral and Gilchrist had been given the day off and had gone on an excursion to Bournemouth. The point is that they say *there was someone in the cottage*. They say they heard sighs and groans. I've queried whether it wasn't a day later but the Mother Superior is quite definite that that couldn't be so. It's all entered up in some book. Was there someone searching for something in the cottage that day, who seized the opportunity of both the women being away? And did that somebody not find what he or she was looking for and come back the next day? I don't set much store on the sighs and still less on the groans. Even nuns are suggestible and a cottage where murder has occurred positively *asks* for groans. The point is, was there someone in the cottage who shouldn't have been there? And if so, who was it? All the Abernethie crowd were at the funeral."

Poirot asked a seemingly irrelevant question:

"These nuns who were collecting in that district, did they return at all at a later date to try again?"

"As a matter of fact they did come again—about a week later. Actually on the day of the inquest, I believe."

"That fits," said Hercule Poirot. "That fits very well."

Inspector Morton looked at him.

"Why this interest in nuns?"

"They have been forced on my attention whether I will or no. It will not have escaped your attention, Inspector, that the visit of the nuns was the same day that poisoned wedding cake found its way into that cottage."

"You don't think— Surely that's a ridiculous idea?"

"My ideas are never ridiculous," said Hercule Poirot severely. "And now, *mon cher,* I must leave you to your questions and to the inquiries into the attack on Mrs Abernethie. I myself must go in search of the late Richard Abernethie's niece."

"Now be careful what you go saying to Mrs Banks."

"I do not mean Mrs Banks. I mean Richard Abernethie's other niece."

ii

Poirot found Rosamund sitting on a bench overlooking a little stream that cascaded down in a waterfall and then flowed through rhododendron thickets. She was staring into the water.

"I do not, I trust, disturb an Ophelia," said Poirot as he took his seat beside her. "You are, perhaps, studying the rôle?"

"I've never played in Shakespeare," said Rosamund. "Except once in Rep. I was Jessica in 'The Merchant.' A lousy part."

"Yet not without pathos. *'I am never merry when I hear sweet music.'* What a load she carried, poor Jessica, the daughter of the hated and despised Jew. What doubts of herself she must have had when she brought with her her father's ducats when she ran away to her lover. Jessica with gold was one thing— Jessica without gold might have been another."

Rosamund turned her head to look at him.

"I thought you'd gone," she said with a touch of reproach. She glanced down at her wrist-watch. "It's past twelve o'clock."

"I have missed my train," said Poirot.

"Why?"

"You think I missed it for a reason?"

"I suppose so. You're rather precise, aren't you? If you wanted to catch a train, I think you'd catch it."

"Your judgement is admirable. Do you know, madame, I have been sitting in the little summerhouse hoping that you would, perhaps, pay me a visit there?"

Rosamund stared at him.

"Why should I? You more or less said goodbye to us all in the library."

"Quite so. And there was nothing—*you* wanted to say to *me?*"

"No." Rosamund shook her head. "I had a lot I wanted to think about. Important things."

"I see."

"I don't often do much thinking," said Rosamund. "It seems a waste of time. But this *is* important. I think one ought to plan one's life just as one wants it to be."

"And that is what you are doing?"

"Well, yes . . . I was trying to make a decision about something."

"About your husband?"

"In a way."

Poirot waited a moment, then he said:

"Inspector Morton has just arrived here." He anticipated Rosamund's question by going on: "He is the police officer in charge of the inquiries about Mrs Lansquenet's death. He has come here to get statements from you all about what you were doing on the day she was murdered."

"I see. Alibis," said Rosamund cheerfully.

Her beautiful face relaxed into an impish glee.

"That will be hell for Michael," she said. "He thinks I don't really know he went off to be with that woman that day."

"How did you know?"

"It was obvious from the *way* he said he was going to lunch with Oscar. So frightfully casually, you know, and his nose twitching just a tiny bit like it always does when he tells lies."

"How devoutly thankful I am I am not married to you, madame!"

"And then, of course, I made sure by ringing up Oscar," continued Rosamund. "Men always tell such silly lies."

"He is not, I fear, a very faithful husband?" Poirot hazarded.

Rosamund, however, did not reject the statement.

"No."

"But you do not mind?"

"Well, it's rather fun in a way," said Rosamund. "I mean,

having a husband that all the other women want to snatch away from you. I should hate to be married to a man that nobody wanted—like poor Susan. Really Greg is so completely wet!"

Poirot was studying her.

"And suppose someone did succeed—in snatching your husband away from you?"

"They won't," said Rosamund. "Not now," she added.

"You mean—"

"Not now that there's Uncle Richard's money. Michael falls for these creatures in a way—that Sorrel Dainton woman nearly got her hooks into him—wanted him for keeps—but with Michael the show will always come first. He can launch out now in a big way—put his own shows on. Do some production as well as acting. He's ambitious, you know, and he really is good. Not like me. I adore acting—but I'm ham, though I look nice. No, I'm not worried about Michael any more. Because it's my money, you see."

Her eyes met Poirot's calmly. He thought how strange it was that both Richard Abernethie's nieces should have fallen deeply in love with men who were incapable of returning that love. And yet Rosamund was unusually beautiful and Susan was attractive and full of sex appeal. Susan needed and clung to the illusion that Gregory loved her. Rosamund, clear-sighted, had no illusions at all, but knew what she wanted.

"The point is," said Rosamund, "that I've got to make a big decision—about the future. Michael doesn't know yet." Her face curved into a smile. "He found out that I wasn't shopping that day and he's madly suspicious about Regent's Park."

"What is this about Regent's Park?" Poirot looked puzzled.

"I went there, you see, after Harley Street. Just to walk about and think. Naturally Michael thinks that if I went there at all, I went to meet some man!"

Rosamund smiled beatifically and added:

"He didn't like that *at all!*"

"But why should you not go to Regent's Park?" asked Poirot.

"Just to walk there, you mean?"

"Yes. Have you never done it before?"

"Never. Why should I? What is there to go to Regent's Park *for*?"

Poirot looked at her and said:

"For you—nothing."

He added:

"I think, madame, that you must cede the green malachite table to your cousin Susan."

Rosamund's eyes opened very wide.

"Why should I? I *want* it."

"I know. I know. But you—you will keep your husband. And the poor Susan, she will lose hers."

"Lose him? Do you mean Greg's going off with someone? I wouldn't have believed it of him. He looks so *wet*."

"Infidelity is not the only way of losing a husband, madame."

"You don't mean—?" Rosamund stared at him. "You're not thinking that Greg poisoned Uncle Richard and killed Aunt Cora and conked Aunt Helen on the head? That's ridiculous. Even *I* know better than that."

"Who did, then?"

"George, of course. George is a wrong un, you know, he's mixed up in some sort of currency swindle—I heard about it from some friends of mine who were in Monte. I expect Uncle Richard got to know about it and was just going to cut him out of his will."

Rosamund added complacently:

"I've always known it was George."

XXIV

THE TELEGRAM came about six o'clock that evening.

As specially requested it was delivered by hand, not telephoned, and Hercule Poirot who had been hovering for some time in the neighbourhood of the front door, was at hand to receive it from Lanscombe as the latter took it from the telegraph boy.

He tore it open with somewhat less than his usual precision. It consisted of three words and a signature.

Poirot gave vent to an enormous sigh of relief.

Then he took a pound note from his pocket and handed it to the dumbfounded boy.

"There are moments," he said to Lanscombe, "when economy should be abandoned."

"Very possibly, sir," said Lanscombe politely.

"Where is Inspector Morton?" asked Poirot.

"One of the police gentlemen," Lanscombe spoke with distaste—and indicated subtly that such things as names for police officers were impossible to remember—"has left. The other is, I believe, in the study."

"Splendid," said Poirot. "I join him immediately."

He once more clapped Lanscombe on the shoulder and said:

"Courage, we are on the point of arriving!"

Lanscombe looked slightly bewildered since departures, and not arrivals, had been in his mind.

He said:

"You do not, then, propose to leave by the nine-thirty train after all, sir?"

"Do not lose hope," Poirot told him.

Poirot moved away, then wheeling round, he asked:

"I wonder, can you remember what were the first words

Mrs Lansquenet said to you when she arrived here on the day of your master's funeral?"

"I remember very well, sir," said Lanscombe, his face lighting up. "Miss Cora—I beg pardon, Mrs Lansquenet—I always think of her as Miss Cora, somehow—"

"Very naturally."

"—She said to me: 'Hullo, Lanscombe. It's a long time since you used to bring us out meringues to the huts.' All the children used to have a hut of their own—down by the fence in the Park. In summer, when there was going to be a dinner party, I used to take the young ladies and gentlemen—the younger ones, you understand, sir—some meringues. Miss Cora, sir, was always very fond of her food."

Poirot nodded.

"Yes," he said, "that was as I thought. Yes, it was very typical, that."

He went into the study to find Inspector Morton and without a word handed him the telegram.

Morton read it blankly.

"I don't understand a word of this."

"The time has come to tell you all."

Inspector Morton grinned.

"You sound like a young lady in a Victorian melodrama. But it's about time you came across with something. I can't hold out on this set-up much longer. That Banks fellow is still insisting that he poisoned Richard Abernethie and boasting that we can't find out how. What beats me is why there's always somebody who comes forward when there's a murder and yells out that they did it! What do they think there is in it for them? I've never been able to fathom that."

"In this case, probably shelter from the difficulties of being responsible for oneself—in other words—Forsdyke Sanatorium."

"More likely to be Broadmoor."

"That might be equally satisfactory."

"*Did* he do it, Poirot? The Gilchrist woman came out with the story she'd already told you and it would fit with what Richard Abernethie said about his niece. If her husband did it, it would involve her. Somehow, you know, I can't visualize that girl committing a lot of crimes. But there's nothing she wouldn't do to try and cover *him*."

"I will tell you all—"

"Yes, yes, tell me all! And for the Lord's sake hurry up and do it!"

ii

This time it was in the big drawing room that Hercule Poirot assembled his audience.

There was amusement rather than tension in the faces that were turned towards him. Menace had materialised in the shape of Inspector Morton and Superintendent Parwell. With the police in charge, questioning, asking for statements, Hercule Poirot, private detective, had receded into something closely resembling a joke.

Timothy was not far from voicing the general feeling when he remarked in an audible *sotto voce* to his wife:

"Damned little mountebank! Entwhistle must be gaga!—that's all I can say."

It looked as though Hercule Poirot would have to work hard to make his proper effect.

He began in a slightly pompous manner.

"For the second time, I announce my departure! This morning I announced it for the twelve o'clock train. This evening I announce it for the nine-thirty—immediately, that is, after dinner. I go because there is nothing more here for me to do."

"Could have told him that all along." Timothy's commentary was still in evidence. "Never was anything for him to do. The cheek of these fellows!"

"I came here originally to solve a riddle. The riddle is solved. Let me, first, go over the various points which were brought to my attention by the excellent Mr Entwhistle.

"First, Mr Richard Abernethie dies suddenly. Secondly, after his funeral, his sister Cora Lansquenet says, 'He was murdered, wasn't he?' Thirdly Mrs Lansquenet is killed. The question is, are those three things part of a *sequence*? Let us observe what happens next? Miss Gilchrist, the dead woman's companion, is taken ill after eating a piece of wedding cake which contains arsenic. That, then, is the *next* step in the sequence.

"Now, as I told you this morning, in the course of my inquiries I have come across nothing—nothing at all, to substantiate the belief that Mr Abernethie was poisoned. Equally, I may say, I have found nothing to prove conclusively that he was *not* poisoned. But as we proceed, things become easier. Cora Lansquenet undoubtedly asked that sensational question at the funeral. Everyone agrees upon *that*. And undoubtedly, on the following day, Mrs Lansquenet was murdered—a hatchet being the instrument employed. Now let us examine the fourth happening. The local post van driver is strongly of the belief—though he will not definitely swear to it—that he did not deliver that parcel of wedding cake in the usual way. And if that is so, then the parcel was left by hand and though we cannot exclude a 'person unknown'—we must take particular notice of those people who were actually on the spot and in a position to put the parcel where it was subsequently found. Those were: Miss Gilchrist herself, of course; Susan Banks who came down that day for the inquest; Mr Entwhistle (but yes, we must consider Mr Entwhistle; he was present, remember, when Cora made her disquieting remark!). And there were two other people. An old gentleman who represented himself to be a Mr Guthrie, an art critic, and a nun or nuns who called early that morning to collect a subscription.

"Now I decided that I would start on the assumption that the postal van driver's recollection was correct. Therefore the little group of people under suspicion must be very carefully studied. Miss Gilchrist did not benefit in any way by Richard Abernethie's death and in only a very minute degree by Mrs Lansquenet's—in actual fact the death of the latter put her out of employment and left her with the possibility of finding it difficult to get new employment. Also Miss Gilchrist was taken to hospital definitely suffering from arsenical poisoning.

"Susan Banks *did* benefit from Richard Abernethie's death, and in a small degree from Mrs Lansquenet's—though here her motive must almost certainly have been security. She might have very good reason to believe that Miss Gilchrist had overheard

a conversation between Cora Lansquenet and her brother which
referred to her, and she might therefore decide that Miss
Gilchrist must be eliminated. She herself, remember, refused
to partake of the wedding cake and also suggested not calling in
a doctor until the morning, when Miss Gilchrist was taken ill
in the night.

"Mr Entwhistle did *not* benefit by either of the deaths—but
he had had considerable control over Mr Abernethie's affairs,
and the trust funds, and there might well be some reason why
Richard Abernethie should not live too long. But—you will say
—if it is Mr Entwhistle who was concerned, why should he come
to *me?*

"And to that I will answer—it is not the first time that a murderer has been too sure of himself.

"We now come to what I may call the two outsiders. Mr
Guthrie and a nun. If Mr Guthrie is really Mr Guthrie, the art
critic, then that clears him. The same applies to the nun, if she
is really a nun. The question is, are these people themselves,
or are they somebody else?

"And I may say that there seems to be a curious—*motif*—one
might call it—of a nun running through this business. A nun
comes to the door at Mr Timothy Abernethie's house and Miss
Gilchrist believes it is the same nun she has seen at Lytchett
St. Mary. Also a nun, or nuns, called here the day before Mr
Abernethie died . . ."

George Crossfield murmured, "Three to one, the nun."

Poirot went on:

"So here we have certain pieces of our pattern—the death of
Mr Abernethie, the murder of Cora Lansquenet, the poisoned
wedding cake, the '*motif*' of the 'Nun.'

"I will add some other features of the case that engaged my
attention:

"The visit of an art critic, a smell of oil paint, a picture post-
card of Polflexan harbour, and finally a bouquet of wax flowers
standing on that malachite table where a Chinese vase stands
now.

"It was reflecting on these things that led me to the truth—
and I am now about to tell you the truth.

"The first part of it I told you this morning. Richard Abernethie died suddenly—but there would have been no reason at all to suspect foul play—had it not been for the words uttered by his sister Cora at his funeral. The whole case for the murder of Richard Abernethie rests upon those words. As a result of them, you all believed that murder had taken place, and you believed it, not really because of the words themselves but because of *the character of Cora Lansquenet herself*. For Cora Lansquenet had always been famous for speaking the truth at awkward moments. So the case for Richard's murder rested not only upon what Cora had *said* but upon Cora herself.

"And now I come to the question that I suddenly asked myself:

"How well did you all know Cora Lansquenet?"

He was silent for a moment, and Susan asked sharply, "What do you mean?"

Poirot went on:

"Not well at all—that is the answer! The younger generation had never seen her at all, or if so, only when they were very young children. There were actually only three people present that day who actually *knew* Cora. Lanscombe, the butler, who is old and very blind; Mrs Timothy Abernethie who had only seen her a few times round about the date of her own wedding, and Mrs Leo Abernethie who had known her quite well, but who had not seen her for over twenty years.

"So I said to myself: 'Supposing it was *not* Cora Lansquenet who came to the funeral that day?' "

"Do you mean that Aunt Cora—*wasn't* Aunt Cora?" Susan demanded incredulously. "Do you mean that it wasn't Aunt Cora who was murdered, but someone else?"

"No, no, it was Cora Lansquenet who was murdered. *But it was not Cora Lansquenet* who came the day before to her brother's funeral. The woman who came that day came for one purpose only—to exploit, one may say, the fact that Richard died suddenly. And to create in the minds of his relations the belief that he had been murdered. Which she managed to do most successfully!"

"Nonsense! Why? What was the point of it?" Maude spoke bluffly.

"Why? To draw attention away from the other murder. From the murder of Cora Lansquenet herself. For if Cora says that Richard has been murdered and the next day *she herself is killed,* the two deaths are bound to be at least considered as possible cause and effect. But if Cora is murdered and her cottage is broken into, and if the apparent robbery does not convince the police, then they will look—where? Close at home, will they not? Suspicion will tend to fall on the woman who shares the house with her."

Miss Gilchrist protested in a tone that was almost bright:

"Oh come—really—Mr Pontarlier—you don't suggest I'd commit a murder for an amethyst brooch and a few worthless sketches?"

"No," said Poirot. "For a little more than that. There was one of those sketches, Miss Gilchrist, that represented Polflexan harbour and which, as Mrs Banks was clever enough to realise, had been copied from a picture postcard which showed the old pier still in position. But Mrs Lansquenet painted always from life. I remembered then that Mr Entwhistle had mentioned there being *a smell of oil paint* in the cottage when he first got there. You can paint, can't you, Miss Gilchrist? Your father was an artist and you know a good deal about pictures. Supposing that one of the pictures that Cora picked up cheaply at a sale was a valuable picture. Supposing that she herself did not recognise it for what it was, but that you did. You knew she was expecting, very shortly, a visit from an old friend of hers who was a well known art critic. Then her brother dies suddenly— and a plan leaps into your head. Easy to administer a sedative to her in her early cup of tea that will keep her unconscious for the whole of the day of the funeral whilst you yourself are playing her part at Enderby. You know Enderby well from listening to her talk about it. She has talked, as people do when they get on in life, a great deal about her childhood days. Easy for you to start off by a remark to old Lanscombe about meringues and huts which will make him quite sure of your identity in case he was inclined to doubt. Yes, you used your knowledge of Enderby well that day, with allusions to this and that, and recalling memories. None of them suspected you were not Cora. You were wearing her clothes, slightly padded, and since she wore a false front of hair, it was easy for you to assume that. Nobody had seen Cora for twenty years—and in twenty years people change so much that one often hears the remark: 'I would never have known her!' But mannerisms are remembered, and Cora had certain very definite mannerisms, all of which you had practised carefully before the glass.

"And it was there, strangely enough, that you made your first mistake. *You forgot that a mirror image is reversed.* When you saw in the glass the perfect reproduction of Cora's birdlike sidewise tilt of the head, you didn't realise that it was actually the *wrong way round.* You saw, let us say, Cora inclining her head to the *right*—but you forgot that actually your own head was inclined to the *left* to produce that effect *in the glass.*

"That was what puzzled and worried Helen Abernethie at the moment when you made your famous insinuation. Something seemed to her 'wrong.' I realised myself the other night when Rosamund Shane made an unexpected remark what happens on such an occasion. Everybody inevitably looks at the *speaker.* Therefore, when Mrs Leo felt something was 'wrong,' it must be that something was wrong with *Cora Lansquenet.* The other evening, after talk about mirror images and 'seeing oneself' I think Mrs Leo experimented before a looking glass. Her own face is not particularly asymmetrical. She probably thought of Cora, remembered how Cora used to incline her head to the right, did so, and looked in the glass—when, of course, the image seemed to her 'wrong' and she realised, in a flash, just what had been wrong on the day of the funeral. She puzzled it out—either Cora had taken to inclining her head in the opposite direction—most unlikely—or else *Cora had not been Cora.* Neither way seemed to her to make sense. But she determined to tell Mr Entwhistle of her discovery at once. Someone who was used to getting up early was already about, and followed her down, and fearful of what revelations she might be about to make struck her down with a heavy doorstop."

Poirot paused and added:

"I may as well tell you now, Miss Gilchrist, that Mrs Abernethie's concussion is not serious. She will soon be able to tell us her own story."

"I never did anything of the sort," said Miss Gilchrist. "The whole thing is a wicked lie."

"It *was* you that day," said Michael Shane suddenly. He had been studying Miss Gilchrist's face. "I ought to have seen it sooner—I felt in a vague kind of way I had seen you before somewhere—but of course one never looks much at—" he stopped.

"No, one doesn't bother to look at a mere companion help," said Miss Gilchrist. Her voice shook a little. "A drudge, a domestic drudge! Almost a servant! But go on, M. Poirot. Go on with this fantastic piece of nonsense!"

"The suggestion of murder thrown out at the funeral was only the first step, of course," said Poirot. "You had more in reserve. At any moment you were prepared to admit to having listened to a conversation between Richard and his sister. What he actually told her, no doubt, was the fact that he had not long to live, and that explains a cryptic phrase in the letter he wrote her after getting home. The 'Nun' was another of your suggestions. The nun—or rather nuns—who called at the cottage on the day of the inquest suggested to you a mention of a nun who was 'following you round,' and you used that when you were anxious to hear what Mrs Timothy was saying to her sister-in-law at Enderby. And also because you wished to accompany her there and find out for yourself just how suspicions were going. Actually to poison *yourself,* badly but not fatally, with arsenic, is a very old device—and I may say that it served to awaken Inspector Morton's suspicions of you."

"But the picture?" said Rosamund. "What kind of a picture was it?"

Poirot slowly unfolded a telegram.

"This morning I rang up Mr Entwhistle, a responsible person, to go to Stansfield Grange and, acting on authority from Mr Abernethie himself" (here Poirot gave a hard stare at Timothy) "to look amongst the pictures in Miss Gilchrist's room and select the one of Polflexan harbour on pretext of having it reframed as a surprise for Miss Gilchrist. He was to take it back to London and call upon Mr Guthrie whom I had warned by telegram. The hastily painted sketch of Polflexan harbour was removed and the original picture exposed."

He held up the telegram and read:

"Definitely a Vermeer. Guthrie."

Suddenly, with electrifying effect, Miss Gilchrist burst into speech.

"I knew it was a Vermeer. I *knew* it. *She* didn't know! Talking about Rembrandts and Italian Primitives and unable to recognise a Vermeer when it was under her nose! Always prating about Art—and really knowing nothing about it! She was a thoroughly stupid woman. Always maundering on about this place—about Enderby, and what they did there as children, and about Richard and Timothy and Laura and all the rest of them. Rolling in money always! Always the best of everything those children had. You don't know how boring it is listening to somebody going on about the same things, hour after hour and day after day. And saying 'Oh yes, Mrs Lansquenet' and 'Really, Mrs Lansquenet?' Pretending to be interested. And really bored—bored—*bored*. . . . And nothing to look forward to. . . . And then—a Vermeer! I saw in the papers that a Vermeer sold the other day for over two thousand pounds!"

"You killed her—in that brutal way—for two thousand pounds?" Susan's voice was incredulous.

"Two thousand pounds," said Poirot, "would have rented and equipped a tea shop. . . ."

Miss Gilchrist turned to him.

"At least," she said. "You *do* understand. It was the only chance I'd ever get. I *had* to have a capital sum." Her voice vibrated with the force and obsession of her dream. "I was going to call it the Palm Tree. And have little camels as menu holders. One can occasionally get quite nice china—export rejects—not that awful white utility stuff. I meant to start it in some nice neighbourhood where nice people would come in. I had thought of Rye. . . . Or perhaps Chichester . . . I'm sure I could have made a success of it." She paused a minute, then added musingly, "Oak tables—and little basket chairs with striped red and white cushions. . . ."

For a few moments the tea shop that would never be, seemed more real than the Victorian solidity of the drawing room at Enderby. . . .

It was Inspector Morton who broke the spell.

Miss Gilchrist turned to him quite politely.

"Oh, certainly," she said. "At once. I don't want to give any trouble, I'm sure. After all, if I can't have The Palm Tree, nothing really seems to matter very much. . . ."

She went out of the room with him and Susan said, her voice still shaken:

"I've never imagined a—*ladylike* murderer. It's horrible."

XXV

"BUT I don't understand about the wax flowers," said Rosamund.

She fixed Poirot with large reproachful blue eyes.

They were at Helen's flat in London. Helen herself was resting on the sofa and Rosamund and Poirot were having tea with her.

"I don't see that *wax flowers* had anything to *do* with it," said Rosamund. "Or the malachite table."

"The malachite table, no. But the wax flowers were Miss Gilchrist's second mistake. She said how nice they looked on the malachite table. And you see, madame, *she* could not have seen them there. Because they had been broken and put away before she arrived with the Timothy Abernethies. *So she could only have seen them when she was there as Cora Lansquenet.*"

"That *was* stupid of her, wasn't it?" said Rosamund.

Poirot shook a forefinger at her.

"It shows you, madame, the dangers of *conversation*. It is a profound belief of mine that if you can induce a person to talk to you for long enough, *on any subject whatever*, sooner or later they will give themselves away. Miss Gilchrist did."

"I shall have to be careful," said Rosamund thoughtfully.

Then she brightened up.

"Did you know? I'm going to have a baby."

"Aha! So that is the meaning of Harley Street and Regent's Park?"

"Yes. I was so upset, you know, and so surprised—that I just had to go somewhere and *think*."

"You said, I remember, that that does not very often happen."

"Well, it's much easier not to. But this time I had to decide about the future. And I've decided to leave the stage and just be a mother."

"A *rôle* that will suit you admirably. Already I foresee delightful pictures in the Sketch and the Tatler."

Rosamund smiled happily.

"Yes, it's wonderful. Do you know, Michael is *delighted*. I didn't really think he would be."

She paused and added:

"Susan's got the malachite table. I thought, as I was having a baby—"

She left the sentence unfinished.

"Susan's cosmetic business promises well," said Helen. "I think she is all set for a big success."

"Yes, she was born to succeed," said Poirot. "She is like her uncle."

"You mean Richard, I suppose," said Rosamund. "Not Timothy?"

"Assuredly not like Timothy," said Poirot.

They laughed.

"Greg's away somewhere," said Rosamund. "Having a rest cure Susan *says?*"

She looked inquiringly at Poirot who said nothing.

"I can't think why he kept on saying he'd killed Uncle Richard," said Rosamund. "Do you think it was a form of Exhibitionism?"

Poirot reverted to the previous topic.

"I received a very amiable letter from Mr Timothy Abernethie," he said. "He expressed himself as highly satisfied with the services I had rendered the family."

"I do think Uncle Timothy is quite awful," said Rosamund.

"I am going to stay with them next week," said Helen. "They seem to be getting the gardens into order, but domestic help is still difficult."

"They miss the awful Gilchrist, I suppose," said Rosamund. "But I daresay in the end, she'd have killed Uncle Timothy, too. What fun if she had!"

"Murder has always seemed fun to you, madame."

"Oh! not really," said Rosamund, vaguely. "But I *did* think it was George." She brightened up. "Perhaps he will do one some day."

"And that will be fun," said Poirot sarcastically.

"Yes, won't it?" Rosamund agreed.

She ate another éclair from the plate in front of her.

Poirot turned to Helen.

"And you, madame, are off to Cyprus?"

"Yes, in a fortnight's time."

"Then let me wish you a happy journey."

He bowed over her hand. She came with him to the door, leaving Rosamund dreamily stuffing herself with cream pastries.

Helen said abruptly:

"I should like you to know, M. Poirot, that the legacy Richard left me meant more to me than theirs did to any of the others."

"As much as that, madame?"

"Yes. You see—there is a child in Cyprus. . . . My husband and I were very devoted—it was a great sorrow to us to have no children. After he died my loneliness was unbelievable. When I was nursing in London at the end of the war, I met someone . . . He was younger than I was and married, though not very happily. We came together for a little while. That was all. He went back to Canada—to his wife and his children. He never knew about—our child. He would not have wanted it. I did. It seemed like a miracle to me—a middle-aged woman with everything behind her. With Richard's money I can educate my so-called nephew, and give him a start in life." She paused, then added, "I never told Richard. He was fond of me and I of him —but he would not have understood. You know so much about us all that I thought I would like you to know this about me."

Once again Poirot bowed over her hand.

He got home to find the armchair on the left of the fireplace occupied.

"Hullo, Poirot," said Mr Entwhistle. "I've just come back from the Assizes. They brought in a verdict of Guilty, of course. But I shouldn't be surprised if she ends up in Broadmoor. She's gone definitely over the edge since she's been in prison. Quite happy you know, and *most* gracious. She spends her time making the most elaborate plans to run a chain of tea shops. Her newest establishment is to be the Lilac Bush. She's opening it in Cromer."

"One wonders if she was always a little mad? But me, I think not."

"Good Lord, no! Sane as you and I when she planned that murder. Carried it out in cold blood. She's got a good head on her, you know, underneath the fluffy manner."

Poirot gave a little shiver.

"I am thinking," he said, "of some words that Susan Banks said—that she had never imagined a *ladylike* murderer."

"Why not?" said Mr Entwhistle. "It takes all sorts."

They were silent—and Poirot thought of murderers he had known. . . .